DEAD SIMPLE & LOOKING GOOD DEAD

Peter James was educated at Charterhouse and then at film school. He lived in North America for a number of years before returning to England. His novels have been translated into twenty-six languages and reflect the author's deep interest in medicine, science, and the paranormal. Peter James lives in London and Sussex.

Also by Peter James

DEAD LETTER DROP
ATOM BOMB ANGEL
BILLIONAIRE
POSSESSION
DREAMER
SWEET HEART
TWILIGHT
PROPHECY
ALCHEMIST
HOST
THE TRUTH
DENIAL
FAITH

Children's novel
GETTING WIRED!

PETER JAMES

DEAD SIMPLE
&
LOOKING GOOD DEAD

PAN BOOKS

Dead Simple first published 2005 by Macmillan.
First published in paperback 2006 by Pan Books.
Looking Good Dead first published 2006 by Macmillan.
First published in paperback 2006 by Pan Books.

This omnibus first published 2008 by Pan Books
an imprint of Pan Macmillan Ltd
Pan Macmillan, 20 New Wharf Road, London N1 9RR
Basingstoke and Oxford
Associated companies throughout the world
www.panmacmillan.com

ISBN 978-0-330-45788-0

1 3 5 7 9 8 6 4 2

A CIP catalogue record for this book is available from
the British Library.

Printed and bound in Great Britain by
Mackays of Chatham plc, Chatham, Kent

DEAD SIMPLE

ACKNOWLEDGEMENTS

Writing is always regarded as a solitary occupation, but for me it is a team effort, and I owe a great debt to several people who have very generously given me their time and input, in so many areas. In particular I want to single out Detective Superintendent Dave Gaylor of Sussex Police, who gave me many suggestions for this novel, tirelessly read and reread the manuscript at many stages, and opened every door that I needed in different divisions of Sussex Police – I could never have written this without him. And I would like to thank the many officers of the Sussex Police Force who were so welcoming and helpful to me, in particular Detective Sergeant Keith Hallett of the Sussex Police Holmes Unit, Detective Inspector William Warner and Senior Scenes of Crime Investigator Stuart Leonard.

I would like to thank also Dr Nigel Kirkham MRCPath and his team at the Brighton and Hove Mortuary, where I long hope to remain a day visitor rather than an overnight guest, my good friend James Simpson – my film and television writing partner, Carina Coleman, who acted as my unofficial editor and gave me some brilliant insights, Mike Harris, Peter Wingate Saul, Alan Tonks, Greg Shackleton, police surgeon and coroner Dr Peter Dean. And Helen Shenston, who gave me the faith and encouragement that kept up my enthusiasm for this book during my bleakest days.

I want to thank also my wonderful new agent, Carole Blake, for her faith in me, and the fantastic team at my new publishers, Macmillan, in particular David North and Geoff Duffield and my editor Stef Bierwerth, who is a total treasure.

Acknowledgements

And both Geoffrey Bailey and Tony Mulliken for their enduring support and belief in me. And, as ever, my faithful hound Bertie and my more recent canine friend Phoebe, who both tolerated my writing – albeit with some reluctance – as tedious interludes between their walks.

Peter James
Sussex, England
scary@pavilion.co.uk
www.peterjames.com

DEAD SIMPLE

1

So far, apart from just a couple of hitches, Plan A was working out fine. Which was fortunate, since they didn't really have a Plan B.

At 8.30 on a late May evening, they'd banked on having some daylight. There had been plenty of the stuff this time yesterday, when four of them had made the same journey, taking with them an empty coffin and four shovels. But now, as the green Transit van sped along the Sussex country road, misty rain was falling from a sky the colour of a fogged negative.

'Are we nearly there yet?' said Josh in the back, mimicking a child.

'The great Um Ga says, "Wherever I go there I am,"' responded Robbo, who was driving, and was slightly less drunk than the rest of them. With three pubs notched up already in the past hour and a half, and four more on the itinerary, he was sticking to shandy. At least, that had been his intention; but he'd managed to slip down a couple of pints of pure Harvey's bitter – to clear his head for the task of driving, he'd said.

'So we are there!' said Josh.

'Always have been.'

A deer warning sign flitted from the darkness then was gone, as the headlights skimmed glossy black-top macadam stretching ahead into the forested distance. Then they passed a small white cottage.

Michael, lolling on a tartan rug on the floor in the back

of the van, head wedged between the arms of a wheel-wrench for a pillow, was feeling very pleasantly woozy. 'I sh'ink I need another a drink,' he slurred.

If he'd had his wits about him, he might have sensed, from the expressions of his friends, that something was not quite right. Never usually much of a heavy drinker, tonight he'd parked his brains in the dregs of more empty pint glasses and vodka chasers than he could remember downing, in more pubs than had been sensible to visit.

Of the six of them who had been muckers together since way back into their early teens, Michael Harrison had always been the natural leader. If, as they say, the secret of life is to choose your parents wisely, Michael had ticked plenty of the right boxes. He had inherited his mother's fair good looks and his father's charm and entrepreneurial spirit, but without any of the self-destruct genes that had eventually ruined the man.

From the age of twelve, when Tom Harrison had gassed himself in the garage of the family home, leaving behind a trail of debtors, Michael had grown up fast, helping his mother make ends meet by doing a paper round, then when he was older by taking labouring jobs in his holidays. He grew up with an appreciation of how hard it was to make money – and how easy to fritter it.

Now, at twenty-eight, he was smart, a decent human being, and a natural leader of the pack. If he had flaws, it was that he was too trusting and on occasions, too much of a prankster. And tonight that latter chicken was coming home to roost. Big time.

But at this moment he had no idea of that.

He drifted back again into a blissful stupor, thinking only happy thoughts, mostly about his fiancée, Ashley. Life was good. His mother was dating a nice guy, his kid brother had just got into university, his kid sister Carly was back-packing in Australia on a gap year, and his business was going incredibly well. But best of all, in three days time he was going to be marrying the woman he loved. And adored. His soul mate.

Ashley.

He hadn't noticed the shovel that rattled on every bump in the road, as the wheels drummed below on the sodden tarmac, and the rain pattered down above him on the roof. And he didn't clock a thing in the expressions of his two friends riding along with him in the back, who were swaying and singing tunelessly to an oldie, Rod Stewart's 'Sailing', on the crackly radio up front. A leaky fuel can filled the van with the stench of petrol.

'I love her,' Michael slurred. 'I sh'love Ashley.'

'She's a great lady,' Robbo said, turning his head from the wheel, sucking up to him as he always did. That was in his nature. Awkward with women, a bit clumsy, a florid face, lank hair, beer belly straining the weave of his T-shirt, Robbo hung to the coat tails of this bunch by always trying to make himself needed. And tonight, for a change, he actually *was* needed.

'She is.'

'Coming up,' warned Luke.

Robbo braked as they approached the turn-off and winked in the darkness of the cab at Luke seated next to him. The wipers clumped steadily, smearing the rain across the windscreen.

'I mean, like I really love her. Sh'now what I mean?'

'We know what you mean,' Pete said.

Josh, leaning back against the driver's seat, one arm around Pete, swigged some beer, then passed the bottle

3

down to Michael. Froth rose from the neck as the van braked sharply. He belched. ''Scuse me.'

'What the hell does Ashley see in you?' Josh said.

'My dick.'

'So it's not your money? Or your looks? Or your charm?'

'That too, Josh, but mostly my dick.'

The van lurched as it made the sharp right turn, rattling over a cattle grid, almost immediately followed by a second one, and onto the dirt track. Robbo, peering through the misted glass, picking out the deep ruts, swung the wheel. A rabbit sprinted ahead of them, then shot into some undergrowth. The headlights veered right then left, fleetingly colouring the dense conifers that lined the track, before they vanished into darkness in the rear-view mirror. As Robbo changed down a gear, Michael's voice changed, his bravado suddenly tinged, very faintly, with anxiety.

'Where we going?'

'To another pub.'

'OK. Great.' Then a moment later, 'Promised Ashley I shwouldn't – wouldn't – drink too much.'

'See,' Pete said, 'you're not even married and she's laying down rules. You're still a free man. For just three more days.'

'Three and a half,' Robbo added, helpfully.

'You haven't arranged any girls?' Michael said.

'Feeling horny?' Robbo asked.

'I'm staying faithful.'

'We're making sure of that.'

'Bastards!'

The van lurched to a halt, reversed a short distance, then made another right turn. Then it stopped again, and Robbo killed the engine – and Rod Stewart with it. '*Arrivé!*' he said. 'Next watering hole! The Undertaker's Arms!'

'I'd prefer the Naked Thai Girl's Legs,' Michael said.

'She's here too.'

Someone opened the rear door of the van, Michael wasn't sure who. Invisible hands took hold of his ankles. Robbo took one of his arms, and Luke the other.

'Hey!'

'You're a heavy bastard!' Luke said.

Moments later Michael thumped down, in his favourite sports jacket and best jeans (not the wisest choice for your stag night, a dim voice in his head was telling him) onto sodden earth, in pitch darkness which was pricked only by the red tail lights of the van and the white beam of a flashlight. Hardening rain stung his eyes and matted his hair to his forehead.

'My – closhes—'

Moments later, his arms yanked almost clear of their sockets, he was hoisted in the air, then dumped down into something dry and lined with white satin that pressed in on either side of him.

'Hey!' he said again.

Four drunken, grinning shadowy faces leered down at him. A magazine was pushed into his hands. In the beam of the flashlight he caught a blurry glimpse of a naked redhead with gargantuan breasts. A bottle of whisky, a small flashlight, switched on, and a walkie-talkie were placed on his stomach.

'What's—?'

A piece of foul-tasting rubber tubing was pushing into his mouth. As Michael spat it out, he heard a scraping sound, then suddenly something blotted the faces out. And blotted all the sound out. His nostrils filled with smells of wood, new cloth and glue. For an instant he felt warm and snug. Then a flash of panic.

'Hey, guys – what—'

Robbo picked up a screwdriver, as Pete shone the flashlight down on the teak coffin.

'You're not screwing it down?' Luke said.

'Absolutely!' Pete said.

'Do you think we should?'

'He'll be fine,' Robbo said. 'He's got the breathing tube!'

'I really don't think we should screw it down!'

''Course we do – otherwise he'll be able to get out!'

'Hey—' Michael said.

But no one could hear him now. And he could hear nothing except a faint scratching sound above him.

Robbo worked on each of the four screws in turn. It was a top-of-the-range hand-tooled teak coffin with embossed brass handles, borrowed from his uncle's funeral parlour, where, after a couple of career U-turns, he was now employed as an apprentice embalmer. Good, solid brass screws. They went in easily.

Michael looked upwards, his nose almost touching the lid. In the beam of the flashlight, ivory-white satin encased him. He kicked out with his legs, but they had nowhere to travel. He tried to push his arms out. But they had nowhere to go, either.

Sobering for a few moments, he suddenly realized what he was lying in.

'Hey, hey, listen, you know – hey – I'm claustrophobic – this is not funny! Hey!' His voice came back at him, strangely muffled.

Pete opened the door, leaned into the cab, and switched on the headlights. A couple of metres in front of them was the grave they had dug yesterday, the earth piled to one side, tapes already in place. A large sheet of corrugated iron and two of the spades they had used lay close by.

The four friends walked to the edge and peered down. All of them were suddenly aware that nothing in life is ever quite as it seems when you are planning it. This hole right now looked deeper, darker, more like – well – a grave, actually.

The beam of the flashlight shimmered at the bottom.

'There's water,' Josh said.

'Just a bit of rainwater,' Robbo said.

Josh frowned. 'There's too much, that's not rainwater. We must have hit the water table.'

'Shit,' Pete said. A BMW salesman, he always looked the part, on duty or off. Spiky haircut, sharp suit, always confident. But not quite so confident now.

'It's nothing,' Robbo said. 'Just a couple of inches.'

'Did we really dig it this deep?' said Luke, a freshly qualified solicitor, recently married, not quite ready to shrug off his youth, but starting to accept life's responsibilities.

'It's a grave, isn't it?' said Robbo. 'We decided on a grave.'

Josh squinted up at the worsening rain. 'What if the water rises?

'Shit, man,' Robbo said. 'We dug it yesterday, it's taken twenty-four hours for just a couple of inches. Nothing to worry about.'

Josh nodded, thoughtfully. 'But what if we can't get him back out?'

'Course we can get him out,' Robbo said. 'We just unscrew the lid.'

'Let's just get on with it,' Luke said. 'OK?'

'He bloody deserves it,' Pete reassured his mates. 'Remember what he did on your stag night, Luke?'

Luke would never forget. Waking from an alcoholic stupor to find himself on a bunk on the overnight sleeper to Edinburgh. Arriving forty minutes late at the altar the next afternoon as a result.

Pete would never forget, either. The weekend before his wedding, he'd found himself in frilly lace underwear, a dildo strapped to his waist, manacled to the Clifton Gorge suspension bridge, before being rescued by the fire brigade. Both pranks had been Michael's idea.

'Typical of Mark,' Pete said. 'Jammy bastard. He's the one who organized this and now he isn't bloody here . . .'

'He's coming. He'll be at the next pub, he knows the itinerary.'

'Oh yes?'

'He rang, he's on his way.'

'Fogbound in Leeds. Great!' Robbo said.

'He'll be at the Royal Oak by the time we get there.'

'Jammy bastard,' Luke said. 'He's missing out on all the hard work.'

'And the *fun*!' Pete reminded him.

'This is fun?' Luke said. 'Standing in the middle of a sodding forest in the pissing rain? Fun? God, you're sad! He'd fucking better turn up to help us get Michael back out.'

They hefted the coffin up in the air, staggered forward with it to the edge of the grave and dumped it down, hard, over the tapes. Then giggled at the muffled 'Ouch!' from within it.

There was a loud thump.

Michael banged his fist against the lid. 'Hey! Enough!'

Pete, who had the walkie-talkie in his coat pocket, pulled it out and switched it on. 'Testing!' he said. 'Testing!'

Inside the coffin, Pete's voice boomed out. 'Testing! Testing!'

'Joke over!'

'Relax, Michael!' Pete said. 'Enjoy!'

'You bastards! Let me out! I need a piss!'

Pete switched the walkie-talkie off and jammed it into the pocket of his Barbour jacket. 'So how does this work, exactly?'

'We lift the tapes,' Robbo said. 'One each end.'

Pete dug the walkie-talkie out and switched it on. 'We're getting this taped, Michael!' Then he switched it off again.

The four of them laughed. Then each picked up an end of tape and took up the slack.

'One . . . two . . . three!' Robbo counted.

'Fuck, this is heavy!' Luke said, taking the strain and lifting.

Slowly, jerkily, listing like a stricken ship, the coffin sank down into the deep hole.

When it reached the bottom they could barely see it in the darkness.

Pete held the flashlight. In the beam they could make out the breathing tube sticking limply out of the drinking-straw-sized hole that had been cut in the lid.

Robbo grabbed the walkie-talkie. 'Hey, Michael, your dick's sticking out. Are you enjoying the magazine?'

'OK, joke over. Now let me out!'

'We're off to a pole-dancing club. Too bad you can't join us!' Robbo switched off the radio before Michael could reply. Then, pocketing it, he picked up a spade and began shovelling earth over the edge of the grave and roared with laughter as it rattled down on the roof of the coffin.

With a loud *whoop* Pete grabbed another shovel and joined in. For some moments both of them worked hard until only a few bald patches of coffin showed through the earth. Then these were covered. Both of them continued, the drink fuelling their work into a frenzy, until there was a good couple of feet of earth piled on top of the coffin. The breathing tube barely showed above it.

'Hey!' Luke said. 'Hey, stop that! The more you shovel on the more we're going to have to dig back out again in two hours' time.'

'It's a grave!' Robbo said. 'That's what you do with a grave, you cover the coffin!'

Luke grabbed the spade from him. 'Enough!' he said, firmly. 'I want to spend the evening drinking, not bloody digging, OK?'

Robbo nodded, never wanting to upset anyone in the group. Pete, sweating heavily, threw his spade down. 'Don't think I'll take this up as a career,' he said.

They pulled the corrugated iron sheet over the top, then stood back in silence for some moments. Rain pinged on the metal.

'OK,' Pete said. 'We're outta here.'

Luke dug his hands into his coat pocket, dubiously. 'Are we really sure about this?'

'We agreed we were going to teach him a lesson,' Robbo said.

'What if he chokes on his vomit, or something?'

'He'll be fine, he's not that drunk,' Josh said. 'Let's go.'

Josh climbed into the rear of the van, and Luke shut the doors. Then Pete, Luke and Robbo squeezed into the front, and Robbo started the engine. They drove back down the track for half a mile, then made a right turn onto the main road.

Then he switched on the walkie-talkie. 'How you doing, Michael?'

'Guys, listen, I'm really not enjoying this joke.'

'Really?' Robbo said. 'We are!'

Luke took the radio. 'This is what's known as pure vanilla revenge, Michael!'

All four of them in the van roared with laughter. Now it was Josh's turn. 'Hey, Michael, we're going to this fantastic club, they have the most beautiful women, butt naked, sliding their bodies up and down poles. You're going to be really pissed you're missing out on this!'

Michael's voice slurred back, just a tad plaintive. 'Can we stop this now, please? I'm really not enjoying this.'

Through the windscreen Robbo could see roadworks ahead, with a green light. He accelerated.

Luke shouted over Josh's shoulder, 'Hey, Michael, just relax, we'll be back in a couple of hours!'

'What do you mean, *a couple of hours*?'

The light turned red. Not enough time to stop. Robbo accelerated even harder and shot through. 'Gimme the thing,' he said, grabbing the radio and steering one-handed around a long curve. He peered down in the ambient glow of the dash and hit the *talk* button.

'Hey, Michael—'

'ROBBO!' Luke's voice, screaming.

Headlights above them, coming straight at them.

Blinding them.

Then the blare of a horn, deep, heavy duty, ferocious.

'ROBBBBBBBBBOOOOOOO!' screamed Luke.

Robbo stamped in panic on the brake pedal and dropped the walkie-talkie. The wheel yawed in his hands as he looked, desperately, for somewhere to go. Trees to his right, a JCB to his left, headlights burning through the windscreen, searing his eyes, coming at him out of the teeming rain, like a train.

2

Michael, his head swimming, heard shouting, then a sharp *thud*, as if someone had dropped the walkie-talkie.

Then silence.

He pressed the *talk* button. 'Hello?'

Just empty static came back at him.

'Hello? Hey guys!'

Still nothing. He focused his eyes on the two-way radio. It was a stubby-looking thing, a hard, black plastic casing, with one short aerial and one longer one, the name '*Motorola*' embossed over the speaker grille. There was also an on–off switch, a volume control, a channel selector, and a tiny pinhead of a green light that was glowing brightly. Then he stared at the white satin that was inches from his eyes, fighting panic, starting to breathe faster and faster. He needed to pee, badly, going on desperately.

Where the hell was he? Where were Josh, Luke, Pete, Robbo? Standing around, giggling? Had the bastards really gone off to a club?

Then his panic subsided as the alcohol kicked back in again. His thoughts became leaden, muddled. His eyes closed and he was almost suckered into sleep.

Opening his eyes, the satin blurred into soft focus, as a roller wave of nausea suddenly swelled up inside him, threw him up in the air then dropped him down. Up again. Down again. He swallowed, closed his eye again, giddily, feeling the coffin drifting, swaying from side to side, floating. The need to pee was receding. Suddenly the nausea wasn't so bad any more. It was snug in here. Floating. Like being in a big bed!

His eyes closed and he sank like a stone into sleep.

3

Roy Grace sat in the dark, in his ageing Alfa Romeo in the line of stationary traffic, rain drumming the roof, his fingers drumming the wheel, barely listening to the Dido CD that was playing. He felt tense. Impatient. Gloomy.

He felt like shit.

Tomorrow he was due to appear in court, and he knew he was in trouble.

He took a swig of bottled Evian water, replaced the cap and jammed the bottle back in the door pocket. 'Come on, come on!' he said, fingers tapping again, harder now. He was already forty minutes late for his date. He hated being late, always felt it was a sign of rudeness, as if you were making the statement, *my time's more important than yours, so I can keep you waiting . . .*

If he had left the office just one minute sooner he wouldn't have been late: someone else would have taken the call and the ram-raid on a jewellery shop in Brighton, by two punks who were high on God-knows-what, would have been a colleague's problem, not his. That was one of the occupational hazards of police work – villains didn't have the courtesy to keep to office hours.

He should not be going out tonight, he knew. Should have stayed home, preparing himself for tomorrow. Tugging out the bottle, he drank some more water. His mouth was dry, parched. Leaden butterflies flip-flopped in his belly.

Friends had pushed him into a handful of blind dates

over the past few years, and each time he'd been a bag of nerves before he'd shown up. The nerves were even worse tonight, and, not having had a chance to shower and change, he felt uncomfortable about his appearance. All his detailed planning about what he was going to wear had gone out of the window, thanks to the two punks.

One of them had fired a sawn-off shotgun at an off-duty cop who had come too close to the jewellery shop – but luckily not quite close enough. Roy had seen, more times than he had needed, the effects of a 12-bore fired from a few feet at a human being. It could shear off a limb or punch a hole the size of a football through their chest. This cop, a detective called Bill Green who Grace knew – they had played rugger on the same team a few times – had been peppered from about thirty yards. At this distance the pellets could just about have brought down a pheasant or a rabbit, but not a fifteen-stone scrum prop in a leather jacket. Bill Green was relatively lucky – his jacket had shielded his body but he had several pellets embedded in his face, including one in his left eye.

By the time Grace had got to the scene, the punks were already in custody, after crashing and rolling their getaway Jeep. He was determined to stick them with an attempted murder charge on top of armed robbery. He hated the way more and more criminals were using guns in the UK – and forcing more and more police to have firearms to hand. In his father's day armed cops would have been unheard of. Now in some cities forces kept guns in the boots of their cars as routine. Grace wasn't naturally a vengeful person, but so far as he was concerned, anyone who fired a gun at a police officer – or at any innocent person – should be hanged.

The traffic still wasn't moving. He looked at the dash

clock, at the rain falling, at the clock again, at the burning red tail lights of the car in front – the prat had his fogs on, almost dazzling him. Then he checked his watch, hoping the car clock might be wrong. But it wasn't. Ten whole minutes had passed and they hadn't moved an inch. Nor had any traffic come past from the opposite direction.

Shards of blue light flitted across his interior mirror and wing mirror. Then he heard a siren. A patrol car screamed past. Then an ambulance. Another patrol car, flat out, followed by two fire engines.

Shit. There had been road works when he'd come this way a couple of days ago, and he'd figured that was the reason for the delay. But now he realized it must be an accident, and fire engines meant it was a bad one.

Another fire engine went past. Then another ambulance, twos-and-blues full on. Followed by a rescue truck.

He looked at the clock again: 9.15 p.m. He should have picked her up three-quarters of an hour ago, in Tunbridge Wells, which was still a good twenty minutes away without this hold-up.

Terry Miller, a newly divorced Detective Inspector in Grace's division, had been regaling him with boasts about his conquests from a couple of internet dating sites and urging Grace to sign up. Roy had resisted, then, when he started finding suggestive emails in his inbox from different women, found out to his fury that Terry Miller had signed him up to a site called U-Date without telling him.

He still had no idea what had prompted him to actually respond to one of the emails. Loneliness? Curiosity? Lust? He wasn't sure. For the past eight years he had got through life just by going steadily from day to day. Some days he tried to forget, other days he felt guilty for not remembering.

Sandy.

Now he was suddenly feeling guilty for going on this date.

She looked gorgeous – from her photo, at any rate. He liked her name, too. Claudine. French-sounding, it had something exotic. Her picture was hot! Amber hair, seriously pretty face, tight blouse showing a weapons-grade bust, sitting on the edge of a bed with a miniskirt pulled high enough to show she was wearing lace-topped hold-ups and *might* not be wearing knickers.

They'd had just one phone conversation, in which she had practically seduced him down the line. A bunch of flowers he'd bought at a petrol station lay on the passenger seat beside him. Red roses – corny, he knew, but that was the old-fashioned romantic in him. People were right, he did need to move on, somehow. He could count the dates he'd had in the past eight and three-quarter years on just one hand. He simply could not accept there might be another Miss Right out there. That there could ever be anyone who matched up to Sandy.

Maybe tonight that feeling would change?

Claudine Lamont. Nice name, nice voice.

Turn those sodding fog lamps off!

He smelled the sweet scent of the flowers. Hoped he smelled OK, too.

In the ambient glow from the Alfa's dash and the tail lights of the car in front, he stared up at the mirror, unsure what he expected to see. Sadness stared back at him.

You have to move on.

He swallowed more water. Yup.

In just over two months he would be thirty-nine. In just over two months also another anniversary loomed. On 26 July Sandy would have been gone for nine years. Vanished into thin air, on his thirtieth birthday. No note. All her belongings still in the house except for her handbag.

After seven years you could have someone declared legally dead. His mother, in her hospice bed, days before she passed away from cancer, his sister, his closest friends, his shrink, all of them told him he should do that.

No way.

John Lennon had said, 'Life is what happens to you when you're busy making other plans.' That sure as hell was true.

By thirty-six he had always assumed Sandy and he would have had a family. Three kids had always been his dream, ideally two boys and a girl, and his weekends would be spent doing stuff with them. Family holidays. Going to the beach. Out on day trips to fun places. Playing ball games. Fixing things. Helping them at nights with homework. Bathing them. All the comfortable stuff he'd done with his own parents.

Instead he was consumed with an inner turbulence that rarely left him, even when it allowed him to sleep. Was she alive or dead? He'd spent eight years and ten months trying to find out and was still no nearer to the truth than when he had started.

Outside of work, life was a void. He'd been unable – or unwilling – to attempt another relationship. Every date he'd been on was a disaster. It seemed at times that his only constant companion in his life was his goldfish, Marlon. He'd won the fish by target shooting at a fairground, nine years ago, and it had eaten all his subsequent attempts to provide it with a companion. Marlon was a surly, anti-social creature. Probably why they liked each other, Roy reflected. They were two of a kind.

Sometimes he wished he wasn't a policeman, that he

did some less demanding job where he could switch off at five o'clock, go to the pub and then home, put his feet up in front of the telly. Normal life. But he couldn't help it. There was some stubbornness or determination gene – or bunch of genes – inside him – and his father before him – that had driven him relentlessly throughout his life to pursue facts, to pursue the truth. It was those genes that had brought him up through the ranks, to his relatively early promotion to Detective Superintendent. But they hadn't brought him any peace of mind.

His face stared back at him again from the mirror. Grace grimaced at his reflection, at his hair cropped short, to little more than a light fuzz, at his nose, squashed and kinked after being broken in a scrap when he'd been a beat copper, which gave him the appearance of a retired prize fighter.

On their first date, Sandy had told him he had eyes like Paul Newman. He'd liked that a lot. It was one of a million things he had liked about her. The fact that she had loved everything about him, unconditionally.

Roy Grace knew that he was physically fairly unimpressive. At five foot, ten inches, he had been just two inches over the minimum height restriction when he'd joined the police, nineteen years back. But despite his love of booze, and an on–off battle with cigarettes, through hard work at the police gym he had developed a powerful physique, and had kept in shape, running twenty miles a week, and still playing the occasional game of rugger – usually on the wing.

Nine-twenty.

Bloody hell.

He seriously did not want a late night. Did not need one. Could not afford one. He was in court tomorrow, and needed to bank a full night's sleep. The whole thought of the cross-examination that awaited him pressed all kinds of bad buttons inside him.

A pool of light suddenly flooded down from above him, and he heard the clattering din of a helicopter. After a moment the light moved forward, and he saw the helicopter descending.

He dialled a number on his mobile. It was answered almost immediately.

'Hi, it's Detective Superintendent Grace speaking. I'm sitting in a traffic jam on the A26 south of Crowborough, there seems to be an accident somewhere ahead – can you give me any information?'

He was put through to the headquarters operations room. A male voice said, 'Hello, Detective Superintendent, there's a major accident. We have reports of fatalities and people trapped. The road's going to be blocked for a while – you'd be best turning around and using another route.'

Roy Grace thanked him and disconnected. Then he pulled his Blackberry from his shirt pocket, looked up Claudine's number and texted her.

She texted back almost instantly, telling him not to worry, just to get there when he could.

This made him warm to her even more.

And it helped him forget about tomorrow.

4

Drives like this didn't happen very often, but when they did, boy, did Davey enjoy them! He sat strapped in the passenger seat next to his dad, as the police car escort raced on in front of them, blue lights flashing, siren *whup, whup, whupping*, on the wrong side of the road, overtaking mile after mile of stationary traffic. Boy, this was as good as any fairground ride his dad had taken him on, even the ones at Alton Towers, and they were about as good as it gets!

'Yeeeha!' he cried out, exuberantly. Davey was addicted to American cop shows on television, which was why he liked to talk with an American accent. Sometimes he was from New York. Sometimes from Missouri. Sometimes Miami. But mostly from LA.

Phil Wheeler, a hulk of a man, with a massive beer belly, dressed in his work uniform of brown dungarees, scuffed boots and black beanie hat, smiled at his son, riding along beside him. Years back his wife had cracked and left from the strain of caring for Davey. For the past seventeen years he had brought him up on his own.

The cop car was slowing now, passing a line of heavy, earth-moving plant. The tow-truck had 'WHEELER'S AUTO RECOVERY' emblazoned on both sides and amber strobes on the cab roof. Ahead through the windscreen, the battery of headlights and spotlights picked up first the mangled front end of the Transit van, still partially embedded beneath the front bumper of the cement truck, then the rest of the van, crushed like a Coke can, lying on its side in a demolished section of hedgerow.

Slivers of blue flashing light skidded across the wet tarmac and shiny grass verge. Fire tenders, police cars and one ambulance were still on the scene, and a whole bunch of people, firemen and cops, mostly in reflective jackets, stood around. One cop was sweeping glass from the road with a broom.

A police photographer's camera flashed. Two crash investigators were laying out a measuring tape. Metal and glass litter glinted everywhere. Phil Wheeler saw a wheel-wrench, a trainer, a rug, a jacket.

'Sure looks a goddamn bad mess, Dad!' Missouri tonight.

'Very bad.'

Phil Wheeler had become hardened over the years, and nothing much shocked him any more. He'd seen just about every tragedy one could possibly have in a motor car. A headless businessman, still in a suit jacket, shirt and tie, strapped into the driver's seat in the remains of his Ferrari, was among the images he remembered most vividly.

Davey, just turned twenty-six, was dressed in his uniform New York Yankees baseball cap the wrong way around, fleece jacket over lumberjack shirt, jeans, heavy-duty boots. Davey liked to dress the way he saw Americans dress, on television. The boy had a mental age of about six, and that would never change. But he had a superhuman physical strength that often came in handy on call-outs. Davey could bend sheet metal with his bare hands. Once, he had lifted the front end of a car off a trapped motor-cycle by himself.

'Very bad,' he agreed. 'Reckon there are dead people here, Dad?'

'Hope not, Davey.'

'Reckon there might be?'

A traffic cop, with a peaked cap and yellow fluorescent waistcoat, came up to the driver's window. Phil wound it down and recognized the officer.

'Evening, Brian. This looks a mess.'

'There's a vehicle with lifting gear on its way for the lorry. Can you handle the van?'

'No worries. What happened?'

'Head-on, Transit and the lorry. We need the van in the AI compound.'

'Consider it sorted.'

Davey took his flashlight and climbed down from the cab. While his dad talked to the cop, he shone the beam around, down at slicks of oil and foam across the road. Then he peered inquisitively at the tall, square ambulance, its interior light shining behind drawn curtains across the rear window, wondering what might be happening in there.

It was almost two hours before they had all the pieces of the Transit loaded and chained onto the flatbed. His dad and the traffic cop, Brian, walked off a short distance. Phil lit a cigarette with his storm-proof lighter. Davey followed them, making a one-handed roll-up and lighting it with his Zippo. The ambulance and most of the other emergency vehicles had gone, and a massive crane truck was winching the front end of the cement lorry up, until its front wheels – the driver's-side one flat and buckled – were clear of the ground.

The rain had eased off and a badger moon shone through a break in the clouds. His dad and Brian were now talking about fishing – the best bait for carp at this time of year. Bored now and in need of a pee, Davey wandered off down the road, sucking on his roll-up, looking up in the sky for bats. He liked bats, mice, rats, voles, all those kinds of creatures. In fact he liked all animals. Animals never laughed at him the way humans used to, when he was at school. Maybe he'd go out to the badger sett when they got home. He liked to sit out there in the moonlight and watch them play.

Jigging the flashlight beam, he walked a short distance into the bushes, unzipped his fly and emptied his bladder onto a clump of nettles. Just as he finished, a voice called out, right in front of him, startling the hell out of him.

'Hey, hello?'

A crackly, disembodied voice.

Davey jumped.

Then he heard the voice again.

'Hello?'

'Shite!' He shone the beam ahead into the undergrowth but couldn't see anyone. 'Hello?' he called back. Moments later he heard the voice again.

'Hello? Hey, hello? Josh? Luke? Pete? Robbo?'

Davey swung the beam left, right, then further ahead. There was a rustling sound and a rabbit tail bobbed, for an instant, in the beam then was gone. 'Hello, who's that?'

Silence.

A hiss of static. A crackle. Then, only a few feet to his right, he heard the voice again. 'Hello? Hello? Hello?'

Something glinted in a bush. He knelt down. It was a radio, with an aerial. Inspecting it closer, with some excitement he realized it was a walkie-talkie.

He held the beam on it, studying it for a little while, almost nervous of touching it. Then he picked it up. It was heavier than it looked, cold, wet. Beneath a large green button he could see the word *talk*.

He pressed it and said, 'Hello!'

A voice jumped straight back at him. 'Who's that?'

Then another voice called out, from some distance away. 'Davey!'

His dad.

'OK, coming!' he yelled back.

Walking on to the road he pressed the green button again. 'This is Davey!' he said. 'Who are you?'

'DAVVVEEEEEYYYY!'

His dad again.

In his panic, Davey dropped the radio. It hit the road hard, the casing cracked and the batteries spilled out.

'COMING!' he shouted. He knelt, picked up the walkie-talkie and crammed it furtively into his jacket pocket. Then he scooped up the batteries and put them in another pocket.

'COMING, DAD!' he shouted again. 'JUST HAD TO TAKE ME A PISS!'

Keeping his hand in his pocket so the bulge wouldn't show, he hurried back towards the truck.

5

Michael pressed the *talk* button. 'Davey?'

Silence.

He pressed the button again. 'Davey? Hello? Davey?'

White-satin silence. Complete and utter silence, coming down from above, rising up beneath him, pressing in from each side. He tried to move his arms, but as hard as he pushed them out, walls pressed back against them. He also tried to spread out his legs, but they met the same, unyielding walls. Resting the walkie-talkie on his chest, he pushed up against the satin roof inches from his eyes. It was like pushing against concrete.

Then, raising himself up as much as he could, he took hold of the red rubber tube, squinted down it, but could see nothing. Curling his hand over it, he brought it to his lips and tried to whistle down it; but the sound was pathetic.

He sank back down. His head pounded and he badly needed to urinate. He pressed the button again. 'Davey! Davey, I need to pee. Davey!'

Silence again.

From years of sailing, he'd had plenty of experience with two-way radios. *Try a different channel*, he thought. He found the channel selector, but it wouldn't move. He pushed harder, but it still wouldn't move. Then he saw the reason why – it had been superglued, so that he couldn't change channels – couldn't get to Channel 16, the international emergency channel.

'Hey! Enough you bastards, come on, I'm desperate!'

With only the most local of movements possible, he held the walkie-talkie close to his ear and listened.

Nothing.

He laid the radio down on his chest, then slowly, with great difficulty, worked his right hand down and into his leather jacket pocket and pulled out the rugged waterproof mobile Ashley had given him for sailing. He liked it because it was different to the common mobiles everyone else had. He pressed a button on it and the display lit up. His hopes rose – then fell again. No signal.

'Shit.'

He scrolled through the directory until he came to his business partner Mark's name.

Mark Mob.

Despite the lack of a signal he pressed the dial button.

Nothing happened.

He tried Robbo, Pete, Luke, Josh in turn, his desperation increasing.

Then he pressed the walkie-talkie button again. 'Guys! Can you hear me? I know you can fucking hear me!'

Nothing.

On the Ericsson display the time showed 11.13.

He raised his left hand until he could see his watch: 11.14.

He tried to remember the last time he'd looked at it. A good two hours had passed. He closed his eyes. Thought for some moments, trying to figure out exactly what was going on. In the bright, almost dazzling light from the torch he could see the bottle wedged close to his neck and the shiny magazine. He pulled the magazine up over his chest, then manoeuvred it until it was over his face and he was almost smothered by the huge glossy breasts, so close to his eyes they were blurred.

You bastards!

He picked up the walkie-talkie and pressed the *talk* button once more. 'Very funny. Now let me out, please!'

Nothing.

Who the hell was Davey?

His throat was parched. Needed a drink of water. His head was swimming. He wanted to be home, in bed with Ashley. They'd be along in a few minutes. Just had to wait. Tomorrow, he would get them.

The nausea he had been feeling earlier was returning. He closed his eyes. Swimming. Drifting. He lapsed back into sleep.

6

In a crappy end to a crappy flight, the whole plane shook with a resounding crash as the wheels thumped the tarmac, exactly five and a half hours later than its scheduled time. As it decelerated ferociously, Mark Warren, worn out and fed up, in his cramped seat, safety belt digging into his belly, which was already aching from too many airline pretzels and some vile moussaka that he was regretting eating, took a final look at the pictures of the Ferrari 360 featured in the road test of his *Autocar* magazine.

I want you, baby, he was thinking. *Want you SO bad! Oh yes I do!*

Runway lights, blurred by driving rain, flashed past his window as the plane slowed down to taxiing speed. The pilot's voice came over the intercom, all charm, and apologies once more, laying the blame on the fog.

Goddamn fog. Goddamn English weather. Mark dreamed of a red Ferrari, a house in Marbella, a life in the sunshine and someone to share it with. One very special lady. If the property deal he had been negotiating up in Leeds came off, he'd be a step nearer both the house and the Ferrari. The lady was another problem.

Wearily, he unclipped his belt, dug his briefcase out from under his legs and shoved his magazine inside it. Then he stood up, mixing with the scrum in the cabin, leaving his tie at half mast, and pulled his raincoat down from the overhead locker, too tired to care how he looked.

In contrast to his business partner, who always dressed

sloppily, Mark usually was fastidious over his appearance. But like his neat, fair hair, his clothes were too conservatively cut for his twenty-eight years, and usually so pristine they looked brand new, straight off the rail. He liked to imagine the world saw him as a gentrified entrepreneur, but in reality, in any group of people, he invariably stood out as the man who looked as if he was there to sell them something.

His watch read 11.48 p.m. He switched on his mobile, and it powered up. But before he could make a call, the battery warning beeped and the display died. He put it back in his pocket. Too damned late now, far too late. All that he wanted now was to go home to bed.

An hour later he was reversing his silver BMW X5 into his underground parking slot in the Van Alen building. He took the lift up to the fourth floor, and let himself into his apartment.

It had been a financial stretch to buy this place, but it took him a step up in the world. An imposing, modern Deco-style building on Brighton seafront, with a bunch of celebrities among the residents. The place had class. If you lived in the Van Alen you were a somebody. If you were a *somebody*, that meant you were rich. All his life, Mark had had just that one goal – to be rich.

The voicemail light was winking away on the phone as he walked through to the large, open-plan living area. He decided to ignore it for a moment as he dumped his briefcase, plugged his mobile into the charger, then went straight to the drinks cabinet and poured himself a couple of fingers of Balvenie whisky. Then he walked over to the window, stared down at the promenade below, still buzzing with people despite the weather and the hour. Beyond that he could see the bright lights of the Palace Pier and the inky darkness of the sea.

All of a sudden his mobile beeped sharply at him. A message. He stepped over and looked at the display. *Shit.* Fourteen new messages!

Keeping it connected to the charger, he dialled his voicemail box. The first message was from Pete, at 7 p.m., asking where he was. The second was from Robbo at 7.45, helpfully telling him they were moving on to another pub, the Lamb at Ripe. The third was at 8.30 from a very drunken-sounding Luke and Josh, with Robbo in the background. They were moving on from the Lamb to a pub called the Dragon, on the Uckfield Road.

The next two messages were from the estate agent concerning the deal in Leeds, and from their corporate lawyer.

The sixth was at 11.05 from a very distressed-sounding Ashley. Her tone startled him. Ashley was normally calm, unflappable.

'Mark, please, please, *please* call me as soon as you get this,' she urged in her soft, distinctive North American accent.

He hesitated, then listened to the next message. It was from Ashley again. Panicky now. And the next, and the next one after that, each at ten-minute intervals. The tenth message was from Michael's mother. She also sounded distraught.

'Mark, I left a message on your home phone, too. Please call me as soon as you get this, doesn't matter what time.'

Mark paused the machine. *What the hell had happened?*

The next call had been Ashley again. She sounded close to hysterics. 'Mark, there's been a terrible accident. Pete,

Robbo and Luke are dead. Josh is on life support in Intensive Care. No one knows where Michael is. Oh God, Mark, please call me just as soon as you get this.'

Mark replayed the message, scarcely able to believe what he had heard. As he listened to it again he sat down, heavily, on the arm of the sofa. 'Jesus.'

Then he played the rest of the messages. More of the same from Ashley and from Michael's mother. *Call. Call. Please call.*

He drained his whisky, then poured out another slug, three full fingers, and walked over to the window. Through the ghost of his reflection he stared down again at the promenade, watching the passing traffic, then out at the sea. Way out towards the horizon he could see two tiny specks of light, from a freighter or tanker making its way up the Channel.

He was thinking.

I would have been in that accident, too, if the flight had been on time.

But he was thinking beyond that.

He sipped the whisky, then sat down on the sofa. After a few moments, the phone rang again. He walked over and stared at the caller display. Ashley's number. Four rings, then it stopped. Moments later, his mobile rang. Ashley again. He hesitated, then hit the *end-call* button sending it straight to voicemail. Then he switched the phone off, and sat down, leaned back, pulling up the footrest, and cradled the glass in his hands.

Ice cubes rattled in his glass; his hands were shaking, he realized; his whole insides were shaking. He went over to the Bang and Olufsen and put on a Mozart compilation CD. Mozart always helped him to think. Suddenly, he had a lot of thinking to do.

He sat back down, stared into the whisky, focusing intently on the ice cubes as if they were runes that had been cast. It was over an hour before he picked up the phone and dialled.

7

The spasms were getting more frequent now. By clenching his thighs together, holding his breath and squeezing his eyes shut, Michael was still just able to ward off urinating in his trousers. He couldn't do this, could not bear the thought of their laughter when the bastards came back and found he had wet himself.

But the claustrophobia was really getting to him now. The white satin seemed to be shrinking in around him, pressing down closer and closer to his face.

In the beam of the torch, Michael's watch read 2.47. *Shit.*

What the hell were they playing at? Two forty-seven. Where the hell were they? Pissed out of their brains in some nightclub?

He stared at the white satin, his head pounding, his mouth parched, his legs knocking together, trying to suppress the pains shooting up through him from his bladder. He didn't know how much longer he could hold off.

In frustration, he hammered with his knuckles on the lid, and hollered, 'Hey! You bastards!'

He looked at his mobile again. No signal. Ignoring that, he scrolled down to Luke's number then hit the dial button. A sharp beep from the machine, and the display on the screen read out *no service*.

Then he fumbled for the walkie-talkie, switched that on and called out the names of his friends again. And then that other voice he dimly remembered.

'Davey? Hello, Davey?'

Only the crackle of static came back to him.

He was desperate for water, his mouth arid and furry. Had they left him any water? He lifted his neck up just the few inches that were available before his head struck the lid, saw the glint of the bottle, reached down. Famous Grouse whisky.

Disappointed, he broke the seal, unscrewed the cap and took a swig. For a moment just the sensation of liquid felt like balm in his mouth; then it turned to fire, burning his mouth, then his gullet. But almost instantly after that he felt a little better. He took another swig. Felt a little better still, and took a third, long swig before he replaced the cap.

He closed his eyes. His headache felt a tiny bit better now. The desire to pee was receding.

'Bastards . . .' he murmured.

8

Ashley looked like a ghost. Her long brown hair framed a face that was as colourless as the patients' in the forest of drip lines, ventilators and monitors in the beds in the ward behind her. She was leaning against the reception counter of the nursing station in the Intensive Care Unit of the Sussex County Hospital. Her vulnerability made her seem even more beautiful than ever, to Mark.

Muzzy from a sleepless night, in a sharp suit and immaculate black Gucci loafers, he walked up to her, put his arms around her, and held her tight. He stared at a vending machine, a drinking water fountain, and a payphone in a perspex dome. Hospitals always gave him the heebie-jeebies. Ever since he'd come to visit his dad after his near fatal heart attack and saw this man who had once been so strong now looking so frail, so damned pathetic and useless – and scared. He squeezed Ashley as much for himself as for her. Close to her head, a cursor blinked on a green computer screen.

She clung to him as if he were a lone spar in a storm-tossed ocean. 'Oh, Christ, Mark, thank God you're here.'

One nurse was busy on the phone; it sounded like she was talking to a relative of someone in the unit, the other one behind the counter, close to them, was tapping out something on a keyboard.

'This is terrible,' Mark said. 'Unbelievable.'

Ashley nodded, swallowing hard. 'If it wasn't for your meeting, you would have been—'

'I know. I can't stop thinking about it. How's Josh?'

Ashley's hair smelled freshly washed, and there was a trace of garlic on her breath, which he barely noticed. The girls had had a hen party last night, arranged in some Italian restaurant.

'Not good. Zoe's with him.' She pointed and Mark followed the line of her finger, across several beds, across the hiss-clunk of ventilators, and the blinking of digital displays, to the far end of the ward, where he could see Josh's wife sitting on a chair. She was dressed in a white T-shirt, tracksuit top and baggy trousers, body stooped, her straggly blonde ringlets covering her face.

'Michael still hasn't turned up. Where is he, Mark? Surely to God you must know?'

As the nurse finished her call, the phone beeped and she started talking again.

'I've no idea,' he said. 'I have absolutely no idea.'

She looked at him hard. 'But you guys have been planning this for weeks – Lucy said you were going to get even with Michael for all the practical jokes he played on the others before they got married.' As she took a step back from him, tossing hair from her forehead, Mark could see her mascara had run. She dabbed at her eyes with her sleeve.

'Maybe the guys had a last-minute change of mind,' he said. 'Sure, they'd come up with all kinds of ideas, like lacing his drink and putting him on a plane to some place, but I managed to talk them out of it – at least I thought I had.'

She gave a wan smile of appreciation.

He shrugged. 'I knew how worried you were, you know, that we'd do something dumb.'

'I was, desperately worried.' She glanced at the nurse, then sniffed. 'So where is he?'

'He definitely wasn't in the car?'

'Absolutely not. I've rung the police – they say that – they say – they—' She began sobbing.

'What did they say?'

In a burst of anger she blurted, 'They won't do anything.'

She sobbed some more, struggling to contain herself. 'They say they've checked all around at the scene of the accident and there's no sign of him, and that he's probably just sleeping off a mighty hangover somewhere.'

Mark waited for her to calm down, but she carried on crying. 'Maybe that's true.'

She shook her head. 'He promised me he wasn't going to get drunk.' Mark gave her a look. After a moment, she nodded. 'It was his stag night, right? That's what you guys do on stag nights, isn't it? You get smashed.'

Mark stared down at grey carpet tiles. 'Let's go and see Zoe,' he said.

Ashley followed him across the ward, trailing a few yards behind him. Zoe was a slender beauty, and today she seemed even more slender to Mark, as he laid his hand on her shoulder, feeling the hard bone beneath the soft fabric of her designer tracksuit top.

'Jeez, Zoe, I'm sorry.'

She acknowledged him with a faint shrug.

'How is he?' Mark hoped the anxiety in his voice sounded genuine.

Zoe turned her head and looked up at him, her eyes raw, her cheeks, almost translucent without make-up, tracked with tears. 'They can't do anything,' she said. 'They operated on him, now we just have to wait.'

He was hooked up to two IVAC infusion pumps, three syringe drivers and a ventilator, which made a steady, soft, eerie hissing sound. A range of data and waveform lines changed constantly on the machine's monitor.

The exit tube from Josh's mouth ended in a small bag, with a tap at the bottom, half filled with a dark fluid. There was a forest of cannulated lines, tagged yellow where they left the pumps and drivers, and tagged with white hand-written labels at the distal end. Wires ran out from the sheets and from his head, feeding digital displays and spiking graphs. What flesh Mark could see was the colour of alabaster. His friend looked like a laboratory experiment.

But Mark was barely looking at Josh. He was looking at the displays, trying to read them, to calculate what they were saying. He was trying to remember, from when he had stood in this same room beside his dying father, which were the ECG, the blood oxygen, the blood pressure readings, and what they all meant. And he was reading the labels on the drip lines. *Mannitol. Pentastarch. Morphine. Midazolam. Noradrenaline.* And he was thinking. Josh had always had it made. Smooth good looks, rich parents. The insurance loss adjuster, always calculating, mapping out his life, forever talking about five-year plans, ten-year plans, life goals. He was the first of the gang to get married, as he wanted to have kids early, so he would still be young enough to enjoy his life after they'd grown up. Marrying the perfect wife, darling little rich girl Zoe, totally fertile, allowed him to fulfil his plan. She'd delivered him two equally perfect babies in rapid succession.

Mark shot a glance around the ward, taking in the nurses, the doctors, marking their positions, then his eyes dropped to the drip lines into Josh's neck and into the back of his hand, just behind the plastic tag bearing his name.

Then they moved across to the ventilator. Then up to the ECG. Warning buzzers would sound if the heart rate dropped too low. Or the blood oxygen level.

Josh surviving would be a problem – he'd lain awake most of the night thinking about that, and had come to the reluctant conclusion it wasn't an option he could entertain.

9

Courtroom One at Lewes Crown Court always felt to Roy Grace as if it had been deliberately designed to intimidate and impress. It didn't carry any higher status than the rest of the courtrooms in this building, but it felt as if it did. Georgian, it had a high, vaulted ceiling, a public gallery up in the gods, oak-panelled walls, dark oak benches and dock, and a balustraded witness stand. At this moment it was presided over by a bewigged Judge Driscoll, way past his sell-by date, who sat, looking half asleep, in a vivid red-backed chair beneath the coat of arms bearing the legend. *'Dieu et mon droit'*. The place looked like a theatre set and smelled like an old school classroom.

Now as Grace stood in the witness stand, dressed neatly as he always was for court, in a blue suit, white shirt, sombre tie and polished black lace-ups, looking good out-wardly, he felt ragged inside. Part lack of sleep from his date last night – which had been a disaster – and part nerves. Holding the Bible with one hand, he rattled his way through the oath, glancing around, taking in the scene as he swore for maybe the thousandth time in his career, by Almighty God, to tell the truth, the whole truth and nothing but the truth.

The jury looked the way all juries did, like a bunch of tourists stranded in a coach station. An untidy, ragbag of a group, gaudy pullovers, open-throat shirts and creased blouses beneath a sea of blank faces, all white, ranked in two rows, behind water jugs, tumblers and a mess of loose-leaf jottings. Haphazardly stacked beside the judge were a video player, a slide projector and a huge tape recorder. Below him, the female stenographer peered primly from behind a battery of electronic equipment. An electric fan on a chair swivelled right then left, not having much impact on the muggy late-afternoon air. The public galleries were heaving with press and spectators. Nothing like a murder trial to pull the punters in. And this was the local trial of the year.

Roy Grace's big triumph.

Suresh Hossain sat in the dock, a fleshy man with a pockmarked face, slicked-back hair, dressed in a brown, chalk-striped suit and purple satin tie. He observed the proceedings with a laconic gaze, as if he owned the place and this whole trial had been laid on for his personal entertainment. Slimeball, scumbag, slum landlord. He'd been untouchable for the past decade, but now Roy Grace had finally banged him to rights. Conspiracy to murder. His victim an equally unsavoury business rival, Raymond Cohen. If this trial went the way it should, Hossain was going down for more years than he would survive, and several hundred decent citizens of Brighton and Hove would be able to enjoy their lives in their homes freed from the ugly shadow of his henchmen making every hour a living hell for them.

His mind drifted back to last night. *Claudine. Claudine bloody Lamont.* OK, it hadn't helped that he'd arrived for his date an hour and three-quarters late. But it hadn't helped either that her photograph on the U-Date website was, charitably, a good ten years out of date; nor that she'd omitted to put on her details that she was a non-drinking, cop-hating vegan, whose sole interest in life appeared to be her nine rescue cats.

Grace liked dogs. He had nothing in particular against cats, but he'd never yet met one that he'd connected with, in the way he almost instantly bonded with any dog. After two and a half hours in a dump of a vegetarian restaurant in Guildford, being lectured and grilled alternately about the free spirits of cats, the oppressive nature of the British police and men who viewed women solely as sex objects, he had been relieved to escape.

Now, after a night of troubled, intermittent sleep and a day of hanging around waiting to be called, he was about to be grilled again. It was still raining this afternoon, but the air was much warmer and clammy. Grace could feel perspiration walking down the small of his back.

The defence silk, who had surprised the court by summoning him as a witness, had the floor now, standing up, arrogant stature, short grey wig, flowing black gown, lips pursed into a grin of rictus warmth. His name was Richard Charwell QC. Grace had encountered him before and it had not been a happy experience, then. He detested lawyers. To lawyers, trials were a game. They never had to go out and risk their lives catching villains. And it didn't matter one jot to them what crimes had been committed.

'Are you Detective Superintendent Roy Grace, stationed at CID headquarters, Sussex House, Hollingbury, Brighton?' the silk asked.

'Yes,' Grace answered. Instead of his usual confident voice, his reply came out of the wrong part of his throat, more like a croak.

'And have you had some dealings with this case?'

'Yes.' Another choked, dry-mouthed sound.

'I now tender this witness.'

There was a brief pause. No one spoke. Richard Charwell QC had the ear of the entire court. A consummate actor with distinguished good looks, he paused deliberately for effect before speaking again, in a sudden change of tone that suggested he had now become Roy Grace's new best friend.

'Detective Superintendent, I wonder if you might help us with a certain matter. Do you have any knowledge about a shoe connected with this case? A brown crocodile-skin slip-on loafer with a gold chain?'

Grace eyeballed him back for some moments before answering. 'Yes, I do.' Now, suddenly, he felt a stab of panic. Even before the barrister spoke his next words, he had a horrible feeling about where this might be going.

'Are you going to tell us about the person to whom you took this shoe, Detective Superintendent, or do you want me to squeeze it out of you?'

'Well, sir, I'm not exactly sure what you are getting at.'

'Detective Superintendent, I think you know very well what I'm getting at.'

Judge Driscoll, with the bad temper of a man disturbed from a nap, intervened: 'Mr Charwell, kindly get to the point, we haven't got all day.'

Unctuously, the silk responded, 'Very well, your honour.' Then he turned back to Grace. 'Detective Superintendent, is it not a fact that you have interfered with a vital piece of evidence in this case? Namely this shoe?'

The silk picked it up from the exhibits table and held it aloft for the entire court to see, the way he might have been holding up a sporting trophy he had just won.

'I wouldn't say I had interfered with it all,' Grace responded, angered by the man's arrogance – but, equally, aware this was the silk's game plan, to wind him up, wanting to rile him.

Charwell lowered the shoe, pensively. 'Oh, I see, you

don't consider that you have interfered with it?' Without waiting for Grace to answer, he went on. 'I put it to you that you have abused your position by removing a piece of evidence and taking it to a dabbler in the dark arts.'

Turning to Judge Driscoll, he continued. 'Your honour, I intend to show this court that the DNA evidence that has been obtained from this shoe is unsafe, because Detective Superintendent Grace has affected the continuity and caused possible contamination of this vital exhibit.'

He turned back to Grace. 'I am correct, am I not, Detective Superintendent, that on Thursday, March 9th of this year, you took this shoe to a so-called medium in Hastings named Mrs Stempe? And presumably we are going to hear from you that this shoe has now been to another world? A rather ethereal one?'

'Mrs Stempe is a lady of whom I have a very high opinion,' Grace said. 'She—'

'We are not concerned with your opinions, Detective Superintendent, just the facts.'

But the judge's curiosity seemed piqued. 'I think his opinions are perfectly relevant in this issue.'

After a few moments of silent stand-off between the defence silk and the judge, Charwell nodded reluctant assent.

Grace continued. 'She has helped me on a number of enquiries in the past. Three years ago Mary Stempe gave me sufficient information to enable me to put a name to a murder suspect. It led directly to his arrest and subsequent conviction.'

He hesitated, aware of the intense gazes of everyone in the room, then went on, addressing the silk. 'If I may respond to your concerns over continuity of the exhibit, sir. If you had checked through the records, which you are entitled to do, and looked at the packaging, you would have seen the label was signed and dated when I removed it and when I returned it. The defence have been aware of this exhibit from the start, which was found outside Mr Cohen's house on the night he disappeared, and have never asked to examine it.'

'So you regularly turn to the dark arts in your work as a senior police officer, do you, Detective Superintendent Grace?'

An audible snigger rippled round the courtroom.

'I wouldn't call it the *dark arts*,' Grace said. 'I would call it an alternative resource. The police have a duty to use everything at their disposal in trying to solve crimes.'

'So would it be fair to say you are a man of the occult? A believer in the supernatural?' the silk asked.

Grace looked at Judge Driscoll, who was staring at him as if it was he himself who was now on trial in this court. Desperately trying to think of an appropriate response, he shot a glance at the jury, then the public gallery, before he faced the silk again. And suddenly it came to him.

Grace's voice notched up a gear, more strident, more confident, suddenly. 'What is the first thing this court required me to do when I entered the witness stand?' he asked.

Before the silk could respond, Grace answered for him. 'To *swear on the Holy Bible*.' He paused for it to sink in. 'God is a supernatural being – the *supreme* supernatural being. In a court that accepts witnesses taking an oath to a supernatural being, it would be strange if I and everyone else in this room did not believe in the supernatural.'

'I have no more questions,' the silk said, sitting back down.

The prosecution counsel, also in a wig and silk gown,

stood up and addressed Judge Driscoll. 'Your honour, this is a matter I want to raise in chambers.'

'It's rather unusual,' Judge Driscoll responded, 'but I'm satisfied that it has been dealt with properly. However,' and now his eyes turned to Grace, 'I would hope cases that come before my court are based on evidence rather than the utterings of Mystic Megs.'

Almost the whole court erupted into laughter.

The trial moved on, and another defence witness was called, a bagman for Suresh Hossain called Rubiro Valiente. Roy Grace stayed to listen while this piece of Italian low-life told a pack of lies, which were exposed in rapid succession by the prosecution counsel. By the afternoon recess, the court was so agog with the audacity of the lies that Roy Grace began to hope the business of the shoe might have been overshadowed.

His hopes were dashed when he went outside into Lewes High Street to get some fresh air and a sandwich. Across the street, the news banner headline of the local paper, the *Argus*, shouted to the world:

POLICE OFFICER ADMITS TO OCCULT PRACTICES

Suddenly, he felt badly in need of a drink and a fag.

10

The hunger wouldn't go away no matter how hard Michael tried to block it from his mind. His stomach reminded him with a steady dull ache as if something were chafing away inside it. His head felt light and his hands shaky. He kept thinking of food, of meaty burgers with thick-cut fries and ketchup. When he pushed those from his mind, the smell of broiling lobsters replaced it; then barbecued corn; grilled garlicky mushrooms; eggs frying; sausages; sizzling bacon.

The lid was pressing down against his face and he began to panic again, snatching at the air, gulping it greedily. He closed his eyes, tried to imagine he was fine, he was somewhere warm, on his yacht – in the Med. Lapping water all around, gulls overhead, balmy Mediterranean air. But the sides of the coffin were pushing in. Compressing him. He fumbled for the torch resting on his chest and switched it on, the battery feeble and rapidly failing now. Carefully unscrewing the cap of the whisky bottle with trembling fingers, he brought the neck to his lips. Then he took one miserly sip, swilling the liquid around his parched, sticky mouth, stretching every drop out as far as it would go, savouring every second. The panic subsided and his breathing slowed.

Only some minutes after he had swallowed, after the warm burning sensation that spread down his gullet and through his stomach had faded away, did he turn his concentration back to the task of screwing the lid back on. Half a bottle left. One sip per hour, on the hour.

Routine.

He switched the torch off to conserve the last dregs of juice. Every movement was an effort. His limbs were stiff and he shivered with cold one moment, then broke out in a clammy, feverish sweat the next. His head pounded and pounded – he was desperate for some paracetamol. Desperate for noise above him, for voices. To get out.

Food.

By some small miracle, the batteries in the walkie-talkie were the same as those in the torch. At least he still had those in reserve. At least there was one bit of good news. The only good news. And the other bit was that in an hour he could have another sip of whisky.

Routine kept the panic attacks at bay.

You kept sane if you had a routine. Five years back he had crewed on a thirty-eight-footer sloop across the Atlantic, from Chichester to Barbados. Twenty-seven days at sea. For fifteen of them they'd had a gale on the nose that not once dropped below a force seven, and at times gusted up to ten and eleven. Fifteen days of hell. Watches four hours on and four hours off. Every wave shook every bone in his body, as they crashed down again and again, every chain rattling, every shackle smacking against the decking or the rigging, every knife, fork and plate clattering in its locker. They had got through that by routine. By measuring each day into groups of hours. And then by spacing those hours with small treats. Bars of chocolate. Sips of drink. Pages of a novel. Glances at the compass. Taking turns pumping the bilges.

Routine gave you structure. Structure gave you perspective. And perspective gave you a horizon.

And when you looked at the horizon, you felt calmer.

Now he measured each hour with a small sip of whisky. Half a bottle left, and his horizon was the hour hand of his watch. The watch Ashley had bought him, a silver-rimmed Longines with luminous Roman numerals. It was the classiest watch he had ever owned. Ashley had great taste. She had class. Everything about her was classy, the kink in her long, brown hair, the way she walked, the confidence with which she talked, her classically beautiful features. He loved walking into a room with her. Anywhere. Eyes turned, stared. Jesus, he loved that! There was something special about her. Totally unique.

His mother said that too, and usually she never approved of his girlfriends. But Ashley was different. Ashley had worked on his mum and charmed her. That was another thing he loved about her, she could charm anyone. Even the most miserable damned client. He fell in love with her the day she walked into the office he shared with Mark, for a job interview. Now, just six months later, they were getting married.

His crotch and thighs itched like hell. Nappy rash. Long back he'd given up on his bladder. Twenty-six hours had passed now.

Something must have happened, but he had no idea what. Twenty-six fucking hours of shouting into the walkie-talkie, dialling his mobile and getting the same damned message. *No service.*

Tuesday. Ashley wanted the stag night to be well before the wedding. *You'll get drunk and feel like shit. I don't want you feeling like that on our wedding day. Have it early in the week to give yourself time to recover.*

He pushed up with his hands for the hundredth time. Maybe the two hundredth time. Maybe even the thousandth time. It made no difference. He had already tried grinding a hole in the lid with the only hard implement he had, the casing of his walkie-talkie. The mobile and the torch were both plastic. But the casing still wasn't tough enough.

He switched on the walkie-talkie again. 'Hello? Is anyone there? Hello?'

Static was there.

A dark thought occurred to him. Was Ashley in on this? Was this why she'd been so insistent that he should have the stag party early in the week, on Tuesday? So he could be locked in here – wherever *here* was – for a whole twenty-four hours, longer, without it causing any problem?

Never. She knew he was claustrophobic, and she didn't have a cruel bone in her body. She always put everyone else first, was always thinking about other people's needs.

The number of presents she had bought for his mother and himself had staggered him. And everything exquisitely appropriate. Her favourite perfume. A CD of her favourite singer, Robbie Williams, a cashmere jumper she had been hankering after. A Bose radio he had coveted. How did Ashley find out all these things? It was a knack, a gift, just one of the endless list of attributes that made her such a special person.

And made him the luckiest man in the world.

The torch beam dimmed, noticeably. He switched it off again to conserve the battery and lay still in the darkness again. He could hear his breathing getting faster. What if?

If they never came back?

It was nearly 11.30. He waited, listening for a gaggle of voices that would tell him his friends were back.

Jesus, when he got out of there they weren't half

going to regret this. He looked at his watch again. Twenty-five to midnight. They would be along soon, any minute now.

They *had* to be.

11

Sandy stood over him, grinning, blocking the sunlight, deliberately provoking him. Her blonde hair swung down either side of her freckled face, brushing his cheeks.

'Hey! I have to read – this report – I—'

'You're so boring, Grace, you always have to read!' She kissed his forehead. 'Read, read, read, work, work, work!' She kissed his forehead again. 'Don't you still fancy me?'

She was wearing a skimpy sun dress, her breasts almost falling out the top; he caught a glimpse of her long, tanned legs, her hem riding up her thighs, and suddenly he felt very horny.

He reached up his arms to cup her face, pulling her down to him, staring into those trusting blue eyes, feeling so incredibly – intensely – deeply – in love with her.

'I adore you,' he said.

'Do you, Grace?' Flirting. 'Do you really adore me more than your work?' She pulled her head back, pouted her lips quizzically.

'I love you more than anything in—'

Darkness suddenly. As if someone had pulled out a plug.

Grace heard the echo of his voice in cold, empty air.

'Sandy!' he shouted, but the sound stayed trapped in his throat.

The sunlight faded into a weak orange glow; street lighting leaking in around the bedroom curtains.

The display on the digital clock said 3.02 a.m.

He was sweating, eyes wide open, his heart tossing around in his chest like a buoy in a storm. He heard the clatter of a dustbin – a scavenging cat or a fox. Moments later it was followed by the rattle of a diesel – probably his neighbour three doors down, who drove a taxi and kept late hours.

For some moments he lay still. Closed his eyes, calmed his breathing, tried to return to the dream, clinging as hard as he could to the memory. Like all the recurring dreams he had about Sandy it felt so real. As if they were still together but in a different dimension. If he could just find some way of locating the portal, crossing the divide, they really would be together again, they'd be fine, they'd be happy.

So damned happy.

A huge swell of sadness rolled through him. Then it turned to dread as he started to remember. The newspaper. That damned headline in the *Argus* last night. It was all coming back. Christ, oh Christ. What the hell were the morning papers going to say? Criticism he could cope with. Ridicule was harder. He already got stick from a number of officers for dabbling in the supernatural. He'd been warned by the previous Chief Constable, who was genuinely intrigued by the paranormal himself, that to let his interests be known openly could harm his promotion prospects.

'Everyone knows you're a special case, Roy – having lost Sandy. No one's going to criticize you for turning over every stone on the damned planet. We'd all do the same in your shoes. But you have to keep that in your box, you can't bring it to work.'

There were times when he thought he was getting over her, when he was getting strong again. Then there were moments like now when he realized he had barely progressed at all. He just wished so desperately he could have put an arm around her, cuddled up against her, talked through the problem. She was a glass-half-full person, always positive, and so savvy. She'd helped steer him through a disciplinary tribunal in his early days in the Force which could have ended his career, when he'd been accused by the Police Complaints Authority of using excessive force against a mugger he'd arrested. He'd been exonerated then, largely through following Sandy's advice. She would have known exactly what he should do now.

He wondered sometimes if these dreams were attempts by Sandy to communicate with him. From wherever she was.

Jodie, his sister, told him it was time to move on, that he needed to accept that Sandy was dead, to replace her voice on the answering machine, to remove her clothes from the bedroom and her things from the bathroom, in short – and Jodie could be very short – to stop living in some kind of a shrine to Sandy, and start all over again.

But how could he move on? What if Sandy was alive, being held captive by some maniac? He had to keep searching, to keep the file open, to keep updating the photographs showing how she might look now, to keep scanning every face he passed in the street or saw in a crowd. He would go on until—

Until.

Closure.

On the morning of his thirtieth birthday, Sandy had woken him with a tray on which was a tiny cake with a single candle, a glass of champagne and a very rude birthday card. He'd opened the presents she had given him, then they had made love. He'd left the house later than usual, at 9.15, and reached his office in Brighton shortly after half past, late for a briefing on a murder case. He'd promised to be home early, to go out for a celebratory meal with another couple – his best friend at the time, Dick Pope, also a detective, and his wife, Leslie, who Sandy got on well with – but it had been a hectic day and he'd arrived home almost two hours later than he had intended. There was no sign of Sandy.

At first he'd thought she was angry with him for being so late and was making a protest. The house was tidy, her car and handbag were gone, there was no sign of a struggle.

Then, twenty-four hours later, her car was found in a bay of the short-term car park at Gatwick Airport. There were two transactions on her credit card on the morning of her disappearance, one for £7.50 at Boots, and £16.42 for petrol from the local branch of Tesco. She had taken no clothes and no other belongings of any kind.

His neighbours in this quiet, residential street just off the seafront had not seen a thing. On one side of him was an exuberantly friendly Greek family who owned a couple of cafes in the town, but they had been away on holiday, and on the other side was an elderly widow with a hearing problem, who slept with the television on, volume at maximum. Right now, at 3.45 a.m., he could hear an American cop drama through the party wall between their semi-detached houses. Guns banged, tyres squealed, sirens *whup-whupped*. She'd seen nothing.

Noreen Grinstead, who lived opposite, was the one person he might have expected to have noticed something. A hawk-eyed, jumpy woman in her sixties, she knew everyone's business in the street. When she wasn't tending to her husband, Lance, who was steadily going downhill with

Alzheimer's, she was forever out front in yellow rubber gloves, washing her silver Nissan car, or hosing and scrubbing the driveway, or the windows of the house, or anything else that did or did not need washing. She even brought stuff out of the house to clean it in the driveway.

Very little escaped her eye. But, somehow, Sandy's disappearance had.

He switched the light on and got out of bed, pausing to stare at the photograph of himself and Sandy on the dressing table. It had been taken in a hotel in Oxford during a conference on DNA fingerprinting, a few months before she disappeared. He was lounging back in a suit and tie, on a chaise longue. Sandy, in an evening dress, was lying back against him, hair up in blonde ringlets, beaming her constant irrepressible grin at a waiter they had sequestered to take the picture.

He went over, picked up the frame, kissed the photo then set it down again, and went into the bathroom to urinate. Getting up in the middle of the night to pee was a recent affliction, a result of the health fad he was on, drinking the recommended minimum eight glasses of water a day. Then he padded, clad only in the T-shirt he slept in, downstairs.

Sandy had such great taste. Their house itself was modest, like all the ones in the street, a three-bedroom mock-Tudor semi, built in the 1930s, but she had made it beautiful. She loved browsing the Sunday supplements, women's magazines and design magazines, ripping out pages and showing him ideas. They'd spent hours together, stripping wallpaper, sanding floors, varnishing, painting.

Sandy got into Feng Shui, and built a little water garden. She filled the house with candles. Bought organic food whenever she could. She thought about everything, questioned everything, was interested in everything, and he loved that. Those had been the good times, when they were building their future, cementing their life together, making all their plans.

She was a good gardener, too. She understood about flowers, plants, shrubs, bushes, trees. When to plant, how to prune. Grace liked to mow the lawn but that was about where his skills ended. The garden was neglected now and he felt guilty about that, sometimes wondering what she would say if she returned.

Her car was still in the garage. Forensics had been through it with a toothcomb after it had been recovered, then he'd brought it back home and garaged it. For years he kept the battery on trickle charge, just in case . . . The same way he kept her slippers out on the bedroom floor, her dressing gown hanging on its peg, her toothbrush in its mug.

Waiting for her return.

Wide awake, he poured himself two fingers of Glenfiddich, then sat down in his white armchair in the all-white lounge with its wooden floor and pressed the remote. He flicked through three movies in succession, then a bunch of other Sky channels, but nothing grabbed his attention for more than a few minutes. He played some music, switching restlessly from the Beatles to Miles Davis to Sophie Ellis-Bextor, then back to silence.

He picked one of his favourite books, Colin Wilson's *The Occult*, from the rows of books on the paranormal that filled every inch of his bookshelves, then sat back and turned the pages listlessly, sipping his whisky, unable to concentrate on more than a couple of paragraphs.

That damned defence barrister strutting around in court today had got under his skin, and was now strutting around inside his mind. Richard bloody Charwell. Pompous sodding bastard. Worse, Grace knew he had been outsmarted by the man. Outmanoeuvred and outsmarted. And that really stung.

He picked up the remote again and punched up the news on Teletext. Nothing beyond the same stories that had been around for a couple of days now and were getting stale. No breaking political scandal, no terrorist outrage, no earthquake, no air disaster. He didn't wish ill on anyone, but he had been hoping for something to fill up the morning's headlines and airwaves. Something other than the murder trial of Suresh Hossain.

His luck was out.

12

Two national tabloids and one broadsheet led with front-page splashes on the murder trial of Suresh Hossain, and all the rest of the British morning papers had coverage inside.

It wasn't the trial itself that was the focus of their interest, but the remarks in the witness box made by Detective Superintendent Roy Grace, who at 8.30 in the morning found himself on the carpet in front of his boss, Alison Vosper, feeling as if the clock had been wound back three decades, and he was back at school, trembling in front of his headmistress.

One of Grace's colleagues had nicknamed her 'No. 27', and it had stuck. No. 27 was a sweet and sour dish on the local Chinese takeaway menu. Conversely, when ordering the dish, it was always referred to as an Alison Vosper. That's exactly what she was, sweet and sour.

In her early forties, with wispy blonde hair cut conservatively short, and framing a hard but attractive face, Assistant Chief Constable Alison Vosper was very definitely sour this morning. Even the powerful floral scent she was wearing had an acrid tinge.

Power-dressed in a black two-piece with a crisp white blouse, she sat behind an expanse of polished rosewood desk, in her immaculate ground-floor office in the Queen Anne police headquarters building in Lewes, with its view out across a trimmed lawn. The desk was bare except for a slim crystal vase containing three purple tulips, framed photographs of her husband (a police officer several years older but three ranks her junior) and her two children, an ammonite pen holder and a stack of the morning's newspapers fanned out like a triumphant poker hand.

Grace always wondered how his superiors kept their offices – and their desks – so tidy. All his working life, his own work spaces had been tips. Repositories of sprawling files, unanswered correspondence, lost pens, travel receipts and out-trays that had long given up on the struggle to keep pace with the in-trays. To get to the very top, he decided, required some kind of paperwork management skill for which he was lacking the gene.

Rumour was that Alison Vosper had had a breast cancer operation three years ago. But Grace knew that's all it would ever be, just rumour, because the Assistant Chief Constable kept a wall around herself. Nonetheless, behind her hard-cop carapace, there was a certain vulnerability that he connected to. In truth, at times he fancied her, and there were occasions when those waspish brown eyes of hers twinkled with humour, and when he sensed she might almost be flirting with him. This morning was not one of them.

No handshake. No greeting. Just a curt nod for him to sit in one of the twin high-backed chairs in front of her desk. Then she launched straight in, with a look that was part reproach, part pure anger.

'What the hell is this, Roy?'

'I'm sorry.'

'*Sorry?*'

He nodded. 'I – look, this whole thing got taken out of context—'

She interrupted him before he could continue. 'You

realize this could bring the whole case crashing down on us?'

'I think we can contain it.'

'I've had a dozen calls from the national press already this morning. You've become a laughing stock. You've made us look like a bunch of idiots. Why have you done this?'

Grace was silent for some moments. 'She's an extraordinary woman, this medium; she's helped us in the past. It never occurred to me anyone would find out.'

Vosper leaned back in her chair, staring at Grace, shaking her head from side to side. 'I had great hopes for you. Your promotion was because of me. I put myself on the line for you, Roy. You know that, don't you?'

Not strictly true, but this wasn't the moment to start splitting hairs. 'I know,' he said, 'and I appreciate it.'

She pointed at the newspapers. 'And this is how you show it? This is what you deliver?'

'Come on, Alison, I've delivered Hossain.'

'And now you've given his defence counsel a crack big enough to drive a coach and horses through.'

'No,' he said, rising to this. 'That shoe had already been through forensics, signed out and signed back in. They can't lay an exhibits contamination charge on me. They might be trying to take a pop at my methods, but this won't have any material effect on the case.'

She raised her manicured fingers and started examining them. Roy could see the tips were black from newsprint ink. Her scent seemed to be getting stronger, as if she were an animal excreting venom. 'You're the senior officer, it's your case. If you let them discredit you it could have a very big effect on the outcome. Why the hell did you do it?'

'We have a murder trial and we don't have a body. We *know* Hossain had Raymond Cohen murdered, right?'

She nodded. The evidence Grace had amassed was impressive and persuasive.

'But with no body there's always a weak link.' He shrugged. 'We've had results in the past from mediums. Every police force in the nation's used them at one time or another. Leslie Whittle, right?'

Leslie Whittle was a celebrated case. Back in 1975 the seventeen-year-old heiress had been kidnapped and vanished into thin air. Unable to find any clues to her whereabouts, the police finally acted on information from a clairvoyant using dowsing techniques, who led them to a drainage shaft, where they discovered the unfortunate girl tethered and dead.

'Leslie Whittle wasn't exactly a triumph of police work, Roy.'

'There have been others, since,' he countered.

She stared at him in silence. Then dimples appeared in her cheeks as if she might be softening; but her voice remained cold and stern. 'You could write the number of successes we've had with clairvoyants on a postage stamp.'

'That isn't true, and you know it.'

'Roy, what I know is that you are an intelligent man. I know that you've studied the paranormal and that *you* believe. I've seen the books in your office, and I respect any police officer who can think *out of the box*. But we have a duty to the community. Whatever goes on behind our closed doors is one thing. The image we present to the public is another.'

'The public *believe*, Alison. There was a survey taken in 1925 of the number of scientists who believed in God. It was forty-three per cent. They did that same survey again in 1998, and guess what? It was still forty-three per cent. The only shift was that there were less biologists who believed, but more mathematicians and physicists. There was another survey, only last year, of people who had had some kind of paranormal experience. It was ninety per cent!' He leaned forwards. 'Ninety per cent!'

'Roy, the Great Unwashed want to believe the police spend ratepayers' money on solving crimes and catching villains through established police procedures. They want to believe we are out scouring the country for fingerprints and DNA, that we have labs full of scientists to examine them, and that we are trawling fields, woods, dredging lakes, knocking on doors and interviewing witnesses. They don't want to think we are talking to Madame Arcata on the end of Brighton Pier, are staring into crystal balls or are shifting upturned tumblers around rows of letters on a bloody Ouija board! They don't want to think we are spending our time trying to summon up the dead. They don't want to believe their police officers are standing on the ramparts of castles like Hamlet talking to his father's ghost. Understand what I'm saying?'

'I understand, yes. But I don't agree with you. Our job is to solve crimes. We have to use whatever means are at our disposal.'

She shook her head. 'We're never going to solve every crime, and we have to accept that. What we have to do is inspire public confidence. Make people feel safe in their homes, and on the streets.'

'That's such bullshit,' Grace said, 'and you know that! You know fine well you can massage the crime statistics any way you want.' No sooner had he said it than he regretted his words.

She gave him a thin, wintry smile. 'Get the Government

to give us another hundred million pounds a year and we will eradicate crime in Sussex. In the absence of that all we can do is spread our resources as thinly and as far as they will go.'

'Mediums are cheap,' Grace said.

'Not when they damage our credibility.' She looked down at the papers. 'When they jeopardize a court case they become more than we can afford. Do you hear me?'

'Loudly, if not clearly.' He couldn't help it, the insolence just came out. She was irritating him. Something chauvinistic inside him that he couldn't help, made it harder for him to accept a dressing-down from a woman than from a man.

'Let me spell it out. You're lucky to still have a job this morning. The Chief is not a happy bunny. He's so angry he's threatening to take you out of the public arena for ever, and have you chained to a desk for the rest of your career. Is that what you want?'

'No.'

'Then go back to being a police officer, not a flake.'

13

For the first time since he had joined the Force, Roy Grace had recently begun wondering whether he should ever have become a policeman. From earliest childhood it was all he had wanted to be, and in his teens he had scarcely even considered any other career.

His father, Jack, had risen to the rank of Detective Inspector, and some of the older officers around still talked about him, with great affection. Grace had been in thrall to him as a child, loved to hear his stories, to go out with him – sometimes in a police car, or down to the station. When he was a child, his father's life had seemed so much more adventurous and glamorous than the dull lives most of his friends' dads lived.

Grace had been addicted to cop shows on television, to books about detectives and cops of every kind – from Sherlock Holmes to Ed McBain. He had a memory that bordered on photographic, he loved puzzles, and he was physically strong. And from all he saw and heard from his father, there seemed to be a teamwork and camaraderie in police life that really appealed.

But now, on a day like this, he realized that being a police officer was less about doing things to the best of your abilities and more about conforming to some pre-ordained level of mediocrity. In this modern politically correct world you could be a law enforcement officer at the peak of your career one moment and a political pawn the next.

His latest promotion, making him the second-youngest Detective Superintendent ever in the Sussex Police Force, and which just three months ago had so thrilled him, was fast turning out to be a poisoned chalice.

It had meant moving from the buzz of Brighton police station in the heart of the town, where most of his friends were, out to the relative quiet of the former factory on an industrial estate on the edge of the city, which had recently been refurbished to house the headquarters of Sussex CID.

You could retire from the force on a full pension after thirty years. No matter how tough it got, if he just stuck it out he would be financially set up for life. That was not how he wanted to view his job, his career. At least, not normally.

But today was different. Today was a real downer. A reality-check day. Circumstances changed, he was thinking, as he sat hunched over his desk, ignoring the pinging of incoming emails on his computer screen, munching an egg and cress brown sandwich, and staring at court transcripts of the Suresh Hossain trial in front of him. Life never stands still. Sometimes the changes were good, sometimes less than good. In little over a year's time he would be forty. His hair was going grey.

And his new office was too small.

The three dozen vintage cigarette lighters that were his prize collection hunched together on the ledge between the front of his desk and the window which, unlike the fine view from Alison Vosper's office, looked down onto the parking lot and the cell block beyond. Dominating the wall behind him was the large, round wooden clock that had been a prop in the fictitious police station in *The Bill*. Sandy had bought him it for his twenty-sixth birthday.

Beneath it was a stuffed seven-pound, six-ounce brown trout he had caught on a visit to Ireland some years ago. He kept it beneath the clock to give him a joke he could crack to detectives working under him, about patience and big fish.

Lined up on either side and slightly cramping it were several framed certificates, and a group photograph captioned 'Police Staff College Bramshill. Management of Serious and Series Crimes. 1997', and two cartoons of him in the police ops room, drawn by a colleague who had missed his true vocation. The opposite wall was taken up by bookshelves bulging with part of his collection of books on the occult, and filing cabinets.

His L-shaped desk was cluttered by his computer, overflowing in- and out-trays, Blackberry, separate piles of correspondence, some orderly, most less so, and the latest edition of the magazine with a bad pun of a title, *Fingerprint Whorld*. Rising from the mess was a framed quotation: 'We don't rise to the level of our abilities, we fall to the level of our excuses.'

The rest of the floor space was occupied by a television and video player, a circular table, four chairs and piles of files and loose paperwork, and his leather go-bag, containing his crime-scene kit. His briefcase sat open on the table, his mobile, dictating machine and a bunch of transcripts he had taken home with him last night all lay beside it.

He dropped half his sandwich in the bin. No appetite. He sipped his mug of coffee, checked the latest emails, then logged back on to the Sussex Police site and stared at the list of files he had inherited as part of his promotion.

Each file contained the details of an unsolved murder. It represented a pile of about twenty boxes of files, maybe even more, stacked on an office floor, or bulging out of cupboards, or locked up, gathering mould in a damp police garage in a station in the area where the murder happened. The files contained scene-of-crime photographs, forensic reports, bagged evidence, witness statements, court transcripts, separated into orderly bundles and secured with coloured ribbon. This was part of his new brief, to dig back into the county's unsolved murders, liaise with the CID division where the crime happened, looking for anything that might have changed in the intervening years that could justify reopening the case.

He knew most of their contents by heart – the benefit of his near photographic memory which had propelled him through exams both at school and in the Force. To him each stack represented more than just a human life that had been taken – and a killer who was still free – it symbolized something very close to his own heart. It meant that a family had been unable to lay its past to rest, because a mystery had never been solved, justice had never been done. And he knew that with some of these files being more than thirty years old, he was the last hope the victims and their relatives probably had.

Richard Ventnor, a gay vet battered to death in his surgery twelve years ago. Susan Downey, a beautiful girl raped and strangled and left in a churchyard fifteen years back. Pamela Chisholm, a rich widow found dead in her wrecked car – but with the wrong kind of injuries for a car accident. The skeletal remains of Pratap Gokhale, a nine-year-old Indian boy found under floorboards at the flat of a suspected paedophile – long vanished. These were just a few of the many cases Grace remembered.

Although they were interred, or their ashes had been scattered a long time ago, circumstances changed for them too. Technology had brought in DNA testing, which threw up new evidence and new suspects. The internet had brought new means of communication. Loyalties had changed. New witnesses had emerged from the woodwork. People had divorced. Fallen out with their friends. Someone who wouldn't testify against a mate twenty years ago now hated him. Murder files never closed. *Slow time*, they called it.

The phone rang. It was the management support assistant he shared with his immediate boss, the Assistant Chief Constable, asking if he wanted to take a call from a detective. The whole political correctness thing irritated him more and more, and it was particularly strong in the Police Force. It hadn't been so long ago when they called them *secretaries*, not bloody *management support assistants*.

He told her to put him through, and moments later heard a familiar voice. Glenn Branson, a bright Detective Sergeant he'd worked with several times in the past, fiercely ambitious and razor sharp – as well as being a walking encyclopedia on movies. He liked Glenn Branson a lot. He was probably the closest friend he had.

'Roy? How you doing? Seen you in the papers today.'

'Yup, well you can fuck off. What do you want?'

'Are you OK?'

'No, I'm not OK.'

'Are you busy right now?'

'How do you define busy.'

'Ever given an answer in your life that isn't a question?'

Grace smiled. 'Have you?'

'Listen, I'm being pestered by a woman – about her fiancé. Seems like some stag-night prank has gone seriously wrong, and he's been missing since Tuesday night.'

Grace had to do a mental check on the date. It was Thursday afternoon now. 'Tell me?'

'Thought you'd be in court today. Tried your mobile, but it's off.'

'I'm having lunch. Got a break from court – Judge Driscoll's having a day in chambers dealing with submissions from the defence.'

One of the major drawbacks of bringing a prosecution to trial was the time it consumed. Grace, as the senior officer, had to be either in court or in close touch during the whole trial. This one was likely to last a good three months – and much of that time was just hanging around.

'I don't feel this is a normal missing persons enquiry – I'd like to pick your brains. You free this afternoon by any chance?' Glenn Branson asked.

To anyone else, Grace would have said no, but he knew Glenn Branson wasn't a time waster – and hell, right now he was pleased to have an excuse to get out of the office, even into this shitty weather. 'Sure, I can make some time.'

'Cool.' There was a moment's pause, then Glenn Branson said, 'Look, could we meet at this guy's flat – I think it would be helpful if you saw it for yourself – I can get the key and meet you there.' Branson gave him the address.

Grace glanced at his watch, then at the diary on his Blackberry. 'How about meeting there at half five? We could go on for a drink.'

'It won't take you three hours to get – oh – I guess a man of your age has to start taking it slowly. See you later.'

Grace winced. He didn't like reminders of his looming big four-O birthday. He didn't like the idea of being forty – it was an age when people took stock of their lives. He'd read somewhere that when you reached forty you'd reached the shape your life was going to be for good. Somehow, being thirty-eight was OK. But thirty-nine meant you were very definitely nudging forty. And it wasn't so long ago that he'd considered people who were forty to be old. Shit.

He looked again at the list of files on the screen. Sometimes he felt closer to these people than to anyone else. Twenty murder victims who were dependent on him to bring their killers to justice. Twenty ghosts who haunted most of his waking thoughts – and sometimes his dreams, as well.

14

He had the use of a pool car, but he chose to drive his own Alfa Romeo 147 saloon. Grace liked the car; he liked the hard seats, the firm ride, the almost spartan functionality of the interior, the fruity noise the exhaust made, the feeling of precision, the bright, sporty dials on the dash. There was a sense of exactness about the vehicle that suited his nature.

The big, meaty wipers swung across the screen, clopping the rain from the glass, the tyres hissing on the wet tarmac, a wild Elvis Costello song playing on the stereo. The bypass swept up over a ridge and down into the valley. Through the mist of rain he could see the buildings of the coastal resort of Brighton and Hove sprawling ahead, and beyond the single remaining landmark chimney from the old Shoreham power station, the shimmering strip of grey, barely distinguishable from the sky, that was the English Channel.

He'd grown up here among its streets and its villains. His dad used to reel off their names to him, the families that ran the drugs, the massage parlours, the posh crooked antique dealers who fenced stolen jewels, furniture, the fences who handled televisions and CD players.

It had been a smugglers' village, once. Then George IV had built a palace just a few hundred yards from his mistress's house. Brighton had somehow never managed to shake off its criminal antecedents nor its reputation as a place for dirty weekends. But these gave the city of

Brighton and Hove its edge over any other provincial resort in England, he thought, flicking his indicator and turning off the bypass.

Grassmere Court was a red-brick block of flats about thirty years old, in an upmarket area of Hove, the city's genteel district. It fronted onto a main road and overlooked a tennis club at the rear. The residents were a mixture of ages, mostly twenty- and thirty-something career singles and comfortably off elderly people. On an estate agent's brochure it would probably have rated *highly des res*.

Glenn Branson was waiting in the porch, wrapped in a bulky parka, tall, black, and bald as a meteorite, talking into his mobile. He looked more like a drug dealer than a copper at this moment. Grace smiled – his colleague's massive, muscular frame from years of serious body-building reminded him of the broadcaster Clive James's description of Arnie Schwarzenegger: that he looked like a condom filled with walnuts.

'Yo, old wise man!' Branson greeted him.

'Cut it out, I'm only seven years older than you. One day you'll get to this age too and you won't find it funny.' He grinned.

They slapped high fives, then Branson, frowning, said, 'You look like shit. Really, I mean it.'

'Not all publicity agrees with me.'

'Yup, well I couldn't help noticing you grabbed yourself a few column inches in the rags this morning . . .'

'You and just about everyone else on the planet.'

'Man, you know, for an old-timer you're pretty dumb.'

'Dumb?'

'You don't wise up, Grace. Keep sticking your head above the parapet and one day someone's going to shoot it clean off. There are some days when I think you are just about the biggest dickhead I know.'

He unlocked the front door of the block and pushed it open.

Following him in, Grace said, 'Thanks, you really know how to cheer someone up.' Then he wrinkled his nose. Blindfolded you would always know if you were in an ageing apartment building. The universal smell of worn carpets, tired paint, vegetables boiling behind one of the closed doors. 'How's the missus?' he asked as they waited for the lift.

'Great.'

'And your kids?'

'Sammy's brilliant. Remi's turning into a terror.' He pressed the button for the lift.

After a few moments, Grace said, 'It wasn't how the press made it seem, Glenn.'

'Man, I know that because I know you. The press don't know you, and even if they did, they don't give Jack Shit. They want stories and you were stupid enough to give them one.'

They emerged from the lift on the sixth floor. The flat was at the end of the corridor. Branson unlocked the door and they went in.

The place was small, with a lounge/diner, a narrow kitchen with a granite worktop and a circular steel sink, and two bedrooms, one of which was used as a study, with an iMac computer and work-desk. The rest of this room/office was filled with bookshelves crammed mostly with paperbacks.

In contrast with the dull exterior and drab common parts of the building, the flat felt fresh and modern. The walls were painted in white, very lightly tinged with grey, and the furnishings were modernistic, with a distinct Japanese influence. There were low sofas, simple prints on the walls, a flat-screen television, with a DVD player beneath, and a sophisticated hi-fi system with tall, slender speakers. In the master bedroom there was an unmade futon bed, with handsome louvred doors on the wardrobe, another flat-screen television, and low bedside tables with starkly modern lamps. A pair of Nike trainers sat on the floor.

Grace and Branson exchanged a glance. 'Nice pad,' Grace said.

'Uh huh,' Branson said. *'Life is Beautiful.'*

Grace looked at him.

'I missed it in the cinema. Caught it on Sky. Incredible film – have you ever seen it?'

Grace shook his head.

'All set in a concentration camp. About a dad who convinces his kid that they're playing a game. If they win the game, they get a real tank. I tell you, it moved me more than *Schindler's List* and *The Pianist.'*

'I've never heard of it.'

'I wonder what planet you're on sometimes.'

Grace stared at a framed photograph by the bed. It showed a good-looking man, in his late twenties, with fair hair, black T-shirt and jeans, arm around a seriously attractive woman also in her late twenties, with long, dark hair.

'This him?'

'And her. Michael Harrison and Ashley Harper. Nice-looking couple, right?'

Continuing to stare at them, Grace nodded.

'Getting married on Saturday. At least, that's the plan.'

'Meaning?'

'Meaning, *if* he shows up. Doesn't look too good right now.'

'You said he hasn't been seen since Tuesday night?' Grace looked out of the window. The view down was across a wide, rain-lashed street backed up with traffic. A bus hove into view. 'What do you know about him?'

'Local boy made good. Property developer. Serious player. Double-M Properties. Has a partner called Mark Warren. Recently built a fuck-off development – an old warehouse on Shoreham Harbour. Thirty-two flats, all sold before they were finished. They've been in business for seven years, done a bunch of stuff in the area, some conversions, some new builds. The chick's Michael's secretary, smart bird, seriously gorgeous.'

'You think he's done a runner?'

Branson shook his head. 'Nope.'

Grace picked up the photograph and stared more closely at it. 'Bloody hell, I'd marry her.'

'That's my point.'

Grace frowned. 'Sorry, I'm slow, had a long day.'

'You'd marry her! If I was a single man, I'd marry her. *Anyone in their right mind would marry her*, right?'

'She's seriously gorgeous.'

'She is, seriously gorgeous.'

Grace stared at him blankly.

In mock exasperation, Branson said, 'Jesus, old timer, you losing your touch or something?'

'Maybe I am,' Grace said, blankly. 'What is your point?'

Branson shook his head. 'My point is exactly that. If you were going to marry this babe on Saturday, would you do a runner?'

'Not unless I was nuts.'

'So if he hasn't done a runner, where is he?'

Grace thought for a moment. 'You said on the phone something about a stag-night prank that might have gone wrong?'

'That's what his fiancée said to me. That was my first thought. Stag nights can be brutal. Even when he didn't show up all of yesterday, that's what I still thought then. But to stay out two nights?'

'Cold feet? Another bird?'

'All possible. But I'd like to show you something.'

Grace followed him into the living area. Branson sat down in front of the computer and tapped the keyboard. He was a wizard on computers. Grace had a good technical mind and was pretty well up to speed with most modern technology, but Branson was light years ahead of him.

A password command came up on the screen. Branson tapped furiously, and within a few seconds, the screen filled with data.

'How did you do that?' Grace asked. 'How did you know the password?'

Branson gave him a sideways look. 'There was no password. Most people see a password request and try to put one in. Why would he need one if he wasn't sharing his computer with anyone else?'

'I'm impressed. You really are a closet geek.'

Ignoring the remark, Branson said, 'I want you to take a close look at this.'

Grace did what he was told, and sat down in front of the screen.

15

Just a couple of miles away, Mark Warren was also hunched in front of his computer. The clock on the flat screen showed 6.10 p.m. His shirt sleeves were rolled up, a neglected Starbucks cappuccino beside him, the froth sunken into a wrinkled skin. His normally tidy desk, in the office he'd shared with Michael for the past seven years, was swamped with piles of documents.

Double-M Properties occupied the third floor of a narrow five-storey Regency terraced townhouse, a short distance from Brighton station, which had been their first property development together. Apart from the office he was in, there was a boardroom for clients, a small reception area and a kitchenette. The furnishings were modern and functional. On the walls were photographs of the three racing yachts they owned together, and through which their success could be charted – from their first boat, a Nicholson-27, to a more substantial Contessa-33, to the distinctly upmarket Oyster-42 which was their current toy.

There were also pictures of their developments. The waterfront warehouse at Shoreham Harbour which they had converted into thirty-two apartments. An old Regency hotel in Kemp Town, overlooking the seafront, which they had converted into ten apartments, and two mews houses at the rear. And their latest, and most ambitious development, an artist's impression drawing of a site in five acres of forest land where they had permission to build twenty houses.

His eyes were raw from two sleepless nights, and, taking a moment's respite from the screen, Mark stared out of the window. Directly opposite was a law firm and a discount bedding store. On sunny days it was a perfect spot to ogle the pretty girls walking down the street – but right now it was pelting with rain, people were hurrying, huddled under umbrellas or wrapped in coats, collars turned up, hands in pockets. And Mark was in no mood for thinking about anything except the task in front of him.

Every few minutes, as he had done all day long, he dialled Michael's mobile number. But each time it went straight to voicemail. Unless the phone was either switched off, or the battery was dead, this indicated Michael was still down there. No one had heard anything. Judging from the time of the accident, they would have buried him about 9 p.m. the night before last. About forty-five hours so far.

The main phone line was ringing. Mark could hear the muted warble and saw the light flashing on his extension. He answered it, trying to mask the nervous quaver that was in his voice each time he spoke.

'Double-M Properties.'

A man's voice. 'Oh, hello, I'm calling about the Ashdown Fields development. Do you have a brochure or prices?'

'I'm afraid not, sir, not yet,' Mark said. 'Be a couple of weeks yet. There is some information up on our website – ah – OK, you checked that already. If you want to leave me your name, I'll have someone get back to you.'

Ordinarily he'd have been pleased to have had such an early enquiry about a development, but sales were the last thing on his mind at the moment.

It was important not to panic, he knew. He'd read

enough crime novels, and seen enough cop shows, to know that it was the guys who panicked that got caught. You just had to keep calm.

Keep deleting the emails.

Inbox. Sent Items. Deleted Folder. All other folders.

It wasn't possible to erase emails totally, they would still be out there, stored on a server somewhere in cyberspace, but surely no one was going to look that far, or were they?

He typed keyword after keyword, doing an Advanced Find on each of them. *Michael. Stag. Night. Josh. Pete. Robbo. Luke. Ashley. Plans! Operation revenge!* Checking every email, deleting any that needed deleting. Covering all the bases.

Josh was on life support, his condition critical, and he almost certainly had severe brain damage. Likely to be a vegetable if he survived. Mark swallowed, his mouth dry. He'd known Josh since they were thirteen, at Varndean School. Luke and Michael, too, of course. Pete and Robbo came later: they'd met in a pub in Brighton one boozy night in their late teens. Like Mark, Josh was methodical and ambitious. And he was good-looking. Women always flocked around Josh the same way they went for Michael. Some people had natural gifts in life, others like himself had to struggle every inch of the way. But even at the young age of twenty-eight, Mark had seen enough of life to know that nothing stays the same for very long. If you were patient, if you bided your time, sooner or later you'd get a lucky break. The best predators were the most patient ones.

Mark had never forgotten a wildlife documentary he'd seen on television, filmed in a bat cave in South America. Some tiny micro-organism fed on the bat guano on the floor of the cave; a maggot ate the micro-organism; a beetle ate the maggot; a spider ate the beetle; then a bat ate the spider. It was a perfect food chain. The bat was smart, all it had to do was shit and wait.

His mobile rang. It was Michael's mother, her third call to him this afternoon and her umpteenth today. He remained as unfailingly polite and friendly as ever. There was still no news of Michael, he told her. It was terrible, he really had no idea what had happened to him, the plan had been simply to go on a pub crawl, he could not imagine where Michael might be now.

'Do you think he could be with another woman?' Gill Harrison asked in her timid, gravelly voice. He'd always got on quite well with her, in as much as it was possible. Her husband had gassed himself before he and Michael had met, and Michael said she had retreated into a shell and stayed there ever since. From the photos of her around the house she had been quite beautiful when younger, a blonde bombshell. But ever since Mark had known her, her hair was prematurely grey, her face dry and creased from chain smoking, her spirit withered.

'I guess anything is possible, Mrs Harrison,' Mark replied. He thought for a moment, choosing his words carefully. 'But he adored Ashley.'

'She's a lovely girl.'

'She is, could do with her back here – the best damned secretary we ever had.' He toyed with his mouse for a moment, moving the cursor idly around the screen. 'But you know drink sometimes makes men do irrational things—'

As the words came out he instantly regretted them. Hadn't Michael once told him that his father had been drunk when he killed himself?

There was a long silence, then she said, very placidly,

'I think he'd have had long enough to sober up by now. Michael's a good and a loyal person. Whatever he might have done drunk, he would never hurt Ashley. Something must have happened to him, otherwise he would have called. I know my son.' She hesitated. 'Ashley is in a terrible state. Will you keep an eye on her?'

'Of course.'

There was another silence then, 'How is Josh?'

'Unchanged. Zoe's staying in the hospital. I'll go back there and sit with her – as soon as I've finished in the office.'

'You'll call me the moment you hear anything?'

'Of course.'

He hung up, stared down at his desk, picked up a document, and something caught his eye beneath it. His Palm.

And as he stared at it, cold fear swept through him. *Oh shit*, he thought. *Oh shit, oh shit, oh shit.*

16

After leaving Detective Superintendent Grace, Glenn Branson headed back across town in the pool car he had taken, a blue Vauxhall that reeked of disinfectant – the result of someone either throwing up or bleeding in it last time it had been used. He parked it back in its space in the lot behind the bland edifice of Brighton police station, and walked into the rear entrance and up the stone staircase, to the office he shared with ten other detectives.

It was 6.20; his shift technically finished every day this week at 6, but he was swamped with paperwork after a major drugs bust on Monday, and had permission to do overtime – and he needed the extra cash. But he was going to do only one hour today, until 7. Ari was going out, on another of her self-improvement courses. Mondays she did evening classes in English literature, Thursdays she did architecture. Ever since their daughter Remi had been born she'd gone into panic mode about her perceived lack of education, and was scared she wasn't going to be able to answer their kids' questions when they grew older.

Although most of the computer screens were off, none of the desks were tidy. Every empty open-plan cubicle looked, as usual, as if its occupant had abandoned it in haste and would be returning shortly.

There were just two colleagues still at work in here, DC Nick Nicholl, late twenties, tall as a beanpole, a zealous detective and a fast football forward, and DS Bella Moy, thirty-five, cheery-faced beneath a tangle of brown hair.

Neither acknowledged him. He walked past Nick Nicholl, who was deep in concentration filling out a form, his lips pursed like a kid in an exam as he wrote in block capitals with a ballpoint. Bella was fixated by something on her screen, her left hand, like an automaton, plucking Maltesers from a box on her desk and delivering them to her mouth. She was a slim woman, yet she ate more than any human being Glenn Branson had ever seen.

As he sat down at his desk, the message light was blinking away, as usual. Ari, his wife, Sammy, his eight-year-old son and Remi, his three-year-old daughter, smiled out at him from a framed photo on his desk.

He glanced at his watch, needing to keep an eye on the time. Ari got mad if he was late and caused her to miss the beginning of her class. And besides, it was no hardship – there were few things he treasured more than spending time with his kids. Then his phone beeped.

It was the front desk. A woman had waited an hour to see him and wasn't leaving. Would he mind having a word with her? Everyone else was busy.

'Right, like I'm not busy?' Glenn said to the receptionist, letting irritation show in his voice. 'What does she want?'

'It's to do with the accident on Tuesday – the missing groom.'

Instantly he mellowed. 'Right. OK, I'll come down.'

Despite her bleached-out complexion, Ashley Harper looked every bit as beautiful in the flesh as she did in the photograph he had just seen of her in Michael Harrison's apartment. She was dressed in designer denims, with a bling belt, and carried a classy handbag. He led her into an interview room, got them each a coffee, closed the door and sat down opposite her. Like all the interview rooms it was small and windowless, painted a drab pea green, with a brown carpet and grey metal chairs and table, and reeked of stale cigarette smoke.

She placed her handbag on the floor. Beautiful grey eyes framed by smudged mascara stared out from a wan face, leaden with grief. Fronds of her brown hair fell across her forehead, the rest swooped in a single wave either side of her face and onto her shoulders. Her nails were perfect, as if she had come straight from a manicure. She looked immaculate, and that surprised him a little. People in her state were usually careless about their appearance, but she seemed dressed to kill.

Equally he knew how hard it was to figure women out. Once, when their relationship was going through a rocky time, Ari had given him the book *Men are from Mars, Women are from Venus*. It had helped him go some way towards understanding the mental gulf between men and women (but not all the way).

'You're a hard man to get hold of,' she said, and tossed her head, flicking her long brown hair away from her eyes. 'I left four messages.'

'Yeah, I'm sorry.' He raised his hands. 'I've two of my team off sick and two away on holiday. I understand how you must feel.'

'Do you? Do you have any idea how I feel? I'm meant to be getting married on Saturday and my fiancé's been missing since Tuesday night. We have the church booked, I've got my dressmaker turning up for a fitting, two hundred guests invited, wedding presents pouring in. Do you have *any* idea how I feel?' Tears rolled down her cheeks. She sniffed, fumbled in her handbag and pulled out a tissue.

'Look, I'm sorry. I have been working on your – Michael

– your fianceé's disappearance since we spoke this morning.'

'And?' She dabbed her eyes.

He cradled his beaker of coffee, which was too hot to drink. Had to let it cool. 'I'm afraid I don't have anything to report, yet.' Not strictly true, but he wanted to hear what she had to say.

'What exactly are you guys doing?'

'Like I said this morning on the phone, ordinarily when someone goes missing—'

She cut him short. 'This isn't *ordinarily*, for God's sake. Michael's been missing since Tuesday night. When we're apart he rings me five, ten times a day. It's now two days. Two fucking days, for Christ's sake!'

Branson studied her face carefully, searching for give-aways. But he found nothing. Just a young woman desperate for news of her loved one. *Or* – ever the cynic – *a fine actress.* 'Hear me out, OK? Two days is not in ordinary circumstances enough for alarm. But I agree, in this situation, it is strange.'

'Something's happened to him, OK? This isn't some normal missing persons situation. His friends did something to him, put him somewhere, sent him somewhere, I don't know what the hell they did to him – I—' She lowered her head as if to hide her tears, fumbled for her bag, found it, pulled out a tissue and dabbed her eyes, still shaking her head.

Glenn was moved. She had no idea, and this wasn't the moment to tell her.

'We're doing everything we can to find Michael,' he said gently.

'Like what? What are you doing?'

Her grief lifted momentarily, as if she was wearing it

like a veil. Then another flood of tears and deep, gulping sobs.

'We've done a search around the immediate vicinity of the accident, and we still have people there – sometimes people get disoriented after an accident, so we're searching all the surrounding area – and we've now put out an all-points alert. All police forces have been informed. Airports and seaports—'

Again she cut him short. 'You think he's done a runner? Jesus! Why would he do that?'

Using a subtle technique he had learned from Roy Grace to tell if someone was lying, he asked her, 'What did you have for lunch today?'

She looked at him in surprise. 'What did I have for lunch today?'

'Yes.' He watched her eyes closely. They moved to the right. *Memory* mode.

Human brains are divided into left and right hemispheres. One contains long-term memory storage, and in the other the creative processes take place. When asked a question, people's eyes almost invariably move to the hemisphere they are using. In some people the memory storage is in the right hemisphere and in some the left; the creative hemisphere the opposite one.

When people are telling the truth, their eyes swing towards the memory hemisphere; when they lie, towards the creative one. Branson had learned to tell which by tracking their eyes in response to a simple *control* question such as the one he had just asked, where there would be no need for a lie.

'I didn't have lunch today.'

Now he judged it was time to tell her. 'How much do

you know about your fiancé's business dealings, Miss Harper?'

'I was his secretary for six months, OK? I don't think there's much I don't know.'

'So you know about his Cayman Islands company?'

Genuine surprise in her face. Her eyes shot to the left. Construct mode. She was lying. 'Cayman Islands?' she said.

'He and his partner' – he paused, pulled out his notebook and flipped through several pages – 'Mark Warren. You're aware of this company they have there? HW Properties International?'

She stared at him in silence. 'HW Properties International?' she echoed.

'Uh huh.'

'No, I know nothing about this.'

He nodded. 'OK.'

The tone of her voice had shifted subtly. Thanks to Roy Grace's teaching he knew what it meant. 'Tell me more?'

'I don't know much more, I was hoping you could tell me.'

Her eyes shot to the left again. Construct mode again. 'No,' she said, 'I'm sorry.'

'It's probably not significant anyway,' he said. 'After all, who doesn't want to avoid the tax man?'

'Michael is shrewd. He's a clever businessman. But he would never do anything illegal.'

'I'm not suggesting that, Miss Harper. I'm trying to establish that perhaps you don't know the full picture about the man you are marrying, that's all.'

'Meaning what?'

Again he raised his hands in the air. It was five to seven.

He needed to go. 'It doesn't necessarily mean anything at all. But it's something we have to be aware of.' He gave her a smile.

It was not returned.

17

On the unstable television screen in the chaotically untidy Portakabin annexed to his dad's house on the edge of Lewes, with its view out on to the yard filled with car wrecks, Davey was watching the American cop show, *Law and Order*. His favourite character, a sharp cop called Detective Reynaldo Curtis, was eyeballing a low-life, holding him by the dewlaps with a clenched fist. 'I'm in your face, know what I'm saying?' Reynaldo Curtis snarled.

Davey, in his baggy jeans, and baseball cap tugged tight over his head, lay back on his beat-up sofa munching a Twinkie bar from a supply that was delivered to him weekly from the States by mail order and shouted out, 'Yeah, scumbag! I'm in your face, know what I'm saying?'

The detritus of Davey's quarterpounder and fries dinner lay on the curled carpet tiles at his feet amid the piles of junk – much of it salvaged during his work with his dad – that covered just about every inch of the floor, shelf and table space of his domain.

Beside him sat the pieces of the walkie-talkie he had found a couple of nights back. He'd been meaning to try to fix it, but hadn't got around to it yet. Idly, he picked the main body of it up and peered at it.

The casing was badly cracked. There was a loose bit of plastic with flanges and two AAA batteries that he had retrieved from the road when he had dropped it. He'd really meant to put it back together but somehow it had slipped his mind. Lots of stuff slipped his mind. Just as fast as most things came into his head, they went out again.

Stuff.

There was stuff all the time that made no sense.

Life was like a jigsaw puzzle where bits were always missing. The important bits. Now there were four bits to the walkie-talkie jigsaw. The cracked box, two batteries and the thing that looked like a lid.

He finished his Twinkie, licked the wrapper, then tossed it onto the floor.

'Know what I'm saying?' he announced to no one. Then he leaned forward, picked up the burger's polystyrene box and rummaged around through the mess of ketchup with his finger. 'Yeah! I'm in your face, know what I'm saying?'

He chuckled. There was a commercial break. Some smarmy media fuckwit talking about building society rates. Growing impatient, Davey said 'Come on, baby, let's get back to the show.'

Instead, another commercial came on. On the screen a baby crawled across the carpet talking in a deep male adult voice. Davey watched for some moments, transfixed, wondering how a baby could learn to speak that way. Then his attention drifted back to the walkie-talkie. There was a telescopic aerial, which he pulled out as far as it would go, then pushed back in again. 'Kerloink!' he said. Then out again. 'Kerloink!'

He pointed it at the television screen, staring down its length, taking aim as if it were a rifle. Then the show came back on.

He looked at his brand new watch, which his dad had given him for his birthday yesterday. It was for timing motor races, and had all kinds of buttons, dials and digital displays that he hadn't quite figured out yet from the instruction book. His dad promised to help him read it, get through the tough words. He needed to have it all working OK for this Sunday, the Monaco Grand Prix, it was important he had it ready for that.

There was a knock on his door, then it opened a few inches. His dad stood there, dressed up in a hunting cap with ear flaps, battered old windcheater and wellington boots. 'Five minutes, Davey.'

'Awww. It's *Law and Order*. Could we make it fifteen?'

Cigarette smoke drifted into the room. Davey saw the red glow as his dad took a drag. 'If you want to come shooting rabbits, we have to leave in five minutes. You must have seen every show of *Law and Order* they ever made.'

The ads ended, the show was coming back on. Davey raised a finger to his lips. Grinning in mock despair, Phil Wheeler backed out of the room. 'Five minutes,' he said, closing the door.

'Ten!' Davey shouted after him, American accent now. 'Compromise! Know what I'm saying?'

Davey turned his focus back on the walkie-talkie, thinking it might be cool to take it out rabbit shooting with him. He peered closely into the battery compartment, figured out which way they were supposed to go in, and inserted the batteries. Then he pushed one of two buttons on the side. Nothing happened. He tried the second button and instantly there was a crackle of static.

He held the speaker part to his ear, listening. Just static. And then, suddenly, a male voice so loud he could have been in the room with him.

'Hello?'

Startled, Davey dropped the walkie-talkie on the floor.

'Hello? Hello?'

Davey stared down at it, beaming with delight. Then

there was another knock on his door and his father called out, 'I've got your gun, let's go!'

Then suddenly afraid his father might get mad if he saw the walkie-talkie – he wasn't supposed to take anything they found around wrecks – Davey crouched down on the floor, pressed the other button, which he assumed to be the *talk* one, and hissed furtively, in his American accent, 'Sorry, can't talk, he's in my face – know what I mean?'

Then he shoved the walkie-talkie under the bed and hurried from the room, leaving the television, and Detective Reynaldo Curtis, having to cope without him.

18

'Hey! Hello! Hello! Hello!'

Silence came back at him from the ivory satin.

'Hey, please, help me!'

Michael, sobbing, stabbed the *talk* button repeatedly. 'Please, help me, please help me!

Just static crackle.

'Sorry, can't talk, he's in my face – know what I mean?'

A strange voice, like some ham actor playing an American gangster. Was this all part of the joke? Michael guided the salty tears down to his dry, cracked lips, and for one fleeting, taunting instant savoured the moisture, before his tongue absorbed them like blotting paper.

He looked at his watch. More hours had gone past: 8.50. For how many more hours was this nightmare going to go on? How could they be getting away with it? Surely to God Ashley, his mother, *everyone*, for Christ's sake, must be on to the boys by now. He'd been down here for – for—

A sudden panic hit him. Was it 8.50 in the morning or evening?

It had been afternoon just a while ago, hadn't it? He'd watched each hour on the hour go past. Surely he could not have been so careless to lose track of a whole twelve-hour chunk? It had to be evening now, night, tonight, not tomorrow morning.

Almost forty-eight hours.

What the hell are you all doing?

He pressed his hands down, pushing himself up for a

moment, trying to get some circulation going into his numb backside. His shoulders hurt from being hunched, every joint in his body ached from lack of movement – and from dehydration – he knew about the dangers of that from sailing. His head throbbed incessantly. He could stop it for a few seconds by levering his hands up to his head and digging his thumbs into his temples, but then it came back just as bad as before.

'*Christ,* I'm getting married on Saturday, you fuckwits! Get me out of here!' he shouted as loudly as he could, then pounded the roof and walls with his feet and hands.

The imbeciles. Friday tomorrow. The day before the wedding. He had to get his suit. Haircut. They were going away on honeymoon on Saturday night to Thailand – he had a ton of stuff to do in the office before then, before going away for two weeks. Had to write his wedding speech.

Oh, come on, guys, there's so much I have to do! You've paid me back now, OK? For all the shit I ever did to you lot? You'd paid me back with interest. Big time!

Dropping his hand to his crotch, he located the torch and switched on for a few precious seconds, rationing the battery. The white satin seemed to be ever closer to him; last time he looked it seemed a good six inches above his face, now no more than three, as if this box, coffin, or whatever it was, was slowly, steadily caving in on him.

He took hold of the tube, dangling limp in front of his face, again squinted, trying to peer up into it, but could see nothing. Then he checked he was pushing the right button on the walkie-talkie. He pressed each one in turn. Listened first to static, then pressed *talk* and shouted as loudly as he could, then pressed the *listen* button again. Nothing.

'*Nada!*' he said out aloud. 'Not a fucking sausage.'

Then an image of a frying pan on his mother's stove came into his mind. A frying pan filled with sausages, eggs, bacon, tomatoes, crackling, fizzing, popping, hissing. He could smell them, dammit, smell the bread too, frying in another pan, the tin of baked beans heating up.

Oh Jesus, I'm so hungry.

He turned his mind away from food, from the pain in his stomach that was so bad it felt its own stomach acids were eating their way through his stomach lining. Somewhere inside his pounding skull his brain was reminding him of something he had read; it was about a breed of frogs – or toads – he couldn't remember which right now, which gestated its babies in its stomach rather than womb. For some reason the stomach acids didn't harm the babies.

What's to stop us humans digesting our own stomachs? he thought, suddenly. His brain was racing now, remembering bits of all kinds of stuff.

He remembered reading some years back a theory about Circadian rhythms. All other living organisms on this planet lived a twenty-four-hour cycle, but not humans – our average was twenty-five and a quarter. Tests had been done putting human beings down into dark places for weeks on end, with no clocks. Invariably they thought they had been down there for a shorter period of time than was the case.

Great, I could be one of their fucking lab rats now.

His mouth was so dry his lips stuck together and it hurt to part them. It felt as if their skin was ripping.

Then he shone the torch straight up, looked at the ever-deepening groove he had made in the wood above his face, picked up his leather belt and again began to rub the corner of the metal buckle backwards and forwards against the hard teak – he knew enough about wood to know this was teak – and that teak was just about the hardest wood – closing his eyes tight, in pain, as specks of sawdust struck them, and gradually the buckle became hotter and hotter until he had to stop to let it cool down.

'Sorry, can't talk, he's in my face – know what I mean?'

Michael frowned. Who the hell was this putting on the fake American voice?

How could any of them think this was funny? What the hell had they told Ashley? His mother?

After a few minutes, he stopped scraping, exhausted. Had to keep going, he knew. Dehydration made you tired. Had to fight the tiredness. Had to get the hell out of this damned box. Had to get out and at those bastards, and there was going to be hell to pay.

He struggled on for a few more minutes, scraping, sometimes catching his knuckles, trying to keep his eyes screwed tight against the sawdust that fell and tickled his face, until he was too tired to go on. His hand dropped down and his clenched neck muscles relaxed their grip. Gently his head dropped back.

He slept.

19

The evening was prematurely dark. Mark parked his car just beyond a bus stop a short way up the road, then waited for some moments. The wide street, lacquered black by the torrential rain, was quiet, a trickle of cars passing. No one seemed to be out walking; no one to notice him.

He pulled on a baseball cap low over his face, then, turning up his anorak collar, ran to the sheltered porch of Michael's apartment block, glancing at each of the parked cars in turn, looking for someone seated in there in the dark. Michael was always telling people that Mark was the detail man in their partnership. Then he would qualify that with a remark that Mark hated. *Mark is incredibly anal.*

But Mark knew that he was right, that was exactly why Double-M Properties was so successful, because he was the one who did all the real work. It was his role to scrutinize every line of the builder's estimates, to be there on site, to approve every single material that was purchased, to watch the schedules and to cost everything down to the last penny. While Michael spent half his time swanning around, womanizing, rarely taking anything too seriously. The success of the business was his, he believed, and his alone. Yet Michael had the majority shareholding, just because he'd had more cash to put in when they had started up.

There were forty-two bells to choose from on the entry-phone panel. He pressed one at random, deliberately on a different floor to Michael's. There was no answer. He tried another, with the name 'Maranello'.

After a few moments a crackly male voice in a thick Italian accent said, 'Hello? Yes? Hello?'

'Delivery,' Mark shouted.

'Delivery what?'

'FedEx. From America, for Maranello.'

'You what? Delivery? I – I not – I – I no—'

There was a moment's silence. Then the sharp buzz of the electric latch.

Mark pushed the door and walked in. He went straight to the lift and took it to the sixth floor, then walked down the corridor to Michael's flat. Michael kept a spare key under the doormat in case he locked himself out – which he had done once, drunk and naked. To Mark's relief it was still there. A single Yale key, covered in fluff.

As a precaution he rang the doorbell and waited, watching the corridor, anxious in case anyone should appear and see him. Then he opened the door, slipped in and quickly closed it behind him, and pulled a small torch from his pocket. Michael's apartment looked out onto the street. There was another apartment block opposite. It was probably safe to turn the lights on, but Mark didn't want to take chances. There *might* be someone out there watching.

Pulling off his sodden cap and coat, he hung them on pegs on the wall, then waited some moments, listening, nervous as hell. Through the party wall he could hear what sounded like marching music, from a television turned up too loud. Then with the aid of the flashlight, he began his search.

He went first into the main room, the lounge/dining area, shining the beam onto every surface. He looked at the pile of unwashed dishes on the sideboard, a half-drunk bottle of Chianti with the cork pushed back in, then the coffee table, with the television remote lying next to a glass bowl containing a large candle, partially burnt. A pile of magazines – *GQ, FHM, Yachts and Yachting*. Beside them a red light winked busily on the answering machine.

He listened to the messages. There was one, left just an hour ago, from Michael's mother, her voice nervy.

'Hello, Michael, I'm just checking in case you are back.'

Another was from Ashley, sounding as if she was on her mobile in a bad reception area. 'Michael darling, just calling to see if by chance you're back. Please, please call me the moment you get this. I love you so much.'

The next was from a salesman asking Michael if he would like to take advantage of a new loan facility Barclays Bank was offering to its card holders.

Mark continued playing the messages right through, but there was nothing of interest. He checked the two sofas, the chairs, the side tables, then went into the study.

On the desk in front of the iMac was just the keypad, cordless mouse, a fluorescent mouse pad, a heart-shaped glass paperweight, a calculator, a mobile charger and a black jar crammed with pens and pencils. What he was looking for was not there. Nor was it on the bookshelves or anywhere in Michael's untidy bedroom.

Shit.

Shit, shit, shit.

He left the apartment, walked down the fire-escape steps and went through the rear exit into the dark of the car park. *Bad news*, he thought to himself as he furtively made his way back to the street. *This was really bad news.*

*

Fifteen minutes later he drove his BMW X5 up the steep hill alongside the huge sprawling complex of the Sussex County Hospital, and pulled into the car park for the Accident and Emergency department. He hurried past a couple of waiting ambulances and into the brightly lit reception and waiting area, familiar to him from his visit the previous day.

He walked past the dozens of people waiting forlornly on the plastic seats, beneath a sign which read 'WAITING TIME – THREE HOURS', and along a series of corridors to the lift, and took that to the fourth floor.

Then he followed the signs to the ICU, the smells of disinfectant and hospital food in his nostrils. He rounded a corner, walked past a vending machine, and a payphone in a perspex dome, then saw ahead of him the reception desk of the Intensive Care Unit. Two nurses stood behind the counter, one on the phone, the other talking to a distressed-looking elderly woman.

He made his way across the ward, past four occupied beds, to the corner where Josh had been last night, expecting to see Zoe at his bedside. Instead, he saw a wizened old man, with wild white hair, sunken, liver-spotted cheeks, cannulated and intubated, with a ventilator beside him.

Mark scanned the rest of the beds, but there was no sign of Josh. Panicking that his health had improved and that he had now been moved to another ward, he hurried back to the reception desk and positioned himself in front of the nurse who was on the phone, a plump, cheery-looking woman of about thirty, with a pudding-basin haircut, and a badge that said 'ITU Staff Nurse, MARIGOLD WATTS'. From her demeanour she seemed to be chatting to her boyfriend.

He waited impatiently, resting his arms on the wooden

counter, staring at the bank of black and white monitors showing every bed, and the colour digital displays beneath each of them. He shifted his position a couple of times in rapid succession, trying to catch her eye, but she seemed to be mainly concerned about her dinner.

'Chinese, I think I fancy Chinese. Peking Duck. Somewhere that does Peking Duck, with the pancakes and—'

Then finally she seemed to notice him for the first time. 'Listen, I have to go. Call you back. Love you too.' She turned to Mark, all smiles. 'Yes, can I help you?'

'Josh Walker.' He pointed across the ward. 'He was over there – ah – yesterday. I'm just wondering which ward he's been moved to?'

Her face froze as if she'd suffered a massive infusion of Botox. Her voice changed, also, suddenly becoming tartly defensive. 'Are you a relative?'

'No, I'm his business partner.' Instantly Mark kicked himself for not saying he was his brother. She would never have known.

'I'm sorry,' she said, as if regretting she had terminated her call for him. 'We can only give information to relatives.'

'You can't just tell me where he has been transferred to?'

A buzzer sounded. She looked up at the screens and a red light was flashing beside one of them. 'I have to go,' she said. 'I'm sorry.'

She rushed from her station across the ward.

Mark took out his mobile. Then he saw a large sign: 'THE USE OF MOBILE PHONES IS STRICTLY FORBIDDEN IN THIS HOSPITAL'.

He backed away, hurriedly retracing his steps to the lift, then took it to the ground floor. Totally gripped with fear he raced through a labyrinth of corridors until he reached the main entrance.

Just as he walked up to the reception desk he heard a loud, near-hysterical voice, and saw Zoe, eyes raw, tears streaming down her cheeks, blonde ringlets totally unkempt.

'You and your friend Michael and all your stupid bloody jokes,' she shouted. 'You stupid, bloody immature jerks.'

He stared at her in silence for some moments. Then she collapsed in his arms, sobbing uncontrollably. 'He's dead, Mark, he just died. He's dead. Josh is dead. Oh God, he's dead. Please help me, what am I going to do?'

Mark put his arms around her. 'I – I thought he was OK, that he was going to pull through,' he said, lamely.

'They said there was nothing they could do for him. They said if he had lived he would have been a vegetable. Oh God. Oh God, please help me, Mark. What am I going to say? How do I tell the children their daddy's never coming home? What do I say to them?'

'Do you – do you want a – a cup of tea or something?'

Through deep gulping sobs she said, 'No I don't want a fucking cup of tea. I want my Josh back. Oh God, they've taken him down to the mortuary. Oh Christ. Oh God, what am I going to do?'

Mark stood in silence, holding her tightly, stroking her back, hoping to hell his relief did not show.

20

Michael woke with a start from a confused dream, tried to sit up, and his head instantly crashed against the coffin lid. Crying out in pain he tried to move his arms, and his shoulders met the unyielding satin first on the left and then the right. He tossed and thrashed in a sudden claustrophobic panic.

'Get me out of here!' he screamed, turning, thrashing, gulping air, sweating and shivering at the same time.

'Oh, please, get me out of here!'

His voice was deadened. Flat. It wasn't going anywhere, it was trapped in here just the same as he was.

His hands fumbled for the torch, unable to locate it for several seconds in his panic. Then he found it, switched it on, stared up and then sideways at the walls of his prison. He looked at his watch: 11.15.

Night?

Tomorrow?

Night, it must still be night, Thursday night.

Rivulets of sweat were running down his body. Making a puddle underneath him. He craned his neck to look over his shoulder, shone his torch down and a reflection shone back. Water.

A whole fucking inch.

He looked down in shock. There was no way. No, absolutely no way that he had sweated this much.

Two fucking inches.

He put his hand down again. Shone the torch. Held his

pinkie upright, like a dipstick. The water came up to just below the second joint. There was no way he had sweated that much. Cupping his hands he scooped some up and drank it greedily, oblivious to its salty, muddy taste. He drank more and more; for several minutes it seemed to him that the more he drank, the thirstier he was.

Then when he had finally finished, a new aspect of the rising water came into the equation. He grabbed the belt buckle and began frantically grinding away at the lid, but within minutes, the buckle became so hot it was burning his fingers.

Shit.

He picked up the whisky bottle. Still a third of its contents left. He struck the top of the bottle hard against the wood above him. Nothing happened. He tried again, heard the dull thud. A tiny sliver of glass sheared off. Tragic to waste it. He put the neck into his mouth, tilted it, swallowed a mouthful of the burning liquid. God, it tasted good, so good. He lay back, up-ended the bottle into his mouth and let it pour in, swallowing, swallowing, swallowing until he choked.

He held the bottle up, squinting at it in the beam, having difficulty focusing now, his head swimming. Only a small amount of whisky remained. Just about—

There was a thump right above his head. He felt the coffin move!

Then another thump.

Like a footstep.

Like someone standing on the lid of the coffin right above him!

Hope sprang every nerve in his body. *Oh Jesus Christ, they are getting me out of here at last!*

'OK, you bastards!' he yelled, his voice more feeble than

he had intended. He took a breath, heard another scrape above him. *At fucking last!*

'What the fuck kept you?'

Silence.

He banged his fist against the lid, slurring his words. 'Hey! What fucking kept you? Josh? Luke? Pete? Robbo? Have you any idea how long I've been down here? This is just so not funny, this really is just so not funny. You hear me?'

Silence.

Michael listened.

Had he imagined it?

'Hello! Hey, hello!'

Silence.

No way had he imagined it. There had been footsteps. A wild animal? No, they had been heavier than that. Human heavy.

He knocked frantically with the bottle and then with his fists.

Then very suddenly, very silently, as if he were watching a magic show on television, the breathing tube slid upwards and disappeared.

A few grains of soil fell down through the hole it vacated.

21

Mark could barely see. The red mist of panic that seized him was blurring his vision, fogging his brain. Michael's voice, he had heard Michael's goddamn muffled voice. Oh Jesus!

He closed the door of his BMW in the darkness of the forest, in the lashing rain, jabbed at the ignition, and tried to get the key in. His boots were heavy and tacky with cloying mud, water was streaming down from his baseball cap onto his face.

With his gloved hands he twisted the key and the headlamps came on in a brilliant white glare as the engine turned over and fired. In their beam he saw the grave and the trees beyond. An animal scurried off into the undergrowth, leaves and plants swayed in the wind and rain, for a moment almost surreally like plants in a current on the ocean floor.

He kept staring at the grave, at the corrugated sheet he had carefully pulled back over, and the shrubbery he had uprooted and laid over it to camouflage it. Then he saw the second spade still sticking in the ground and cursed. He climbed down from the car, ran across and grabbed it, and shoved it inside the tailgate. Then he climbed back in, slammed the door, scanning the scene, checking it as well as his blurred vision could.

He was thinking. No construction was due to start here for at least another month, there were still planning issues to be sorted and finalized. No reason for anyone to come here. The planning committee had made their inspection, everything now was on hold for the formal rubber stamp.

Shaking uncontrollably, he put the car in gear and headed back down the track, over the two cattle grids again that had been put there, presumably by the Forestry Commission, to stop deer getting out onto the road.

As he pulled out onto the road he switched on the radio, hitting button after button in search of some music. There was news. Talking. A commercial. He hit the CD button, surfed each of the CDs in turn, but none of them worked for him. He switched the machine off.

Minutes later, as he drove around a curve, the beam of the headlights picked up a row of wreaths on the verge. The sight churned his stomach. Headlights came the other way, passed. Then more headlights. He gripped the wheel tightly, his head swimming, trying to concentrate, trying to think clearly. Then he came to another curve, even sharper, and he was going much too fast. Panicking, he braked sharply, too sharply, felt the judder as the ABS anti-skid kicked in and heard a thump as the breathing tube shot forward off the passenger seat beside him and into the footwell.

Somehow he got around the bend, then saw a lay-by ahead and pulled in. He pressed the SatNav command button, then dialled in *Arlington Reservoir*. After a few moments the system's disembodied female voice announced, 'The route is being calculated.'

Twenty-five minutes later he pulled up at the start of the wooden jetty on the deserted hard of the yacht club of the five-mile-long reservoir and switched off the engine. Grabbing his flashlight, he climbed down and stood in the darkness, listening. The only sound was the clacking of rigging flailing in the wind. No lights on anywhere. The clubhouse was silent. He glanced at his watch. Ten after midnight.

He took the breathing tube from the footwell, then the two shovels from inside the tailgate and walked down to the end of the jetty. He and Michael had begun their sailing here, as kids, before they had become more adventurous and started ocean sailing. From his memory the water here was about twenty feet deep. Not perfect, but it should be adequate. He dropped the breathing tube and then the shovels into the inky, rippled surface and watched them disappear. Then he pulled off his boots and dropped them in too. They sank instantly.

Then he padded back to the car, pulled on the moccasin loafers he had brought and headed home, feeling suddenly very weary. He drove slowly, carefully, not wanting to get clocked by any speed cameras, nor attract the attention of any cop car.

His first task in the morning was going to be to drive straight to a car wash he knew, near Hove station. A place that was always busy, that local cab drivers used, where filthy cars were the norm, where there was always a queue, where no one would take the slightest notice of a BMW X5 caked in mud.

22

Grace took the smouldering stub of his cigar out of his mouth, yawned, then replaced the stub, gripping it with his teeth in a sudden burst of concentration as he scooped up his five cards off the rumpled green baize cloth. A small pile of fifty-pence chips lay in the centre of the table, the antes from each player. In front of him were tumblers of whisky, glasses of wine, piles of cash and chips, and a couple of overflowing ashtrays, surrounded by fragments of crisps and sandwich crumbs. There was a fug of smoke in the room, and outside rain and wind lashed the tall windows, which overlooked the English Channel and the lights of the Palace Pier.

They always played Dealer's Choice, and each time it was his turn, Bob Thornton, a long-retired Detective Inspector, always chose Draw – the poker game Grace liked least of all. He glanced at his watch: 12.38 a.m. Following the tradition of their weekly Thursday-night poker games, the last full round had started at half past midnight, and there would be just two more hands after this one.

It had not been a good night for him; despite wearing his lucky turquoise socks and his lucky blue-striped shirt, he'd had unremittingly lousy cards, made a couple of bad calls, and had been seen on an expensive bluff. The whole game had gone the same way as just about everything else this week: south. One hundred and fifty quid down so far, and the last round was often the most vicious.

He glanced fleetingly at his cards, while concentrating

on the reactions of his five colleagues to their own, and suddenly perked up a little. Three tens. The first decent hand he'd picked up in at least two hours. But a dangerous hand too – good enough that he'd be daft not to play it, but it was no slam-dunk.

Bob Thornton was a hard guy to read. In his mid-seventies, he was a big, energetic man who still played regular squash, with a hawkish face and liver-spotted hands that looked almost reptilian. He wore a green cardigan over a tartan open-neck shirt, corduroy trousers and tennis plimsolls. By a wide margin he was the oldest of the hard core of ten regular players, from whom enough to cobble together a game turned up to play every Thursday, week in, week out, year in, year out, each player taking it in turn to host the evening.

The game had been going on long before Grace had joined the Force. Bob had told them, more than once, that when he had joined the group decades ago he had been the youngest player. Thinking about his looming thirty-ninth birthday, Grace wondered if, like Bob, he would one day end up himself as the old fart of the group.

But age clearly brought some advantages. Bob was sharp as a tack, hard to read and a wily and very aggressive player. Grace could not remember many occasions over the years when Bob had not gone home with a profit – and true to form there was mountain of chips and cash in front of the man right now. Grace watched him hunch his shoulders as he inspected and sorted his cards, keeping them close to his chest, peering at them through his glasses with alert, greedy eyes. Then he opened and shut his mouth, flicking his tongue along his lips in a serpent-like manner, and Grace knew immediately he didn't have to worry about Bob's hand – unless he got lucky in the pick-up.

It was Grace's turn to open the betting. He eyed the rest of his companions.

Tom Allen, thirty-four years old, a detective in Brighton CID, with a serious, boyish face and a mop of curly hair. Dressed in a sweatshirt over a T-shirt, he peered at his cards impassively. Grace always found him hard to read.

Next to Tom sat Chris Croke, a motorcycle cop in Traffic – or *Road Policing*, as the department was now called. With lean and wiry good looks, short blond hair, blue eyes and a quick-fire charm, Croke was a consummate ladies' man, who seemed to live the lifestyle more of a playboy than of a cop. He was hosting tonight's game in his flash, fifth-floor apartment in the coolest apartment block in Brighton, the Van Alen. Ordinarily a cop living such a ritzy lifestyle would have aroused suspicions in Grace, but it was well known that Croke's ex-missus was a socialite heiress to a vast football pools fortune.

Croke had met her when he'd stopped her for speeding and it was his boast that, despite giving her a ticket, she had still married him. Whatever the truth, that was now history, but there was no question he had done well out of the marriage, because when she had finally got tired of the erratic hours that were the lot of any cop's spouse, she had settled a pile of loot on him.

Croke was reckless and unpredictable. In seven years of playing with him, Grace found his body language hard to decipher. He never seemed to care whether he won or lost; it was much easier to read people who had something at stake.

Grace turned his focus on Trevor Carter, a quiet, balding man who worked in IT at Brighton police station. Dressed conservatively in a grey shirt, sleeves rolled up, unfashionably large glasses and drab brown trousers,

Carter was a frugal, family man, who played the game as if the welfare of his four children depended on it. He rarely bluffed, rarely raised and as a result rarely finished any evening up. Carter's giveaway was a nervous twitch of his right eye – the sure-fire signal that he had a strong hand. It was twitching now.

Lastly he looked at Geoff Panone, a Drugs Squad detective of thirty, dressed in a black T-shirt, white jeans and sandals, with near-shoulder-length black hair and a gold earring, who was puffing away on a massive cigar. Grace had learned from watching him over the past couple of years that when he had a good hand at Draw poker, he systematically rearranged the cards in his hand, and when he had a lousy hand, he didn't. Worryingly, he was now rearranging his cards.

'Your bet, Roy,' Bob Thornton told him.

The limit was always the pot on the table. No one could bet higher, which kept the stakes to an affordable level. With six of them putting in a total ante of three pounds, that was the opening ceiling. Not wanting to give anything away, and at the same time wanting to keep everyone in, Grace opened with one pound. All of them came in until Trevor Carter, who raised by three pounds, the twitching of his eye even more pronounced now.

Geoff tossed in a further two pounds. Bob Thornton hesitated just for a fraction, just enough for Grace to know that he definitely did not have a good hand so far and was taking a chance because it was the last round. He decided to press his opportunity and raised by a further three pounds.

Everyone looked at him. They knew he'd had a bad night and this was a giveaway. But it was already too late to do anything about that.

Tom threw his cards down and shook his head. Chris hesitated for some moments, then tossed in five pounds. Trevor and Geoff upped their bets to match also. Bob Thornton followed.

'How many cards?' Bob asked Grace.

Changing two would have revealed he had three of a kind. But changing two would have given him better odds. Grace decided his strategy and changed just one, dumping his three of clubs, retaining a seven of spades. He picked up a seven of hearts.

His heart leapt. *A full house!* Not a top one, but a seriously strong hand. Tens on sevens. Now he was in business!

Certain from watching the change of cards of the others that he had the strongest hand, Grace decided to seize his opportunity and bet the ranch. To his dismay, each of the next three players in turn dropped out and he realized he'd pushed it too hard. But then to his relief Trevor Carter came in and raised him.

Confidently pulling out his wallet, Grace raised him further. Trevor then raised him several more times in succession, until Grace finally lost his nerve, peeled some more banknotes from his wallet and saw him.

Then he puffed nervously on his cigar as Carter flipped over his cards, one by one.

Oh shit, oh shit, oh shit.

A running flush – 7,8,9,10, Jack on the bounce.

'Bloody brilliant!' Croke said.

''Well played!' Bob Thornton exclaimed. 'My God, that was well hidden!'

'I picked them up,' a near-ecstatic Trevor Carter said. 'I picked them up!'

Grace sat back in dismay. It was a hand in a million – maybe even longer odds than that. Impossible to have predicted. And yet he should have realized, from the uncharacteristic strength of Trevor's betting, that Trevor knew he had him beat – and seen him much sooner.

'I reckon your supernatural powers need a bit of topping up, Roy,' chirped Croke.

Everyone laughed.

'Fuck off!' retorted Grace more good-naturedly than he felt. Assistant Chief Constable Alison Vosper was right. People *were* laughing at him. Here it was light-hearted, among friends. But there were others in the Force for whom there was no joke. If he wasn't careful his career could be stalled and he could find himself sidelined.

And right now he was down the best part of three hundred quid.

And by the time the remaining three games had been played, Grace had managed to increase his losses for the evening to four hundred and twenty-two pounds and fifty pence.

He was not a happy bunny as he took the lift down to the underground car park of the block. As he walked towards his Alfa Romeo parked in the visitors' section, he was still so cross with himself and his friends that he barely noticed the mud-streaked BMW X5 that was driving in.

23

'Yeeha!' Davey, soaking wet, unlocked the door of his Por-takabin, then kicked it wide open and strutted in. 'Yeeha!' he announced to the television screen, which was always on, to all his buddies who hung around on the screen. He paused, water trickling down his baseball cap and off his oilskins and muddy wellingtons onto the foam carpet, to check them out. James Spader was in an office, talking to some chick he did not recognize.

'Wasted 'bout two hundred of them darned vermin. Know what I'm saying?' Davey said to James Spader in his best Southern drawl.

But Spader simply ignored him, kept on talking to the chick. Davey picked the remote off his bed and pointed it at the television. 'Yeah, well, I don't need you either, know what I'm saying?' He changed channels. Now he saw two guys he did not know, face to face, arguing with each other. Click.

James Gandolfino was walking through the cars in a Mercedes-Benz dealership, towards a handsome woman with long black hair.

Davey zapped him and he was gone.

He surfed through a whole bunch of channels, but there didn't seem to be anyone interested in talking to him. So he walked over to the fridge. 'Just gonna git me a beer from the minibar,' he announced, pulled out a Coke, flipped it open with one hand, drained half the can, then sat on the bed and belched. His watch said 2.21.

He was wide awake. Wanted to talk to someone, to tell them about all the rabbits he and his dad had shot tonight.

'Here's the thing,' Davey said, then he belched again. He checked the pockets of his oilskins, pulled out a couple of live shotgun cartridges, then hung the oilskins on their hook on the door. He sat on the edge of his bed, wearily, the way he'd seen Clint sit when he was easing off his boots, and dropped his wellingtons one after the other onto the floor.

Then he fondled the two unspent cartridges. 'They've got your name on them,' he informed Sean Penn, who was walking towards him. But Sean Penn wasn't in the mood for conversation either.

Then Davey remembered. There was someone who would talk to him. He knelt down on the floor, reached under the bed for the walkie-talkie, then pulled out the aerial as far as it would go. *Kerloink!*

He pressed the *listen* button and heard the crackle of static. Then he tried the *talk* button.

24

Michael, wide awake, was crying. He did not know what to do, he felt so utterly helpless. It was after two in the morning, Friday morning, he was meant to be getting married tomorrow. There were a million things that needed to be done.

Who or what the hell had taken the breathing tube? Could it have been a badger taking something to its lair? What would a badger want with a length of rubber tubing? Besides, the footsteps had been too heavy. It had been a human, for sure.

Who?

Why?

Where was Ashley, his beloved, darling, gorgeous, caring Ashley? What was she thinking right now, what was going through her mind?

He kept hoping, every moment, that this was some terrible nightmare and in a minute he would wake and be in his bed with Ashley beside him. It just did not make any sense.

There was a sudden sharp hiss, stark and clear. The walkie-talkie!

Then a voice, in a thick Southern drawl said: 'You have any idea how much damage they do? Huh? You got yourself any idea?'

Frantically, Michael scrabbled in the darkness for his torch.

The voice continued, 'Y'know, most folk ain't got no

idea. You git them durn conservationalists talking 'bout protecting the wildlife, but them guys, they don't know shit, know what I'm saying?'

Michael found the torch, switched it on, located the walkie-talkie and pressed the *talk* button. 'Hello?' he said. 'Hello? Davey?'

'Uh huh, I'm talking to ya! Bet you don't have no idea, right?'

'Hello, who are you?'

'Hey dude, you don't need to worry 'bout who I am. Thing is five danged rabbits eat near enough the same amount of grass as one sheep. Go figure.'

Michael gripped the black box, totally confused, wondering if he was hallucinating. What the hell was going on? 'Can I speak to Mark? Or Josh? Or Luke? Or Pete? Robbo?'

There was silence for some moments.

'Hello?' Michael said. 'Are you still there?'

'Ma friend, I ain't going nowhere.'

'Who are you?'

'Maybe I'm the Man With No Name.'

'Listen, Davey, this joke's gone on too long, OK? Too fucking long. Please get me out of here.'

'You gotta be impressed with two hundred rabbits, right?'

Michael stared at the walkie-talkie. Had everyone gone totally insane? Was this the lunatic who had just taken out the breathing tube? Michael tried desperately to think clearly.

'Listen,' he said. 'I've been put here as a joke by some friends. Can you get me out of here, please?'

'You in some kind of bad shit?' the American voice said.

Still unsure whether this was some kind of game, Michael said, 'Bad shit, you got it.'

'What do you think about two hundred rabbits?'

'What do you want me to think about two hundred rabbits?'

'Well dude, what I want you to think is that any dude wastes two hundred rabbits, he's gotta be an OK kind of a dude, know what I'm saying?'

'Totally,' Michael said. 'I totally agree with you.'

'OK, we're on the same page, that's cool.'

'Sure is. Cool.'

'Don't get much cooler, right, dude?'

'You got it,' Michael said, trying to humour him. 'So maybe you could lift the lid off for me and we could have a discussion about this face to face?'

'I'm kinda tired now. Think I'm going to hunker down, get me some shut-eye, know what I'm saying?'

Panicking, Michael said, 'Hey, no, don't do that, let's keep talking. Tell me more about the rabbits, Davey.'

'Told ya, I'm the Man With No Name.'

'OK, Man With No Name, you don't happen to have a couple of Panadols, because I've one mother of a headache?'

'Panadols?'

'Yes.'

There was silence. Just the crackle of static.

'Hello?' Michael said. 'You still there?'

There was a chuckle. 'Panadol?'

'Come on, please get me out of here.'

After another long silence the voice said, 'Guess that depends where *here* is.'

'I'm in the goddamn coffin.'

'You're shittin' me.'

'No shit.'

Another chuckle. 'No shit, Sherlock, right?'

'Right! No shit, Sherlock.'

'I have to go now, it's late. Shut-eye!'

'Hey, please wait – please—'

The walkie-talkie went silent.

In the fading beam of the flashlight Michael saw that the water had risen considerably just in the past hour. He tested the depth again with his hand. An hour ago it had reached the knuckle of his index finger.

Now it covered his hand completely.

25

Roy Grace, in a white short-sleeve shirt and sombre tie, his collar loose, stared at the text message on his phone, and frowned:

Can't stop thinking about you! Claudine xx

Claudine?

Sitting in his office shortly after 9 a.m., in front of his computer screen, which was pinging with new emails every few moments, feeling dog tired and with a blinding headache, he was cold. It was tipping down with rain outside and there was an icy draught in the room. For some moments he watched it running down his window, staring at the bleak view of the alley wall beyond, then he unscrewed the cap of a bottle of mineral water he'd bought at a petrol station on his way in, rummaged in a drawer of his desk and took out a packet of Panadol. He popped two capsules from the foil, swallowed them, then checked the time the message had been sent: 2.14 a.m.

Claudine.

Oh God. Now it registered.

His cop-hating, vegan blind date from U-Date of Tuesday night. She'd been horrible, the evening had been a disaster, and now she was texting him. Terrific.

He held his mobile phone in his hand, toying with whether to reply or just delete it, when his door opened and Branson walked in, dressed in a crisp brown suit, a violent tie and two-tone brown and cream correspondent's shoes, holding a capped Starbucks coffee in one hand and two paper bags in the other.

'Yo, man!' Branson greeted him, breezily, as usual, plonking himself in the chair opposite Grace and setting the coffee and paper bag down on his desk. 'Still own a shirt, I see.'

'Very funny,' Grace said.

'You win last night?'

'No, I did not sodding well win.' Grace was still smarting at his loss. Four hundred and twenty quid. Money wasn't a problem for him, and he had no debts, but he hated losing, especially losing heavily.

'You look like shit.'

'Thanks.'

'No, I mean, really. You look like absolute shit.'

'Nice of you to come all this way to tell me.'

'You ever see *The Cincinatti Kid?*'

'I don't remember.'

'Steve McQueen. Got wiped out in a card game. Had a great ending – you'd remember, the kid in the alley challenging him to a bet, and he tosses his last coin at him.' Branson peeled the lid off, spilling coffee onto the desk, then removed an almond croissant, dropping a trail of icing sugar next to the coffee spill. He proffered it to Grace. 'Want a bite?'

Grace shook his head. 'You should eat something more healthy for breakfast.'

'Oh really? So I get to look like you? What did you have? Organic wheat grass?'

Grace held up the Panadol packet. 'All the nourishment I need. What are you doing here in the sticks?'

'Got a meeting in ten minutes with the Chief. I've been drafted onto the Drugs Performance committee.'

'Lucky you.'

'It's all about profile, isn't that what you told me? Stay visible to your chiefs?'

'Good boy, you remembered. I'm impressed.'

'But actually that's not why I'm here to see you, old-timer.' Branson pulled a birthday card out of the second bag and laid it in front of Grace. 'Getting everyone to sign – for Mandy.'

Mandy Walker was in the Child Protection Unit in Brighton. At one time Grace and Branson had both worked with her.

'She's leaving?' Grace said.

Branson nodded, then mimed a pregnant belly. 'Actually, thought you'd be in court today.'

'Adjourned to Monday.' Grace signed alongside a dozen other names on the card; the coffee and pastry suddenly smelled good. As Branson took a bite of croissant he reached out a hand, took the other croissant from its bag and tore a mouthful off, savouring the instant hit of sweetness. He chewed slowly, peering at Branson's tie, which had such a sharp geometric pattern it almost made him dizzy, then handed back the card.

'Roy, that flat we went to on Wednesday, right?'

'Down The Drive?'

'There's something I don't get. I need the wisdom of your years. You got a couple of minutes?'

'Do I have any choice?'

Ignoring him, Branson said, 'Here's the thing.' He took another bite of his croissant, icing sugar and crumbs falling onto his suit and tie. 'Five guys on a stag night, right? Now—'

There was a rap on the door, then it opened, and Eleanor Hodgson, Grace's management support assistant, brought in a sheaf of papers and files. A rather prim, efficient middle-aged woman, with neat black hair and a plain, slightly old-fashioned face, she always seemed nervous of just about everything. At the moment she looked nervous of Glenn Branson's tie.

'Good morning, Roy,' she said. 'Good morning, DS Branson.'

'How you doing?' Glenn replied.

She put the documents down on Roy's desk. 'I've got a couple of forensics reports back from Huntingdon. One's the one you've been waiting for.'

'Tommy Lytle?'

'Yes. I've also got the agenda and briefing notes for your budget meeting at eleven.'

'Thanks.' As she was leaving the room he quickly sifted through the pile and pulled the Huntington report to the top. Huntingdon, in Cambridge, was one of the forensic centres that Sussex Police used. Tommy Lytle was Grace's oldest 'cold case'. At the age of eleven, twenty-seven years ago, Tommy had set out from school on a February afternoon, to walk home. He'd never been seen again. The only lead at the time had been a Morris Minor van, seen by a witness who had had the presence of mind to write down the number. But no link to the owner, a weirdo loner with a history of sex offences on minors, had ever been established. And then, two months ago, by complete coincidence, the van had showed up on Grace's radar, when a classic car enthusiast who now owned it got stopped for drunken driving.

The advances in forensics from twenty-seven years back were beyond quantum. With modern DNA testing, police forensic scientists boasted, not without substance, that if a human being had ever been in a room, no matter how long ago, given time, they could find evidence. Just one skin cell that had escaped the vacuum cleaners, or a hair, or a clothing fibre. Maybe something one hundred times smaller than a pinhead. There would be a trace.

And now they had the van. And the original suspect was still alive. And forensics had been through that van with microscopes!

Despite his fondness for Branson, suddenly Grace could not wait for him to leave, so he could read the report. If he solved this, it would be the oldest cold case ever solved in the country.

Popping the remains of the croissant in his mouth and talking while he chewed, Branson said, 'Five guys go on a stag night, right? The groom is a real joker – he's pulled a stunt on each of the guys in the past – handcuffed one poor sod to a seat on the night train to Edinburgh when he was meant to be getting married in Brighton the next morning.'

'Nice guy,' Grace said.

'Yes, just the kind of fun bloke you want for your best friend. So. Let's look at what we have: Five of them start out. Somewhere along the line they lose the groom, Michael Harrison. Then they are in an RTA, three of them dead at the scene, the fourth in a coma and he died last night. Michael has vanished, no one has heard a word. It is now Friday morning and he's due to be married in a little over twenty-four hours.'

Branson sipped some coffee, stood up for a moment and walked around the office. He stopped and stared for a moment at the SASCO flip chart, on which a draft rota for something had been written in blue ink. He flipped it over, then picked up a pen and drew on the board.

'We got Michael Harrison.' He wrote his name and drew a circle around it. 'We got the four dead mates.' He drew a second circle. 'Then we have the fiancée, Ashley Harper.' He drew a third circle around her. 'Then the business partner, Mark Warren.' He drew a fourth circle. 'And . . .'

Grace looked at him quizzically.

'We have what we dug out of his computer yesterday, yeah?'

'A bank account in the Cayman Islands.'

Still holding the pen, Branson sat down in front of Grace again.

Grace continued. 'The business partner wasn't at the stag do, you said.'

Branson never failed to be impressed by Grace's memory for detail. He always seemed to retain everything. 'Correct.'

'Because he was stuck out of town on a delayed flight.'

'That's the story so far.'

'So what does he say? Where does he think Michael Harrison went? Did he fuck off to the Cayman Islands?'

'Roy, you have seen his bird. And we agreed no bloke in his right mind would ditch her and run away – she is drop-dead gorgeous, and smart with it. And . . .' Branson pursed his lips.

'And what?'

'She lies. I did your NLP stuff on her, the eye trick. I asked her if she knew about the Cayman Islands account and she said she didn't. She was lying.'

'She was probably just being protective. Covering her boss – and fiancé's arse.' Grace was distracted for an instant by the ping of another incoming email. Then he thought hard. 'What is your take so far?'

'The following possible scenarios: Could be his mates have been paying him back and they've tied him up somewhere. Or he might have had an accident. Or he's got cold feet and done a runner. Or the Cayman Islands features in this somewhere.'

Grace clicked open one of the emails that was flagged as urgent and was from his boss, Alison Vosper. She asked if he was free for a brief meeting at 12.30. He typed back that he was, while he talked to Branson. 'The guy's business partner, Mark Warren, he'd know if they had been planning a prank, like tying him to a tree, or something.'

'Ms Harper says he knows they were planning something, but doesn't know what they decided on.'

'Have you checked out the pubs they visited?'

'Doing that today.'

'CCTV footage?'

'Starting on that, too.'

'Have you checked out the van?'

From the look of sudden panic on Branson's face, Grace saw he hadn't. 'Why the hell not? Isn't that the first place to look?'

'Yeah, you're right. I haven't got fully into gear on this yet.'

'Have you done an all-ports?'

'Yeah, his picture's being circulated this morning. We've put out a missing persons alert.'

Grace felt as if a dark cloud had slipped overhead. *Missing persons.* Every time he heard the phrase it affected him, brought it all right to the front of his mind again. He thought of this woman, Ashley, Branson had described. The day before her wedding and her man gone missing. How must she feel?

'Glenn, you said this guy is a joker – any chance this a prank he's pulling and he's about to turn up, with a big grin on his face?'

'With four of his best mates dead? He'd have to be pretty sick.' Branson looked at his watch. 'What you doing for lunch?'

'Unless I get a call from Julia Roberts, I may be free – oh – subject to No. 27 not detaining me for more than half a hour.'

'How is the delightful Alison Vosper?'

Grace gave him a bleak stare and raised his eyebrows. 'More sour than sweet.'

'Ever thought of shagging her?'

'Yes, for about one nano-second – or perhaps even a femto-second – isn't that the smallest unit of time that exists?'

'Could be a good career move.'

'I can think of a better one.'

'Like?'

'Like not trying to shag the Assistant Chief Constable.'

'Did you ever see Susan Sarandon in *Moonlight Mile*?'

'I don't remember it.'

'She reminds me of Susan Sarandon in that movie. I liked that movie, it was good. Yeah. Want to take a ride out to the car pound with me, lunchtime – talk some more on the way? I'll buy you a pint and slap-up sandwich.'

'Lunch at the car pound? Wow, proves what I thought the moment I saw that tie. You really do have style.'

26

The water was still rising, Michael calculated, at one inch every three hours. It was now just below his ears. He was shivering from cold, getting feverish.

He had worked frantically through the night, sawing with the glass, and he was now on the last fragment of the whisky bottle and his arms ached with exhaustion. He had made a deep groove in the lid, but had still not yet broken through to the outside of it.

He was pacing himself now, two hours on, half an hour off, imagining he was sailing. But he was losing. The water was rising faster than the hole was widening. His head would be underwater before the hole was wide enough to get through.

Every fifteen minutes he pressed the *talk* button on the walkie-talkie. Each time all he got was static back.

It was now 11.03 a.m. Friday.

He ground away, powdered glass and wet soil pouring steadily down, the last fragment of glass shrinking with every minute he worked, thinking, all the time thinking. When the glass was finished he still had the belt buckle. And when that was finished what other instruments did he have to grind away at the wood with? The lens of the torch? The batteries?

A sharp hiss as the walkie-talkie came to life, then a phoney American accent again. 'Hi, buddy, how ya doin'?' This time he recognized it.

Michael pressed the *talk* button. 'Davey?' he said. 'Is that you?'

'Just watching the news on TV,' Davey informed him. 'They're showing an auto wreck I went to with my dad on Tuesday! Boy that was some accident! All of 'em dead – and there's one guy missing!'

Michael suddenly gripped the walkie-talkie with deep intensity. 'What was it, Davey? What was the car?'

'Ford Transit. Boy was it trashed!'

'Tell me more, Davey.'

'There was one guy sticking right out through the wind-shield, half his head missing. Jeez, could see his brains coming out. Knew right away he was a goner. Only one survivor, but he died too.'

Michael began shaking uncontrollably. 'This guy who is missing. Do you know who he is?'

'Uh huh!'

'Tell me who he is?'

'I have to go in a minute, help my dad.'

'Davey, listen to me. I may be that guy.'

'You shittin' me?'

'What's his name, Davey?'

'Uh – dunno. They're just saying he's meant to be get-ting married tomorrow.'

Michael closed his eyes. *Oh no, oh Christ, oh no.* 'Davey, was this accident – ah – this auto wreck – about nine o'clock on Tuesday night?'

'That's about the size of it.'

With new urgency, Michael held the walkie-talkie up close to his mouth. 'Davey, I'm that guy! I'm that guy who is getting married tomorrow!'

'You shittin' me?'

'No, Davey. Listen to me carefully.'

'I have to go – can talk to you later.'

Michael shouted at him, 'DAVEY, DON'T GO, PLEASE DON'T GO. YOU ARE THE ONLY PERSON WHO CAN SAVE ME.'

Silence came back at him. Just the crackle of static to tell him Davey was still on the other end.

'Davey?'

'I have to go, know what I'm saying?'

'Davey, I need your help. You are the only person in the world who can help me. Do you want to help me?'

Another long silence. Then, 'What did you say your name was?'

'Michael Harrison.'

'They just said your name on television!'

'Do you have a car, Davey? Can you drive?'

'My dad has a truck.'

'Can I speak to your dad?'

'Uh – I dunno. He's pretty busy, you know, we have to go out and tow in a wreck.'

Michael thought, desperately hard, how to get through to this character. 'Davey, would you like to be a hero? Would you like to be on television?'

The voice became giggly. 'Me on television? You mean like, me be a movie star?'

'Yes, you could be a movie star! Just get your dad to speak to me and I'll tell him how you could be a movie star. Why don't you get him, put him on the walkie-talkie? How about that?'

'I dunno.'

'Davey, please get your dad.'

'Like here's the problem. My dad don't know I have this walkie-talkie, you see he'd be pretty mad at me if he knew I had this.'

Humouring him, Michael said, 'I think he'd be proud of you, if he knew you were a hero.'

'You reckon?'

'I reckon.'

'I have to go now. See ya! Over and out!'

The walkie-talkie fell silent again.

Pleading with all his heart, Michael was calling: 'Davey, please, Davey, don't leave me, please get your dad, please, Davey!'

But Davey had gone.

27

Ashley, sitting bleakly in an old, deep armchair in the tiny sitting room of Michael's mother's bungalow, stared blankly ahead through a blur of tears. She looked with no appetite at the untouched plate of assorted biscuits on the coffee table, then across at the colour photograph, on the mantelpiece above the fake-coal electric fire, of Michael, aged twelve, on a bicycle, then out through the net curtains at the view across the rain-lashed street to playing fields just below Brighton racecourse.

'I have the dressmaker coming at two,' she said. 'What do you think I should do?' She sipped her coffee then dabbed her eyes with a tissue. Bobo, Gill Harrison's tiny white shih-tzu dog with a bow on its head, looked up at Ashley and gave a begging whine for a biscuit. She responded by stroking the soft hair of its belly.

Gill Harrison sat on the edge of the sofa opposite her. She was dressed in a shapeless white T-shirt, shell-suit trousers and cheap white trainers. A thin ribbon of smoke trailed from a cigarette gripped between her fingers. Light glinted off a diamond engagement ring that was far too large to be real, next to a thin gold wedding band. A bracelet hung loose on her wrist.

She spoke in a gravelly voice, tinged with a coarse Sussex accent, and her strain showed through it. 'He's a good boy. He never let anyone down in his life – that's what I told the policeman what came round. This is not him, not Michael.' She shook her head and took a heavy drag on her cigarette. 'He likes a joke—' She gave a wry laugh. 'When he was a kid he was a terror at Christmas with a flippin' whoopee cushion. Always giving people a fright. But this is not him, Ashley.'

'I know.'

'Something's happened to him. Them boys done something to him. Or he's had an accident as well. He hasn't run out on you. He was round here Sunday evening, we had tea together. He was telling me how much he loved you, how happy he was, bless him. You've made him so happy. He was telling me about this house you've found out in the country that you want to buy, all his plans for it.' She took another drag on her cigarette, then coughed. 'He's a resourceful boy. Ever since his dad—' She pursed her lips, and Ashley could see this was really difficult for her. 'Ever since his dad – he told you?'

Ashley nodded.

'He stepped into his dad's shoes. I couldn't have coped without Michael. He was so strong. A rock, to myself and Carly – you'll like Carly. He sent her the money for her ticket back from Australia so she could be here for the wedding, bless him. She should be arriving here any minute. She phoned me from the airport a couple of hours ago.' She shook her head, in despair.

Ashley, in baggy brown jeans and a ragged white shirt, smiled at her.

'I met Carly just before she went to Australia – she came into the office.'

'She's a good girl.'

'If she's your daughter she must be!'

Gill Harrison leaned forward and stubbed out her cigarette. 'You know, Ashley, all his life Michael has worked so hard. Doing a newspaper round when he was a child to help me and Carly, and then his business with Mark. Nobody ever appreciates him. Mark's a nice boy but—'

'But what?'

Gill shook her head.

'Tell me?'

'I've known Mark since he was a child. Michael and he were inseparable. But Mark's always hung on to his coat tails. I sometimes think Mark's a bit jealous of him.'

'I thought they made a good team,' Ashley said.

Gill pulled a pack of Dunhills from her handbag, shook another cigarette out and stuck it in her mouth. 'I've always told him to watch out for Mark. Michael's innocent, he trusts people too easily.'

'What are you saying?'

She pulled a cheap plastic lighter from her bag and lit the cigarette. 'You have a good influence on Michael. You'll make sure he's all right, won't you?'

Bobo started whining again for a biscuit. Ignoring it, Ashley responded, 'Michael's strong. He's all right, he's fine.'

'Yeah, course he is.' She shot a glance across at the telephone on a table in the corner. 'He's all right. He'll call any time now. Those poor boys. They were so much a part of Michael's life. I can't believe—'

'I can't either.'

'You have your appointment with your dressmaker, dear. You should keep it. The show must go on. Michael will turn up, you do believe that, don't you?'

After a brief hesitation, Ashley said, 'Of course I do.'

'Let's speak later.'

Ashley stood up, walked over to her future mother-in-law, and hugged her hard. 'It's all going to be OK.'

'You're the best thing that ever happened to him. You

are a wonderful person, Ashley. I was so happy when Michael told me that – that—' She was struggling now, emotion choking her words. 'That you – the two of you—'

Ashley kissed her on the forehead.

28

Grace sat, tight-lipped, in the blue Ford, holding the edges of his seat, watching the unfolding country road ahead nervously through the wipers and the heavy rain. Oblivious to his passenger's fear, Glenn Branson swept tidily through a series of bends, proudly demonstrating the skill he had recently acquired from a high-speed police driving course. The radio, tuned to a rap station, was far too loud for Grace.

'Doing it right, aren't I?'

'Uh – yep,' Grace said, deciding the less conversation, the less distraction to Branson, which in turn meant longer life expectancy for both of them. He reached forward and turned the volume down.

'Jay-Z,' Branson said. 'Magic, isn't he?'

'Magic.'

They entered a long right-hander. 'They tell you to keep hard to the left, to open up the view; that's a good tip, isn't it.'

A left-hander was coming up and in Grace's view they were going too fast to get round it. 'Great tip,' he said, from somewhere deep in his gullet.

They got round it, then down into a dip.

'Am I scaring you?'

'Only slightly.'

'You're a wuss. Guess it's your age. Do you remember *Bullitt*?'

'Steve McQueen? You like him, don't you?'

'Brilliant! Best car chase ever in a movie.'

'It ended in a bad car smash.'

'Brilliant, that film,' Branson said, missing his point – or more likely, Grace thought, deliberately ignoring it.

Sandy used to drive fast too. That was part of her natural recklessness. He used to be so scared that Sandy would have a bad accident one day, because she never seemed to be able to get her head around the natural laws of physics that determined when a car would make it around a corner and when it would not. Yet in all the seven years they were together she never once crashed, or even scratched, her car.

Ahead of them, to his relief, he saw the sign – 'BOLNEY CAR POUND' – fixed to tall sheet-metal fencing, topped with barbed wire. Branson braked hard and turned in, past a guard dogs warning sign, into the forecourt of a large modern warehouse building.

Grabbing an umbrella from the boot, and huddling beneath it, they rang the bell on the entryphone beside a grey door. Moments later it was opened by a plump, greasy-haired man of about thirty, wearing a blue boiler suit over a filthy T-shirt, and holding a half-eaten sandwich in a tattooed hand.

'Detective Sergeant Branson and Detective Superintendent Grace,' Branson said. 'I rang earlier.'

Chewing a mouthful, the guy looked blank for a moment. Behind him, several badly wrecked cars and vans sat in the warehouse. His eyes rolled pensively. 'The Transit, yeah?'

'Yup', Branson said.

'White? Came in Tuesday from Wheeler's?'

'That's the one.'

'It's outside.'

They signed in, then followed him across the warehouse floor and out through a side door, into an enclosure that was a good acre in size, Grace estimated, filled with wrecked vehicles as far as the eye could see. A few were under tarpaulins, but most were exposed to the elements.

Holding the umbrella high, just clearing the top of Branson's head, he looked at a Rentokil van that was burnt out after a bad frontal collision – it was hard to imagine anyone had survived in it. Then he noticed a Porsche sports car, compacted to little more than ten feet in length. And a Toyota saloon with its roof cut off.

The place always gave him the heebie-jeebies. Grace had never worked in the Traffic Division, but in his days as a beat copper he'd attended his share of traffic accidents and it was impossible not to be affected by them. It could always happen to anyone. You could set out on a journey, happy, full of plans, and moments later, in the blink of an eye, maybe through no fault of your own, your car was turned into a monster that smashed you to pieces, cut your limbs off and maybe even broiled you alive.

He shuddered. The vehicles that ended up in this place, under secure lock and key, were the ones in the region that had been involved in serious or fatal accidents. They were kept here until the Crash Investigation Unit and sometimes Crime Scene Investigators had obtained all the information they required, before going to a breaker's yard.

The fat man in the boiler suit pointed at a twisted mass of white, with part of its roof cut away, the cab, with the windscreen gone, sheared jaggedly away from the rest of the van, and much of the interior was covered in white plastic sheeting. 'That's the one.'

Both Grace and Branson stared at it in silence. Grace couldn't help his mind dwelling for several uncomfortable moments on the sheer horror of the image. The two of them walked around the van. Grace noticed mud caked on the wheel hubs, and more, heavy mud on the sills and splashes of it up the paintwork, slowly dissolving in the rain.

Handing the umbrella to his colleague, he wrenched open the buckled driver's door, and immediately was hit by the cloying, heavy stench of putrefying blood. It didn't matter how many times he experienced it, each new occasion was just as bad. It was the smell of death itself.

Holding his breath to try to block it out he pulled back the sheeting. The steering wheel had been hacked off and the driver's part of the front bench seat was bent right back. There were blood stains all over the front seat, the floor and the dash.

Covering them with the sheeting, he climbed in. It felt dark and unnaturally silent. It gave him the creeps. Part of the engine had come through the flooring and the pedals were raised in an unnatural position. Reaching across, he opened the glove compartment, then pulled out an owner's manual, a pack of parking vouchers, some fuel receipts and a couple of unlabelled tape cassettes. He handed the cassettes to Glenn.

'Better have a listen to these.'

Branson pocketed them.

Ducking under the jagged cut in the roof, Grace climbed into the back of the van, his shoes echoing on the buckled floor. Branson pulled open the rear doors, letting more light in. Roy stared down at a plastic fuel can, a spare tyre, a wheel-wrench and a parking ticket in a plastic bag. He took the ticket out, and saw it was dated several days before the accident. He handed it to Branson for bagging. There was a solitary, left-foot Adidas trainer which he also passed to Branson, and a nylon bomber jacket. He felt in the pockets, pulling out a pack of cigarettes, a plastic lighter and a dry-cleaning ticket stub with an address in Brighton. Branson bagged each item.

Grace scanned the interior carefully, checking he had missed nothing, thinking hard. Then climbing back out and sheltering under the umbrella, he asked Branson, 'So who owns this vehicle?'

'Houlihan's – the undertakers in Brighton. One of the boys who died worked there – it was his uncle's firm.'

'Four funerals. Should get a nice quantity discount,' Grace said grimly.

'You're a real sick bastard sometimes, you know that?'

Ignoring him, Grace was pensive for a moment. 'Have you spoken to anyone at Houlihan's?'

'Interviewed Mr Sean Houlihan, the owner, himself yesterday afternoon. He's pretty upset as you can imagine. Told me his nephew was a hard-working lad, eager to please.'

'Aren't they all? And he gave him permission to take the van?'

Branson shook his head. 'No. But says it was out of character.'

Roy Grace thought for a moment. 'What's the van ordinarily used for?'

'Collecting cadavers. Hospitals, hospices, old folk's homes, places like that where they'd be spooked to see a hearse. You hungry?'

'I was before I came here.'

29

Ten minutes later they sat at a wobbly corner table in an almost deserted country pub, Grace cradling a pint of Guinness and Branson a Diet Coke, while they waited for their food to come. There was a cavernous inglenook fireplace beside them piled with unlit logs, and a collection of ancient agricultural artefacts hung from the walls. It was the kind of pub Grace liked, a genuine old country pub. He loathed the theme pubs with their phoney names that were insidiously becoming part of every town's increasingly characterless landscape.

'You've checked his mobile?'

'Should have the records back this afternoon,' Branson said.

'Number twelve?'

Grace looked up to see a barmaid holding a tray with their food. Steak and kidney pudding for him, swordfish steak and salad for Glenn Branson.

Grace pierced the soft suet with his knife and instantly steam and gravy erupted from it.

'Instant heart attack on a plate that is,' Branson chided. 'You know what suet is? Beef fat. Yuk.'

Spooning some mustard onto his plate, Grace said, 'It's not what you eat, it's worrying about what you eat. Worry is the killer.'

Branson forked some fish into his mouth. As he started chewing, Grace continued. 'I read that the levels of mercury in sea fish, from pollution, are at danger level. You shouldn't eat fish more than once a week.'

Branson's chewing slowed down and he looked uncomfortable. 'Where did you read that?'

'It was a report from *Nature*, I think. It's about the most respected scientific journal in the world.' Grace smiled, enjoying the expression on his friend's face.

'Shit, we eat fish like – almost every night. *Mercury*?'

'You'll end up as a thermometer.'

'That's not funny – I mean—' Two sharp beeps in succession silenced him.

Grace tugged his mobile from his pocket and stared at the screen.

Why no reply to my text, Big Boy? Claudine XX

'God, this is all I need,' he said. 'A frigging bunny boiler.'

Branson raised his eyebrows. 'Healthy meat, rabbit. Free range.'

'This one isn't healthy and she doesn't eat meat. I mean bunny boiler as in that old movie with Glenn Close.'

'*Fatal Attraction?* Michael Douglas and Anne Archer, 1987. Great movie – it was on Sky on Sunday.'

Grace showed him the text.

Branson grinned. '*Big Boy*, eh?'

'It never got that far and it's never going to.'

Then Branson's mobile rang. He pulled it from his jacket pocket and answered. 'Glenn Branson. Yeah? OK, great, I'll be there in an hour.' He ended the call and left his phone on the table. Looking at Grace, he said, 'The Vodafone log from Michael Harrison's phone just came in. Want to come to the office and help me with it?'

Grace thought for a moment, then checked his diary on his Blackberry. He'd kept the afternoon clear, intending to clear up some paperwork relating to the Suresh Hossain trial that Alison Vosper had requested at their 12.30 meeting, then read the report on the Tommy Lytle case. But that had waited twenty-seven years, and another day would not make much difference either way. Whereas Michael Harrison's disappearance was urgent. Although he did not know the characters, he felt for them. Particularly for the fiancée; he knew just how wrenching it was when a loved one went missing. At this moment, if there was any way he could be of help, he should do it.

'OK,' he said. 'Sure.'

Branson ate his salad, and left the rest of his fish untouched, while Grace tucked into his steak and kidney pudding with relish. 'I read a while ago,' he told Branson, 'that the French drink more red wine than the English but live longer. The Japanese eat more fish than the English, but drink less wine and live longer. The Germans eat more red meat than the English, and drink more beer, and they live longer, too. You know the moral of this story?'

'No.'

'It's not what you eat or drink – it's speaking English that kills you.'

Branson grinned. 'I don't know why I like you. You always manage to make me feel guilty about something.'

'So let's go find Michael Harrison. Then you can enjoy your weekend.'

Branson pushed his fish to the side of his plate and drained his Diet Coke.

'Filled with Aspartame, that stuff,' Grace said, looking disapprovingly at his glass. 'I read a theory on the web that it can give you Lupus.'

'What's Lupus?'

'It's far worse than mercury.'

'Thanks, Big Boy.'

'Now you're just jealous.'

*

As they entered the tired-looking, six-storey building that housed Brighton police station from the parking lot at the rear, Grace felt a pang of nostalgia. This building had a reputation as being the busiest police station in Britain. The place hummed and buzzed and he had loved his time – almost fifteen years – working here. It was the buzz that he missed most about his recent posting to the relatively quiet backwater of the CID headquarters building on the outskirts.

As they climbed up the cement stairs, blue walls on either side of them, the familiar noticeboards with events and procedures pinned to them, he could smell that he was still in a busy police station. It wasn't the smell of hospitals, or schools, or a civil service building, it was the smell of energy.

They went on up past the third floor, where his old office had been, and then along a corridor on the fourth floor, past a large sign dominating an entire noticeboard, with the wording 'OVERALL CRIME DETECTION RATE. APRIL. 27.8%'. Then he followed Branson into the long, narrow office his colleague was setting up as the incident room for Michael Harrison. Six desks, each with a computer terminal. Two of them were occupied, both by detectives he knew and liked – DC Nick Nicholl and DS Bella Moy. There was a SASCO flip chart on an easel and a blank whiteboard on the wall, next to a large-scale map of Sussex, on which was a pattern of coloured pins.

'Coffee?' Branson offered.

'I'm fine for the moment.'

They stopped at Bella's desk, which was covered in neat wodges of paper, among which stood an open box of Maltesers. Pointing at the papers, she said, 'I have Michael Harrison's Vodafone log from Tuesday morning up until nine o'clock this morning. I also thought it would be a good idea to get the ones of the other four with him.'

'Good thinking,' Branson said, impressed with her initiative.

She pointed at her computer screen, on which there was a map: 'I've plotted here all the masts of the mobile networks the five of them used, Orange, Vodaphone and T-Mobile. Orange and T-Mobile operate on a higher frequency than Vodafone – which Michael Harrison is on. The last signal from his mobile came from the base station at the Pippingford Park mast on the A22. But I've found out we cannot rely on the fact that this is the nearest, because if the network is busy it will hand off signals to the next available mast.'

She was going to go far, this young lady, Grace thought. Studying the map for a moment, he asked, 'What's the distance between the masts?'

'In cities it is about five hundred metres. But out in the country, it is several miles.'

From previous experience, Grace knew that the mobile phone companies used a network of radio masts that acted as beacons. Mobiles, whether on *standby* or *talk* mode, sent constant signals out to the nearest beacon. It was a simple task to plot the movements of any phone user from this information. But this was obviously a lot easier in cities than in the countryside.

Bella stood up and walked across to the map of Sussex on the wall. She pointed at a blue pin in the centre of Brighton, surrounded by green, purple, yellow and white pins. 'I've marked Michael Harrison's phone with blue pins. The other four with him have different colours.'

Grace followed her finger as she talked. 'We can see all five pins remained together from seven in the evening until nine.' She pointed to three different locations. 'There is a pub in each of these places,' she said. 'But this is where it gets interesting.' She pointed to a location some miles north of Brighton. 'All five pins close together here. Then we only have four. Here.'

Branson said, 'Green, purple, yellow and white. No blue.'

'Exactly,' she said.

'What movement on the blue pin after that?'

'None,' she said, emphatically.

'So they parted company,' Grace said, 'at – about – eight forty-five?'

'Unless he dropped his phone somewhere.'

'Of course.'

'So we're talking about a radius of five miles, about fifteen miles north of Brighton?' Glenn Branson said.

'Is his phone still giving off signals?' Grace said, distracted by Bella's combination of smart mind and good looks. He'd met her before but had never really *noticed* her before. She had a really pretty face, and unless she was wearing rocks inside her bra, she had seriously large breasts – something that had always turned him on. He switched his mind off her and back to business. Then he shot a glance at her hand to see if she was wearing any rings. One sapphire band, but not on the marriage finger. He filed it away.

'The last signal was at eight forty-five Tuesday night. Nothing since.'

'So what's your view, Bella?' Grace asked.

Bella thought for a moment, fixing him with alert blue eyes. But her expression bore nothing more than businesslike deference to a superior. 'I spoke to a technician at the phone company. He says his mobile is either switched off, and has been since Tuesday night, or it is in an area of no signal.'

Grace nodded. 'This Michael Harrison is an ambitious and busy businessman. He's due to get married tomorrow morning to a very beautiful woman, by all accounts. Twenty minutes before a fatal car smash that killed four of his best friends, his phone went dead. During the past year he has been stealthily transferring money from his company to a Cayman Islands bank account – at least one million pounds that we know about. And his business partner, who should have been on that fatal stag night, for some reason was not there. Are my facts right so far?'

'Yes,' Glenn Branson said.

'So he could be dead. Or he could have pulled a smart vanishing act.'

'We need to check out the area Bella has ring-fenced. Go to all the pubs he might have visited. Talk to everyone who knows him.'

'And then?'

'Facts, Glenn. Let's get all the facts first. If they don't lead us to him, then we can start to speculate.'

The phone on Bella's desk rang. She answered it, and almost instantly her expression conveyed that it was significant.

'You're certain?' she said. 'Since Tuesday? You can't be sure it was Tuesday? No one else could have taken it?' After a few moments, she said, 'No, I agree. Thank you, that could be very significant. May I take your number?'

Grace watched while she wrote down on a pad '*Sean*

Houlihan', followed by a number. 'Thank you, Mr Houli-han, thank you very much, we'll get back to you.'

She hung up and looked at Grace then Branson. 'That was Mr Houlihan, the owner of the undertakers where Robert Houlihan, his nephew, worked. They've just discovered that they are missing a coffin.'

30

'Missing a coffin?' Glenn Branson said.

'Not something people ordinarily steal, is it?' Bella Moy said.

Grace was silent for a moment, distracted by a blue-bottle that buzzed noisily around the room for a moment, then batted against a window. Forensics was on the floor below. Bloodstained clothes and artefacts were a magnet for bluebottles. Grace hated them. Bluebottles – or *blowflies* – were the vultures of the insect world. 'This character, Robert Houlihan, borrowed the undertaker's van without permission. Seems possible he might have borrowed a coffin without permission too.' He looked quizzically at Branson then Bella, then at Nick Nicholl. 'Do we have one very sick prank on our hands?'

'Are you suggesting his mates might have put him in a coffin?' Glenn Branson said.

'Do you have a better theory?'

Branson smiled, edgily. 'Work on the facts. Right?'

Looking at Bella, subconsciously thinking how attractive she was, Grace said, 'How sure is this Houlihan fellow that his coffin has been taken and they haven't just misplaced it?'

'People misplace their front door keys – I don't think people misplace coffins,' Branson said, a tad facetiously.

Bella interrupted, 'He's very sure. It was the most expensive coffin in his range, Indian teak, says it would last for hundreds of years – but this one had a flaw – the wood had warped or something – wasn't sealing tight at the bottom – he was having a ding-dong with the manufacturers in India about it.'

'I can't believe we have to import coffins from *India*! Don't we have carpenters in England?' Branson said.

Grace was staring at the map. He traced a circle with his finger. 'This is a pretty big area.'

'How long could someone survive in a coffin?' Bella asked.

'If the lid was on properly it would depend on if they had air, water, food. Without air, not long. A few hours, maybe a day,' Grace replied.

'It's now three days,' Branson said.

Grace remembered reading about a victim who had been pulled out alive from the ruins of his home twelve days after an earthquake in Turkey. 'With air, at least a week, maybe longer,' he said. 'We'd have to assume if they have done some damned stupid prank on him they would have left him with air. If they didn't, then we're looking for a body.'

He looked at the team. 'Presumably you've talked to Mark Warren, the business partner?'

'He's also his best man,' Nicholl said. 'Says he has no idea what happened. They were going on a stag-night pub crawl and he was stuck out of town and missed it.'

Grace frowned, then glanced at his watch, acutely aware of time slipping away. 'There's one thing going on a stag-night pub crawl, there's another thing taking a coffin with you. You don't decide to take a coffin with you on the spur of the moment – do you?' He stared pointedly at each of them in turn.

All three shook their heads.

'Someone's talked to all the girlfriends, wives?'

'I did,' Bella said. 'It's hard because they're in shock, but one of them was very angry – Zoe . . .' She picked up her notepad and flipped over some pages. 'Zoe Walker – widow of Josh Walker. She said that Michael was always playing stupid pranks, and she was certain they had been planning revenge.'

'And the best man didn't know anything about it? I don't buy that,' Grace said.

'I'm pretty convinced he didn't know anything. Why would he have any reason to lie?' Nicholl said.

Grace was worried by the young detective's naivety. But he always believed in giving juniors opportunities to show their abilities. He let it ride for the moment, but logged it firmly in his mind to come back to later today.

'This is one hell of an area to search,' Branson said. 'It's heavily wooded; it could take a hundred people days to comb this.'

'We have to try to narrow it down,' Grace responded. He picked up a marker pen from Bella's desk, and drew a blue circle on the map, then turned to DC Nicholl. 'Nick, we need a list of every pub in this circle. This is where we need to start.' He turned to Branson. 'Do you have photographs of the lads in the van?'

'Yes.'

'Good boy. Two sets?'

'I have a dozen sets.'

'We'll divide in two, DS Branson and I will take one half of the pubs, you two take the other. I'll see if we can get the helicopter to cover the area – although it's very wooded, they've a better chance of seeing something from the air.'

*

An hour later, Glenn Branson pulled his car up on the deserted forecourt of a pub called the King's Head, on the Ringmer Road, on the perimeter of the circle. They climbed out of the car and went up to the door. Above it was a sign saying, 'John and Margaret Hobbs, landlords'.

Inside, the saloon bar was deserted and so was the drab restaurant area off to the left. The place smelled of furniture polish and stale beer. A fruit machine flashed and winked away in a far corner, near a dartboard.

'Hello?' Branson called out. 'Hello?'

Grace leaned over the bar and saw an open trap door. He lifted a flap in the counter, went behind it, kneeled and shouted down into the cellar, which was illuminated by a weak bulb. 'Hello? Anyone there?'

A gruff voice came back. 'Be up in a moment.'

He heard a rumbling sound, then a grey beer barrel, with 'HARVEY'S' stamped on the side, gripped by a pair of massive, grimy hands, appeared, followed by the head of a burly, red-faced man, in a white shirt and jeans, sweating profusely. He had the bulk and the broken nose of an ex-boxer. 'Yes, gents?'

Branson showed him his warrant card. 'Detective Sergeant Branson and Detective Superintendent Grace of the Sussex Police. We're looking for the landlord. Mr Hobbs?'

'You've found him,' he wheezed, climbing out, then hauling himself up on to his feet and staring at them warily. He stank of body odour.

'Wonder if you'd mind taking a look at these photographs and see if you recognize any of the faces. They might have come in here last Tuesday night.' Branson laid the photographs on the counter.

John Hobbs studied each of the photographs in turn. Then he shook his head. 'No, never saw them before.'

'Were you working here on Tuesday night?' Grace asked him.

'I'm here every sodding night,' he said. 'Seven days a week. Thanks to your bloody lot.'

'Our lot?' Grace said.

'Your Traffic Division. Not easy to make a living running a rural pub, when your chums in Traffic sneak around outside, breathalysing all my customers.'

Ignoring the comment, Grace said, 'Are you absolutely sure you don't recognize them?'

'I get ten people in here on a mid-week night, it's Fat City. If they'd been here, I'd have seen them. I don't recognize them. Any reason why I should?'

It was moments like this that made Roy Grace very angry at the Traffic Division. For most people, being stopped for speeding, or to take a breathalyser check, was the only contact they ever had with the police. As a result, instead of viewing the police as their friends and guardians of the peace, they regarded them as an enemy.

'Do you watch television? Read the local papers?' Grace asked.

'No,' he said. 'I'm too busy for that. Is that a crime?'

'Four of these boys are dead,' Glenn Branson said, riled by the man's attitude. 'They were killed in a traffic accident on Tuesday night.'

'And you walk in here with your big swinging dicks, looking for some poor sodding landlord to blame for plying them with drink?'

'I didn't say that,' Grace replied. 'No, I'm not. I'm looking for this lad who was with them.' He pointed at Michael's photograph.

The landlord shook his head. 'Not in here,' he said.

Looking up at the walls, Branson asked, 'Do you have CCTV?'

'That meant to be a joke? Like I have money to buy fancy security gizmos? You know the CCTV I use?' He pointed at his own eyes. 'These. They come free when you're born. Now, if you'll excuse me, I have a barrel to change.'

Neither of them bothered to reply.

31

Michael shivered. Something was crawling through his hair. It was progressing steadily, determinedly, towards his forehead. It felt like a spider.

In panic, dropping the belt buckle, he jerked his hands up, sweeping furiously at his hair, fingers raw and bloody from scraping away at the lid.

Then it was on his face, crossing his cheek, mouth, chin.

'Jesus, get off, you fuckwit!' He smacked at his face with both hands, then felt something small and sticky. It was dead, whatever it had been. He wiped what remains he could feel off the thick, itchy growth of his stubble.

He had always been fine with most creatures, but not spiders. When he was a kid, he'd read a story in the local newspaper about a greengrocer who got bitten by a tarantula that was concealed in a bunch of bananas and had nearly died.

The beam of the torch was very faint now, giving a dark amber glow to the interior of the coffin. He was having to hold his head up to stop the rising water washing over his cheeks and into his eyes and mouth. Something else had bitten him on the ankle a while back, some insect, and it was stinging.

He shook the torch. For a moment the bulb died altogether. Then a tiny strip of filament glowed for a few seconds.

He was freezing cold. Working away at the lid was the

only thing stopping him from getting even colder. He still hadn't broken through. He had to, *had to*, before the water – he tried to shut the unthinkable from his mind, but he couldn't. The water kept rising, it covered his legs and part of his chest. With one hand he was having to cradle the walkie-talkie in the gap between his chest and the lid to prevent it from getting immersed.

Despair, like the water, was steadily enveloping him. Davey's words went round and round inside his mind.

There was one guy sticking right out through the windshield, half his head missing. Jeez, could see his brains coming out. Knew right away he was a goner. Only one survivor, but he died too.

A Transit van in a smash at a time and place that fitted. Pete, Luke, Josh, Robbo – could they really all be dead? And that was the reason no one had come to find him? But Mark must have known what they were planning, he was his best man, for Christ's sake! Surely Mark was out there, leading a team looking for him? Unless, he thought bleakly, something had happened to him, too. Maybe he'd joined them at the next pub and been in the van with them?

It was ten past four, Friday afternoon. He tried to imagine what was happening right now. What was Ashley doing? His mother? Was everything still going forward for tomorrow as planned?

He raised his head, so his mouth was up a few precious inches closer to the lid, and shouted, as he did regularly, 'Help! Help me! Help!'

Nothing but numbing silence.

I have to get out.

There was a fizz, then a crackle that for a moment

Michael thought was splintering wood, until he heard the familiar hiss of static. Then a disembodied Southern drawl: 'You mean that, what you said, 'bout me being on television?'

'Davey?'

'Hey pal, we just got back – that was a real wreck, boy! You didn't want to be in that automobile, I tell you. Took 'em two hours to cut the driver out, he was in pretty bad shape. Better shape than the woman in the other car, though, you know what I'm saying?'

'Yes I do,' Michael said, trying the tack of humouring him.

'Not sure about that. I'm saying she's dead. Y'all understand?'

'Dead? Yes, I understand that.'

'You can tell y'know, just by looking, who the dead ones are and who the ones gonna survive are. Not all the time. But wow, I'm tellin' you something!'

'Davey, that wreck you went to on Tuesday night, can you remember how many young men were in it?'

After some moments of silence, Davey said, 'Just counting the ambulances. Bad accidents you get one ambulance for each person. There was one leaving when we arrived, one still there.'

'Davey, you don't by any chance know the names of the victims?'

Almost instantly, surprising Michael, Davey rattled them off to him. 'Josh Walker, Luke Gearing, Peter Waring, Robert Houlihan.'

'You have a good memory, Davey,' Michael said, trying to encourage him. 'Was there anyone else? Was someone called Mark Warren in that wreck, also?'

Davey laughed. 'Never forget a name. If Mark Warren

had been in that wreck, I'd have known about it. Remember every name I ever heard, remember where I heard it, and the time. Ain't ever been a shitload of use.'

'Must have been good for history at school.'

'Mebbe,' he said noncommittally.

Michael fought the temptation to shout at him from sheer frustration. Instead, keeping his patience, he said, 'Do you remember where the accident happened?'

'A26. Two point four miles south of Crowborough.'

Michael felt a ray of hope brightening inside him. 'I don't think I'm very far from there. Can you drive, Davey?'

'You mean like an automobile?'

'Yup, that's exactly what I mean.'

'Guess that would depend on how you define *drive*.'

Michael closed his eyes for some moments. There had to be some way to connect properly with this character. *How?* 'Davey, I need help, really badly. Do you like games?'

'You mean like computer games? Yeah! Do you have a Play-Station-2?'

'No not here, not actually with me.'

'We could connect online maybe?'

Water slopped into Michael's mouth. He spat it out, panicking. Christ it was rising quickly now. 'Davey, if I give you a phone number, could you dial it for me? I need you to tell someone where I am. Could you get someone on the line while you are talking to me?'

'Houston, we have a problem.'

'Tell me the problem?'

'The phone's in my dad's house, you see. He doesn't know I have this walkie-talkie – I shouldn't have it. It's our secret.'

'It's OK, I can keep a secret.'

'My dad would be pretty mad at me.'

'Don't you think he'd get even madder if he knew you could have saved my life and you let me die? I think you might be the only person in the world who knows where I am.'

'It's OK, I won't tell anyone.'

More water lapped into Michael's mouth; filthy, muddy, brackish water. He spat it out, his arms, shoulders, neck muscles all aching from trying to keep his head clear of the rising level. 'Davey, I'm going to die if you don't help me. You could be a hero. Do you want to be a hero?'

'I'm going to have to go,' Davey said. 'I can see my dad outside – he needs me.'

Michael lost it, and screamed at him. 'No! Davey, you are not fucking going anywhere. You have to help. YOU HAVE TO FUCKING HELP ME.'

There was another silence, a very long one this time, and Michael worried he'd pushed too far. 'Davey?' he said, more gently. 'Are you still there, Davey?'

'I'm still here.' Davey's voice had changed. His voice suddenly was meek, chastised. He sounded like a small, apologetic boy.

'Davey, I'm going to give you a phone number. Will you write this down and make the call for me? Will you tell them that they need to speak to me on your walkie-talkie – and that it is very, very urgent. Will you do that for me?'

'OK. Tell them it's very, *very* urgent.'

Michael gave him the number. Davey told him he would go and make the call then radio him back.

Five agonizingly long minutes later, Davey's voice

came back on the walkie-talkie. 'I just got voicemail,' he said.

Michael clenched his hands in frustration. 'Did you leave a message?'

'No. You didn't tell me to do that.'

32

The landlady of the Friars, in Uckfield, was a tall, blowsy lady in her late forties, with spiky blonde hair, who looked like she'd been around the block a few times. She greeted Grace and Branson with a friendly smile and studied the photographs Grace laid on the counter carefully.

'Uh huh,' she said. 'They were in here, all five of them. Let me think . . . About eight o'clock on Tuesday.'

'You're sure?' Glenn Branson said.

She pointed at the photograph of Michael. 'He was looking a bit wrecked, but was very sweet.' She pointed at Josh's photograph. 'He was the one buying the drinks. He ordered a round of beers, I think, and some chasers. This chap' – again she pointed at Michael – 'told me he was getting married on Saturday. He said I was the most beautiful woman he had ever seen, and if he'd met me sooner, he'd have been marrying me.'

She grinned at Branson, then gave Grace a distinctly flirtatious smile. She clearly knew how to play the police, he thought. No doubt she had the local law in her pocket. No problems over staying open beyond closing time here.

'Did you by any chance hear them talking about their plans?' Grace asked.

'No, love. They were all in a sunny mood. We weren't busy, they were all sitting in that corner.' She pointed across the empty lounge to an alcove table and chairs, above which hung several horse brasses. 'I didn't pay much attention, had one of my regulars talking about his marital problems. You know how it is.'

'Yep,' said Grace.

'So you don't know where they were going next?' Branson asked.

She shook her head. 'Seemed like they were on a bender. Downed their drinks and were off.'

'Do you have closed-circuit television here?'

She gave Grace another deeply flirtatious smile. 'No, love. Sorry.'

As they left the pub, and hurried across the forecourt to their car, ducking against the teeming late-afternoon rain, Grace heard the distant sound of a helicopter. He looked up but could see nothing, as Branson unlocked the car. He sat inside and slammed the door shut against the elements, then called up Bella and Nick.

'How are you guys doing?'

'Goose eggs,' Nicholl said. 'No joy. We've two pubs to go. You?'

'Three more,' Grace said.

Branson started the car. 'Bit of a tasty old slapper,' he said to Grace. 'Think you could be in there.'

'Thanks,' Grace said. 'After you.'

'I'm a happily married man. You ought to go with the flow a bit.'

Roy Grace looked down at his mobile. At the text messages from Claudine, the cop-hating vegan from Guildford. 'You're lucky,' he said. 'Seems to me that half the women who aren't married are insane.'

He fell silent for some moments, then he said, 'The accident happened just after nine. This might have been the last pub they went to before they put him in the coffin.'

'They could have fitted in one more.'

They went to the next three pubs, but no one remembered the boys. Nick and Bella had found one more publican who recognized them. They left at around 8.30. All apparently very drunk. That pub was about five miles away. Grace was despondent at the news. From the information they had received, they were no nearer to pinpointing where Michael Harrison might be than when they had started.

'We should go and talk to his business partner,' Grace said. 'If he's the best man he *has* to know something. Don't you think?'

'I think we should organize a search of the area.'

'Yes, but we need to narrow it down.'

Branson started the car. 'You said to me some while back that you know a geezer who does some kind of thing with a pendulum?'

Grace looked at him in surprise. 'Yes?'

'Don't remember his name. You said he can find things that are lost, just by swinging a pendulum over a map.'

'I thought you didn't believe in that? You're the one who always tells me I'm an idiot for dabbling in that terrain. Now you are suggesting I go and see someone?'

'I'm getting desperate, Roy. I don't know what else to do.'

'We press on, that's what we do.'

'Maybe he's worth a try.'

Grace smiled. 'I thought you were the big sceptic.'

'I am. But we have a guy meant to be walking down the aisle in church tomorrow at two – and we have – ' he checked his watch ' – just twenty-two hours to get him there. And about fifty square miles of forest to search, with about four hours of daylight left. What say you?'

Privately, Grace believed that Harry Frame was worth a

try. But after the fiasco in court on Wednesday, he wasn't sure it was worth risking his career over it, if Alison Vosper were to find out. 'Let's exhaust all our other avenues, first, then we'll see, OK?'

'Worried what the boss might say?' Branson taunted.

'You get to my age, you start thinking about your pension.'

'I'll bear that in mind, in about thirty years' time.'

33

Ashley Harper's address was a tiny Victorian terraced house close to a railway line in an area that had once been a working-class area of Hove, but now was an increasingly trendy – and expensive – enclave for singles and first-time buyers. The quality of the cars parked in the street and the smart front doors were the giveaway.

Grace and Branson climbed out of the car, walked past a Golf GTI and a convertible Renault, and rang the door-bell of number 119, which had a silver Audi TT parked outside.

After a few moments the door was opened by a very beautiful woman in her mid-twenties. She gave Branson a sad smile of recognition.

'Hello, Ashley,' Branson said. 'This is my colleague, Detective Superintendent Grace. Can we have a chat?'

'Of course, come in. Do you have any news?' She looked at Grace.

Grace was struck by the contrast of the interior of the house with the outside. They had entered an oasis of cool minimalism. White carpet, white furniture, grey metal Venetian blinds, a large framed Jack Vettriano print of four dudes in sharp suits on the wall, which Grace recognized, pin-pricks of coloured lights jigging on a wall-mounted sound system. The hands of a faceless clock on a wall read 6.20 p.m.

She offered them drinks. Branson was given a mineral

water in a smart glass tumbler and Grace, seated beside him on a long sofa, a black coffee in an elegant white mug.

'There were three confirmed sightings of your fiancé on Tuesday night at pubs in the Ashdown Forest area,' Glenn Branson told her. 'Each of them also confirmed he was with four companions – the ones you know. But we have no information on what they were up to, other than getting drunk.'

'Michael isn't a drinker,' she said bleakly, holding a large glass of red wine in both hands.

'Tell me about Michael,' Grace asked, watching her intently.

'What sort of things?'

'Anything. How did you meet him?'

She smiled, and for an instant visibly relaxed. 'I came for a job interview to his firm. Michael and his partner.'

'Mark Warren?' quizzed Grace.

A fleeting hesitation, so small it was barely noticeable. But Grace had seen it. 'Yes.'

'Where did you work before? he asked.

'I was working for a real estate firm in Toronto, Canada. I only came back to England just before I got this job.'

'Back?'

'I'm from England originally – my roots are here.' She smiled.

'What firm in Toronto?'

'You know Toronto?' she asked, a little surprised.

'I did a week there with the RCMP about ten years ago – at their murder lab.'

'Right. It was a small firm – part of the Bay group.'

Grace nodded. 'So Michael Harrison and Mark Warren hired you?'

'Uh huh, that was last November.'

'And?'

'It was a great job – good pay – I wanted to learn about the property business, and they seemed like really nice guys. I – um – I' – she blushed – 'I thought Michael was very attractive, but I was sure he was married or had a girl-friend.'

'Excuse me for being personal,' Grace said, 'but when did you and Michael become an item?'

After a brief pause she said, 'Very quickly – within a couple of months. But we had to keep it secret, because Michael was concerned about Mark finding out. He thought it would be difficult for Mark if he was – you know – having a thing with me.'

Grace nodded. 'So when did Mark find out?'

She reddened. 'He came back to the office one day when we weren't expecting him.'

Grace smiled. He felt for her, she had a vulnerability about her that he knew would make almost all men feel protective towards her. He felt the same way himself, already, and he'd only known her for a few minutes. 'And then?'

'It was a little bit awkward for a while. I told Michael I thought I should quit, but he was very persuasive.'

'And Mark?'

Grace noticed the minutest flinch. A barely visible tightening of her facial muscles. 'He was OK about it.'

'So it didn't affect your business relationship?'

'No.'

Watching her eyes closely, Grace asked, 'Did you know they have a business offshore, in the Cayman Islands?'

Her eyes shot to Branson then back to Grace. 'No – I – I don't know about it.'

'Did Michael ever talk to you about tax shelters for himself and Mr Warren?'

Anger flashed in her face, so harshly and so suddenly that Grace was startled. 'What is this? Are you policemen or are you from the Inland Revenue?'

'If you want to help us find your fiancé, you have to help us get to know him. Tell us everything, even the stuff you think is totally irrelevant.'

'I just want you to find him. Alive. Please God.'

'Your fiancé didn't talk about his stag night with you?' Grace questioned, thinking back to his own stag night, when he'd given Sandy a detailed itinerary and she'd rescued him, in the early hours of the following morning, when he'd been abandoned in a back street of Brighton, stark naked apart from a pair of socks, on top of a pillar box.

She shook her head. 'They were just going out for a few drinks, that's all he told me.'

'What are you going to do if he hasn't turned up by the time of your wedding tomorrow?' Branson asked.

Tears rolled down her cheeks. She went out of the room and returned holding an embroidered handkerchief, which she used to dab her eyes. Then she started sobbing. 'I don't know. I really don't know. Please find him. I love him so much, I can't bear this.'

After waiting for her to calm down, and watching her eyes again intently, Grace asked, 'You were secretary to both of them. Didn't Mark Warren tell you what they had planned?'

'Just a boys' night out. I was having a girls' night out, you know, a hen party. That was all.'

'You know that Michael has a reputation as a practical joker?' Grace asked.

'Michael has a great sense of humour – that's one of the things I love about him.'

'You don't know anything about a coffin?'

She sat bolt upright, almost spilling her wine. 'A coffin? What do you mean?'

Gently, Branson explained. 'One of the boys, Robert Houlihan – you knew him?'

'I met him a few times, yes. A bit of a loser.'

'Oh really?'

'That's what M – Michael said. He sort of hung on to their crowd but wasn't really part of it.'

'But part of it enough to be included in the stag night?' Branson persisted.

'Michael hates to hurt anyone. I think he felt Robbo had to be included. I suppose because he'd made the other guys ushers, but not Robbo.'

Grace drank some coffee. 'You didn't have any falling-out with Michael? Nothing to make you think he might have got cold feet about the wedding?'

'Christ,' she said. 'No. Absolutely not. I – he—'

'Where are you going on your honeymoon?' Grace asked.

'The Maldives. Michael's booked a fantastic place – he loves water – boats, scuba diving. It looks like paradise.'

'We have a helicopter out looking for him. We have drafted in one hundred special constables, and if he hasn't turned up by tonight we are going to start a full search of the area where he was last seen. But I don't want to tie up hundreds of valuable police man-hours only to find he's sunning himself in the Cayman Islands, courtesy of the British taxpayer. Do you understand?'

Ashley nodded. 'Loud and clear,' she said bitterly. 'This is about money, not about finding Michael at all.'

'No,' Grace said, softening his tone. 'This is not about money. I'm prepared to authorize whatever it costs to find Michael.'

'Then please start now.' Hunching her thin shoulders, she stared pitifully down at her glass of wine. 'I recognize you, from the *Argus* piece on you. And the *Daily Mail* yesterday. They were trying to ridicule you for going to a medium, right?'

'Yes.'

'I believe in all that. Don't you know somebody? You know – with your contacts? Aren't there mediums, psychics – who can locate missing people?'

Grace shot a glance at Branson, then looked at Ashley. 'There are, yes.'

'Couldn't you go to someone – or put me in touch with someone you can recommend?'

Grace thought carefully for a moment. 'Do you have anything belonging to Michael?' He was aware of Glenn Branson's eyes boring into him.

'Like what?'

'Anything at all. Some object. An item of clothing? Jewellery? Something he would have been in contact with?'

'I can find something. Just give me a couple of minutes.'

'No problem.'

34

'Are you out of your tree?' Branson said as they drove away from Ashley's house.

Holding the copper bracelet Ashley had given him in his hand, Grace replied, 'You suggested it.' There was a deep bass boom, boom, boom from the radio. Grace turned the volume down.

'Yeah, but I didn't mean for you to ask her.'

'You wanted us to nick something from his pad?'

'*Borrow*. Man, you live dangerously. 'What if she talks to the press?'

'You asked me to help you.'

Branson gave him a sideways look. 'So what do you make of her?'

'She knows more than she's telling us.'

'So she's trying to protect his arse?'

Grace turned the bracelet over in his hands. Three thin bands of copper welded together, each ending in two small roundels. 'What do you think?'

'There you go again – your usual, answering a question with a question.'

Grace said nothing for a while, thinking. In his mind he was recalling the scene inside Ashley Harper's house. Her anxiety, her answers to the questions. Nineteen years in the Police Force had taught him many lessons. Probably the most important one was that the truth is not necessarily what was immediately apparent. Ashley Harper knew more than she was saying, of that he was certain. The reading of her eyes told him that. Probably, he assessed, in her grief-stricken state she was concerned about whatever tax scam Michael Harrison might be involved with in the Cayman Islands getting out in the open. And yet he felt this was not the whole story.

*

Twenty minutes later they parked on a yellow line on the Kemp Town promenade, elevated above the beach and the English Channel, and climbed out of the car.

Rain was still pelting down, and, apart from the grey smudge of a tanker or freighter on the horizon, the sea was empty. A steady stream of cars and lorries sluiced past them. Over to the right, Grace could see the Palace Pier with its white domes, tacky lights and the helter-skelter rising like a pillar at the end.

Marine Parade, the wide boulevard that ran along a mile of handsome Regency facades with sea views, teemed with traffic sluicing past in both directions. The Van Alen was one of its few modern apartment buildings, a twenty-first-century take on Art Deco. A beady voice answered the bell of apartment 407 on the high-security entry panel within moments. 'Hello?'

'Mark Warren?' Glenn Branson said.

'Yes, who is this?'

'The police – may we have a word with you about Michael Harrison?'

'Sure. Come up – the fourth floor.' There was a sharp buzz and Grace pushed the front door open.

'Weird coincidence,' he said to Branson as they entered the lift. 'I was here last night on one of my poker nights.'

'Who do you know here?'

'Chris Croke.'

'Chris Croke – that git in Traffic?'

'He's all right.'

'How can he afford a pad in a place like this?

'By marrying money – or rather, by divorcing money. He had a rich missus – her dad was a lottery winner he told me once – and a good divorce lawyer.'

'Smart bastard.'

They stepped out on the fourth floor, walked down a plushly blue carpet and stopped outside 407. Branson pressed the bell.

After a few seconds the door was opened by a man in his late twenties, dressed in an open-neck white business shirt, pin-stripe suit trousers and black loafers with a gold chain. 'Gentlemen,' he said, affably, 'please come in.'

Grace looked at him with faint recognition. He had seen this man before, somewhere, recently. Where? Where the hell had he seen him?

Branson dutifully showed him his warrant card, but Mark Warren barely glanced at it. They followed him through a small hallway into a huge open-plan living area, with two red sofas forming an L-shape and a long, narrow black lacquer table acting as a border for a kitchen and dining area.

The place was similar in its minimalistic style, Grace noted, to Ashley Harper's, but considerably more money had been lavished here. An African mask sat on top of a tall black plinth in one corner. Classy, if impenetrable, abstract paintings lined the walls, and there was a picture window looking directly out at the sea with a fine view of the Palace Pier. A news programme, muted, played on a flat screen Bang and Olufsen television.

'Can I get you a drink?' Mark Warren asked, wringing his hands.

Grace observed him carefully, watching his body language, listening to the way he spoke. The man exuded anxiety. Unease. Hardly surprising, considering what he must be going through. One of the biggest problems for survivors of any disaster, Grace knew from past experience, was coping with guilt.

'We're fine, thanks,' Branson said. 'We don't want to keep you long – just a few questions.'

'Do you have any news of Michael?'

Grace told him about their trawl of pubs, and about the missing coffin. But there was something about the way he responded that ran up a flag in Grace's mind. Just a small flag, barely more than a minuscule fluttering pennant.

'I can't believe they'd do anything like taking a coffin,' Mark Warren said.

'You should know,' Grace retorted. 'Isn't it the role of the best man to organize the stag night?'

'So I read in the stuff I downloaded from the net,' he replied.

Grace frowned. 'So you weren't involved in the plans? At all?'

Mark looked flustered. His voice was awkward as he started speaking, but rapidly calmed. 'I – no, that's not what I'm saying. Like I mean – you know – we – Luke – wanted to organize a strippergram, but that's kind of so yesterday – we wanted something more original.'

'To pay back Michael Harrison for all his practical jokes?'

Flustered again for a moment, Mark Warren said, 'Yes, we did discuss that.'

'But you didn't talk about a coffin?' Roy Grace asked, locked on to his eyeballs.

'Absolutely not.' There was indignation in his voice.

'A teak coffin,' Grace said.

'I – I don't know anything about any coffin.'

'You're saying to me that you were his best man, but you didn't know anything about the plans for his stag night?'

A long hesitation. Mark Warren shot long glances at each of the police officers in turn. 'Yes,' he answered finally.

'I don't buy that, Mark,' Grace said. 'I'm sorry, but I don't buy it.' Instantly he detected the flash of anger.

'You're accusing me of lying to you? I'm sorry, gentlemen, this meeting is over. I need to talk to my lawyer.'

'That's more important to you than finding your business partner?' Grace quizzed. 'He's meant to be getting married tomorrow. You are aware of that?'

'I'm his best man.'

Watching Mark Warren's face closely, Grace suddenly remembered where he had seen him before. At least, where he *thought* he had seen him before. 'What car do you drive, Mark?' he asked.

'A BMW.'

'Which model? A 3-Series? 5-Series? 7-Series?'

'An X5,' Mark said.

'That's a four-wheel drive?'

'Yes, it is.'

Grace nodded and said nothing; his brain was churning.

35

Standing in the corridor, waiting for the lift, Branson watched Mark Warren's front door, making sure it was shut, then he said, 'What was that about – the business with the car?'

As they stepped inside the lift, Grace pressed the bottom button, marked 'B'. Still deep in thought, he didn't reply.

Branson watched him. 'Something's not right with that dude. You read that?'

Still Grace said nothing.

'You should have pressed "G" for the ground floor – that's the way we came in.'

Grace stepped out into the underground garage and Branson followed. The place was dry, dimly lit, with a faint smell of engine oil. They walked past a Ferrari, a Jaguar saloon, a Mazda sports car and a small Ford saloon, then a couple of empty bays until Grace stopped in front of a gleaming silver BMW X5 off-roader. He stared hard at the car. Droplets of rainwater still lay on the paintwork.

'Cool machines, these,' Branson said. 'But they don't have much room in the rear. Much more in a Range Rover or a Cayenne.'

Grace peered at the wheels, then knelt down and looked under a door sill. 'When I was here last night,' he said, 'and came down here for my car about quarter to one in the morning, this BMW drove in, covered in mud. I noticed it because it seemed a little unusual – you don't often see a dirty four-wheel drive in the centre of Brighton, they're mostly used by mothers doing the shopping run.'

'You sure it was *this* car.'

Grace tapped the side of his own head. 'The number plate.'

'Your photographic memory – still working at your advanced age . . .'

'Still working.'

'So what's your take?'

'What's yours?'

'A missing coffin. A forest. A mud-caked car. A best man who is the only survivor, who wants to speak to his lawyer. A bank account in the Cayman Islands. Something smells.'

'It doesn't smell, it stinks.'

'So what happens next?'

Grace pulled the copper bracelet out of his pocket and held it up. 'This happens next.'

'Is that what you really think?'

'You have a better idea?'

'Take Mark Warren in for questioning.'

Grace shook his head. 'The guy's smart. We need to be smarter.'

'Going to a flaky pendulum dowser is smarter?'

'Trust me.'

36

You had to stay awake. That was how you survived. Hypothermia made you sleepy, and when you fell asleep you would sink into a coma and then you died.

Michael was shivering, near-delirious. Cold, so, so cold; he heard voices, heard Ashley whispering into his ear; reached up to touch her and his knuckles struck hard teak.

Water slopped into his mouth and he spat it out. His face was squashed tight against the lid of the coffin. The flashlight didn't work any more, he tried keeping the walkie-talkie above the water, but his arm was hurting so much it was not going to be possible for much longer.

He wedged his mobile phone, which was useless, into the back pocket of his jeans. It made it uncomfortable, but it gave him another inch and a half height. For whatever good that would do. He was going to die; he did not know how much longer he had but it wasn't long.

'Ashley,' he said weakly. 'Ashley, my darling.'

Then more water filled his mouth.

He rubbed away at the ever-widening and deepening groove in the lid with the casing of the flashlight. He thought of the wedding tomorrow. His mum showing him the dress she had bought, and the hat and the shoes and the new handbag, wanting his approval, wanting to know she looked good for his special day, wanting him to be proud of her, wanting Ashley to be proud of her. He remembered the phone call from his kid sister, from

Australia, so excited by the ticket he had paid for. Carly would be here now, staying with his mother, getting ready.

His neck hurt so badly, he didn't know how much longer he could stand the pain; every few minutes he had to relax, sink back, holding his breath, let the water wash over his face, then push himself up. Soon that would not be possible any more.

Crying with frustration and terror he lashed out at the lid, pummelled it. He pressed the *talk* button again. 'Davey! Davey! Hey, Davey?'

He spat more water out.

Every molecule in his body shivered.

Static came back at him.

His teeth clicked in his mouth. He swallowed a mouthful of the muddy water, then another mouthful. 'Please, oh please, somebody, please, please, oh please, help me.'

He tried to calm himself down, to think about his speech. Had to thank the bridesmaids. Propose a toast to them. Must remember to thank his mother first. Finish with the toast to the bridesmaids. Tell funny stories. There was a great joke Pete had given him. About a couple going on honeymoon and—

Honeymoon.

It was all booked. They were flying tomorrow night, at nine o'clock, to the Maldives. First class – Ashley didn't know about that bit, that was his secret treat.

Oh get me out of here, you idiots. I'm going to miss my wedding, my honeymoon. Come on! Now!

37

The clock on the dash of the Ford read 7.13 p.m. as Branson drove Grace along past the elegant Regency townhouse faces of Kemp Town, then onto open road, high above the cliffs, past the vast neo-Gothic buildings of Roedean girls' school and then past the Art Deco building of St Dunstan's Home for the Blind. The rain lashed down and the wind buffeted the car, crazily. It hadn't stopped for days now. Branson turned the radio up, drowning out the intermittent crackle of the police two-way radio, swaying to the beat of a Scissor Sisters track.

Grace tolerated it for some moments, then turned the volume down again.

'What's the matter, man – this group is so cool,' Branson said.

'Great,' Grace said.

'You want to pull a bird, yeah? You need to get with the culture.'

'You're my culture guru, right?'

Branson shot him a sideways glance. 'I ought to be your style guru, too. Got a great hairdresser you should go to – Ian Habbin at The Point. Get him to sharpen up your hair – I mean, like, you are looking so *yesterday*.'

'It's starting to feel like yesterday,' Grace responded. 'You asked me to have lunch with you. It's now past teatime and heading for supper. At this rate we'll be having breakfast together.'

'Since when did you have a life?' Almost as the words

came out, Branson regretted saying them. He could see the pain in Grace's face without even turning to look at him. 'Sorry, man,' he said.

They drove through the smart, cliff-top village of Rottingdean, then along a sweeping rise, dip, followed by another rise, past the higgledy-piggledy suburban sprawl of post-war houses of Saltdean, then Peacehaven.

'Take the next left,' Grace said. Then he continued to direct Branson through a maze of hilly streets, crammed with bungalows and modest detached houses, until they pulled up outside a small, rather shabby-looking bungalow, with an even shabbier-looking camper van parked outside.

They hurried through the rain into a tiny porch, with wind chimes pinging outside, and rang the doorbell. After a few moments it was answered by a diminutive, wiry man well into his seventies, with a goatee beard, long grey hair tied back in a pony tail, wearing a kaftan and dungarees, and sporting an ankh medallion on a gold chain. He greeted them effusively in a high-pitched voice, a bundle of energy, taking Grace's hand and staring at him with the joy of a long-lost friend. 'Detective Superintendent Grace! So good to see you again.'

'And you, my friend. This is DS Branson. Glenn, this is Harry Frame.'

Harry Frame gripped Glenn Branson's hand with a strength that belied both his years and his size and stared up at him with piercing green eyes. 'What a pleasure to meet you. Come in, come in.'

They followed him into a narrow hallway lit by a low-watt bulb in a hanging lantern and decorated in a nautical theme, the centrepiece of which was a large brass porthole on the wall, and through into a sitting room, the shelves crammed with ships in bottles. There was a drab three-piece suite, its backs covered in antimacassars, a television, which was switched off, and a round oak table with four wooden chairs by the window, to which they were ushered. On the wall Branson clocked a naff print of Anne Hathaway's cottage and a framed motto which read, 'A mind once expanded can never return to its original dimensions.'

'Tea, gentlemen?'

'Thank you,' Grace said.

Looking at Grace for his cue, Branson said, 'That would be very nice.'

Harry Frame hurried busily out of the room. Branson stared at a lit, solitary white candle in a glass holder on the table, then at Grace, giving him a *What is this shit?* expression.

Grace smiled back at him. *Bear with it.*

After a few minutes a cheery, dumpy, grey-haired lady, wearing a heavy-knit roll-neck, brown polyester trousers and brand new white trainers, carried out a tray containing three mugs of tea and a plate of Bourbon biscuits, which she set down on the table.

'Hello, Roy,' she said familiarly to Grace, and then to Branson, with a twinkle in her eye she said, 'I'm Maxine. *She Who Must Be Obeyed!*'

'Nice to meet you. Detective Sergeant Branson.'

She was followed by her husband, who was carrying a map.

Grace took his mug, and noticed the tea was a watery-green colour. He saw Branson eyeing his dubiously.

'So, gentlemen,' Harry said, seating himself opposite them, 'you have a missing person?'

'Michael Harrison,' Grace said.

'The young man in the *Argus*? Terrible thing, that accident. All so young to be called over.'

'Called over?' Branson quizzed.

'Obviously the spirits wanted them.'

Branson shot Grace a glance which the Detective Superintendent resolutely ignored.

Moving the biscuits and the candle over to one side, Frame spread out an Ordnance Survey map of East Sussex on the table.

Branson ate a biscuit. Grace fished in his pocket and gave the medium the copper bracelet. 'You asked me to bring something belonging to the missing person.'

Frame took it, held it tight and closed his eyes. Both police officers stared at him. His eyes remained closed for a good minute, then, finally, he started to nod. 'Umm,' he said, his eyes still closed. 'Umm, yes, umm.' Then he opened his eyes with a start, looking at Grace and Branson as if surprised to find them still in the room. He moved closer to the map, then pulled a length of string, with a small lead weight attached, from his trouser pocket.

'Let's see what we can find,' he said. 'Yes, indeed, let's see. Is your tea all right?'

Grace sipped his. It was hot and faintly sour-tasting. 'Perfect,' he said.

Branson sipped his too, dutifully. 'Good,' he said.

Harry Frame beamed, genuinely pleased. 'Now, now . . .' Resting his elbows on the table, he buried his face in the palm of his hands as if in prayer, and began to mutter. Grace avoided Branson's eye.

'Yarummm,' Frame said to himself. 'Yarummmm. Brnnnn. Yarummm.'

Then he sat bolt upright, held the string over the map

between his forefinger and thumb, and let the lead weight swing backwards and forwards, like a pendulum. Then, pursing his lips in concentration, he swung it vigorously in a tight circle, steadily covering the map inch by inch.

'Uckfield?' he said. 'Crowborough? Ashdown Forest?' He looked quizzically at each man. Both nodded.

But Harry Frame shook his head. 'No, I'm not being shown anything in this area, sorry. I'll try another map, smaller scale.'

'We're pretty sure he is in this area, Harry,' Roy Grace said.

Frame shook his head determinedly. 'No, the pendulum is not telling me that. We need to look wider.'

Grace could *feel* Branson's scepticism burning like a furnace. Staring at the new map, which showed the whole of East and West Sussex, he saw the pendulum swinging in a narrow arc over Brighton.

'This is where he is,' Frame murmured.

'Brighton? I don't think so,' Grace responded.

Frame produced a large-scale street map of Brighton and set the pendulum swinging over it. Within moments it began to make a tight circle over Kemp Town. 'Yes,' he said. 'Yes, this is where he is.'

Grace stared at Branson now, as if sharing his thoughts. 'You are wrong, Harry,' he said.

'No, I don't think so, Roy. This is where your man is.'

Grace shook his head. 'We've just come from Kemp Town – we've been to talk to his business partner – are you sure you aren't picking up on that?'

Harry Frame picked up the copper bracelet. 'This is his bracelet? Michael Harrison?'

'Yes.'

'Then this is where he is. My pendulum is never wrong.'

'Can you give us an address?' Branson asked.

'No, not an address – the housing is too dense. But that's where you must look, that is where you will find him.'

38

'Fucking weirdo,' Branson said to Grace as they drove away from Harry Frame's house.

Grace, deep in thought, did not say anything for a long while. In the past hour the rain had finally stopped, and streaks of late-evening sunlight pierced the net of grey cloud that sagged low over the sea. 'Let's assume he's right for a moment.'

'Let's get a drink and something to eat,' Branson said. 'I'm starving; I'm about to keel over.'

The clock read 8.31 p.m.

'Good idea.'

Glenn called his wife on his mobile. Grace listened to Branson's end of the conversation. It sounded pretty heated and finished with him hanging up in mid-call. 'She's well pissed off.'

Grace gave him a sympathetic smile. He knew better than to make an uninformed comment on someone else's domestic situation.

A few minutes later, in the bar of a cliff-top pub called the Badger's Rest, Grace cradled a large Glenfiddich on the rocks, noticing that his companion was making short work of a pint of beer, despite the fact he was driving.

'I went into the Force,' Branson said, 'so I'd have a career that would make my kids proud of me. Shit. At least when I was a bouncer, I had a life. I'd get to bath my Sammy and put him to bed and had time to read him a story before I went off to work. Do you know what Ari just said to me?'

'What?' Grace stared at the specials on the blackboard.

'She said Sammy and Remi are crying 'cause I'd promised to be home and read them stories tonight.'

'So go home,' Grace said gently, meaning it.

Branson drained his pint and ordered another. 'I can't do that, you know I can't. This isn't a fucking nine-to-five job. I can't just walk out of the office like some dickhead civil servant, and do a Piss Off Early Tomorrow's Saturday stunt. I owe it to Ashley Harper and to Michael Harrison. Don't I?'

'You have to learn when to let go,' Grace said.

'Oh really? So when exactly do I let go?'

Grace drained his whisky. It felt good. The burning sensation first in his gullet, then in his stomach. He held his glass out to the barman, ordered another double, then put a twenty-pound note down and asked for change for the cigarette machine. He hadn't had a cigarette for several days, but tonight his craving for one was too strong.

The pack of Silk Cut dropped into the tray of the machine. He tore off the cellophane and asked the barman for some matches. Then he lit a cigarette and drew the smoke deeply, gratefully, down into his lungs. It tasted beyond exquisite.

'I thought you'd quit,' Branson said.

'I have.'

He received his new drink and clinked glasses with Glenn. 'You don't have a life and I'm destroying mine. Welcome to a career in the police.'

Branson shook his head. 'Your friend Harry Frame is one weird dude. What a flake!'

'Remember Abigail Matthews?'

'That kid a couple of years ago? Eight years old, right?'

'Right.'

'Kidnapped outside her folks' home. You found her in a crate in a hangar at Gatwick Airport.'

'Nigerian. She'd been sold into a child sex ring in Holland.'

'That was great detective work. Wasn't that part of the reason you got promoted so fast?'

'It was. Except I never told anyone the truth about how I found her.' The whisky was talking now, rather than Roy Grace. 'I never told anyone, because—'

'Because?'

'It wasn't great detective work, Glenn, that's why. It was Harry Frame who found her, with his pendulum. OK?'

Branson was silent for some moments. 'So that's why you believe in him.'

'He's been right in other cases, too. But I don't shout about him. Alison Vosper and her brass cronies don't like anything that doesn't fit into their boxes. You want a career in the police, you have to be seen to play by the rules. You have to be *seen*, OK? You don't actually have to play them, just so long as they *think* you are playing by them.' He drained the second whisky far faster than he had intended. 'Let's get some grub.'

Branson ordered scampi. Grace chose a distinctly unhealthy gammon steak with two fried eggs and French fries, lit another cigarette and ordered another round of drinks.

'So what do we do next, old wise man?'

Grace squinted at Branson. 'We could get smashed,' he said.

'That's not exactly going to help us find Michael Harrison, is it? Or have I missed something?'

'You haven't missed anything – not that I can see. But it is now about . . .' Grace checked his watch. 'Nine on a

Friday night. Short of heading out into Ashdown Forest with a shovel and a flashlight, I'm not sure what else we can achieve.'

'There must be something that we're missing.'

'There's always something, Glenn. What very few people understand is the importance of serendipity in our job.'

'You mean luck?'

'You know the old joke about the golfer?'

'Tell me.'

'He says, "It's a strange thing . . . the more I practise, the luckier I get."'

Branson grinned. 'So maybe we haven't practised enough.'

'I think we've practised enough. Tomorrow's the big day. If Mr Michael Harrison is playing the joke of all jokes, then tomorrow will be the moment of truth.'

'And if he's not?'

'Then we go to Plan B.'

'Which is what?'

'I have no idea.' Grace squinted at him across the top of his glass. 'I'm just your lunch date. Remember?'

39

Ashley, in her white towelling dressing gown, was slouched on her bed watching a *Sex in the City* repeat playing on the plasma television screen, when the telephone rang. She sat up with a start, nearly spilling some of the Sauvignon Blanc in the glass she was holding. Her alarm clock said 11.18 p.m. It was late.

She answered it with a nervous, near-breathless, 'Yeshello?'

'Ashley? I hope I haven't woken you, love?'

Ashley put her wine glass down on her bedside table, grabbed the remote and muted the sound. It was Gill Harrison, Michael's mother. 'No,' she said. 'Not at all. I can't sleep anyhow. I haven't slept a wink since – Tuesday. I'm going to take a pill in a little while – the doctor gave me some – said they would knock me out.' In the background she heard Bobo, Gill's little white shih-tzu, barking.

'I want you to think again, Ashley. I really think you must cancel the reception tomorrow.'

Ashley took a deep breath. 'Gill – we discussed it all yesterday and today. We can't get anything refunded cancelling this late; we have people coming from all over the place – like my uncle from Canada who's giving me away.'

'He's a nice man,' Gill said. 'Poor fellow's come all this way.'

'We adore each other,' Ashley said. 'He took the whole week off just so he could be at the rehearsal on Monday.'

'Where's he staying?'

'In London – at the Lanesborough. He always stays at the best.' She was quiet for a moment. 'Of course, I've told him, but he said he would come down anyway to give me support. I've managed to stop my other girlfriends in Canada – four of them were coming over – and I have other friends in London I've convinced not to come – the phone's been ringing off the hook for the past couple of days.'

'Here, too.'

'The problem is Michael has friends and colleagues invited from all over England – and the Continent. I've tried to contact as many people as possible, and so has Mark – but – we need at least to look after those who do turn up. And I still think Michael might.'

'I don't think so, love, not now.'

'Gill, Michael played all kinds of pranks on his friends when they got married – two of them only made it to the church minutes before the wedding began, because of what he did to them. Michael could still be somewhere, locked up or tied up, not knowing anything about what has happened. He *might* still be planning – or trying – to make it.'

'You're a lovely girl, and you are a kind person – it's going to be devastating for you to be at the church and he doesn't arrive. You have got to accept that something has happened to him. Four people are dead, love. Michael must have heard about them – if he is OK.'

Ashley sniffed, then began to sob. For some moments she cried inconsolably, dabbing her eyes with a tissue she had plucked from a box on her bedside table. Then, sniffing hard, she said, 'I'm trying so damned hard, but I'm not coping. I just – I – keep – praying he's going to turn up – every time the phone rings I think it's going to be him –

you know – that he'll be laughing, explaining it's all been some dumb joke.'

'Michael's a good boy,' Gill said. 'He's never been cruel – this is too cruel. He wouldn't do this; it's not in him.'

There was a long silence. Finally Ashley broke it. 'Are you OK?'

'Apart from being worried sick about Michael, yes, I'm OK, thanks. I've got Carly here.'

'She's arrived?'

'Yes, a couple of hours ago from Australia. I think she'll be a bit jet-lagged tomorrow.'

'I should come over to say hello.' She was silent for a moment. 'You see what I mean – all these people coming from all over the place – we just have to at least be at the church to meet them – and offer them some food. Can you imagine if we weren't there and Michael then turned up?'

'He would understand – that you cancelled out of respect for the boys who died.'

Sobbing even harder, Ashley said, 'Please, Gill, please let's go to the church and see.'

'Take that pill and get some sleep, love.'

'I'll call you in the morning.'

'Yes. I'll be up early.'

'Thanks for calling.'

'Night night.'

'Night!' Ashley said.

She replaced the receiver then, charged with a burst of energy, rolled over, her breasts spilling out of the open front of her dressing gown, and gazed down at Mark, who was lying naked under the bedclothes beside her. 'Stupid cow, doesn't have a clue!' Her lips burst into a massive grin, her whole face alight with joy. 'Not a clue!'

She put her arms around his neck, held him tightly and kissed him passionately, on the mouth at first, before working her way slowly, steadily, with maximum possible torture, further and further down his body.

40

He was sweating under the duvet. Too hot, far too hot, somehow it had worked its way right over his head and he could barely breathe. Rivulets of water ran down his face, down his arms, legs, the small of his back. He pushed the duvet off, sat up, felt a numbing crack to his skull, sank back.

Splash.

Oh Jesus.

Water slopped all around him. And felt as if it were inside him too, as if the blood in his veins and the water in which he lay were interchangeable. Some word for it. Some word he grasped for, and it eluded him, slipped from his grasp each time he closed on it. *Like soap in a bathtub*, he thought.

Cold now. Unbearably hot an instant ago, now cold. So cold. Oh so teeth-chattering-cold-cold-cold. His head was splitting. 'Just going to check and see if there are any paracetamol in the bathroom cabinet,' he announced. To the silence that came back at him he said, 'Won't be long. Just popping out to the chemist.'

The hunger had gone away some hours ago, but now it was back with a vengeance. His stomach burned as if the acids had now turned on the lining for want of anything else to break down. His mouth was parched. He put a hand out and scooped water into his mouth, but despite his thirst it was an effort to drink it.

Osmosis!

'OSMOSIS!' in a burst of elation he shouted the word out at the top of his voice, repeating it over and over. 'Osmosis! Gotcha! *Osmosis!*'

Then suddenly he was hot again. Perspiring. 'Someone turn the thermostat down!' he shouted out in the darkness. 'For Christ's sake, we're all boiling down here; what do you think we are, lobsters?'

He started giggling at his remark. Then, right above his face, the lid of the coffin began to open. Slowly, steadily, noiselessly, until he could see the night sky, alive with comets racing across it. A beam of light shone out from him, dust motes drifted lazily through it, and he realized all the stars in the firmament were projected there from the light. The sky was his screen! Then he saw a face drift across, through the beam, through the dust motes. Ashley. As if he were looking up at her from the bottom of a swimming pool, and she was drifting face-down over him.

Then another face drifted over – his mother. Then Carly, his kid sister. Then his father, in the sharp brown suit, cream shirt and red silk tie that Michael remembered him in best. Michael did not understand how his father could be in the pool but his clothes were dry.

'You're dying, son,' Tom Harrison said. 'You'll be with us soon now.'

'I don't think I'm ready yet, Dad.'

His father gave a wry smile. 'That's the thing, son, who is?'

'I found that word I was looking for,' Michael said. '*Osmosis.*'

'That's a good word, son.'

'How are you, Dad?'

'There are good deals to be had up here, son. Terrific deals. Heck of a lot better. You don't have to fart around trying to hide your money in the Cayman Islands up here. What you make is what you keep – like the sound of that?'

'Yes, Dad—'

Except it wasn't his father any more he was talking to, but the vicar, Reverend Somping, a short, supercilious man in his late fifties, with greying wavy hair and a beard that only partially masked the ruddy complexion of his cheeks – ruddy not from a healthy outdoors lifestyle, but from broken veins from years of heavy boozing.

'You're going to be very late, Michael, if you don't haul yourself out of there. You do realize that if you don't reach the church by sunset, I cannot marry you, by law?'

'I didn't, no – I—'

He reached up to touch the vicar, to seize his hand, but he struck hard, impenetrable teak.

Darkness.

The slosh of water as he moved.

Then he noticed something. Checking with his hands, the water was no longer up to his cheeks, it had subsided, to the top of his neck. 'I'm wearing it like a tie,' he said. 'Can you wear water like a tie?'

Then the shivers gripped him, clenched his arms so that his elbows banged against his ribs, his feet knocked, his breathing got faster, faster until he was hyperventilating.

I'm going to die, I'm going to die, here, alone, on my wedding day. They are coming for me, the spirits, they are coming down here into the box and—

He put his jerking hands together over his face. He could not remember the last time he had prayed – it was sometime long before his dad had died. Tom Harrison's death had been the final confirmation to him that there was no God. But now the words of the Lord's Prayer poured into his head and he whispered them into his hands, as if not wanting to be overheard.

A crackle of static broke his concentration. Then a burst of twangy country and western music. Followed by a voice. 'Well, good morning, sports fans, this is WNEB Buffalo bringing you the latest in sports, news and weather on this rainy ole Saturday morning! Now last night in the play-offs . . .'

Frantically, Michael fumbled for the walkie-talkie. He knocked it off his chest and into the water. 'Oh shit, no, oh shit, shit shit!'

He fished it out, shook it as best he could, found the *talk* button and pressed it. 'Davey? Davey, is that you?'

Another hiss and crackle. 'Hey, dude! You the dude with the friends in the wreck on Tuesday, right?'

'Yes.'

'Hey, good to talk to you again!'

'Davey, I really need you to do something for me. Then you could make a big announcement on your radio station.'

'Depends what other news there is on the day,' Davey said, dismissively.

'OK.' Michael fought the urge to snap at him. 'I need you either to get someone on the phone that I can speak with via your walkie-talkie, or for you and your dad to come and rescue me.'

'I guess that would depend on whether y'all are in an area we cover, know what I'm saying?'

'I do, Davey. I know exactly what you are saying.'

41

Later, lying naked in bed with a dozen scented candles burning around them in the room, and Norah Jones singing on the stereo, Ashley lit a cigarette, then held it up to Mark's lips. He took a deep drag.

'Gill's right,' Mark said. 'I don't think you should go to the church, and you definitely should not go ahead with the reception.'

Ashley shook her head vigorously. 'We absolutely should. Don't you see? I'll turn up there at the church . . .' She paused to take a drag, then blew the smoke out slowly, deliciously, towards the ceiling. 'Everyone will see me, the poor abandoned bride, and they'll all feel so sorry for me.'

'I'm not sure I agree; it could backfire.'

'How?'

'Well – they might think you're insensitive, insisting on going ahead – that you're not respecting Pete, Luke, Josh and Robbo. We both need to be seen to be acting as if we care about them.'

'You and I have been in touch with their families. We've both written them all letters, we're doing all the right things there. But we've been discussing the wedding for the past three days. *We are going ahead!* We have to pay the bloody caterers whatever we do, so we might as well look after those people who make the effort to turn up. It probably won't be many – but surely that's the least we can do?'

Mark took the cigarette from her and drew hard, inhaling the smoke deep into his lungs. 'Ashley, people would understand. You've battered me with your logic for three days and you haven't listened to me. I think this is a huge mistake.'

'Trust me,' Ashley said. She gave him a fierce look. 'Don't start wimping out on me now.'

'Christ, I'm not wimping out – I just—'

'Want to bottle out?'

'This is not about bottling out. Come on, partner, be strong!'

'I am being strong.'

She wormed her way down his body, nuzzling her face in his pubic hairs, his penis limp against her cheek. 'This is not what I call strong,' she said mischievously.

42

Grace started his weekend the way he liked, with an early-Saturday-morning six-mile run along Brighton and Hove seafront. Today it was again raining hard, but that did not matter; he wore a baseball cap with the peak pulled down low to shield his face, a lightweight tracksuit and brand new Nike running shoes. Powering along at a good, fast pace, he soon forgot the rain, forgot all his cares, just breathed deep, went from cushioned stride to cushioned stride, a Stevie Wonder song, 'Signed, Sealed, Delivered', playing over in his head, for some reason.

He mouthed the words as he ran past an old man in a trenchcoat walking a poodle on a leash, and then was passed by two Lycra-clad cyclists on mountain bikes. It was low tide. Out on the mudflats a couple of fishermen were digging lugworms for bait.

With the tang of salt on his lips, he ran alongside the promenade railings, on past the burnt-out skeleton of the West Pier, then down a ramp to the edge of the beach itself, where the local fishermen left their day boats dragged up far enough to be safe from the highest of tides. He clocked some of their names – *Daisy Lee, Belle of Brighton, Sammy* – smelled bursts of paint, tarred rope, putrefying fish as he ran on past the still-closed cafes, amusement arcades and art galleries of the Arches, past a windsurfing club, a boating pond behind a low concrete wall, a paddling pool, then underneath the girdered mass of the Palace Pier – where seventeen years back he and

Sandy had had their first kiss, and on, starting to tire a little now, but determined to get to the cliffs of Black Rock before he turned round.

Then his mobile phone beeped with the message signal.

He stopped, pulled it from his zipped pocket and looked at the screen.

You can't tease a girl like this, Big Boy. Claudine XX

Jesus! Leave me alone. You spent the whole evening attacking me for being a cop, now you're driving me nuts. So far his only experience at internet dating wasn't working out too well. Were they all like Claudine? Aggressive, lonely women with a screw loose? Surely not, there had to be some normal women out there. Didn't there?

He pocketed the phone and ran on, knowing he owed her a reply, but wondering if it was better to just continue ignoring her. What could he say? *Sod off and stop bothering me? It was nice meeting you but I've decided I'm gay?*

Eventually he decided he would send her a text when he got back. He would take the coward's route: *Sorry, I've decided I'm not ready for a relationship.*

His relaxing mind turned to work, to the paper mountain that seemed to be forever building and building. The Nigerian trafficking of young women; the trial of Suresh Hossain; the cold case of little Thomas Lytle; and now the disappearance of Michael Harrison.

This really bugged him. And one thought in particular had woken him during the night and stayed with him. He reached the under-cliff walk, ran along below the white chalk bluffs, high above the Marina with its rows of pontoons and forest of masts, its hotels and shops and restaurants, and on for two more miles.

Then he turned, feeling the burn in his lungs, his legs high from the exertion, and ran back until he reached the point where he was near the Van Alen building. He ran up the ramp onto the promenade, waited for a gap in the busy traffic of Marine Parade and crossed over. He made his way down the narrow street along the side of the building, and stopped by the entrance to the underground car park.

His luck was in. Within moments, the gates swung open and a dark blue Porsche Boxter drove out, a predatory-looking blonde in dark glasses – despite the dull, wet day – at the wheel. He slipped in before the gates closed. It was good to be out of the rain.

He breathed in the dry, engine-oil-laced air as he ran down the hard concrete, past a red Ferrari he remembered from before, and several other cars he recalled, and then stopped in front of the gleaming, mint-clean BMW X5 off-roader.

He stared at the number plate. W796 LDY. Then he looked around, scanning the area. It was deserted. He walked up closer, knelt beside the front nearside wheel, then lay down on his back, wormed himself under the sill and peered up at the inside of the wheel arch. It was covered in mud.

He pulled his handkerchief out of his pocket, opened it out in the palm of his left hand, then with his right hand scraped at the dry mud until several pieces of it fell into his handkerchief.

Carefully he closed it, knotted it and replaced it in his pocket. Then he hauled himself back up, walked to the garage entrance and waved his hand across the infra-red beam. Moments later, with a loud clank and a busy whirr, the doors opened for him.

He walked out, checked the street in both directions, then resumed his homeward run.

43

At 9.30, showered and after a relaxed breakfast of scrambled eggs and grilled organic tomatoes – organic was a current fad he was going through at home, to counteract all the junk food he often had to eat when working, along with drinking quantities of mineral water – he enjoyed a leisurely read of the *Daily Mail*, followed by a drool over a road test of the latest Aston Martin in *Autocar*. Then Grace went into the study he had created in a small back room of the house overlooking his tiny, increasingly overgrown garden, and the almost embarrassingly neat gardens of his neighbours on either side, sat down at his desk in front of his computer screen and rang Glenn Branson's home phone number. His handkerchief, containing the soil he had scraped from Mark Warren's car, lay on the desk inside a small plastic bag.

Ari, Branson's wife, answered. Although he had clicked with Glenn from the day he had met him, Grace found Ari quite hard to get on with. She was often brittle with him, almost as if she suspected that, because he was single, he might be trying to lead her husband astray.

Over the years Grace had worked hard to charm her, always remembering their kids' birthdays with cards and generous presents, and taking her flowers on the few occasions he had been invited round for a meal. There were moments when he thought he was making progress with her, but this morning was not one of them. She sounded less than pleased to hear him. 'Hi, Roy', she said curtly, 'you want to speak to Glenn?'

No, actually, I want to speak to the Man in the Moon, he nearly said, but didn't. Instead, a tad lamely, he asked, 'Is he around?'

'We're in rather a hurry,' she said. In the background he heard the sound of a kid screaming. Then Ari shouting, 'Sammy! Give it to her, you've had your turn, now give it to your sister!' Then the screaming got louder. Finally Branson came on the line.

'Yo, ole wise man, you're up early.'

'Very funny. What was it you said you were doing today?'

'Ari's sister's thirtieth birthday party – in Solihull. Seems I have the choice – find Michael Harrison or save my marriage. What would you do?'

'Save your marriage. Be grateful for your sad-old-git friends who have no life and can spend their weekends doing your work for you.'

'I'm grateful. What are you doing?'

'I'm going to a wedding.'

'You're such a sentimentalist. 'Top hat? Tails? All cleaned and pressed?'

'Anyone ever tell you what a bitch you are?'

'The wife I nearly don't have any more.'

Grace felt a twinge of pain. He knew that Glenn did not mean any malice, but the words stung. Every night, even if it was late, and even if it meant hassle, Glenn at least went home to loving kids and to a beautiful warm woman in his bed. People who had that were incapable of understanding what it meant to live alone.

Solitude.

Solitude could be crap.

Was crap.

Grace was tiring of it – but did not know what to do about it. What if he found someone? Fell in love with a woman, big time? And then Sandy turned up? What then?

He knew in his mind she wasn't ever going to turn up, but there was a part of his heart that refused to go there, as if it was stuck like some old-fashioned record needle, in an eternal groove. Once or twice every year, when he was low, he would go to a medium, trying to make contact with her, or at least trying to eke out some clue about what might have happened to her. But Sandy remained elusive, a photographic negative that lay for ever black and featureless in the hypo fluid of the developing tray.

He wished Branson a good weekend, envying him his life, his demanding wife, his gorgeous kids, his damned normality. He washed up his breakfast things, staring out of his kitchen window at Noreen Grinstead across the street, in a brown polyester trouser suit, apron and yellow rubber gloves, a plastic hat over her head to shield her from the rain, busily soaping her silver Nissan on the driveway. A black and white cat darted across the road. On the radio the presenter, on *Home Truths*, was interviewing a woman whose parents had not spoken one word to each other throughout her childhood.

Nineteen years in the police had taught him never to underestimate the weirdness of the human species. Yet barely a day went by when it didn't seem to be getting even weirder.

He went back into the study, dialled Brighton police station and asked if any of the Crime Scene Investigators were in. Moments later he was put through to Joe Tindall, a man he rated highly.

Tindall was meticulous, hard-working and endlessly

resourceful. A short, thin, bespectacled, man, with thinning wiry hair, he could have been a mad professor drawn straight from Central Casting. Before joining the police, Tindall had worked for several years for the British Museum as a forensic archaeologist. Joe was the man he was working with on the Tommy Lytle cold case.

'Hey, Joe!' Grace said. 'No weekend off?'

'Ha! I'm having to do the ballistics testing on the jewellery shop raid – everyone else has buggered off. And I've got the stabbing on Wednesday to deal with, thank you very much.'

Grace remembered there had been a man stabbed to death in Brighton late on Wednesday night. No one knew yet whether it was a mugging or a tiff between two gay lovers.

'Joe, I need some help. I have a sample of soil I've taken from a suspect vehicle. How can I find out, very quickly, what part of Sussex this soil is from? How specific could anyone get for me?'

'How specific do you need?'

'Within a few square feet.'

'Very funny, Roy.'

'I'm not smiling.'

'Do you have a sample from the suspect area? I could get tests run and see if they match. We have chalk, clay, gravel and sand in Sussex.'

'The suspect area is Ashdown Forest.'

'The soil there is predominantly sand and clay. We can get matches from pollen, fossils, seeds, animal droppings, grasses, water, all kinds of stuff. How specific can you get?'

'Within a few square miles.'

'You'd have to do a lot better than that. There are areas all over England that would match Ashdown Forest.'

'How long would it take you to get a match without a sample from the specific area?'

'We're talking weeks – and I'd need a huge team – and one hell of a budget.'

'But you could do it?'

'Given unlimited resources and enough time, I could give you a match in a small area.'

'How small?'

'That would depend. A few hundred square feet, perhaps.'

'OK, thanks. I have something I want to bring over to you – are you in the office for a while?'

'All day, Roy.'

44

An hour later, dressed in a blue suit, white shirt and a bright tie, Grace drove onto the sprawling, hilly Hollingbury industrial estate on the outskirts of Brighton, past an ASDA store, an ugly 1950s low-rise, and then slowed as he reached the long, low Art Deco Sussex House, headquarters of Sussex CID.

Originally built as a factory, it had been bought by the police a few years back and transformed. If it wasn't for the dominant police insignia on the facade, a passer-by could have mistaken it for a swanky, hip hotel. Painted gleaming white against red brickwork, with a long grass bank running its full length, it wasn't until you passed the security guard and drove through the high, railed gates into the rear car park, filled with police vehicles, skips and with a formidable cell block beyond, that it became less glamorous.

Grace parked underneath the building between a police off-roader and a police van, walked up to the rear entrance, held his ID card against the electronic panel to open the door and entered the building. He flashed his card at the security officer behind the front desk and made his way up the plushly carpeted stairs, past ancient truncheons in patterns mounted on blue boards and two more large blue boards halfway up the stairs on which were pinned photographs of some of the key police personnel working in this section of the building.

He knew all the faces. Ian Steel and Verity Smart, of

the Specialist Investigations Branch, David Davison of the Crime Policy and Review Branch, Will Graham and Christopher Derricott in the Scientific Support Branch, James Simpson in the Operations and Intelligence Branch, Terrina Clifton-Moore of the Family Liaison Unit, and a couple of dozen more.

Then he walked through a wide open-plan area filled with desks, few of them attended today, and offices on either side labelled with their occupants' names and the Sussex Police badge.

He passed the large office of Detective Chief Superintendent Gary Weston, who was the Head of Sussex CID. Reaching another door, he held his card up against the security panel and entered a long, cream-painted corridor lined with red noticeboards on either side, to which were pinned serious crime detection procedures. One was labelled 'Diagram – Common Possible Motives', another, 'Murder Investigation Model', another, 'Crime Scene Assessment'.

The place had a modern, cutting-edge feel, which he liked. He had spent much of his career in old, inefficient buildings that were like rabbit warrens; it was refreshing to feel that his beloved Police Force, to which he had dedicated his life, was truly embracing the twenty-first century. Although it was marred with one flaw that everyone here moaned about – there was no canteen.

He walked further along, past door after door flagged with abbreviations. The first was the Major Incident Suite, which housed the incident room for serious crimes. It was followed by the Disclosure Officers Room, the CCTV Viewing Room, the Intelligence Office Room, the Outside Enquiry Team Office, and then the stench hit him, slowly at first, but more powerful with every step.

The dense, cloying, stomach-churning reek of human putrefaction, which had become too familiar to him over the years. Much too familiar. There was no other stench like it; it enveloped you like an invisible fog, seeping into the pores of your skin, deep into your nostrils and your lungs and your stomach, and the fibres of your hair and clothes, so that you carried it away with you and continued on smelling it for hours.

As he pushed open the door of the small, pristine Scene of Crimes Office, he saw the cause: the Crime Scene Investigators' photographic studio was in action. A Hawaiian shirt, torn and heavily bloodstained, lay under the glare of bright lights, on a table, on a sheet of brown background paper. Nearby, in plastic bags, he could see trousers and a pair of camel loafers.

Peering further into the room, Grace saw a man, dressed in white overalls, who he did not recognize for a moment, staring intently into the lens of a Hasselblad mounted on a tripod. Then he realized Joe Tindall had had a makeover since he'd last seen him a few months back. The mad-professor hairstyle and large tortoiseshell glasses had gone. He now had a completely shaven head, a narrow strip of hair running from the centre of his lower lip down to the centre of his chin and hip rectangular glasses with blue-tinged lenses. He looked more like a media trendy than a scientific boffin.

'New woman in your life?' Grace asked, by way of a greeting.

Tindall looked up at him in surprise. 'Roy, good to see you! Yes, as a matter of fact – who told you that?'

Grace grinned, looking at him more closely, almost expecting to spot an earring as well. 'Young, is she?'

'Actually – yes – how do you know?'

Grace grinned again, staring at his newly shaven pate, his trendy glasses. 'Keeping you young, isn't she?'

Then Tindall understood and grinned sheepishly. 'She's going to kill me, Roy. Three times a night every night.'

'You *try* three times a night or succeed?'

'Oh, fuck off!' He stared Grace up and down. 'You're looking sharp, for a Saturday. Hot date yourself?'

'A wedding, actually.'

'Congratulations – who's the lucky girl?'

'I have a feeling she's not that lucky,' Grace retorted, placing a small plastic bag containing the earth he had retrieved from Mark Warren's BMW down on the table, next to the shirt. 'I need you to pull out some stops.'

'You always need me to pull out some stops. Everyone does.'

'Not true, Joe. I gave you the Tommy Lytle material and told you there was all the time you need. This is different. I have a missing person – how fast you get this analysed might determine whether he lives or dies.'

Joe Tindall held the bag up and peered at it. He shook it gently, peering at it all the time. 'Quite sandy,' he said.

'What does that tell you?'

'You mentioned Ashdown Forest on the phone?'

'Uh huh.'

'This might be the kind of soil you'd find there.'

'*Might?*'

'The UK is knee-deep in sandy soil, Roy. There's sandy soil in Ashdown Forest – but there's sandy soil in a million other places, too.'

'I need an area that's about seven foot long and three foot wide.'

'Sounds like a grave.'

'It is a grave.'

Joe Tindall nodded, peering closely at the earth again. 'You want me to locate a grave in the middle of Ashdown Forest from this little bag of earth?'

'You're catching on.'

The SOCO officer removed his glasses for some moments, as if that would give him clarity of vision, then put them on again. 'Here's the deal, Roy. You locate the grave and I'll get you an analysis on whether this soil matches or doesn't.'

'Actually, I need it to be the other way around.'

Tindall held up the plastic bag. 'I see. Who do you think I am? David Blaine? Derren Brown? I swing this in the air and somehow magic up a grave in the middle of a ten-thousand-hectare forest?'

'You have a problem with that?'

'Actually, yes, I do have a problem with that.'

45

A few hours later, Grace cruised slowly up a steep hill past All Saints' church in Patcham Village, where a certain wedding had been scheduled to happen at two o'clock this afternoon – in exactly three-quarters of an hour.

This was his own personal favourite church in the area. A classic Early English parish church, intimate, simple, with unadorned grey stonework, a small tower, a fine stained-glass window behind the altar and tombstones going back centuries in the overgrown graveyard out the front and along the sides.

The heavy rain had eased to a light drizzle as he sat in his Alfa, parked close to the entrance, on a grass bank opposite the church, giving him a commanding view of all the arrivals. No sign of anyone yet. Just a few pieces of sodden confetti on the wet tarmac, from an earlier wedding, probably this morning.

He watched an elderly woman in a hooded PVC raincoat wheel a shopping basket down the pavement and pause to exchange a few words with a huge man in an anorak with a tiny dog on a leash, who was walking up in the opposite direction. The dog cocked its leg on a lamppost.

A blue Ford Focus pulled up and a man with a couple of cameras slung around his neck climbed out. Grace observed him, wondering whether he was the official wedding photographer, or press. Moments later a small brown Vauxhall pulled up behind it, and a young man in

an anorak emerged, carrying a distinctive reporter's notebook. The two men greeted each other and began chatting,
both looking around, waiting.

After ten minutes he saw a silver BMW off-roader pull
up. Because of its tinted glass windows and the rain, he
could not make out who was inside, but he recognized
immediately Mark Warren's number plate. Moments later,
Warren, in a dark raincoat, jumped down and hurried up
the path to the main entrance of the church. He disappeared inside, then came out almost immediately and
hurried back to his car.

A taxi pulled up, and a tall, distinguished-looking
man with silver hair, dressed in a morning suit with a red
carnation in the buttonhole, and holding a grey top hat,
closed the rear door and walked towards the church. The
taxi had evidently been paid to wait. Then a silver Audi TT
sports car pulled up. Grace remembered seeing one like it
parked in front of Ashley Harper's house.

The driver's door opened, and Ashley, holding a small
umbrella, emerged, in a smart white, wedding dress, her
hair up. An older woman appeared from the passenger
door, in a white-trimmed blue dress and neatly coiffed
silver-grey hair. Ashley waved acknowledgement to the
BMW, then huddled under the umbrella. The pair hurried
up the path and disappeared into the church. Mark Warren
followed.

Then, at five to two, Grace saw the vicar cut across the
graveyard and enter, and decided it was time to make his
move. He left his car, tugging on his Tommy Hilfiger blue
and yellow anorak. As he crossed the road the young man
with the notebook approached him. He was in his mid-
twenties, sharp-faced, wearing a cheap grey suit with his

tie knotted massively but slackly, so the top button of his white shirt showed above it, and chewing gum.

'Detective Superintendent Grace, isn't it?'

Grace eyeballed him, used to being recognized by the press, but wary all the same. 'And you are?'

'Kevin Spinella, the *Argus*. Just wondering if you have any update on Michael Harrison for us?'

'Nothing yet, I'm afraid. We'll be waiting to see if he turns up to his wedding.'

The reporter glanced at his watch. 'Cutting it a bit fine, isn't he?'

'It wouldn't be the first time a groom has been late.' Grace smiled and eased past Spinella.

Hurrying after him, the reporter asked, 'Do you think Michael Harrison is alive or dead, Detective Superintendent?'

Stopping for one moment, Grace said, 'We're regarding this as a missing persons enquiry.'

'For the moment?'

'I don't have any further comment, thank you.' Grace pushed open the heavy door, stepped into the gloom of the porch and closed the door behind him.

Whenever he entered a church, Grace always felt a sense of conflict. Should he unhook a kneeler, get down on the floor and pray, the way most people did? The way he did as a kid alongside his mother and father, most Sunday mornings of his childhood. Or should he just sit down on a pew, letting the God he was no longer sure he believed in know his anger? For a long time after Sandy's disappearance he had gone to church and had prayed for her return. Sometimes he had attended services, but mostly he had gone into an empty church. Sandy had never been a believer, and during the past few years, with his prayers unanswered, he had increasingly become an agnostic. It no longer felt right, praying.

Give me Sandy back, then I'll pray my heart out to you. But not until then, Mr God, OK?

He walked past a row of dripping umbrellas, a criss-crossed noticeboard and a stack of service sheets with *Michael John Harrison and Ashley Lauren Harper* printed on the front, then into the church itself, instantly breathing in the familiar smells of dry, old wood, old cloth, dust and a hint of burning wax. The place was beautifully bedecked with flowers, but there was no hint of their perfume.

About a dozen people stood in the aisle and nave, all of them silent, expectant, as if they were extras on a film set waiting for the director's command to move.

Grace took in the group rapidly, nodding at Ashley, who was sheet-white and clutching the arm of the tall man in the black morning coat, presumably her father. Next to her stood the woman he had seen emerging from the car with Ashley, a handsome woman in her fifties but with the strained look of someone who has been through a sustained rough time. Mark Warren, in a navy suit, sporting a white carnation, stood beside a good-looking young couple in their early thirties.

He realized everyone was looking at him. In a faltering voice Ashley broke the ice by thanking him for coming and introduced him first to Michael's mother, who seemed distraught, and then to the handsome, distinguished-looking man he had thought was her father, but turned out to be her uncle. He gave Grace a warm handshake, introducing himself as Bradley Cunningham, staring Grace straight back in the eye and saying, 'Good to meet you, Detective Superintendent.'

Picking up on his North American accent, Grace asked, 'Whereabouts in the States are you from?'

The man frowned as if insulted. 'Actually, I'm Canadian, from Ontario.'

'I apologize.'

'No problem, it's a common mistake you Limeys make.'

'I guess you might have problems differentiating regional accents across Britain,' Grace said.

'Actually, you are right.'

Grace smiled, eyeing his morning coat approvingly. 'It's good to see someone properly dressed for a wedding.'

'Actually the pants are killing me,' Cunningham confessed. 'Rented this lot from your wonderful Moss Bros, but I think I got given the wrong pants!' Then his face became grave. 'Still, this is a terrible thing, isn't it?'

'Yes,' Grace said, distracted suddenly. 'Terrible.'

Ashley interrupted them, introducing Grace to the vicar, the Reverend Somping, a short, bearded man in white robes and a dog collar, with rheumy, bloodshot eyes, who looked distinctly angry.

'I told Miss Harper we should have cancelled this completely,' the Reverend Somping said. 'It is ridiculous to put someone through this agony – and what about the guests? This is such a nonsense.'

'He *will* turn up,' Ashley blubbed. 'He will, I know he will.' She looked imploringly at Grace. 'Please tell him that Michael is on his way.'

Grace stared at the bride, so sad and vulnerable-looking, and almost had to restrain himself from reaching out his arms and hugging her. She looked so forlorn, so desperate. He felt like punching the arrogant vicar in the face.

'Michael Harrison might yet turn up,' he said.

'He's going to have to turn up pretty smartly,' the vicar said, coldly. 'I have another wedding here at four.'

'I thought this was a church,' Grace said, angry at his insensitivity to Ashley. 'Not a supermarket.'

The Reverend Somping attempted, without success, to glare Grace out. Then he said, defensively, 'I work for the Lord. He gives me his timetable.'

After a few moments Grace snapped back, 'In that case I suggest you ask your boss to produce the groom, pronto.'

46

At twenty past two, quite unnecessarily considering the small number of people present, the Reverend Somping climbed up the steps into the pulpit with all the labour of a man scaling Everest the hard way. He placed his palms on the wooden rails, leaned forward with an expression leaden with gravitas and announced:

'I have been asked by the bride, Miss Ashley Harper, and by the mother of the groom, Mrs Gillian Harrison, to inform you that this wedding is delayed, indefinitely, pending the presence of Michael Harrison. What should be a joyous occasion, the union of two young, loving people, in the eyes of our Lord, has been curtailed by the absence of Michael. None of us knows what has happened to him, but our thoughts and prayers are with him, his family and with his bride-to-be.'

He paused, staring challengingly at the group of people, before continuing. 'Miss Harper and Mrs Harrison have generously suggested that even though no wedding has taken place, you should at least enjoy the refreshments which have been laid on for the reception, in the Queen Mary Room of the Brighton Pavilion. They would appreciate it if you would join them there after we have said a prayer for Michael's well-being.'

He launched into a brief, hurried prayer. Then someone opened the church doors.

Grace watched the people filing out in silence. It had all the atmosphere of a funeral. Sometime in the next week several of the guests here would be attending four funerals. And he hoped that the no-show by Michael Harrison didn't mean it could be five. But it was not a good sign, it was a very bad sign indeed. Any prospect that Michael Harrison was playing a prank could now be discounted.

And there was something else bothering him.

*

An hour later at the reception, in the Queen Mary Room at the Royal Pavilion, with fine oil paintings in gilded frames hung on its pink walls, there was none of the cheery buzz of a party, but instead a number of stilted conversations punctuated the silence. Only a few of the twenty tables, beautifully laid for 200 guests, and decorated with orchids, were being used. Two chefs in white coats and toques manned the laden buffet tables with an army of waiters and waitresses, and the tiered wedding cake sat in a space of its own, an almost unwelcome reminder of the reason everyone was here. All the same, several people seemed to be tucking into platefuls of food and swigging down the champagne and wines.

Grace, who had been invited by Ashley, had been delayed talking on his phone to DC Nicholl and DS Moy about increasing the team. There was a rookie female detective constable Bella rated highly and who was free, called Emma-Jane Boutwood. Grace backed Bella's judgement by suggesting Emma-Jane be brought into the team immediately.

Now at the reception, he watched Ashley and Mark Warren keenly. Despite her eyes being tear-stained and streaked with mascara, she was putting on a brave face, seated at a table, with a young man on one side and a woman the other that Grace did not recognize from the church. It seemed several more people had turned up here, told by Ashley that the reception was still on for anyone who would like to come.

'He'll turn up,' Grace heard her saying. 'There's a reason behind this.' Then she continued, 'This is just so bizarre – isn't your wedding day meant to be the happiest day of your life?' before breaking down in a flood of tears.

On another table, Grace singled out Michael's mother and Ashley's uncle seated next to each other. He watched Bradley Cunningham for some moments, thoughtfully. Then he was interrupted by Mark Warren, sporting a white carnation in his buttonhole, holding an empty champagne flute, his voice slurred. He pushed his face close up against Grace's.

'Detective Sergeant Grace?' he quizzed.

'Detective *Superintendent*,' Grace corrected him.

'S-shorry – didn't realize you'd been promoted.'

'I haven't, Mr Warren.'

Mark stood back a moment, then squared up to him, eyeballing him as levelly as he could, except the alcohol was making him squint. His presence was clearly making Ashley uncomfortable – Grace saw her look up from her table.

'Can't sh'you leave thish young lady alone? Do you have any idea what she is going through?'

'That's why I'm here,' Grace said calmly.

'You should be out, trying to find Michael, not hanging around, freeloading here.'

'Mark!' Ashley cautioned.

'Fuck it,' Mark said, brushing her aside, and eyeballing Grace again. 'What the fuck are you doing about this situation?'

Angered by his attitude, but remaining calm, Grace said, 'My team are doing everything they can.'

'Doesn't much look like it to me. Should you be drinking on duty?'

'It's mineral water.'

Mark squinted at Grace's glass.

Standing up and joining them, Ashley said, 'Why don't you circulate, Mark?'

Grace clocked the edge in her voice. Something very definitely did not feel right but he couldn't place quite what.

Then Mark Warren jabbed him in the chest. 'You know your problem? You don't give a fuck, do you?'

'Why do you think that?'

Mark Warren gave him an asinine grin, raising his voice. 'Come on. You don't like rich people, do you? We can go fuck ourselves, can't we? You're too busy looking at speed cameras, trapping motorists. Why should you give a fuck about some poor rich sod who's the victim of some prank that's gone wrong, hey? When you could be out earning a fat bonus from trapping motorists?'

Grace deliberately lowered his voice, almost to a whisper, which he knew would force Mark Warren to lower his voice, also. 'Mr Warren, I don't have any connection with the Traffic Division. I'm here to try to help you.'

Mark leaned closer, straining to hear him. 'Sorry, I missed that. What did you say?'

Still speaking deliberately quietly, Grace said, 'When I was at Police Training College we had to do a parade and be inspected. I'd buffed my belt buckles to a shine like a mirror. The Chief made me take the belt off and held up the back for everyone to see. I hadn't polished that at all and I felt ashamed. It taught me a lesson – it's not just what you can see that matters.' He gave Mark a quizzical look.

'What exshacktly ish that meant to mean?'

'I'll leave you to think about that, Mr Warren – next time you have your BMW washed.'

Grace turned and walked away.

47

Back in his car, with the rain pattering down on the windscreen, Grace was deep in thought. So deep, it was several moments before he even noticed the parking ticket tucked under the wiper.

Bastards.

He climbed out of the car, grabbed the ticket and tore it from its cellophane wrapping. Thirty-quid fine for being five minutes over the time on his voucher – and no chance of putting it through expenses. The Chief had clamped down firmly on that.

Hope you appreciate this, Mr Branson, having your nice weekend break in Solihull. He grimaced, tossing the ticket into the passenger footwell in disgust. Then he turned his mind back to Mark Warren. Then back five years to the fortnight's course in forensic psychology he had done at the FBI training centre in Quantico in the USA. It had not been enough to make him an expert, but it had taught him the value of his instincts, and it had taught him how to read certain aspects of body language.

And Mark Warren's body language was all wrong.

Mark Warren had lost four close friends. His business partner was missing, maybe dead. Very likely dead. He ought to be in shock, numb, bewildered. Not angry. It was too soon for anger.

And he had noticed the reaction to his remark about the car wash. He had touched a nerve there very definitely.

I don't know what you are up to, Mr Mark Warren, but I'm making it my business to find out.

He picked up his phone, dialled a number, listened to it ringing. On a Saturday afternoon he was expecting to get the answering machine, but instead he got a human voice. Female. Soft and warm. Impossible for anyone to guess from her voice what she did for a living.

'Brighton and Hove City Mortuary,' she said.

'Cleo, it's Roy Grace.'

'Wotcher, Roy, how you doing?' Cleo Morey's ordinarily quite posh voice was suddenly impish.

Involuntarily, Grace found himself flirting with her over the phone. 'Yes, OK. I'm impressed you're working on a Saturday afternoon.'

'The dead don't know what day of the week it is.' She hesitated. 'Don't 'spose the living care much, either. Most of them anyhow,' she added as an afterthought.

'*Most* of them?'

'Seems to me most living people don't really know what day of the week it is – they give the impression they do, but they don't really. Don't you think?'

'This is heavy philosophy for a wet Saturday afternoon,' Grace said.

'Well I'm doing my Open University degree in philosophy, so I've got to practise my arguments on someone – and I don't get much response from the lot in here.'

Grace grinned. 'So how are you?'

'OK.'

'You sound a bit – low.'

'Never felt better, Roy. I'm tired, that's all. Been here on my own all week – short-staffed – Doug's on holiday.'

'Those lads who were killed on Tuesday night – are they still in the mortuary?'

'They're here. And so is Josh Walker.'

The one who died afterwards, in hospital?'

'Yes.'

'I need to come over, take a look at them. Would now be OK?'

'They're not going anywhere.'

Grace always enjoyed her dark humour. 'I'll be there in about ten minutes,' he said.

*

The Saturday-afternoon traffic was heavier than he had expected and it was nearly twenty minutes before he entered the busy gyratory system, then turned right, past a sign saying 'BRIGHTON & HOVE CITY MORTUARY' and through wrought iron gates attached to brick pillars. The gates were always open, twenty-four hours a day. Like a symbol, he reflected, that the dead didn't have much respect for business hours.

Grace knew this place far too well. It was a bland building with a horrible aura. A long, single-storey structure with grey pebbledash rendering on the walls and a covered drive-in on one side deep enough to take an ambulance or a large van. The mortuary was a transit stop on a one-way journey to a grave or a crematorium oven, for people who had died suddenly, violently or inexplicably – or from some fast-onset disease like viral meningitis, where a post-mortem might reveal medical insights that could one day help the living.

Yet a post-mortem was the ultimate degradation. A human being who had been walking, talking, reading, making love – or whatever – just a day or two earlier being cut open and disembowelled like a pig on a butcher's slab.

He didn't want to think about it, but he couldn't help

it; he'd seen too many post-mortems and knew what happened. The scalp would be peeled back, then the cap of the skull sawn off, the brain removed and sliced into segments. The chest wall would be cut open, all the internal organs taken out and sliced and weighed and some bits sent off for pathological analysis, the rest crammed into a white plastic bag and stitched back inside the cadaver like giblets.

He parked behind a small blue MG sports car, which he presumed was Cleo's, and hurried through the rain over to the front entrance and rang the bell. The blue front door with its frosted glass panel could have come straight from a suburban bungalow.

Moments later, Cleo Morey opened it, smiling warmly. No matter how many times he saw her, he could never quite get used to the incongruity of this immensely attractive young woman, in her late twenties, with long blonde hair, dressed in a green surgical gown, with a heavy-duty green apron over the top and white wellington boots. With her looks she could have been a model, or an actress, and with her brains she could have probably had any career she set her mind to – and she chose this. Booking in cadavers, preparing them for post-mortems, cleaning up afterwards – and trying to offer crumbs of comfort to the families of the bereaved, invariably in shock, who came to identify the bodies. And for much of the time she worked alone here.

The smell hit Roy immediately, the way it always did, that sickly sweet reek of disinfectant that permeated the whole place and made something squirm in his guts.

They took a left off the narrow entrance hall into the undertaker's office, which doubled as reception. It was a small room with a blower heater on the floor, pink Artexed walls, a pink carpet, an L-shaped row of visitor chairs, and a small metal desk on which sat three telephones, a stack of small brown envelopes printed with the words 'PERSONAL EFFECTS', and a large green and red ledger bearing the legend 'MORTUARY REGISTER' in gold block lettering.

There was a light box on one wall, as well as a row of framed 'PUBLIC HEALTH AND HYGIENE' certificates, and a larger one from the 'BRITISH INSTITUTE OF EMBALMERS', with Cleo Morey's name inscribed beneath. On another wall was a closed-circuit television camera, which showed, in a continual jerky sequence, views of the front, back, then each side of the building, then a close-up on the entrance.

'Cup of tea, Roy?'

Her clear bright blue eyes engaged with his for just a fraction longer than was necessary for the question. Smiling eyes. Incredibly warm eyes.

'I'd love a cup of tea.'

'English breakfast, Earl Grey, Darjeeling, China, camomile, peppermint, green leaf?'

'I thought this was the mortuary, not Starbucks,' he said.

She grinned. 'We also have coffee. 'Espresso, latte, Colombian, mocha—'

He raised a hand. 'Builder's tea, perfect.'

'Full fat milk, semi-skimmed, with lemon—'

He raised both his hands. 'Whatever milk you have open. Joe not here yet?'

He had asked Joe Tindall, from SOCO, to attend.

'Not yet, do you want to wait until he gets here?'

'Yes, we should.'

She flicked a switch on the kettle and disappeared into the locker room opposite. As the kettle began burbling, she returned with a green gown, blue overshoes, a face mask and white latex gloves, which she handed to him.

While he pulled them on, she made his tea for him and opened a tin containing digestive biscuits. He took one and munched it. 'So you've been here on your own all week? Doesn't it get you down? No conversation?'

'I'm always busy – we've had ten admissions this week. Eastbourne was going to send over someone from their mortuary, but they got too busy as well. Must be something about the last week in May.'

Grace pulled the band of the mask over his head, then let the mask hang loose below his chin; the young men had not been dead long enough to smell too bad, in his experience. 'You've had the families of all the four young men up?'

She nodded. 'And has the guy who was missing, the groom, turned up yet?'

'I've just come from the wedding,' Grace said.

'I thought you were looking a bit smart for a Saturday, Roy.' She grinned. 'So at least that's resolved itself?'

'No,' he replied. 'That's why I'm here.'

She raised her eyebrows but didn't comment. 'Anything in particular you want to see? I can get you copies of the pathologist's reports to the Coroner's office.'

'What I want to start with when Joe gets here,' he replied, 'are their fingernails.'

48

Followed by Joe Tindall, who was tugging on his gloves, Grace followed Cleo along the hard, speckled floor, watching her streaked blonde hair swinging against the neck of her green gown, past the glass window of the sealed infection chamber, into the main post-mortem room.

It was dominated by two steel tables, one fixed, one wheeled, a blue hydraulic hoist and a row of fridges with floor-to-ceiling doors. The walls were tiled in grey and the whole room was surrounded by a drain gulley. Along one wall was a row of sinks and a coiled yellow hose. Along another was a wide work surface, a metal cutting board and a glass-fronted cabinet filled with instruments and some packs of Duracell batteries. Next to the cabinet was a chart itemizing the name of each deceased, with columns for the weights of their brain, lungs, heart, liver, kidneys and spleen. A man's name, Adrian Penny, with his grim recordings was written in blue chinagraph pen.

Seeing what Grace was looking at, she said cheerfully, 'A motorcyclist we did a PM on yesterday. Overtook a lorry and didn't notice a steel girder sticking out the side – sliced the poor sod's head clean off at the neck.

'How the hell do you remain sane?' he asked.

Grinning, she replied, 'Who said I'm sane?'

'I don't know how you do your job.'

'It's not the dead who harm people, Roy, it's the living.'

'Good point,' he said. He wondered what her views were about ghosts. But this was not the time to ask.

The room felt cold. There was a hum from the refrigeration system, and a sharp clicking sound from overhead, from one fluorescent light that hadn't come on properly. 'Any preference who you want to see first?'

'No, I'd like to see all of them.'

Cleo marched up to the door marked '4' and pulled it open. As she did so there was a blast of icy air, but it wasn't the cold that instantly sent a chill through Grace. It was the sight of the human form beneath the white plastic sheets on each of the four tiers of metal trays on rollers.

The mortician wheeled the hoist up close, cranked it up, then pulled the top tray out onto it and closed the fridge door. Then she pulled back the sheet to reveal a fleshy white male, with lank hair, his body and waxy white face covered in bruises and lacerations, his eyes wide open, conveying shock even in their glassy stillness, his penis shrivelled and limp lying in a thick clump of pubic hairs like some hibernating rodent. Grace looked at the buff tag tied around his big toe. The name read 'Robert Houlihan'.

Grace's eyes went straight to the young man's hands. They were big, coarse hands, with very grimy nails. 'You have all their clothes here?'

'Yes.'

'Good.' Grace asked Tindall to take scrapings from the nails.

The SOCO officer selected a sharp tool from the instrument rack, asked Cleo for a specimen bag, then carefully scraped part of the dirt from each of the nails into the bag, labelled and sealed it.

The hands of the next body, Luke Gearing, were badly mangled from the accident, but apart from blood under them, the nails, bitten to the quick, were reasonably clean. There was no grime on Josh Walker's hands either. But

Peter Waring's were filthy. Tindall took scrapings from his nails, and bagged them.

Next he and Grace carefully examined all their clothes. There was mud on all their shoes, and plenty of traces of it on Robert Houlihan and Peter Waring's clothes. Tindall bagged all of these items separately.

'Are you going back to the lab now with these?' Grace asked him.

'I was planning to go home – be quite nice to see it before the weekend is over and have a life – or some pretence of one.'

'I hate to do this to you, Joe, but I really need you to start work on these now.'

'Great! You want me to cancel my U2 concert tickets for tonight, which I paid fifty fucking quid each for, stand my date up and haul my sleeping bag out of the office cupboard?'

'U2 – she really is young, isn't she?'

'Yes, and you know what, Roy, she has a short fuse. She's high maintenance.'

'There might be a man's life at stake here.'

His anger rising, Tindall said, 'I want the price of my tickets back from your budget.'

'It's not my case, Joe.'

'Oh – so whose is it?'

'Glenn Branson's.'

'And where the hell is he?'

'At a birthday party in Solihull.'

'It gets better all the time.'

By the row of lockers Tindall peeled off and binned his protective clothing and said, 'Have a nice sodding evening, Roy – go and ruin someone else's weekend next time.'

'I'll come over and keep you company.'

'Don't bother.'

Tindall slammed the door behind him. Moments later Grace heard the angry revving of a car engine. Then he noticed that, in his pique, the forensic expert had left behind the black bin liner containing his bags of evidence. He debated whether to run out after him, then decided to drive it over himself and try to calm the man down. He could understand his being hacked off – he would have been too, in the same circumstances.

He ducked into the sitting area, helped himself to another digestive biscuit and drained the remains of his tea, which had gone cold. Then he picked up the bin liner and Cleo walked him to the door. As he was about to step out into the rain he turned to her.

'What time are you finishing work today?'

'Another hour or so, with luck – assuming no one dies this afternoon.'

Grace stared at her, thinking she really did look incredibly lovely – and suddenly feeling a bag of nerves as he glanced at her hands and saw no rings. Of course she could have taken them off for work. 'I—' he said. 'I – just wondered – do you – you know – I mean – have any plans for this evening?'

Her eyes lit up. 'Actually I have a date to go to the cinema,' she said. Then added, as if for reassurance, 'With a friend – an old girlfriend who's going through a traumatic divorce.'

All his usual confidence deserting him, Grace said, 'I didn't know – whether you were married – or had a fellow – I—'

'Neither,' she said, giving him a long, friendly, expectant gaze.

'Would you – sometime – maybe – like to have a drink one night?'

Continuing to gaze at him, her lips slowly breaking into a broad smile, she said, 'I'd like that a lot.'

He walked on air across the tarmac to his car, oblivious to the pelting rain. Just as he pressed the remote to unlock the doors, Cleo called out to him. 'Roy! I think you forgot something!'

He turned and saw she was holding the black bin liner in her hand.

49

'You idiot,' Ashley said to Mark, who was slumped raggedly in the back of the limousine beside her. 'I can't believe your behaviour – why the hell did you have to be so aggressive to that cop?' She leaned forward and checked the glass partition to the chauffeur was firmly shut.

Mark put a hand on her ankle, and worked his way up her leg, beneath her wedding dress. She pushed him away sharply.

'Behave!' she said, sharply. 'For Christ's sake.'

'He'sh a jerk.'

'You're pissed out of your skull. What the hell did you think you were doing, having a go at him about speed cameras?'

Mark squinted at her. 'Putting him off the scent.'

Through the window she could see they were approaching the Van Alen building. It was half past five. 'How exactly is that *putting him off the scent*?'

'Wouldn't expect me to be rude if I had somesing to hide, would he?'

'So what exactly did he mean about having your BMW washed?'

'No idea.'

'You must have some idea – what did he mean?'

The intercom suddenly clicked and the driver's voice said, 'Front entrance?'

'Sh'fine,' Mark said. Then he turned to Ashley. 'Want to come up for a drink?'

'I don't know what I want. I could kill you.'

'What a charade thash wash.'

'It was a good charade – until you almost blew it.'

Mark spilled out of the car, almost falling on his face onto the pavement. It was only Ashley's steadying hand that saved him. Several people walking past stared, but she ignored them, her one goal to get Mark inside before he did anything else incriminating.

She dismissed the driver and helped Mark up to the front entrance, where he stared, bleary-eyed, at the door panel then managed to punch in his entry code accurately.

A few minutes later they were inside his apartment. Mark closed the door and slid the safety catch in place.

'I can't stay, Mark,' she said.

He began pawing at her clothes. She pushed his hands away. 'Let's have some coffee, and then I want you to tell me what the detective meant about having your car washed.'

Mark stared at her. She was wearing her white lace wedding dress, the veil pushed up. He lunged forward and kissed her on the mouth. She allowed him to kiss her on the lips and gave him a half-hearted kiss back, then pulled away. 'I mean it, I can't stay. I have to go round to Michael's mother and play the role of the grieving stood-up bride – or whatever fucking role I'm meant to be playing. God, what an afternoon. What a nightmare.'

Mark staggered over towards the open-plan kitchen, opened a cupboard and pulled out a jar of coffee. He stared at it with a puzzled expression, put it back in the cupboard, opened the fridge and removed a bottle of Cristal champagne.

'I think we should have a proper toast to your wedding day,' he said.

'That's not amusing – and you've had more than enough to drink.'

Holding the unopened bottle, Mark slumped onto a sofa, then patted the cushion beside him, by way of an invitation.

After some moments of haughty hesitation, Ashley sat at the far end of the sofa, as far from Mark as possible, tugged off her veil, then crossed her legs and kicked her shoes off. 'Mark, I want to know what Grace meant about your having the BMW washed.'

'I have no idea.'

She was silent.

'Do you love me?'

Shaking her head in despair she stood up. 'Yes, I love you. I have no idea why at this moment, but I do. And Michael's mother is waiting for me to turn up and blub my bloody eyes out, which is what I am about to go and do.'

'Have a drink first.'

'Christ, Mark.'

He pushed himself up from the sofa, staggered towards her and took her in his arms. Then he nuzzled her neck. 'You know – if the accident hadn't happened – the wedding would've gone ahead. You'd be Mrs Michael Harrison now.'

She nodded, melting a fraction.

He stared into her eyes. 'You'd have been on your way to the Savoy in London. You'd have made love to him tonight, wouldn't you?'

'That's what wives are meant to do on their wedding night.'

'And how would you have felt?'

Cupping his face in her hands, she said, 'I would have imagined it was you.'

'Would you have gone down on him? Sucked his dick?'

She pulled away from him. 'Mark!'

'Would you?'

'No way.'

'Come on!'

'We had an agreement, Mark.'

He took the bottle over to the sink, removed the foil then took two glasses from the cabinet. He popped the cork then filled the glasses and handed one to her.

She took it reluctantly and chinked glasses with him. 'We had it all planned,' she said to him.

'We had Plan A. Now we're into Plan B.' He drank a large gulp, draining half his glass. 'Wash wrong wish shat?'

'The first is that you are pissed. The second is that I now don't happen to be Mrs Michael Harrison. Which means I don't get to participate in his half of Double-M Properties.'

'His two-thirds, actually,' Mark said.

'So?'

'So I do, under our shareholders' agreement, and our key man insurance policy.'

'Provided he's dead.'

'Why do you say that? *Provided?*'

'You plugged the air hole properly, didn't you? You used superglue like I told you?'

Squirming, he said, 'Yesh.'

She was staring hard at him, seeing through him. 'Are you sure?'

'Yesh. That lid was screwed down. I pulled the tube out and I put a ton more earth down on top. If he was alive he'd have made contact, wouldn't he?'

She gave him a strange look.

'You want me to go and stick a fucking stake through his heart?'

She drank some champagne, then walked over to the

stereo and looked at the CD rack. 'How much do you love me?'

'How much? More than I could ever put into words.'

She pulled a CD out of its container, put it on the player and pressed the *play* button. Moments later, 'Love is All Around' filled the room. She put her glass down, took Mark's and put that down, then put her arms around him and began to lead him in a dance to the music. Pressing her lips against his ear she said, 'If you love me, you'll always tell me the truth, won't you?'

They danced for some moments, then he said, 'There'sh shomething that's been bothering me for the past few daysh.'

'Tell me?'

'You know that Michael and I both use Palms for picking up email when we're out of the office. We've been careful not to copy him in on any emails about his stag night – but I think I might have messed up.'

'What do you mean?'

'I think I copied him on one by mistake. And he has it with him.'

She pulled back from him, her eyes sharp as tacks. 'Are you saying he has it with him?'

'Possibly.'

'How *possibly*?'

'I can't find it anywhere in his office – or in his flat.'

'It's in the grave with him?'

'It might be.'

'*Might* be?'

Mark shrugged.

'You'd better make bloody sure, Mark.'

He stared at her in silence. 'I'm just telling you because—'

'Because?'

'Because it could be a risk.'

'You'd better get it back, hadn't you?'

'We're OK so long as no one finds him.'

Ashley sat down on a sofa and drank some of her champagne. 'I don't believe what I'm hearing. Why didn't you tell me this before?'

Mark shrugged. 'I thought – I—'

'You what?'

Mark joined her and attempted to clink glasses. Ashley withdrew hers, sharply.

'You'd better get it back,' she said. 'Pretty damned sharply. Like tonight. *Capisce?*'

50

As he drove back out towards the CID headquarters, Grace
plugged his mobile into the hands-free and rang Glenn
Branson. 'How's Solihull?' he asked.

'Pissing with rain. How's Brighton?'

'Pissing with rain.'

'And Ari's sister's gone to bed with a migraine.'

'So it's going to be a great birthday party.'

'I've collected plenty of brownie points for turning up,
though. How was the wedding?'

'A bit like your birthday party's going to be. No show
from the host.'

'No surprise there. Tell me – how many of Ashley
Harper's relatives turned up?'

'Just one that I saw,' Grace said. 'An uncle.' He halted at
a traffic light. 'I wanted to ask you, have you checked on
Michael Harrison's bank account and credit cards?'

'Got a constant monitor on them. Nothing since Tuesday afternoon. Same with his mobile. Any developments
your end?'

'The helicopter's been up again but seen nothing.
Nicholl and Moy are working over the weekend – they're
getting Michael's photograph circulated to the press, and
they're collecting all the CCTV camera footage in the suspect area – I have a team starting work viewing it. We're
going to have to make a decision about calling in specials
and getting a full-blown search of the area. And I'm getting

unhappier by the minute with his business partner, Mark Warren.'

'Tell me?'

'Nothing specific yet, but I think he knows something he isn't telling. We need to run some background checks on him.'

'I have the Holmes team doing that already.'

'Good boy. Hang on—' Grace concentrated for a moment as he pulled away from the lights. 'I think we should take a close look at their company, Double-M Properties. See what their insurance policies are.'

'I have that under way, too – and I'm having their Cayman Islands company checked out. What do you make of Ashley?'

'I don't know,' Grace said. 'I don't have a view. She's giving a convincing performance. I think we should check her out, too. You know what's odd about her?'

'This no relatives thing? You ever see that movie *The Last Seduction*, with Linda Fiorentino?' The phone signal weakened suddenly and Branson's voice became crackly.

'I don't remember it.'

'Bill Pullman was in it, too.'

'Doesn't ring a bell.'

'She was in *Men in Black* too.'

'OK.'

'Worth seeing – *The Last Seduction*. Had a predatory woman. Dark ending. She kind of reminds me of Ashley.'

'I'll check it out.'

'Get it on DVD. Play.com – great value.'

'How many twenty-seven-year-olds do you know that don't have relatives? You're twenty-seven, you are getting married, the biggest day of your life, and you can only produce one relative to turn up to your big day.'

'She could be an orphan. We need to check her background out.'

'I'll go and talk to Michael's mother – she must know about her future daughter-in-law.'

'Mine knew more about Ari than I did before I got hitched.'

'Precisely,' Grace said.

*

Ten minutes later Grace was walking along the corridor of the Major Incident Suite of the CID headquarters, lugging the black plastic bag from the mortuary. He stopped by a white sheet pinned to a red board which was headed 'DIAGRAM – COMMON POSSIBLE MOTIVES'. It was helpful, sometimes, to refresh his mind from these charts, although most of it was ingrained in his brain. He read the chart:

> Sexual. Jealousy. Racism. Anger/fright. Robbery.
> Power control. Maintain active lifestyle. Gain.
> Payment. Homophobia. Hate. Revenge. Psychotic.

He moved on to the next board, which was headed, 'FAST TRACK'. Below was printed:

1. Identify suspects
2. Intelligence opportunities
3. Scene forensics
4. Crime scene enquiries
5. Witness search
6. Victim enquiries
7. Possible motives
8. Media
9. Post-mortems
10. Significant witness interview
11. Other critical actions

Media, he thought. This was a good story for the media. He would phone his contacts, start getting the story out. Maybe that would get the ball rolling. He walked on and entered the small, pristine SOCO Suite. He would phone the *Argus* reporter Kevin Spinella for starters, he decided.

Joe Tindall was ready for him in the first of the two rooms, known as the *wet room*. There was a cluster of brown paper sacks on the floor, each labelled, in black print 'Evidence Bag', a roll of brown paper on a worktop, a sink and a tall air box.

'Thanks,' Joe Tindall said, as he handed him the bag, his tone a lot less friendly than when they had met earlier, but at least he was calmer.

The SOCO officer opened the black bin liner and pulled out the individual bags of soil, then the bags of clothes. Most of the clothes were heavily bloodstained. The stench of putrefaction began to rise from the clothes bags. 'These soil samples taken from the victims' finger-nails and shoes,' he said. 'You want to see if we can establish a match with the soil sample you brought in earlier?'

'From the suspect vehicle, yes. How quickly could you do this?'

'The person to do this is Hilary Flowers – appropriate name, don't you think?'

Grace smiled. 'I've used her before. She's good.'

'She's a genius on pollens. She's got me several results from pollen scrapings from victims' nostrils. But she's expensive.'

Grace shook his head in frustration. When he had first joined the police it was about solving crimes. These days, with everything farmed out to private companies, it was more about budgets. 'How quick is she?'

'She normally works on about two weeks' turnaround.'

'I don't have two weeks – we're talking about someone who might be buried alive. Every hour counts, Joe.'

Tindall looked at his watch. 'Twenty past six on a Saturday night. You're going to be lucky.' He picked up the phone and dialled. Grace watched his face, anxiously. After some moments, Tindall shook his head and whispered back, 'Voicemail.'

He left a message, asking her to call him back, urgently, then replaced the receiver. 'That's all I can do, Roy. If there's a match, she'll find it. Pollen, insect larvae, fossils, soil composition, you name it.'

'Nobody else you can think of?'

Joe Tindall looked at his watch again. 'It's Saturday night, Roy. If I leave now and drive like the clappers, I might just make the second half of the U2 concert – and get a shag afterwards. I think you're going to find that everyone else on this planet who might be able to identify soil samples also has plans for tonight.'

'My guy who's buried alive had plans for today, Joe. He was meant to be getting married.'

'Bummer.'

'You could say that.'

'I don't mean to be frivolous. But I have worked one hundred and ten hours this week, so far.'

'Join the club.'

'I can't do anything, Roy. Nothing. You know me well enough – if there was anything at all that I could suggest, I would tell you. If there was anyone, anywhere in England right now who could give us the analysis on this soil tonight, I'd get in the car and drive to them. But I don't know anyone else. Hilary is the woman. I'll give you her number and you can keep trying. That's all I can say.'

Grace wrote the number down.

51

As he climbed back into his Alfa, his mobile beeped with a text message.

> *Who's talking about a relationship?*
> *I'm just talking about sex. XXX*

Grace shook his head, despairing of ever understanding women. On Tuesday night Claudine had been vile to him, berating him about the police for the best part of three hours. Now in response to his text this morning she wanted to sleep with him?

And the worst part of it was that he actually felt horny. For the first time in years. Claudine was no beauty, but she wasn't a paper-bag job either. With another empty Saturday night stretching out ahead of him, the prospect of driving to Guildford and making out with this cop-hating vegan was almost appealing.

But not appealing enough. And at this moment, his head was full of more prosaic thoughts, listing everything he needed to do in the search for Michael Harrison.

*

Shortly after seven o'clock, with the rain easing, accompanied by Linda Buckley, a uniformed WPC in her mid-thirties with short blonde hair and a kind but alert face, he walked from his car up the path of the neat front garden of Gillian Harrison's bungalow and rang the doorbell. It triggered a loud yapping sound from within. Moments later the door opened and a small white dog, with a pink bow on its head, rushed out and began worrying his shoes.

'Bobo! Come here! Bobo!'

He flashed his warrant card at the woman he recognized from the aborted wedding this afternoon. 'Mrs Harrison? Detective Super-intendent Grace from Brighton CID, and this is the Family Liaison Officer we have assigned to you and Miss Harper, WPC Buckley. If there is anything you need, she will help you.'

Shoeless, her silvery blonde hair elegantly coiffed, wearing a smart blue dress with white trim and reeking of cigarette smoke, she gave a fleeting smile to the WPC, then a fearful look at Grace that instantly made him feel sorry for her. 'Yes, I remember you – you were at the reception this afternoon.'

'Is it possible to have a word with you?'

Her eyes were tear-stained and streaked with mascara. 'Have you found him? Have you found my son?'

He shook his head. 'I'm afraid not, no, I'm sorry.'

After a moment's hesitation she said, 'Would you like to come in?'

'Thank you.'

He followed her into the small sitting room, then sat down in the armchair she indicated, beside an unlit fake coal fire. 'Would you like something to drink? A glass of wine? Coffee?'

'A glass of water would be fine,' he said.

'Nothing at all for me,' said the WPC. 'Would you like me to help you?'

'No, thank you, that's kind of you.'

The dog looked up at him and gave a begging whine.

'Bobo, quiet!' she commanded. The dog followed her, slavishly, out of the room.

Grace stared around. There was a framed print of *The Haywain* on the wall and another print, of the Jack and Jill windmills at Clayton, a large framed photograph of Michael Harrison, in a tuxedo, with his arm around Ashley Harper, in a long evening dress, clearly taken at some function, another photograph of a much younger Michael Harrison, in short trousers, astride a bicycle and a black and white wedding photograph of Gill Harrison and her late husband, he presumed, from the information Glenn Branson had given him. He could see the resemblance between Michael Harrison and his father – a tall, good-looking man with long brown hair touching his shirt collar. From his huge lapels and wide trousers he guessed it was taken in the mid-seventies.

Gill Harrison returned, followed by the dog, with a tumbler of water in one hand and a wine glass in the other. She gave Grace the tumbler then sat down on the sofa opposite him.

'I'm very sorry about today, Mrs Harrison, it must have been very distressing for you,' he said, taking the glass, and sipping the cold water gratefully.

A young woman walked into the room. She had a sun-tanned, slightly beaky face, long, ragged blonde hair, and was dressed in a singlet and jeans. She sported rings on her lips and ears and a stud in her tongue.

'This is Carly, my daughter. Carly – this is Chief Inspector Grace of the CID, and WPC Buckley,' Gill Harrison said. 'Carly flew back from Australia for the wedding.'

'I saw you at the reception, but we didn't get a chance to speak,' he said, standing up to shake her reluctant hand, then sitting down again.

'Nice to meet you, Carly,' the WPC said.

Carly sat on the sofa right next to her mother and put a protective arm around her shoulder.

'Where were you in Australia?' Grace asked, trying to be polite.

'Darwin.'

'I haven't been there. I've been to Sydney.'

'I have a daughter who lives there,' said Linda Buckley breezily, trying to break the ice.

Carly shrugged, indifferently.

'I wanted to cancel the wedding and reception completely,' Gill Harrison said. 'It was Ashley who insisted. She felt—'

'She's a stupid bitch,' Carly said.

'Carly!' her mother exclaimed.

'Excuse me,' Carly said. 'Everyone thinks she's' – and she made a cutesy, Barbie doll flutter with her hands – 'so sweet. But I think she's a calculating little bitch.'

'Carly!'

Carly gave her mother a kiss on the cheek. 'I'm sorry, Mum, but she is.' Turning to Grace she said, 'Would you have insisted on the reception going ahead?'

Grace, watching them both, thought carefully before responding. 'I don't know, Carly. I guess she was caught between a rock and a hard place.'

'My brother is the sweetest guy in the world,' she said. 'Yeah.'

'You don't seem to like Ashley,' he said, seizing the chance.

'No, I don't like her.'

'Why not?'

'I think she's a lovely girl,' Gill Harrison butted in.

'Oh crap, Mum! You're just desperate to have grand-children. You're just pleased that Michael isn't gay.'

'Carly – that's not a nice thing to say.'

'Yeah, well, it's the truth. Ashley's a manipulative ice queen.'

Grace, suddenly feeling excited, tried to remain impassive. 'What gave you that impression, Carly.'

'Don't listen to her,' Gill Harrison said. 'She's tired and emotional with jet-lag.'

'Bullshit,' Carly said. 'She's a gold-digger.'

'How well do either of you know her?' Grace asked.

'Met her once – that was once too often,' Carly said.

'I think she's a delightful girl,' Gill answered. 'She's intelligent, domesticated – you can talk to her, have a proper conversation with her. She's been very good to me.'

'Have you met her family?' Grace asked.

'Poor thing hasn't got any family apart from her very lovely Canadian uncle,' Gill said. 'Her parents were killed in a car crash on holiday in Scotland when she was three. She was brought up by foster parents who were complete bullies. In London at first, then they moved to Australia. Her foster father tried to rape her repeatedly during her teens. She left them when she was sixteen and went to Canada – Toronto – where her uncle and aunt took her in – her aunt died quite recently, I gather, and she's very upset about that. I think Bradley and his wife were the only people who ever showed her kindness. She's had to make her own way in the world. I really admire her.'

'Phoeey!' said Carly.

'Why do you say that?' Grace asked.

''Cause I didn't think she was real when I met her. And after seeing her today, I think she's even less real. I can't explain it – but she doesn't love my brother. I know that. She might have been desperate to get married to him, but that's not the same as loving him. If she genuinely loved him, she'd never have gone through this charade today, she'd have been too upset.'

Grace looked at her with growing interest.

'You see?' Carly said. 'That's a woman talking. Maybe a jet-lagged woman, like my mum says. But a woman. A caring woman who loves her bro. Unlike his bitch-queen-from-hell fiancée.'

'Carly!'

'Oh fuck off, Mum.'

52

After Ashley left the flat, still furious at him, Mark switched on the television, hoping to catch the local news. He tried the radio too, but it was just gone seven and he had missed it.

Changed into jeans, trainers, a sweatshirt and a light anorak, with a baseball cap tugged low over his forehead, he was shaking from nerves and from an overdose of caffeine. He'd already downed two mugs of strong coffee in his attempt to sober up and was now finishing off a third. He drained the last dregs, then walked to the front door of his apartment. Just as he reached it the phone rang.

Hurrying back into the living area, he looked at the caller display. *Private number.* After a moment's hesitation he picked up the receiver.

'This is Kevin Spinella from the *Argus.* I'd like to speak to Mr Mark Warren.'

Mark cursed. If he'd been thinking more clearly he might have told the man that Mark Warren was out, but instead he found himself saying, 'Yes, speaking.'

'Mr Warren, good evening, sorry to trouble you on a Saturday evening. I'm calling about your business partner, Michael Harrison. I went along to the wedding that should have taken place this afternoon at All Saints' church, Patcham. You were the best man – I didn't feel it appropriate to intrude at the church – but I wonder if I could have a few words with you now?'

'Um – yes – yes, of course.'

'I understand Michael Harrison disappeared on his stag night, when there was that terrible accident. I'm curious to know why you, as best man, weren't there?'

'On the stag night?'

'Exactly.'

'I should have been, of course,' Mark said, calmly, trying to sound friendly, to make it all sound perfectly natural. 'I was out of town – up north on a business meeting – had it all scheduled to be back in good time, but my flight was delayed by fog,' Mark said.

'Where was that?'

'Leeds.'

'Ah right. These things happen – that's the problem with this country.'

'Absolutely!' Mark said, feeling they were starting to bond.

'I understand from the police that you have no knowledge of what was planned for the stag night. Is that right?'

Mark was silent for a moment. Thinking. *Careful.* 'No,' he said. 'That's not strictly true. I mean – that's not true at all. We had planned to go on a pub crawl.'

'A pub crawl! Right, OK. But isn't it usual for the best man to arrange the stag night?'

'Yes, so I believe.'

'But you didn't organize this stag night?'

Mark tried to focus his thoughts. Alarm bells were ringing. 'Yes, I did – Michael didn't want anything too elaborate – just to go to a few pubs with his mates. I had fully intended to be there.'

'What exactly did you plan?'

'We – ah – were going to do the usual stuff, you know – a bunch of pubs, get Michael wrecked, then deliver him home. We were going to hire a minibus and have a

designated driver, but one of our crowd said he had access
to a van and that he didn't mind not drinking, so we went
along with that.'

'Where did the coffin fit into this plan?'

Shit. Mark felt himself getting deeper into mire. 'Coffin,
did you say?'

'I understand you arranged for a coffin.'

'I don't know anything at all about a coffin!' Mark
exclaimed. 'That's a new one on me.' Trying to sound really
surprised he said again, for emphasis, '*Coffin?*'

'Do you think your friends organized this in your
absence?' the journalist asked.

'Absolutely. Must have done. One of them, Robert
Houlihan, works – worked – for his uncle, an undertaker –
but we never discussed a coffin. Are you sure about this?'

'I'm informed by the police they believe there was a
coffin in the van – before the accident. Can you think what
might have happened to Michael Harrison?'

'No, I have no idea. I'm desperately worried.'

'I spoke yesterday to the widow of one of your friends.
Mrs Zoe Walker. She said you were all planning to get
revenge on Michael Harrison because he regularly played
pranks on the rest of you. Might the coffin have something
to do with that?'

'As I said, I don't know anything about the coffin. It
sounds like some last-minute idea.'

'Do you think your mates might have put Michael Harrison into the coffin and that he's stuck somewhere?'

Mark thought hard before responding. 'Listen, you
know how it is when a bunch of guys get drunk. Sometimes
they do crazy things.'

'Been there myself.'

They both chuckled. Mark felt a tad relieved.

'Well, thank you for your time. If you hear anything, perhaps you'd be kind enough to let me know, if I give you my number?'

'Of course,' he said, looking around for a pen.

As Mark stood in the lift a few minutes later, he was thinking about the conversation, hoping to hell he hadn't said anything stupid, and worrying how Ashley would react if she saw him quoted in the paper. She'd be furious that he'd even spoken to them. But what choice did he have?

Driving up the ramp of the car park, he turned cautiously into the street, made a left turn, then eased out into the heavy Saturday-evening traffic, being careful to keep his speed down, knowing he must be over the legal limit. The last thing he needed was to be stopped and breathalysed.

Twenty minutes later he reached the car park of the garden centre at the back of Newhaven, the Channel port ten miles from his apartment. With little time to spare before its 8 p.m. closing time, he made a rapid dash through the store, buying a spade, screwdriver, hammer, chisel, small Maglite flashlight, rubber gardening gloves and a pair of gum boots. By eight he was back in his car, in the almost deserted lot. The sky was surprisingly clear and it would be a good couple of hours yet before it was completely dark – if then.

Two hours that he had to kill.

He knew he should eat something, but his stomach was all knotted up. He thought about a burger, a Chinese, an Indian. Nothing appealed. Ashley was angry at him; he'd never seen her angry before and it distressed and scared him. It was as if some connection between them had been switched off. He had to switch it back on and the only way was to appease her. Do what she said. Do what he had known for several days that he needed to do.

He wanted to call her, tell her he loved her, hear her tell him she loved him back. But she wasn't going to do that, not now, not yet. She was right to be mad at him; he'd been an idiot, nearly blown everything. Christ, why the hell had be been so stupid with that cop?

He started the engine and the radio came on. Eight o'clock. The local station news. First an international story, more bad stuff about Iraq. Then an item about Tony Blair and the European Union. Then his ears stiffened as the chirpy newscaster said, 'Sussex Police are stepping up their search for Brighton property developer Michael Harrison. His fiancée, Ashley Harper, and their guests were tragically disappointed when he failed to turn up at All Saints' church, Patcham, this afternoon for his wedding, confirming suspicions that he is incapacitated following the stag night prank that left four of his best friends dead. Detective Superintendent Roy Grace of the Sussex CID, who is now leading the enquiry into Michael Harrison's whereabouts, said this morning that the police were upgrading their search from a missing persons enquiry into a Serious Incident Investigation.'

Mark turned the volume of the radio up louder, and caught the Detective Superintendent's voice.

'We believe that Michael Harrison may be the victim of a prank that has gone very tragically wrong, and we would like all persons who believe they may have information about the events surrounding last Tuesday evening to contact the Incident Suite at Sussex CID urgently.'

Mark's vision blurred; the whole parking lot seemed to be vibrating and there was a muzzy sound in his ears as if he were in an aircraft that was taking off, or diving deep underwater. He pinched his nostrils, blew and his ears popped. His hands were wet with perspiration – then he realized his whole body was wet; he could feel the droplets of water running down his skin.

Breathe deeply, he remembered. That was the way to deal with stress. Ashley had taught him that just before he'd been to see a particularly tricky client.

So he sat in his car in the falling light, listening to the rhythm of his pounding heart, and breathed deeply.

For a long while.

53

Once any investigation – such as a murder, kidnapping, rape, armed robbery, fraud or missing persons enquiry – was elevated to Major Incident status it was awarded a code word.

All major incidents were now being handled from CID headquarters at Sussex House, which was why at twenty past eight on Saturday night, when most normal people who had a life were either at home or out enjoying themselves, Roy Grace, now officially in charge of the investigation, found himself climbing the stairs of Sussex House, past the framed photographs of the key team members and the displays of truncheons on the walls.

He had taken the decision – and the appropriate action – to upgrade the Michael Harrison missing persons enquiry to a Major Incident within minutes of leaving Gill Harrison's house. It was a big decision, with huge cost and police time implications, one that he was going to be required to justify to the Chief Superintendent and to Alison Vosper. No doubt he'd have a tough time doing that – he could already imagine some of the withering questions she would throw at him.

DC Nick Nicholl and DS Bella Moy, their Saturday-night plans long in tatters anyway, were on their way over here, along with their new recruit to the team, Emma-Jane Boutwood, bringing everything that they'd had in the Incident Room at Brighton police station – which was not much, so far.

Entering the Major Incident Suite, he walked through the green-carpeted, open-plan area lined with desks that housed the support staff of the senior officers of the CID. Each senior officer had his own room flanking this area, with his or her name printed on blue and yellow photochromatic card on the door.

On his left, through a wide expanse of glass he could see into the impressive office of the man who was technically his immediate boss – although Alison Vosper in practice was – Detective Chief Superintendent Gary Weston. Gary Weston and Roy Grace went back a long way – they had been partnered up when Grace had first joined the CID as a rookie constable, and Weston had not been much more experienced.

There was only a month's age difference between the two men, and Grace wondered, a little enviously sometimes, how Gary had achieved quite such a meteoric rise compared to his own, and would doubtless end up as a Chief Constable somewhere in Britain very soon. But in his heart he knew the answer. It wasn't that Gary Weston was a better cop or academically any brighter – they'd sailed through many of the same advancement courses together – it was simply that Gary was a better political animal than he would ever be. He didn't resent his former partner for this – they had remained good friends – but he could never be like him, never keep his opinions to himself the way Gary so often had to.

No sign of Gary in his office now, at 8.30 on a Saturday night. The Detective Chief Superintendent knew how to live the good life, mixing home, pleasure and work with ease. The framed photographs of greyhounds and race-horses that lined his walls were evidence of his passion for the tracks, and the stand-up framed photographs of his attractive wife and four young children strategically placed on every flat surface left visitors to his office in no doubt about his priorities in life.

Gary would probably be at a greyhound track tonight, Grace imagined. Having a cheery meal with his wife and friends, placing bets, relaxing, looking forward to a family Sunday. He saw the spectral reflection of his own face in the glass and walked on across the deserted room, past winking message lights on desks, silent fax machines, screensavers playing their eternal loops. Sometimes – at moments like this when he felt so disconnected from the real world – he wondered if this was what it was like to be a ghost, drifting unseen past everyone else's lives.

Holding his security card up to the panel at the end of the room, he pushed open the door, entering a long, silent, grey-carpeted corridor that smelled of fresh paint. He passed a large red felt-faced noticeboard headed 'OPERATION LISBON' beneath which was the photograph of an oriental-looking man, with a wispy beard, surrounded by several different photographs of the rocky beach at the bottom of the tall cliffs of local beauty spot Beachy Head, each with a red circle drawn on it.

This unidentified man had been found dead four weeks ago at the bottom of the cliff. At first he was assumed to be another jumper, until the post-mortem had revealed to the pathologist that he was already dead at the time he took his plunge.

On the opposite wall was 'OPERATION CORMORANT', with a photograph of a pretty teenage brunette who had been found raped and strangled on the outskirts of Brighton.

Grace passed the Outside Enquiry Team office on his left, a large room where detectives drafted in on major incidents would base themselves for the duration, then entered the door immediately opposite, marked 'INTEL ONE'.

The Intelligence Office Room was the new nerve centre for all major incidents. As he entered it, everything about it felt new, smelled new, even the attitude of the people working in here – apart from a distinct odour of Chinese food tonight. Despite opaque windows too high to see out of, the room, with its fresh white walls, had an airy feel, good light, good energy, very different to the messy buzz of police station incident rooms that Grace had grown up with.

It had an almost futuristic feel, as if it could as easily have housed Mission Control at Houston, and was a large, L-shaped room, divided up by three principal work stations, each comprising a curved, light-wood desk with space for up to eight people to sit, and massive white-boards, one marked 'OPERATION CORMORANT', one marked 'OPERATION LISBON' and one 'OPERATION SNOW-DRIFT', each covered in crime scene photographs and progress charts. Another would shortly be labelled 'OPERA-TION SALSA', the random name the police headquarters computer in Scotland Yard had thrown out for his Michael Harrison investigation.

Mostly the names had nothing to do with the investigations themselves, and occasionally they had to be changed. He remembered one time when the name 'OPER-ATION CAUCASIAN' had been given to the investigation of a black man who had been found dismembered in the boot of a car. It had been changed to something less controversial. But with Operation Salsa, the dumb computer had by chance struck a right chord. Grace had the very definite feeling of being involved in a song and dance.

Unlike the work stations in most police offices, there was no sign of anything personal on the desks or up on the walls. No pictures of families, footballers, no fixture lists, no jokey cartoons. Every single object in this room, apart from the furniture and the business hardware, was related to the matters under investigation. Apart from the Pot Noodle a weary-looking, long-haired Detective Inspector Michael Cowan was tucking into with a plastic fork at the end of one of the work stations.

Heading another of the work stations, glued to a flat computer screen, with a beaker of Coke in his hand, sat Jason Piette, one of the shrewdest Detective Inspectors that Grace had ever worked with. He would have been happy to place money on Piette one day becoming head of the Met – the top police job in the country.

Each of the work stations was manned by a minimum team of an office manager, normally a Detective Sergeant or Detective Inspector, a system supervisor, normally a lesser-ranking police officer, an analyst, an indexer and a typist.

Michael Cowan, wearing a loose checked shirt over jeans, greeted Grace cordially. 'How you doing, Roy? You're looking a bit smart.'

'Thought I should dress up for you boys – obviously I didn't need to bother.'

'Yeah, yeah!'

'What crap are you eating?' Grace responded. 'You have any idea what's in that stuff?'

Michael Cowan rolled his eyes, grinning. 'Chemicals, they keep me going.'

Grace shook his head. 'Smells like a Chinese takeaway in here.'

Cowan jerked his head up at the whiteboard beside

him, headed 'OPERATION LISBON'. 'Yup, well, you can take my Chinese problem away from me any time you feel like. I've given up a hot date to be here.'

'I'll trade with you gladly,' Grace said.

Michael Cowan looked at him inquisitively. 'Tell me?'

'You don't want to know, believe me.'

'It's that bad?'

'Worse.'

54

In the beam of the headlamps, Mark could see a whole cluster of wreaths at the roadside, on the apex of a right-hand curve. Some lay on the grass verge, some were propped against a tree and the rest against a hedge. There were several more than the last time he had passed here.

Taking his foot off the accelerator, he slowed to a crawl, a shiver rippling through him, deep inside him, deep inside his soul. He continued to watch them as they receded in the glow of his tail lights, until they vanished into the darkness, into the night, vanished, were gone, had never been there. *Josh, Pete, Luke, Robbo.*

Himself, too, if the plane had not been delayed.

Then of course the problem would have been different. Covered in goose pimples, he floored the accelerator, wanting to get away from here; it was giving him the creeps. His mobile beeped, then began to ring. Ashley's number on caller display appeared on the panel on the dash.

He answered it on the hands-free, glad to hear her, badly in need of human company. 'Hi.'

'Well?' She sounded as frosty as when she had left his apartment.

'I'm on my way.'

'Only now?'

'I had to wait for it to get dark. I don't think we should talk on mobiles – shall I come and see you when I get back?'

'That would be really stupid, Mark.'

''Yes. I – I – how is Gill?'

'Upset. How do you expect her to be?'

'Yup.'

'*Yup?* Are you OK?'

'Sort of.'

'Are you sober now?'

'Of course,' he said, tetchily.

'You don't sound good.'

'I don't feel good, OK?'

'OK. But you're going to do it?'

'That's what we agreed.'

'Will you call me after?'

'Sure.'

He hung up. It was misty ahead, and a film of moisture covered the windscreen. The wipers arced twice, the rubber blades were shrieking. He switched them off. The shrubbery at the edge of the forest was looking familiar, and he slowed down, not wanting to overshoot the turn-off.

Moments later he rattled over the first cattle grid, then the second, the headlight beams stretching out ahead through the mist like twin lasers, the car lurching on the potholed track as he accelerated, driving too fast, scared of the trees that seemed to be pressing threateningly in on either side, and glancing in his mirror, just in case . . .

Just in case what, exactly?

He was getting close now. A low murmur of chatter from the radio distracted him, and he switched it off, dimly aware that his breathing was getting faster, that perspiration kept pouring down his temples, his back. The nose dipped steeply as the front wheels plunged into a puddle, and water, sounding as hard as pebbles, spattered the windscreen. Switching the wipers on again, he slowed right down. Jesus, it was deep; he hadn't realized how much rain there'd been since he was last here. And then – *shit, oh shit, no!*

The wheels had lost traction in the mire.

Pressing the accelerator harder made the BMW vibrate, slide a few feet sideways, then slip back again.

Oh, Christ, no!

He could not get stuck, could not, could not. How the hell could he explain this, half-ten at night, out here?

Breathe deeply . . .

He breathed in, peering out fearfully at the darkness, at every shadow in front of him, to the side of him, behind him, then pressed the central locking, heard the *clunk*, but felt no better. Then he switched on the dome light and looked down at the controls. There were settings for off-road conditions, a lower gear ratio, a differential lock; he'd seen them a hundred times and never bothered to read up about them.

Reaching over, he pulled the handbook out of the glove compartment, frantically scrambled through the index, then turned to the relevant pages. He pushed a lever, pressed a button, put the book down beside him, and tentatively tried the accelerator. The car lurched, then, to his relief, powered forwards.

He kept going at a steady ten miles per hour, the car much more surefooted now, moving forward through more puddles as if it was on a conveyor belt. Then he made the right fork which would take him to the clearing. A baby rabbit hopped out in front of him, turned and ran back, then scampered forward, right beneath him. He had no idea whether he hit it or not, didn't care, just wanted to press on, maintain his speed, his momentum, his grip on the mud.

The small glade of scrubby mosses and grasses was right ahead now, and to his relief the sheet of corrugated iron, beneath the camouflage of uprooted plants he had strewn over it, was still in place.

He drove up onto the relatively firm soil, not wanting to risk the car bogging itself down while it was parked, then, switching off the engine but leaving the headlamps on full beam, he tugged on his new gum boots, grabbed the Maglite and climbed down onto the squelchy soil.

There was an instant of total silence. Then a faint rustle in the undergrowth which made him turn, stabbing the beam of the Maglite into the forest in fear. Holding his breath, he heard a crackle, then a rattle like a coin in a tin, and a large pheasant careened clumsily off between the trees.

He swung the beam from right to left, sick with fear, opened the tailgate of the car, pulled on the rubber gloves, then pulled out the tools he had bought and carried them over to the edge of the grave.

He stood still for some moments, staring down at the corrugated iron sheet, listening. The car engine pinged. Droplets of water fell all around him in the forest, but otherwise silence. Total silence. A snail had attached itself to one section of the corrugated iron, its shell rising like a barnacle on a wreck. Good. This sheet looked like it had lain here undisturbed for years.

Placing his tools and the Maglite down in the wet grass, he grabbed an end of the sheet, and pulled it back. The grave appeared like a dark crevasse. Gripping the flashlight, he stood up, but remained rooted to the spot, trying to pluck up the courage to step forward.

As if Michael might be crouching in there, ready to grab him.

Slowly, small step by small step, he inched towards the edge, then in a panicky thrust he pointed the beam down into the long, rectangular hollow.

And breathed out.

Everything was as he had left it. The earth still heaped, undisturbed. For some moments he stared, guiltily. 'I'm sorry, partner,' he whispered. 'I—'

There wasn't anything to say. He went back to the car and turned the lights off. No sense in advertising his presence, just in case there was anyone out in the woods at this hour, which he doubted – but you never knew.

It took almost an hour of hard digging before the spade struck the wood of the coffin lid. There was much more earth than he had thought – OK, he had added quite a bit the other night, but even so . . . He continued to scrape away until he could see the whole lid clearly and the brass screws in each corner. The tiny hole where the breathing tube had been, which he had plugged with earth, had been widened; it seemed a little larger – or was it his imagination?

Reaching up, he put the spade on the ground, grabbed the screwdriver and set to work on each of the screws in turn. Then came the bit he hadn't quite worked out: the coffin fitted tightly into the hole, and there was no gap beside it – the only place to stand was on the lid, and that made it impossible to remove it.

He climbed out, then clenching the Maglite in his teeth, still holding the screwdriver, prostrated himself and wriggled forwards over the edge of the grave, and reached down. He could touch the lid of the coffin easily.

Then he began trembling. What the hell was he

going to find? Removing the flashlight from his mouth he called, softly, 'Michael?' Then louder. 'Michael? Hello? Michael?'

Then he rapped several times on the lid with the handle of the screwdriver – although he knew that if Michael was alive – and conscious – he would have heard his footsteps and the scraping of the shovel on the lid. Except he might be too weak to have responded.

If he was still alive.

A big *if*. It was four days now – and he clearly had no air. He stuck the barrel of the Maglite back in his mouth and clenched hard. *He had to do this. Had to do this fucking thing. Had to be here to get the goddamn Palm back from Michael.* Because one day someone was going to find this grave and open it up and find the corpse, and find the goddamn Palm with all the emails on it, and that cop, Detective Superintendent Graves or whatever his name was, would find the email he had sent Michael on Monday, telling him they all had a real treat in store for him, and giving him cryptic clues – too cryptic for Michael to have figured out in advance what they were going to do to him, but a total giveaway to the cop.

Mark eased the blade of the screwdriver under the lid, then levered it up a few inches, until he could get his fingers in. Taking the strain with his left hand, he put the screwdriver down on the ground above him, then lifted the heavy lid as high as he could, barely registering the deep, jagged groove that had been carved on the inside.

Inky water shimmered back at him, the soggy remnants of a magazine floating on the surface, large bare breasts just visible in the bright beam.

Mark screamed and the Maglite fell from his teeth, splashed into the water and struck the bottom of the coffin with a dull thud.

There was no one inside.

55

The lid fell down with a bang like a gunshot. Mark scrambled to his feet, tripped and went sprawling in the muddy soil. He hauled himself to his knees, swivelled in a complete circle, his eyes scanning the darkness, whimpering, panting, his brain seized up in his panic, wondering which way to run. To the car? Into the woods?

Oh sweet Jesus. Christ. Christ.

Still on all fours he backed away from the grave and spun around in a complete circle again. Was Michael out there, watching him, about to strike?

About to blind him with a flashlight beam?

He stood and ran to the car, wrenched open the door, climbed in and the bloody interior lights all came on, fucking floodlighting him! He slammed the door shut, hit the central locking button, twisted the ignition key, rammed the gear lever into *drive*, snapped on the lights and floored the accelerator, swinging the car round in a wide arc, the beam of the lights traversing the trees, shadows leaping, fading; he continued round in a circle, then another circle, then a third.

Oh Jesus.

What the hell had happened?

He hadn't got the fucking Palm. Had to go back and check. Had to.

How the hell could . . . ?

How could he have got out? Screwed the lid back down? Put the earth on top?

Unless?

He'd never been there?

But if he hadn't been there, why didn't he turn up to the wedding?

Thoughts hurtled round his brain. All jumbled. He wanted to call Ashley, and, oh sure, he knew the first thing she would ask him.

Did you get the Palm?

He drove up to the edge of the grave, sat in the car, waiting, watching. Then he opened the door, jumped down, flat on his stomach, and without bothering to roll up his sleeves plunged his hands into the cold water. Hit the soft, satin bottom. Felt the padded sides, then the bottom again. Found the torch and retrieved it. No longer working. His hands hit something small, round, metallic; his fingers clasped around it and pulled it out too, holding it up to the beam of the headlights. It looked like the cap of a whisky bottle.

He turned and stared fearfully at the woods all around. Then he plunged his arms back into the coffin, working his way from one end to the other. The sodden page of a magazine wrapped itself around his hand. Nothing else. Nothing at all. The damned thing was empty.

He stood up, replaced the corrugated iron sheet, half-heartedly throwing some grasses over it, then got back into the safety of his car. He slammed the door and hit the central locking button again, then turned and headed back down the track, accelerating hard, crashing through the ruts and puddles until he rumbled over the two cattle grids and reached the main road.

Then he switched the diff lock off and pushed the gear lever back to normal high-gear drive and turned back towards Brighton, staring into his rear-view mirror, fearful of every pair of headlights that appeared behind him, wanting desperately to call Ashley but too confused to know what to say to her.

Where the hell was Michael?

Where?

Where?

He drove back past all the wreaths, glancing at the orange glow of the dash, then at the road, then into his mirror. Had he imagined it? Hallucinated it? *Come on, guys, what's your secret? What do you know that I don't? You put an empty coffin in the ground? OK, so what did you do with Michael?*

As he drove on he began to calm down a fraction, starting to think more clearly, convincing himself it was unimportant now. Michael was not there. There was no dead body. No one had anything on him.

Clenching the steering wheel with his knees, he pulled his rubber gloves off and dropped them in the passenger footwell. Of course, this was Michael all over. It had all his hallmarks. Michael the joker. Had Michael set this whole damned thing up?

Missing his wedding day?

Wild thoughts began going through his mind now. Had Michael twigged about himself and Ashley? Was this part of his revenge? He and Michael had known each other for a long time. Since they were thirteen. Michael was a smart guy, but he had his own way of dealing with problems. Possible that he had twigged – although he and Ashley had been incredibly careful.

He thought back as he drove. To the day Ashley had first come to the office in response to an ad they had put in the *Argus* for a PA. She had walked in, so smart, so beautiful, streets ahead of all the others they had interviewed before and after her. She was in a whole different league.

Having just split up with a long-term girlfriend, and being free, he'd fancied her in a way he'd never fancied anyone before. They'd connected from that first moment, although Michael had seemed blind to it. By the end of her second week working for them, unknown to Michael, they started sleeping together.

Two months into their secret relationship, she told Mark that Michael had the hots for her and had invited her out to dinner. What should she do?

Mark had felt angry, but had not revealed that to Ashley. All his life, ever since he had met Michael, he had lived in his shadow. It was Michael who always pulled the best-looking girls at parties, and it was Michael who somehow charmed his bank manager into giving him a loan to buy the first run-down property that he had made a big return on, while Mark had struggled on a meagre salary in a small accountancy practice.

When they had decided to go into business together, it was Michael who had the cash to fund it – and took two thirds of the shares for doing that. Now they had a business worth several million pounds. And Michael had the lion's share.

When Ashley had walked in that day, it was the first time that a woman had looked at him first.

And then the shit had dared to ask her out.

What happened next had been Ashley's idea. All she had to do was marry Michael and then engineer a divorce. Just set him up with a hooker and have a hidden cameraman. She'd settle for half his shares – and with Mark's thirty-three per cent, that would give them a majority holding. Control of the company. Goodbye, Michael.

Dead simple, really.

Murder had never been on the agenda.

56

Ashley, in a white towelling dressing gown, her hair down and loose over her shoulders, opened the front door of her house and stared at the mud-spattered figure of Mark with a mixture of disbelief and anger.

'Are you insane, coming here?' she said as a greeting. 'And at this hour. It's twenty past twelve, Mark!'

'I have to come in. I couldn't risk phoning you. We have to talk.'

Startled by the desperate tone of his voice, she relented, first stepping out and looking carefully down the quiet street in both directions. 'You weren't followed here?'

'No.'

She looked down at his feet. 'Mark, what the hell are you doing? Look at your boots!'

He stared down at his filthy gum boots, pulled them off, then carried them inside. Still holding them, he stood in the open-plan living area, watching the winking lights from the silent wall-mounted stereo.

Closing the front door, she stared at him fearfully. 'You look terrible.'

'I need a drink.'

'I think you had enough earlier today.'

'I'm too bloody sober now.'

Helping him off with his anorak she asked, 'What would you like? A whisky?'

'Balvenie if you have some. Otherwise anything.'

'You need a bath.' She headed towards the kitchen. 'So, tell me, was it awful? Did you get the Palm?'

'We have a problem.'

Ashley spun round as if she'd been shot. 'What kind of a problem?'

Mark stared at her helplessly. 'He wasn't there.'

'Not there?'

'No – he – I don't know – he—'

'You mean *he* wasn't there? The *coffin* wasn't there?'

Mark told her what had happened. Ashley's first reaction was to go to each of the windows and draw the blinds tightly, then she poured him a whisky and made herself a black coffee. Then they sat down on opposite sofas.

'Is it possible you went to the wrong place?'

'You mean – like there's two different coffins? No. I was the one who suggested that spot in the first place. We were going to leave him with a porno magazine and a bottle of whisky – both of those are in there – well the cap of the bottle is.'

'And the coffin lid was screwed down – with earth on top?' Clasping her coffee with both hands, she blew steam away from the top and sipped it. Mark watched as her dressing gown opened and part of her large white breasts was visible through the gap. And they made him want her, now, despite everything, despite all his panic; he just wanted to seize her in his arms and make love to her.

'Yes – it was exactly how it was on Thursday when I—'

'Took the breathing tube?'

He gulped some whisky. She was giving him a sympathetic smile now. Maybe he could at least get to stay an hour or two. Make love. He needed some release from this nightmare.

Then her expression darkened. 'How sure are you that he was in there when you took the tube?'

'Of course he was bloody in there. I heard him shout. Christ!'

'You didn't imagine it?'

'Imagine him shouting?'

'You were in a pretty bad state.'

'You would have been too. He was my business partner. My best friend. I'm not a bloody murderer – I—'

She gave him a richly cynical look.

'I'm only doing this – because – because I love you, Ashley.' He drank some more whisky.

'He could be out there right now,' she said. 'Prowling in the dark, watching, couldn't he?'

Mark shook his head. 'I don't know. If he wasn't in the coffin, why didn't he come to the wedding? But he was – or someone was – there are marks inside the lid; someone had been trying to scrape their way out.'

Ashley took the news impassively.

'Maybe he knows about us – that's all I can think. That he fucking *knows* about us.'

'He doesn't,' Ashley said. 'He has no idea. He talked to me a lot about you, how much you wanted to settle down with the right woman and have kids, and that you never seemed to be able to find a steady girlfriend.'

'Oh great, he always gave my ego a real boost.'

'Not in a nasty way, Mark. He cares about you.'

'You're being very defensive about him.'

'He is my fiancé.'

'Very funny.' Mark set his glass down on the square coffee table, then buried his face in his hands.

'You need to pull yourself together. Let's look at this logically, OK?'

Still with his face in his hands, he nodded.

'Michael was there on Thursday night. You took the tube, plugged the air hole, right?'

Mark made no comment.

'We know he is a big practical joker. So, somehow he gets out of the coffin, and he decides to make it look as if he is still in there.'

Mark stared at her, abjectly. 'Great joke. So he's out and he knows I took the breathing tube – and there could only be one reason why I did that.'

'You're wrong. How would he know it was you? Could have been anyone out walking in the woods.'

'Come on, Ashley, get real. Someone walking in the woods stumbles across a grave, with a breathing tube sticking out of the coffin, removes the tube and heaps a ton more earth on top of the coffin?'

'I'm just trying to throw thoughts out.'

Mark stared at her, the thought suddenly going through his mind that perhaps Ashley and Michael had hatched something between them. To trap him.

Then he thought about all those days and evenings he had spent with Ashley over the past months, the things she had said to him, the way they had made love, planned – and the scornful way she always spoke about Michael, and he dismissed that thought completely.

'Here's another idea,' she said. 'The others – Pete, Luke, Josh and Robbo – all knew you were going to be arriving late. Perhaps they were setting up a practical joke on you – with Michael – and it backfired?'

'OK,' he said. 'Even supposing Michael wasn't in that coffin when I went there, and I imagined him calling out, then where the hell is he? Where has he been since

Tuesday night? Why hasn't he been in touch; why didn't he turn up to the wedding? Can you answer me that?'

'No. Unless the others were pulling a stunt on you and him – and he's tied up or locked up in some other place.'

'Or done a runner?'

'He hasn't done a runner,' Ashley said. 'I can tell you that.'

'How can you be sure?'

Her eyes rested on Mark's. 'Because he loves me. He really, genuinely loves me. That's why I know he hasn't done a runner. Did you put everything back as it was?'

Mark hesitated, then lied, not wanting to admit he'd fled in panic. 'Yes.'

'So either we have to wait,' she said. 'Or you go find him – and deal with him.'

'Deal with him?'

Her look said it all.

'I'm not a killer, Ashley. I might be a lot of things—'

'You might not have a choice, Mark. Think about it.'

'He won't be able to nail anything on me. Nothing that he can stick.' He fell silent, thinking. 'Can I wait here?'

She stood up and walked over to him, placed her hands on his shoulders and gently massaged his back. Then she kissed his neck. 'I would love you to stay,' she whispered. 'But it would be madness. How do you think it would look if Michael turned up? Or the police?'

Mark turned his head and tried to kiss her on the lips. She allowed him one quick peck then pulled away. 'Go,' she said. 'Vamoosh! Find Michael, before he finds you.'

'I can't do that, Ashley.'

'You can. You already did it on Thursday night. It might not have worked, but you proved you *can* do it. So *go* do it.'

He padded dejectedly across the floor to get his boots,

and Ashley brought over his sodden, muddy anorak. 'We need to be careful what we say over the phone – the police are getting nosy. We should start assuming the phones are tapped,' she said. 'OK?'

'Good thinking.'

'Talk to you in the morning.'

Mark opened the door warily, as if expecting to find Michael there with a gun or a knife in his hand. But there was just the glow of the streetlamps, the dull shine of silent cars and the still of the urban night punctuated only by the distant screech of two fighting cats.

57

Every couple of months, Roy Grace took his eight-year-old goddaughter, Jaye Somers, out for a Sunday treat. Her parents, Michael and Victoria, both police officers, had been some of his and Sandy's closest friends, and they had been hugely supportive in the difficult years following her disappearance. With their four children, aged two to eleven, they had become almost a second family to him.

Today he'd had to disappoint Jaye by explaining when he collected her that he could only spare a couple of hours, as he had to go back to work to try to help someone who was in trouble.

He never told Jaye in advance what the treat would be, so she always enjoyed the guessing game for the first few minutes of their car journey.

'I think we are going to see animals today!' Jaye said.

'Do you?'

'Yes.'

She was a pretty child, with long silvery blonde hair, a cherubic, happy face and an infectious laugh. Today she was smartly dressed, as usual, in a green frock with white lace trim and a tiny pair of pink trainers on her feet. Sometimes her expressions, and the things she said, could seem incredibly grown-up. There were moments when Grace felt he was out with a miniature adult, not a child.

'So what makes you think that?'

'Umm, let me see.' Jaye leaned forward and twiddled the dials on Grace's car radio, selected the CD and punched

a number. The first track of a Blue album began to play. 'Do
you like Blue?'

'Uh huh.'

'I like the Scissor Sisters.'

'Do you?'

'They're cool. Do you know them?'

Grace remembered that Glenn Branson was into them.
'Of course.'

'We're definitely going to see animals.'

'What sort of animals do you think we're going to see?'

She turned the music up, swaying her arms to the beat.
'Giraffes.'

'You want to see giraffes?'

'Giraffes don't dream much,' she informed him.

'Don't they? You talk to giraffes about their dreams?'

'We have a project in school about animals dreaming.
Dogs dream a lot. So do cats.'

'But not giraffes?'

'No.'

He grinned. 'OK, so how do you know that?'

'I just do.'

'How about llamas?'

She shrugged.

It was a fine late-spring morning, the sun bright and
warm and dazzling through the windscreen, and Grace
pulled his sunglasses out of the glove compartment. There
was a hint, today at any rate, that the long spell of bad
weather might be over. And Jaye was a sunny person, he
enjoyed her company a lot. He normally forgot his troubles
during the few precious hours he was with her.

'So what else have you been up to at school?'

'Stuff.'

'What kind of stuff?'

'School's boring at the moment.'

Grace drove extra carefully with Jaye on board, slowly heading out of Brighton into the countryside. 'Last time we went out you said you were really enjoying school.'

'The teachers are so stupid.'

'All of them?'

'Not Mrs Dean. She's nice.'

'What does she teach?'

'Giraffe dreams.' She burst into giggles.

Grace pulled up as the traffic queued for a roundabout. 'That's all she teaches?'

Jaye was quiet for a moment, then said suddenly, 'Mummy thinks you should get married again.'

Surprised, he said, 'Does she?'

Jaye nodded very definitely.

'And what do you think?'

'I think you'd be happier if you had a girlfriend.'

They reached the roundabout. Grace took the second exit, onto the Brighton bypass. 'Well,' he said, 'who knows?'

'Why don't you have a girlfriend?' she asked.

'Because . . .' He hesitated. 'Well – you know – finding the right person is not always that easy.'

'I have a boyfriend,' Jaye announced.

'You do? Tell me about him.'

'His name is Justin. He's in my class. He told me he wants to marry me.'

Grace shot her a sideways glance. 'And do you want to marry him?'

She shook her head vigorously. 'He's yuck!'

'He's your boyfriend, but he's *yuck*? What kind of a boyfriend is that?'

'I'm thinking of ending it,' she said, deadly serious.

This was another reason why Grace loved his days out

with Jaye, because he felt she kept him in touch with the young world. Now, for a moment, he felt totally lost. Did he ever have a girlfriend at eight? No way . . .

His mobile, lying in his door pocket, rang. He picked it up and held it to his ear rather than use the hands-free in case it was bad news which might upset Jaye. 'Roy Grace,' he said.

A young female voice said, 'Hello? Detective Superintendent Grace?'

'Speaking.'

'It's DC Boutwood.'

'Emma-Jane? Hi, welcome to the team.'

She sounded nervous. 'Thank you. I'm at Sussex House – DC Nicholl asked me to call you – there's been a development.'

'Tell me?'

Even more nervous now, she said, 'Well, sir, it's not very good news. Some ramblers have found a body in Ashdown Forest, about two miles east of Crowborough.'

Right in the heart of the suspect area, Grace thought instantly.

'A young man,' she continued. 'Late twenties or early thirties. Sounds like he fits Michael Harrison's profile.'

Glancing at Jaye, he said, 'What condition is he in?'

'I don't have that information. Dr Churchman is on his way there now. DC Nicholl wants to know if you will be able to attend?'

Grace glanced at Jaye again. There was no option. 'I'll be there in an hour.'

'Thank you, sir.'

As he hung up, Jaye informed him, 'Mummy said that people mustn't use their mobile phones when they are driving. It is very dangerous.'

'Your mummy is quite right. Jaye, I'm sorry, I'm going to have to take you back home.'

'We haven't seen the giraffe yet.'

He switched on his indicator, to pull off the road at the next exit and turn back. 'I'm sorry. There is a young man who has gone missing and I have to help find him.'

'Can I help too?'

'Not this time, Jaye, I'm sorry.' He picked up his phone and dialled Jaye's home number. Fortunately her parents were in. Grace gave an edited version of the events to her mother and reversed the car. He promised to take her out again next Sunday, instead. They would go and see a giraffe, for sure.

Ten minutes later, holding his hand, she trotted back alongside him up to the front door of her house, her disappointment palpable.

He felt like a heel.

58

A mud-spattered police patrol car was waiting at the side of the main road, marking the start of the track into the forest for him. Grace pulled up alongside, then the constable at the wheel led the way for a good mile.

The waterlogged, potholed track was barely driveable in his car, the sump bottoming, the front wheels slithering and spinning as they lost traction. Mud exploded over the bonnet, spattering the windscreen with large brown flecks. Grace, who had just taken the Alfa to a pricey car wash before picking up Jaye, cursed. Then a clump of gorse scraped the side, sounding as hard as nails. He cursed again, more loudly, his nerves wound up, upset that he'd disappointed Jaye, but far more upset about the news of the body.

It wasn't necessarily Michael Harrison, he thought. But he had to admit it was hard to escape the coincidence. Michael Harrison was last seen in exactly this area. Now a body matching his age, height and build turns up.

Did not sound good.

As they rounded a bend he saw a cluster of vehicles ahead, and a strip of yellow crime-scene tape sealing off the area. There were two police cars, a white SOCO van, a plain green van – probably belonging to an undertaker – and a convertible Lotus Elise sports car which he knew belonged to Nigel Churchman, the local consultant pathologist who had a penchant for boy's toys. How had he got that up here?

He pulled up and opened his door, expecting the sickly stench of death to fill his nostrils. But all he smelled were pine, flowers, earth, the scents of the forest. Whoever it was had not been dead long, he thought, climbing out, his moccasin loafers instantly sinking into the boggy woodland soil.

He removed his white protective suit and overshoes from a bag in the boot of his car and pulled them on, then made his way over, ducking under the tape. Joe Tindall, also dressed in white protective clothing and white boots, turned towards him, holding a large camera.

'Hi!' Grace greeted him. 'You're having a great weekend!'

'You and me,' Tindall said sourly, nodding at the undergrowth yards behind him. 'You know my mother wanted me to be an accountant?'

'Never figured you for a bean counter,' Grace replied.

'Apparently, most accountants have a life,' he retorted.

'But what kind of a life?'

'One where they get to spend their Sundays at home with their wife and kids.'

'All the people I know with kids,' Grace replied, 'can't wait to get rid of them for the day. Especially on Sundays.' He patted his colleague on the back. 'One man's Sunday in his garden is another man's hell.'

Tindall jerked his head over at the body, barely visible in the dense undergrowth. 'Well, he's not having a great Sunday, whichever way you slice it.'

'Probably not the best metaphor under the circumstances,' Grace said, walking over towards the corpse, a dozen or more bluebottles hovering over it. Churchman, a handsome, fit-looking man with a boyish face, wearing a white oversuit, was kneeling beside it, holding a small tape recorder.

Grace saw a slightly overweight young man with short spiky fair hair, wearing a checked shirt, baggy jeans and brown boots, lying on his back, mouth open, eyes shut, his skin waxy white. There was a small gold earring in his right ear. The rounded face, frozen in death, had boyish looks.

He tried to recall the photographs of Michael Harrison that he had seen. The hair colouring was the same, the features could have been his, but he had seemed better-looking than this. Equally, Grace knew that people's looks changed after death, as the skin contracted and the blood dried.

Nigel Churchman looked up at him. 'Roy,' he said. 'Hi, how are you?'

'I'm OK, you?'

The pathologist nodded.

'What have we got?'

'I'm not sure yet – too early to tell.' With his rubber-gloved hands he gently lifted the young man's head. Grace swallowed as dozens of the small flies flew angrily off. There was a deep, uneven dent in the back of the cranium, covered in knotted hair and dark, congealed blood.

'He's had a violent blow from some blunt instrument,' Churchman said. Then with his typical dry humour he added, 'Wasn't good for his health.'

'You know, you get sicker every time I meet you.'

Churchman grinned broadly, as if it were a compliment. 'You sound like my wife.'

'I thought you got divorced?'

'I did.'

They were interrupted by a sharp fizz, crackle, then a burst of speech from the police radio of one of the constables behind him. Grace turned and saw the police officer talk into his two-way radio, giving a report. Then he looked down at the corpse, studying it carefully, noting again the face, the clothes, the cheap watch and the even cheaper-looking plastic strap. The green string bracelet on his right wrist. He swept his hand across the corpse's face, brushing away the hovering flies. Yes, the corpse was definitely in the right place, but could they be sure this was Michael Harrison?

'There's nothing on him at all? No credit card or paper?'

'Not that we've found.'

Looking down at the young man again, Grace wondered, was this how he would have dressed for his stag night? The image he had of Michael Harrison was altogether someone more classy-looking. This man looked like a spiv. But whoever he was, he did not deserve to be lying here, being pecked away by blowflies, with the back of his head stove in.

'Any sense of how long he's been here?' Grace asked.

Churchman stood up, to his full six-foot height. 'Tough one. Not long. No sign of first-generation larvae infestation; no discolouration on the skin – in the conditions we've had, several days of warm and damp air, we would expect rapid deterioration. He's been here twenty-four hours max, possibly less.'

Grace's brain was churning, thinking about all the young males aged twenty to thirty who had been reported missing in the past couple of weeks. He knew the statistics only too well, from all his years of searching for Sandy. Two hundred and fifty thousand people a year in England alone went missing. Of those, one-third were never seen again. Some were dead, their bodies disposed of so efficiently they would never be found. Others had run away, beyond the reach of the best efforts of the police. Or else they had gone overseas and changed their identities.

He only ever saw just a fraction of the missing person enquiries: those who had gone in suspicious circumstances; the ones the police were looking into and the tiny percentage of those he got asked to review.

The timescale fitted. The looks sort of fitted. *Sort of.* There was only one sure way to find out.

'Let's get him to the mortuary,' he said. 'See if we can get someone to identify him.'

59

Naked apart from the towel around his midriff, Mark padded out of the shower into the locker room of the sports club. He'd worked up a sweat, but it had been a lousy game of tennis. He had played badly against his regular Sunday-morning opponent, an olive-skinned half-Danish, half-American investment banker with a wiry determination called Tobias Kormind. He didn't usually beat Tobias, but he normally took one set off him. Today, distracted and unable to focus, he had only taken a couple of games in the entire match.

Mark liked Tobias because he had never been part of Michael's tight clique of old friends. And Tobias, who had a creative brain and was well connected in the London banking world, had given Mark some smart ideas on how to develop Double-M Properties beyond the confines of Brighton, and build it into an international property empire. But Michael had never wanted to know. He never saw the reason to take gambles; he just wanted to continue down the plodding path they were on, doing one development at a time, selling it, then moving to the next.

Tobias gave him a friendly pat on the back. 'Guess your mind wasn't on the game this morning, huh?'

'I guess not, I'm sorry.'

'Hey, you know, you've had terrible things happen to you this week. You lost four of your best friends, and your business partner has vanished.' Tobias, standing naked, towelled his hair vigorously. 'So what are the police doing?

You have to get behind them, you know, push them – like everybody else. They are probably all overworked and will respond best to the people who push them.'

Mark smiled. 'Ashley's a pretty tenacious girl – she's giving them hell.'

'How is she doing?'

'Bearing up – just about. It was tough for her yesterday – some people she hadn't been able to reach showed up for the wedding.'

Tobias had never met either Michael or Ashley, so he was not able to add much. 'Sounds bad, if he didn't show for the wedding.'

Mark nodded, inserting his key into his locker door. As he pulled it open his mobile, which he had left inside, beeped twice. The display informed him that he had four messages.

Apologizing to Tobias, and stepping a few paces away from him, he played them back. The first was from his mother, asking if there was any news, and reminding him not to be late for Sunday lunch today as she was going to a concert in the afternoon. The next was from Ashley, sounding worried. 'Mark? Mark? Oh, guess you are on court. Call as soon as you get this.' Then another one from Ashley. 'It's me, trying you again.' The fourth was also from Ashley. 'Mark – please call, it's really urgent.'

Moving further away from Tobias, he felt the blood draining from his head. *Had Michael turned up?*

All night he had been thinking, trying to figure out how Michael had got out of the coffin and what he would say to Michael if confronted by him. Would Michael believe that he did not know the plan? All it needed was one email on Michael's Palm. Mark – and the others – had sent him several, teasing him about the stag night.

He rang Ashley, fearing the worst. She sounded distressed, and at the same time strangely formal – he presumed for the benefit of anyone who might be tapping the phones.

'I – I don't know exactly what's going on,' she said. 'About half an hour ago I had a phone call from a young woman detective called Emma-Jane something – um . . .' She was silent for moment. Mark heard a rustle of paper and then her voice again. 'DC Boutwood. She asked me if Michael wore an earring. I told her he did when I first started going out with him, but I made him take it off because I thought it was bad for his image.'

'You were right,' Mark replied.

'Do you think he might have put it on for his stag night?'

'It's possible; you know he's always liked dressing up a bit wildly for an evening out. Why?'

'I've just had a call back from this Detective Constable. They've found a body that matches Michael's description – in the woods near Crowborough.' She began crying. It was a great performance if anyone was listening to their conversation.

'Oh Jesus,' Mark said. 'Are they sure it's him?'

In between deep, gulping sobs she said, 'I don't know. Michael's mother has been asked to go to the mortuary to identify the body. She's just rung to ask if I'll go with her. They want us to go over as soon as we can.'

'Do you want me to come? I could drive you both?'

'Would you mind? I – I don't think I could cope with driving, and Gill can't, she's on the floor. Oh God, Mark, this is so terrible.' Then she began crying again.

'Ashley, I'll be there as soon as I can. I'll pick Gill up first as she's nearest to me, then you. Be with you in half an hour.'

Ashley was crying so hard he wasn't even sure if she heard him.

60

Grace, driving back towards Brighton, phoned Jaye and apologized to her that he had had to cut short their day out.

'What's his name, the lost boy?' she asked.

Grace hesitated, then could see no harm in telling her. 'Michael.'

'Why is he hiding, Uncle Roy? Has he been naughty?'

He smiled; children saw the world so much more simply than adults. But it was a good question. He had learned a long time ago in police work never to take anything at face value; turn over every stone, open every door, always think out of the box. It was important to consider Michael Harrison as an active participant in his disappearance, as much as a passive one. Despite the corpse that should already be at the mortuary by now.

'I'm not sure,' he answered.

'What happens if you don't ever find Michael?'

It was an innocent question, but it hit home with his emotions. 'I think we will find him.' He didn't want to say anything about the corpse.

'But what happens if you don't?' she persisted. 'How long will you keep looking?'

He smiled sadly at her innocence. She'd been born a year after Sandy had disappeared and had no idea of the poignancy of her questions. 'For as long as it takes.'

'That could be a long time, if he's hidden really well. Couldn't it?'

'It's possible.'

'So that means we might not get to see a giraffe for years and years?'

After he had finished his conversation with her, he immediately dialled Emma-Jane Boutwood in the Incident Room. 'What did you find out about the earring?'

'Michael Harrison used to wear one all the time – a small gold ring, until his fiancée stopped him. But it's possible he was wearing it for his night out.'

Not good news, Grace thought. 'OK. Mobile phones. We should have the mobile phone numbers of Mark Warren and Ashley Harper on file by now – I want you to get on to the companies and get copies of their logs from – ' he thought for a moment, ' – last Saturday.'

'I might not get much joy until tomorrow, sir. I've had problems getting anything out of phone companies at weekends before.'

'Do your best.'

'Yes, sir.'

*

Ten minutes later, for the second time this weekend, Grace drove up to the long, low building that housed the Brighton and Hove City Mortuary. The bright May sunlight made no impact on its grim exterior, as if the grey pebbledash walls were there to ward off any therms of warmth that might dare try to enter. Only cold corpses and even colder souls were permitted inside.

Cleo Morey excepted.

He hoped she was on duty again today. *Very much* hoped, as he walked over to the entrance and rang the bell. Moments later, to his delight, Cleo opened the door. Dressed as usual in her uniform of green gown, green apron and white boots – the only kit he had ever seen her in – she greeted him with a bright smile, seeming genuinely pleased to see him.

And for a moment he stood, tongue-tied, like a kid on his first date with a girl he knows in his heart is out of his league. 'Hi!' he said, and then added, 'We can't go on meeting like this.'

'I prefer you walking in, than to have you come in feet first,' she said.

He shook his head, grinning. 'Thanks a lot.'

She ushered him in to her tiny office with its pink walls. 'Can I offer you some tea? Coffee? A cold drink?'

'Can you do a full Cornish cream tea?'

'Sure – scones with strawberry jam and clotted cream?'

'And toasted tea cakes?'

'Of course.' She tossed her blonde hair back, her eyes never leaving his, very definitely flirting with him. 'So, this is your idea of a relaxing Sunday afternoon?'

'Absolutely. Doesn't everyone take a Sunday afternoon drive out into the country?'

'They do,' she said, switching on the kettle. 'But most people go to enjoy the flowers and the wildlife – not to look at corpses.'

'*Really?*' he feigned. 'I knew there was something wrong with my life.'

'Mine too.'

There was a silence between them. An opportunity, he knew. The kettle made a faint hissing sound. He saw a trickle of steam from the plastic spout. 'You told me you weren't married – have you ever been?' he asked. 'Do you have a family?'

She turned to look at him, resting her eyes on his, a warm, friendly, relaxed gaze. 'You mean do I have an ex-husband, two-point-two children, a dog and a hamster?'

'That sort of thing.' Grace smiled at her, his colly-wobbles gone, feeling comfortable with her. Extremely comfortable.

'I have a goldfish,' she said. 'Does that count as family?'

'You do? Me too.'

'What's she called.'

'It's *he*. Marlon.'

She burst out laughing. 'That's an absurd name for a goldfish.'

'Luckily, he doesn't know that,' Grace responded.

She shook her head, grinning broadly as the kettle came to the boil. 'Actually, I think it's great.'

'So what's yours called?'

She teased him with her eyes for some moments, before saying, coyly, 'Fish.'

'*Fish?*' Grace echoed. 'That's its name?'

'*Her* name.'

'OK. Guess that's easy to remember. *Fish.*'

'Not as smart as *Marlon,*' she said.

'It's OK, I like it. It has a certain something about it.' Then he seized his chance, although the words came out clumsily. 'Don't suppose you'd like to meet up for that drink some time this week?'

The warmth of her reply took him by surprise. 'I would *love* to!'

'Great. OK. When's good – ah – I mean – how's tomorrow?'

'Monday's are good for me,' she said.

'Great. Terrific! Um . . .' He was racking his brains, thinking of somewhere to go. Brighton was full of cool bars, but right now he couldn't think of one. Should they go to a quiet bar? A buzzy place? A restaurant? Monday nights were quiet. Maybe just a pub first time, he thought. 'Whereabouts do you live?' he asked.

'Just up off the Level.'

'You know the Greys?'

'Of course!'

'How about there – about eight?'

'I'll see you there.'

The kettle shrieked and they both grinned. As she began pouring water into the pot, the doorbell rang. She went out of the room and came back in accompanied by the beanpole-tall frame of DC Nicholl, dressed in weekend casuals. 'Good afternoon, Roy,' he said, greeting his boss.

'Want some tea. Great service here today.'

'Earl Grey?' Cleo asked. 'Green leaf? Camomile? Darjeeling?'

Looking confused, the young DC, who was always very serious, very earnest, asked, 'Do you have any ordinary tea?'

'One builder's tea coming up,' Cleo said.

'So what do we think?' Grace asked, getting to the point.

'Gillian Harrison – Michael Harrison's mother – is on her way here to identify the body,' Nick informed him.

'I've made him look presentable,' Cleo said.

'It was one of her skills, to take a body – however badly marked or mangled – and make it look as intact and peaceful as possible for when a loved-one or relative came to identify someone. Sometimes it was never going to be possible. But as they walked through to the back of the mortuary, to the small, carpeted viewing room, with its perennial silver vase containing a small spray of plastic flowers, which doubled as a multidenominational chapel for the many people who wanted that solace, Grace could see she had done a good job on this body.

The young man had been placed on his back, his head resting on a plastic pillow which cleverly concealed the fact that the rear of his cranium was stove in. Cleo had washed the mud and grime off his face and hands, tidied his spiky hair and arranged his clothes. If it wasn't for his alabaster complexion, he could have been just another young man enjoying a quiet Sunday afternoon kip after a few jars in a boozer, Grace thought.

'Emma-Jane is on the case on the mobile phone numbers,' Nick Nicholl told him.

'We need to see which way the wind blows before deciding on any more action,' Grace said, looking at the body. 'Let's find out first if this is our man.' Then he heard the distant ring of the front entrance bell.

'I think we're about to find out now,' Cleo said, walking off.

Moments later she returned, followed by an ashen Gill Harrison, and Ashley Harper, stiff-faced, holding her hand. PC Linda Buckley, the Family Liaison Officer, stood a few steps behind. Michael Harrison's mother looked a wreck, as if she had just come in from gardening. Her hair was dishevelled; she wore a grubby windbreaker over a white sleeveless vest, brown polyester trousers and scuffed mules. Ashley, by contrast, in a navy suit and starchy white blouse, looked as if she was dressed in her Sunday best.

Both women acknowledged Grace with a silent nod, then he stepped aside to let them past. He watched them carefully as Cleo led them up to the viewing window, and for a moment his eyes were drawn to Cleo. She said few words to the two women, yet conveyed exactly the right balance of sympathy and professionalism. The more he saw of her, the more he liked her.

Gill Harrison said something and turned away, sobbing.

Ashley shook her head and turned away too, putting a comforting arm around her fiancé's mother.

'You are absolutely sure, Mrs Harrison?' Cleo asked.

'It's not my son,' she sobbed. 'It's not him, not Michael. It's not him.'

'It's not Michael,' Ashley confirmed to Cleo. Then she stopped in front of Grace and said, 'That's not Michael.'

Grace could see both women were telling the truth. Gill Harrison's bewildered expression was understandable. But he was surprised Ashley Harper did not look more relieved.

61

Two hours later, Grace, Glenn Branson, who had just arrived back from Solihull, Nick Nicholl, Bella Moy and Emma-Jane Boutwood sat at the work station which Operation Salsa had been allocated.

Grace smiled to reassure their new recruit, Emma-Jane, a slim, attractive girl with an alert face and long fair hair scooped up in a bun, then started to read out loud to them the report he had dictated since leaving the mortuary, and which Emma-Jane had just typed up. This was the way he liked to run all his investigations – keeping everything under constant review.

'The time is six-fifteen p.m., Sunday May 29th,' he read out. 'This is the first review of Operation Salsa, the investigation into the disappearance of twenty-nine-year-old male Michael Harrison, conducted on day five of his disappearance. I will now summarize the incident.'

For some minutes, Grace reviewed the events leading up to Michael's disappearance. Then he discussed possible suspects. 'At this time we have no evidence a crime has been committed. However, I am uncomfortable about Michael Harrison's business partner, Mark Warren, and his fiancée, Ashley Harper. I am also uncomfortable about Ashley's uncle from Canada, Bradley Cunningham, because I have a hunch he is not who he says he is – just a hunch at this stage.'

He paused to drink some water, then continued. 'Resourcing. East Downs Division has been very positive in offering manpower. We instigated a search of the vicinity of the accident last Tuesday night and have been upgrading the level of this further over the past few days. I'm now bringing in the Sussex Police Underwater Search Unit, and will have the USU team drag all local rivers, lakes and reservoirs. We will also request a further helicopter sweep – the visibility from the improved weather conditions may be helpful.'

He went on through the headings. 'Meeting cycles': Grace announced there would be a daily 8.30 a.m. and 6.30 p.m. briefing. He reported that the Holmes computer team had been up and running since Friday. He read out the list under the heading 'Investigative Strategies', which included 'Communications/Media', reporting that Michael Harrison's disappearance was scheduled to feature in this week's *Crimewatch* television programme if he hadn't turned up by then.

Next was 'Forensics'. Grace reported that soil samples from Mark Warren's car were being analysed along with soil samples recovered from the clothing and hands of the four dead boys. There should be an initial report some time tomorrow from Hilary Flowers, the forensic geologist they had consulted.

Then he reached the heading 'Any Concerns Raised by SIO', and there read out his detailed issues about the attitudes and anomalies in Mark Warren's and Ashley Harper's behaviour – and the disclosure of the Cayman Islands bank account of Double-M Properties.

When he reached the end of the report, he summed up: 'The alternative scenarios as I see them are as follows:

'One. Michael Harrison has been incarcerated somewhere and cannot escape.

'Two. Michael Harrison is dead – either as a result of his incarceration or has been unlawfully killed.

'Three. Michael Harrison has deliberately disappeared.'

Then he asked his team if they had any questions. Glenn Branson raised his hand and asked whether the body of the as yet unidentified man found in the woods had any bearing on the events.

'Unless there's a serial killer in Ashdown Forest targeting twenty-nine-year-old males, I don't think so.'

Grace's reply raised a titter despite the seriousness of the situation.

'Who's going to own this murder victim?' Branson asked.

'East Downs Division,' Grace said. 'We have enough on our plate.'

'Roy, any thoughts of putting tails on Ashley Harper and Mark Warren?' Branson asked.

It was an option he had been considering, but to put an effective twenty-four-hour surveillance watch on anyone could take as many as thirty people – three teams working in eight-hour shifts – on a simple job. More if it was complicated. The drain on manpower was astronomical, and Grace knew from experience that his chiefs would only sanction surveillance when absolutely necessary – such as on a potential major drugs bust or when there was a life at stake. If they made no headway soon, he might have to make the request.

'Yes,' he said. 'But park that for now. But what I do want is a scan on all the CCTV footage in Brighton and Hove last Thursday, from dawn until one a.m. Friday morning. Mark Warren was out in his car, a BMW off-roader – the details are on the file. I'd like to know where he went.' Then he added, 'Oh yes, and Michael Harrison has a yacht he keeps at the Sussex Motor Yacht Club. Someone should make sure it's still there. We'll look like dickheads organizing a manhunt if we find he's buggered off to sea on his boat.'

He looked at DC Boutwood. 'You can narrow the CCTV footage down from the mobile phone cell logs – you just need to pick the cameras in the area they throw up. Have you made any progress?'

'Not yet, sir. I'll be on it first thing in the morning – no one can help me today.'

Grace looked at his watch. 'I have to be in court tomorrow at ten – I may or may not be needed there all day. So we meet here at eight-thirty first.' He turned to Branson. 'Our liaison at the East Downs is Detective Inspector Jon Lamb. He's already got his team started – be good if you speak to him.'

'I'll call him in a few minutes.'

Grace fell silent, scanning the pages of the review, checking he had not missed anything. He needed to know more about the character of Michael Harrison and about his business relationship with Mark Warren, and also about Ashley Harper. Then he looked up at his team. 'It's now almost seven-thirty, on a Sunday evening. I think you should go home, get some rest – I think we're going to have a full week ahead of us. Thanks for giving up your Sunday.'

Branson, wearing fashionably baggy slacks and a sharp, zip-up cotton top, walked out to the car park with him. 'What's your sense, old wise one?' he asked.

Grace dug his hands in his pocket and said, 'I've been too close to this for the past couple of days – what's yours?'

Branson slapped his hands against his sides in frustration. 'Man! Why are you always doing this to me? Can't you just answer my questions?'

'I dunno. Tell me?'

'Shit, you really piss me off sometimes!'

'Oh, so you had a nice weekend away with your family, leaving me to do your job, and that pisses you off?'

Indignant, Branson exclaimed 'A *nice* weekend with my family. You call driving three hours up the M1 and three hours back, with a bolshy wife and two screaming kids, a *nice* weekend? Next time you drive them to Solihull, and I'll stay here and do whatever crap job you want me to do. Deal?'

'Bargain.'

Grace reached his car. Branson hovered. 'So, what is your sense?'

'It's not all as it seems, Horatio, that's my sense.'

'Meaning?'

'I can't put it any more clearly – yet. I have a bad feeling about Mark Warren and about Ashley Harper.'

'What kind of bad feeling?'

'A *very* bad feeling.'

Grace gave his friend a warm pat on the back, then climbed into his car and drove to the security gate. As he pulled out on the main road, with its panoramic view across Brighton and Hove, right down to the sea, with the sun still high above the horizon in the cloudless cobalt sky, he punched the CD button for Bob Berg's *Riddles*, and as he drove he began to chill. And for a few delicious moments his thoughts turned away from his investigations, to Cleo Morey.

And he smiled.

Then his thoughts turned back to work: to the long drive to south London and back he had ahead. If he was lucky, he might be home by midnight.

62

Mark, in sweatshirt, jeans and socks, paced around his apartment, a glass of whisky in his hand, unable to settle or to think clearly. The television was on, the sound mute, the actor Michael Kitchen striding, steely-faced, through a war-torn southern England landscape that looked vaguely familiar – somewhere near Hastings, he thought he recognized.

He had locked his door from the inside, bolted the safety chain. The balcony was safe, impenetrable, four floors up, and besides Michael had a fear of heights.

It was almost fully dark outside now. Ten o'clock. In just over three weeks it would be the longest day of the year. Through the glass doors to the balcony he watched a single light bobbing out at sea. A small boat, or yacht.

It had been weeks since he and Michael had taken out *Double-MM*, their racing sloop. He had planned to go to the Marina today and do some work on her. You could never leave a boat for long; there was always something leaking, corroding, tearing or peeling.

In truth, the boat was a damned chore for him. He wasn't even sure he needed the hassle, and rough seas petrified him. Sailing was a big part of Michael's life, always had been ever since Mark had known him. If he wanted to be Michael's business partner, then sharing the boat with him went with the territory.

And sure, they had fun, lots of fun; plenty of good, wind-blown days out sailing under a brilliant sky, plenty of weekends down the coast to Devon and Cornwall, and sometimes across to the French coast or the Channel Islands. But if he never stepped on a yacht again, it wouldn't bother him.

Where the fuck are you, Michael?

He drank some more whisky, sat on the sofa, leaned back, crossed his legs, feeling so damned confused. Michael and Ashley should have been jetting away on their romantic honeymoon today. He had not figured how he was going to cope with that, Ashley making love to Michael, loads of times probably. He would have expected that on a damned honeymoon, unless she feigned something – she had promised him she was going to feign something, but how could she keep that up for a fortnight?

And besides, he knew she and Michael had already slept together, it was part of their plan. At least she had told him Michael was lousy in bed.

Unless that was a lie.

He shook the ice cubes around in the glass and drank some more. He'd rung Pete's, Luke's and Josh's widows, and Robbo's father, each time on the pretext of finding out about the funeral plans – but in reality to pick their brains, to see if any of them had let anything slip before they'd gone out on Tuesday night. Anything that could incriminate him, or that could give him a clue to what they had been planning.

Michael had been there Thursday night, for sure. He had not imagined it. No way. So, he was there Thursday night, but not last night. The coffin lid was screwed down tight. And Michael was not Houdini.

So if Michael had been there Thursday and was not there now, someone must have let him out. And then screwed back the lid. But why?

Michael's humour?

And if he had got out why didn't he show up for the wedding?

Shaking his head he arrived back at his starting point. Michael was not in the coffin and he had imagined the voice. Ashley was convinced of that. There were moments when he convinced himself. But not strongly enough.

He needed to talk this through with Ashley some more. What if Michael had somehow got out and discovered their plans?

Then surely he would have confronted one or the other of them by now.

He stood up, wondering if he should go over to Ashley's. She was worrying him, behaving so damned coldly towards him, as if this whole thing was his bloody fault. But he knew what she would say to him.

He stood up and paced around the room again. If Michael was alive, if he had got out of the coffin, what could he find out from the emails on his Palm?

Mark suddenly realized in the panic of the past few days he had overlooked one very simple way of checking. Michael always backed up the contents of his Palm onto the office server.

He went into his study, flipped open the lid of his laptop and logged on. Then cursed. The damned server was down.

And there was only one way to get it back up and running.

63

Max Candille was almost impossibly good-looking, Roy Grace always thought on each occasion he met him. In his mid-twenties, with bleached blond hair, blue eyes and striking features, he was a modern Adonis. He could surely have been a top model, or a movie star. Instead, in his modest semi-detached house in the suburban town of Purley, he had chosen to make his *gift,* as he called it, his career. Even so, he was quietly becoming a rising media star.

The bland exterior of the house, with its mock-Tudor beams, neat lawn and a clean Smart parked in the driveway, gave few clues about the nature of its occupant.

The whole interior of the house – the downstairs at least, which was all Grace had ever seen – was white. The walls, the carpets, the furniture, the slender modern sculptures, the paintings, even the two cats which prowled around like bonsai versions of Siegfried and Roy's cheetahs, were white. And seated in front of him, in an ornate rococo chair, with a white frame and white satin upholstery, sat the medium, dressed in a white roll-neck, white Calvin Klein jeans and white leather boots.

He held his china demitasse of herbal tea delicately between his finger and thumb and spoke in a voice that was borderline camp.

'You look tired, Roy. Working too hard?'

'I apologize again for coming so late,' Grace said, sipping the espresso Candille had made for him.

'The spirit world doesn't have the same time frames as the human one, Roy. I don't consider myself a slave to any clock. Look!' He put down his tea, held up both his hands, and pulled each sleeve back to reveal he wore no watch. 'See?'

'You're lucky.'

'Oscar Wilde is my hero when it comes to time. He was always unpunctual. One time when he arrived exceptionally late for a dinner party the hostess angrily pointed at the clock on the wall and said, "Mr Wilde, are you aware what the time is?" And he replied, "My dear lady, pray tell me, how can that nasty little machine possibly know what the great golden sun is up to?"'

Grace grinned. 'Good one.'

'So, are you going to tell me what brings you here today, or should I guess? Might we be concerned with something to do with a wedding? Am I warm?'

'No prizes for that one, Max.'

Candille grinned. Grace rated the man. He didn't always get things right, but his hit rate was high. In Grace's long experience, he didn't believe that any medium was capable of always getting everything right, which is why he liked to work with several, sometimes cross-checking one against another.

No medium he had worked with so far had been able to tell him what had happened to Sandy – and he had been to many. In the months following her disappearance he visited every medium he could find who had any kind of a reputation. He had tried a few times with Max Candille, who had been honest enough at their very first meeting to tell him that he simply did not know, that he was unable to make a connection with her. Some people left a trail behind, all kinds of vibrations in the air, or in their belongings, Max had explained. Others, nothing. It was as if, Max told him, Sandy had never existed. He couldn't explain it. He couldn't say whether she had covered her own tracks, or if someone had done it for her. He didn't know whether she was alive or not.

But he seemed very much more definite about Michael Harrison. Taking the bracelet Ashley had given Grace, he thrust it back at the police officer within seconds, as if it was burning his hand. 'Not his,' he said, emphatically. 'Absolutely not his.'

Frowning, Grace asked, 'Are you sure?'

'Yes, I'm sure, absolutely.'

'It was given to me by his fiancée.'

'Then you need to ask her and yourself *why*. This absolutely does not belong to Michael Harrison.'

Grace wrapped the bracelet back in a tissue and carefully pocketed it. Max Candille was emotional – and *not* always accurate. However, combining his comments on the bracelet with Harry Frame's, something did not feel right about it.

'So what can you tell me about Michael Harrison?' Grace asked.

The medium sprang up from his chair, went out of the room, pausing to blow kisses at the cats, then returned moments later holding a copy of the *News of the World*. 'My favourite paper,' he informed Grace. 'I like to know who's screwing who. Far more interesting than politics.'

Grace enjoyed reading it himself, sometimes, but wasn't about to admit that now. 'I'm sure,' he said.

The medium folded back a couple of pages then held the paper up so Grace could see the headline, with Michael Harrison's photograph beneath. 'MANHUNT FOR AWOL FIANCE'.

Then the medium looked at it himself for some moments. 'Well, see, you are even quoted in here. '"We are now regarding Michael Harrison's disappearance as a Major Incident,' said Detective Superintendent Roy Grace of Sussex Police, 'And are stepping up police manpower to comb the area he is believed to be in . . .'"'

Then he looked up at Grace again. 'Michael Harrison's alive,' he said. 'Definitely alive.'

'Really? Where? I need to find him – that's what I need your help for.'

'I see him somewhere small, dark.'

'Could it be a coffin?'

'I don't know, Roy. It's too blurred. I don't think he has much energy.' He closed his eyes for some moments and slowly swivelled his head from left to right. 'No, very little there. The battery's almost flat, poor thing.'

'What do you mean?'

The medium closed his eyes again. 'He's weak.'

'How weak?' Grace asked, concerned.

'He's fading, his pulse is low, much too low.'

Grace watched him, wondering. *How did Max know this?* Was he connected across the ether? Just making a guess on a hunch? 'This small dark place – is it in the woods? In a town? Under ground or above ground? On water?'

'I can't see, Roy. I can't tell.'

'How long has he got?' Grace asked.

'Not long. I don't know if he's going to make it.'

64

'You see, here's the thing, Mike. Not everyone gets to have a lucky day on the same day. So we have a sort of irregular situation here – this is your lucky day and it's my lucky day. How lucky is that?'

Michael, weak, shivering from fever and near-delirious, stared up, but all he could see was darkness. He did not recognize the man's voice; it sounded a hybrid of Australian and south London, spoken quickly, with fast, nervy inflections. Davey with another of his accents? No, he did not think so. His brain swirled. Confused. He did not know where he was. In the coffin?

Dead?

His head pounded, his throat was parched. He tried to open his mouth, but his lips would not part. Ice squirmed through his veins.

I'm dead.

'You were in a horrible wet coffin, getting all soggy and rheumatoid, now you're in a nice, dry, cosy cot. You were going to die. Now maybe you aren't going to die – but I want to stress that's a pretty big *maybe*!'

The voice receded into the darkness. Michael was sinking, going down a lift shaft, down, down, the walls rushing past. He tried to call out, but his lips would not move. There was something pressing tightly around his mouth. All he could do was make a panicky grunt.

Then the voice again, really close, as if the man was in

the lift with him. 'Do you know about Schrödinger's Cat, Mike?'

They were still going down. How many floors? Did it matter?

'Did you study physics when you were at school?'

Who was this? Where was he? 'Davey', he tried to say, but all that came out was a murmur.

'If you know anything about science, Mike, you'd know about it. Schrödinger's Cat was inside a box, and was both alive and dead at the same time. That's like you now, my friend.'

Michael felt consciousness slipping away. The lift was swaying on ropes now; darkness seemed to be racing past him, round and round. He closed his eyes. Then felt a blast of heat and saw red through his eyelids. He opened his eyes, then immediately squeezed them shut against a blinding glare of light.

'I don't think you should be going to sleep; you need to keep awake now, Mike. Can't let you die on me, I went to a lot of trouble. I'll give you more water and glucose in a while, got to introduce foods to you slowly. I got trained in all this stuff, you're in good hands. Jungle training. I know how to survive, and help others survive. You're lucky it was me who came along. Need to keep you awake. We'll chat to each other for a while, get to know each other a little better – bond a little, OK?'

Michael tried to speak again. Just a murmur came out. He was trying to remember, the sensation of being lifted from the coffin, of being on something soft in a van – but was that on the stag night? Was this maybe one of his mates? Weren't they dead? Mark? He just wanted to close his eyes and sleep now.

Cold water lashed his face, startling him. His eyes sprang open, blinking into watery darkness.

'I'm just keeping you awake, no offence meant, mate.' The voice sounded more Australian than south London now.

Michael shivered; the water had sharpened him a fraction. He tried to move his arms, to see if he was still in the coffin, but he couldn't move them. He tried to move his legs, but they wouldn't move either; it was as if they were bound together. He tried to raise his head, to touch the lid, but he barely had the strength to raise it a couple of inches.

'Guess you're wondering who I am and where you are?'

Michael closed his eyes tightly again as a blast of light dazzled him, hurting his retinas like sunburn. He emitted another grunt.

'It's OK, Mike, don't bother to try to talk back. It's duct tape – hard to say anything through that. I'll do the talking and you just do the listening – until you're better, that is. We have a deal?'

Michael felt bewildered; but at the same time deeply apprehensive. Nothing was making any sense – he wondered if he was dreaming or hallucinating.

'First, Mike, I'm going to give you the house rules. You don't ask my name and you don't ask where we are. You got that?'

Michael grunted again.

'I'll remind you later, anyway. You ever see that Stephen King film, *Misery*?'

Michael heard the question through his drifting mind, but was unsure whether it was directed at him or someone else. *Misery*. He seemed to recall it. Kathy Bates. He tried to ask if Kathy Bates was in it, but his damned lips wouldn't move. 'Mnhhhh,' he said.

'That was some movie. Remember, James Caan got caught by his crazy fan, Kathy Bates, who smashed his legs with a sledgehammer so he couldn't run away? But that wasn't faithful to the novel, you know, Mike? Did you know that?'

'Mnhhhh.'

'In the novel she actually cut one leg off, then cauterized it with a blow torch. You got to be pretty weird to do that, wouldn't you think, Mike?'

Michael stared into the darkness, trying to make out his features, to put a face to the voice, to check if this voice was coming from above him, below him, inside him.

'You would, wouldn't you, Mike?'

'Mnhhhh.'

'I've been listening to you for five days, Mike. You and your buddy, Davey. Figured you were getting pretty frustrated with him – I would have been too, in your shoes.' The man laughed. 'I mean, that's pretty tough shit. You get trapped and the only person in the whole world who knows you're alive is a fucking moron!' He was silent for some moments, then he continued. 'Of course, I was there with you, Mike, as well, but I just didn't want to interrupt. Breakers' code, don't butt in on someone else's conversation. Well, that's my code anyway. How you doing?'

Michael's head was throbbing, darkness swirling all around him even faster now.

'You're doing OK. Another twenty-four hours in that grave and you might as well have stayed there. But you'll be OK now. I'll get your strength up; you're lucky, I was trained in the Australian SAS. Signals. I know all about survival; you couldn't be in better hands, Mike. I'd say that was worth a lot, wouldn't you? I'm talking about money, Mike. Big money! Moolah!'

'Mnhhhh.'

'But I'm afraid I'm going to need some bona fides, Mike. Understand what bona fides are? Proof it's you – are you on my bus?'

Michael squeezed his eyes shut against another burst of light. Then he opened them again and caught a glint of steel.

'This will hurt a little, but you don't have to worry, Mike. I'm not doing a Kathy Bates on you – I'm not crazy; I'm not about to cripple you. Just need some bona fides, that's all.'

Then Michael, through his delirium, felt an excruciating pain in his left index finger. He bellowed in agony, a tornado of air hurtling up his windpipe and screeching through the duct tape like a banshee.

65

Arriving back in Brighton shortly before midnight, Roy Grace was wide awake. The large espresso Candille had made him seemed to be having an effect like rocket fuel on his energy level. For no particular reason he decided to make a small detour and swing past the offices of Double-M Properties, in the street just below Brighton station.

As he approached he was surprised to see Warren's BMW parked right outside. He pulled up in front of it, climbed out and looked up. He could see on the third floor that the lights were on, and again, purely on a whim, he walked up to the front entrance and pressed the Double-M button on the panel.

After some moments he heard a crackly, very wary-sounding Mark Warren. 'Hello?'

'Mr Warren – Detective Superintendent Grace.'

There was a long silence. Then Mark Warren said, 'Come on up.' There was a sharp rasping sound from the lock, and Grace pushed open the door, then climbed three steep, narrow flights of stairs.

Mark opened the glass-panelled door into the reception area, looking sheet-white and, in Grace's opinion, very uneasy. 'This is a bit of a surprise, officer,' he said clumsily.

'I was just passing, saw the lights were on – wondered if we could have a quick chat. I thought you might like an update.'

'Um – yes, thank you.'

Mark shot a nervous glance at an open door behind

him, which led into an office where he was clearly working. He then steered Grace in a different direction, into a cold, windowless boardroom, switched on the lights and pulled out a chair for him at the highly polished conference table.

But before he sat down, Grace fished in his pocket and pulled out the bracelet he'd been given by Ashley. 'I found this on the staircase – does it belong to anyone who works here?'

Mark stared at it. 'On the staircase?'

Grace nodded.

'Actually, yes, this is mine – it has tiny magnets at each end – I wear it for my tennis elbow. I – I don't know how it got there.'

'Lucky I spotted it,' Grace said.

'Indeed – thank you.' Mark seemed very confused.

Grace noted a row of framed photographs on the walls: a warehouse at Shoreham Harbour, a tall Regency terraced house and a modern office block, which he recognized as being on the London Road, on the outskirts of Brighton. 'These all yours?' he asked.

'Yes.' Mark fiddled with the bracelet for some moments, then pulled it onto his right wrist.

'Impressive,' Grace said, nodding at the photographs. 'Seems like you have a good business.'

'Thank you. It's going well.'

Mindful of the blasting he'd had from Ashley after being rude to the Detective Superintendent yesterday at the wedding, Mark was now making a big effort to be polite. 'Can I get you a coffee or anything?'

'I'm fine, thanks all the same,' Grace said. 'Equal shares – you and Michael Harrison?'

'No – he has the majority.'

'Ah. He put up the money?'

'Yes – well, two thirds. I put up the rest.'

Watching his body language carefully, Grace asked, 'And there are no issues between you, over this imbalance?'

'No, officer – we get on well.'

'Good. Well . . .' Grace stifled a yawn. 'We're stepping up our search of the area in the morning. As you may have heard, we had a false alarm today.'

'The body of the young man. Who was he?'

'A local chap – a young man who I'm told was a bit backward. Quite a few of the local police knew him, apparently – his dad's got a tow-truck and crash repair business – does quite a lot of work for the Traffic Division.'

'Poor sod. He was murdered?'

'It seems likely,' Grace said guardedly. Then, watching Mark again closely, he said, 'Am I correct that you and Michael Harrison have a bank account in the Cayman Islands?'

Without flinching, Mark replied, 'Yes, we have a company there, HW Properties International.'

'Two-thirds – one-third split?'

'Correct.'

Grace remembered there was at least one million pounds in that account. More than a tidy sum. 'What kind of insurance do you and Michael have? Do you have life insurance policies on each other, as business partners?'

'We have the usual key-man insurance – do you want to see the policy?'

'Not at this moment, but at some point I'd like to, yes. Perhaps you could fax a copy over to the Incident Room for me tomorrow?'

'No problem.'

Grace stood up. 'Well, I won't trouble you any more tonight. Busy are you? Often work on a Sunday night?'

'I like to catch up on my paperwork at the weekend. Only chance I get when the phones aren't ringing.'

Grace smiled. 'I know the feeling.'

Mark watched the detective's head disappear down the stairwell, then closed the door, making sure the latch was down, then returned to his office, switched his computer back on, and began the arduous task he had started a couple of hours earlier, of reading every day's back-up of Michael's Palm, going back weeks, and deleting any references to the stag night.

Ashley had been spending this afternoon doing the same on the laptops of Peter, Luke, Josh and Robbo, on the pretext to their families that she was looking for clues about Michael's whereabouts.

Downstairs, Grace closed the front door behind him and walked across the pavement to his car. But it was some moments before he climbed back into it. Instead, he leaned against the passenger door, staring up at the third-floor window, thinking. Thinking.

He did not like Mark Warren. The man was a liar – and he was nervous as hell about something. Ashley Harper was a liar, also. She had deliberately given him a bracelet that did not belong to Michael.

And what exactly was Mark Warren's bracelet doing in her house?

66

'Jesus, oh Jesus.' Michael was crying in pain, holding up his left hand as far as the duct tape wound right around his body, pinioning both arms to his side, would allow. Blood gouted from the stump of his forefinger, cut off at the first joint. He stared up into the blinding lights. 'What is this; what the hell are you doing?'

'It's OK, Mike, relax!'

His arm was held by a thin, hairy hand with an iron grip, the wrist sporting a heavy diver's watch. And he could see his assailant's head now, shadowy against the dazzling lights, two eyes behind slits in a black hood.

Then he saw white cream oozing from the neck of a tube, and the next moment it felt as if ice had been put on his finger. He cried out again, the pain almost unbearable.

'I know what I'm doing, Mike. You don't have to worry; it won't go septic. I'd like you to call me Vic. Understand? Vic?'

'Vhrrrr,' Michael gasped.

'That's good, you and me on first-name terms. We're business partners, see? We should be on first-name terms.'

His assailant pulled out a long white bandage and wound it tightly around the bloody tip of the finger, then on down, tighter and tighter until it was acting as a tourniquet. Then he wound sticking plaster around it to hold it. 'See, Mike, the way I look at it, I saved your life – so that's got to be worth something, hasn't it? And from what I read in the papers and saw on television, it seems like you're loaded. I'm not, you see, that's the difference. Want some water?'

Michael nodded. He was trying to think straight but the numbing, throbbing pain in his finger made that hard.

'If you want to drink, I have to take the tape off your mouth. I do that on condition you don't shout. Is that a deal, Mike?'

He nodded his head.

'My word has always been my bond. Is it yours?'

Again Michael nodded.

An arm reached down. The next instant Michael felt as if half the skin on his face had been ripped away. His mouth gasped open, his chin and cheek stinging like hell. Then the man reached down again holding a plastic mineral water bottle with the top removed and tilted some of the contents into Michael's mouth. It tasted cold and good as he gulped it down greedily, some spilling over and dribbling down his chin and neck. Then some went down the wrong way and he began to choke.

The bottle was withdrawn. He carried on coughing. When the fit finally stopped, he felt more alert. He could smell dank air and engine oil as if he was in some kind of underground car park. Looking up at the eye slits he asked, 'Where am I?'

'You have a short memory, Mike. I told you never to ask where you are, or who I am.'

'You – you said Vic – your name.'

'I'm Vic to you, Mike.'

There was a silence between them.

In his rapidly clearing brain Michael was starting to feel

more scared of this man that he had been in the coffin. 'How – how did you find me?'

'I spend all week out in my camper van, Mike – see, I check on mobile phone masts around the south of England, for the phone companies. Listen to the old Citizens' Band radio, chat to a few mates around the globe. When there's no one to chat to, I scan all the radio bands, sometimes listen in to the police chatter. With my kit I can listen to just about any conversation I want – mobile phones, anything. Told you I was in Signals in the Australian Marines.'

Michael nodded.

'So, Wednesday, I was sitting around in the evening after work and I stumbled across Davey and you having a cosy chat. I stayed tuned to the channel and picked up some subsequent chats between you. Saw the news coverage, heard about the coffin. So I pulled on my thinking hat and I thought to myself, if I was going to take my best mate on a pub crawl why would I take a coffin? Maybe to hide you somewhere? Bit of a sick prank? So I went along to the local Planning Office in Brighton and looked up your company – and lo! – I discover you're applying for planning consent on forest land you bought last year, right in the area where you were having your pub crawl. I figured was that a coincidence, or was that a coincidence? And I also figured, out on a pub crawl, your mates would all be lazy bastards. They wouldn't want to carry you too far. You'd be close to a track you could get a vehicle down.'

'Is that where I was?' Michael asked.

'That's where you'd still be, mate. Now tell me about this money you have stashed away in the Cayman Islands.'

'What do you mean?'

'I told you, I pick up chatter on the police radios. You've

got money in the Cayman Islands, haven't you? North of a million, I understand. Wouldn't that be a reasonable reward for saving your life? Cheap at twice the price, Mike, if you ask me.'

67

At 7.20 the next morning, Grace arrived at Sussex House. The sky was dark blue, with wispy trails of cloud like strips of rags. One cop he'd been out on the beat with years back knew all about cloud formations and could predict the weather from them. From memory, the clouds up there this morning were cumulonimbus. Dry weather. Good for the search today.

In most police stations he could have got a good fry-up, which was what he needed for energy, he thought as he walked along the corridor to the bank of vending machines. He pushed a coin in the hot drinks dispenser, then waited for the plastic cup to fill with white coffee. Carrying it back to his office, he realized how weary he felt. All night he'd tossed and turned, switched the light on, made a note, switched it off, then back on again. Operation Salsa drip-fed its facts and anomalies to him relentlessly, drip by drip by drip, until grey light had begun to seep around the curtains, and the first tentative chatter of dawn birdsong had begun.

The bracelet. The BMW arriving back so late in the parking lot, covered in mud. Mark Warren working in his office at midnight on a Sunday. Ashley Harper's Canadian uncle, Bradley Cunningham. Ashley Harper's expression and behaviour at the mortuary today. Forensic results on the soil due today. CCTV results, possibly.

He looked at his in-tray, piled with post from last week he had not yet dealt with, then switched on his computer and looked at an even bigger stack of emails in his in-box. Then his door opened and he heard a chirpy, 'Good morning, Roy.'

It was Eleanor Hodgson, his management support assistant, who he had asked to come in especially early today. She held a sheet of paper in her hand.

'How was your weekend?' he asked.

'Very nice, I went to my niece's wedding on Saturday, then had a houseful of relatives yesterday. And you?'

'Managed to get out in the country yesterday.'

'Good!' she said. 'You needed a break and some fresh air.' She peered at him more closely. 'You look very pale, you know.'

'Tell me about it.' He took the sheet of paper, already knowing what it was – his agenda for the week. She had produced it every Monday morning for him, for as long as he could remember.

He sat down, the smell of the coffee tantalizing, but the liquid as yet too hot to drink, and scanned the agenda, needing to clear his diary of everything non-essential now he was the SIO on the case.

At ten this morning he was due to attend court for the continuation of the Suresh Hossain trial, and he would have to do that. At 1 p.m. he had a dentist's appointment in Lewes – which would have to be cancelled. At 3 o'clock tomorrow he had a meeting scheduled with South Wales CID for an exchange of information on a known Swansea villain found dead with a snooker cue sticking through his eye on a waste tip near Newhaven. That would have to be rescheduled. On Wednesday he was due at the Police Training College at Bramshill for an update on DNA fingerprinting. Thursday's highlight was the Sussex Police headquarters cricket team – of which he had landed

himself the unwelcome headache of being Hon. Sec. –
AGM. Friday was clear at the moment, and on Saturday
there was a terrorist attack training exercise at Shoreham
Harbour – in which he was not involved.

It would have been a nothing week, if it weren't for
the Hossain trial and now Operation Salsa. But, then, in
his experience, few weeks finished the way he expected
them to.

He told Eleanor to reschedule everything except his
trial attendances, then rummaged through his post, dictating replies to the most urgent on the pile. He scanned
his emails and because time was short and he was a slow
typist, dictated replies to those, too. Then he walked along
the maze of corridors to the Incident Room. It was already
beginning to feel like home to him.

*

The 8.30 a.m. Operation Salsa briefing meeting was short.
There had been no new developments overnight – apart
from what he had gleaned from Max Candille, which he
kept to himself, and from his visit to Double-M's offices.
Hopefully by their next meeting at 6.30 p.m. there might be
some news.

Grace drove into Lewes, stopping at a petrol station on
the way to buy an egg and bacon sandwich, which he was
still munching as he walked up the courthouse steps at
9.50. It was already beginning to feel like a very long day.

The morning proceedings were taken up with in-
camera submissions to the Judge by the prosecuting
counsel, and all Grace could do was hang around in
the waiting room, giving Eleanor some dictation over the
phone and speaking to Glenn Branson a couple of times.
There was not enough time to get to the office and back

during the lunch recess, so instead he went along to his dental appointment after all, for his six-monthly check-up, and to his relief his teeth were fine, although he received a reprimand from the dentist about not brushing his gums carefully enough. But at least no fillings – he dreaded them, always had.

Returning to court at 2 p.m., he discovered he was not going to be needed for the rest of the day, and went back to his office. With the time Operation Salsa was now consuming, a massive backlog was building up on the rest of his paperwork, and he did his best to deal with the most urgent of it.

It was an uneventful afternoon for him, right up until his arrival at the 6 p.m. briefing in the Incident Room. He could tell instantly from the team's faces that there had been a development. It was Bella Moy who told him the news.

'I've just had a call from a Phil Wheeler, Roy – the father of the murdered lad found this afternoon.'

'Tell me?'

'He said he didn't know if it was significant, but apparently his son told him that he'd been chatting with Michael Harrison on a walkie-talkie radio – since – Thursday.'

68

Ashley walked up behind Mark, who was hunched over his desk in front of his computer screen, trying to catch up on his work. He badly owed the architect, the quantity surveyor and the construction company responses to a whole raft of emails on issues that had been raised by the Planning Department over the company's most ambitious project to date, the new Ashdown development of twenty houses.

She slipped her arms around his neck, leaned forward and nuzzled his cheek. He breathed in the heady scents of her fresh, summery cologne and the faint citrus tang of her hair.

Bleary-eyed, he lifted his arms up and cupped her cheeks in his hands. 'We're going to be OK,' he said.

'Of course. We don't do *not OK*, right?'

'Right.'

Leaning further over, she kissed him on the forehead.

Mark shot a glance across the office at the open doorway, wary every second of the day and night of who might walk through it.

She kissed him again. 'I love you,' she said.

'I love you too, Ashley.'

'Do you? You haven't shown me much affection the past few days,' she chided.

'Oh, right, like you've been all over me?'

'Let's put that behind us.' She nibbled his ear, then, unbuttoning his shirt front, slipped her hands inside and began to tease his nipples with her fingers and thumbs. She felt him react almost instantly, heard his sharp intake of breath, felt his chest tighten. Slipping her hands out, she reached around him, clicked his mouse to exit the program, then whispered into his ear, 'Fuck me.'

'Here?'

'Here, now!'

Mark stood up, a little panicky, and glanced at his watch. 'The cleaners come around six-thirty – they'll be—'

Ashley unbuckled his suit trousers, and jerked down his zip. Then she pulled down his trousers and underpants together in one swift tug. 'So we'll just have to have a quickie, won't we?' She stopped and stared for a moment, as if in appreciation, at his engorged penis, then said, 'Well, somebody seems pleased to see me!'

Then she took him in her mouth.

Mark stared out of the window. They were in full view of the windows across the street. He tried to step sideways and almost tripped over his trousers and pants. He leaned down, fumbled with the buttons on Ashley's blouse, got his hands inside, unhooked her bra. Within a couple of minutes, naked except for his shoes and socks, he was lying on top of her, deep inside, the dusty, nylon smell of the hard carpet mingling with Ashley's scents in his nostrils.

Then there was a sharp buzz from the intercom.

'Shit!' he said, panicking. 'Who the fuck's that?'

Ashley pulled him tighter into her, her nails raking his back. 'Ignore it,' she said.

'What if it's Michael? Checking if anyone is in?'

'You're such a wuss!' she said, releasing him.

Ignoring the remark, Mark hauled himself to his feet and hobbled out of the room and over to the reception desk which Ashley normally manned and stared at the small black and white CCTV monitor. He could see a man in a motorcycle helmet, holding a package, standing outside the front door in the street. Mark pressed the *speak* button. 'Hello?'

'Package for Mr Warren, Double-M Properties.'

'Do you want to just put it through the letter box?'

'I need a signature.'

Mark cursed. 'I'll be down in a moment.'

He pulled his clothes back on, stuffing his shirt tails into his trousers, and blew Ashley a kiss. 'Back in two secs.'

'Don't worry about me,' she said unsmiling. 'I'll carry on without you.'

He hurried downstairs, opened the door and took a small Jiffy bag, with a printed label addressed to him but no information where it was from, from a stocky hulk of a man in leathers with 'FAST TRACK COURIERS' embossed on the front. He signed the docket, was given a duplicate copy then closed the door and climbed back up the staircase.

The sender's handwritten name on the docket read, 'JK Contractors'. Mark had no idea what was inside it. There was so much damned paperwork on the planning applications that he was steadily sinking under the mountain. This was probably a bunch of technical drawings from the quantity surveyor. Typically extravagant to send them by courier when post would have been fine. He would open it later. Right now there was just one thing on his mind, Ashley, lying naked on his office floor. And he was feeling crazily, dizzily, rampantly horny.

Then, totally unexpectedly, within seconds of lying back on top of her it was all over.

'Sorry,' he said, taking his weight on his elbows. 'I—'

'Get turned on by motorcycle couriers, do you?' she asked, seemingly only partly in jest.

'Oh sure.'

'A lot of men are gay and don't realize it. You know, bikers in leather can be a pretty erotic thing for guys.'

'What is this?'

'What do you think it is? You leave me here naked and on the verge of coming; you go down and see a guy in leathers and the next moment you shoot your bolt before you've barely got back inside me.'

He rolled off and sat up beside her on the floor, a wave of gloom washing through him. 'I'm sorry,' he said. 'I just have a shitload of stuff going on in my head at the moment.'

'And I don't?'

'Maybe you're better at handling this than I am.'

'I don't know what you're capable of handling, Mark. I thought you were the strong guy and Michael was the weak one.'

He leaned forward and placed his face in his hands. 'Ashley, we're both tense, OK.'

'You shouldn't be tense, you just had a great orgasm.'

'OK, OK, OK. I have apologized. You want me to work on you? I'll make you come – you know – by hand.'

She stood up abruptly, picking up some of her clothes as she did. 'Forget it, I'm not in the mood any more.'

They both dressed in silence. It was Ashley, putting on some lipstick, who finally broke it. 'You know what they say, Mark? Good sex is one per cent of a relationship; bad sex is ninety-nine per cent.'

'I thought we had great sex – normally.'

She checked her lipstick in her compact mirror, as if she was about to go out on a date. 'Yes, well, I did, too.'

Mark walked over and put an arm around her. 'Ashley, darling, come on, I apologized – I'm so damned stressed. We should go away for a few days.'

'Sure, that would look good, wouldn't it.'

'I mean when this is all over.'

She gave him a sharp look. 'When exactly will it all be over?'

'I don't know.'

She put her mirror away in her handbag. 'Mark, darling, it can never be over while Michael is alive. We both know that. We burnt our bridges on Thursday night when you took out the breathing tube.' She gave him a peck on the cheek. 'See you in the morning.'

'Are you going?'

'Yes, I'm going. I always go at the end of the day; something wrong with that? I thought we were supposed to be keeping up appearances?'

'I guess, yes – I mean . . .'

She looked at him for a couple of seconds. 'Pull yourself together, for Christ's sake. Understand?'

He nodded lamely. Then she was gone.

He stayed on for another hour, working on his emails, then, with the noise of the cleaners driving him to distraction, he decided to quit for the day and take the rest of his work home.

On his way to the door, he picked up the package he had signed for earlier and tore it open. There was something inside, a small object, tightly wrapped in cellophane then bound with tape.

Frowning, he wondered what it was. A replacement sim card for a mobile? A computer part?

He pulled a pair of scissors out of the desk drawer and snipped one end open, squeezed it, and peered inside.

At first he thought it was a joke, one of those plastic fake fingers you can buy in novelty shops. Then he saw the blood.

'No,' he said, feeling giddy suddenly. 'No. NO.'

The severed fingertip fell from the pack and landed noiselessly on the carpet.

Stepping back away from it in horror, Mark saw there was an envelope inside the packet.

69

Grace turned off the main road and onto a country lane, barely beyond the outskirts of Lewes. He passed a farm-shop sign, a telephone booth, then saw a tall mesh fence topped with barbed wire, some of it erect, some in a state of collapse, ahead on his left. There were two gates, wide open, that didn't look as if they had been closed in a decade. Fixed to one of them was a faded, cracked painted sign which read 'WHEELER'S AUTO RECOVERY'. Beside it was another, much smaller warning sign, reading 'GUARD DOGS!'

The appearance of the place was about as near to a hillbilly homestead as Grace had ever experienced. It was beyond ramshackle; it was beyond the most untidy place he had ever seen in his life.

The yard was dominated by a large blue tow-truck, parked amidst a dozen or so partially or totally cannibal-ized carcasses of vehicles, some smashed, some badly rusted, and one, a small Toyota, just looking as if it had been parked and someone had nicked everything it was possible to nick from it.

There were piles of sawn and unsawn logs, a wooden trestle, a rusting bandsaw, a decrepit Portakabin, against which was a faded chalked sign which read 'XMAS TREES SALE', and a wood-framed bungalow that looked as if it could collapse at any moment.

As he drove in and switched the engine off, he heard the fierce, deep barking of a guard dog shattering the quiet stillness of the warm evening, and remained prudently in the car for some moments, waiting for a hound to appear. Instead, the front door of the bungalow opened, and a hulk of a man came out. In his fifties, he had thinning, greasy hair, a heavy five-o'clock shadow and a massive beer belly barely restrained by a string vest and bulging over the buckle of his brown dungarees like an overhang of snow about to avalanche.

'Mr Wheeler?' Grace said, approaching, still wary of the sound of the barking dog, which was getting even louder and deeper.

'Yes?' The man had a gentle face with big sad eyes, and massive, grimy hands. He smelled of rope and engine grease.

Grace pulled out his warrant card and held it up for him to see. 'Detective Superintendent Grace from Sussex CID. I'm very sorry to hear about your son.'

The man stood still, impassively, then Grace saw he was starting to tremble. His hands clenched tight, and a tear rolled down from the corner of each eye. 'You want to come in?' Phil Wheeler said, in a faltering voice.

'If you have a few minutes, I'd appreciate it.'

The inside of the house was pretty much like the outside and the reek of the place indicated a heavy smoker. Grace followed the man into a dingy sitting room with a three-piece suite and a large old television. Almost every inch of the floor and furniture was covered in motorbiking magazines, country and western magazines and vinyl record sleeves. There was a photograph of a fair-haired woman resting her hands on the shoulders of a small boy on a scooter, on the sideboard, and a few cheap-looking china ornaments, but nothing at all on the walls. A clock on the mantelpiece, set into the belly of a chipped porcelain racehorse, indicated the time at ten minutes past seven. Grace was surprised, checking it against his own watch, that it was more or less accurate.

Scooping several record sleeves off an armchair, Phil Wheeler said, by way of an explanation, 'Davey liked this stuff, used to play it all the time, liked to collect—'

He broke off and walked out of the room. 'Tea?' he called.

'I'm fine,' Grace said, unsure what kind of hygiene went on in the kitchen.

This level of interview would have been delegated to someone junior by most SIOs, but Grace had always been a firm believer in getting out in the field himself. It was his style of operating – and it was one of the aspects of police work that he found most interesting and rewarding if sometimes, like now, challenging.

After a couple of minutes, Phil Wheeler lumbered back into the room, swept a pile of magazines and some more record sleeves off the settee and eased himself down, then pulled a tobacco tin out of his pocket. He prised open the tin with his thumbnail, removed a packet of cigarette papers, then proceeded, one-handed, to roll himself a cigarette. Grace couldn't help watching; it had always fascinated him how people could do this.

'Mr Wheeler, I understand your son told you he had some conversations on a walkie-talkie radio with a missing person, Michael Harrison.'

Phil Wheeler ran his tongue along the paper and sealed the cigarette. 'I can't understand why anyone would want to hurt my boy. He was the friendliest person you could meet.' Holding his unlit cigarette, he bicycled his hand in the air. 'Poor kid had – you know – water on the brain, encephalitis. He was slow, but everyone liked him.'

Grace smiled in sympathy. 'He had a lot of friends in the traffic police.'

'He was a good lad.'

'So I understand.'

'He was my life.'

Grace waited. Wheeler lit the cigarette from a box of Swan Vesta matches and moments later the sweet smoke wafted across to Grace. He breathed in deeply, enjoying the smell, but not enjoying this task. Talking to the newly bereaved had always been, in his view, the single worst aspect of police work.

'Can you tell me a bit about the conversations he had? About this walkie-talkie?'

The man inhaled, smoke spurting from his mouth and nostrils as he spoke. 'I got pretty angry with him on – I don't know – Friday or Saturday. I didn't know he had the damned thing. He finally told me he'd found it near that terrible wreck on Tuesday night with the four lads.'

Grace nodded.

'He kept talking about his new friend. To be honest I didn't take much notice. Davey lived in – how do you put it – his own little world most of the time – always off having conversations with people inside his head.' He put the cigarette down in a tin ashtray, then blotted his eyes with a scrunched up handkerchief and sniffed. 'He was always chatting. I sometimes had to switch off, otherwise he could drive me nuts.'

'Can you remember what he said about Michael Harrison?'

'He was very excited – I think it was Friday – he'd been told he could be a hero. You see, he loved American cop shows on the telly – he always wanted to be a hero. He was going on about knowing where someone was, and that he was the only person in the world who knew, you see, and this was his chance to be a hero. But I didn't take much notice; had a busy day with two wrecks we had to bring in – I didn't make the connection.'

'Do you have the radio?'

He shook his head. 'Davey must have taken it with him.'

'Did Davey drive?'

He shook his head. 'No. He liked to steer the truck sometimes, I let him do that on a quiet road – you know – like one hand on the wheel? But no, he could never drive, didn't have the ability. He had a mountain bike, that was all.'

'He was found about six miles away from here – do you think he went off to find Michael Harrison? To try to be a hero?'

'I had to pick up a car on Saturday afternoon. He didn't want to come with me, told me he had important business.'

'Important business?'

Philip Wheeler gave a sad shrug. 'He liked to believe he mattered.'

Grace smiled, thinking privately, *we all do*. Then he asked, 'Did you glean anything from Davey about where Michael Harrison might be?'

'No, it didn't occur to me to make any connection – so I didn't take much notice of what he said.'

'Would it be possible to see your son's room, Mr Wheeler?'

Phil Wheeler jabbed a finger, pointing past Grace. 'In the Portakabin. Davey liked it there. You can go across – please don't mind if I don't – I—' He pulled his handkerchief out.

'That's fine, I understand.'

'It's not locked.'

Grace crossed the yard and walked up to the Portak-abin. The dog which he had still not yet seen, which he thought had to be on the far side of the bungalow, began barking again, even more aggressively. Fixed to the wall beside the front door was a warning sign to intruders reading 'ARMED RESPONSE!'

He tested the door handle, then pulled the door open and stepped inside onto carpet tiles, several of which were curling at the edges, but most of which were covered in either socks, underpants, T-shirts, sweet wrappers, a McDonald's burger container lying open, the lid smeared with congealed ketchup, car instruments, hub caps, old American licence plates and several baseball caps. The room was even more untidy than the bungalow, and had a rank odour of cheesy feet, which reminded him of a school locker room.

Much of the space in the room was taken up by a bed and an unstable television flickering between colour and black and white, on which he saw the credits running for *Law and Order*. Grace never liked watching British cop shows – they always managed to irritate him by showing wrong procedures or stupid decisions by the investigating officers. US cop shows seemed more exciting, more together. But maybe that was because he didn't know US police procedures well enough to be critical.

Glancing around, he saw adverts which looked like they had been torn from magazines plastered all over the walls. Looking more closely, he identifed all of them as being for things American – cars, guns, food, drink, vacations.

Stepping past the burger container, he looked down at

a very old Dell computer, with a floppy disk protruding from the front of the processor, sharing a work surface that sufficed for a desk with a carton of Twinkie bars, a six-inch-tall plastic Bart Simpson and a large scrap of lined notepaper on which there were ballpoint jottings in child-like handwriting.

Grace looked carefully at the jottings and realized it was a crude diagram. Beside two sets of parallel lines was scrawled: '*A 26. NORTH KROWBURG. DUBBLE KATTLE GRYD. 2 MYLES. WITE COTIDGE.*'

It was a map.

Below it, he saw a sequence of numbers: *0771 52136*. It looked like a mobile number, and he tried dialling it, but nothing happened.

He spent another twenty minutes rummaging through everything in the room, opening every drawer, but he found nothing else of interest. Then he took the sheet of paper back to the bungalow and showed it to Phil Wheeler.

'Did Davey talk to you about this?'

Phil Wheeler shook his head. 'No.'

'Do the directions mean anything to you?'

'Double cattle grid, two miles, white cottage? No, don't mean anything.'

'The number? Do you recognize this?'

He looked at the number, reading out each digit aloud. 'No, not any number I know.'

Grace decided he had got about as much out of the man as he was going to get tonight. He stood up, thanked him, and told him again how sorry he was about his son.

'Just catch the bastard who did it, Detective Superintendent. Do that at least, for me and Davey, will you?'

Grace promised to do his best.

70

Mark Warren, dripping with perspiration, jigged the key in the front door lock of his apartment, panicking for a moment that the lock was jammed. Then he pushed the door open fearfully, stepped inside, closed it, locked it and engaged the safety chain.

Ignoring the bundle of post awaiting him, he set down his briefcase, ripped off his tie, unbuttoned his shirt collar, then slung both his jacket and the tie on the sofa. He poured himself four fingers of Balvenie, chinked some ice cubes out of the fridge straight into the glass, then gulped down some of the whisky.

He opened his leather laptop bag and removed the Jiffy bag that had arrived earlier, holding it at arm's length, hardly daring to look at it. He put it on a black lacquered table on the far side of the room, took out the note which he had already looked at earlier, in the office, then walked over to the coffee table, took another deep gulp of his whisky and sat down.

The note was short, printed off a computer on blank A4 paper. It said: 'Have the police check the fingerprints out and you'll find it is your friend and business partner. Every 24 hours I will cut an increasingly bigger bit off him. Until you do exactly what I tell you.'

There was no signature.

Mark drank some more whisky, draining the glass. He refilled it – another four fat fingers but the same ice cubes, and read the note again. Then again. He heard a siren somewhere outside and flinched. Then the door intercom buzzed, throwing him into a flat spin of panic. Marching across to the CCTV panel, he desperately hoped it was Ashley. Her phone had been off when he tried to call her from the office and it had still been off when he had called her again minutes ago coming up in the lift.

But it wasn't Ashley; it was the face of a man he was starting to see too much of, for his liking, Detective Superintendent Grace.

For some moments he wondered whether to ignore him, let him go away, come back some other time. But maybe he had news.

He picked up the receiver and told Grace to come in, then pressed the button for the electronic door catch.

It seemed only seconds later that Grace was knocking on his door, and he'd barely had time to scoop up the note and the Jiffy bag and stuff them in a cupboard.

'Good evening, officer,' Mark said as he opened the door, conscious suddenly that he was feeling a tad muzzy from the drink and that his voice was affected, too. He kept a full arm's length as he shook Grace's hand, so that the policeman wouldn't notice the alcohol on his breath.

'Mind if I come in for a few minutes, or are you busy?'

'Never too busy for you, officer – I'm around to help you seven-two-four. What news do you have? Can I get you a drink?'

'A glass of water, please,' Grace said, feeling parched.

They sat down opposite each other on the deep leather sofas, and Grace watched him for a little while. The man looked in a bad state of nerves; he seemed a little uncoordinated and smelled strongly of alcohol. Watching his eyes carefully, Grace asked him, 'What did you have for lunch today?'

Mark's eyes shot to the left momentarily and then back to the centre. 'I had a turkey and cranberry sandwich, from a deli just around the corner. Why?'

'It's important to eat,' Grace said. 'Particularly when you are stressed.' He gave Mark a smile of encouragement then sipped some water from the tall, expensive-feeling glass he had been given. 'Got a bit of a mystery, Mark, which I wonder if you could help me with?'

'Of course – I'll try.'

'A couple of CCTV cameras picked up a BMW X5 registered in your name, late Thursday night, heading into Brighton from the direction of Lewes . . .' Grace paused to pull his Blackberry out of his pocket. 'Yes, at 12.29 a.m. and again at 12.40 a.m.' Grace decided for the moment to say nothing about the results of the soil analysis that he'd been given at the briefing meeting, earlier. Like a lion closing in on a kill, he leaned forward. 'You went for a late-night drive in Ashdown Forest, perhaps?'

Now he watched Mark's eyes rigidly. Instead of going back to the left, to the same side as when Mark answered his question about the sandwich, to the memory side, they swung wildly, right, then left, then right again, very definitely settling right now. *Construct* mode. He was intending to lie his way out of this one.

'I may have done,' he replied.

'You *may* have done? Isn't driving in a forest at midnight a little bit of an unusual thing to do? Wouldn't you remember a bit more clearly?'

'It's not unusual for me,' Mark responded, seizing his drink, his entire body language changing suddenly. It was Grace's turn to feel uneasy now, wondering what was going on. Mark leaned back, swirled the whisky around in his glass, the ice cubes chinking. 'You see, that's where we are doing our new big property development. We got outline planning permission a couple of months back for twenty new houses on a five-acre site in the heart of the forest, and now we're working on the details – because we're getting a lot of hostility from the environmental groups. I go back and forward to the forest all the time, day and night – I have to check out the environmental factors, and a big part of that is the impact on the wildlife at night time. I'm working up a whole report to support our application.'

Grace's heart sank; he felt as if a rug had just been pulled away, quickly and very smartly, from beneath him. He'd just wasted the best part of a thousand pounds of his budget on the soil analysis, and he felt an idiot. Why hadn't he known this? Why hadn't Glenn or anyone on the team known it?

His brain was spinning and he tried to slow it down and get some traction on this thoughts. Mark Warren still looked a wreck and he just did not get the impression it was from worrying about his business partner. The aggression he had shown at the wedding indicated something else altogether, but he didn't know what.

Then, for about the third time in the past ten minutes, he saw Mark Warren's eyes flick across to a point on the far side of the room, as if someone was standing there. Grace deliberately dropped the cover of his Blackberry on the floor and, in leaning down to get it, glanced back in the direction Mark kept looking at. But he couldn't see anything of significance. Just the smart hi-fi set, some interesting modern art and a few cupboards.

'I read about that young man – in the mortuary. Saw the piece in the paper today. Very sad,' Mark said.

'Might even have been on your land,' Grace said, testing.

'I don't know exactly where it happened.'

Fixing on his eyes again, and remembering the words on the sheet of notepaper in Davey's bedroom, Grace said, 'If you take the A26 outside Crowborough just past a white cottage, then over a double cattle grid. Is that where you are?'

Mark didn't need to respond. Grace could see all he needed to know from the rapid swivelling of his eyes, the furrowing of his forehead, the hunching of his entire frame and the change in tone of his face colour.

'It could be – possibly – yes.'

Now it was all starting to come clear to Grace. 'If a bunch of you were going to bury your mate alive in a coffin, it would make sense to do it on land you own, wouldn't it? Somewhere familiar to you?'

'I – I suppose . . .'

'You're still insisting you had no idea of any plan to bury Michael Harrison in a coffin?'

His eyes were all over the place for a few seconds. 'Absolutely. Nothing at all.'

'Good, thank you.' Grace studied his Blackberry for a moment. 'I also have a number I wonder if you could help me with, Mark?'

'I'll try.'

Grace read out the number that had been written on the same diagram.

'0771 52136,' Mark repeated. His eyes shot instantly to the left. Memory mode. 'That sounds like Ashley's mobile with a couple of digits missing. Why do you ask?'

Grace drained his water and stood up. 'It was found in Davey Wheeler's home – the murdered boy. Along with the directions I just gave you.'

'What?'

Walking over to the window, Grace slid open the patio door and stepped out on to the teak decking that covered the balcony. Steadying himself on the metal guard rail, he looked down four floors at the bustling street below. It wasn't far, but it was enough for him; he had always suffered from vertigo, never had any head for heights.

'How did this boy get Ashley's phone number and the directions to our land?' Mark asked.

'I'd also like to know that very much.'

Once again Mark's eyes shot across the room. Grace wondered, was it the cupboard? Something in there? What?

Grace had such bad feelings about this man, and about Ashley Harper, that he wanted to get search warrants and take their homes – and office – apart. But to do that was not easy. Magistrates required convincing to sign warrants, and to convince them you needed evidence. The bracelet she had given him wouldn't be enough. Right now, on both Mark Warren and Ashley Harper all he really had were gut feelings. No evidence.

'Mark, is this land of yours easy to find? The directions – the white cottage, the cattle grid?'

'You have to know the turn-off – it's not marked, other than by a couple of stakes – we didn't want to draw attention to it.'

'Sounds to me that that's the place to look for your partner, pretty damned quick, wouldn't you say?'

'Absolutely.'

'I'll liaise with the Crowborough police, who are already doing a full search of the area, but it sounds like it would be vital for you to be there – at least point them to the right area. If I arrange to get you picked up in the next half-hour?'

'Fine. Thank you. Ah – how long do you think I'll be needed?'

Grace frowned. 'Well – all I need is for you to show us the entrance – the turn-off – and to take us to where your land begins. Maybe an hour altogether. Unless you want to join in the search yourself?'

'Sure – I mean – I'll do what I can.'

71

Mark closed the door on Grace, ran into the bathroom, knelt down and threw up into the toilet bowl. Then he threw up some more.

He stood up, pressed the flush lever, then rinsed his mouth with cold water; his clothes were wringing wet with perspiration, his hair plastered to his head. With the tap running, he nearly didn't hear the landline phone ringing.

Grabbing the receiver off the hook, he just caught it on the last ring before it would have diverted to voicemail. 'Hello?'

A male voice with an Australian accent said, 'Is that Mark Warren?'

Something about the voice made Mark instantly wary. 'This is an ex-directory number. Who am I speaking to?'

'My name's Vic – I'm with your friend, Michael – he gave me your number. Actually he'd like to have a quick word with you; shall I put him on?'

'Yes.' Mark gripped the receiver hard against his ear, trembling. Then he heard Michael's voice, very definitely Michael, but making a sound unlike Mark had ever heard before. It was a bellow of pain that seemed to start deep within Michael's soul then burst, like a train from a tunnel, into a crescendo of utter, unbearable agony.

Mark had to pull the phone away from his ear. The roar died away then he heard Michael whimpering then screaming again. 'No, please, no, no. NO NO NO NO!'

Then he heard Vic's voice again. 'Bet you're wondering

what I'm doing to your mate, don't you, eh Mark? Don't worry, you'll find out when it arrives in tomorrow's post.'

'What do you want?' Mark asked, straining his ears, but he could hear no sound from Michael now.

'I need you to transfer some money in your Cayman Islands bank to an account number I'm going to give you shortly.'

'It isn't possible – even if I was willing to do it. Two signatures are needed for any transaction, Michael's and mine.'

'In your safe in your company office you have documents signed by both of you, giving power of attorney to a lawyer in the Cayman Islands; you put it there last year when you both went off sailing for a week, and you were hoping to close on a property deal in the Grenadines that then didn't happen. You've forgotten to destroy those documents. Just as well, I'd say.'

How the hell did the man know this, Mark wondered.

'I want to speak to Michael – I don't want to hear him in pain, I'd just like to talk to him, please.'

'You've talked to him enough today. I'm going to leave you to think about this, Mark, and we'll catch up later, have a cosy chat. Oh, and Mark, not a word of this to the police – that could really make me angry.'

The line went dead.

Immediately Mark hit the last number recall button. But it was no surprise that the automated voice came up with, 'I'm sorry, we do not have the caller's number.'

He tried Ashley's number again. To his relief she answered.

'Thank God,' he said. 'Where have you been?'

'What do you mean, where have I been?'

'I've been trying to get hold of you.'

'I went to have a massage, actually. One of us has to keep a cool head, OK? Then I popped in to see Michael's mum and now I'm on my way home.'

'Can you swing by here – like now, this second?'

'Your voice is slurred – have you been drinking?'

'Something's happened, I *have* to speak to you.'

'Let's talk in the morning.'

'It can't wait.'

The imperative in his voice got through. Reluctantly she said, 'OK – I just don't know if it's a good idea coming to you – we could meet somewhere neutral – how about a bar or a restaurant?'

'Great, somewhere the whole world can hear us?'

'We'll just have to talk quietly, OK? It's better than me being seen coming over to your apartment.'

'Jesus, you are paranoid!'

'Me? You're a fine one to talk about paranoia. Name a restaurant.'

Mark thought for a moment. A police car would collect him in half an hour. It was about half an hour's drive out to the site. Maybe just ten minutes there, then half an hour back. It was eight o'clock on Monday night; places would be quiet. He suggested meeting at ten at an Italian restaurant near the Theatre Royal, which had a large upstairs dining area that would almost certainly be empty tonight.

*

It wasn't. To his surprise, the restaurant was heaving – he had forgotten that after the Brighton Festival the city was still in full swing, its bars and restaurants crowded every night. Most of the tables upstairs were taken as well, and he was squeezed into a cramped table behind a rowdy party table of twelve. Ashley wasn't there yet. The place was typically Italian: white walls, small tables with candles jammed in the top of Chianti bottles and loud, energetic waiters.

The ride out to Crowborough and back had been uneventful: two young detectives in an unmarked car, who had spent most of the way out there arguing about football players, and most of the way back discussing cricket. They showed no interest in him at all other than to tell him they should both have gone off duty an hour ago and were in a hurry to get back. Mark viewed that as good news.

He directed them to the start of the track, with the double cattle grid, then sat and waited as they radioed for the local search team to join them. After a short while several minibuses, headed by a police Range Rover, arrived in convoy.

Mark got out of the car, explained how far up they had to drive, but did not volunteer to join them. He did not want to be there when they found the grave – and they would find it for sure.

He needed a drink badly, but was not sure what he wanted. He was thirsty, so he ordered a Peroni beer to tide him over, then stared at the menu as a distraction from his thoughts. Moments later, Ashley arrived.

'Still drinking?' she admonished, by way of a greeting, and without kissing him, squeezed in opposite him, throwing a disapproving glance at the rowdy group beside them, who were guffawing at a joke, then put her very bling pink Prada handbag on the table.

She looked more beautiful than ever, Mark thought, dressed in a fashionably ragged cream blouse, which gave her breasts considerable, and very erotic, exposure, and a small choker; she had her hair up. She looked fresh and relaxed, and smelled of a gorgeous perfume he recognized but could not name.

Smiling at her, he said, 'You look stunning.'

Her eyes were darting around the room impatiently, as if seeking a waiter. 'Thanks – you look like shit.'

'You'll understand why in a moment.'

Semi-ignoring him, she raised a hand, and when a waiter finally scuttled over, she imperiously ordered a San Pellegrino.

'Want some wine?' Mark said. 'I'm going to have some.'

'I think you should have water, too – you're drinking far too much just recently. You need to stop, get a grip. OK?'

'OK. Maybe.'

She shrugged. 'Fine, you do what you want.'

Mark slipped his hand across the table towards hers, but she withdrew her hands, sitting bolt upright, arms firmly crossed.

'Before I forget, tomorrow is Pete's funeral. Two o'clock, the Good Shepherd, Dyke Road. Luke's is on Wednesday; I haven't got the time yet – and I don't know about Josh and Robbo yet. So what's this big latest thing you have to tell me?'

The waiter came with her water, and they ordered. Then when the waiter had moved away Mark began by telling her about the finger.

She shook her head, sounding shocked. 'This cannot be true, Mark.'

Mark had put the finger in the Jiffy bag into the fridge in his apartment, but he'd brought the note with him and gave it to her.

Ashley read it carefully, several times, mouthing the words as if in total disbelief. Then suddenly there was anger in her eyes and she looked at him accusingly. 'This isn't your doing, Mark?'

It was Mark's turn to be shocked. He mouthed the word before he said it. 'What? You think I have Michael hidden somewhere and I cut his finger off. I might not like him too much but—'

'You're happy to let him die of asphyxiation in a coffin – but you wouldn't ever do something nasty to him, like cut a finger off? Come on, Mark, what kind of bullshit is this?'

He glanced around, alarmed at the way she had raised her voice. But no one was taking any notice.

Mark could not believe the way she seemed to be turning on him. 'Ashley, come on, this is me. Jesus Christ, what's got into you? We're a team, you and I – isn't that the deal? We love each other; we're a team, right?'

She softened, glanced around, then reached forward, took his hand and brought it to her lips, planting a gentle kiss on it. 'My darling,' she said, her voice lowered. 'I love you so much – but I'm just in shock.'

'Me too.'

'I suppose we all handle shock, stress – you know – in different ways.'

He nodded, pulled her hand towards his mouth and kissed it tenderly. 'We have to do something for Michael.'

She shook her head. 'It's perfect, don't you see? We just do nothing! This man – Vic – he's going to think you care because you're Michael's partner.' She grinned. 'It's an incredible situation!'

'It's not; I haven't told you everything.' He drained his beer and looked around, wondering if the wine was on its way. Then he told her about the phone call from Vic and the sound of Michael screaming.

Ashley listened in silence. 'Christ, poor Michael – he—'

She bit her lip and a tear rolled down her cheek. 'I mean – oh shit, oh shit.' She closed her eyes for some moments, then opened them again, staring directly into Mark's. 'How – how the hell – how did this man find Michael?'

Mark decided not to mention the visit from Grace at this moment; Ashley was already distressed enough. 'All I can think is he must have stumbled across the grave – it wasn't exactly well concealed. Hell, the boys only planned to be away a max of an hour or two. I camouflaged it a bit – but it wouldn't have been hard – a rambler could easily have seen it.'

'A rambler's one thing,' she said bleakly. 'This guy's not a rambler.'

'He's a chancer, maybe. Finds Michael, figures out from all the press and media coverage that this is the rich guy everyone's looking for – it's the chance of a lifetime. He takes him off to another location and sends us a ransom note – and proof that he has Michael.'

Ashley said, her voice faltering, 'How – how do – you – we – anyone – I mean – how do we know it's Michael's finger?'

'About three weeks ago Michael and I were on the boat, doing some maintenance work on her, on a Saturday afternoon – remember?'

'Vaguely.'

'The heads door slammed shut on Michael's index finger. He was hopping around, cursing, running it under a cold tap. He showed me a few days later a black band right across the nail.' He paused. 'The finger that arrived has a black band. OK?'

A hearty plate of avocado, mozzarella and tomatoes arrived for Ashley. And a large bowl of minestrone was set down in front of Mark. When the waiter went away again,

Ashley said, 'Do you want to call the police, Mark? Tell the bloodhound Detective Superintendent about this?'

Mark churned that over in his mind, letting his soup cool while Ashley began eating. If they told the police and the man carried out his threat to kill Michael, that was one elegant solution to the situation. Except the bellow of pain from Michael had got to him. None of this had seemed quite real before. All the boys dead in the wreck. Going up to the grave and taking the air tube. Even when Michael had shouted out in the coffin, it hadn't affected him, not really. Not the way the sound of him in pain was affecting him now.

'Michael must have his Palm. If he gets out alive he is going to know that I knew where he was being buried.'

'Since the accident there's never been any question of him getting out alive,' she said. Then after a moment's hesitation added a testy, 'Has there?'

Mark was silent. His mind, normally so orderly and focused, was a messed-up jumble at this moment. They'd never intended to harm Michael with the stag-night prank – that was just the payback for all his jokes. And the original plan he'd hatched with Ashley had never involved hurting Michael either, surely? Ashley was going to marry him, and get half his shares in Double-M Properties. When the ink was dry on the certificates, Mark and she would have enough votes between them to take control of the company. They would vote Michael off the Board of Directors, and then he would be a minority shareholder – and wouldn't have much option but to let them buy him out at a low price.

Why the hell had he kept quiet the night he had arrived home from Leeds and heard about the accident. Why? Why?

But of course he knew the real reason why. Pure jealousy. It was because he had never been able to bear the thought of Ashley going off on honeymoon with Michael – and the solution had fallen into his lap.

'Has there, Mark?' Ashley's persistent voice cut through his thoughts.

'Has there what?'

'Duh! Hello! Has there ever been any question of him getting out alive?'

'No, of course not.'

She stared at him, a firm, steady gaze.

He stared back, replaying the terrible screams of pain over and over inside his head, thinking, *Ashley, you didn't hear them.*

72

Michael lay in the bitumen-black darkness, his heart thudding, his head pounding, his index finger throbbing, and excruciating spikes of pain from his balls shooting deep up into his belly. It was – he didn't know how long ago, maybe an hour, maybe more, maybe less – from when that hooded bastard had clipped callipers to them and fired electric shocks into them.

But the pain was nothing compared to the dark, cold fear that stalked his mind. He was remembering the movie, *The Silence of the Lambs*, which he had seen some years back, and again more recently on television with Ashley. A girl, a senator's daughter, had been kept in the bottom of a well by the serial killer who skinned his victims. He couldn't help it; he was shivering, trying to focus his thoughts, determined, somehow, to survive.

To get back to Ashley. To take her down the aisle. That was all he wanted.

God, how he pined for her!

He couldn't move his arms or his legs. After spooning him tinned stew and bread, his captor had sealed his mouth again with duct tape and he had to breathe just through his nose, which was partially blocked. He sniffed, suddenly panicking that it was getting completely blocked. Sniffed again, harder, deep, rapid sniffs, setting his heart racing.

He tried to work out where he might be. The place smelled dank, musty, there was still a faint reek of engine oil. He was lying on a hard surface and something sharp was digging into the base of his spine, hurting like hell, getting worse by the minute.

He felt stronger, despite the pain, much stronger than he had earlier. The food was having an effect. *I am not fucking staying here and dying. I haven't done everything in life to end up here. No way. No absolutely no absolutely no, no no fucking way.*

He struggled against his bonds. Breathed in deeply, trying to shrink his body, then out, trying to expand. And felt something give. Some tiny hint of slack. In again, pulled his arms in tight, tight, tight, out, in, out. Oh sweet Jesus he could move his right arm. Only a tiny amount. But he could move it! He pushed against his bonds, constricted, pushed again, constricted. More slack for his right arm.

Then more still!

He rolled over onto his side, then his stomach. His nostrils filled with the reek of engine oil now; he was lying face down in the slimy stuff, but it didn't matter, because at least the pain in the base of his spine had stopped.

He wriggled his hand round, further round, and then touched something.

OhmyGod!

He was touching the top of his Ericsson mobile!

Got his hand on it, pulled, and it came out of the back pocket of his trousers.

His heart kicked into overdrive. It had been there in the coffin, underwater. Even though it was supposed to be waterproof he doubted it would work. All the same, he ran his fingers over its surfaces as if he was caressing the best friend he had ever had in his life. Found the power button at the top, pushed it. Listened.

There was the faintest beep. Then a dim glow of light, enough that he could see steep walls either side of him. He was in a space about six feet wide and maybe five feet high, covered with a door of some kind. And suddenly he was alert, his brain sharp and focused. He tried to move his hand, to slip it free of the bonds and bring the phone up to his face, but nothing he did succeeded. The bonds were too tight, too well wound around his arms.

Yet.

He had to think this through.

Text.

He could try to send a text.

Think! You switch the phone on and what happens? First is a request for the pin code. Like most people, he used a simple code: 4–4–4–4, his lucky number.

He ran his finger across the key pad – 4 was far left, second row. He tapped it and heard a beep; then another beep each time he tapped the next three. Incredible! The thing had been submerged in the coffin but it was working. Enough to send a text?

The next part was going to be much harder. He had to work out the letters on the keys. On key number 1 he remembered there were no letters. Key number 2 had ABC. He did some maths in his head – the whole alphabet was in groups of three letters except for two numbers, where there were four. Which numbers? Shit, he had used text so much, it must be imprinted in his brain, if he could just access it.

It had to be the least popular letters in the alphabet, Q and – X or Z?

Taking it slowly, counting very carefully, he tried to recall the sequence on his phone. The *menu* button was top left. One tap took you to *messages*. The second tap took you to *write message*. The third tap took you to the blank screen. Then he tapped out what he hoped were the right letters. *Alive. Call police.*

The next tap, he hoped he remembered correctly, took you to *send*.

The one after that to *phone number*.

He tapped in Ashley's number.

The one after that should be *send*.

He pressed, and to his incredible relief heard a confirmation beep. The message had gone!

Then he felt a stab of panic. Even if the message had gone successfully, what use would it be to her, or the police? How the hell would they be able to find him from a text? Within moments he was engulfed in despair darker than the blackness that surrounded him.

But he refused to give up. There had to be a way. *Think! Think!*

His fingers moved along the keys, counting, 1–2–3–4–5–6–7–8–9.

He pressed 9–9–9. Then he pressed the send button. Moments later he heard a faint ringing sound. Then a female voice, very faint also.

'Emergency, which service?'

He tried desperately to speak, but all he could make was his feeble grunting sound. He heard the voice say, 'Hello? Caller? Hello? Is everything all right? Hello, Hello, caller, can you identify yourself? Hello? Caller, are you in trouble? Can you hear me, caller?'

There was a silence.

Then her voice again. 'Hello, caller, are you there?'

He hung up, dialled again. Heard another female voice speak almost identical words. He hung up again. They would have to understand if he kept doing this. Surely they would understand?

73

In the saloon bar of the pub, Grace ordered Cleo Morey her second Polstar vodka and cranberry, and himself a Diet Coke. One large Glenfiddich had been enough – he was going to have to return to the Incident Room later this evening and needed all his wits.

They sat on cushioned seats at a corner table. With less than a dozen other people in the pub the place was not very busy. A one-armed bandit at the far end of the room winked and blinked away forlornly like an old tart in a windswept alley.

Cleo looked stunning. Her hair, freshly washed and shining, hung down over her shoulders. She wore a classy-looking light suede jacket over a beige tank top, white jeans of fashionable three-quarter length, revealing her slender ankles, and plain white mules.

Grace had dashed from Mark Warren's apartment to the Incident Room to get copies of Davey's diagram faxed out to the team, and from there went straight on to the pub, still arriving an hour and twenty minutes late. Of course he had had no time to change or even tidy himself up. He was wearing the plain navy suit he had put on early this morning in case he had to appear in court, with a white shirt and plain navy tie – now slackened and hanging at half mast with his top button open. Compared to Cleo he was feeling very dowdy.

'I've never seen you in civvies before,' he joked.

'Would you have felt more comfortable if I'd turned up in my green gown and wellies?'

'I guess it would have had a certain *je ne sais quoi* about it.'

She beamed at him, and raised her glass. 'Cheers!'

She had a great figure. He loved her blue eyes, her small, pretty nose, her almost rosebud lips, her dimpled chin, her lean body. And she smelled stunning too, as if she had been marinated in some very classy perfume. Some difference to the reek of Trigene disinfectant that he normally associated her with – tonight she radiated femininity, her eyes sparkled with fun, and every man in the pub was ogling her. Grace wondered if they would still be ogling if they knew what she spent her days doing.

He poured some more Coke over the ice cubes and lemon and raised his glass back. 'Good to see you.'

'And you, too. So, tell me about your day?'

'You don't want to hear about my day!'

She leaned closer, all her body language receptive to him. If she came any closer still she would be snuggling up to him. He felt very good, very comfortable sitting here with her, and for a moment all his cares were parked in another space. 'I do,' she said. 'I want a blow-by-blow account of every minute!'

'How about the edited version? I got up, had a shower, went out, met Cleo for a drink. That enough?'

She laughed. 'OK, that's a start. Now talk me through the bits you edited out.'

He gave her a brief summary, mindful of the time. It was a quarter past nine – in an hour he had to be back in the Incident Room. He shouldn't have come on this date at all, he ought to have cancelled because of everything he had to do, but hell, didn't he have the right to enjoy himself just once in a while?

'Must be tough, interviewing the bereaved,' she said. 'In seven years I should have got used to seeing people, often within a few hours of getting the news that their loved one is dead; but I still dread every single one of those moments.'

'It might sound callous,' Grace said, 'but catching the bereaved within a few hours is the best chance we have of getting them to talk. When people have just lost someone, their first automatic response is to go into shock. While they are in that state they will talk. But within twelve hours or so, with family and friends gathering around, they start to close ranks, and clam up. If you are going to get anything useful, in my experience, you have to do it in those first hours.'

'You like what you do?' she asked.

He sipped his Coke. 'I do. Except – when I run up against people in my organization with limited minds.'

Cleo poked around in her drink with a cocktail stick as if looking for something, and for a moment the intensity of her gaze reminded Grace of her at work in the post-mortem room, when she was taking a tissue sample. He wondered what it would be like if he ever made love to her. Would the sight of her naked body remind him of all the naked cadavers he had looked at with her? Would he be put off by knowing that beneath her beautiful skin were the same hideous, slimy, fat-coated internal organs that all humans – and all mammals – shared in common?

'Roy, there's something I've been wanting to ask you for a long time. And of course I saw that stuff in the papers last week. How did you get interested in the supernatural?'

It was his turn to probe his drink. With the plastic

cocktail stick he squeezed the lemon flesh, releasing some of the juice into the Coke. 'When I was a kid, my uncle – my dad's brother – lived on the Isle of Wight – in Bembridge. I used to go and stay every summer for a week – and loved it. They had two sons, one slightly older than me, the other slightly younger – I kind of grew up with them from about the age of six. I don't know if you've ever been to Cowes?'

'Yes, Daddy's taken me sailing there during Cowes Week lots of times.'

Mimicking her posh accent, Grace said, 'Ew, Deeaddy would.'

Grinning and blushing, she gave him a friendly prod in the arm. 'Don't be mean! Carry on with your story.'

'They had a tiny terraced cottage, but right opposite was quite a grand house – a townhouse, four storeys high. There were two very sweet old ladies who lived there, and they were always sitting in a big bay window on the top floor, and they'd wave at us every time we saw them. When I was fourteen my aunt and uncle sold their house and emigrated to New Zealand, and I didn't go back there for about eight years. Then, in the spring of the summer that Sandy and I got married, I was taking her on one of those kind of *meet the ancestors* tours – and I thought it would fun to show her Cowes and the place where I'd spent so many happy holidays as a kid.'

He paused to light a cigarette, clocking Cleo's frown of surprise, then continued. 'When we got to my uncle's house, the beautiful townhouse opposite was in the process of being demolished – to make way for an apartment building. I asked the workmen what had happened to the two old ladies and they introduced me to the property developer – he'd lived in Cowes all his life and knew just about everyone. He told me the house had been empty for over forty years.'

He paused to drag on his cigarette. 'There had been two old ladies, sisters – both had lost their husbands in the First World War, the story goes. They became inseparable, then one was diagnosed with cancer and the other decided she didn't want to go on living alone. So they both gassed themselves in that top room, sitting in the bay window. That was in 1947.'

Cleo sat for some moments, thinking. 'You never saw the old ladies outside?'

'No – I was young – just a kid. I suppose at the time it never occurred to me that they were always indoors. I supposed that some old people did just stay indoors.'

'And your uncle and aunt?'

'I spoke to them about it afterwards – called them in New Zealand. They said they used to wave at this blank window just to humour us – they thought these two old ladies were our imaginary friends!'

'And they were real to you?'

'I looked them up in the newspaper archives. There were photographs of both of them – unmistakeable. Absolutely no question in my mind – these were the two old ladies I had waved at – and who had waved at me every day for a week, for ten years of my childhood.'

'Amazing! That's a pretty convincing story,' she said. 'So what is your explanation?'

He noticed her glass was empty. 'Another?'

'Oh, why not!' she said. 'But it's my turn to buy.'

'I kept you waiting and hour and twenty minutes – I'm buying the drinks. No argument!'

'So long as I can buy them on our next date – deal?'

They locked eyes, both smiling. 'Deal.'

Then she tapped the table impatiently with her manicured finger. 'So, come on, what is your explanation?'

Grace ordered Cleo Morey a third vodka and cranberry, then said, 'I have several theories about ghosts.' After a brief pause, he added, 'What I mean is, I believe there are different types of ghosts—'

He was interrupted by the beeping of his phone.

Apologizing to Cleo, he answered with a curter than usual, 'Grace speaking.'

It was DC Boutwood in the Incident Room. 'Sorry to bother you, sir. There has been a development. Are you on your way back yet?'

He looked at Cleo Morey, loath to tear himself away, and said with more than a trace of reluctance, 'Yes, I'll be there in fifteen minutes.'

74

In the studious atmosphere of the Incident Room time barely intruded. At five past ten, when Grace walked back in, all the desks were almost fully manned. At the Operation Salsa work station, Nick forked his way through a Chinese takeaway, Bella munched on an apple, and Emma-Jane sat glued to her computer screen, sipping a carton of Ribena through a straw. For a moment none of them noticed him.

'Hi,' he said. 'What's up?'

Immediately all three of them looked up. Bella Moy said, through a mouthful of apple, 'Glenn's had to rush home – some problem with the babysitter. He'll be back shortly.'

'Great! Is that the development you wanted to tell me about?'

DC Boutwood looked at him nervously; the junior on the team, she hadn't yet spent enough time with him to know when he was being funny and when he was in a temper. She was wise to be cautious – at this moment it was borderline and he was very tired. 'Sir, they've found a coffin in a concealed grave on land owned by Double-M Properties – from the diagram you brought in.'

'Brilliant! Fantastic news!'

Then he was aware of all three pairs of eyes on him, and that there was something wrong. 'Yes?'

'I'm afraid it's not such good news, sir. There's no one in it.'

'Just an empty coffin? In a proper grave?'

'As I understand, sir, yes.' She was getting increasingly nervous.

'Was there anyone in it – I mean – had there been anyone in it?'

'Apparently on the lid – the inside – there were signs of it, yes – sir.'

'Cut the *sir*, OK? Call me Roy.'

'Yes, sir – I – I – mean – *Roy*.'

He gave her a fleeting smile of reassurance. 'What kind of signs inside the lid?'

'Evidence of someone trying to scrape – cut – their way out of it.'

'And Michael Harrison, or whoever it was, succeeded?'

'The lid was off, sir – Roy – but apparently the grave was covered with a corrugated iron sheet and someone had put shrubs and mosses on top. Sounds like they were trying to conceal it.'

Grace leaned his arms wearily on the work-station surface. 'So who the hell are we dealing with here? Houdini?'

'It doesn't make much sense,' added Nicholl.

'The guy – Michael Harrison – has a reputation as a practical joker. It makes plenty of sense,' Grace retorted testily. He was starting to feel very tired and very grumpy and wished he wasn't here at all, but back in the pub, chatting with the warm and lovely Cleo Morey.

Realizing his blood sugar must be running low – he'd not eaten anything since a sandwich at lunchtime, and was now starving – he went out, down the corridor to a vending machine, and bought himself a double espresso, a bottle of water and a Mars Bar.

When he returned to the Incident Room, already

munching on the Mars, Emma-Jane was holding a telephone receiver up for him.

'Ashley Harper – she's insisting on speaking to you and says it is very urgent.'

Grace swallowed his mouthful, and took the receiver. 'This is Detective Superintendent Grace,' he said.

'It's Ashley Harper,' she said, sounding frantic. 'I've just had a text message from Michael. He's alive!'

'What does he say?'

'*Alive, call police.* I think that's what it says.'

'You think?'

'The spelling's a bit strange – text messages come out a bit oddly sometimes, don't they?'

'That's all it says?'

'Yes.'

Thinking fast, Grace asked, 'From his own mobile?'

'Yes, his normal number.'

He could have dispatched Nick or Bella over to her, but he decided he wanted to see Ashley himself.

'Stay there. I'm coming over right now.'

75

Mark stared at his gloomy reflection in the smoked-glass mirror in the lift that was sweeping him up to the fourth floor of the Van Alen building. Everything seemed to be unravelling around him.

Less than a week ago he'd sat on the aeroplane flying back from Leeds, reading the road test on the Ferrari 360 and trying to decide whether he would buy one in red or in silver, and whether it should have Formula-One-style gear-shift paddles, or a conventional lever on the floor.

Now that car was fast receding towards the horizon, without him. And everything else seemed to be, too.

What was Ashley's problem? For months they had been so incredibly close, as close as he could ever imagine two human beings could be. They shared the same humour, the same taste in food, drink, the same interests; they fancied each other like crazy, making love whenever they could snatch a few precious moments – and on a couple of occasions coming perilously close to being caught by Michael. She was an amazing girl, smart, super-bright and yet so loving and caring. He had never met anyone remotely like her, and could not imagine life without her.

So why was she being so short with him now? OK, it had been stupid to get drunk at the wedding and to be rude to the smartarse cop. But all this talk about killing Michael really worried him. Murder had never been on the agenda. Ever. Now she was talking like it had been all the time. Her words of half an hour ago in the trattoria echoed in his head.

There's never been any question of him getting out alive, has there?

And yes, he'd gone along with her plan. Not actually to murder Michael – just to – to – to—

Not murder. Definitely not murder.

Murder was when you planned things, wasn't it? Premeditated? This had all just been circumstance. Burying Michael alive, then the accident. He had no love for Michael. Michael was always first in every fucking thing. At school, Michael won the 100 metres and just about every damn thing else. He was the one who got to score the goals in football; he was the first of their group to lose his virginity – women always gravitated to him, always, always. Mark would find himself standing next to Michael in a crowded bar, and a couple of beautiful girls would come up to Michael, and he would say, 'This is my friend, Mark!' And the girls would smile and say, 'Hi, Mark!' and then turn their backs on him for the entire evening. It didn't happen once, it happened time and time again.

It had been the same with Ashley, in the beginning. In that first interview six months back it had been Michael, as usual, who had done all the talking and Ashley had seemed captivated by him, barely even casting Mark a glance. (Later she'd told Mark that it was all an act, because she had so desperately wanted the job and had been tipped off that it was Michael who really controlled the company.)

During the first month or so, Mark had been able to see how interested Michael was in Ashley. He knew his friend well enough to read the signs – he was flirting with her through his jokes, questions, flattery, stories about himself, exactly the way he flirted with all the women he fancied, and Mark had watched Michael's continuing flirtation with her with huge amusement – and satisfaction. It was the first time ever he had pulled a girl that Michael had fancied – and it felt terrific, liberating, as if finally, after fifteen years of their friendship, he no longer felt under Michael's thumb.

The plan had been Ashley's idea. Mark had had no qualms about any of it, except the notion of Ashley and Michael on honeymoon. That he had found so hard to bear. That, he knew in his heart, had been the reason he'd driven out into the forest last Thursday night and removed the air tube.

But now to let this madman torture and mutilate his friend? To death? He wasn't sure he had the stomach to do that.

He unlocked his front door, and as he stepped inside, the landline phone rang. He slammed the door shut, ran across the room, glanced at the display, but there was no caller number showing.

'Hello?' he answered.

The same Australian voice he had heard before said, 'Hi, mate, Vic here. I'm a little curious about the copper who popped round to see you earlier. Thought I told you about not speaking to the cops.'

'I didn't,' Mark said. 'This is a Detective Superintendent investigating Michael's disappearance – I had no idea he was coming.'

'I don't know if I believe you or not, mate. Want to have another chat with Mike about it, or are we cool?'

Trying to follow what he meant, Mark said, 'I think we're cool.'

'So you are going to do what I tell you?'

'I'm listening.'

'Just go to your office right now, open the safe, take out the documents signed by you and Mike giving power of attorney to a lawyer in the Cayman Islands called Julius Grobbe and fax it to him. At the same time you phone Julius Grobbe and tell him to transfer one million, two hundred and fifty-three thousand, seven hundred and twelve pounds from your bank account there to the numbered account in Panama I have already faxed to him. I'll phone you back here in exactly one hour and you can tell me how you got on. If you don't pick up the receiver, your friend loses another bit of his body, and this bit will *really* hurt him. Copy?'

'Copy.'

One million, two hundred and fifty-three thousand, seven hundred and twelve pounds was the exact total Mark and Michael had in their joint account.

76

Roy Grace and Glenn Branson – who had arrived back at Sussex House just as Grace was leaving – sat down in Ashley's cool, minimalistic sitting room and studied the very badly texted message on her dinky Sony Ericsson phone.

*aliVe. *£ cAlll ponlice*

Ashley sat opposite them, wringing her hands, her face pale, eyes watery. She looked as if she had been out somewhere, Grace thought, staring at her ragged cream blouse, her hair, linen skirt, and smelling the powerful aroma of perfume she exuded. *Where? With whom?*

He ought to be feeling sorry for her, he knew. Her fiancé had vanished, their wedding had been called off and tonight, instead of being somewhere on honeymoon, she was sitting crying in her house in Brighton. But he didn't feel sorry, couldn't feel sorry. All he could feel was deep suspicion.

'Have you tried calling him back?'

'Yes, and I've texted him. The line just rings and goes to voicemail.'

'That's better than before,' Grace said. 'It didn't ring before, just went straight to voicemail.'

Branson was fiddling with the phone – as he was much better with gadgets than Grace. 'It was sent by Michael Harrison, phone number plus 44797 134621,' he announced, then pressed a button with his thumb whilst

sucking in his lower lip in concentration. 'At 22.28, today.'
Both Grace and Branson checked their watches. Just over
an hour ago.

Twenty minutes before she rang, Grace thought. *Why
did she wait twenty minutes?*

Glenn Branson dialled the number and held the phone
to his ear. Grace and Ashley watched him, expectantly.
After some moments, Branson said, 'Hello, Michael Harrison, this is Detective Sergeant Branson of Brighton CID
responding to your text to Ashley Harper. Please call or text
me on 0789 965018. The number again is 0789 965018.'
Then he ended the call.

'Ashley, does Michael normally text you?'

She shrugged. 'Not a huge amount, but yes – you know
– little love messages, that sort of thing.' She smiled suddenly, and in the warmth it brought to her face, and the
beauty it seemed to animate, Grace could see her melting
almost any heart she chose.

Branson grinned. 'Has he always been a crap texter?'

'Not usually, no.'

Grace stared again at the words. *aliVe. *£ cAlll ponlice*

It looked like an infant had texted them, not a grown
man. Unless of course he had done them in a hurry, or
while driving.

'What information can you get from this?' Ashley
asked.

Grace was about to tell her, then decided not to. He
surreptitiously touched Branson's leg with his own as
a signal not to contradict him. 'Not a lot really, I'm afraid.
It's good news in one respect, in that we know he's alive,
but it is bad news, because he is clearly in trouble. Unless
it is part of a hoax.'

Her eyes were all over the place, Grace noticed; he had

been watching every inch of her body language since she had appeared at the door; everything was considered, all done after a pause, nothing spontaneous.

'You can't still believe Michael is doing some kind of a hoax?' she said incredulously. Grace noticed something very forced and theatrical about the way this came out. He told her about the discovery of the coffin – all the details.

'So he's escaped – is that what you think?'

'Maybe,' Grace said. 'Or maybe he was never there.'

'Oh, right, so he like scratched the inside of the lid himself?'

'I think that's one possible scenario, yes. It is not necessarily the right one.'

'Oh, come on, get real! This text message is desperate and you are sitting here giving me a bullshit theory about a hoax?'

'Ashley, we are very real,' Grace said calmly. 'We have an entire team in the Major Incident Suite; we have over one hundred officers out searching for Michael Harrison; we are getting national media coverage – we are doing all we possibly can.'

She looked contrite suddenly, a little girl lost and scared. She stared meekly at the two police officers, eyes wide, and dabbed them with a handkerchief. 'I'm sorry,' she sniffed, 'I didn't mean to have a go at you; you have been so brilliant, both of you. I'm just so – so—' She began to shake, her face scrunched up against a flood of tears.

Grace stood up awkwardly, and Branson followed.

'It's OK,' Grace said. 'We'll see ourselves out.'

77

He made the call. But it took five attempts for the damned fax to go through. The first time, trying to do it too quickly, he hadn't loaded the letter in straight and it had jammed. He'd spent ten precious minutes trying to unjam it without tearing the letter.

He'd driven, which was stupid considering the amount he'd drunk, but it was too far to walk to the office and back in the time, and he hadn't wanted to risk not being able to get a taxi.

Now, bursting in through the door of his apartment with less than three minutes to the deadline, he made straight for the drinks cabinet, poured himself three fingers of Balvenie and gulped it straight down. He felt the burn in his gullet, then winced as it burnt his stomach even harder, closing his eyes for a moment.

His mobile beeped. A text message signal.

He pulled it out of his pocket and stared at the display.

Well done, mate! Just made it.

The phone was jigging in his hand from nerves. Where the hell was this man, Vic? He punched the *options* button, trying to see the source of the text. It was a number he did not recognize. Clumsily, he typed back, *Are we OK now?* Then pressed the *send* button. Instantly there was a soft beep, indicating the text had been sent.

The whisky wasn't working, at least not on his nerves. He walked unsteadily over towards the drinks cabinet. But before he reached it, the phone beeped again. Another incoming text.

> *Walk out onto your balcony, mate.*
> *Look down at the street below!*

Mark made straight for the patio doors, unlocked them and stepped out onto the teak decking, then crossed the narrow balcony, past two sun-loungers, placed his hands on the rail and looked down. Music pounded from a gay nightclub a few yards down the street, and he could see the bald domes of the two bouncers. A couple walked along arm in arm. Three drunk girls were staggering along, bumping into each other, giggling. A steady stream of cars drove past.

He looked at the far side of the street, wondering if that was where Vic meant, but all he could see was a couple snogging. Holding his phone in the palm of his hand, he tapped out, *I cannot see you.* And sent it. Again he scanned the street.

Moments later, there was another beep. The reply on his screen read: *I'm right behind you!*

But before he had a chance to turn, one strong hand grabbed the rear of his belt, and another his shirt collar. A fraction of a second later, both his feet were in the air. He dropped his phone, desperately trying to grab the balcony rail, but he was too high up, and his fingers clawed at nothing but air.

Before he even had time to shout, he was launched like a javelin over the rail and plunged down towards the pavement.

He landed flat on his back, with an impact that broke his spine in seven places and shattered his skull with the impact of a coconut hit by a sledgehammer.

One of the drunk girls screamed.

78

Grace and Branson heard the call on the police radio in Grace's car minutes before they arrived back at Sussex House. An apparent suicide jumper at the Van Alen building on the Kemp Town seafront.

They looked at each other. Grace pulled his blue light from the glove compartment, clipped it to the roof, and hit the accelerator. They raced through a speed camera which flashed at them, but he didn't care; he could sort that one out.

Seven minutes later he was forced to slow to a crawl as he drove onto Marine Parade. Ahead he could see a whole circus of flashing blue lights, a crowd of people and two ambulances.

After double parking, both of them leaped out of the car, pushed their way through the crowd and reached two uniformed constables who were busily putting up a tape barrier bearing the wording 'POLICE LINE, DO NOT CROSS'.

Flashing their warrant cards, they ducked under the tape and saw two paramedics standing uselessly by the crumpled heap of a man on the ground, with a dark pool of blood stained with yellow seeping from his head and another, larger, darker stain from his torso.

Under the amber glare of the street lighting Grace could see the man's face. It was Mark Warren, no question. Fighting the rising bile in his throat, he turned to one of the constables and showed him his warrant card.

'What happened?'

'I – don't know, sir. I just spoke to a witness – she was walking along with her friends when he landed, almost at their feet. She's in the far ambulance – bad shock.'

Grace glanced at Branson, who was looking unsteady, then down at the clearly lifeless body. Mark Warren's eyes were wide open, as if in shock.

Christ. Only a few hours ago he had been talking to the man. He had reeked of alcohol and seemed a nervous wreck. Suddenly Grace thought about Cleo. How she would be busy in about an hour's time at the mortuary, making him look presentable for some relative to come and identify him. He didn't envy her that one bit.

'Does anyone know who this man is?' said a voice.

'Yeah, I know him,' said another voice. 'On my floor. He's my neighbour!'

Grace heard a siren, coming closer. 'I know him too,' he said. Then corrected himself. 'Knew him.'

Robert Allison, a tough Detective Inspector – and former Sussex Police snooker champion – who Grace knew well, emerged from the front door of the building and Grace, followed by Branson, walked over to him.

'Roy! Glenn!' Robert Allison greeted them. 'What are you two stop-outs doing here?'

'Thought we'd swing by to catch some sea air,' Grace said.

'Dangerous thing to do around here,' the Detective Inspector said, nodding at the corpse. 'He thought he'd step out on his balcony and catch some sea air, too.' A police surgeon had arrived, and a police photographer. Allison spoke to them both briefly then returned to Grace and Branson.

'Any information about what happened?' asked Grace.

'Not yet.'

'I know him,' Grace said. 'I interviewed him earlier this evening. About eight o'clock. He's the business partner of the young man who's missing – the wedding prank – the four lads killed last week.'

Allison nodded. 'Right.'

'Can we get into his apartment?'

'I've just been up there – the porter has a key. Want me to come with you?'

'Yes, sure, why not?'

A few minutes later Grace, Branson and Detective Inspector Allison entered the apartment. The porter, a muscular-looking man in his fifties, wearing shorts and a singlet, waited outside.

Grace strode into the sitting area, with which he was already a little familiar, and walked over towards the balcony, which he had stepped out onto a few hours back. He went out again and looked down at the scene below. He could see the small crowd, the two ambulances, the police cars, the flashes of the police photographer's camera, the tape cordoning off the crumpled figure of Mark Warren, the dark stains like shadows leaking from his body and head.

He thought back to the wedding, when Mark had come up to him so aggressively. Then tonight when he was a drunken wreck. Grace knew from his experience that survivors of accidents in which others had died often got chewed up with guilt that they had survived; it could destroy some people. But had Mark Warren jumped over the balcony for that reason?

That night he had come back late to this apartment with mud on his car – had that been a guilt trip to the scene of the accident he should have died in with his friends? Possibly. But what was the damned aggression about at the wedding? That bit did not fit. He hadn't had a good feeling about Mark Warren. The best man who didn't know what the stag night plans were.

How likely was that?

He went back inside pensively. 'Let's just take a good look around for a few minutes,' he said, and began by walking over to the cupboard door Mark had kept staring at earlier. But all it contained were two dusty flower vases and an empty box of Cohiba Robusto cigars.

Steadily he worked his way through each cupboard, opening every door and drawer. Glenn Branson began doing the same, while Allison watched. Then Grace reached the fridge in the open-plan kitchen and opened the door. Casting his eye across the cartons of skimmed milk, yoghurt pots, clumps of fashionable salad leaves and several bottles of white burgundy and champagne, he almost missed the Jiffy bag on the third shelf.

He pulled it out and peered inside, frowning. Then he tipped the small plastic bag it contained out on the black marble kitchen work surface.

'Jesus,' Branson said, staring at the fingertip.

'OK,' Robert Allison said. 'Now this starts to make sense. I found it on the victim when I was looking for ID.' He pulled a folded sheet of A4 paper from his pocket and handed it to Grace.

Grace and Branson both read it.

'Check the fingerprints out and you'll find it is your friend and business partner. Every 24 hours I will cut an increasingly bigger bit off him. Until you do exactly what I tell you.'

Grace read it again, and then a third time. 'I think this tells us two things,' he said.

Both detectives looked at him, but they had to wait some while before he spoke, finally.

'The first is that I don't think we're looking at a suicide here. And secondly, if I'm right in that assumption, we'll be lucky to find Michael Harrison still alive.'

79

The phone was ringing again! The third time! Each time before he had hit the buttons, trying to stop it in case Vic heard. Then he had fumbled with the keyboard, dialling 901. And each time got the same damned woman's voice. 'You have no messages.'

But now her voice said something different. 'You have one new message.' Then he heard, 'Hello, Michael Harrison, this is Detective Sergeant Branson of Brighton CID responding to your text to Ashley Harper. Please call or text me on 0789 965018. The number again is 0789 965018.'

It was the sweetest sound Michael had ever heard in his life.

Again he fumbled with the keys, trying to text a reply in the dank darkness: *A'88m breing h$ld*—

Then dazzling, blinding white light.

Vic.

'Got a mobile you didn't tell me about, have you, Mikey? Naughty boy, aren't you? Think I'd better take that off you before you get yourself into trouble.'

'Urrrr,' Michael said through the duct tape.

The next moment he felt the phone being ripped from his hand. Followed by Vic's reproachful voice.

'That's not playing the game fair, Mike. I'm very disappointed in you. You should have told me about the phone. You really should have done.'

'Urrrr,' Michael mumbled again, shimmying in terror.

He could see eyes glinting through the hood above him, inches from his face, bright green eyes like a feral cat.

'You want me to hurt you again? Is that what you'd like, Mikey? Let's see who you were calling, shall we?'

Moments later Michael heard the police officer's faint voice through the phone's speaker again.

'Well, fancy that,' the Australian said. 'How sweet. Calling your fiancée. Sweet, but naughty. I think it's time for a punishment. Would you like me to cut off another finger – or clip the callipers back on your bollocks?'

'Noorrrrrrr.'

'Sorry, mate, you'll need to articulate better. Talk me through what you'd like best. It's all the same to me – and by the way, your mate Mark is a rude bastard. Thought you'd like to know he never said goodbye.'

Michael blinked against the light. He didn't know what the man was talking about. Mark? Dimly he wondered where it was that Mark had gone.

'Here's something for you to think about, Mikey. That one million, two hundred thousand pounds you have salted away in the Cayman Islands. That's one hell of a nest egg, wouldn't you say?'

How much did this man know about him and his life, Michael wondered. Was that what he was after? He could have it, every damned penny, if he would just let him go. He tried to tell him. 'Urrrrrrr. Ymmmgghvvvvvit.'

'That's sweet of you, Mikey, whatever it is you're trying to tell me. I really appreciate all the efforts you are making. But here's the thing, you see. Your problem is, I already have it. And that means I don't need you any more.'

80

Shortly before midnight, Grace drove back into the car park of Sussex House, giving a weary nod to the security guard. They had said little on the drive back from the Van Alen building; Grace and Branson were both wrapped in their thoughts.

As Grace pulled the car up, Branson yawned noisily. 'Think we can go home, go to bed, get some sleep?'

'No stamina, youth?' Grace chided.

'And you're wide awake, full of beans? Firing on all cylinders, yeah? I've heard when you get past a certain age you start needing less sleep; which apparently is just as well, since you spend half the night getting up to piss.'

Grace smiled.

'I don't look forward to old age much,' Branson said. 'Do you?'

'To be honest, I don't think about it. I see a guy like Mark Warren, lying all broken, leaking his brains out on the pavement, and I remember he and I were talking just a few hours before; things like that make me believe in just living one day at a time.'

Branson yawned again.

'I'm going back to work,' Grace said. 'You can fuck off home if you want.'

'You know, you can be such a bitch at times,' Branson said, reluctantly following him to the main entrance, through the doors and up the staircase past the displays of truncheons.

Emma-Jane Boutwood, wearing a white cardigan tied around her neck and a pink blouse, was the only person still in the Incident Room. Grace walked over to her, then gestured at the empty work stations. 'Where's everyone, E-J?'

She leaned forward as if to read some small print on her computer screen and said distractedly, 'I think they've all gone home.'

Grace stared at her tired face, and gave her a light pat on her shoulder, his hand touching the soft wool of the cardigan. 'I think you should go home too; it's been a long day.'

'Can you just give me one minute, Roy? I have something I think is going to interest you – both of you.'

'Anyone like a coffee?' Grace asked. 'Water? Coke?'

'You buying?' Branson said.

'No, the ratepayers of Sussex are buying this time. They want us working at midnight, they can buy us coffee. This one's going on expenses.'

'I'll have a Diet Coke,' Branson said. 'Actually, no, change that. Make it a full-strength Coke; I need the sugar hit.'

'I'd love a coffee,' Emma-Jane said.

Grace walked out, along the empty corridor to the rest area with its kitchenette and vending machines. Fumbling in his pocket he pulled out some change, bought a double espresso for himself, a cappuccino for Emma-Jane and a Coke for Branson, then carried them back to the Incident Room on a plastic tray.

As he walked in, the young detective constable was pointing at something on her computer screen, and Branson, leaning over her shoulder, seemed engrossed. Without turning his head, he said, 'Roy, come and take a look at this!'

Emma-Jane turned to Grace. 'You asked me to check up on Ashley Harper's background—'

'Uh huh. What have you found?'

Almost swelling with pride she said, 'Actually, quite a lot.'

'Tell me.'

She flipped a couple of pages on a notepad covered in her neat handwriting, checking her notes as she spoke. 'The information you gave me was that Ashley Harper was born in England, and her parents were killed in a car crash in Scotland when she was three; that she was subsequently brought up by foster parents, in London first, then they moved to Australia. When she was sixteen she went to Canada and stayed with her uncle and aunt – and that her aunt died recently. Her uncle's name was Bradley Cunningham – I don't have her aunt's first name.'

Still reading from her pad she went on: 'Ashley Harper returned to England – to her roots – about nine months ago. You said that previously she had worked in real estate in Toronto, Canada and that her employers were a subsidiary of the Bay group.' Then she looked up to Grace and Branson as if for confirmation.

Grace replied. 'Yes, that's right.'

'OK,' she said. 'Earlier today I spoke to the head of Human Resources for the Bay group in Toronto – as you may know they are one of the largest department store chains in Canada. They do not have a real estate subsidiary, nor have they ever had an Ashley Harper work for them. I did some further checking and found there are no real estate firms anywhere in Canada with the name "The Bay" in them.'

'Interesting,' Branson said, flipping the ring-pull of his Coke. There was a sharp hiss.

'It gets even more interesting,' she said. 'There is no Bradley Cunningham listed in any phone directory for Toronto, nor for anywhere else in the whole of Ontario. I haven't had time to check out the rest of Canada yet. But . . .' she paused to sip some chocolate-covered froth off the top of her cappuccino, 'I have a journalist friend on the *Glasgow Herald* in Scotland. She's checked back in the archives of all the principal Scottish papers. If a three-year-old girl was orphaned in a car crash, it would have made the news, right?'

'Usually,' Grace said.

'Ashley claims to be twenty-eight. I've had her go back twenty-five years, and then five years either side of that. The name Harper has not come up.'

'She could have taken the name of her foster parents,' Branson said.

'She could,' agreed Emma-Jane Boutwood. 'But what I'm about to show you reduces that possibility.'

Grace looked admiringly at the young DC. She seemed to be growing in confidence in front of his eyes. She was exactly the kind of new blood the police force so badly needed. Smart, hard-working youngsters with determination.

'I had the name Ashley Harper run through the Holmes network, as you requested,' she said, addressing Grace.

Holmes-2 was the second phase in a computerized database of crimes, linking all police forces throughout the UK and Interpol and, more recently, other police networks overseas.

'Nothing showed up under the name Ashley Harper,' she said. 'But this is where it gets interesting. Taking the initials "AH", and linking them to a broad category heading of "property", Holmes came up with the following. Eighteen months ago a young lady called Abigail Harrington married a wealthy property developer in Lymm, Cheshire, called Richard Wonnash. He was big into free-fall parachuting. Three months after their wedding, he died when his parachute failed to open during a jump. Four years ago, in Toronto, Canada, a woman called Alexandra Huron married a real estate developer called Joe Kerwin. Five months after their wedding he drowned in a sailing accident on Lake Ontario. Seven years ago, a woman called Ann Hampson married a property developer in London called Julian Warner. He was a high-profile society bachelor, with big holdings in London docklands around the time of the early 1990s property crash. Six months and two days after their wedding, he gassed himself in an underground car park in Wapping.'

She took another sip of her froth.

'Same initials,' Branson said. 'But what does that prove?'

'A lot of con artists keep the same initials when they change their names,' she said. 'I read about this at police training college. In itself it proves nothing. But here's where it gets better.' She tapped her keyboard and a black and white newspaper photograph of a young woman with close-cropped dark hair appeared. The face belonged to Ashley Harper – or her double.

'This is from the *Evening Standard* article on the death of Julian Warner,' she said.

There was a long silence while Grace and Branson studied the photograph. 'Shit,' Branson said. 'Certainly looks like her.'

Saying nothing, she tapped the keyboard again.

Another photograph, also in black and white, appeared. This showed a woman with shoulder-length fair hair. Her face looked even more like Ashley Harper. 'This is from the *Toronto Star*, four years ago, reporting on the death of Joe Kerwin.'

Grace and Branson said nothing. Both were stunned.

'This next one is from the *Cheshire Evening Post*, eighteen months ago, in an article about the death of Richard Wonnash. Abigail Harrington was the beautiful grieving widow.' She tapped her screen and a new photograph appeared, in colour. The hair was red, styled in an elegantly short razor cut. The face yet again was, almost beyond doubt, Ashley Harper's.

'Bloody hell!' Branson exclaimed.

Grace stared at the face, pensively, for a long time. Then he said, 'Emma-Jane, well done.'

'Thank you – Roy.'

Grace turned to Glenn Branson. 'So,' he said. 'It's twenty minutes to one. Which magistrate do you feel brave enough to wake up?'

'For a search warrant?'

'You worked that all out by yourself did you?' Ignoring Branson's grimace, Grace stood up. 'Emma-Jane, go home; get some sleep.'

Branson yawned. 'How about me? Do I get some sleep?'

Grace clapped a hand on his shoulder. 'I'm afraid, my friend, your day's only just begun.'

81

A few minutes later, Grace was on the phone to a very sleepy-sounding magistrates' clerk, who asked if this couldn't wait until the morning.

'We're investigating a possible abduction, and it's a potential life-or-death situation,' Grace informed her. 'I need an evidential warrant and I'm afraid it absolutely cannot wait.'

'OK,' she said reluctantly. 'The duty magistrate is Mrs Quentin.'

Grace smiled to himself. Hermione Quentin was one magistrate he particularly disliked, having had a run-in with her some months back in court over a suspect he had wanted to hold in custody; she had refused. She was the worst kind of magistrate in his view, married to a wealthy stockbroker, living in a vulgar ostentatious house, a middle-aged glamour queen with no experience of the real world and some kind of zealous personal agenda to change the way the police in general viewed criminals. It would give him the sweetest pleasure to get her out of bed to sign the warrant in the small hours of the morning.

Grace and Branson then spent a further ten minutes on the phone, organizing a team to assemble at Sussex House at 5 a.m. Then, taking pity on Branson, Grace sent him home to get a couple of hours' kip.

Next he rang DC Nicholl, and apologized for disturbing him, then instructed him to head for Ashley Harper's house and keep watch on it for any movement.

At 2 a.m., with the signed warrant in his hand, Grace arrived back at his home, set his alarm for 4.15, and crashed out.

*

When he hit the alarm button and jumped automatically out of bed in the dark room, he could hear the first twitterings of the dawn chorus, reminding him as he stepped into the shower that, although summer had not yet begun, they were less than a month shy of the longest day, 21 June.

At 5 a.m. he was back at Sussex House, feeling remarkably perky on his two and a bit hours' sleep. Bella and Emma-Jane were already there, as was Ben Farr, a round-faced, bearded Sergeant in his late forties who was to be the Exhibits Officer, and Joe Tindall. Glenn Branson arrived a few minutes later.

Over cups of coffee, Grace briefed them. Then, shortly after half past five, all wearing protective waistcoats, they set off in a police Transit van and a marked car, which Branson drove, Grace in the passenger seat.

Reaching Ashley's street, Grace told Branson to pull up alongside Nick's unmarked Astra, and wound his window down.

'All quiet,' Nicholl reported.

'Good boy,' Grace said, noting that Ashley Harper's Audi TT was in its usual place outside her house. He told Nicholl to cover the street behind, then they drove on.

There were no free spaces in the street, so they double parked beside the Audi. Grace gave Nick Nicholl a couple of minutes to get in place, then, leading the posse, marched up to the front door, in full daylight now, and rang the bell.

There was no response.

He rang again, then, after a minute, rang yet again. Then he nodded to Ben Farr, who went over to the Transit and removed a heavy-duty ram, the size of a large fire extinguisher. He hefted it up to the front door, swung it hard and the door flew open.

Grace went in first. 'Police!' he shouted. 'Hello? Police!'

The silent, winking lights of the hi-fi system greeted him. Followed by the rest of his team, he walked up the stairs and paused on the first-floor landing. 'Hello!' he called out again. 'Miss Harper?'

Silence.

He opened one door, onto a small bathroom. The next door was to a small, bland spare bedroom that didn't look as if it had ever been used. He hesitated, then pushed the remaining door, which opened onto a master bedroom, with a double bed that had clearly not been slept in. The curtains were drawn shut. He found the light switch and turned it on, and several ceiling spots lit up the room.

The place had a deserted feel, like a hotel room waiting for its next occupant. He saw an immaculate duvet over a queen-size bed, a flat-screen television, a clock radio plus a couple of Hockney swimming pool prints on the wall.

No Ashley Harper.

So where the hell was she?

Feeling a stab of panic, Grace exchanged glances with Glenn Branson. They both knew that somewhere along the line they had been outsmarted, but where and how? For a moment all he could think of was the bollocking he would get from Alison Vosper if it turned out he had woken a JP in the middle of the night to get a search warrant for no good reason.

And there could be all kinds of good reasons why Ashley Harper wasn't here tonight. For a moment he felt angry at his friend. This was all Glenn's fault. He'd suckered him into this damned case. It wasn't anything to do with him, not his problem. Now he owned the fucking problem and it was getting deeper.

He tried to recap, to think how he would cover his arse if No. 27 hauled him in. There was Mark Warren's death. The note. The finger in the fridge. Emma-Jane's findings. There was a whole ton of things that were not right. Mark Warren, so belligerent at the wedding reception. Bradley Cunningham, so smooth, so upmarket at the wedding.

'Actually the pants are killing me . . . rented this lot from your wonderful Moss Bros, but I think I got given the wrong pants!'

From the time he had spent in the United States and in Canada, and the conversations Grace had had about the differences in their language, he knew that classy Americans and Canadians might call ordinary trousers 'pants', but they would called dressier trousers 'trousers'. It had been an instant giveaway that Bradley Cunningham might not be who he made himself out to be.

Not that that slender hypothesis would satisfy Alison Vosper.

'Take this place apart,' he told his team wearily. 'Look under every bloody stone. Find out who owns this place. Who owns the televisions, the hi-fi, the Audi outside, the carpets, the wall sockets. I want to know every damned detail about Ashley Harper. I want to know more about her than she knows herself. Everybody understand?'

*

After two hours of searching, so far no one had found anything. It was as if Ashley Harper had been through the place with some kind of super-Hoover. There was nothing other than the furniture, a bio yoghurt pot in the fridge together with some soya milk, a bunch of radishes and a half-drunk bottle of Sainsbury's own-label Scottish mineral water.

Glenn Branson came up to Grace, who was busy lifting the mattress off the spare bed. 'Man, this is so weird – it's as if she knew we were coming, know what I mean?'

'So why didn't we know she was leaving?' Grace asked.

'There you go again. Another question.'

'Yes,' said Grace, tiredness making him snappy now. 'Maybe that's because you're always giving me questions instead of fucking answers.'

Branson raised a hand in the air. 'No offence, man.'

'None taken.'

'So where the fuck is she?'

'Not here.'

'I figured that one.'

'Roy! Take a look at this – I don't know if it's of any use?' DC Nicholl came into the room holding a small piece of paper, which he showed to Grace.

It was a receipt from a company called Century Radio on Tottenham Court Road. On the receipt was printed: 'AR5000 Cyber Scan, £2,437.25'.

'Where was this?' Grace asked.

'In the dustbin in the back yard,' Nick replied, with pride.

'Two thousand, four hundred and thirty-seven pounds for a scanner?' Grace asked. 'What kind of scanner costs that much? Some kind of computer scanner?' After a few moments thought, he added, 'Why would anyone throw away the receipt? Even if you couldn't charge the scanner to your business, sure as hell you would keep the receipt in case it went wrong. Wouldn't you?'

'I sure as hell would,' Branson agreed.

Grace looked at the date on the receipt. Last Wednesday. Time of purchase showed as 14.25. On Tuesday night, her fiancé disappears. On Wednesday afternoon she goes out and buys a two-and-a-half-thousand-quid scanner. This didn't make sense – yet. His watch showed that two hours had elapsed so far, it was now just past 8 a.m. 'I don't know what time Century Radio opens – but we need to find out about that scanner,' he said.

'You have some thoughts about it?' Branson asked.

'Plenty,' Grace replied. 'Too many. Far too many.' Then he added. 'I have to be at Lewes Crown Court by quarter to ten.'

'For your good friend Suresh Hossain?'

'I'd hate to think he was missing me. How about some breakfast? A big fry-up – the works?'

'Cholesterol, man, bad for your heart.'

'You know what? Right now everything's bad for my heart.'

82

As Grace entered the large, bustling waiting area for the three courtrooms housed in the handsome Georgian Lewes Crown Court building with plenty of time to spare, he switched his phone to silent. At least Claudine seemed to have got the message and had stopped texting him.

He yawned, his body feeling leaden, the massive fry-up he'd just eaten sapping his energy rather than fuelling it. He just wanted to lie down somewhere and have a kip. It was strange, he thought. A week ago this trial had dominated his life, his every waking thought. Now it was secondary; finding Michael Harrison was all that mattered.

But this trial did matter a lot, too. It mattered to the widow and children of Raymond Cohen, the man beaten to a pulp with a spiked stick, either by Hossain or by his thugs. It mattered to every ordinary decent person in the City of Brighton and Hove, because they had a right to be protected from monsters like him, and it mattered a very great deal to Grace's credibility. He had to shed his tiredness and concentrate.

Finding a quiet corner in the room, he sat down and returned a call to Eleanor, who was dealing with his post and email for him. Then he closed his eyes, grateful for the rest it gave them, and cradled his head in his hands, trying to catnap, trying to block from his ears the swinging of doors opening and closing, the cheery banter of greetings, the clicks of briefcase locks, the murmured voices between lawyers and clients.

After a couple of minutes he took two deep breaths, and the oxygen hit gave him an instant small boost. He stood up and looked around. In a moment he might find out whether he would be needed or not today. Hopefully not, and he could get back to Sussex House, he thought, looking around for the person he needed to speak to, Liz Reilly from the Crown Prosecution Service.

There were a good hundred people in the room, including several gowned barristers and assistants, and he spotted Liz at the other end of the room, a smartly dressed, conservative-looking woman in her early thirties, holding a clipboard and deep in conversation with a barrister he did not recognize.

He walked across and stood near them, catching her signal that she would be with him in a moment. When she finally broke away from the barrister, she looked excited. 'We have a possible new witness!'

'Really? Who?'

'A call-girl from Brighton. She rang the CPS last night saying she's been following the trial in the papers, and alleging that Suresh Hossain beat her up during a session with her. The sex session was on the night of February 10th last year, in Brighton.'

February 10th was the night of the murder for which Suresh Hossain was on trial.

'Hossain has a cast-iron alibi that he was at dinner in London with two friends that night. Both have testified,' Grace said.

'Yes he has, but they are both employees of Hossain. This girl isn't. She's terrified of him – the reason she hasn't come forward before is she's been threatened with her life if she does. And there's a problem, which is she doesn't trust the police. That's why she rang us, rather than the police.'

'How credible do you think she is?'

'Very,' she said. 'We'd need some high-level witness protection for her.'

'Whatever she wants. Anything!' Grace wrung his hands in excitement. He wanted to hug Liz Reilly. This was wonderful news. *Wonderful!*

'But someone's going to have to go and convince her that the police won't bust her for – you know – her trade.'

'Where's she now?'

'At her home.'

Grace looked at his watch. 'I could go and see her right away. Is that possible?'

'Go in an unmarked car.'

'Yes, and I'll take a WPC with me who can stay with her. We don't want to give Hossain any chance of getting at her. I want to go and see her and persuade her to come in right away.'

'If you play her carefully, you'll be pushing on an open door.'

Suddenly, Grace wasn't tired any more.

83

It was shortly after midday when he arrived back in the Incident Room. The witness, Shelley Sandler, was good, he thought. Mid-twenties, intelligent, articulate, vulnerable, she'd be highly credible in court. Just so long as she didn't panic and change her mind at the last minute, as so often happened. But she seemed determined to get back at Hossain. Very, very determined.

This was such good news. After a shaky few days last week, it now looked to Grace as if getting the verdict he so badly wanted was going to be achievable.

The full team were at the work station, plus two new assistants, a young male constable and a middle-aged female assistant, so he called a briefing meeting, telling them all to stay seated.

Keeping his voice low, as the other work stations were occupied also with teams hard at work, Nick Nicholl spoke first. 'Roy, the receipt we took earlier this morning from Miss Harper's house, two thousand, four hundred and thirty-seven pounds for a scanner?'

'Uh huh.'

'I got all the information on it from Century Radio.' He handed a few printed sheets off a web page to Grace. 'The rest of us have seen this.'

Grace looked at it.

AR5000 Receiver 'Cyber Scan'. Incredible 10Khz–2600Mhz Frequency Range! The AR5000 advances the frontiers of performance, providing excellent strong signal handling, high sensitivity and wide frequency coverage with microprocessor facilities to match including 5 independent VFOs, 1,000 memory channels, 20 search banks, Cyber Scan fast scan and search – including all mobile frequencies. Scanning and search speed is 45 channels or increments per second . . .

He turned to Branson. 'You're the best techie I know. I think I have already guessed what this thing is – can you confirm?'

'It's a state-of-the-art radio frequency scanner. It's the kind of thing used by Citizens' Band radio nuts to find new friends, to eavesdrop on police radio networks or on mobile calls.'

Grace nodded. Then to Emma-Jane Boutwood he said, 'Do we have any evidence that Ashley Harper was ever into Citizens' Band radio either in her current incarnation or any previous one?'

'We don't,' she said. 'No.'

He looked at the colour picture of the scanner. A large silver box on its own legs, with a dial on the front, and the same perplexing array of knobs and buttons you'd find on any complex piece of radio kit. 'So, on Tuesday night her fiancé disappears. Wednesday afternoon at two-thirty she legs it to London and buys a radio scanner for two and a half thousand quid. Any good theories why? And how the hell did she knew how to use it?'

'Desperation?' volunteered Nick Nicholl.

'I don't buy that,' Grace said.

'She obviously genuinely did not know where he was,' Bella Moy suggested.

Grace nodded distractedly. That made sense, but to him it did not fit.

'She might have known that Michael Harrison had a walkie-talkie. Perhaps it was to try to communicate with him?' Emma-Jane Boutwood said. 'Or – how about – to listen in to who else he might be communicating with?'

Grace was impressed. 'Yes, good thinking.' He looked around. 'Any more theories? OK, let's park this for a moment. Any other progress?'

'Yes,' Nick Nicholl said. 'After you left Ashley Harper's house, Joe Tindall started pulling up floorboards. We discovered an envelope full of receipts behind a chest of drawers we moved – it might have fallen there accidentally or it might have been hidden. Most of the receipts don't seem that interesting to us, but there is one here you should see.'

It was for £1,500 from a company with a Maddox Street, London W1 address, called Conquest Escorts. Underneath the name was the legend 'Discreet, charming male and female escorts for every occasion'. Two dates were shown – the previous Saturday, the intended day of Ashley Harper's wedding, and the previous Monday.

'Turn it over, Roy,' Nick Nicholl said. 'Take a look at the other side.'

Grace turned it over and saw written in ballpoint pen the name Bradley Cunningham.

His mind shot back to the conversation he had had with Ashley, in her house, on Friday night. He could remember her sitting there so dejectedly, talking about her Canadian uncle, saying, 'We adore each other . . . he took the whole week off just so he could be at the rehearsal on Monday.'

'She's faked an uncle?' he said, puzzling.

'She's faked a whole lot more than just an uncle – E-J

will tell you in a minute,' Glenn Branson said. 'Take a look at this first.'

He handed Grace a photocopied sheet of A4 paper. It was a faxed instruction to Bank Hexta, registered on Grand Cayman Island, to transfer the sum of £1,253,712 to a numbered account at Banco Aliado in Panama. The instruction was signed by both Michael Harrison and Mark Warren, and the date and time at the top showed 11.25 p.m., the previous day.

Grace read it through twice then frowned at Branson. 'This is about twenty minutes before he went off his balcony.'

'Yes, correct.'

Grace thought about the note found in Mark Warren's pocket. 'So he went and transferred the money in order to save his friend's life. Then he goes and tops himself?'

'Maybe they had some big debt to pay. Panama could be tied up with Colombia – the Colombian mafia – maybe they got themselves into shit on a loan? They pay it off, and Mark Warren then tops himself?'

'It's a reasonable theory,' Grace said. 'But these two guys have been doing pretty well. They have this huge development at Ashdown – twenty houses – that could make them several million. Why top himself for – what would his share be – a few hundred thousand pounds?'

'So he makes the transfer and then is killed.'

'That's a more elegant theory,' Grace said. 'I spoke to Cleo Morey at the mortuary just now. There's a Home Office pathologist on his way down. We might have a bit more information later today.'

DS Bella Moy then told Grace she had some information from the phone company. Vodafone had logged activity from Michael Harrison's mobile between 10.22 p.m. and

11 p.m. the previous night, and there had been several 999 emergency calls made from Michael Harrison's phone, but on each occasion the operator could not hear anyone at the other end and got no response to her questions.

'What about the cell mast?'

'I was just coming to that, Roy. Vodafone have been very helpful this morning, and we already have from them the location of the closest cell radio mast to Michael Harrison's phone,' she said.

'Where is it?'

Her face fell a little. 'This is not such good news – it's in the town centre of Newhaven, and the one mast covers the entire town.'

'Well, it's some help,' Grace said. 'Any coincidence that Newhaven is a Channel seaport?'

'I've already put out an all-ports alert,' she said.

'For what?'

'For Ashley Harper and for Alexandra Huron – that's the name she was using in Canada four years ago.'

She clearly had more to say, so Grace let her go on.

'I checked on her Audi TT car. It was leased by her, in her own name, from a dealer in Hammersmith a year ago. All payments are up to date and kosher. Same with her house, leased, but the lease expires at the end of this month.'

'To coincide with her wedding?' Branson suggested.

'Quite possible,' Emma-Jane said. 'Then on a hunch I had our new recruits do a trawl of all the car and van rental firms in the area, and gave them all of Ashley Harper's previous names in addition to her own. Nothing showed up under the name Ashley Harper,' she said. 'But at ten past midnight – this morning – a woman called Alexandra Huron rented a Mercedes saloon from a local Avis at

Gatwick Airport, using a Toronto Dominion Bank of Canada credit card. The assistant who dealt with the customer has now positively identified her from photographs as Ashley Harper.'

'CCTV cameras,' Grace said. 'What I—'

Glenn Branson raised a hand. 'We're already on the case. We're already having every camera checked between Gatwick and Newhaven from the time she picked up the car.'

'She left her house about an hour before you went there, Nick,' Grace said to DC Nicholl.

'Yes.'

'Do we know how she got to the airport?'

'No.'

Grace fell silent. For a few moments no one had anything to say. He was busy thinking through all the timings last night – when he had been to see Mark Warren, when he and Glenn Branson had visited Ashley. Mark Warren being taken out to the forest to help locate the grave. The money being transferred. Mark Warren's death. Ashley renting the car under a different name.

Now he knew what her game was; that was clear enough. And he knew that they needed to find her. Absolutely nothing else mattered at this moment than to do that.

And quickly.

If it wasn't already too late.

84

'Strewth, woman, four fucking suitcases – what's the matter with you, Alex?'

'What do you mean?'

'I'm not helping you lug four fucking suitcases, that's what I mean.'

'So we'll get a porter.'

'And what about the excess baggage charge?'

'We're travelling Club, Vic; they have a big baggage allowance. Relax.'

'Fucking relax? Why can't you just leave all this shit behind, buy new stuff in Sydney – they have shops there, you know!'

Ashley, in a Prada denim trouser suit and high heels, standing between her suitcases in the living room of the small detached house in Newhaven, placed her hands defiantly on her hips and stared out of the window. The view from the rented house's remote hill-top position took in almost the whole of the town, and much of the port that was part of it.

She watched the Seacat cross-Channel ferry slipping past the harbour mole, heading out to sea. It was a flat, grey day, and humid; she was perspiring, which added to her bad mood, and her period was about to start, which made it even worse.

She turned on him, her voice rising in acidity. 'Really? They have shops in Sydney? You mean shops you can walk into and buy things from?'

'Oh, fuck off, you stupid cow – don't speak to me like I'm some fucking servant.'

'You fuck off! Why should I leave all this stuff behind? This is my life.'

'What do you mean *this* is your life?'

At five foot, seven inches, Vic stood barely half an inch taller than Ashley, but he had always seemed to her to be much taller. He had the wiry, muscular build and the persona of a fighting man, with tattooed arms, crew-cut hair and a rough-hewn, handsome face. His clothes added to his military persona; at this moment he was dressed in a combat jacket over a black T-shirt, baggy khaki chinos and what could have been black marching boots.

'Do you mean Michael is your life? Mark? These two gits have been your life, is that what you mean? Have I got something wrong here – I thought I was your life, you stupid bitch.'

'I thought you were too,' she said tightly, holding back tears.

'So what the fuck does that mean?'

'Nothing,' she said.

He grabbed her by the shoulders and turned her round to face him. 'Alex, relax, OK. We're nearly there, home free; let's just calm right down.'

'I'm perfectly calm,' she said. 'You're the one who's all wired.'

He pulled her towards him. Stared into her green eyes. Then tenderly pushed some stray strands of her hair back up her forehead. 'I love you,' he said. 'I love you so much, Alex.'

She put her arms around his neck, pulled his lips up against hers and kissed him passionately for some moments. 'I love you too, Vic. I always have.'

'And yet you happily went off and screwed Mark, then Michael. And a whole bunch of guys before them.'

She stepped back angrily and almost fell over a suit-case. 'Jesus Christ, what's got into you?'

'What's got into me? We've fucked up this time, that's what. OK?'

'We haven't fucked up, Vic; we have a result.'

'A lousy one-point-two million quid? Half a year of our lives for that?'

'Neither of us could have foreseen what was going to happen – the crash.'

'We should have played it differently. You could have got Michael out, gone through with the wedding, and then we'd have had half his money, and his partner's.'

'And that would have taken months, Vic – maybe years. They still have some planning issues on their big develop-ment. As it is, we got a quick result. And if you hadn't gambled away half our goddamn money, we wouldn't have even needed to be here at all in the first place, OK?'

Sheepishly, he looked at his watch. 'We have to get going if we're going to make the flight.'

'I'm ready.'

'You don't have any idea how fucking painful this stuff is for me, Alex, do you? What we do? My sitting on the sidelines, knowing this year you're screwing Michael and Mark, before that you were screwing that jerk Richard in Cheshire, not to mention Joe Kerwin and Julian Warner.'

'I can't believe I'm hearing this, Vic. I did what I did because that was my part of our bargain, OK?'

'No, not OK.'

'You've always had your sweet revenge on them in the

end – so what's your problem? And this way, I get to spare you and me from a honeymoon with Michael.'

He looked at his watch again, anxiously. 'We'll talk in the car – I have one more thing to do before we leave.' He lugged her suitcases out into the hall, then went back into the sitting room and moved the sofa right across the room. Then he knelt down and peeled back a corner of the carpet.

'Vic,' she said.

He looked up. 'What?'

'Can't we just leave him?'

'Leave him?'

'He's not going anywhere, is he? He's not going to get out – he can't even speak, you said.'

'I'm going to finish him off, put him out of his misery.'

'Why not just leave him? No one's ever going to find him.'

'Take me ten seconds to crush his neck.'

'But why?'

He glared at her. 'You are sweet on him, bitch, aren't you?'

Blushing she said, 'I am absolutely not sweet on him.'

'You were never worried about me getting rid of any of the others. What's so special about Mikey boy?'

'Nothing's special about him.'

He let the carpet fall back in place, stood up, and rolled the sofa back to where it had been. Then he repositioned the coffee table. 'You've got a point, Alex, about him not getting out. Why show any mercy on the little bastard by putting him out of his misery? We'll just let him starve to death all on his own in the darkness. Happy with that?'

She nodded. 'Have you checked today's papers?'

'No, I've been cleaning the place out. Got all yesterday's – nothing to worry about. We'll check today's at the airport.' He grinned. 'Then after that, no worries, right?'

Five minutes later the Mercedes was packed with Ashley's four suitcases and Vic's large holdall. He locked the front door and pocketed the keys.

'Do you think we should drop them back in to the agency?'

'We have five more months to run on the lease, woman! You want people going in there and sniffing around? Because I tell you one thing, it ain't going to smell too good in there in a week or two.'

She said nothing as she clipped on her seatbelt, watching the house out of the window for the last time. It was a strange house, perfect for their purposes because of its isolation – the nearest neighbour was a quarter of a mile away – and in fact doubly perfect in the light of events last Tuesday night. You could never in a million years call it a pretty or stylish house. Built on scrubby wasteland – which hadn't changed – in the 1930s, it looked like one truncated half of a pair of semi-detached houses, as if the other side of it had never been built. Originally there had been an integral garage, but some years back that had been converted into what was now the sitting room.

He started the car. In an hour they would be at Gatwick Airport. Tomorrow, or later today – she always had a problem with the time zones – they would be back in Australia. Home. Specks of drizzle pattered onto the windscreen. Regardless, she slipped on her new Gucci sunglasses. Vic had cropped her hair – no time to go to a salon – then she had put on this morning a short, dark wig. If there was any search at all at the airport, they would be watching for Ashley Harper. There was just the smallest possibility they might be looking for Alexandra Huron. But as she looked at the passport in her handbag, which still had two years to run, she smiled. Certainly no one would be looking for Anne Hampson.

Vic put the gear lever into *drive*, then fumbled around. 'Where's the fucking brake?'

'It's a handle; you pull it.'

'Why the fuck do they have a handle? Why didn't you rent a normal car?'

'How much more normal than a Mercedes can you get?'

'One with a proper parking brake!'

'For Christ's sake!'

He slid down his window and shouted out, 'Bye, fuckwit. Have a nice rest of your life!'

'Vic?'

'Yeah?' He accelerated away fiercely down the potholed road, which the council seemed to have forgotten. 'What's the matter, missing your lover boy's dick already?'

'You know something? It's bigger than yours!'

He lunged out at her, slapping her face, the car swerving onto the overgrown grass verge, then back onto the road, lurching through a pothole.

'Does that make you feel good, hitting me?'

'You are just a fucking slapper.'

They reached a T-junction and turned right by a modern housing development, the trees still saplings.

'And you're just a bully, Vic. You're a sadist, you know that? Does that make you feel good? Is that how you really get your rocks off, tormenting someone like Michael?'

'And you get your rocks off by screwing him and knowing that one day you are *really* going to screw him?' He turned to glare at her, then pulled out onto the main road.

It happened so fast, all she saw was what felt, for an instant, like a sudden change in the light. There was a tremendous bang; she felt a fierce jerk; her ears went numb; and the interior of the car filled with what looked like feathers, and reeked of cordite. At the same time the horn began to blare.

'Oh shit, oh shit, shit, shit!' Vic hammered on the steering wheel with his fists; the driver's air bag hanging like a spent condom from the wheel boss, and another air bag limp beside his head.

'Are you all right?' he asked Ashley.

She nodded, staring at the bonnet of the car, which was raised jaggedly up in front of her, the Mercedes star that had been on the end now invisible. There was another car, white, stopped at a crazy angle in the middle of the road a few yards away.

Vic tried to open his door, and seemed to be having difficulty. Then he threw his weight against it and, with a scream from the hinges, it opened.

Ashley's door opened without a problem. She unclipped her belt and stepped out shakily, then pinched her nose and blew hard to clear her ears. She could see a bewildered-looking grey-haired woman behind the wheel of the other car, a Saab, with much of its nose crumpled.

Vic inspected the damage to the Mercedes. The offside front wheel was crushed and buckled and pushed right into the engine compartment. There was no chance of the car being driveable.

'You stupid fucking bitch!' Vic yelled, above the blare of the Mercedes horn, at the Saab.

Ashley could see another car coming up the road, and a van coming from the opposite direction. And she could see a young man running towards them. 'Vic,' she shouted urgently, 'we need to do something, for Christ's sake!'

'Yeah, right, we need to do something. What do you fucking suggest?'

85

Back at the Incident Room, Nick Nicholl suddenly yelled at Grace. 'Roy! Line seven, pick it up, pick it up!'

Grace stabbed the button and lifted the receiver to his ear. 'Roy Grace,' he said.

It was a Detective Sergeant from Brighton police station called Mark Tuckwell. 'Roy,' he said, 'the Mercedes you have an alert out on, blue saloon, Lima-Juliet-Zero-Four-Papa-X-Ray-Lima?'

'Yes.'

'Its just been involved in a RTA in Newhaven. The occupants, one male, one female, have hijacked a vehicle.'

Grace sat bolt upright, the phone clenched to his ear, adrenaline exploding. 'Have they taken hostages?'

'No.'

'Do we have descriptions of the two people?'

'Not great ones so far. Man stocky, Caucasian, cropped hair, mid-forties; the woman has short dark hair, late twenties, early thirties.'

Grabbing a pen, he asked, 'What are the details of the vehicle they've taken?'

'A Land Rover Freelander, green, Whisky-Seven-Nine-Six-Lima-Delta-Yankee.'

Scribbling this down, Grace asked, 'Any contact with this car so far?'

'Not yet.'

'Exactly how long ago was it taken?'

'Ten minutes.'

Grace thought for a moment. Ten minutes. You could get a long damned way in ten minutes. He thanked the Detective Sergeant and told him he would call him back in a couple of minutes and to keep his line clear.

Then Grace quickly briefed his team. Handing the vehicle details to Nick Nicholl he said, 'Nick, circulate the vehicle details to all the surrounding counties – Surrey, Kent, Hampshire – and also the Met. Now!'

He thought for a moment. The roads to the east of Newhaven went to Eastbourne and Hastings. To the north were the fast roads to Gatwick Airport and to London. To the west was Brighton. Most likely, if they stayed with the Land Rover, they would head north. Turning to DS Moy he said, 'Bella, get the helicopter up. On the assumption they are heading away from the area, get it positioned to cover the roads ten to fifteen miles north of Newhaven.'

'Right.'

'When you've done that, get a watch put on all CCTV at the railway stations in the area, in case they try to ditch the vehicle and get a train.'

He drank a swig of water. 'Emma-Jane, call the Road Policing Department and get some vehicles up on the A23 on look-out for this car immediately. When you've done that, alert the police at Newhaven Harbour and Gatwick and Shoreham Airports.'

He ran through a mental checklist: *stations, seaports, airports, roads.* Often, he knew, when people hijacked cars they would only drive them a short distance, ditch them and take a different car. 'Glenn,' he said, 'get the whole surrounding area of Newhaven flooded – we want to make sure they haven't abandoned the car yet. Also get a couple of our patrol cars here on standby.'

'I'll do it now.'

Grace rang through to the Ops Room and informed them he was taking command of the incident. The clerk there told him there was one update that had just come in. A car matching the description had sideswiped several cars at a traffic light as it had cut past them on the pavement to get over the Newhaven swing bridge seconds before it opened. This information was just two minutes old.

86

Vic Delaney stabbed the brake pedal hard as they came into a right-hander on the winding country road that was much sharper than he had realized. The front wheels locked and for a sickening moment they carried straight on, towards a poplar tree, while he wrestled with the chunky steering wheel. Ashley screamed, 'Viiiic!'

The car lurched violently to the right, the front slewing round, the rear wheels breaking way, then he over-corrected and they were heading at another poplar. Then back, the top-heavy car swinging like a weighted sack, their luggage crashing around in the rear. Then they were back under control.

'Slow down, Vic, for God's sake!'

There was a massive truck ahead, crawling along, and in a moment they were on its tail, with no room to pass. 'Oh, fucking Jesus!' he said, braking, hammering the steering wheel in frustration.

It had all gone wrong. *The story of my life*, he thought. His dad had died of drink when he'd been in his teens. Shortly before his eighteenth birthday he'd beaten up his mother's lover because the guy was a punk and treated her like shite. And his mother had responded by throwing him, Vic, out.

He'd drifted into the services in search of adventure, and instantly felt at home in the Marines, except he'd also acquired a taste for money. Lots of money. In particular he liked fancy clothes, cars, gambling and tarts. But above all else he liked the feeling he got – all that respect – when he walked into a casino in a sharp suit. And what better massage for a man's pride could there be than to get comped at a casino for a steak dinner, maybe a room, too.

A lucky streak in the casinos during his second year in the Marines netted him some big loot, then an unlucky streak wiped him out.

He'd then teamed up with a bent Quartermaster called Bruce Jackman, in charge of the ordnance supplies, and found an easy way to make fast money by selling off guns, ammunition and other military supplies via a website. When that was in the process of being rumbled, he'd garrotted Bruce Jackman, and left him hanging in his bedroom with a suicide note. And had never lost a night's sleep over it since.

Life was a game, *survival of the sharpest.* In his view humans made the mistake of trying to pretend they were any different to the animal world. All life was the law of the jungle.

That didn't mean you couldn't love someone. He'd been deeply, crazily, besottedly in love with Alex from the moment he had first seen her. She had it all: real class, style, stunning beauty, a great body, and she was a dirty cow in bed. She was everything he had ever wanted in a woman and way more. And she was the only woman he had met who was more ambitious than himself – and who had a game plan to achieve her simple goals: make a fortune when you are young, then spend the rest of your life enjoying it. Dead simple.

Now all they had to do was get to Gatwick Airport and catch a plane.

The interior of the Freelander stank of diesel fumes from the exhaust of the massive lorry in front of him, crawling at less than 30 mph. He pulled out to see if he could pass, then pulled back in sharply as a truck thundered past in the opposite direction. Increasingly impatient, they followed the truck through a sweeping, dipping, S-bend, past a quarry sign, then up a hill, the truck slowing even more. He slipped his left hand over into Ashley's lap, found her hand, squeezed it. 'We'll be all right, angel.'

She squeezed his hand back, by way of a reply.

Then a blue sparkle in the mirror caught his eye. And a cold sliver of fear whiplashed through his belly.

He watched the mirror carefully. Tarmac, grass and trees unspooled behind them. Then the sparkle of blue again and this time there was no mistaking it. *Shit.* Any second it would come into sight around the corner.

Pulling out again, he suddenly saw to his right a wooden public-footpath signpost, and a wide track, and in one swift jerk of the wheel, swung the Freelander right across the path of an oncoming van and onto the bumpy, overgrown track, the car crashing into a deep, water-filled pothole, then out the other side. In his mirror he saw a police car flash past in the opposite direction, much too fast, he hoped, to have seen them.

'Why have you turned off?'

'Police.' He accelerated, felt the wheels spinning, gripping, the car lurching forward, sliding up the ruts, then down again. They passed a farmyard, with an empty horse-box outside and a silent tractor, and a corrugated iron structure filled with empty sheep pens.

'Where does this go?' Ashley asked.

'I don't fucking know.'

At the end of the track he turned left onto a metalled lane; they drove past several cottages, then reached a very busy main road. Vic, winding down his window and dripping with perspiration, said, 'This is the A27 – it takes us to the A23 – straight up to Gatwick, right?'

'I know. But we can't go on the main road.'

'I'm thinking – the best way—'

Both of them heard the clatter of the helicopter. Vic stuck his head out of the window and looked up. He saw a dark blue helicopter bearing down out of the sky straight towards them. As it arced round, the sound even louder, it was low enough for him to read the stencilled white 'POLICE' beneath the cockpit.

'Bastards.' There was no break in the traffic, so he judged it too risky to go straight over. Instead he made a left turn, accelerating hard out in front of a Jaguar, which proceeded to flash him with its lights and hoot, both of which he ignored, staring fixedly ahead, his brain in panic mode. The traffic was slowing down ahead. Shit, it was coming to a standstill! Pulling out to the right a fraction and peering past the traffic, he could see the reason for the jam, despite part of his view being obscured by a tall caravan.

A police car had blocked off the road, and there was a large blue 'POLICE STOP' barrier either side of it.

87

'They just rammed through a police barrier at the Bed-
dingham roundabout,' the Ops Clerk, Jim Robinson,
informed Grace, 'and are now proceeding west on the A27.
Their next turn-off options are the roundabout in one mile,
where they have a choice of a right turn towards Lewes or
left towards Kingston village.'

'Have we got anyone at the roundabout?'

'A bike on its way – might just get there in time.'

'A bike's no use. We need to get them boxed in. At least
they're not in a fast car, so we can catch them. We need four
cars – where are the nearest four located?'

'We have two heading for the A23 junction, one on its
way from Lewes, ETA four minutes, one on its way over
from Shoreham, ETA three minutes to the A23/A27 junction, two here at Sussex House ready to go, and one coming
in from Haywards Heath, ETA two minutes.'

'The helicopter still has them in sight?'

'Right above them.'

Grace closed his eyes a moment, visualizing the road.
Right now the villains, whoever they were – and he had the
strongest suspicions about who one of them was – had
made the error of picking the road on which he drove to
and from work every day, and knew better, probably, than
any other road on the planet. He knew every turn-off, every
opportunity, adding in the fact they were in a vehicle with
off-road capabilities, and although the ground was fairly
soggy from all the recent rainfall, there would be plenty of

opportunities to get off the road and across farmland if they wanted.

'Can we get a couple of police off-roaders into the mix as well?' Grace said. 'Position them as close to the A27/A23 junction as you can.'

He looked at his watch. A quarter to two. Tuesday. There would be a fair amount of traffic on the move and one consideration was other road users. The police had had a lot of bad press in recent years over reckless car pursuits and some tragic deaths of innocent people in the process. He needed to keep this pursuit as safe as was possible in the circumstances.

Boxing them in would be best: a car in front, a car behind, one either side and slowly bring their speed down. That would be the textbook happy ending.

Except he hadn't known too many happy endings since he'd grown too old to enjoy fairy tales.

88

Barrelling down a long, curving hill in the fast lane, with the speedometer needle flickering past 125 mph, Vic knew the A23 junction would be coming up in a minute or so, and he was going to have to make a decision. For the past couple of minutes, aware of the constant shadow of the helicopter, his mind had been occupied with one thought: *If I was a cop what bases would I be covering right now?*

Airports were not going to be an option. Nor ferry-ports. But there was one thing that the cops probably had not considered – probably because they didn't even know about it. But to get to it they needed to lose the damned chopper. And there was a place, just a few miles ahead, where he could do that.

The dual carriageway rose dramatically uphill, with undulating open Downland countryside to his right, and the vast urban sprawl of Brighton and Hove to his left. And ahead, some miles yet, the tall chimney landmark of his intended destination, Shoreham Harbour. But that wasn't going to be his first stop.

'Why've you carried on, Vic?' Ashley asked nervously. 'I thought we were going to Gatwick.'

Vic did not reply. A little old man was pottering along in the inside lane in a bronze four-door Toyota that looked a good ten years old. Perfect!

The tunnel was coming up any moment now. From memory it was about a quarter of a mile long, cutting through the Downs. They passed the 'No Overtaking' warning sign and entered the dimly lit gloom of the tunnel doing a good 110 mph. Instantly, Vic swerved into the inside lane and stamped on the brakes, slowing the car down to a crawl and putting on his hazard flashers.

'Vic – what the hell—'

But he was ignoring her, staring in the mirror, watching a line of cars flash past. And now the Toyota was approaching. Vic tensed, knowing he had to get his timing absolutely right. The Toyota indicated that it was going to pull out to overtake, and began moving out, but instantly there was a flash of lights and the blare of a horn as a Porsche hurtled past, and the Toyota, braking hard, swerved back into the inside lane.

Beaut!

Vic jerked on the Land Rover's handbrake as hard as he could, knowing it would stop the car without the brake lights showing. 'Brace yourself!' he shouted, releasing the brake and accelerating.

There was a scream of tyres behind, but by the time the Toyota struck them, they already had some forward momentum again. There was a small impact, just a tiny jolt that he barely felt, and the sound of breaking glass.

'Out!' yelled Vic, hurling open his door, jumping down, running back and surveying the damage. All he was concerned with was the front of the Toyota. It looked fine – the grille was stove in and a headlamp gone, but no oil or water was spewing out.

'Get the fucking bags!' he yelled at Ashley, who was walking, startled, towards him. 'The fucking bags, woman!'

He wrenched open the driver's door of the Toyota. The driver was even more frail than he had looked when he had driven past, well north of eighty, with a liver-spotted face, wispy hair and spectacles with bottle-glass lenses.

'Hey, what – what do you think – what—?' the old man said.

Vic unclipped his seatbelt, aware that a car was pulling up behind them, then removed his glasses to disorient him. 'I'll get you into the ambulance, mate.'

'I don't need a bloody—'

Vic hauled the man out, hefted him over his shoulder and placed him on the rear seat of the Land Rover, then shut the door. A pot-bellied, middle-aged man who had just climbed out of a Ford people-carrier that had pulled up behind the Toyota came running up to Vic. 'I say, do you need any help?'

'Yes, poor bloke, I think he's had a stroke – was swerving all over the place.'

A lorry thundered past, then two motorbikes. Ashley shouted out, 'For God's sake help me, Vic, I can't manage these bloody cases on my own!'

'Leave the fucking things!'

'One has all my papers in it—'

Vic saw the pot-bellied man looking at Ashley oddly and decided the fastest solution was to deck him. He knocked him out cold with one punch, and propped him up against the front of his Ford.

Then they hastily loaded Vic's holdall and two of Ashley's cases into the Toyota and jumped in. Vic found *reverse*, then, with a grinding noise coming from what he presumed was the fan belt, he eased the car back several feet, then he found *drive*, and the car juddered. He checked his mirror, then accelerated, pulling out past the Land Rover, and accelerated as fast as the distinctly clapped-out old Toyota would go towards the rapidly widening light at the far end of the tunnel.

Ashley was staring at him in shock. 'That was clever,' she said.

'Can you see the fucking chopper?' he asked, squinting as they came back out into bright light.

She squirmed around in her seat, craning her neck upwards through first the front windscreen, then the rear. 'It's not following!' she exclaimed. 'It's hovering over the front of the tunnel – wait – great – now it's going back to the rear!'

'Fucking A!'

Vic took the first exit off the dual carriageway, which came up a mile on. It took them down into the mixed urban and industrial sprawl of Southwick, the suburb separating the city of Brighton and Hove from Shoreham. They had a few minutes' head start before the police got an ident on this car, and maybe with a bit of luck the old git who owned it couldn't remember the licence number, Vic hoped.

'OK, so where the hell are we going, Vic?'

'To the one place the police aren't looking at.'

'Which is?'

'Michael and Mark have a boat, right, a proper yacht. You've been on it?'

'Yes, I've told you – I've been out on it a few times.'

'It's big enough to cross the Channel, right?'

'The guy they bought it from sailed it across the Atlantic.'

'That's fine. You and I know how to sail.'

'Yes.' Ashley remembered several sailing holidays they'd had in Australia and in Canada, chartering a yacht, going off on their own. Some of the few happy and peaceful moments of her life.

'So now you know where we're going. Unless you have a better idea?'

'Take their boat?'

'We'll sail after dark.'

They were now on a busy main road, with semi-detached houses on each side, set well back. He slowed down as they approached a red light and could see a shopping parade ahead on both sides of the road. Then, as he halted, his face fell. Brilliant white light filled the rear-view mirror. He heard the sharp blast of a two-tone siren. Saw a blue flashing light, heard the blip of a loud throttle; then a police motorcyclist pulled alongside his window, signalling for him to get out.

Instead, he floored the accelerator and shot straight over the lights, right across the path of a heavy truck.

'Oh shit,' Ashley said.

Moments later, siren on, the motorcycle was alongside again, the cop signalling sternly for him to pull over. Instead, Vic turned the wheel sharply to the right, deliberately striking the bike, sending it hurtling over on its side; in his mirror he caught a fleeting glimpse of the cop, unseated, rolling across the road.

Panicking, Vic saw a pillar box ahead, and a quiet-looking side-street. He turned sharply into it, hearing the sound of the bags sliding across the back seat, then accelerated down the tree-lined avenue. It was starting to rain again, and he fumbled around with the switches until he found the wipers and got them working. They reached a T-junction, with a church ahead.

'Do you know where we are?'

'The harbour can't be far,' he said. He drove on, through a maze of quiet residential streets, then suddenly they came out into a narrow, bustling high street, with traffic crawling down it. 'There!' Vic pointed ahead. 'That's the harbour!'

At the bottom of the high street, they came to the junction with the main coast road that ran all the way along Brighton and Hove seafront, past Shoreham Harbour and then along the banks of the River Adur.

'Which way's the boat?'

'It's at the Sussex Motor Yacht Club,' she said. 'You have to go left.'

There was a bus coming, quickly. He was going to wait to let it pass when a glint of white light in his mirror caught his eye; almost in disbelief, he saw a police motorbike weaving through the jammed traffic behind him. The same damned cop he had just knocked off his machine?

He pulled out in front of the bus, tyres screeching. Then, moments later, out of nowhere, a black BMW with a flashing blue light on the dash and more flashing blue lights inside its rear windscreen, hurtled past the bus and his Toyota, cutting in front of him, forcing him to brake sharply. Above its rear bumper the words, in flashing red lights, appeared: 'STOP POLICE'.

In complete blind panic he swung the car round in a U-turn, accelerating back the other way, weaving through the traffic, which was slowing down ahead at a roundabout. The motorbike was right behind him, siren howling. Putting two wheels on the pavement, jamming his hand on the horn, making pedestrians leap out of the way, Vic squeezed past the line of cars and a van and reached the roundabout. There were three choices: right seemed to go back into the maze of houses; straight on the traffic was clogged up. Left went over a metal-girdered bridge spanning the river.

He turned left, the motorbike glued to his tail as he accelerated as hard at the Toyota would go, the fan grinding, shrieking, the noise getting worse every second. Below, the tide was right out, the river just a slack brown trickle between the mud banks, with moored boats lying on their sides, many of them barely looking as if they were capable of floating when the tide came back in.

On the far side of the bridge the road was clear. But within moments the BMW was coming up fast behind him. The motorbike suddenly whipped in front of him and then decelerated, trying to force him to slow. 'Thought I fucking gave you a lesson already,' Vic muttered, accelerating, trying to ram it, but the rider was too quick for him, darting forward as if anticipating this.

Vic, trying desperately to think straight, looked at the landscape to either side. On the left was a garage, a parade of shops and what looked like a large residential area. Over to his right he could see the flat expanse of Shoreham Airport, used mostly by private aircraft and a few small Channel Islands airlines. The entrance was coming up.

Without signalling he swung right, onto the narrow road. There was a concrete wall on his left, and the open expanse of the airfield to his right, dotted with hangars, with small planes and helicopters parked in front, and the white Art Deco control tower building, in need of a lick of paint. The thought now going through his head was that if he could just shake off the cops for a few minutes, they could hijack a light aircraft, like the twin-engined Beechcraft he could see coming in now – just drive straight over to it, grab the pilot.

As if anticipating exactly that, the BMW pulled alongside, then swung into him, forcing him into the concrete wall. Ashley screamed as the car slammed against it, grating along it with sparks showering past them. 'Vic, for Christ's sake do something!'

He sat, gripping the wheel for dear life, clenched up in

concentration, knowing they were hopelessly underpow-ered against the BMW and the bike. There was a tunnel coming up ahead. He could guess exactly what the BMW had in mind – to go in it ahead of him and then stop. So he stamped on the brakes. Caught by surprise, the BMW shot past, and instantly he swerved behind it, off the road and onto the airfield itself.

The bike stayed with him, and moments later, the BMW was behind him as well. He drove across the bumpy grass straight towards the first row of parked aircraft, weav-ing wildly in between them, trying to shake off the cops behind him, trying to spot someone walking to a plane or getting out of one. Then, as he headed for a gap between a Grumman executive jet and a Piper Aztec, the BMW suddenly rammed him hard, jolting them both forward, Ashley, despite her seatbelt, cracking her head on the windscreen and crying out in pain.

He heard the BMW revving. The runway was right in front of him, and he could see the twin-engined plane bearing down, yards away from touching down. He floored the accelerator, lurched across the runway, right through the shadow of the plane. And then, for a brief moment, no bike and no BMW in his mirror! He kept going, flat out, the car lurching, the grating from the engine getting worse and accompanied by an acrid smell of burning now, straight toward the perimeter fence and the narrow road beyond that.

'We need to get out and hide, Vic. We're not going to outrun them in this thing.'

'I know,' he said grimly, panic gripping him again as he couldn't see a gap anywhere in the fence. 'Where's the fucking exit?'

'Just go through the fence.'

Taking her advice, he continued driving flat out at the fence, slowing just before they struck it, the wire mesh making a dull clanging sound, and ripping like cloth. Then he was on the perimeter road, with the mudflats of the river to his right and the airfield to his left, and the bike and the car were right behind him. A Mercedes sports was coming the other way. Vic kept going. 'Out the fucking way!' At the last moment the Mercedes pulled over onto the verge.

They were coming up to a T-junction with a narrow road that was little more than a lane. To the left there was a removals lorry parked outside a cottage, unloading, blocking the road completely.

He turned right, flooring the pedal, watching in his mirror. At least this lane was too narrow for the BMW to get past. The bike was getting in position. Any moment it would whip past. Vic swerved out to warn it off. They were doing seventy, seventy-five, eighty, approaching a wooden bridge over the river.

Then, just as he reached the bridge, two small boys on bicycles appeared at the far end, right in the middle of the road. 'Shiiiiiiiit, oh shiiit, oh shiiit,' Vic said, stamping on the brakes, thumbing the horn, but there was no time; they were not going to stop, and there was no room to get past them. Ashley was screaming.

The car slewed right, left, right. It struck the right-hand barrier of the bridge, veered over and struck the left, pinballed off it, doing a half pirouette, then rolled over onto its roof, bounced in the air, clearing the safety barrier, bursting through the wooden side of the bridge's superstructure, splintering it like matchsticks, and plunging, upside down, the rear doors flying open, and the suitcases hurtling alongside the car towards the mudflats below, which were as soft and treacherous as quicksand.

The motorcyclist dismounted and, limping from his leg injury from when he had been knocked off his machine only a few minutes earlier, hobbled over to the hole in the side of the bridge and peered down.

All he could see protruding from the mud was the grimy black underbelly of the Toyota. The rest of the car had sunk into it. He stared at the metal floor pan, the exhaust and silencer, the four wheels still spinning. Then, in front of his eyes, the mud bubbled all around the car, like a cauldron brewing, and moments later the underbelly and the wheels slipped beneath the surface and the mud closed over it. There were some deep bubbles which broke the surface, as if the underwater lair of some monster had been disturbed. Then nothing.

89

The incoming tide was hampering their efforts. A wide cordon had been thrown around the whole area where the car had gone in, canvas sheeting only partially obscuring the view from a swelling crowd of curious onlookers on the far bank. A fire engine, two ambulances, half a dozen police vehicles, including a crash recovery tender, were all parked down the lane.

A crane had been driven onto the elderly bridge despite concerns about how much weight it could stand. Grace stood on the bridge himself, watching the recovery proceedings. Police frogmen were working hard to get the hooks of the lifting gear dangling from the crane onto secure fixings on the Toyota. The sky, which had been delivering spots of rain on and off all day, had lightened in the last hour and the sun was trying to break through.

The tightly packed mud had made it impossible for the frogmen to get down any further, and the only hope that the occupants were alive rested on the windows having stayed intact and that there was air trapped inside the car. The amount of shards of glass strewn over the bridge made this seem more than a long shot.

Two suitcases had been recovered from the abandoned Land Rover Freelander, but all they contained were women's clothes; not one scrap of paper that could give a clue to Michael Harrison's whereabouts. Grace had a grim feeling this car would yield something.

Glenn Branson, standing next to Grace, said, 'You know

what this reminds me of? The original *Psycho* – 1960. When they winch the car with Janet Leigh's body in out of the lake. Remember?'

'I remember.'

'That was a cool movie. The remake was shit. I dunno why people bother with remakes.'

'Money,' Grace said. 'That's one of the reasons why you and I have a job. Because people do an awful lot for money.'

After a few more minutes the hooks were in place. Then the lifting began. Against the deafening roar of the crane's engine, Grace and Branson barely heard the sucking and gurgling sounds of the mud, beneath the waters of the rising tide, yielding its prize.

Slowly, in front of their eyes, and washed clean by the water, the bronze Toyota rose up in the air, its boot-lid open and hanging. Mud oozed slowly out of all of the window frames. The car looked badly smashed and the roof pillars were buckled. It didn't look as if one single window had remained in place.

And as the mud fell out, some in slabs, some in squitty streaks, at first just the silhouettes of the two occupants became visible, and then, finally, their inert faces.

The crane swung the car over onto the bank, lowering it on its roof a few yards from a rotting houseboat. Several fireman, police officers and workmen who had come with the crane, unhooked the lifting gear then slowly righted the car. As it rolled back onto its wheels, the two figures inside jerked like crash-test dummies.

Grace, with trepidation, followed by Branson, walked down to it, squatted and peered in. Even though there was some mud still stuck to her face, and her hair was much shorter than the last time he had seen her, there was no question it was Ashley Harper, her eyes wide open, unblinking. Then he shuddered in revulsion as a scrawny, long-legged crab crawled across her lap.

'Jesus,' Branson said.

Who the hell was the man next to her, in the driving seat? Grace wondered. His eyes were open also, a powerful, thuggish-looking man with a shocked death mask.

'See what you can find on her,' Grace said, wrenching open the driver's door, and checking the man's sodden, muddy clothing for ID. He pulled out a heavy leather wallet from inside his jacket and opened it. Inside was an Australian passport.

The photograph was the man in the car, no question. His name was Victor Bruce Delaney and he was forty-two years old. Under *emergency contact* was written the name *Mrs Alexandra Delaney*, and an address in Sydney.

Glenn Branson wiped mud from a yellow handbag, unzipped it and after a few moments also pulled out a passport, this one British, which he showed to Grace. It contained a photograph that was, without doubt, Ashley Harper, but with close-cropped black hair, and it bore the name Anne Hampson. Under *emergency contact* nothing had been written.

There were credits cards both in the man's wallet and in a purse inside the handbag, but nothing else. Not a clue about where they had come from or where they might be headed.

'Houston, we have a problem,' Glenn Branson said quietly to Grace, but there was no humour in his tone.

'We do.' Grace stood up and turned away. 'It's suddenly a whole lot bigger than it was two hours ago.'

'So how the hell are we going to find Michael Harrison now?'

After a moment's silence Grace said, 'I have an idea, but you're not going to like it.'

Glancing uncomfortably at the occupants of the car, Glenn Branson said, 'I don't like anything much at the moment.'

90

An hour and a half later, Grace helped buckle the diminutive, wiry figure of Harry Frame into the front seat of the pool Ford Mondeo he and Branson had used this afternoon.

The pony-tailed, goatee-bearded medium, reeking of patchouli oil and wearing his trademark kaftan and dungarees, had a street map of Newhaven laid out in his lap, and held a metal ring on a length of string in his right hand.

Grace had decided to leave Glenn Branson out of this. He didn't want any negative vibes, and he knew that Harry Frame's energy was sensitive at best.

'So did you bring me something, as I requested?' Harry Frame asked Grace as he climbed behind the wheel of the car.

Grace dug a box out of his pocket and handed it to the medium. Frame opened it and removed a pair of gold cufflinks.

'These are definitely Michael Harrison's,' Grace said. 'I took them from his flat on my way here.'

'Perfect.'

It was only a short distance along the coast from Harry Frame's Peacehaven home to Newhaven. As they drove past the seemingly endless sprawl of shops and takeaway restaurants, Harry Frame was holding the cufflinks in his closed palm. 'Newhaven, you said?'

'There was a car we were interested in that was involved in an accident in Newhaven earlier today. And

Newhaven is where Michael Harrison's mobile signal came from. I thought we'd drive to that spot and you could see if you pick anything up. Is that a good idea?'

In his effusive, high-pitched voice, the medium said, 'I'm already picking up something. We're near, you know. Definitely.'

Grace, following the directions he had been given, began to slow down. Some tyre marks, a spill of oil on the road and a few sparkling shards of safety glass showed him where the Mercedes had been in the accident, and he turned right into a modern housing development of small, detached houses with immature gardens, then immediately pulled over and stopped.

'OK,' he said. 'This is where the accident happened this morning.'

Harry Frame, holding the cufflinks in his left hand, began to swing the pendulum over the map, taking increasingly deep breaths. He closed his eyes tightly and after a few moments said, 'Drive on, Roy, just drive straight on. Slowly.'

Grace did as he was instructed.

'We're getting closer!' Frame said. 'Definitely. I see a turn-off to the left coming up shortly – might not even be a road, just a track.'

After about a hundred metres, there was indeed a track going up to the left. It had been metalled, very many years ago, but had fallen into a state of total disrepair. It went uphill, through wind-blown, scrubby wasteland, and it did not seem from here, at least, that it was going to lead to anything.

'Make a left turn, Roy!'

Grace looked at him, wondering if he was cheating by peeping through his eyelids. But if Harry was looking anywhere, it was down into his lap. Grace turned onto the track and drove up it for a quarter of a mile, then a squat, ugly detached house came into view just on the crest of the hill. It had fine views over Newhaven and the harbour beyond, but little else to recommend it.

'I see a house, all on its own. Michael Harrison is in this house,' Frame said, excitement raising his voice even higher.

Grace pulled up outside. The pendulum was swinging fast in a tight circle, and Harry Frame, eyes still tight shut, was juddering as if he had been plugged into an electrical socket.

'Here?'

Without opening his eyes, Harry Frame confirmed, 'Here.'

Grace left him in the car, then stopped at the front gate, staring at the neglected front lawn and the flower beds, which were a tangle of bindweed. There was something odd about the house, which he couldn't immediately figure out. It looked as if it had been built in the 1930s, or maybe early 1950s, and the design was strange, lopsided.

He walked up a path of concrete slabs with weeds sprouting between the cracks, and pressed the cracked plastic front-door bell. There was a shrill ring, but no one came to the door. He tried again. Still no answer.

Then he did a circuit around the house, peering into each window as he went. It had a forlorn, neglected air about it, both inside and out. All the furnishings looked twenty or thirty years old, as did the design of and appliances in the kitchen. Then he noted, to his surprise, that there was a stack of newspapers on the kitchen table.

He looked at his watch. It was just gone 6 p.m. He ought to get a search warrant, he knew. But that would take another couple of hours – and with every minute that passed the chances of finding Michael Harrison alive were shrinking.

How much did he trust Harry Frame? The medium had been right on several occasions in the past – but he had been wrong on just as many.

Shite.

The thought of what Alison Vosper would say to him if he was caught breaking into a house without a warrant bothered him.

He didn't have enough to back his judgement up, but it would have to do. Time was running out for Michael Harrison.

With a loose brick from the garden, he smashed a kitchen window pane, then wrapping his hand in his handkerchief, he removed the pieces of glass that remained lodged in the putty, found the window catch, opened it and crawled in.

'Hello!' he shouted. 'Hello! Anyone home?'

The place felt and smelled dingy. The kitchen was clean, and other than some newspapers, all bearing yesterday's date, there was no sign of anyone having lived here recently. He checked out each of the downstairs rooms. The large sitting room was drab as hell, with a couple of framed prints of seascapes on the walls. He noticed there were lines on the carpet, as if someone had recently moved the sofa. He moved on into a dark dining room, with an oak table and four chairs, and flock wallpaper, then on to a small lavatory, with a 'God Bless This House' cross-stitch hanging on the wall.

Upstairs felt equally unloved and unlived in. There were three bedrooms, all the beds stripped to bare mattresses with old, yellowing pillows, without slips, lying on them, and a small bathroom, with a geyser boiler and stained washbasin and bath.

Above the bed in the smallest room was a loft hatch. By placing a chair, precariously, on the mattress, then standing on it, he was able to push open the hatch and peer in. To his surprise there was a light switch just inside the hatch, which worked, and he could see in an instant there was nothing up here. Just a small water tank, an old carpet sweeper and a rolled-up rug.

He opened every cupboard and cabinet door. Upstairs, all the bed linen and bath towels were folded away in the cupboards. Downstairs, the kitchen cupboards contained basics – coffee, tea, a few tins, but nothing else. It could easily have been a year or two since anyone had been here. No sign of Michael Harrison. Nothing.

Nowhere.

He checked the hall cupboard, in case there was a cellar entrance in there, although he knew that few houses after the Victorian era had cellars. He needed to find out who owned this place and when it was last lived in. Maybe the owners had died and it was in the hands of executors? Maybe a cleaning lady came up here occasionally?

A cleaning lady who read every national newspaper?

Grace let himself out of the back door and walked around to the side of the house, where there were two dustbins. He lifted the lid of the first one, and instantly he had a different story. There were egg-shells, used tea bags, an empty skimmed milk carton bearing a sell-by date of today and a Marks and Spencer lasagne carton bearing a sell-by date that had not yet been reached.

Thinking hard, he walked round to the front of the house, trying again to work out what it was that was wrong with the design. Then he realized. Where there was now an ugly plastic-framed window to the right of the front door, there should have been an integral garage. He could see it now, clearly; the tone of the bricks didn't match the rest of the house. At some point someone had converted this into a living room.

And suddenly it reminded him of something from his childhood: his dad, tinkering with things. He liked to do his own servicing on his car, changing the oil, doing the brake linings, *staying out of the hands of the rip-off merchants,* as his dad called garages.

He remembered the inspection pit in their garage, where he had spent many happy hours of his childhood helping his dad service the succession of Fords he always bought, getting covered in oil and grease – not to mention the occasional spider.

And he thought about the lines on the carpet in the sitting room that he had just seen, where the sofa had been moved.

On just a hunch, no more than that, he went back into the house and straight to the sitting room. He lifted the coffee table aside, then pushed back the sofa along the tracks in the green floral carpet that had been made previously.

Then he noticed that one corner of the carpet was slightly curled up. He knelt and gave it a tug, and it lifted easily. Far too easily. And instead of dust and fluff beneath there was a thick underlay that was not like any conventional carpet underlay. He knew exactly what it was. Soundproofing material.

His excitement mounting, he glanced over his shoulder, then peeled the heavy grey material back, and saw beneath it a large sheet of plywood. He worked his fingers under the edges, with some difficulty, as it fitted flush into a groove in the floor, then prised it up, and pulled it aside.

Instantly he gagged from the stench that hit his nostrils.

A horrendous reek of body odour, urine and excrement.

Holding his breath and scared of what he was going to find, he peered into the six-foot-deep garage inspection pit and saw a shadowy figure at the bottom, bound hand and foot and across the mouth with duct tape.

At first he thought the figure was dead. Then the eyes blinked. Frightened eyes.

Oh sweet Jesus, he was alive! Grace felt an almost uncontainable feeling of joy erupt through him. 'Michael Harrison?'

A muffled 'Mnhhhh' greeted him.

'Detective Superintendent Grace of Sussex CID,' Grace said, lowering himself into the pit, oblivious to the smell now, just desperately anxious to see what condition the young man was in.

Kneeling beside him, Grace gently peeled the duct tape away from his lips. 'Are you Michael Harrison?'

'Yes,' he croaked. 'Water. Please.'

Grace squeezed his arm gently. 'I'll get you some right away. And I'll get you out of here. You're going to be fine.'

Grace scrambled up out of the pit, hurried into the kitchen and ran the tap, radioing for an ambulance at the same time. Then he climbed back down into the pit clutching a pint tumbler of water.

He tilted it into Michael Harrison's mouth, who drank it down in one long, greedy draught, with only a few drops spilling down his chin. Then, as he removed the glass, Michael looked at him and asked, 'How's Ashley?'

Grace stared back at him, thinking hard, then gave him a gentle, reassuring smile. 'She's safe,' he said.

'Thank God.'

Grace squeezed his arm again. 'Want more water?'

Michael nodded.

'I'll get you some, then I'll cut this tape off you.'

'Thank God she's safe,' Michael said, his voice weak and trembling. 'She's all I've thought of, all I – I . . .'

Grace climbed back out of the pit. At some point he was going to have to tell Michael everything, but this didn't feel like the time or the place.

And he didn't know how to begin.

LOOKING GOOD DEAD

TO HELEN

ACKNOWLEDGEMENTS

I owe a massive debt to the recently retired Chief Superintendent Dave Gaylor of Sussex Police, who has given me so much
help in the writing of this novel, quite apart from generously
acting as role model for the character of Roy Grace, and never
tiring of reading and rereading the manuscript, and opening
more doors for me in the police forces in the UK – and abroad
– than I could have ever dared to hope for.

And a heartfelt thank you to very many other members of
the Sussex Police who have been immensely tolerant of my
intrusions and so welcoming and helpful. In particular to
Chief Constable Ken Jones for his very kind sanction. And to
Detective Sergeant Paul Hastings, Ray Packham of the High
Tech Crime Unit, High Tech Crime Investigator John Shaw,
and all the team at the High Tech Crime Unit who have been
so very enthusiastically supportive and have helped to shape
a key part of this story. Thanks also to Detective Superinten-
dent Kevin Moore, Inspector Andy Parr, Chief Superintendent
Peter Coll, Detective Sergeant Keith Hallet of the Sussex Police
Holmes Unit, Brian Cook, Scientific Support Branch Manager,
Detective Inspector William Warner, and Senior Scenes of
Crime Investigator Stuart Leonard. Family Liaison Officer DC
Amanda Stroud, Family Liaison Officer DS Louise Pye, Senior
Support Officer Tony Case of the HQ Criminal Investigation
Department, and IT Support Officer Daniel Salter.

I've had great help from Essex Coroner Dr Peter Dean,
pathologist Dr Nigel Kirkham and Home Office Pathologist
Dr Vesna Djurovic; and a special thanks for the invaluable

Acknowledgements

support from the wonderfully cheery team at Brighton and Hove Mortuary, Elsie Sweetman, Sean Didcott and Victor Sindon.

I am grateful also for help with farming and chemical queries from Tony Monnington and Eddie Gribble, my helicopter mentor, Phil Homan, law information from Sue Ansell, and my human back-up service, Chris Webb, without whom I would have been sunk when my laptop was stolen at Geneva airport. And thank you to Imogen Lloyd-Webber, Anna-Lisa Lindeblad and Carina Coleman, who read the manuscript in varying stages and provided me with quite brilliant insights.

Thanks are owed to my fabulous agent, Carole Blake, for her tireless hard work and sound advice (and her great shoes!), and to Tony Mulliken, Margaret Veale and all at Midas, and the quite fantastic team at my publishers, Macmillan. Everyone there has been amazingly supportive, and I am deeply touched. To single out a few names, thank you to Richard Charkin, David North, Geoff Duffield, Anna Stockbridge, Ben Wright, Ed Ripley, Vivienne Nelson, Liz Johnson, Caitriona Row, Claire Round, Claire Byrne, Adam Humphrey, Marie Gray, Michelle Taylor, Richard Evans, and my totally wonderful editor Stef Bierwerth, who is just the all-time greatest! And across the Channel I have to say a huge 'Danke!' to the team at my German publishers, Scherz, for their incredible support. Especially Peter Lohmann, Julia Schade, Andrea Engen, Cordelia Borchardt, Bruno Back, Indra Heinz, and the quite awesome Andrea Diederichs, editor, tour guide, shopping adviser!

Thank you as ever to my faithful hounds Bertie and Phoebe, who always seem to sense when I need a walk – but haven't yet learned to mix me a martini . . .

And penultimate but biggest thank you to my darling

Acknowledgements

Helen – whose unflagging support helped boost me so many times along the way.

The last thanks is to all you readers of my books. Thank you for all your mail, and all your encouragement. It is everything.

Peter James
Sussex, England
scary@pavilion.co.uk
www.peterjames.com

LOOKING GOOD DEAD

1

The front door of the once-proud terraced house opened, and a long-legged young woman, in a short silk dress that seemed to both cling and float at the same time, stepped out into the fine June sunshine on the last morning of her life.

A century back, these tall, white villas, just a pebble's throw from Brighton's seafront promenade, would have served as weekend residences for London toffs. Now, behind their grimy, salt-burned facades, they were chopped up into bedsits and low-rent flats; the brass front-door knockers had long been replaced with entry-phone panels, and litter spewed from garbage bags onto the pavements beneath a gaudy riot of letting-agency boards. Several of the cars that lined the street, shoehorned into not enough parking spaces, were dented and rusting, and all of them were saturation-bombed with pigeon and seagull shit.

In contrast, everything about the young woman oozed class. From the careless toss of her long fair hair, the sunglasses she adjusted on her face, the bling Cartier bracelet, the Anya Hindmarsh bag slung from her shoulder, the toned contours of her body, the Mediterranean tan, her wake of Issey Miyake tanging the rush-hour monoxide with a frisson of sexuality, she was the kind of girl who would have looked at home in the aisles of Bergdorf Goodman, or at the bar of a Schrager hotel, or on the stern of a fuck-off yacht in St-Tropez.

Not bad for a law student scraping by on a meagre grant.

But Janie Stretton had been too spoiled by her guilty father, after her mother's death, to ever contemplate the idea of merely *scraping by*. Making money came easily to her. Making it from her intended career might be a different matter altogether. The legal profession was tough. Four years of law studies were behind her, and she was now in the first two years as a trainee with a firm of solicitors in Brighton, working under a divorce lawyer, and she was enjoying that, although some of the cases were, even to her, weird.

Like the mild little seventy-year-old man yesterday, Bernie Milsin, in his neat grey suit and carefully knotted tie. Janie had sat unobtrusively on a corner chair in the office as the thirty-five-year-old partner she was articled to, Martin Broom, took notes. Mr Milsin was complaining that Mrs Milsin, three years older than himself, would not give him food until he had performed oral sex on her. 'Three times a day,' he told Martin Broom. 'Can't keep doing it, not at my age, the arthritis in me knees hurts too much.'

It was all she could do not to laugh out loud, and she could see Broom was struggling also. So, it wasn't just men who had kinky needs. Seemed that both sexes had them. Something new learned every day, and sometimes she didn't know where she gained the most knowledge from – Southampton University Law School or the University of Life.

The beep of an incoming text broke her chain of thought just as she reached her red and white Mini Cooper. She checked the screen.

2night. 8.30?

Janie smiled and replied with a brief *xx*. Then she waited for a bus followed by a line of traffic to pass, opened the door of her car, and sat for a moment, collecting her thoughts, thinking about stuff she needed to do.

Bins, her moggie, had a lump on his back that was steadily getting bigger. She did not like the look of it and wanted to take him to the vet to get it checked. She had found Bins two years ago, a nameless stray, scrawny to the point of starving, trying to lift the lid of one of her dustbins. She had taken him in, and he had never shown any inclination to leave. So much for cats being independent, she thought, or maybe it was because she spoiled him. But hell, Bins was an affectionate creature and she didn't have much else in her life to spoil. She would try to get a late appointment today. If she got to the vet by 6.30 that should still leave plenty of time, she calculated.

In her lunch break she needed to buy a birthday card and present for her father – he would be fifty-five on Friday. She hadn't seen him for a month; he'd been away in the USA on business. He seemed to be away a lot these days, travelling more and more. Searching for that one woman who might be out there and could replace the wife, and mother of his daughter, he had lost. He never spoke about it, but she knew he was lonely – and worried about his business, which seemed to be going through a rough patch. And living fifty miles away from him did not help.

Pulling on her seat belt and clicking it, she was totally unaware of the long lens trained on her, and the quiet whirring of the digital Pentax camera, over two hundred yards away, not remotely audible against the background hubbub of traffic.

Watching her through the steady cross hairs, he said into his mobile phone, 'She's coming now.'

'Are you sure that's her?' The voice that replied was precise, and sharp as serrated steel.

She was real eye candy, he thought. Even after days and nights of watching her, 24/7, inside her flat and outside, it was still a treat. The question barely merited an answer.

'I am,' he said. 'Yes.'

2

'I'm on the train,' the big, overweight, baby-faced dickhead next to him shouted into his mobile phone. 'The train. T-R-A-I-N!' he repeated. 'Yeah, yeah, bad line.'

Then they went into a tunnel.

'Oh fuck,' the dickhead said.

Hunched on his seat between the dickhead on his right and a girl wearing a sickly sweet perfume on his left, who was texting furiously, Tom Bryce suppressed a grin. An amiable, good-looking man of thirty-six, in a smart suit, with a serious, boyish face lined with stress and a mop of dark brown hair that flopped incessantly over his forehead, he was steadily wilting in the stifling heat, like the small bunch of flowers, rolling around on the luggage rack above him, which he had bought for his wife. The temperature inside the carriage was about ninety degrees and felt even hotter. Last year he had travelled first class and those carriages were marginally better ventilated – or at least less jam-packed – but this year he had to economize. Although he still liked to surprise Kellie with flowers once a week or so.

Half a minute later, emerging from the tunnel, the dick-head stabbed a button, and the nightmare continued. 'JUST WENT THROUGH A TUNNEL!' he bellowed, as if they were still in it. 'Yeah, fucking INCREDIBLE! How come they don't have a wire or *thing*, you know, to keep the connection? Inside the tunnel, yeah? They got them on some motorway tunnels now, right?'

Tom tried to tune him out and concentrate on the emails on his wobbling Mac laptop. Just another shitty end to another shitty day at the office. Over one hundred emails yet to respond to, and more downloading every minute. He cleared them every night before he went to bed – that was his rule, the only way to keep on top of his workload. Some were jokes, which he would look at later, and some were raunchy attachments sent by mates, which he had learned not to risk looking at in crowded train carriages, ever since the time he had been sitting next to a prim-looking woman and had double-clicked on a PowerPoint file to reveal a donkey being fellated by a naked blonde.

The train clicked and clacked, rocking, shaking, then vibrating in short bursts as they entered another tunnel, nearing home now. Wind roared around the edges of the open window above his head, and the echo of the black walls howled with it. Suddenly, the carriage smelled of old socks and soot. A briefcase skittered around on the rack above his head and he glanced up nervously, checking it wasn't about to fall on him or crush the flowers. On a blank advertising panel on the wall opposite him, above the head of a plump, surly-looking girl in a tight skirt who was reading *Heat* magazine, someone had spray-painted SEAGULLS WANNKERS in clumsy black letters.

So much for football supporters, Tom thought. They couldn't even spell *wankers*.

Beads of sweat trickled down the nape of his neck, and down his ribs; more trickled down all the spaces where his tailored white shirt wasn't already actually glued by perspiration to his skin. He'd removed his suit jacket and loosened his tie, and he felt like kicking off his black Prada loafers, which were pinching his feet. He lifted his clammy face from the screen as they came out of the tunnel, and instantly the air changed, to sweeter, grass-scented Downland air; in a few minutes more it would be carrying a faint tinge of salt from the English Channel. After fourteen years of commuting, Tom could have told when he was nearing home with his eyes shut.

He looked out of the window at fields, farmhouses, pylons, a reservoir, the soft, distant hills, then back at his emails. He read and deleted one from his sales manager, then replied to a complaint – yet another key customer angry that an order hadn't arrived in time for a big summer function. Personalized pens this time, printed golfing umbrellas previously. His whole ordering and shipping department was in a mess – partly from a new computer system and partly because of the idiot running it. In an already tough market this was hurting his business badly. Two big customers – Avis car rentals and Apple computers – lost to competitors in one week.

Terrific.

The business was creaking under the weight of debts. He'd expanded too fast, was too highly geared. Just as he was over-mortgaged at home. He should never have let Kellie convince him to trade up houses, not when the market was moving down and business was in recession. Now he was struggling to stay solvent. The business was no longer covering its overheads. And, despite all he told her, there was still no let-up in Kellie's obsession with spending money. Almost every day she bought something new, mostly on eBay, and because it was a bargain in her logic it didn't count. And besides, she told him, he was always buying expensive designer clothes for himself, how could he argue? It didn't seem to matter to her that he only bought his clothes during the sales and that he needed to look sharp in his line of work.

He was so worried he'd even discussed her spending problem recently with a friend of his, who had been through counselling for depression after his divorce. Over a few vodka martinis, a drink in which Tom was increasingly taking solace in recent months, Bruce Watts told him there were people who were compulsive spenders and they could be treated. Tom wondered if Kellie was bad enough to warrant treatment – and if so, how to broach it.

The dickhead started again. 'Hello, BILL, it's RON, yeah. Ron from *PARTS*. YEAH, THAT'S RIGHT! JUST THOUGHT I'D GIVE YOU A QUICK HEADS-UP ON— Oh fuck. BILL? HELLO?'

Tom raised his eyes without moving his head. No signal. Divine providence! Sometimes you really could believe there was a God. Then he heard the wail of another phone.

His own, he suddenly realized, feeling the vibration in his shirt pocket. Glancing surreptitiously around he pulled it out then, checking the caller's name, answered it in as loud a voice as he could muster. 'HELLO, DARLING,' he said. 'I'M ON THE TRAIN! T-R-A-I-N! IT'S RUNNING LATE!' He smiled at the dickhead, relishing a few moments of deliciously sweet revenge.

While he continued talking to Kellie, lowering his voice to a more civilized level, the train pulled into Preston Park station, the last stop before his destination, Brighton. The dickhead, gripping a tiny, cheap-looking holdall, and a couple of others in the carriage got off, then the train moved on. It wasn't until some moments after he had ended the call that Tom noticed the CD lying on the seat beside him which the dickhead had just vacated.

He picked it up and examined it for any clues as to how to reach its owner. The outer casing was opaque plastic, with no label or writing on it. He popped it open and removed the silver-coloured disc, turning it over and inspecting it carefully, but it yielded nothing either. He would load it into his computer and open it up and see if that provided anything, and, failing that, he planned to hand it in to Lost Property. Not that the dickhead really deserved it . . .

A tall chalk escarpment rose steeply on either side of the train. Then to his left it gave way to houses and a park. In moments they would be approaching Brighton station. There wasn't enough time to check the CD out now; he would have a look at home later tonight, he decided.

If he could have had the smallest inkling of the devastating impact it was going to have on his life, he would have left the damned thing on the seat.

3

Squinting against the low evening sun, Janie eyed the clock on the dash of her Mini Cooper in panic, then double-checked it against her wristwatch. 7.55 p.m. Christ. 'Almost home, Bins,' she said, her voice tight, cursing the Brighton seafront traffic, wishing she'd taken a different route. Then she popped a tab of chewing gum into her mouth.

Unlike his owner, the cat had no hot date tonight and was in no hurry. He sat placidly in his wicker carrying basket on the front passenger seat of the car, staring a tad morosely out through the bars at the front – sulking perhaps, she thought, from having been taken to the vet. She put out a hand to steady the basket as she turned, too fast, into her street, then slowed down, looking for a parking space, hoping to hell she was going to be lucky.

She was back a lot later than she had intended, thanks to her boss keeping her on in the office – today of all days – to help draft briefing notes for a conference with counsel in the morning on a particularly bitter divorce case.

The client was an arrogant, good-looking layabout who had married an heiress and was now going for as much of her money as he could get. Janie had loathed him from the moment she first met him, in her boss's office some months back; in her view he was a parasite, and she secretly hoped he would not get one penny. She had never confided her opinion to her boss, although she suspected he felt much the same.

Then she had been kept over half an hour in the vet's

waiting room before finally being ushered in with Bins to see Mr Conti. And it really had not been a successful consultation. Cristian Conti, young and quite hip for a vet, had spent a lot of time examining the lump on Bins's back and then checking elsewhere. Then he had asked her to bring the cat back in tomorrow for a biopsy, which had immediately panicked Janie into worrying that the vet suspected the lump was a tumour.

Mr Conti had done his best to allay her fears and had listed the other possibilities, but she had carried Bins out of the surgery under a very dark shadow.

Ahead she saw a small space between two cars, a short way down from her front door. She braked and put the car into reverse.

'You OK, Bins? Hungry?'

In the two years since they had become acquainted, she had grown very attached to the ginger and white creature, with his green eyes and huge whiskers. There was something about those eyes, about his whole demeanour, the way one moment he would nuzzle up to her, purring, sleeping with his head on her lap when she watched television, and another moment he was giving her one of those looks that seemed so damned human, so adult, so all-knowing. He was so right, whoever it was who had said, 'Sometimes when I am playing with my cat, I wonder if perhaps it is not my cat who is playing with me.'

She reversed into the space, making a total hash of it, then tried again. Not perfect this time either, but it would have to do. She closed the sunroof, picked up the cage and climbed out of the car, pausing to check her watch one more time, as if somehow, miraculously, she had read it wrong last time. She hadn't. It was now one minute to eight.

Just half an hour to feed Bins and get ready. Her date was a control freak, who insisted on dictating exactly how she looked each time they met. Her arms and legs had to be freshly shaven; she had to put on exactly the same measure of Issey Miyake and in the same places; she had to wash her hair with the same shampoo and conditioner, and apply exactly the same make-up. And her Brazilian had to be trimmed to within microscopic tolerances.

He would tell her in advance what dress to wear, what jewellery, and even where in the flat he wanted her to be waiting. It all went totally against the grain; she had always been an independent girl, and had never allowed any man to boss her around. And yet something about this guy had got to her. He was coarse, eastern European, powerfully built and flashily dressed, whereas all the men she had dated previously in her life had been cultured, urbane smoothies. And after just three dates she felt in his thrall. Just even thinking about him now made her moist.

As she locked the car and turned to walk towards her flat she did not even notice the only car in the street not caked in pigeon and seagull guano, a shiny black Volkswagen GTI with blacked-out windows, parked a short way ahead of her. A man, invisible to the outside world, sat in the driver's seat, watching her through a tiny pair of binoculars and dialling on his pay-as-you-go mobile phone.

4

Shortly after half past seven Tom Bryce drove his sporty silver Audi estate past the tennis courts, then the open, tree-lined recreation area of Hove Park, which was teeming with people walking dogs, playing sports, lazing around on the grass, enjoying the remnants of this long, early summer day.

He had the windows down, and the interior of the car was filled with gently billowing air carrying the scent of freshly mown grass and the soothing voice of Harry Connick Junior – who he loved, but Kellie thought was naff. She didn't care for Sinatra either. Quality singing just didn't do it for her; she was into stuff like house, garage, all those weird beaty sounds he did not connect to.

The longer they were married, the less it seemed they had in common. He couldn't remember the last movie they'd agreed on, and *Jonathan Ross* on a Friday night was about the only TV show they regularly sat down to watch together. But they loved each other, that he was sure of, and the kids came above everything. They *were* everything.

This was the time of each day he enjoyed the most, the anticipation of getting home to the family he adored. And tonight the contrast between the vile, sticky heat of London and the train, and this pleasant moment now seemed even more pronounced.

His mood improving by the second, he crossed the junction with swanky Woodland Drive, nicknamed Millionaires' Row, with its long stretch of handsome detached houses, many backing onto a copse. Kellie hankered to live there one day, but it was way out of their price league for the moment – and probably always would be, the way things were headed, he thought ruefully. He continued west, along the altogether more modest Goldstone Crescent, lined on either side with neat semi-detached houses, and turned right into Upper Victoria Avenue.

No one was quite sure why it had been named Upper since there was no Lower Victoria Avenue. His elderly neighbour, Len Wainwright – secretly nicknamed the Giraffe by Kellie and himself, as he was nearly seven foot tall – had once announced in one of his many moments of not exactly blinding erudition across the garden fence that it must be because the street went up a fairly steep hill. It wasn't a great explanation, but no one had yet come up with a better one.

Upper Victoria Avenue was part of a development which was thirty years old but still did not yet look as if it had reached maturity. The planes in the street were still tall saplings rather than full trees, the red brick of the two-storey semi-detached houses still looked fresh, the mock-Tudor wood beams on the roof facings hadn't yet been ravaged by woodworm or the weather. It was a quiet street with a small parade of shops near the top, mostly lived in by youngish couples with kids, apart from Len and Hilda Wainwright, who had retired here from Birmingham on their doctor's suggestion that the sea air would be good for Hilda's asthmatic chest. Tom held the view that cutting down on her forty fags a day might have been a better option.

He pulled his Audi into the tight space in his carport, alongside Kellie's rusting Espace, pocketed his mobile phone and climbed out, grabbing his briefcase and the flowers. The newsagent across the street was still open, as was the small gym, but the hair salon, ironmonger and estate agency were closed for the day. Two teenage girls stood at the bus stop a short way down, dolled up for a night out, miniskirts so short he could see the start of their buttocks. Feeling a distinct prick of lust, his eyes lingered on them for a moment, following their bare legs up as they shared a cigarette.

Then he heard the sound of the front door opening, and Kellie's voice calling out excitedly, 'Daddy's home!'

As a marketing man, Tom had always been good with words, but if anyone had asked him to describe how he felt this moment, every weekday night, when he arrived home to the greeting from the people that meant everything in the whole world to him, he doubted he could have done it. It was a rush of joy, of pride, of utter love. If he could freeze one moment of his life, it would be this, now, as he stood in the open doorway, feeling his kids' tight hugs, watching Lady, their Alsatian, holding her lead in her mouth, hope on her face, stamping a paw on the ground, tail the size of a giant redwood swinging wildly. And then seeing Kellie's smiling face.

She stood in the doorway in denim dungarees and a white T-shirt, her face, framed by a tangle of blonde ringlets, all lit up with her wonderful smile. Then he gave her the pink, yellow and white bouquet of flowers.

Kellie did what she always did when he gave her flowers. Her blue eyes sparkling with joy, she turned them around in her hands for a moment, going 'Wow, oh wow!' as if they genuinely were the most beautiful bunch she had ever seen. Then she brought them to her nose – her tiny, pert little nose he had always loved – and sniffed them.

'Wow! Look at these. Roses! My favourite flowers in my favourite colours. You are so thoughtful, my darling!' She kissed him.

And on this particular evening her kiss was longer, more lingering than usual. Maybe he'd get lucky tonight? Or, God forbid, he thought for a moment as a cloud momentarily slid across his heart, she was prepping him for news of some insane new purchase she had made today on eBay.

But she said nothing as he went in, and he could see no box, no packing case, no crate, no new gadget or gizmo. And, ten minutes later, relieved of his sticky clothes, showered and changed into shorts and a T-shirt, his see-sawing mood resumed its steady, if temporary, upward trend.

Max, seven years, fourteen weeks and three days old 'xactly', was into Harry Potter. He was also into rubber bracelets and proudly sported white MAKE POVERTY HISTORY, and black and white anti-racism STAND UP–SPEAK UP ones.

Tom, pleased that Max was taking an interest in the world even if he didn't fully understand the significance of the slogans, sat on the chair beside his son's bed in the little room with its bright yellow wallpaper. He was reading aloud, making his way through the books for the second time, while Max, curled up in his bed, his head poking out of his Harry Potter duvet, blond hair tousled, his large eyes open, absorbed everything.

Jessica, four, had toothache and had gone into a sudden strop, and was not interested in a story. Her bawling, coming through the bedroom wall, seemed impervious to Kellie's efforts at calming her down.

Tom finished the chapter, kissed his son goodnight,

picked a Hogwarts Express carriage off the floor and put it on a shelf next to a PlayStation. Then he turned off the light, blowing Max another kiss from the door. He went into Jessica's pink room, a shrine to Barbie World, saw her scrunched-up face, puce and sodden with tears, and received a helpless shrug from Kellie, who was trying to read her *The Gruffalo*. He attempted to calm his daughter himself for a couple of minutes, to no avail. Kellie told him Jessica had an emergency appointment with the dentist in the morning.

He retreated downstairs, treading a careful path between two Barbie dolls and a Lego crane, into the kitchen where there was a good smell of cooking, and then almost tripped over Jessica's miniature tricycle. Lady, in her basket, gnawing tendrils from a bone the size of a dinosaur's leg, again looked up at him hopefully and her tail gave a sloppy wag. Then she jumped out of her basket, walked across the room and rolled onto her back, tits in the air.

Giving them a rub with his foot whilst her head lolled back with a goofy smile, her tongue falling out between her teeth, he said, 'Later, you old tart, I promise. Walkies later. OK. Deal?'

It had been this kitchen that had sold Kellie on the house. The previous owners had spent a fortune on it, all marble and brushed steel, and Kellie had subsequently added just about every gadget a creaking credit limit could buy.

Through the window he could see the sprinkler whirring in the centre of the small, rectangular garden, and a blackbird on the lawn standing under the falling water, raising a wing and rubbing itself with its beak. Tiny, brightly coloured clothes hung on the washing line.

Beneath them a plastic scooter lay on the grass. In the little greenhouse at the end, tomatoes, raspberries, strawberries and courgettes he was nurturing himself were coming along.

It was the first year he had ever tried to grow anything and he felt inordinately proud of his endeavours – so far. Above the fence he could see the Giraffe's long, mournful face bobbing along. His neighbour was out there at all hours, clipping, pruning, weeding, raking, watering, up and down, up and down, his frame angled and bent like a tired old crane.

Then he glanced at the watercolour and crayon drawings and paintings almost entirely covering one wall – efforts from both Max and Jessica – checking for anything new. Apart from Harry Potter, Max was car mad and much of his art had wheels on. Jessica's had weird-looking people and even weirder animals, and she always drew the sun shining brightly somewhere in every picture. She was normally a cheery girl, and it upset him to see her crying tonight. There was no new artwork for him to admire today.

He mixed himself a stiff Polstar vodka and cranberry juice, grinding in crushed ice from the dispenser on their swanky American fridge – another one of Kellie's 'bargains' – with a television screen built into the door, then carried his glass into the living room. He debated whether to go through into the little conservatory, which had the sun on it now, or even go and sit out on the bench in the garden, but decided to watch television for a few minutes instead.

He picked up the remote and settled down in his sumptuous recliner armchair – an internet bargain he had actually bought for himself – in front of Kellie's most recent extravagant e-purchase, a huge flat-screen Toshiba television. This took up half the wall, not to mention half his income when the payment instalments 'holiday' expired in a year's time – although he had to admit it was great to watch sport on. As usual, the QVC Shopping Channel was on the screen, with Kellie's keyboard plugged in and lying on the sofa.

He flicked through some channels, then found *The Simpsons* and watched that for a little while. He always liked this show. Homer was his favourite – he empathized with him. Whatever Homer did the world always dumped on him.

Sipping his drink he felt good. He loved this chair, loved this room with its dining area at one end and open-air feel with the conservatory at the other. Loved the photos of the kids and of Kellie all around, the framed abstract prints of a deckchair and of the Palace Pier on the walls – inexpensive art that he and Kellie had actually agreed on – and the glass cabinet filled with his small collection of golf and cricket trophies.

Upstairs he could hear Jessica's crying was finally sub-siding. He drained the vodka and was mixing himself another one when Kellie came down into the kitchen. Despite her worn-out expression, no make-up and having given birth to two kids, she still looked slender and beau-tiful. 'What a day!' she said, raising her arms in a dramatic arc. 'Think I could do with one of those, too.'

That was a good sign; drink always made her amorous. He had been feeling randy on and off all day. He'd woken around 6 a.m. feeling horny, as he did most mornings, and as usual he'd rolled over in bed and straddled Kellie in the hope of a quickie. And as usual he had been foiled by the sound of the door opening and the patter of tiny feet. He was becoming convinced Kellie had a secret panic button that she hit to bring the kids running into the bedroom at the first hint of an attempt at sex.

In many ways there was an increasingly clear pattern to his life, he thought: constant crap at the office, mounting debts at home and a permanent stiffy.

He began mixing Kellie a massive drink as she gave the chicken casserole a stir, watching her, in admiration, simultaneously lifting the lid of a saucepan full of potatoes and checking something inside the oven. She multi-tasked in the kitchen in a way that was totally beyond his abilities. 'Is Jess OK now?'

'She's being a little madam today, that's all. She's fine. I gave her something from the doctor which'll get rid of the pain. How was your day?'

'Don't even ask.'

She cupped his face in her hands and gave him a kiss. 'When did you last have a good day?'

'I'm sorry, I don't mean to moan.'

'So, talk about it. I'm your wife; you can tell me!'

He stared at her, cupped her face in his own hands and kissed her forehead. 'Over supper. You look so beautiful. Every day you look more beautiful.'

She shook her head, grinning. 'Nah, just your eyesight – happens with age.' Then she took a step back and pointed at herself. 'Do you like these?'

'What?'

'These dungarees.'

Gloom momentarily enveloped him again. 'Are they new?'

'Yes – they came today.'

'They don't look new,' he said.

'They're not supposed to! They're Stella McCartney. Really cool, aren't they?'

'Paul's daughter?'

'Yes.'

'I thought her stuff was expensive.'

'It is usually – these were a bargain.'

'Of course.' He continued mixing her drink, not wanting an argument tonight.

'I've been checking the Web for holiday bargains. I have the dates when Mum and Dad could take the kids – the first week in July. Would that work?'

Tom dug his Palm out of his pocket and checked the calendar. 'We have an exhibition at Olympia the third week – but early July would be fine. But it's going to have to be something really cheap. Maybe we should just go somewhere in England?'

'The prices on the net are unbelievable!' she said. 'We could have a week in Spain cheaper than staying at home! Check out some of the sites – I've written them down. Take a look after supper. Holly, down the road, has a friend who got a week in St Lucia for two hundred and fifty pounds on the net. Wouldn't the Caribbean be great?'

He put the Palm down, took her in his arms and kissed her. 'I thought I might give my computer a break tonight – and concentrate on you.'

She kissed him back. 'I'd hate to think of the withdrawal symptoms you'd suffer.' She smiled mischievously. 'And there's a Jamie Oliver programme I want to watch. You can't stand him. You'd be much happier for half an hour on your little machine upstairs.'

Handing Kellie her drink, he said, 'Where would you most like to go if we could afford it?'

'Anywhere they don't have screaming kids.'

'You really don't mind leaving them? Haven't changed

your mind?' Are you certain?' Kellie had never before wanted to be apart from their kids.

'At this moment, I'd happily sell them,' she said, and drained half her sea breeze in one gulp.

*

An hour later, shortly after nine o'clock, Tom went upstairs and into his small den, with its view out across the street. It was still full daylight; he loved the long summer evenings, and for a few more weeks they would continue getting longer. He could see a small blue triangle of distant English Channel, between two roofs of the flats above the shops opposite him. Above them a flock of starlings darted into view then was gone again. The smell of a neighbour's barbecue wafted in through the window, tantalizing him even though he had just eaten.

Inside the gym he could see some poor sod doing bench presses, the trainer standing beside him. It reminded him that apart from taking Lady for short walks around the block, he'd done little exercise for months. Too many business lunches, too much booze and now some of his favourite clothes were getting too tight. Kellie was always telling him he was daft, living across the road from a gym and not using it. But it was yet another expense.

Maybe he'd just take Lady for a longer walk on these fine summer evenings. Perhaps get back into swimming. Golf once a week just wasn't doing it for his waistline; he hated seeing all those men with flaccid beer bellies in the golf club locker room, and was uncomfortably aware he was close to developing one of his own. As if signalling to himself, he pummelled his stomach with his fists. *Going to make you into a six-pack by the time we go on holiday!*

He sipped his third large vodka, feeling mellow now,

the cares of his day receded into a pleasant alcohol haze, and set the glass down beside him, glancing at the webcam on its stalk mount on his desk, through which he had the occasional communication with his brother in Australia, then tapped a command on his laptop and ran his eyes down his in-box. Almost immediately he came to a message from his old boss at the Motivation Business, Rob Kempson, with whom he had remained friendly.

> *Tom*
> *Check out the gazonkas on this one!*
> *Rob*

Instead of clicking, Tom took the CD the dickhead had left on the train out of its case, and inserted it into his laptop. His virus protection software kicked in, but when the CD icon finally stabilized on his desktop there was still no clue to its identity. He double-clicked on it.

Moments later his entire desktop went blank. A small window appeared on the screen with the message:

> Is this Mac address correct?
> Click YES to continue. NO to exit.

Assuming it was a normal Windows-to-Apple Mac problem, Tom clicked YES.

Moments later another message appeared.

> Welcome, subscriber. You are being connected now.

Then the words appeared:

> A SCARAB PRODUCTION

Almost instantly, they faded. At the same time the

screen steadily lightened into a grainy colour image of a bedroom, as if he was viewing it through a security camera.

It was a good-sized room, feminine-looking, with a small double bed covered with a duvet and scattered cushions, a plain dressing table, a long antique wooden mirror that might have come from a dressmaker's shop, a wooden chest at the end of the bed, a couple of deep-pile rugs on the floor, and closed vertical blinds. Two bedside lamps lit the room, and there was another light source from a bathroom door, partially open. A couple of black and white Helmut Newton photographs of nudes hung on the walls. Opposite the bed were large mirrored cupboard doors, and reflected in them was a door leading, presumably, to a corridor.

A young, slender woman emerged from the bathroom, adjusting her clothes, glancing at her watch, looking a little nervous. Elegant and beautiful, with long fair hair and wearing a slinky black dress with a single strand of pearls around her neck, she was holding a clutch bag as if on her way to a party. She reminded Tom a little of Gwyneth Paltrow, and for one fleeting moment he wondered if it was her; then she turned her head and he could see it wasn't, although she looked quite similar.

She sat, perched on the edge of the bed, and to Tom's surprise kicked off her high-heeled shoes, seeming totally unaware of the camera. Then she stood up again and began unbuttoning her dress.

Moments later the bedroom door opened behind the woman, and a short, powerfully built man, a hooded balaclava over his face and dressed entirely in black, came in and closed the door behind him with a gloved hand. The woman either had not heard him or was ignoring him. As he walked slowly across the room towards her, she began unfastening her pearl necklace.

The man pulled something from inside his leather jacket which glinted in the light, and Tom craned forward in surprise when he saw what it was: a long stiletto blade.

In two quick strides the man reached her, jerked an arm around her neck, and plunged the stiletto between her shoulder blades. Frozen by the surreality, Tom watched the woman's gasp of shock, unsure whether she was acting or this was for real. The man pulled the blade out, and it was covered in what appeared to be blood. He stabbed her again, then again, blood spraying from the wounds.

The woman fell to the floor. The man knelt, tore away her dress, then slit her bra strap with the blade, pulled the bra away, and brutally rolled her onto her back. Her eyes were rolling, her large breasts falling to one side. He slashed through the top of her black tights, then pulled them completely off, stared down at her naked, exquisite body for some moments, then plunged the knife into her belly just above her Brazilian-cut pubic hair.

Tom stared, sickened, about to exit the site, except curiosity kept him watching. Was she acting, was the knife fake, was the blood gouting from her belly stage blood? The man plunged the knife in again and again, savagely.

Then Tom jumped as the door behind him opened.

He spun round in his chair to see Kellie standing there, holding her wine glass, clearly tipsy.

'Did you find us anywhere nice, darling?' she asked.

He swivelled back round, and slammed down the lid of the computer before she could see what was on the screen.

'No,' he said, his voice quavering. 'Nothing, no. I . . .'

She put her arms around his neck, slopping some wine onto the laptop. 'Ooops, sshorry!'

He tugged out his handkerchief and dabbed it off. As he did so, Kellie slid her free hand down inside his shirt and began to tease a nipple. 'I've decided you've done enough work for today. Come to bed.'

'Five minutes,' he said. 'Give me five minutes.'

'I might be ashhleep in five minutes.'

He turned and kissed her. 'Two minutes, OK?'

'One!' she said, and retreated from the room.

'I haven't walked Lady.'

'She had a long walk this afternoon. She's fine; I already let her out.'

He grinned. 'One minute, OK?'

She raised a mischievous finger. 'Thirty seconds!'

The moment she closed the door, he opened the lid of his computer and tapped a key to wake it up.

On the screen appeared the words:

Unauthorized access. You have been disconnected.

For some moments he sat, thinking. What the hell had he just seen? It had to have been a movie trailer, it *must* have been.

Then his door opened again and Kellie said, 'Fifteen seconds – or I'll start without you.'

5

It was the best birthday present ever, in all her life, in all fifty-two years of it! Nothing had ever come close before, not within a million miles. Not the MG sports car wrapped up in a pink bow that Don had given her for her fortieth (which he hadn't really been able to afford) nor the silver Cartier watch he'd given her for her fiftieth (which she knew he couldn't really afford either) nor the beautiful tennis bracelet he'd just given her yesterday for her fifty-second.

Nor the week at Grayshott Hall health farm that her two sons Julius and Oliver had clubbed together to buy her – fabulous indulgence but did they think she was overweight or something?

Whatever. Hilary Dupont was beyond caring, she was walking on air, all twelve stone of her, floating out the front door, jangling Nero's lead, proclaiming to herself, 'A handbag, Mr Worthing? A *handbag*?'

Peacehaven, the suburb where Hilary lived, was part of the eastern urban sprawl of Brighton, a wide cross-hatch of residential streets stretching back from the cliff-top coastal road to the edge of the rural South Downs, densely filled with bungalows and detached houses all built since the First World War.

A wide expanse of farmland began just one row of houses back from Hilary's street. Any neighbour chancing to glance out of their window shortly before ten o'clock on this cloudy June morning would have seen an overweight but strikingly handsome blonde woman, dressed in a smock over a spotted leotard, her feet clad in green gumboots, talking and gesticulating to herself, being followed by a rather plump black Labrador zigzagging from lamp post to lamp post, and pissing on each one.

Hilary turned left at the end of the street, following the road round, warily watching her dog for a moment as a double-glazing delivery van roared by, then she crossed the road, went up to a gate that led through into a field of brilliant yellow rape, and called out to Nero – who was about to do a dump in someone's driveway – in a stentorian voice that could have silenced the whole of Wembley stadium without a microphone, 'Nero! Don't you dare! COME here!'

The dog raised his head, saw the open gate, trotted joyfully towards it, then broke into a loping sprint and was off, away up the hill, and lost to her sight among the rape in seconds.

She closed the gate behind her, then repeated yet again, 'A handbag, Mr Worthing? A *handbag*?'

She was glowing, she was on fire; she'd already called Don, Sidonie, Julius, Oliver and her mother telling them the news, the *incredible* news, the best news ever: the phone call, just half an hour ago, from the Southern Arts Dramatic Society, telling her she had got the part of Lady Bracknell, the top role! The star!

After twenty-five years of amateur acting, mostly for the Brighton Little Theatre Group, always hoping to be discovered, finally she had a real break! The Southern Arts Dramatic Society was semi-professional, putting on an open-air play every summer, first on the ramparts of Lewes Castle, then touring all over the UK, right down to

Cornwall. It was famous; it would get reviewed in the press; she was bound to get noticed! *Bound* to!

Except, oh God, the nerves were already starting to kick in. She had been in the play before, years ago, in a minor role. But she still knew chunks of it by heart.

Striding off up the hill, around the edge of the field, thrusting with her arms as she spoke, she proclaimed, at the top of her voice, what she considered one of the most dramatic and funny lines of the play. If she could get that line right, she would have captured the character. 'A *handbag*, Mr Worthing? You were found in a *handbag*?'

An airliner circled low overhead, positioning itself for its final approach to Gatwick, and she had to raise her voice a little to hear herself. 'A handbag, Mr Worthing? *You* were found in a handbag?

'A handbag, Mr Worthing? You were *found* in a handbag?'

She carried on walking, repeating the line over and over, each time changing the inflexions and trying to think who else she could phone and tell. Only six weeks to the opening night, not long. God, so much to learn!

Then doubts started. What if she wasn't up to it?

What if she froze or corpsed in front of such a big audience? That would be the end, completely the end!

She would be OK; she would somehow get through. After all she came from a theatrical family. It was in her blood; her mother's parents had been music hall artistes before they'd retired and bought a bed and breakfast business near the sea in Brighton.

As she crested the brow and saw the next hill unfurling for a mile ahead of her, and wide open farmland to either side broken by just a few solitary trees and mesh fences, she could see no sign of Nero. A strong breeze was blowing, bending the rape and the long green wheat sheaves. She cupped her hands over her mouth and shouted, 'NERO! Come on, boy. NERO!'

After a few moments she saw a wide ripple in the rape, something zigzagging through it – Nero seemed incapable of ever running in a straight line. Then he broke cover, and came bounding towards her, holding something white and dangly in his mouth.

A rabbit, she thought at first, and hoped at least the poor thing was dead. She couldn't bear it when he brought a live, wounded one and plopped it proudly at her feet, wriggling and screeching in fright, which he was fond of doing.

'Come on, boy, what's that you've got there? Drop! Drop!'

Then her own mouth dropped.

A shiver rippled all the way through her as she took one nervous step forward, staring down at the motionless white object.

Then she began to scream.

6

Roy Grace did not enjoy holding press conferences. But he was well aware the police were paid public servants, and therefore the public had a right to be kept informed. It was the spin that journalists put on everything that he hated. It seemed to him that journalists weren't interested in informing the public; that their job was to sell newspapers or attract viewers or listeners. They wanted to take news and slant it into stories, the more sensational the better.

And if there wasn't anything sensational in the story, then why not have a pop at the police themselves? Few things grabbed the public's attention better than a whiff of police negligence, racism or heavy-handedness. Car chases going wrong had been a particular hobby horse in recent years, especially if members of the public were injured or killed by reckless police driving.

Like yesterday, when two suspects being chased in a stolen car had crashed off a bridge and drowned in a river.

Which was why he was here now, standing in the Briefing Room, facing an open-centred rectangular table with not enough chairs for all the press present, his back to a large, smart, curved board bearing an artistic display of five police badges on a blue background, with the www.crimestoppers.co.uk number printed prominently beneath each of them.

He guessed there were about forty media people crammed in here – newspaper, radio and television reporters, photographers, cameramen and sound recordists – most of them familiar, among them some young fresh-faced ones working for the local press and stringing for the nationals, hoping for their big break, and some old, weary ones just waiting to get out of here and into a pub.

Flanking him, more to show that the police were taking this seriously than to actually contribute much to the conference, was the Assistant Chief Constable, Alison Vosper, a handsome but hard-looking woman of forty-four with blonde hair cropped short, standing in for the Chief, Jim Bowen – away at a conference – and Grace's immediate superior, Gary Weston, the Chief Superintendent.

Weston was a relaxed-looking thirty-nine-year-old Manchester man with charismatic charm, with whom Grace had been mates when they were both beat coppers, and they remained good friends now. Although almost the same age as Grace, Weston had played the politics, cultivated influential friends, his eyes firmly set on a chief constable career path – and with his abilities, maybe even the top job at the Met, Grace thought frequently with a tinge of admiration but no envy.

Being politically astute, Gary Weston was keeping quiet today, letting Roy Grace do all the talking, seeing whether the Detective Superintendent was going to dig himself even deeper into the murky brown stuff.

An acidic young female reporter whom none of the police officers had seen before got her question in: 'DS Grace, I understand that a woman was injured in a car accident in Newhaven, then an elderly gentleman was injured in an accident on the Brighton bypass, and a few minutes later a police officer was knocked off his motorbike. Can you explain your reasons for permitting the chase to continue?'

'The accident in Newhaven took place before the police began pursuit,' Grace responded, choosing his words carefully. 'The accused persons hijacked a Land Rover immediately following this accident. They then rammed a Toyota saloon driven by an elderly gentleman in a tunnel and hijacked his vehicle. We knew that at least one of the accused was armed and dangerous, and that an innocent member of the public's life depended on us apprehending them, and I took the view that the public were more endangered by letting them go, which is why I made the decision to keep them in sight.'

'Even though that ended in their deaths?' she went on.

Her tone infuriated him, and he had to hold back the very strong urge to swear at her, to tell her the two who had died were monsters, that drowning in a muddy river was better justice for all the people they'd wronged and harmed and killed than being given some pathetic jail sentence by a bleeding-heart liberal judge. But he also had to be very careful not to give the assembled company something they could twist into a sensational headline.

'The cause of their deaths will be established in due course by an inquest,' he said, far more calmly than he felt.

His response provoked an angry murmur, a flurry of hands in the air and about thirty questions all at once. Glancing at the clock, relieved to see the minute hand had clicked forward, he stood firm. 'I'm sorry,' he said, 'that's all we have time for today.'

*

Back in his small, almost brand-new office, in the huge, recently refurbished two-storey art deco building which had originally been built in the 1950s as a hospital for contagious diseases and which now housed the headquarters of Sussex CID, Grace sat down in his swivel chair. Like almost every item of furniture in the room it was almost fresh out of its box, and didn't yet feel familiar or comfortable.

He wriggled around in the chair for a moment, played with the toggle levers, but it still wasn't great. He had liked his old office down at Brighton police station much better. The room had been bigger, the furniture beat-up, but the place was in the centre of town and had a buzz. These new premises were on an industrial estate on the edge of the city and felt soulless. Miles of long, silent, freshly carpeted and painted corridors, office after office filled with new furniture, and no canteen! Nowhere to get a cuppa apart from a do-it-yourself or a bloody vending machine. Nowhere to even get a sandwich – you had to walk across the road to the Asda hypermarket. So much for design committees.

He stared fondly for a moment at his prized collection of three dozen vintage cigarette lighters hunched together on the ledge between the front of his desk and the window, and reflected that for weeks his work schedule had prevented him from pursuing one of his favourite pastimes – something he used to share with his wife, Sandy, and in which he now found great solace – trawling antique markets and car boot sales in search of old gadgets.

Dominating the wall behind him was the large, round wooden clock that had been a prop in the fictitious police station in *The Bill*, which Sandy had bought in happier times at an auction, for his twenty-sixth birthday.

Mounted in glass beneath it was a seven-pound, six-ounce brown trout he'd picked up at a stall in the Portobello Road. Its location beneath the clock was no accident – it enabled him to use a tired old joke when briefing new detectives about patience and big fish.

The rest of the floor space was occupied by a television and video player, a circular table, four chairs and piles of loose paperwork, his holdall containing his crime-scene kit, and small towers of files.

Each file on the floor stood for an unsolved murder. He stared at one green envelope, its corner obscured by a whorl of carpet fluff. It represented a pile of about twenty boxes of files either stacked on an office floor, or bulging out of a cupboard, or locked up, gathering mould in a damp police garage in a station in the area where the murder had happened. It was the open file on a gay vet called Richard Ventnor, battered to death in his surgery twelve years ago.

It contained scene-of-crime photographs, forensic reports, bagged evidence, witness statements, transcripts – all separated into orderly bundles and secured with coloured ribbon. This was part of his current brief, to dig back into the county's unsolved murders, liaise with the CID division where the crime had happened, looking for anything that might have changed in the intervening years that could justify reopening the case.

He knew most of each file's contents by heart – a benefit of the memory that had propelled him through exams both at school and in the force. To him, each stack represented more than just a human life that had been taken – and a killer who was still free – it symbolized something very close to his own heart. It meant that a family had been unable to lay its past to rest because a mystery had never been solved, justice had never been done. And he knew that with some of these files being more than thirty years old, he was the last hope the victims and their relatives probably had. There was just one case where he was currently making some real progress. Tommy Lytle's.

Tommy Lytle was Grace's oldest cold case. At the age of eleven, twenty-seven years ago, Tommy had set out from school on a February afternoon, to walk home. He'd never been seen again. The only lead at the time had been a Morris van, seen by a witness who had had the presence of mind to write down the number. But no link between the owner, a weirdo loner with a history of sex offences on minors, and Tommy had ever been established. And then, two months ago, by complete coincidence, the van had showed up on Grace's radar when the classic car enthusiast who now owned it got stopped for drunken driving.

The advances in forensics from twenty-seven years back were beyond quantum. With modern DNA testing police forensic scientists boasted, not without substance, that if a human being had ever been in a room, no matter how long ago, then given time they could find evidence to prove it. Just one skin cell that had escaped the vacuum cleaner, or a hair, or a clothing fibre. Maybe something one hundred times smaller than a pinhead. There would be a trace.

And now they had the van.

And the original suspect was still alive.

Forensics had been through that van with microscopes, but so far, as a disappointing lab report Grace had read last night at home informed him, they had found nothing to link the van to the victim. The forensic Scenes of Crime team had found a human hair, but the DNA was not a match.

But they would find something in that damned van, Grace was determined, if he had to pull the vehicle apart millimetre by millimetre himself with a pair of tweezers.

He took a swig from his bottle of mineral water, grimacing at the taste – or lack of taste – the sheer, faintly metallic nothingness of the stuff he was drinking in an effort to wean himself off his usual gallon of coffee a day. Then, replacing the cap, he stared at the gathering rain clouds, heavy as suet, suspended low above the grey slab of the Asda roof across the road that was most of his view, thinking about tomorrow.

It was Thursday tomorrow and he had a date – not like the last, disastrous bunny boiler of a blind date from an internet agency – but a real one with a beautiful woman. He was both looking forward to it and nervous at the same time. He was fretting about what to wear, about where to take her, whether he'd have enough to say to her.

And he was concerned about Sandy. About what she would think about him dating another woman. Absurd, he knew, to be thinking these thoughts after almost nine years, but he couldn't help it. Just as he could not help wondering, almost every moment of his waking life, where she was, what had happened to her. Whether she was alive or dead.

Clutching the plastic Evian bottle he took another long swig, then stared over the top of the piles of out-of-control paperwork on his desk at his computer screen, then down at a stack of this morning's papers. The headlines of the top one, the local paper the *Argus*, screamed out at him: TWO DEAD IN SUSSEX POLICE CHASE.

He dumped the newspapers on the floor and scanned the latest deluge of emails. He was still just getting the hang of the new Vantage software for the force's system, which was a lot easier to use than the GreenScreen it replaced. Grace checked the incident reports log to see what had happened during the night, which normally he would have done first thing, but today he'd had to prepare for the press conference.

There was nothing out of the ordinary, just the usual detritus of a Brighton midweek night and morning. A handful of muggings, break-ins, car thefts, a hold-up at an all-night grocery store, a pub fight, a domestic, a bunch of RTAs – no fatalities – a call-out to farmland near Peacehaven to investigate a suspicious object. No major incidents, no serious crimes, nothing to grab his interest.

Good. He'd been out of the office most of the past week, apart from some hours he had had to spend in preparation and in court on the ongoing trial of a local villain, and needed a few days to catch up on his paperwork.

He synced his Blackberry with the computer and checked his diary. It was still clear. His secretary, Eleanor Hodgson – or Management Support Assistant as the political correctness Politburo now dictated she be called – had wiped all his appointments to let him concentrate on his case and the trial. But his diary would fill up soon enough, he rued.

Almost immediately there was a rap, then his door opened and Eleanor came in. Prim and nervy, fifty-something, she looked the kind of backbone-of-England woman Grace imagined one would meet at a vicar's tea party – not that he had ever actually been to one. And after three years of working for him, Eleanor was still unfailingly polite and a tad formal, as if she was nervous of upsetting him, although he could not imagine why.

She stood holding a wodge of newspapers at arm's length as if concerned they might pollute her. 'Oh, Roy,' she said. 'I, er . . . these are later editions of some of the morning papers; I thought you might want to see them.'

'Anything new?'

'More of the same. The *Guardian* has a quote from Julia Drake at the Independent Police Complaints Commission.'

'I didn't think it would be long before they started. Self-righteous fucking cow.'

Eleanor flinched at his swear word, then smiled nervously. 'Everyone's being a bit harsh on you, I think.'

He glanced at his water, suddenly craving a cup of coffee. And a cigarette. And a drink. It was nearly lunchtime and he usually tried to avoid drinking until the evening, but he had a feeling he was going to break that rule today. The Independent Police Complaints Commission. Terrific. How many hours of his life was that going to consume over the coming months? He had known it was inevitable they would get involved, but having it confirmed seemed, suddenly, to make everything worse.

His phone rang. He answered it as Eleanor stood there, and heard the Chief Superintendent's crisp Mancunian accent.

'Well done, Roy,' Gary Weston said, sounding even more like his superior than ever. 'You handled yourself well.'

'Thanks. We've now got the IPCC to deal with.'

'We'll sort them. Are you free at three?'

'Yes.'

'Come to my office – we'll work on a report for them.'

Grace thanked him. The moment he hung up, the phone rang again. This time it was the Force Control Room. A civilian dispatcher called Betty Mallet, who had been there as long as he could remember, said, 'Hello, Roy, how you doing?'

'Been better,' he said.

'I've a request from Peacehaven CID for a senior officer to attend an investigation scene right away; are you free?'

Grace groaned silently. Why couldn't she have called someone else? 'What can you tell me about it?'

'A local resident was walking her dog this morning up on farmland between Peacehaven and Piddinghoe village. The dog ran off and came back with a human hand in its mouth. The CID have gone up there with tracker dogs and they've located more human body parts – apparently very recent.'

Like all detectives, Grace kept a leather holdall at the ready containing a protective suit, overshoes, gloves, torch and other essential items of crime-scene kit. 'OK,' he said, resignedly staring at his bag on the floor, not needing this, not needing it at all. 'Give me the exact location – I'll be there in twenty minutes.'

7

They were laughing at him as he walked up the street. The Weatherman could feel it in his bones, the way some people could feel the cold or the damp in their bones. Which was why he avoided eye contact with all and everyone.

He could sense them all stopping, staring, turning, pointing, whispering, but he did not care. He was used to it; they'd been laughing at him all his life, or certainly for as far back into his twenty-eight years on this particular planet that he could remember. He was pretty sure it had been different on his previous planet, but *they* had blocked his memory of that.

'Viking, North Utsire, South Utsire, south-west four or five, veering north-west five to seven for a time, occasionally,' he said to himself as he walked, indignant at being summoned out of the office and having to give up his lunch hour. 'Gale eight in Viking, showers, dying out. Moderate or good. Forties, cyclonic five to seven, becoming north-west seven to severe gale nine, backing south-west four or five later. Showers then rain later. Moderate or good,' he continued.

He talked quickly, his mind not really on the forecast and his brain busy crunching through algorithms for a new program he was designing for work. It would make half the current system redundant, and there were people who would be pissed off at that. But then they shouldn't have spent all that taxpayers' money on crap hardware without knowing what they were doing in the first place.

Life was a learning curve, you had to understand how to deal with it. Q in *Star Trek* had it sussed. 'If you can't take a little bloody nose, maybe you ought to go back home and crawl under your bed. It's not safe out here. It's wondrous, with treasures to satiate desires both subtle and gross. But it's not for the timid.'

The Man Who Was Not Timid continued his journey, marching uphill through the lunchtime throng of Brighton's North Street, past a Body Shop, a Woolwich Building Society, then SpecSavers.

Thin and pasty-faced, he had a gawky frame, a clumsy haircut and eyebrows furrowed in fierce concentration behind unfashionably large glasses. Dressed in a fawn anorak, a white nylon shirt over a string vest, grey flannel trousers and vegan sandals, he carried a small rucksack on his back containing his laptop and his lunch. He walked, pigeon-toed, in a loping stride, stooped forward with an air of determination as if forcing his way through the steadily increasing south-westerly blowing in from the Channel. Despite his age, he could have passed for an insolent teenager.

'Cromarty, Forth, Tyne, Dogger, north-west seven to severe gale nine, backing south-west four or five, occasionally six later. Showers then rain later. Moderate or good.'

He continued reciting aloud the updated regional shipping forecast for the British Isles which had been broadcast at 05.55 hours this morning, Greenwich Mean Time. He had learned them by heart, four times a day, seven days a week, since he was ten. It was, he had discovered, the best way to get from A to B – just recite the shipping forecast all the way, it stopped the heat from everyone's stares from burning his skin.

And he had found it a good way to stop other kids laughing at him at school. Also whenever anyone had wanted to know the shipping forecast – and it was surprising how often the other pupils at Mile Oak school *had* wanted to know – he was always able to tell them.

Information.

Information was currency. Who needed money if you had information? The thing was most people were completely crap at information. Crap at pretty well everything really. That's why they weren't *chosen*.

His parents had taught him that. He didn't have much to thank them for, but at least he had that. All the years they had drummed it into him. *Special. Chosen by God. Chosen to be saved.*

Well, they hadn't got it quite right. It wasn't actually God, but he had long given up trying to tell them that. Wasn't worth the hassle.

He passed an amusement arcade, then turned left at the Clock Tower into West Street, passing Waterstone's bookshop, a Chinese restaurant and a FlightCentre, heading down towards the sea. A few minutes later he pushed his way through the revolving doors in the fine Regency facade of the Grand Hotel, entered the foyer and walked across to the front desk.

A young woman in a dark suit, with a gold badge pinned to the lapel engraved with the name ARLENE, watched him warily for a moment, then gave him a dutiful smile. 'Can I help you?' she said.

Staring down at the wooden counter, avoiding eye contact, he focused on a plastic dispenser full of American Express application forms.

'Can I help you?' she asked again.

'Umm, well, OK.' He looked even harder at the forms, feeling even more indignant now he was here. 'Can you tell me which room Mr Smith is in?'

After checking a computer screen she replied, 'Mr Jonas Smith?'

'Um, right.'

'Is he expecting you?'

Yes, he sodding well is. 'Um, right.'

'May I have your name, sir. I will phone his room.'

'Um, John Frost.'

'One minute please, Mr Frost.' She lifted a receiver and dialled a number. Moments later she said into the phone, 'I have Mr John Frost in reception. May I send him up?' After a brief pause she said, 'Thank you,' and replaced the receiver. Then she looked at the Weatherman again. 'Number seven one four – on the seventh floor.'

Staring down again at the American Express forms, he bit his lower lip, nodded, and then said, 'Um, OK, right.'

He took the elevator to the seventh floor, walked along the corridor and rapped on the door.

It was opened by the Albanian, whose real name was Mik Luvic but who the Weatherman had to call Mick Brown – all in his view part of a ridiculous charade in which all of them, including himself, had to go under assumed names.

The Albanian was a muscular man in his thirties with a lean, hard face set in a cocksure expression, and gelled spikes of short, fair hair. He was dressed in a gold-spangled black singlet, blue slacks and white loafers, and sported a heavy gold chain around his neck. His powerful bare shoulders and forearms were covered in tattoos, and he was mashing gum with sharp little incisors that reminded the Weatherman of a piranha fish he had once seen in the local aquarium.

Staring down at the eau de Nil carpet, the Weatherman said, 'Oh, hi. I've come to see Mr Smith.'

The Albanian, who had once made a living by illegal bare-knuckle and cage fighting but now had a cushier gig, stared at him for several seconds in silence, chewing continuously with his mouth open, then gestured him into a large suite which reeked of cigar smoke and was furnished in plush, ersatz Regency, and closed the door swiftly behind them. Pointing disinterestedly towards an open doorway, the Albanian turned his back on the Weatherman, strutted across the room, sat down on a chair and resumed watching a football game on a television.

The Weatherman had met the Albanian on several occasions now, and had yet to hear him speak. He wondered sometimes if he was deaf and dumb, but didn't think so. Walking through the doorway as he was bid, he entered a much larger room in the centre of which the grossly overweight Mr Smith was seated on a sofa, his back to the French windows which overlooked the sea, concentrating on a bank of four computer screens on the coffee table in front of him and biting at a fingernail as if he was chewing a chicken bone.

He was dressed in a Hawaiian shirt open to the navel, revealing folds of hairless, pale flesh that made him look as if he had breasts. The top of his blue slacks stretched across stubby legs the width of mature tree trunks. By contrast, his tiny feet, in monogrammed velvet Gucci slippers, without socks, seemed dainty, like dolls' feet, and his head, coiffed with immaculate silver, wavy hair bunched into a short pigtail at the back, was even more out of proportion, as if it belonged to someone twenty sizes smaller. He had so many chins that until his minuscule mouth opened and the muscles around came into play it was hard for the Weatherman to see where his face ended and his neck began.

'You want lunch, John?' Jonas Smith said, in a sharp Louisiana drawl that contained not an ounce of warmth. He jabbed a porcine finger, the skin around the nails bitten raw in places, across at a room-service trolley laden with plates of sandwiches and aluminium food covers.

Staring down at the eau de Nil carpet, the Weatherman said, 'Actually, I have my sandwich.'

'Huh. You want a drink? Order yourself a drink and sit down.'

'Thanks. Um, OK. Right. I don't need a – um, drink. I – um . . .' the Weatherman looked at his watch.

'Then fucking sit down.'

The Weatherman hesitated for a moment, contained his anger and moved towards the nearest chair.

The American resumed gnawing on his nail and fixed his small, piggy eyes on the Weatherman, who unhitched his rucksack and perched himself on the edge of a chair, his eyes scanning the pile of the carpet as if searching for a pattern that was not there.

'Coke? You want a Coke?'

'Umm, actually, umm.' The Weatherman looked at his watch again. 'I have to be back by two.'

'You'll go back when I fucking tell you.'

The Weatherman was hungry. He thought about his tofu and bean-shoot sandwich in the plastic box inside his rucksack. But the problem was he didn't really like people watching him eat. He took a deep breath and closed his eyes, which helped with his anger. 'Fisher, German Bight, south-west four or five, veering north-west, six to gale eight. Showers. Moderate or good.' Opening his eyes again, he noticed a glass ashtray, containing a half-smoked cigar that had gone out, on the table next to the sofa.

'What's that?' Mr Smith said. 'What d'you say there?'

'Shipping forecast. You might need it.'

The American, whose real name was Carl Venner, stared at the geek, well aware that he was part genius, part two chips short of a circuit board. A hostile little fuckwit with a major attitude problem. He could handle that; he'd handled worse shit in his life. The thing was to remember that right now he was useful, and when he stopped being useful, nobody would miss him.

'Appreciate you coming at such short notice,' Venner said, his mouth forming a brief smile, but there was no thaw in his voice.

'Um, right.'

'We have a problem, John.'

Nodding his head, the Weatherman said, 'OK, right.'

There was a long silence. Sensing someone behind him, he turned his head to see the Albanian had entered the room and was standing in the doorway, his arms crossed, watching him. Two other men had joined him, flanking him. The Weatherman knew they were both Russian, although he had never been introduced to them.

They seemed to materialize out of the walls for every meeting he had with Venner but he hadn't figured out where they fitted in. They were unsmiling, lean, sharp-faced, with topiaried hair and sharp black suits; business associates of some kind. They always made him feel uncomfortable.

'You told me that our site was not hackable,' Mr Smith said. 'So you want to explain to Mr Brown and myself how come we got hacked last night?'

'We have five firewalls. No one can hack us. I had an automatic alert come through within two minutes that we had someone making an illegal access, and I disconnected them.'

'So how did he make that access?'

'I don't know; I'm working on it. At least,' he added petulantly, 'I was until you interrupted me and called me here. Could be a software glitch.'

'I was eleven years head of network monitoring for Europe for US Military Intelligence, John. I know the difference between a software glitch and footprints. I'm looking at footprints here. Come and take a look.' He pointed at one of the computer screens.

The Weatherman walked round until he could see the screen. Rows of digits, all encrypted, ran down and across it. One group of letters was blinking. Studying the screen for some moments, he then carefully studied the other three screens. Then back to the first one, to the steady blink-blink-blink.

'Um, there could be a number of reasons for this.'

'There could be,' the American agreed, impatiently. 'But I've eliminated them. Which leaves us with just one possibility – someone unauthorized has gotten hold of a subscriber disc. So what I need you to do is provide us with the name and address of the subscriber who lost it, and this person who found it.'

'I can give you the user ID of the subscriber – that will

be on the login details. Um, the person who found it – er – um, might not be that easy.'

'If he was able to find us, you'll be able to find him.' Mr Smith folded his hands, and his lips parted into a fleshy smile. 'You have the resources. Use them.'

8

Roy Grace was in a muddy field, waist-high in rape, in a white paper suit pulled on over his clothes, and protective overshoes. For some moments he just stood in the rain-spotted wind and watched an ant steadfastly making its way across the female human hand that was lying, palm down, among the stalks of brilliant yellow rape.

Then he knelt and sniffed the flesh, flapping away a bluebottle. No smell came from the hand, which told him that it must be fresh – in this summer warmth probably less than twenty-four hours old.

Years back, as a fledgling detective attending a murder scene – a young woman found raped and strangled in a churchyard in the centre of Brighton – he had been approached by an attractive young red-headed journalist on the *Argus* who had been hanging around outside the police cordon. She had asked him if he felt emotions when he attended a murder, or whether he regarded it as just doing his job, the way anyone else did any other kind of job.

Although happily married to Sandy at the time, he had enjoyed his flirtatious chat with her and had not wanted to confess that this was actually the first murder he had ever attended. So, trying to be all macho he had told her that yes, it was a job, just a job, that was how he coped with the horror of murder scenes.

Now he was thinking back to that moment.

To that bravado lie.

The truth was that the day he turned up to a murder scene and it felt no more than just doing a job, the day he did not care deeply for the victim, would be the day he would quit the force and do something else. And that day was still a long way off. Maybe it would eventually happen to him, the way it had happened to his dad and the way it seemed to happen to many of the old sweats on the force, but right now he was feeling a whole bellyful of the same emotions he had each time he came to a murder scene.

It was a potent mixture of fear at what he was going to have to look at, and the awesome burden of responsibility that fell on his shoulders as Senior Investigating Officer – the knowledge that this dead woman, whoever she was, had parents, maybe siblings, maybe a husband or lover, maybe children. One of her loved ones would have to identify the body, and all of them, in a state of grief and shock, would have to be interrogated and eliminated from enquiries.

The hand was elegant, long fingers, well kept nails, the bright pink varnish contrasting vividly with flesh that had turned the colour of alabaster, except for a long strip of dark, congealed blood in a gash that ran along the leading edge of her thumb and into her wrist. It looked like a defence wound. He wondered who she was, what kind of a person she was, what had led to this.

The first twenty-four hours in a murder enquiry were key. After that, detection became increasingly slow and laborious. Over the following hours and days he knew he would have to drop just about everything else in his life for this enquiry. He would get to know as many details of her life and death as her body, her home, her personal effects, her family and friends could yield. It was likely he would end up knowing more about her than anyone who had known her when she was alive.

The enquiry would be invasive and at times brutal. Death alone did a pretty thorough job of stripping away human dignity, but it had nothing on a police forensic investigation. And there was always the haunting sense that this dead person's soul might – just might – be watching him.

'This is where we think the hand came from, Roy.' The bulky figure of Bill Barley, the local Detective Inspector from East Downs Division, made even bulkier-looking by his white oversuit billowing in the wind, stood beside him, pointing a latex-gloved finger across the field which he had diligently cordoned off at a site where several SOCO members, also in white suits, were busy erecting a square white tent.

Beyond, at the edge of the field where he had parked, Grace could see yet another vehicle joining the cluster of marked and unmarked police cars, the dog-handler's van, the photographer's van and the tall, square truck-sized shape of the Major Incident Vehicle dwarfing everything.

The Coroner's black van hadn't been summoned yet. Nor had the press been notified, but it wouldn't be long before the first reporter arrived. Just like the blowflies.

Barley was a true old sweat, in his fifties, with a bluff Sussex accent and a rubicund face lined with broken veins. Grace was impressed by the speed with which he had secured the area. The worst nightmare was to arrive at a murder scene where inexperienced officers had already trampled most of the evidence into the ground. The DI appeared to have this scene well under control.

Barley covered the hand with some heavy-duty sheeting, then Grace followed him, stepping carefully in his tracks to disturb the ground as little as possible, glancing every few moments at a police Alsatian loping gracefully through the rape in the distance, until they reached the area where most of the activity was concentrated. Grace could see immediately why. In the centre, flattening a small area of the crop, was a large, crumpled black bin liner, with torn shreds jigging in a gust of wind, and several bluebottles flying around it.

Grace nodded greetings at one of the SOCO officers, Joe Tindall, who he knew well. In his late thirties, Tindall used to look like a mad scientist, with a thatch of dull hair and bottle-lensed glasses, but had had a makeover since falling in love with a much younger girl. Now, inside his hooded white suit, he sported a completely shaven head, a quarter-inch-wide vertical strip of beard running from the centre of his lower lip down to the centre of his chin, and hip rectangular glasses with blue-tinted lenses. He looked more like a drugs dealer than a boffin.

'Morning, Roy.' Tindall greeted him in his usual sarcastic tone. 'Welcome to "One Thousand and One Things to Do with a Bin Liner on a Wednesday Morning in Peacehaven".'

'Been shopping, have you?' Grace asked, nodding at the black plastic.

'You can't believe the things you can get with your Nectar points these days,' Tindall said. Then he knelt and very carefully opened out the liner.

Roy Grace had been in the police for nineteen years, the past fifteen of which he had spent investigating serious crimes, mostly murders. Although every death disturbed him, there wasn't much any more that really shocked him. But the contents of the black bin liner did.

It contained the torso of what had been clearly a young,

shapely woman. It was covered in congealed blood, the pubic hairs so matted he couldn't tell their colour, and almost every inch of her flesh had been pierced by some sharp instrument, probably a knife he thought, in a frenzy of stabbing. The head was absent and all four limbs had been severed. One arm and both legs were in the bag along with the body.

'Jesus,' Grace said.

Even Tindall's humour had dried up. 'There's some really sick bastard out there.'

'Still no head?'

'They're looking.'

'A pathologist's been called?'

Tindall waved away a couple of bluebottles. Some more appeared and Grace flapped those away, angrily. Bluebottles – blowflies – could smell decaying human flesh from five miles away. Short of a sealed container, it was impossible to keep them away from a body. But sometimes they were useful. Bluebottles laid eggs, which hatched into larvae, which became maggots and then bluebottles. It was a process which took only a few days. On a body that had not been discovered for weeks it was possible to work out roughly how long it had been dead from the number of generations of insect larvae infestation.

'Someone's called for a pathologist, I presume, Joe?'

Tindall nodded. 'Bill has.'

'Nadiuska?' Grace asked, hopefully.

There were two Home Office pathologists who tended to be sent to murder scenes in this area, because they lived reasonably locally. The police favourite was Nadiuska De Sancha, a statuesque Spaniard of Russian aristocratic descent who was married to one of Britain's leading plastic surgeons. She was popular because not only was she good at her job, and extremely helpful with it, but she was wonderful to look at. In her late forties, she could easily pass for a decade younger; whether her husband's craftsmanship had had anything to do with that was a matter of constant debate among all who worked with her – the speculation fuelled even more by the fact she invariably wore roll-neck tops, winter and summer.

'No, luckily for her – Nadiuska doesn't like multiple stabbings – it's Dr Theobald. And there's a police surgeon on his way as well.'

'Ah,' Grace said, trying not to let the disappointment show in his voice. No pathologist liked multiple stab wounds because each one had to be painstakingly measured. Nadiuska De Sancha was not just eye candy, she was fun to work with – flirtatious, a big sense of humour and fast in her work. By contrast, Frazer Theobald was, by general consensus, about as fun to be around as the corpses he examined. And slow. So painfully slow. But his work was meticulous and could never be faulted.

And suddenly, out of the corner of his eye, Grace could see the man's diminutive frame, all in white and clutching his large bag, striding across the field towards them, his hooded head not that far above the top of the rape.

'Good morning, all,' the pathologist said, and exchanged latex-gloved handshakes with the trio.

Dr Frazer Theobald was in his mid-fifties. A stockily built man a tad under five foot two inches tall with beady, nut-brown eyes, he sported a thick Adolf Hitler moustache beneath a Concorde-shaped hooter of a nose and an untidy, threadbare thatch of wiry hair. It would not have needed much more than a large cigar for him to have gone to a fancy dress party as a passable Groucho Marx. But Grace doubted Theobald was the kind of man ever to have contemplated attending something as frivolous as a fancy dress party. All he knew about the man's private life was that he was married to a lecturer in microbiology, and that his main relaxation was solo dinghy sailing.

'So, right, Detective Superintendent Grace,' he said, his eyes fixing first on the remains inside the flapping sheets of the bin liner, then on the ground around. 'Can you bring me up to speed?'

'Yes, Dr Theobald.' It was always formal with the pathologist for the first half-hour or so. 'So far we have this dismembered torso of what looks like a young woman with multiple stab wounds.' Grace looked at Barley as if for confirmation and the DI took over.

'East Downs police were alerted by an emergency call made earlier this morning by a woman walking her dog. The dog found a human hand, which we have left in situ.' The DI pointed. 'I cordoned off the area, and a search by police dogs discovered these remains here, which I have left untouched, other than to further open up the bin liner.'

'No head?'

'Not yet,' the DI said.

The pathologist knelt, set down his bag and, carefully folding back the bin liner, studied the remains in silence for some moments.

'We need a fingerprint and DNA test right away to see if we can get an ident,' Grace said. He stared downhill across the field to the streets of houses. And beyond them, a mile or so distant, he could see the grey water of the English Channel, barely distinguishable from the grey of the sky.

Addressing the DI, Grace continued, 'We should also start a house-to-house enquiry in the area, ask for reports of anything suspicious in the past couple of days. See if there are any missing persons in the area – if not broaden that out to the whole of Brighton and then Sussex. Are there any CCTV cameras, Bill?'

'Only in some of the local shops and some other businesses.'

'Make sure they're told to keep all tapes for the past seven days.'

'Right away.'

Nodding down, Grace said, 'Any idea how these remains might have got here? Any tyre marks?'

'We have a trail of footprints. Heavy-duty boots of some kind, from the patterns. They look sunk in deep; I think she must have been carried,' Bill Barley said, pointing along a narrow band of soil and rape between two strips of police tape stretching into the distance.

Theobald had his bag open now, and was carefully examining the bloody hand lying there.

Who is she? Grace wanted to know. *Why was she killed? How did she get here?* Anger boiled in him.

Anger and something else.

It was the awful knowledge, the one he refused ever to face, that this young woman's fate could have been his own wife's fate also. Nine years ago Sandy had disappeared off the face of the earth, and not a trace of her had appeared since. She could have been murdered and dumped somewhere. Killed and savagely butchered. If you wanted to get rid of a body and make sure it would never, ever be found it was easy – there were dozens of ways to do it.

And that was what bothered him now. Someone had gone to the trouble of butchering this girl and removing her head. But if they had really wanted to make it hard to identify her, they would have taken her hands as well. So why hadn't they?

Why had they dumped her remains here in the middle of this field, where she was bound to be discovered quickly? Instead of putting her even in a shallow grave?

Could it be, he wondered, because whoever had done this had wanted her to be discovered?

9

Kellie, dressed in a purple jogging suit, squatted on the floor of the living room, keyboard on her lap, leaning against the sofa, munching her way through a tube of salt-and-vinegar flavoured Pringles. Not exactly the healthiest lunch, but they were low fat – wouldn't do her figure any harm, she thought.

Logged on to the Web, she stared at the purple crystal Swarovski bracelet on the television screen, then double-clicked on the image to make it larger. Guiltily, she thought how well it would go with the outfit she had on. A bit bling, perhaps, a bit chav. But Swarovski costume jewellery was definitely classy; she loved their stuff. The RRP, it showed, was £152.00 and the highest bid showing so far was just £10.75. With only three hours, forty-two minutes of auction time remaining!

That was nothing! She entered a bid of twelve pounds. That wouldn't make an appreciable dent in their finances – and if she could get it for close to that price then in a few weeks she could put it back on at a higher price and make a profit!

She watched the screen for several minutes more, and no further bids appeared. So far, so good. She reached out her arm, picked up the bottle of Smirnoff – the one from her secret stash that she kept hidden from Tom at the back of her underwear drawer in the bedroom – unscrewed the cap and took just a little nip. It was only her third drink of the morning, she rationalized, ignoring the fact it had been a new bottle and was now a third empty.

Outside, rain was pelting down. Lady trotted into the room, lead in her mouth, cocked her head and whined.

'You want your walk, my darling, don't you? Have to wait for the rain to ease off, OK?'

The dog whined again, louder.

She put the bottle down and raised her arm. Lady nuzzled up to her then rolled over, clumsily, onto her back.

'Typical woman, aren't you?' Kellie slurred affectionately, the buzz from the vodka lifting her midday blues. 'Just want your tits caressed.'

She stroked the dog's belly for some moments, then crooked her arm around her neck and kissed her on the head, breathing in the animal's strong, warm, furry smell. 'Love you, Lady.'

Hearing some noise outside, Lady suddenly jumped back to her feet, growled, and prowled out into the hall. She barked, and moments later Kellie heard the thump of the dog flap in the kitchen as Lady ran off into the garden, no doubt to chase off some bird that had dared to land on the lawn.

Her bid on eBay still stood unchallenged.

One day she would get this online auction thing right. There had been an article in the *Daily Mail* a couple of weeks ago, which she had cut out and kept, about all the people who had made fortunes selling things on eBay. She had tried telling Tom – but he just didn't seem to understand – that all she was doing was trying, in her own way, to make them some money. But she just wasn't any good at it. She would be, though; she would get the hang of it.

Then she looked at the bottle. Maybe just one more small mouthful?

She closed her eyes, thinking. *What the hell is wrong with me? With my life? Is it crap genes?*

Kellie thought about her parents. Her father with all his dreams, whom she adored, was now housebound with advanced Parkinson's at just fifty-eight years old. She remembered as a child all the different business ventures he had tried and failed at. He had driven a cab in Brighton and had started his own limousine hire service. That had gone under. He'd bought a franchise selling a health drink which was going to make his fortune. That had cost them their house.

Her mother had supplemented their income by work-ing long, tough hours at Gatwick Airport, promoting perfumes in the duty-free section, until she had had to leave to look after her father. They now lived, in a state of permanent fear of vandals, burglars and muggers, in a council flat in Whitehawk, the roughest estate in Brighton. Two days ago, when she had gone to visit them, she had left her old Espace outside for just an hour. When she had come out, the hubcaps had been stolen.

She remembered when she had first met Tom, at the twenty-first party of a girlfriend from teacher training college in Brighton. She had been struck by how much he reminded her of her father – the father she wanted to remember, the young, handsomely boyish man with immense charm, passion for life and such enthusiasm. Tom had had such great vision, such amazing plans, and unlike her father's, his had been carefully thought out. He wanted to get experience working for one of the most successful companies in his field and then start out on his own.

And she had believed in him. It had seemed impos-sible to her that Tom could fail. All her friends had liked him immediately. Her parents adored him. She had fallen in love with him that night. Two nights later she had slept with him, in his tiny basement flat just off Hove seafront, with a Scott Joplin CD playing on repeat for hours. They had barely spent a night apart since.

For the first few years of their marriage everything had been brilliant. Tom had started his own business and it had really taken off. They had moved to a larger flat, and then to this house. It had started to go wrong when she had left her job teaching in a primary school shortly before Max was born. She grew bored, then she'd suffered a long bout of post-natal depression. She had found it tough being at home all day with a baby, while Tom left early to go to London and arrived home late, usually too tired to talk. It would not be for ever, he had promised her. He just needed to put in the hours now, investing in their future.

Then Jessica had been born. And the same lonely struggle had repeated itself. Only Tom's business had got harder. He worked even longer hours and talked to her less. She had started taking Max to school, made a new bunch of friends. All the other women seemed to have successful husbands, great clothes, nice cars, swanky homes, wonderful holidays.

This whole business with eBay that Tom just did not seem to understand had started because she was trying to help him. OK, there were *some* things that she did buy for herself, but mostly it was bargains she bought with the intention of selling again at a profit.

But she never seemed to get bids anywhere close to the prices she had paid.

There was another reason for her spending, both on eBay and on the QVC Shopping Channel, which she could never tell Tom: it masked the forty pounds a week out of her housekeeping that her vodka habit was costing her.

It was just a phase, a way of getting through the stress. She wasn't an alcoholic, she told herself. She was just coping with a small crisis she was going through, her own way. As if to convince herself, she picked up the *Argus* and turned to the jobs section. That would be the best solution – find something part time. Make a contribution to the housekeeping, at least. And have some cash to buy the occasional drink – not that she really needed it.

Her mobile phone rang. It was out in the kitchen, where she had left it.

Cursing, she scrambled to her feet and walked, a little unsteadily, out of the room, glanced at the caller display, saw it was her best friend Lynn Cottesloe, and answered it.

'Hi,' she said, 'how're you?' conscious that her voice was a little slurred.

'I'm sitting in Orsino's restaurant. Where are you?'

'Oh, shit,' Kellie said. 'I'm – sho shorry.'

'Are you OK?'

Shit, Kellie thought. *Shit, shit, shit!* She had totally forgotten they were meant to be having lunch today. She looked at her watch. It was 1.15 p.m.

'Kellie, are you OK?'

'OK? Me? Absolutely,' she said breezily.

10

In the narrow room that doubled as the London office and showroom of BryceRight Promotional Merchandise Limited, Tom Bryce sat gloomily at his desk, his shirt-sleeves rolled up and his tie at half-mast. He was shivering and thinking about putting his jacket back on. Bloody English weather. Yesterday it had been almost unbearably hot, today it was freezing.

The place gave off the right image; it was a smart address, and although not big, the room was elegantly proportioned with large windows, and had the original stucco work on the ceiling. There was just enough space for desks for the five of them, a waiting area which was also the display area, and a tiny kitchenette behind a partition at the far end.

The company name had been Kellie's idea. A tad corny he had thought at the time, but as she had pointed out it was a name people would easily remember. BryceRight supplied business gifts and promotional clothing to companies and clubs. Its product lines ranged from over-printed pens, calculators, mouse pads and executive desk toys, to T-shirts, baseball caps, sportswear and trophies.

After graduating from business school in Brighton, Tom had worked for one of the largest companies in the field, the Motivation Business, and then, a decade ago, supported by Kellie, had mortgaged himself up to the hilt and set up on his own. He had operated from his den and the two spare bedrooms in their home until shortly after

Max was born, when he had accumulated enough capital to take on the lease at this prestigious, if cramped, address just off Bond Street, as well as a warehouse close to Brick Lane in east London.

For the first six years the business boomed. He was a natural salesman, his customers liked him, everything was rosy. Then 9/11 had happened and for two days the phone had not rung. And it never really seemed to have rung with any consistency since.

He employed four salesmen, two of whom were based here in London, one in the north of England and one in Scotland. Additionally his secretary, Olivia, was in this office, as well as his admin clerk, Maggie, who was in charge of customer liaison and product sourcing. He employed another four people at the warehouse, an order chaser, a quality control supervisor and two dispatch clerks. And that was where he had a lot of problems – probably from not being there enough himself.

BryceRight had a blue-chip customer base, with some of the largest household names as clients. They supplied Weetabix, Land Rover, Legal and General Insurance, Nestlé, Grants of St James's, as well as many much smaller clients.

For the first few years he used to really enjoy coming into work, and he'd even relished the post-9/11 challenge for a time, but more recently with the latest economic downturn and ever-increasing competition his turnover had plunged to the point where he was no longer making enough money to cover his overheads. He was losing customers to the competition, existing customers were placing smaller orders, and just recently there had been a spate of fuck-ups which had lost him even more business.

The in-tray on his desk was stacked with bills, some

more than ninety days old. Yet again at the end of this month it was going to be a tough balancing act between the receivables and the debts to ensure the wage cheques did not bounce. And there would be, as always, the Kellie spending factor in that equation, also.

She was smiling out from the silver frame on his desk, along with Max and Jessica, all three of them responding to something the photographer had said. It was a great photograph, in flattering soft focus, giving them a slightly dreamlike quality. Staring at her fondly, he hoped to God there were going to be no more unwelcome surprises from her for a while.

How could he break it to her if they had to sell the house and downsize? And to what? A flat? How could he tell Max and Jessica that they might not have a garden any more?

He stared out of his second-floor window through the pouring rain at the windows across the road. Conduit Street was narrow, and the tall buildings made it feel like a gully. Even on a sunny day his office was in permanent shade.

Glancing down he could see the lunchtime stream of people, the sea of umbrellas and the line of cars, taxis and vans waiting to cross the lights at the intersection with Bond Street. In particular he watched a new maroon Bentley Continental. Ever since they had first come out he had hankered after one, but at this moment the gulf separating him from something so expensive seemed as big as the gulf that separated a snail on his garden fence from Mars.

He disconsolately munched his sandwich of tuna and sweetcorn on rye bread. He wasn't crazy about the combination of tuna and sweetcorn, and he disliked the sharp caraway seeds in rye, but this morning he had woken up more determined than he had been in a long while to eat more healthily – and this stuff was supposed to be low fat, low everything. He would have preferred his usual bacon and egg, or cheddar and pickle any day. It was Kellie, in bed last night playfully prodding his stomach and calling him 'Tubs', that had been the final straw.

He glanced at the first page of the trade magazine *Promotions and Incentives* and saw that one of his competitors, whose business was booming, was preparing for a stock market flotation. What was their secret?' he wondered. What the hell had they done so right that he had done so wrong?

He took another bite, and watched the techie, Chris Webb, a tall, laconic forty-year-old with floppy hair and a solitary earring, who he called in for all his computer problems – and who treated him like a retarded child – prodding around with a screwdriver in the entrails of his Mac laptop. Every few moments Tom looked over at the blank screen, hoping against hope it would spring back to life.

And thinking about what he had seen last night.

He had not been able to get the image of the girl being stabbed out of his mind, and it had given him such a vivid nightmare he had woken screaming at three in the morning. It must have been a movie or a movie trailer of some kind.

But it had seemed somehow so damned real.

'Your data's gone, mate, I'm afraid,' Chris Webb said, irritatingly cheerily.

'Yes, that's what I told you,' Tom said. 'I need you to retrieve it.'

As the techie busied himself with the machine again,

Tom, feeling lost without his computer and unable to concentrate on the magazine, stared at the displays of some of his company's products, thinking they were all looking a bit tired, had been there too long, needed sharpening up.

He studied the Team Jaguar glass showcase, displaying an anorak, baseball cap, polo shirt, ballpoint pen, key fob, driving gloves, tie and headsquare, all in the Jaguar livery. There were some newer designs they had produced which should be in there, he thought. Then he turned his attention to another display – of mouse pads, pens, calculators and umbrellas all bearing the Weetabix logo. That needed bringing up to date also.

Olivia, his secretary, an attractive twenty-something who lurched from one man-crisis to the next, came into the room holding a Pret a Manger bag, mobile phone pressed to her ear in deep conversation. Behind her empty desk sat his best salesman, Peter Chard, in one of his trademark sharp suits, his hair slick, a doppelgänger for the actor Leonardo DiCaprio, engrossed in a motoring magazine and forking his way through a pot noodle. At the desk next to him sat Hong Kong-born Simon Wong, a quiet, ambitious thirty-year-old, busy filling out an order form. It was a new client and a decent-sized order; some small cheer, Tom thought.

A phone started ringing. Olivia, still engrossed on her mobile, seemed oblivious to it. Peter and Simon didn't seem to hear it either. Maggie was out of the office at lunch.

'SOMEONE ANSWER THE FUCKING PHONE!' Tom shouted.

His secretary raised an apologetic arm and strode over to her desk.

'So talk me through exactly what happened again,'

Chris Webb said, sounding exasperated as if he were addressing the class imbecile.

Both salesmen looked at Tom.

'I opened my computer on the train this morning and it wouldn't boot up. It was dead,' he said.

'It's booting up fine,' the techie said. 'But there's no data, is there? That's why you're not getting anything up on the screen.'

Lowering his voice in an attempt to lose his audience, Tom said, 'I don't understand.'

'There isn't much to understand, mate. Your database is wiped clean.'

'Not possible,' Tom said. 'I mean – I haven't *done* anything.'

'You've either had a virus or you've been hacked.'

'I thought Macs don't get viruses.'

'You did what I told you, didn't you – please tell me you did. You didn't hook this up to the office server?'

'No.'

'Lucky for that – it would have trashed your entire database.'

'So there's a virus.'

'You've got *something* in there. Nothing's wrong with your hardware. I just can't believe you were so stupid – putting in a CD you found on a train. Jesus, Tom!'

Tom glanced past him. The rest of his team seemed to have lost interest. 'What do you mean, *stupid*? It's a computer, right? That's what it does. It's got all the anti-virus software – which you installed. It plays CDs. It ought to be able to play *any* CD.'

Webb held up the CD. 'I've had a read of this, away from any machine it could harm. It's spyware – it will reconfigure your software and plant God knows what kind of stuff in your system. You found it on a train?'

'Last night.'

'Serves you right for not handing it in to Lost Property right away.'

Sometimes Tom couldn't believe he actually paid this guy to *help* him. 'Thanks a lot. I was trying to be helpful – thought I might find an address on it I could send it to.'

'Yeah, well next time it happens send it to me and I'll look at it for you. So, apart from this, have you opened up any attachments you didn't recognize?'

'No.'

'Are you sure?'

'I never do – you warned me not to, years ago. Only the ones that come from people I know.'

'Porn?'

'Jokes, porn, the usual stuff.'

'I suggest you wear a condom next time you surf the net.'

'That's not even funny.'

'That wasn't a joke. You've picked up a very nasty virus; it's extremely aggressive. If you'd logged on to your office server this morning, you'd have wiped that clean, and all your colleagues' computers as well. And the backup.'

'Shit.'

'Good word,' Chris Webb said. 'Couldn't have put it better myself.'

'So how do I get rid of it?'

'By paying me a lot of money.'

'Great.'

'Or you can buy a new computer.'

'You really know how to cheer someone up, don't you?'

'You want the facts, I'm giving them to you.'

'I don't understand. I thought Macs didn't get viruses.'

'They don't very often. But there are some floating around. You might have just been unlucky. But most likely it's from this CD. Of course there is another possibility.' He looked around, found the mug of tea he had put down a while ago, and swigged some down.

'And what's that?' Tom asked.

'It might be someone who is pissed off with you.' After a few moments, Webb added, 'Flash tie you're wearing.'

Tom glanced down; it was lavender with silver horses. Hermès. Kellie had recently bought it on the internet in some closing-down offer – her idea of economizing.

'It's for sale,' he said.

11

Shortly after half past four in the afternoon, at the end of three hours of painstaking scrutiny, the dismembered remains of the young woman beneath the awning in the rain-lashed field of rape had come close to yielding as much as they were going to out here, the Home Office pathologist decided.

He completed the primitive but effective technique of pressing Sellotape against every inch of her flesh in the hope of trapping more fibres, tweezered off a few fibres that had lodged in her pubic hair, carefully bagging each of them, then ran his eye once more over the body parts and the ground immediately around them, concentrating fiercely, checking just one more time for anything he might have missed.

Grace would have preferred the pathologist to go straight to the mortuary and perform the post-mortem this evening, which was normal practice, but Theobald informed him apologetically that he was already committed to a PM in Hampshire on a suspicious yachting death.

In an ideal world all post-mortems on murder victims would be carried out in situ, as there was such a risk in moving them of losing some vital clue, perhaps invisible to the naked eye. But a muddy, wind-blown, rain-swept field did not constitute an ideal world. Bodies were seldom found in places that were post-mortem friendly. Some pathologists preferred to spend a minimal amount of time at the crime scene and return to the relatively pleasant working environment of the mortuary. But Dr Frazer Theobald was not one of them. He could be at a scene late into the night, indeed all through the night, if necessary, before declaring himself satisfied that the remains were ready to be removed to the mortuary.

Grace looked at his watch. His mind was partly on his date tomorrow night. It would be good to get off before the shops shut today. He knew it was wrong to be thinking this way, but for years his sister, and everyone else, had been telling him to get a life. For the first time since Sandy had gone he had met a woman that he really was interested in. But he was worried that his wardrobe was crap, and he needed some new summer clothes. Then he tried to put his date out of his mind and concentrate on his work.

The young woman's head had still not yet been found. Roy Grace had called in a POLSA, a Police Search Adviser, and several police vans had already arrived filled with constables, many of them Specials, and begun a line search of the area. The driving rain was hampering visibility, and a helicopter droned low overhead, covering a slightly wider area. Only the police Alsatians, bounding away in the distance, seemed unfazed by the elements. To the farmer's chagrin, a sixty-deep line of policemen, wearing fluorescent jackets in an even brighter yellow than the crop, was systematically trampling every square inch of his field.

Grace had spent much of the time on his phone, organizing the search, arranging a workspace for the team he would be assembling in the Major Incident Suite, obtaining an incident code name from the Sussex Police computer, and listening to the profiles of the handful of young women who had been reported missing in the past few days. There was only one missing person report within a five-mile radius that was a major cause for concern, a further three within the whole of Sussex, and another six in the entire south-east of England.

So far the taciturn Dr Theobald had been unable to give him much of a description, beyond light brown hair, gleaned from her pubic hair colouring, and a guess that she was either in her twenties or her early thirties.

Four women fitted that description.

Grace was well aware of the grim statistic that 230,000 people went missing in England every year. And that 90 per cent of those who turned up would do so within thirty days. More than 30 per cent of those 230,000 would never be seen again. Normally, only children and elderly people prompted immediate action. For all other missing person reports the police ordinarily waited a minimum of twenty-four hours, and usually more, depending on the circumstances.

Every missing person enquiry touched a nerve deep in Roy Grace's soul. Each time he heard the words he gave a silent shudder.

Sandy was a *missing person.* She had disappeared off the face of the earth on his thirtieth birthday, just under nine years ago, and had never been seen since.

There was no evidence that the majority of those 70,000 people who vanished had died. People went missing for a raft of reasons. Mostly it was a breakdown in family relationships – husband or wife walking out, kids running away from home. Psychiatric problems. But some – and Roy Grace always hated to acknowledge this to himself – went on that list for an altogether more sinister reason. Either they were murdered, or, in rarer instances, held captive against their will. Grisly cases came to light from time to time, in the UK and in just about every other country in the world, of people being held for years, sometimes decades. Sometimes in his worst, darkest moments of despair he imagined Sandy being held chained in a cellar somewhere by a maniac.

He still believed she was alive, whatever the reason for her disappearance. Over the past nine years he had consulted almost more mediums than he could remember. Every time he heard about a medium with a good reputation he would go and see them. Whenever one came to Brighton and performed in public, he would be there in the audience.

And in all this time none of them, not one, had claimed to be in touch with his dead wife, or to have a message from her.

Grace had no unswerving belief in mediums, any more than he had in doctors, or scientists. He possessed an open mind. He believed the dictum of one of his favourite characters in fiction, Sherlock Holmes. 'When you have eliminated the impossible, whatever remains, *however improbable*, must be the truth.'

His thoughts were interrupted by the chirrup of his mobile phone. He looked at the display but the number was withheld – most likely it was a colleague, standard practice among police officers. Answering it he said, 'Roy Grace.'

'Yo, old wise man!' said a familiar voice.

'Fuck off, I'm busy,' Grace said with a grin. After three hours trying to make conversation with the miserably silent Dr Frazer Theobald, it was good to hear a friendly voice. Glenn Branson was a Detective Sergeant with whom he was close mates. They had worked together on and off for several years, and he was the first person Grace had recruited onto his Major Incident Team for this murder.

'Well you can fuck off too, old-timer. While you're lounging around on your second brandy after a long lunch, I'm working my butt off doing your job for you.'

The unpleasant taste of a sardine and tomato sandwich, Grace's lunch which seemed like an aeon ago, still lingered in his memory. 'Chance would be a fine thing,' he said.

'Saw a well brilliant film last night. *Serpico.* Al Pacino playing this "tec" routing out bent cops in the New York Police Department. Ever see it?' Branson was a total movie buff.

'I saw it about thirty years ago, when I was in my cradle.'

'It was made in 1973.'

'Films take a long time to reach your local picture house, do they?'

'Very witty. You should see it again – it's so good. Al Pacino, he's the man.'

'Thanks for this valuable piece of information, Glenn,' he said, stepping out of the awning and out of earshot of the pathologist, a police photographer named Martin Pile, and Dennis Ponds, the senior Sussex Police Public Relations Officer, who had just arrived and was waiting to be briefed by Grace for the press. From his experience, at this stage in a major incident it was best to say very little. The less information the press printed about what had actually been found, the state of the body or body parts and the location, the easier it would be to weed out crank phone calls and time wasters – and to tell when there was a caller with genuine information.

At the same time the police had to recognize the

wisdom of maintaining a good working relationship with the media – although in Grace's case that had been souring fast over the past couple of weeks. He'd been pilloried in today's news over the death of two suspects, and he'd been savaged last week for admitting in court, during a murder trial, that he had consulted a medium.

'I'm standing on a hill in the pissing rain. How exactly does this help our enquiry?'

'It doesn't; it's for your education. All you ever watch is crap.'

'Nothing wrong with *Desperate Housewives.*'

'Tell me about it, I live with one. But I have some information for you.'

'Uh huh?'

'A trainee solicitor – an articled clerk. Just come in.'

'Well that would be a loss,' Grace said sarcastically.

'You know, man, you're sick.'

'No, just honest.'

Like most of his police colleagues, Roy Grace disliked the legal profession, criminal lawyers in particular, for whom the law was just a game. Every day police officers risked their lives trying to catch criminals; their lawyers made good livings trying to outwit the law and free them. Sure, Grace knew, innocent people who were arrested had to be protected. But it was still early days in Glenn's career – he wasn't long enough in the tooth as a cop yet. He hadn't experienced enough human scum escaping justice thanks to smart lawyers.

'Yeah, whatever. She didn't turn up for work today. One of her friends checked her flat. She's not there; they're well worried.'

'So? When was she last seen?'

'At work yesterday afternoon. She had an important

client meeting this morning and she never showed. Never phoned. Her boss said this isn't in character. Her name's Janie Stretton.'

'I've got a list of four other names, Glenn. What makes this one special?'

'Just a hunch.'

'Janie Stretton?'

'Yep.'

'I'll add her to the list.'

'Put her at the top.'

The rain was permeating his suit, and dripping down his face. Grace stepped back into the shelter of the tented awning. 'We still don't have a head,' he said. 'And I have a feeling we're not going to find it for a very good reason. We've already run a fingerprint test, which is negative. We're sending off for a priority DNA to Huntingdon labs, but that will be a couple of days.'

'I've found her,' Glenn Branson said. 'I'll put money on it.'

'Janie Stretton?' Grace said.

'Janie Stretton.'

'She's probably in bed, shagging some three-grand-an-hour brief.'

'No, Roy,' the Detective Sergeant insisted. 'I think you're looking at her.'

12

Tom spent the afternoon at the offices of a major new client, Polstar Vodka, shaving his prices – and profit margin – down to the bone to avoid a competitor getting the business. Further handicapped by not having his laptop with him, he left glumly with an order for 50,000 engraved martini glasses and overprinted silver coasters which he had originally been banking on to give him a good profit. Now he would be lucky to even cover his costs. At least it was turnover to show the bank, but he was painfully aware of the old adage, 'Turnover is vanity, profit is sense.'

With luck it would lead to more profitable business in time, he hoped.

Arriving back at the office shortly before five o'clock, he was relieved to see his laptop up and running again. But at a cost of seven hours of the techie's expensive time that he could ill afford. Peter Chard's desk was empty and Simon Wong was on the phone; Maggie was also busy on the phone. Olivia brought him over a pile of letters to sign.

He dealt with them then turned his attention to Chris Webb, who had managed to retrieve some data. He talked him through the system upgrade he had done and the new anti-virus software he had installed – at further expense, of course. But he was still unable to explain where the virus that had wiped the database had come from other than from the disc Tom had found on the train, which he was going to take away to analyse further.

After Chris had left, Tom spent half an hour catching up

on his emails. Then out of curiosity he opened his Explorer Web browser, and went to the recent history section, which showed him all the websites he had looked at in the past twenty-four hours. There were a couple of visits to Google, several to ask.co.uk and one to Railtrack when he had looked up train times yesterday. There was also one to the Polstar Vodka site he had visited yesterday, in order to brief himself for this afternoon's meeting. Then there was one he did not recognize at all.

It was a long, complex string of letters and slashes. Chris Webb's parting words as he had left were that he should not log on to any unfamiliar website, but Tom had been using the internet for years and years now and had a good understanding of it. He knew that you could pick up a virus from opening an attachment, but he just did not accept you could get one from a website. Cookies, yes. He knew that many retailers used the unscrupulous trick of sending a cookie when you logged on to their site. The cookie would sit in your system and report back to them everything you subsequently looked at on the net. That way they could build individual customer profiles on their database and learn what products people were interested in. But viruses? No way.

He clicked on the address.

Almost instantly the message came up on his screen:

Access denied. Unauthorized login attempt.

'Anything else you need tonight, Tom?'

He looked up. Olivia, holding her handbag, was standing by his desk.

'No, that's fine, thanks.'

She was beaming. 'Got a hot date. Have to go to the hairdresser!'

'Good luck!'

'He's the marketing director for a magazine group. Could be some business there.'

'Go kill!'

'I will!'

He looked back at the screen and clicked on the address again.

Within moments the same message appeared.

Access denied. Unauthorized login attempt.

*

Later that evening – after a larger martini than usual, dinner and almost an entire bottle of a particularly yummy Australian Margaret River Chardonnay, instead of his usual couple of glasses – Tom sat down in his den, opened his laptop, went to his email in-box and started working. More emails came in every few minutes.

Two in succession contained decent repeat orders, which pleased him. One was from the marketing director of one of their major clients, thanking him personally for all his help in making their recent half-centenary such a success.

Feeling distinctly cheered, he scanned the rest of the emails, filing some, deleting some and replying to others. Then another new one appeared.

Dear Mr Bryce

Last night you accessed a website you were unauthorized to visit. Now you have tried to access it again. We do not appreciate uninvited guests. If you inform the police about what you saw or if you ever try to access this site again, what is about to happen to your computer will happen to your wife, Kellie, to your son, Max, and to your daughter, Jessica. Take a good look, then have a hard think.

Your friends at Scarab Productions

Barely before he had time to register the words, they vanished from the screen. Then all the rest of his emails began to vanish, also, as if they were being dissolved in acid.

Within a minute, maybe less, as he watched helplessly, his brain too paralysed to think about switching the machine off, everything on his computer vanished.

He tapped at the keys. But there was nothing, just a blank, black screen.

13

Dennis Ponds, the senior Sussex PRO, had been given the sobriquet Pond Life by many officers. Too many stories got leaked to the press, and the prime suspect was always his office.

A former journalist, he looked more like a City trader than a newspaper man. In his early forties, with slicked-back black hair, mutantly large eyebrows and a penchant for sharp suits, he had the tough task of brokering the increasingly fragile relations between police and public.

Roy Grace, swigging a bottle of mineral water, stared at him across his desk, feeling empathy with the man. Ponds wasn't trusted by many police and the press were always suspicious of his motives. It was not a job anyone could win at. One police PRO had ended up in a sanatorium; another, Grace remembered well, sipped from a hip flask all day long.

Ponds had just laid the entire collection of morning newspapers on Grace's desk and was now sitting in front of him, wringing his hands. 'At least we managed to keep it off the front page, Roy,' he said apologetically, his eyebrows rising like two crows preparing for flight.

They'd been lucky; a Charles and Camilla story took most of the front-page splashes. It was a reflection of modern times that the headless torso story made just a few lines on the inside pages of some papers, and was not mentioned at all in others. But, like the entire half-page of the

Daily Mail open in front him, TWO DEAD AFTER POLICE CAR CHASE had made every single national paper.

'You did your best,' Grace said. Unlike many of his colleagues he recognized the importance of public relations.

'You handled the conference well,' Pond Life said. 'The best thing we can do is build on the torso story today. I've set a con for two. You up for that?'

'Ready to slay 'em,' Grace retorted.

'Can you give me anything for them, in advance?'

Grace fiddled with the bottle cap, screwing it on then unscrewing it again. 'No matches from the fingerprints. We're waiting for a DNA report from the labs. Meantime we're checking through the missing persons lists.'

'Are we telling them the head's missing?'

'I don't want anyone to know that yet. I'm just going to say that the body was badly mutilated, which is hampering the identification.'

'I thought I was the one who doctored the truth for you guys.'

Grace smiled. 'You've obviously been a good teacher.'

The eyebrows now flexing like wings in flight, Ponds asked, 'Any hot leads?'

'Come on, Dennis. Now you're sounding like a journalist.'

'I'd like to throw them a bone.'

'There are several possible matches.'

'Yes, but I hear the most likely is a Brighton girl, a trainee solicitor. Is that right?'

Stunned at this information, Grace asked, 'Where did you hear that?'

The PRO shrugged. 'Word on the street.'

'What street? Who the hell told you that?'

Ponds stared at the Detective Superintendent. 'Three different journalists have already rung my office.'

Grace remembered his conversation with Glenn Branson over his mobile phone yesterday afternoon, when Glenn was speculating who the young woman might be. Had someone listened in? That was near impossible – the new phones sent digitized signals, scrambled. With anger rising inside him and jabbing his bottle at the ceiling, Grace said, 'Who the fuck talked to them? Dennis, that dead girl, whoever she is, has a family. Maybe a husband, maybe a mother, maybe a father, maybe kids, who all loved her. We're not in any state to start speculating.'

'I know that, Roy. But we can't lie to the press, either.'

Thinking as ever about Sandy, Grace said, 'Look, can't you understand that everyone who has a missing loved one who fits her description is going to be glued to every word that's printed, to everything that's said on television and on the radio? I'm not in the business of raising hopes, I'm in the business of finding criminals.'

Dennis Ponds jotted furiously on a shorthand pad. 'That's good,' he said. 'That last line. Can I use that in our press release?'

Grace stared at the man for a moment. So typical of a press officer that. Sound bites. That's all Ponds ever wanted, really. He nodded and looked at his watch, wanting to get over to the Incident Room and brief his team there. Then he needed to get to the post-mortem, which would start at 10 a.m.

There was another reason why he was anxious to attend the post-mortem, and it had nothing to do with the poor young woman whose butchered remains were now being further butchered by the pathologist. It had everything to do with another young woman in the mortuary, with whom he had a date tonight.

Underneath the mountain of newspapers on his desk was the men's style magazine *FHM*. Grace had hoped to grab a few minutes this morning to scan the magazine and see what the hottest men's fashions were. Glenn Branson kept ribbing him about his clothes, his haircut, even his damned watch. His trusty old Seiko – which Sandy had given him – was too small, apparently, too *yesterday*; gave out the wrong signals about him. Probably even gave out the wrong kind of time.

How the hell could you be cool? At nearly thirty-nine was it even worth trying? Then he thought about Cleo Morey, and his stomach did a sort of backflip into wet cement with excitement. And yes, he realized it was. It was *hugely* worth trying.

Dennis Ponds stayed nattering for what felt an eternity, but Grace tolerated it because he knew he needed Ponds onside at the moment, and this was good bonding. Besides, Ponds passed on some interesting gossip about the Chief Constable, the Assistant Chief, Alison Vosper, and then had a moan about Chief Superintendent Gary Weston, Grace's immediate boss, who, Ponds said, seemed to be more interested in horse races and dog tracks than in policing, and that people were starting to notice and talk.

Whatever the truth, it wasn't smart of his ambitious boss to let his reputation slip. As a friend, he ought maybe to say something – but how to? And besides, Grace knew – but did not want to admit to himself – that he sometimes felt a little jealous of Gary Weston's lifestyle, his adoring family, his easy social graces, his effortless rise up through the ranks. He was trying to remember who it was who had said, 'Every time a friend of mine succeeds, something inside me dies.' Because, sadly, it was true.

Finally Dennis Ponds left. As the door closed Grace picked up the magazine and began to browse through it. Within minutes his gloom had returned. There were twenty different fashion looks on twenty different pages. Which would make him look modern and smart for his date? And which a total loser?

There was only one way to find out, he thought, resigning himself to a serious loss of face.

14

Grace left his office and walked through into the Management Support Assistants' area, where Eleanor was stationed along with three other MSAs. Together these four women provided the secretarial backup for all the senior CID officers in CID headquarters, apart from Gary Weston, who had his own full-time assistant.

One of his dislikes about the building was its depersonalizing sense of uniformity. Perhaps simply because it was fairly newly refurbished, or perhaps because it was away from the city itself, the building felt sterile. It didn't have the chunks out of the walls made in scuffles with villains or by someone in a hurry with a metal object, or the threadbare patches of carpet, or the nicotine-stained ceilings of most police stations. There were no cracked windows, busted chairs, wonky desks – all the patina of use that gave a place character – although, admittedly, not always welcome character.

Eleanor had a spray of violets on her desk in a dinky china vase, a photograph of her four kids but curiously not one of her husband, a half-filled-out Sudoku puzzle torn from a newspaper and her plastic lunch box.

She looked up with her habitual nervous smile at him, a cardigan hanging neatly over the back of her chair. After several years of working together there were certain things she knew to do automatically. One was to clear his diary whenever he was the SIO on a major incident.

She told him briefly about three committee meetings

at which she had cancelled his attendance, one on internal procedures, one on the combined UK police forces Cold Case Review Board, and one on the fixture list for the Sussex Police rugby team.

He then received a call on his mobile from Emily Gaylor at the Brighton Trials Unit, his case administrator for the Suresh Hossain trial, telling him he definitely would not be needed in court today. Hossain was a local property villain accused of murdering a business rival.

Clutching his briefcase with his *FHM* magazine securely tucked away inside it, he walked through the green-carpeted, open-plan area lined with desks housing the support staff of the senior officers of the CID. On his left through a wide expanse of glass he could see into the impressive office of Detective Chief Superintendent Gary Weston. For once, Gary was actually there, busy dictating to his assistant.

Reaching the doorway at the far end, Grace held his security card up to the grey Interflex eye, then pushed open the door, entering a long, silent, grey-carpeted corridor which smelled of fresh paint. He passed a large red felt-faced noticeboard headed OPERATION LISBON beneath which was a photograph of a Chinese-looking man with a wispy beard, surrounded by several different photographs of the rocky beach at the bottom of the tall cliffs of local beauty spot Beachy Head, each with a red circle drawn on them. This unidentified man had been found dead four weeks ago at the bottom of the cliff. At first he was assumed to be another jumper, until the post-mortem had revealed that he was already dead at the time he took his plunge.

Grace passed the Outside Enquiry Team office on his left, a large room where detectives drafted in on major incidents would base themselves for the duration, then a door on his left, marked SIO, which would be the temporary office he would move into for this enquiry. Immediately opposite was a door marked MIR ONE, which he entered.

MIR One and MIR Two were the nerve centres for major incidents. Despite opaque windows too high to see out of, One, with its fresh white walls, had an airy feel, good light, good energy. It was his favourite room in the entire head-quarters building. While in other parts of Sussex House he missed the messy buzz of police station incident rooms that he had grown up with, this room felt like a power-house.

It had an almost futuristic feel, as if it could as easily have housed NASA Mission Control in Houston. An L-shaped room divided by three principal workstations, each comprising a long, curved desk with space for up to eight people, it contained massive whiteboards, one marked OPERATION CORMORANT, one marked OPERATION LISBON, one OPERATION SNOWDRIFT, each covered in crime-scene photographs and progress charts. And there was a new one, fresh as of yesterday afternoon, labelled OPERATION NIGHTINGALE, the random name the Sussex Police computer had thrown out for the dismembered torso investigation.

Unlike the workstations in the rest of the building, there was no sign at all of anything personal on the desks or up on the walls in this room. No pictures of families or footballers, no fixture lists, no jokey cartoons. Every single object in this room, apart from the furniture and the business hardware, related to the matters under investigation. There was no banter, either. Just the silence of fierce concentration, the muted warble of phones, the *clack-clack-clack* of paper shuffling from laser printers.

Each of the workstations was manned by a minimum

team of an office manager, normally a detective sergeant or detective inspector, a system supervisor, an analyst, an indexer and a typist. Grace knew most of the faces, but people were too busy to be distracted by the niceties of greetings in here.

No one looked up as he walked across to his own team except for Detective Sergeant Glenn Branson, six foot two inches tall, black and bald as a meteorite, who greeted him with a raised hand. He was dressed in one of his customary sharp suits, today a brown chalk-stripe that made him look more like a prosperous drug dealer than a cop, a white shirt with a starched collar, and a tie that looked like it had been designed by a colour-blind chimpanzee on crack.

'Yo, old-timer!' Glenn Branson said, in a voice loud enough to cause everyone in the room to look up for a moment.

Grace glanced down at the rest of his eight core team members with a brief smile. He had taken most of them straight from his last case, which meant they hadn't had much of a break, if any, but they were a good bunch and had worked well together. From years of experience he had learned that if you had a good team, it was worth keeping it intact if at all possible.

The most senior was Detective Sergeant Bella Moy, cheery-faced beneath a tangle of hennaed brown hair, an open box of Maltesers, as ever, inches from her keyboard. He watched her typing in deep concentration, every few moments her right hand moving from the keyboard as if it were some creature with a life of its own to pluck a chocolate and deliver it to her mouth. She was a slim woman yet ate more than any human being Grace had ever come across.

Next to her sat Detective Constable Nick Nicholl, in his late twenties, short-haired and tall as a beanpole, a zealous detective and a fast football forward who Grace was encouraging to take up rugby, thinking he would be perfect to play in the police team he had been asked to be president of this coming autumn.

Opposite him, reading her way through a thick wodge of computer printout, was rookie DC Emma-Jane Boutwood. A pretty young woman with long blonde hair and a perfect figure, Grace had initially thought her a lightweight when she had first joined his team on the last case. But she had rapidly proved herself a feisty officer, and he had a feeling she had a brilliant future in the force, if she stayed.

'So?' Glenn Branson said. 'I've changed my hunch. How do I convince you my new hunch is right? Teresa Wallington.'

'Who she?' Grace asked.

'A Peacehaven girl. Engaged. Never turned up to her engagement party last night.'

The words twisted something cold deep inside Grace. 'Tell me.'

'I spoke to her fiancé. He's real.'

'I don't know,' Grace said. His instincts told him it was too soon, but he did not want to dampen Glenn Branson's enthusiasm. He studied the photographs of the crime scene on the wall, which had been rushed through at his request. He looked at a close-up of the severed hand, then the grisly shots of the butchered torso in the black bag.

'Trust me, Roy.'

Still looking at the photographs, Grace said, 'Trust you?'

'There you go doing it again!' Branson said.

'Doing what?' Grace asked, puzzled.

'Doing what you always do to me, man. Answering with a question.'

'That's because I never understand what the hell you are on about!'

'Bulllllll-shit!'

'How many missing women do we have who are not yet eliminated?'

'No change from yesterday. Still five. From a reasonable radius of our area. More if we include nationwide.'

'No word from the lab on the DNA yet?' Grace asked.

'Tonight, by six o'clock, they hope they'll know whether the victim is on their database,' DC Boutwood interjected.

Grace glanced at his watch. Fifteen minutes then he needed to go straight on to the mortuary. He did some quick mental arithmetic. According to Frazer Theobald's best guess in the field yesterday, the woman had been dead for less than twenty-four hours. It was not uncommon for someone to go AWOL for one day. But two days would start causing real concern among friends, relatives and work colleagues. Today was likely to be productive in at least establishing a shortlist of who the victim might be.

Addressing DC Nicholl he said, 'Have we got a cast of the footprints?'

'It's being done.'

'*Being* done is not good enough,' Grace said a little testily. 'I said at this morning's briefing I wanted two officers out with casts, going round outdoor clothing stores in the area seeing if there's a match. Chances are someone bought boots for the occasion. If they did, they may be on a CCTV camera. There can't be that many stores that sell heavy-duty boots in the area – make sure I have a report for our six thirty p.m. briefing.'

DC Nicholl nodded and immediately picked up his phone.

'It's the second day she hasn't contacted him,' Branson pressed.

'Who?' Grace said distractedly.

'Teresa Wallington. She's living with her fiancé. There doesn't sound like any reason why she failed to turn up.'

'And the other four on our list?'

'None of those have been seen today either,' he admitted grudgingly.

Although thirty-one, Branson had only been a cop for six years, after a somewhat false start in life as a nightclub bouncer.

Grace liked him a lot; he was smart and caring, and he had great hunches. Hunches were important in police work but they had a downside – they could lead officers to jump to conclusions too quickly, without properly analysing other possibilities, and then subconsciously select evidence to fit their hunch. Sometimes Grace had to curb Branson's enthusiasm for his own good.

But at this moment it wasn't just Branson's hunch on the case that Grace needed him for. It was on something distinctly extracurricular.

'Want to take a drive to the mortuary with me?'

Branson stared at him with raised eyebrows. 'Shit, man, is that where you take all your dates?'

Grace grinned. Branson was closer to the mark than he realized.

15

Tom Bryce was seated in a long, narrow ground-floor boardroom in a small office block on an industrial estate close to Heathrow airport – so close that the jumbo he could see out of the window seemed to be on a flight path that would land it slap in the middle of this room. It screamed overhead, flaps lowered, wheels down, passing over the roof like the shadow of a giant fish, with what seemed like inches to spare.

The room was tacky. It had brown suede walls decorated with framed posters of horror and science fiction films, a twenty-seater bronze meeting table that looked as if it had been looted from a Tibetan temple, and extremely uncomfortable high-back chairs, no doubt designed to keep meetings short.

His customer, Ron Spacks, was a former rock promoter, wheezy and nudging sixty. Sporting a toupee that looked as if it hadn't been put on properly and teeth that were far too immaculate for his age and his substance-ravaged face, Spacks sat opposite Tom, dressed in a very faded and threadbare Grateful Dead T-shirt, jeans and sandals, sifting through the BryceRight catalogue and muttering 'Yeah' to himself every few moments when he alighted on something of interest.

Tom sipped his beaker of coffee and waited patiently. Gravytrain Distributing was one of the largest DVD distributors in the country. The gold medallion around Ron

Spacks's neck, the rhinestone rings on his fingers, the black Ferrari in the lot outside, all testified to his success.

Spacks, as he had proudly told Tom on previous occasions, had started with a stall off the Portobello Road, flogging second-hand DVDs when no one even knew what DVDs were. Tom had little doubt that much of the man's empire had been founded on pirated merchandise, but he was in no state to make moral choices about his customers. In the past Spacks had ordered large, and always paid on the nail.

'Yeah,' Spacks said. 'You see, Tom, my customers don't want nothing fancy. What you got new this year?'

'CD beer mats – on page forty-two, I think. You can have them overprinted.'

Spacks turned to the page. 'Yeah,' he said, in a tone of voice that said quite the reverse. 'Yeah,' he repeated. 'So how much would a hundred thousand cost – get 'em down to a quid, could yer?'

Tom felt lost without his computer. It was at the office, once more being resuscitated by Chris Webb. All the costings for his products were on that machine, and without them he daren't start discounting – particularly on a potential order of this size.

'I'll have to get back to you. I can email you later today.'

'Have to be a quid max, yeah,' Spacks said, and popped open a can of Coke. 'I'm really looking for close to seventy pence.'

Tom's mobile rang. Glancing at the display he saw it was Kellie and pressed to terminate the call.

Seventy pence was no go, he knew that for sure – they cost him more than that – but he decided not to tell Spacks for the moment. 'I think that would be tight,' he said tactfully.

'Yeah. Tell you something else I'm interested in. About twenty-five gold Rolexes, yeah.'

'Gold Rolexes? Real ones?'

'Don't want no copy rubbish – the real deal. Want 'em etched with a logo. Can you get me a price? Need 'em quickly. Middle of next week.'

Tom tried not to show his surprise, particularly after Spacks had told him he didn't want anything fancy. Now he was talking about watches that cost thousands of pounds each. Then the phone rang again.

It was Kellie once more, and this worried Tom; ordinarily she would just have left a message. Maybe one of the kids was ill? 'Mind if I answer?' he said to Spacks. 'My wife.'

'She who must be obeyed must be answered. The Oyster – that's the classic Rolex, innit?'

Tom, who knew about as much of the world of gold Rolexes as he did about chicken farming in the Andes, said, 'Yep, definitely.' Then with a nod to Spacks he picked up the phone and accepted the call. 'Hi, honey.'

Kellie sounded strange and vulnerable. 'Tom, I'm sorry to bother you, but I've had a phone call that's spooked me.'

Standing up and moving away from Spacks, Tom said, 'Darling, what happened? Tell me.'

'I went out to have my nails done. About five minutes after I got back in the phone rang. A man asked if I was Mrs Bryce, and I – I said yes. Then he asked was I Mrs Kellie Bryce, and I said yes. Then he hung up.'

Outside it was a damp, rain-flecked day and the air conditioning made this room unnecessarily cold. But suddenly something far colder squirmed deep inside him, cupping hard, icy fingers around his soul.

The threat last night? The threat in those seconds

before his computer memory had been erased. Was this call connected with that email he had received?

If you inform the police about what you saw or if you ever try to access this site again, what is about to happen to your computer will happen to your wife, Kellie, to your son, Max, and to your daughter, Jessica.

Except of course he had not informed the police or tried to access the site again. He tried to think through the possibilities. 'Did you try and do a ring-back? One four seven one?'

'Yes. It said number withheld.'

'Where are you now, darling?' he asked.

'Home.'

He looked at his watch and saw his hand was shaking. It was just past midday. 'Listen, it's probably nothing, probably just a wrong number. I don't know. Maybe someone checking an eBay delivery or something? There could be a ton of reasons,' he said, trying to sound reassuring, but not doing a good job of convincing himself. In his mind all he could see was the beautiful long-haired young woman in the room, being butchered by the man.

'I'm just in a meeting. I'll call you back as quickly as I can.'

'I love you,' she said.

Glancing at Spacks, who was thumbing through more pages of the catalogue, he said, 'Me too. I'll be five minutes, ten max.'

'Wimmin!' Spacks said sympathetically when he hung up.

Tom nodded.

'Can't win with wimmin.'

'No,' Tom agreed.

'So. Rolex watches. I need a price for twenty-five men's gold Rolex watches. With a small engraving on them. Delivery end of next week.'

Tom was so concerned about Kellie that the potential value of the request barely registered. 'What kind of engraving?'

'A microdot. Tiny.'

'Leave it with me. I'll get back to you. I'll get you the best price.'

'Yeah.'

16

Glenn Branson's driving had always made Grace uneasy, but since Branson had taken his advanced police driving course, as part of his application to transfer to the National Crime Squad, it scared him witless. To make things worse, his colleague always had the car radio tuned to a rap station, with the volume loud enough to make Grace's brain feel like it was inside a blender.

The APD course enabled drivers to take part in high-speed pursuits, so in order to show off his prowess, Branson had chosen the only route that took them along a stretch of road where it would be possible to have a really bad high-speed smash without trying too hard. It was a mile-and-a-half-long stretch of two-lane tarmac, which ran like a spine across the open Downland countryside that lay between the industrial estate where CID head-quarters was and central Brighton.

It was like a racetrack. Grace could see the road for a mile ahead: the two gentle bends, the straight, the sharp right-hander at the end of it, and then half a mile on the sharp left-hander where there had last been a fatal smash less than a week ago. He eyed a lorry heading towards them and then looked at Branson, hoping he had noticed that they would probably hit the right-hander at about the same time. But Branson was concentrating on the fast, sweeping left-hander coming up.

The speedometer showed an illegal 95 mph and was climbing. Drops of drizzle flecked the windscreen. 'See, man!' Branson shouted above the hammering voice of Jay-Z. 'You move out to the right, gives you the best view around the bend, then you clip the apex. That's how they do it in Formula One.'

Grace whistled through his teeth as they clipped the apex as well as a chunk of mud, grass and nettles from the verge. The car lurched alarmingly. His shirt felt clammy.

The lorry was getting nearer.

Grace checked the tensioning on his seat belt, then the speedometer. The unmarked police Vectra was now doing 110 mph. He considered asking whether his colleague was going to brake at all before they reached the ninety-degree right-hander now only a few hundred yards ahead, but he was nervous that any conversation might distract Branson. Up on a windy knoll to his left, Grace saw two men pulling golf trolleys.

He wondered if his last moments on earth would be spent in the mangled wreckage of a police Vauxhall that smelled of stale burgers, cigarettes and someone else's sweat, being gawped at through the busted windscreen by two helpless old geezers in golfing gear while a rapper he had never met shouted abuse at him.

'So, my hunch,' Branson said, right on the apex of the bend, the front of the massive truck just a hundred yards in front of them.

Grace gripped both sides of his seat.

Defying all the laws of physics, the car somehow made it around the bend, still pointing in the right direction. Now there was just one more dangerous bend and then they would be in a 40 mph zone and relative safety.

'I'm all ears.'

'All I can hear is your heartbeat,' Branson said with a grin.

'I'm lucky to still have one.' Grace turned the radio down. As if in response, Branson slowed the car down.

'Teresa Wallington, she's living with her fiancé, right. So they plan an engagement party at Al Duomo restaurant for Tuesday night – has to be midweek cos he works strange shifts. Got relatives and friends from all over the country to come down, right?'

Grace said nothing. Although they were in the calmer waters of a 40 mph limit they were not out of danger yet. While Branson was talking, and fiddling with the radio at the same time, the car was drifting steadily across the road into the path of an oncoming bus. Just as Grace was about to grab the wheel in panic, Branson appeared to notice the bus and unhurriedly manoeuvred the car back on to the left-hand side of the road.

'Then she doesn't show,' Branson said. 'No phone call, no text, *nada*.'

'So the fiancé murdered her?'

'I've got him coming in this afternoon. Thought we'd put him in the suite, take a look at him.'

There was a small Witness Interview Suite at Sussex House, which could be monitored through a camera from an adjoining room. Its main purpose was to talk to vulnerable witnesses. By watching and filming them officers were able to study their body language and generally assess their credibility. But sometimes Grace found it a helpful place to perform the first interview on someone who might turn out to be a suspect – often as not the husband or lover of a murder victim.

In the comfortable red armchairs of the Witness Interview Suite people were more likely to give something away than on the hard old upright chairs in the grim interview rooms at Brighton police station. The videotapes could be given to a psychologist for profiling in some cases. It was for this same reason that spouses, partners or lovers of murder victims were sometimes put on television as quickly as possible – to see what body language they used.

'So you've gone off your trainee solicitor? I thought you were sweet on her,' Grace teased.

'Spoke to her best friend. She told me she's done this before – vanishing off the radar for a couple of days, without explanation. The only thing different is she's never been absent from work before.'

'You're saying she's flaky?'

Branson, fiddling with the radio again, said, 'Sounds to me.'

Grace wondered if Branson had noticed the traffic backed up ahead at a red light – and that they were heading, far too rapidly, towards the back of a garbage truck. This time he did something. 'GLENN!'

Branson's response was to stamp on the brakes, prompting a screech of tyres from behind. Grace turned his head to see a small red car snaking to a halt, inches from rear-ending them.

'What was that driving course thing you went on?' Grace asked. 'Remind me about it? Did they hand out the notes in Braille?'

'Oh fuck off,' Glenn replied. 'You're a wimp of a passenger, you know that? A real back-seat driver.'

Grace decided he would feel a lot safer in the back seat.

The engine stalled and Branson restarted it. 'Remember the start of *The Italian Job*, when he drives that Lamborghini into the tunnel and – boom!'

'In the remake?'

'No, tosspot, that was crap. The original. The Michael Caine one.'

'I remember the coach at the end. Hanging over the edge of the cliff. That's what your driving reminds me of.'

'Yeah, well, you drive like an old woman.'

Grace took the copy of *FHM* out of his case. 'Can you pull over for a sec; I need your advice.'

When the lights turned green, Branson drove a short distance then pulled into a bus stop. Grace opened the magazine and showed him a double-page spread of male models in different fashions.

Branson gave him a strange look. 'You turning gay or something?'

'I have a date.'

'With one of these?'

'Very witty. I have a date tonight, a serious date. You seem to be the Sussex Police style guru; I need some advice.'

Branson stared at the photographs for a moment. 'I told you already, right, you should do something about your hair.'

'Easy for you to say as you don't have any.'

'I shave my head, man, because it's well cool.'

'I'm not shaving mine.'

'I told you before, I know a great hairdresser. Ian Habben at The Point. Get some highlights put in, keep your sides short, but grow a bit on top and get it all gelled up.'

'I don't have time to grow it by eight o'clock tonight. But I do have time to get some kit.'

Branson suddenly gave his friend a really warm smile. 'You're serious, man; you really do have a hot date! I'm pleased for you.' He squeezed Roy's shoulder. 'It's about time you started getting yourself a life again. So who is she? Anyone I know?'

'Maybe.' Grace was touched by his friend's reaction.

'Cut the mystery crap. Who is she? Not that Emma-Jane? She's well fit!'

'No, not her – anyhow she's far too young for me.'

'So who? Bella?'

'Just tell me what I should wear.'

'Not the old git suit you're wearing now.'

'Come on, what do you think?'

'So where are you taking her?'

'Out for an Italian. Latin in the Lanes.'

'That's the old lady's favourite restaurant! Ari loves the seafood mixed grill.' He beamed. 'Hey, you're spending serious dosh on her!'

Grace shrugged. 'What do you think I should do, take her to McDonald's?'

Ignoring the comment, Glenn Branson said, 'Watch how she eats.'

'Why's that?'

'You can tell from how a woman eats how she is going to be in bed.'

'I'll remember to watch.'

Then Branson was silent for some moments, studying the magazine. He flipped over a few pages. 'For someone of your age, I wouldn't try to look too young.'

'Thanks.'

Branson pointed at a model wearing an unstructured casual beige jacket over a white T-shirt, jeans and brown loafers. 'That's you. Can see you in that. Mr Cool. Go to Luigi's in Bond Street; they'll have something like that.'

'Want to come with me after the mortuary – help me choose something?'

'Only if I get to date you afterwards.'

There was a loud blast on a horn. Branson and Grace both turned to see the nose of a bus filling the rear window.

Branson put the car in gear and drove on. A few minutes later they were driving downhill into the busy gyratory system, past a giant Sainsbury's supermarket to their right and then a strategically placed undertaker's. Then they turned sharp left in through wrought-iron gates attached to brick pillars bearing the small, unwelcome sign, BRIGHTON AND HOVE CITY MORTUARY.

Grace had no doubt that there were worse places in the world, and in that respect he had led a sheltered life. But for him this place was about as bad as it got. He remembered an expression he had once heard, 'the banality of evil'. And this was a banal place. It was a bland building with a grim aura, a long, single-storey structure with grey pebbledash rendering on the walls and a covered drive-in on one side high enough to take an ambulance.

The mortuary was a transit stop on the one-way journey to a grave or crematorium oven for those who had died suddenly, violently or inexplicably – or from some fast-onset disease like viral meningitis where a post-mortem might provide medical insights that could one day help the living. Normally he found himself shuddering involuntarily as he passed through these gates, but today was different.

Today he felt positively elated. Not because of the dead body he was coming to study, but because of the woman who worked here. His date for tonight.

But he wasn't about to tell Glenn Branson that.

17

Tom carefully reversed his Audi out of the bay in the Gravy-train Distributing parking lot, nervous of hitting Ron Spacks's Ferrari, then stuck his phone into the hands-free cradle and dialled Kellie, deep in thought.

That image of the woman being butchered was chilling him, going round and round in his mind. It was a movie, must have been – there were hundreds of movies he had never seen – just a scene from a thriller. Or maybe a trailer for one. You could create all kinds of effects these days. It *was* a film.

It had to have been.

But he knew he was just trying to convince himself. The trashing of his computer, the threatening email? He shivered as if a dark cloud had slipped across his soul. Just what the hell had he really seen on Tuesday night?

Then he heard Kellie's voice, a tad more cheery now. 'Hiya,' she said.

'Darling?' he said. 'Sorry about that, I was with a very difficult customer.'

'No, it's OK, it's probably just me. It's just – you know – it was spooky.'

As he drove along past a row of factory and warehouse units, another plane was coming in to land, and he raised his voice above the din. 'Tell me exactly what happened.'

'It was just a phone call. The man asked if this was the Bryce residence, then if I was Mrs Kellie Bryce, and when I told him I was, he hung up.'

'You know what it is?' Tom said. 'It's probably one of those con men. I read about them in the paper the other day – there's a whole ring operating. They call up people pretending to be from their bank, saying it's a security check; they get them to confirm a whole load of stuff about their house, their passwords, then their bank details and credit cards. It could have been one of those interrupted in mid-flow.'

'Maybe.' She did not sound any more convinced than he felt. 'He had a strange accent.'

'What kind of an accent?'

'Sort of European, not English.'

'And he didn't say anything else at all?'

'No.'

'Are you expecting any deliveries?'

There was an awkward silence. 'Not exactly.'

Shit. She *had* bought something. 'What do you mean *not exactly*, darling?'

'The bidding hasn't closed.'

Tom didn't even want to know what today's extravaganza might be. 'Listen, I'll try to get home early. I have to go into town and collect my laptop – it's being fixed again.'

'Still wrong?'

'Yes, some glitch that won't go away. How's the weather?'

'Brightening up.'

'Maybe if I get down in time we could have a barbecue with the kids?'

Her response was strange, almost evasive, he thought as he pulled out onto the main road, looking for the signs to London at a roundabout a short distance ahead. 'Yes,' she said. 'Well, OK, maybe.'

All the way, on the slow crawl along the M4 bottleneck,

thanks to John Prescott's cursed bus lane (for which many times Tom could have boiled the Deputy PM's testicles in oil), he was trying to work out all the reasons someone might have made that call and then hung up. And the most likely was a delivery driver who got cut off. Simple as that. Nothing to get worried about.

Except he did worry, because he loved Kellie and Max and Jessica just so damned much.

His parents had been killed in a car smash in fog on the M1, when he was twenty, and his only sibling, his brother Zack, five years younger than him, who had never really got over it, was a dope-head dropout living in Bondi Beach in Sydney, doing odd jobs and a bit of surfing. Apart from Zack and a maternal uncle who lived in Melbourne who he had not seen since he was ten – and who hadn't bothered to come to his parents' funeral – Kellie, Max and Jessica were all the family he had, and that made them even more precious still.

Just as the motorway ended and became Cromwell Road, his phone rang. No number showed in the caller display.

Tom pressed the button to answer it. 'Hello?'

A male voice with a strong eastern European accent asked, 'Is that Tom Bryce speaking?'

Guardedly he said, 'It is, yes.'

Then the man hung up.

18

The remains of the dead woman lay on a steel trolley in the sterile post-mortem room, bagged in translucent plastic like frozen produce from a supermarket.

The torso was wrapped in one sheet; the two legs and the hand that had been recovered from the field of rape were each parcelled separately. The hand was in a small bag, and there was a separate bag tied over each of the feet – this was done to protect any fibres or skin or soil particles that might be lodged under the nails. Then one large sheet had been wrapped around everything.

It was this outer plastic sheet that Dr Frazer Theobald was very carefully removing, painstakingly checking for anything, however microscopic, that might have fallen from the dead woman's skin or hair, which could have come from her killer.

Grace had been to this place more times than he cared to remember. The first time had been some twenty years back, when he was a rookie cop attending his first post-mortem. He could still recall it vividly, seeing a sixty-year-old man who had fallen off a ladder, laid out stark naked, devoid of all human dignity with two tags bearing his name – one buff and one green – hanging from his big toe.

When the mortician had cut around the back of the scalp, just beneath the hairline, then had peeled it forward so that it hung down over the face, exposing the skull, and the pathologist, wielding a rotary bandsaw, began to grind into the top of the skull, Grace had done what more than a few rookie cops do, which was to turn a horrible shade of green, stagger out to the toilet and throw up.

He didn't throw up any more, but the whole place still weirded him every time he came here. In part it was the reek of Trigene disinfectant that you carried away with you, in every pore of your skin, for hours after you had left the building; in part the diffused light that came in through the opaque windows, giving this room an ethereal quality. And then there was always the sense that the mortuary was a depot, a repository, a brutal halfway house between dying and resting in peace.

Bodies were kept here until the cause of death was ascertained, and in some cases until they had been formally identified, then they would be released to an undertaker under the directions of relatives. Occasionally bodies were never identified. There was one, of an elderly man, in a fridge in the back storage room, which had been there for nearly a year. He had been found dead on a park bench, but no one had claimed him.

Grace wondered sometimes, in his darker moments, if that might happen to him one day. He had no wife, no kids, no parents – just his sister, and if he outlived her? But he never dwelt on that too much – he had enough problems just with living – although he did think about death a lot. Particularly in here. Sometimes, staring at a body on a trolley or at the freezer locker doors, a chill would seep deep through his veins as he wondered how many ghosts this building contained.

Cleo Morey, the Chief Mortician or Senior Pathology Technician, to give her her formal title, helped Dr Theobald lift the large outer sheet away and then carefully folded it for storage; it would be sent to a forensics laboratory if the body yielded no clues. Grace let his eyes linger on her for some moments. Even in her working clothes she looked strikingly beautiful, he thought, a view shared by everyone who met her.

Then the Home Office pathologist unwrapped the torso and began the laborious task of measuring and recording the dimensions of each of the thirty-four stab wounds.

The flesh looked paler than yesterday, and although much of it, including the dead woman's breasts, was lacerated into strips of crimson pulp, he could see the first signs of marbling starting to occur.

The room was dominated by two steel post-mortem tables, one fixed, the other, on which the remains of the woman lay, on castors. There was a blue hydraulic hoist and a row of fridges with floor-to-ceiling doors. The walls were tiled in grey and a drain gully ran all the way round. Along one wall was a row of sinks and a coiled yellow hose. Along another was a wide work surface, a metal cutting board and a glass-fronted display cabinet filled with instruments, some packs of Duracell batteries and grisly souvenirs that no one else wanted – mostly pacemakers – removed from victims.

Next to this was a wallchart itemizing the name of the deceased, with columns for the weights of each brain, lungs, heart, liver, kidneys and spleen. All that was written on it so far was ANON. WOMAN.

It was a sizeable room but it felt crowded this morning. In addition to the Home Office pathologist and the Chief Mortician, there was Darren, the Assistant Mortician, a sharp, good-looking and pleasant-natured lad of twenty with fashionably spiky black hair, Joe Tindall, the senior

SOCO officer, who was photographing the ruler in position on each stab wound, Glenn Branson and himself.

The visitors wore protective green gowns with white cuffs and either plastic overshoes or white wellington boots. The pathologist and the two morticians wore blue pyjamas and heavy-duty green aprons, and the pathologist had a mask hanging loosely below his chin. Grace looked at Cleo Morey, caught her eye, then the brief but very definite grin she gave him, and his nerves jangled.

He felt like an excited kid. And it was wrong, it was unprofessional – every ounce of his concentration should be on this case right now – but he couldn't help it. Cleo Morey was distracting him and that was a fact.

They had already been out on a date just a few days ago. Well, it had been a date of sorts – a quick drink in a pub which got cut even shorter by a phone call calling him urgently back to work.

God, she was gorgeous, he thought. And however many times he saw her, he could never quite square this young, leggy woman in her late twenties with her long blonde hair, English-rose face and quick brain, with working in this place, doing one of the grimmest jobs in the world. With her looks she could have been a model or an actress, and with her brains she could probably have had any career she set her mind to – and she had chosen this. Long hours on call day and night. At a moment's notice she would get summoned to a riverbank, to a burned-out warehouse, to a shallow woodland grave to recover a body. To prepare the body for the pathologist to carry out the post-mortem, then to reassemble it as well as possible, no matter how burned or decomposed, for identification by relatives, and to offer them some succour, some glimpse of hope that their loved one's death had not been quite as bad as the body indicated.

As he watched Dr Theobald press a ruler against the fifth stab wound, right above the young woman's belly button, he did not envy Cleo her task on this one. With luck, identification would be done by DNA, he thought; no parent should ever have to see this sight. Yet, he knew only too well just how important it was to some people to see for themselves. Often, despite all efforts to dissuade them, loved ones would insist on a viewing, just to see them one more time, to say goodbye.

Closure.

Something he'd never had. And that helped him to understand the need for it. Without closure you had no hope of moving on. Which was why he'd been stuck in a state of limbo since Sandy's disappearance. There was a hot young medium coming to Brighton tomorrow, performing to just a small audience at a holistic health centre, and Grace had bought a ticket. It would probably turn out to be another blank, he knew, but the British and international police had exhausted every conventional avenue.

Cleo shot him a glance, a warm, definitely flirty glance. Careful to check first that Branson wasn't watching, he shot her back a wink.

Christ, you are so gorgeous! he thought, heavy-hearted and feeling so damned guilty about Sandy. It was as if still, after all these years, he was being unfaithful to her by dating another woman.

His mobile phone beeped, signalling a text message. He pulled it from his inside pocket and glanced at the display. It was from DC Nicholl back at the Major Incident Suite.

Teresa Wallington eliminated.

Immediately Grace sidled up to Branson and motioned him over to the rear of the room. 'I think you need to work on your hunch technique,' Grace said to him. Then he held up the phone for his colleague to read the message.

'Shit. I had a feeling – like I *really* had a feeling about this,' the Detective Sergeant said. He looked so despondent Grace felt sorry for him.

Giving him a pat of encouragement, he said, 'Glenn, in the movie *Se7en* Morgan Freeman had a hunch that didn't turn out quite right either.'

Glancing sideways at him, Branson said, 'Are you implying this is some trait common to black cops?'

'Nah, he's an actor.' Grace eyed Cleo again, watching her streaked blonde hair swinging, incongruously pretty, against the green apron strap around her neck. 'Maybe it's just common to big, bald gorillas.' He gave him another friendly pat.

Then he dialled Nick from the landline phone on the work surface beside him. The new digital phones the police were being issued with scrambled all conversations, but at present their conventional mobile phones were simple to eavesdrop on, so he avoided using them on anything sensitive.

'She got cold feet about the wedding,' Nick Nicholl explained. 'Did a runner. Now she's come back very contrite.'

'Sweet,' Grace said sarcastically. 'I'll tell Glenn. He loves a good weepie with a happy ending.'

Silence down the phone. DC Nick Nicholl possessed a good brain but a sense of humour bypass.

They ran through the remaining shortlist of missing

women who fitted the description, and Grace told Nicholl to make sure the police had something that DNA could be extracted from, from each of the four women. Nicholl updated him on the state of the continuing inch-by-inch grid search of the area surrounding where the body had been found, for the girl's head and left hand. Privately, Grace did not expect them to turn up. The hand possibly, because a dog or a fox might have run off with it. But he doubted they would ever find the head.

He made another quick call, to check on the progress of the trial of Suresh Hossain – a case which had become very personal to him. It was a difficult case; the Crown Prosecution Service had made some blunders, and he hadn't handled it as well as he should have done. He'd been stupid in taking a piece of evidence, a shoe belonging to the murdered man, to a medium. The defence counsel had found out about it and humiliated him in court.

Dr Frazer Theobald was making his usual slow but thorough progress. His examination of the dead woman's stomach indicated she had not eaten in the immediate hours before she was killed, which would give some help in gauging when she might have died – early in the evening rather than late, if she had not had an evening meal. There was no smell of alcohol either – which would have been present after just a couple of drinks – which meant it was unlikely although not impossible that she had been to a bar.

Shortly after half past twelve, when Grace stepped away again, this time to call Dennis Ponds to check on the 2 p.m. press conference, Glenn Branson walked over to him, looking uncharacteristically shaken and bilious.

'You'd better come and look at this, Roy.'

Grace killed the call he was about to make and followed him across the room. Everyone was standing around the table in what looked to him like shocked silence. As he approached he could smell the vile stench of excrement and bowel gases.

The woman's torso had been opened up, her ribcage was exposed and he could see that her heart, lungs and the rest of her vital organs had been removed, and lay waiting to be bagged and put back inside her chest when the post-mortem was finished, leaving an empty carcass.

On the metal-edged dissecting tray, raised some inches above her, was a length of pale brown tube which looked like a long sausage. It was about an inch in diameter, lying in a mess of blood, excrement and mucus. Dr Theobald had made an incision in it, which he was holding open with forceps for everyone's benefit.

The pathologist turned to him, his moustachioed face even more serious than usual. Then he pointed. 'I think you should take a look at that, Roy.'

Anatomy had never been Grace's strong point, and sometimes when peering at the organs of a cadaver it took him some time to orient himself and figure out what was what. He looked down, trying to work out what this might be. Part of the intestines, he thought. Then, as he was look-ing, Dr Theobald used the forceps to open the incision he had made further, and now Grace could see something in there.

Something that everyone else in the room had already seen.

Something that made him stare, for some moments, in complete, mind-boggled shock.

Then he took an involuntary step back as if he wanted to get away from it.

'Jesus,' he said, closing his eyes for an instant, feeling the blood draining from his head. His stomach was boiling in shock and revulsion.

'OhmyGod.'

19

It was a shiny, fat, black beetle, an inch long, with spiny feet and a ribbed back, and it had a single curved horn protruding from its head.

Frazer Theobald picked it up, delicately, with a pair of tweezers and held it aloft for all to see. The creature was motionless.

Grace who had never cared for beetles, took another step back. In truth he was not good at creepy-crawlies in general; he had been scared of spiders all his life and was very definitely wary of beetles. And this was – oh Jesus – one seriously horrible-looking creature.

He caught Cleo's eye and saw a flash of revulsion in her face.

'That's what, exactly?' Branson said, his voice quavering, pointing down at the dissecting table, involuntarily rescuing Grace from asking a potentially dumb question.

'Her rectum, of course,' the pathologist said dismissively.

Branson turned away, looking repulsed. Then he watched as Theobald brought the beetle towards his nostrils, the long fronds of his moustache twitching, close to becoming entwined in the hair-like spines on the beetle's legs.

The pathologist sniffed deeply. 'Formaldehyde,' he announced. Then he proffered the insect to Grace for verification. The Detective Superintendent fought his revulsion and sniffed also. Instantly he caught the whiff that reminded him of his school biology dissection classes.

'Yes,' he agreed. Then he looked down again at the dissection table.

'That's why I didn't detect it on a visual examination of the rectum – it had been inserted too far up.'

Grace stared at the neck of the tube on the table, the dead young woman's sphincter. 'In your view, Frazer, inserted before or after her death?'

'I can't tell.'

Then he asked the question that was on everyone's lips. 'Why?'

'That's for you lot to figure out,' Theobald said.

Branson was standing on the far side of the room, leaning against the work surface adjoining the sink. 'Remember *Silence of the Lambs*?'

Grace remembered it well. He had read the novel, one of the few books that had genuinely scared him, and had seen the film.

'The victims all had a moth stuffed down their throats,' Branson said. 'It was a death's head moth.'

'Yes,' Grace said. 'It was the killer's signature.'

'So maybe this is *our* killer's signature.'

Grace stared at the beetle, which the pathologist was still holding aloft. He could swear for an instant that its legs were twitching, that the thing was still alive. 'Anyone know what kind of beetle it is?' he asked.

'A stag beetle?' Cleo Morey suggested.

'Not with that horn.' Darren, the Assistant Mortician interjected. 'I studied entomology as part of my course. I don't remember anything like that in the UK. I don't think it's native.'

'Someone's imported it?' Grace said. 'They've gone to

the trouble of importing it, then inserted it up her rectum? Why?'

There was a long silence. Finally the pathologist inserted the insect in a plastic bag and labelled it. 'We need to find out all we can about it,' he said.

Grace was thinking hard. Over the years he had from necessity read as much as he could find on the mentality of murderers. Most murders were domestic, perpetrated by people who knew their victims. These were one-offs, frequently crimes of passion committed in the heat of the moment. But a small percentage of murderers were the truly warped ones who killed for gratification and thought they could outwit the police – sometimes to the extent of playing games with them.

These were the killers who often left some kind of signature. A taunt. *This is my clue; catch me if you can, you dumb mother of a cop!*

Grace looked at his watch. There was one person he knew who could tell him, probably instantly, what kind of beetle this was. Whether that would be of any real help or not, he had no idea, but just maybe it would yield a clue.

'We need to keep this from the press,' he said. 'Total radio silence on this, everyone, OK?'

All nodded. They understood his reasoning. With a clue as unusual as this they would know instantly that if a caller claiming to be the killer could describe this, he was their man. It could save them hours, if not days, of sifting through false leads.

Grace told Branson to get one of the team at the Incident Room to trawl the UK for any other murder victims where there had been a beetle found at the scene. Then he asked the pathologist a stupid question. He knew it was stupid, but it still needed to be asked. 'The beetle was definitely dead before it was inserted?'

'I doubt anyone would keep a supply of formaldehyde up their rectum,' the pathologist replied, just very slightly sarcastically. He pointed at a small glass vial on the dissecting tray which contained a murky-looking fluid. 'There is no trace in there – that's the bowel lining mucus.'

Grace nodded and did a quick mental calculation. If he left straight after the press conference there would be time to show the beetle to the one man he was certain would be able to identify it.

20

'Viking north-west, veering south-east five or six, becoming variable three or four later. Showers. Good. North Utsire, South Utsire, north-west, four or five first in South Utsire, otherwise variable three or four,' the Weatherman said.

He was driving his car, a crappy little white Fiat Panda with terminal rust. On the radio, some plonker, who seriously did not know what he was talking about, was explaining how easy it was to perform identity theft. But driving along the road beside Shoreham Harbour, the commercial port adjoining the City of Brighton and Hove, made the shipping forecast definitely relevant.

On his left was the Sussex Motor Yacht Club, followed by a warehouse, on his right a row of terraced houses. He was on his way again to see Jonas Smith – or Carl Venner, his real name – and the fat man was beginning to piss him off. He had only hooked up with Venner to get revenge on the people he worked for, who really pissed him off big time. Now he had to drop everything each time *Venner* summoned him, because *Venner* refused to communicate by phone or email, like any *normal* person. There always had to be a ridiculous charade to go through, either meeting him in a hotel room, like the last time, in case he was followed, or on very rare occasions in his office, like now.

At the end of the row of houses he passed a yacht chandlery, then pushed the indicator into right-turn mode, waited for a gap in the traffic and accelerated, the engine spluttering under the sudden load, across into the Portslade Units industrial estate. It was easy to spot the building he was heading for; it was the one with the helicopter, like a mutant black insect, parked on the roof. Venner's private helicopter.

He drove past an antiques depot, then pulled into the carport of a massive modern warehouse alongside a large black Mercedes which he knew was one of the cars that belonged to Venner. The sign on the wall said OCEANIC & OCCIDENTAL IMPORT/EXPORT.

He killed the engine, but continued to listen to Radio Five Live, wondering whether to use his mobile phone to call in and correct the plonker. But he was short of time; he needed to get back to the office. Muttering to himself, 'Forties, Cromarty, Tyne, Dogger, north-west seven to severe gale force nine,' he climbed out of the car, locked it and checked each door methodically, walked up to the side entrance and, showing his face to the lens of the security camera, pressed the buzzer.

There was a *klunk* followed by a rasping buzz as the lock released. He pushed open the heavy-duty door and entered a ground-floor space, the size of a football pitch, filled with massive grey sea containers. Two surly eastern Europeans in overalls, one bald with a tattooed head, the other with a long mane of black hair, watched him, gave a brief nod of recognition and turned their attention back to a container being hoisted into the air on a vast mobile lift.

The Weatherman had hacked into the company's computer system and read the manifests. He knew what was inside the containers. Half had legitimate goods, mostly machine parts and agricultural chemicals, the other half contained stolen exotic cars for Russia and the Middle

East, military equipment destined for Syria and North Korea, and out-of-date pharmaceuticals for Nigeria.

But he wasn't about to tell Venner he knew that. It was just useful knowledge. He just wanted to see him, tell him what he had found out, then get back to the office. And tonight he had a date with Mona – well, a date on an internet chat site. His third with her. Mona worked for an IT company in Boise, Idaho in America; they talked mostly about the environment.

But the big thing about her was she had read Robert Anton Wilson, and they had so much else in common. She agreed with the Weatherman that quite soon people would be able to download their brains into computers and live a virtual existence, freed from all the crap restraints of being a biological human being.

He rode the industrial-sized, bare elevator up to the floor above. 'Decreasing in East Forties and East Dogger,' he informed Mick Brown, who was standing there to greet him as the doors opened, wearing a grey Prada tracksuit and white loafers.

The Albanian had never heard the UK shipping forecast. He had no idea what the Weatherman was on about, and didn't care. He chewed a piece of gum for some moments with his mouth open, revealing most of his tiny, white incisors to the Weatherman, staring at him, taking in his limp expression, his limp hair, his limp white shirt, beige trousers, his clumsy grey shoes. He was checking for signs of a weapon, not that he thought the weird Mr Frost would be capable of carrying one, but it was something he was paid to do, so he checked all the same.

Frost had no muscles; he looked weak. It was going to be easy to kill this one when the time came. But no sport either. The Albanian preferred fighters; it was good to knock someone about a little while they were trying to knock you back, especially women. 'Mobile?' he said in his guttural accent.

'I didn't bring it.'

'Left? In car or office?'

'Office,' he lied. 'That's what I was told.'

Directly opposite the elevator was a solid-looking door with a security keypad and a closed-circuit camera. The Albanian pulled a card from his pocket, pressed it to the pad, then pushed open the door, beckoning the Weatherman to follow.

Instantly, as he entered, Frost smelled the familiar reek of stale cigar smoke. They went into a small, stark, windowless room, cheaply carpeted wall to wall. It was furnished with an old metal desk that looked like it had come from a closing-down sale, a swivel chair, a wall-mounted plasma television on which a football match was showing, and five monitors, one showing outside the office door, the other four giving 360-degree coverage of the exterior of the building.

'You wait.' The Albanian walked to the rear of the office, opened another door, stepped inside and closed the door behind him. Moments later the Weatherman heard raised voices. Venner was shouting, but the sound was too muffled to hear what was being said.

He stared at the television screen. It was lunchtime, another reason he was irritated, the second lunchtime this week he had been summoned by Venner. Staring at the floor, fixating on a tiny piece of silver foil trapped in the carpet fibres, he wondered how to pluck up the courage to tell him that he didn't want to work for him any more. Then he glanced up at the screen, wishing it was *Star Trek* instead of football. *Star Trek* gave him courage, inspiration.

He imagined himself as several of the characters, from time to time. Boldly going . . .

'Hrmmm,' The Man Who Was Not Timid said, clearing his throat and his mind, thinking, wondering again how to pluck up the courage. Carl Venner was not going to be happy—

Then his thread was interrupted by the sound of Venner's door opening and the voice of the fat man yelling in his squeaky Louisiana drawl, 'Just get the fucking little bitch outta my sight – she fucking bit me, fucking bitch!'

Moments later a small, frightened-looking girl staggered out of the room, wearing a bewildered expression. She had eastern European features, long brown hair and a slim figure, and wore vivid lipstick that was badly smudged. She was dressed in tarty shoes, a low-cut top and a miniskirt so short it was barely street-legal. Under her right eye was a fresh weal which looked set to come out as a shiner; her left cheek had an equally fresh blow which had broken the skin and was drizzling blood. There were large bruises running the length of both her arms.

The Weatherman reckoned she was not a day older than twelve.

She caught his eye for a moment as if pleading for help, but he just looked away, searching for that bit of silver foil on the carpet, feeling bad about her but helpless, and even more determined to tell Venner to stick it, except of course he hadn't been paid yet.

The Albanian spoke sharply to the girl in a language the Weatherman did not understand. The girl answered Mr Brown back in a raised voice, feisty for her young years, looked back at the Weatherman again, desperately, but he was staring at the carpet and muttering silently to himself.

Then the Weatherman felt an arm around his

shoulders, and smelled the sour reek of cigar smoke combined with body odour, only slightly masked with Comme des Garçons 'Homme' cologne – he had recently learned by heart the smell of all the colognes in a Gatwick Airport duty free shop, as a way of killing time before a flight.

'She doesn't like it up the ass, John. What do you think about that?' Carl Venner asked; his five-foot-five-inch, twenty-six-stone frame looked in a dishevelled state, and he had a fresh scratch on his cheek. His normally immaculately coiffed wavy silver hair was awry and his pigtail had been partially pulled free of its band. He wore an emerald shirt wide open, with half the buttons torn off, revealing the massive rolls of loose flesh of his midriff and a hairless white belly overhanging his shiny belt.

His face was a blotchy red with exertion or anger and dry patches of psoriasis, which the Weatherman had noticed before, showed on his forehead; the man was wheezing so hard he wondered if he was about to have a heart attack.

'She doesn't like being fucked up the ass,' Venner said, rephrasing slightly. 'Can you believe that?'

The Weatherman didn't really have an opinion on the subject. Feeling himself propelled forward by the short, dense mass of Carl Venner, he simply said, 'Ummmm.'

They stopped for a moment and Venner turned his head back to Mr Brown. 'Do what you want with her, then get rid of the little bitch.'

Putting up with this, and being party to it, was not part of his deal, but then the Weatherman had never understood the true nature of his contractor until he had started looking into Venner's background by hacking into his private files.

He had first encountered Venner on an internet chat-line for techies, where information was exchanged and technical conundrums posited and worked out. Venner had set him a challenge which the Weatherman had thought at the time was hypothetical. The challenge was whether it was possible to put up a website on the internet that would be completely and permanently untraceable. The Weatherman had already designed the system. He had thought of offering it to the British intelligence services, but then he had been pissed off about the Iraq war. And anyway he distrusted all government bodies, everywhere. In fact he distrusted just about everything.

Venner propelled him through into his cavernous office, which comprised most of the upstairs floor of the warehouse. It was a vast, windowless and soulless place, carpeted in the same cheap material as the front office and almost equally sparsely furnished, apart from one area at the far end taken up with several racks of computer hardware – which the Weatherman knew inside out, as he had installed it all himself.

Venner's desk, on which sat four open laptops and nothing else other than a glass ashtray with two crushed cigar butts and a glass bowl full of chocolate bars, was a clone of the one outside. There was an old executive black leather armchair behind it, and a long brown leather sofa, in poor condition, near the desk. On the carpet just in front of it the Weatherman noticed a crumpled pair of skimpy lace knickers. Above him, raindrops were pattering down on the metal warehouse roof.

As ever, Venner's two silent Russian colleagues, in their black suits, materialized from nowhere and flanked the fat man, silent and unsmiling, giving the Weatherman just faint nods of acknowledgement.

'You know, she really did fucking bite me. Look!' Venner

exhaled a blast of cigar-laced halitosis and held up a fat, stubby index finger, nail gnawed to the quick.

The Weatherman could see deep puncture marks just above the first knuckle. Peering at them he said, 'You'll need a tetanus jab.'

'Tetanus?'

The Weatherman fixated on the knickers on the carpet, rocking backwards and forwards in silence, deep in thought.

'Tetanus?' the American repeated, worried.

Still staring at the knickers Frost said, 'The bacterial inoculum of human bite wounds is worse than any other animal. Do you have any idea how many organisms thrive in human oral flora?'

'I don't.'

Still rocking, the Weatherman said, 'Up to one million per millilitre – with over one hundred and ninety different bacterial species.'

'Terrific.' Venner stared dubiously at his wound. 'So . . .' He strutted agitatedly around the floor in a small circle, then closed his hands together, his expression indicating a complete change of mood and subject. 'You have the information?'

'Ummm.' The Weatherman continued to stare at the knickers, still rocking. 'What is going to, umm – going to, ummm – to the girl? Happen to her?'

'Mick's taking her home. What's your problem?'

'Ummm – no I, umm – good. OK, great.'

'Do you have what I asked you to bring? What I'm fucking paying you for?'

The Weatherman unbuttoned the back pocket of his trousers and pulled out a small, lined sheet of paper torn from a notebook and folded twice. He handed it to Venner, who took it with a grunt. 'You are one-hundred-per-cent sure?'

'Yes.'

This seemed to satisfy Venner, who waddled over to his desk to read it.

Written on it was the address of Tom and Kellie Bryce.

21

Professor Lars Johansson was a man who, in Grace's opinion, looked more like an international banker than a scientist who had spent much of his life crawling through bat caves, swamps and hostile jungles around the globe in search of rare insects.

Over six foot tall, with smooth blond hair and suave good looks, attired in a three-piece chalk-striped suit, the Anglo-Swede exuded urbane charm and confidence. He sat at his large desk, in his cluttered office on the top floor of London's Natural History Museum, with his half-moon tortoiseshell glasses perched on the end of his nose, surrounded by display cases and bell jars filled with rare specimens, a microscope, and a raft of medical implements, rulers and weights. The entire room could have come straight from the set of an Indiana Jones movie, Grace thought.

The two men had met and become friends a few years back at the International Homicide Investigators Association Convention, an event hosted in different US cities, which Grace attended annually. Ordinarily Grace would have sent one of his team to see Johansson, but he knew he'd get quicker answers by coming in person.

The entomologist removed the plastic bag containing the beetle from the buff-coloured police evidence bag. 'It's been swabbed, Roy?' he asked in his cultured English accent.

'Yes.'

'So it is OK to take it out?'

'Absolutely.'

Johansson carefully extracted the inch-long beetle with a pair of tweezers and laid it on his blotter pad. He studied it in silence for some moments with a large magnifying glass while Grace sipped gratefully on a mug of black coffee, thinking ruefully for a moment about the date with Cleo he had had to cancel tonight, in order to first be here and then get back to Sussex House for a late briefing of his team. He had been looking forward to it more than anything he could remember in a very long time and felt gutted he was not going to see her. But at least they had made a new date, for Saturday, just two days away. And the bonus was that that would give him time to buy some new gear.

'It's a good specimen, Roy,' he said. 'Very fine.'

'What can you tell me about it?'

'Where exactly did you find this?'

Grace explained, and the entomologist, to his credit, barely raised an eyebrow.

'That would fit,' he said. 'Very sick but very apt.'

'Fit?' Grace asked.

'It is an appropriate location – for reasons that will become clear to you.' He gave a wry smile.

'I'm all ears.'

'Do you want the full Year Two university biology class lecture on this little fellow? Or the short summary.'

'Just the simpleton download – I'll have to pass it on to some people who are even bigger numskulls than myself.'

The entomologist smiled. 'His name is *Copris lunaris*, and he's about average length – they are normally fifteen to twenty-five millimetres. He's indigenous to southern Europe and North Africa.'

'Are they found here at all?'

'Not outside a zoo.'

Grace frowned, thinking about the ramifications of this.

The Professor continued: 'It was considered a sacred creature by the ancient Egyptians, and is also known as a dung beetle or Scarab.'

Now Grace understood. '*Dung* beetle?'

'Exactly. The best-known are the subspecies called dung-rollers. They use their head and front legs to scrape up the dung and shape it into a ball, then they roll it along until they find a suitable place to bury it, so it can mature and break down.'

'Sounds delicious,' Grace said.

'I think I prefer Swedish meatballs.'

Grace thought for a moment. 'So putting this beetle up the woman's rectum has some significance.'

'It would seem a warped one, but yes.'

A siren *whupped* past in the street below. 'I think it's a fair assumption that we're dealing with someone who has a different value set to you and me,' Grace said with a grimace. 'What exactly is the connection with the ancient Egyptians, Lars?'

'I'll print it out for you; it's really quite fascinating.'

'Will it help me find my killer?'

'He's clearly someone who knows about symbolism. I would think it is important for you to understand as much about this as possible. You haven't been to Egypt, Roy?'

'No.'

The Professor was starting to look quite animated. 'If you go to Luxor, the Valley of the Kings or any of the temples, you'll see scarabs carved everywhere; they were a fundamental part of Upper and Lower Egyptian culture. And of course they were significant in funeral rites.'

Grace sipped some more of his coffee, running through in his mind all he had to do this evening, while the Professor worked on his keyboard for a few moments.

Twenty minutes ago DC Emma-Jane Boutwood had phoned to tell him the DNA results were in and there was no match on the database. No more body parts had yet been found. One more of the missing women had been eliminated in the past hour. DNA from the rest had been couriered up to the lab and hopefully – for the police, at any rate – there would be a match. If not they would have to immediately widen their search.

Suddenly, a printer spat a sheet of paper out inches from where he was sitting, startling him.

'Funeral rites?'

'Yes.'

'What was the significance of these beetles in funeral rites, Lars?'

'They'd be put in the tombs to ensure eternal resurrection.'

Grace thought about it for some moments. Were they dealing with a religious fanatic? A game player? Clearly it was someone intelligent – cultured enough to have read up on ancient Egypt – the placing of this particular beetle in the woman's rectum was no random act. 'Where would someone get hold of a scarab beetle in England?' he asked. 'Only in a zoo?'

'No, there are a few importers of tropical insects who would deal in them. I don't doubt they are available on the internet as well.'

Grace made a mental note to have someone list and

visit every tropical insect supplier in the UK and do a trawl on the Web.

The entomologist returned the beetle to the evidence bag. 'Is there anything else I can help you with on this, Roy?'

'I'm sure there will be. I can't think of anything more at the moment. And I really appreciate your staying on late to see me.'

'It's not a problem.' Lars Johansson nodded towards the window and the view out over Exhibition Road. 'Turned out to be a fine evening. Are you heading back down to Sussex?'

Grace nodded.

'Let me buy you a drink – one for the road?'

Grace glanced at his watch. The next fast train down to Brighton was in about forty minutes. He did not have time for a drink, but he sure felt in need of one. And as the Professor had been helpful to him so many times in the past, he thought it would be rude to decline. 'Just a quick one,' he said. 'Then I'll have to run.'

Which was why, thirty minutes later, at a street table outside a crowded pub, he found himself wondering just exactly what the hell was wrong with his life. He should have been out on a date tonight with one of the most beautiful women he had ever seen. Instead he was drinking his second pint of warm beer, having first had a fifteen-minute lecture on the digestive system of the scarab beetle, and now a lengthy analysis from the increasingly maudlin Lars Johansson of all that was wrong with the man's marriage.

22

The Thursday-night rush-hour traffic out of London had been worse than usual. And tonight being a fine, balmy night, it seemed every Londoner was escaping into the countryside. Tom normally travelled by train to avoid this hell, but he'd had to take the car today to get out to Ron Spacks's office, and afterwards he'd had to drive back into central London to collect his laptop.

His plans to get home early and have a barbecue supper in the garden with his family had been shot to ribbons by Chris Webb arriving late to fix his computer and then taking much longer than he had thought. It was almost half past four in the afternoon by the time Chris had finished, freeing Tom to start his journey at the worst possible time.

Normally in the car he would catch up on phone calls or listen to the radio – in London he particularly liked David Prever on Smooth FM, otherwise he listened to the Radio 4 news or Jazz FM – but this evening, apart from one call to Ron Spacks to say he had his team working on prices for the Rolex Oyster watches – that was potentially a dream order he just had to get – he had driven in silence, just with his own sombre thoughts.

Is that Tom Bryce speaking?
The strong eastern European accent.
His conversation with Kellie earlier.
What kind of an accent?
Sort of European, not English.

The same person?

Last night you accessed a website you were unauthorized to visit. Now you have tried to access it again. We do not appreciate uninvited guests. If you inform the police about what you saw or if you ever try to access this site again, what is about to happen to your computer will happen to your wife, Kellie, to your son, Max, and to your daughter, Jessica. Take a good look, then have a hard think.

Tom had had no intention of informing the police about what he had seen on Tuesday night. The internet was a sewer; you could find anything you wanted on it, however erotic or gross. He'd been to a website that was either a movie trailer or some gratuitously violent site for sickos and would have left it at that. It wasn't his job to police the sewer.

But that threatening email implied there was something more to that site.

He was approaching the South Downs now; the traffic, although heavy, was moving quickly. Over to his left, half a mile across meadows, he saw a glint of light in reflected glass. A train. Forgetting the cramped, stuffy conditions for a brief moment, he envied its passengers the relative ease of their journey. However, he'd be home in fifteen minutes, and he was looking forward to a large, stiff drink.

He looked out through the windscreen at the brilliant yellow ball of sun sinking low in the cobalt sky. Beyond the hills was his home, his sanctuary. But he didn't feel safe; something was shaking his insides, mixing up all his emotions, pouring a cocktail of confused fears into him.

He didn't want to tell Kellie that he'd had the same call, and yet they had always been so open and honest with each other, he wondered if it would be wrong not to tell her. Except it would only make her even more nervous. And then he'd have to explain the CD.

And then?

The threat in the email was clear. *If* he informed the police. *If* he attempted to visit the site again.

Well the fact was he intended to do neither. So they should be fine.

So why the calls? Maybe he'd been stupid to make that second visit to the website, he realized.

*

As he turned into his street and drove up the hill, an alarm bell rang inside him. Ahead he could see Kellie's old maroon Espace parked out in the street. She normally put it in the carport. Why was it out on the street? he wondered.

Moments later as he pulled up outside the house he saw the reason. Almost every square inch of the carport was taken up by a crate. It was one of the biggest crates he had ever seen in his life. It could easily have housed a full-grown elephant, with room for it to swing a cat from its trunk.

The thing was taller than the garage door, for Chris-sake.

And instead of the front door opening wide, and Kellie, Max, Jessica and Lady bursting out through it to greet him, the door opened just a few inches and Kellie's face peered round, warily, before she emerged wearing a baggy white T-shirt over cut-off denim shorts and flip-flops. Some-where at the back of the house he could hear Lady barking in furious excitement. No sign of the kids.

'It's a little bigger than I expected,' Kellie said, meekly, by way of a greeting. 'They're going to come back tomorrow to put it together.'

Tom just stared at her for a moment. She looked so vulnerable suddenly. Scared of the phone call or of him? 'Wh— what is it?' he asked. All he could think was that whatever was in there had to have cost serious money.

'I just had to buy it,' she said. 'Honestly, it was such good value.'

Jesus. Trying desperately to hold on to his fast-unravelling patience. 'What is it?'

She gave a little shrug and said, trying to sound non-chalant and not succeeding, 'Oh, it's just a barbecue.'

Now he understood the reticence in her voice when he had suggested earlier today that they had a barbecue this evening. 'A barbecue? What the hell do you barbecue in a thing that size? Whales? Dinosaurs? An entire fucking herd of Aberdeen Angus?'

'The list price new is over eight thousand pounds. I got it for *three thousand*!' she exclaimed.

Tom turned away, his temper just a few threads from fraying completely. 'You're unbelievable, my darling. We've already got a perfectly decent kettle barbecue.'

'It's rusting.'

'So, you could get a brand-new one from Homebase for about seventy quid. You've spent *three thousand*? And where the hell are we going to put it – the thing'll take up half the garden.'

'No, I don't – it's not – not that big when it's assembled. It just looks so cool!'

'You'll have to send it back.' Then he paused, looking around. 'Where are the kids?'

'I told them I needed to speak to you before you saw them. I warned them that Daddy might not be too pleased.'

She slipped her arms around him. 'Look, there's something I haven't told you – I sort of wanted it to be a surprise.' She gave him a kiss.

Christ, he wondered, what now? Was she going to tell him she was pregnant?

'I've got a job!'

The words actually jolted a smile out of him.

*

Half an hour later, after he had read Jessica several pages of *Poppy Cat Loves Rainbows*, then Max a chapter of *Harry Potter and the Goblet of Fire*, and had watered his tomatoes in the greenhouse, and the raspberry canes, strawberries and courgettes in the strip of soil beside it, he was seated with Kellie at the wooden table on their terrace, with a massive vodka martini in his hand, catching the last rays of the evening sun on their garden. They clinked glasses. Near his feet, Lady crunched contentedly on a bone.

Len Wainwright's head was visible, through the wisteria Kellie had trained along the top of the fence to give them added privacy, moving along, down towards his shed. Len had spent a lot of time, time that Tom could not afford, talking him through the various stages in the construction of this shed. But he had never actually explained its purpose. Kellie had once suggested that he was going to murder his wife and put her underneath. It had seemed funny at the time; Tom wasn't smiling any more.

The air smelled sweet and was still, other than the busy evening chatter of birds. It was a time of year he normally loved, a time of day when he normally unwound and began enjoying life. But not this evening. Nothing seemed to calm the undefined fear that just went round and round inside him.

'I – I didn't know you . . . I – I mean I thought you weren't keen on, you know, being apart from the kids, working?' he said.

'Jessica's now started at nursery school, so I have time,' she replied, sipping her wine. 'It's a new hotel started up in Lewes – I've been offered a job on the front desk, flexi-hours, starting Monday week.'

'Why hotel work? You've never done hotel work. Why don't you go back to teaching if you want to work again?'

'I feel like doing something different. They'll train me. There's nothing to it. It's mostly dealing with stuff on the computer.'

Giving you the opportunity to stay on eBay all day long, Tom thought, but said nothing. He took a gulp of his drink and started doing some mental calculations. If Kellie could earn enough just to cover her purchases that would be a considerable help. But three thousand pounds off her credit card today for the damned monster barbecue . . . It would take her months to earn that. Meantime he was going to have to fund it. Then his mobile phone, which he had left in his den, began to ring.

They caught each other's eyes. He saw the flash of fear in Kellie's, and wondered if she saw it in his own, also.

He hurried upstairs, and saw with relief on the caller display it was Chris Webb.

'Hi, Chris,' he said. 'Have you found out anything from the disc?'

The techie's voice was sour. 'No, and it doesn't look like I'm going to.'

'How come?'

'I got home and my whole place has been ransacked. Someone's been through everything, and I mean every-thing. It'll take a week to sort this lot out.'

'Christ. Have you had much taken?'

'No,' he said, 'I haven't.' There was a long pause during which Tom heard the click of what sounded like a cigarette lighter and a sharp inhalation. 'In fact there seems to be only one damned thing missing.'

'What's that?'

'Your CD.'

23

Alison Vosper, the Assistant Chief Constable, was the boss to whom Roy Grace ultimately had to answer. She possessed a mercurial temper, turning her from sweetness and light one moment to very sour the next. Some years back she had been given the sobriquet No. 27 by a wag in the force, naming her after a sweet-and-sour dish at a local Chinese takeaway. It had stuck, although it seemed to Grace it was probably time to change it, as he could not remember the last time she had actually been in a sweet mood.

And she most certainly was not in one today.

Nine o'clock on this Friday morning found him standing on the deep pile carpet of Vosper's office, in front of her desk, with that same sick feeling in the pit of his stomach he used to get when told to report to the headmaster's office at school. It was ridiculous for a man of his age to be nervous of a superior, but Alison Vosper had that effect on him, as indeed she did on everyone, whether they cared to admit it or not.

He had been summoned here ostensibly to give her a private briefing in advance of the daily press conference, but there wasn't a whole lot to say. Nearly forty-eight hours on, they did not know who the victim was and they had no suspect.

One thing Grace had learned in his years as a police officer was how much importance senior officers attached to letting the public feel they were getting results. From the standpoint of trying to make the great unwashed feel all warm and fuzzy about the police, Grace had the feeling that the superiors sometimes considered on balance that it was better to bang somebody into custody, however innocent they might be, and at least show they were doing something, than to have to admit lamely to a room full of journalists trying to flog column inches that they hadn't a clue.

Unlike the modern, soulless building of the CID head-quarters at Sussex House where he was now based, the big cheeses were all housed in this handsome Queen Anne mansion, at the centre of the untidy cluster of buildings that comprised Sussex Police headquarters, on the edge of the ancient county town of Lewes.

The building's fine original features had been left intact in most of the grander offices, in particular the delicate stucco work and the ornate ceilings. Alison Vosper's was a fine example. Her ground-floor room was immaculate, with a fine view out over a manicured lawn, and it was furnished with elegant antiques which gave a sense of both authority and permanence.

The centrepiece was a large expanse of polished rose-wood desk on which sat a black-edged blotter, a slim crystal vase containing three purple tulips, framed photo-graphs of her husband – a police officer several years older but three ranks her junior – and her two children, a boy and a girl, immaculate in their school uniforms, an ammonite pen holder, and as always a stack of the morning's papers fanned out. Mercifully Grace did not feature on any of the front pages.

Assistant Chief Constable Alison Vosper was not only sour this morning, she was extremely frosty, an effect enhanced by her starchy-looking high-necked blouse the colour of ice, cinched at the front by an equally icy-looking diamanté brooch. Even her perfume had an acidic tang to it.

As usual Vosper did not invite him to sit down – a technique she had long used on all juniors as a way of keeping meetings short and to the point. Grace informed her of everything that had happened since yesterday's very late briefing. The only visible reaction he got was when he came to the beetle – enough revulsion to show that beneath her hard carapace Alison Vosper was still human.

'So we have three possibles among the women reported missing in the past few days?' she said. Her accent was a flat Midlands Brummie, which made her sound even harder.

'Yes, and we've couriered material collected from their homes up to Huntingdon for DNA analysis – I've called in a favour there. We'll get a match sometime today.'

'And if there is no match?'

'We'll have to go wider.'

Her phone rang. She pressed a button, held it down and snapped, 'I'm busy.' Then she looked up at the Detective Superintendent again. 'You know there's a lot riding on this for you, Roy?'

He shrugged. 'More than any other case?'

She gave him a long, hard, silent look. 'I think we both know that.'

Grace frowned, unsure what was coming next and uncomfortable at her words.

She twisted her gold wedding band around on her finger for a moment, and it seemed to soften her. 'You've been lucky, spending your career so far in one area, Roy. A lot of police officers have to move around, constantly, if they want to get promotion. Like me. Birmingham's my home, but I've spent just three years in my whole career in Brum. I've been all over the place – Northumberland, Ipswich, Bristol, Southampton. It's different to your dad's day. He spent all his career with the force in Brighton, didn't he?'

'If you include Worthing as well.'

She gave a thin smile. Worthing was only a few miles down the coast. Then her demeanour hardened again. 'Your father was a well-loved and respected man, so I am told. But it doesn't seem to many people that you are your father's son.'

She left the words hanging in the air. Roy felt them like a sting in his heart. It was as if he had been lanced and his energy was now leaking out. He stared back at her, confused and suddenly feeling very vulnerable indeed. 'I – I know I have my critics,' he said, and he was aware, too late, how lame that sounded.

She shook her head, then this time pulled her wedding band right off, holding it out in front of her, as if symbolizing that nothing was permanent, that she could flick him out of her life as easily as she could flick the gold band into a bin. 'It's not your critics I'm worried about, Roy. The Chief is worried about the damage you've done to Sussex Police. You nearly caused a mistrial a couple of weeks ago by taking a piece of evidence to a medium – and you got splashed all over the nation's headlines as a result, making you and us a laughing stock. You've lost a lot of respect among colleagues for dabbling in the supernatural. Then you allowed two suspects to get killed during a pursuit.'

Grace tried to interrupt, thinking she was being totally unreasonable, but she raised a hand, blocking him.

'Now we're forty-eight hours into a murder enquiry, you can't name the victim, you don't have a suspect; all you have is the life history of a damned beetle found at the scene.'

Now he was getting angry. 'I'm sorry; this is just not fair, and you know it.'

'This is not about what's fair, Roy; this is about the police being seen to be competent, protecting the public.'

'Those two who died in the car – they were guilty as hell, and they were dangerous. They'd driven through roadblocks, they hijacked two cars, they knocked an officer off his motorcycle. Would you rather we had just let them go?' He shook his head in exasperation.

'What I'm saying to you, Roy, is that it might be better to move you to an area where you aren't known. Up north somewhere, perhaps. Somewhere busy that can use your skills. Somewhere like Newcastle. I've been asked by one of my colleagues there for the services of an experienced SIO for a sensitive investigation that could take several months, maybe a year. And I think you are the right person for that.'

'You've got to be joking. This is my home. I don't want to be transferred anywhere. I'm not even sure I'd want to stay in the force if that happened.'

'Then pull yourself together and make sure it doesn't. I'm drafting in another officer to share your cold-case workload as I don't think you are making as much progress there as you should. He's a former Detective Inspector from the Met, and we've promoted him to the same rank as you.'

'Do I know him?'

'His name is Cassian Pewe.'

Grace thought for a moment, then groaned inwardly. *Detective Inspector Cassian Pewe*, now to be *Detective Superintendent Cassian Pewe*. Grace had had a run-in with him a couple of years ago, when the Met had sent in reinforcements to help police Brighton during the Labour Party conference. He remembered him as deeply arrogant. 'He's coming here?'

'He starts on Monday. He'll be working out of an office here. Do you have a problem with that?'

Yes, he wanted to say, his brain spinning. *Of course, teacher's pet*. Where else would she station him? Here was perfect, so that she and Pewe could have regular cosy chats – about how and where to undermine pain-in-the-arse Roy Grace.

But he had no choice but to say, 'No.'

'Your card is marked, Roy. OK?'

He felt so choked he could only nod his reply. Then his phone rang. She signalled for him to answer it.

He stepped away from her desk and looked at the display. It was from the Major Incident Suite. 'Roy Grace,' he answered.

It was DC Nicholl, calling him excitedly to tell him they had heard back from the lab at Huntingdon. They had a positive DNA match for the body.

24

'I can't believe your music, man,' Branson said. 'It's crap, it's just total crap. There's no other word for it.'

They were on a long stretch of downhill dual carriageway heading west, past the grassy expanse of the old World War II fighter base, down to their left, that had now become Shoreham Airport, a busy base for private aircraft and commercial flights to the Channel Islands, and in the direction of Southampton.

Shoreham was the extreme western suburb of Brighton, and Grace always felt a strange mixture of relief and loss when he left it behind him. Loss, because Brighton was where he really felt at home, and anywhere else felt like uncharted waters where he was out of his depth, a little insecure. And relief, because all the time he was in the Brighton and Hove City conurbation he felt a sense of responsibility, and away from it he could relax.

After his years in the force it was his second nature to subconsciously assess every pedestrian and the occupants of every car on the street. He knew most of the local villains, certainly all of the street drug dealers, and some of the muggers and burglars; knew when they were in the right place and when in the wrong place. That was one of the things so ridiculous about Alison Vosper's threat to transfer him. A lifetime of knowledge and contacts down the pan.

Roy Grace had decided to drive, because his nerves wouldn't take another journey with Branson showing off his high-speed pursuit skills. Now he wasn't sure his nerves could take any more of the Detective Sergeant's poking about with the CD player. But Branson wasn't finished with him yet.

'The *Beatles*? Who the hell listens to the Beatles in their car these days?'

'Me, I like them,' Grace said defensively. 'Your problem is you can't differentiate between loud noise and good music.' He brought the Alfa Romeo to a stop at a red light, the junction with the Lancing College road. He had decided to take his own car because it hadn't had a long run in a while and the battery needed a good charge. More importantly, if he had taken a pool car, Branson would probably have insisted on driving and been hurt if he hadn't let him.

'That's well funny, coming from you,' Branson said. 'You just don't *get* music!' Then suddenly changing the subject, he pointed at a pub across the road. 'The Sussex Pad. Do good fish there, went there with Ari. Yeah, it was good.' Then he turned his attention back to the CD player. 'Dido!'

'What's wrong with Dido?'

Branson shrugged. 'Well, if you like that kind of thing, I suppose. I hadn't realized how sad you were.'

'Yeah, well I do like that kind of thing.'

'And – Jesus – what's this? Something you got free with a magazine?'

'Bob Berg,' Grace said, getting irritated now. 'He happens to be a seriously cool modern jazz musician.'

'Yeah, but he's not *black*.'

'Oh, right, you have to be black to be a jazz musician?'

'I'm not saying that.'

'You are! Anyhow he's dead – he was killed in a crash a

few years ago and I love his stuff. Just an awesome tenor saxophonist. OK? Want to pull anything else apart? Or shall we talk about your *hunch*?'

A tad sullenly, Glenn Branson switched on the radio and tuned it into a rap station. 'Tomorrow, right, I'm taking you clothes shopping? Well I'm going to take you music shopping as well. You get a hot date in this car and she sees your music, she's going to be looking in the glove locker for your pension book.'

Grace tuned him out, turning his mind back to the immediate task ahead of them and all the other balls he had to keep in the air simultaneously.

His nerves were frayed this morning, both from his meeting with Alison Vosper, which had left him feeling very down, and from the task that was facing him in about an hour's time. Ordinarily, Grace could have said with complete honesty that he liked almost every aspect of police work – except for one thing, and that was breaking the news of a death to a parent or loved one. It wasn't something he had to do very often these days as it was a task for family liaison officers, detectives who were specially trained. But there were some situations, like the one he was going to now, where Grace wanted to be present himself to gauge the reaction, to glean as much information as he could in those key early moments after the news was broken. And he was taking Glenn Branson because he thought it would be good training for him.

Newly bereaved people followed an almost identical pattern. For the first few hours they would be in shock, totally vulnerable, and would say almost anything. But rapidly they would start to withdraw, and other members of the family would close ranks around them. If you wanted information, you had to tease it out within those first few hours. It was cruel but almost always effective, and otherwise you were stuffed for weeks, maybe months. Newspaper reporters knew that, too.

*

He recognized the two family liaison officers, DC Maggie Campbell and DC Vanessa Ritchie, sitting in their car, a small grey unmarked Volvo parked over on the grass verge of the lane outside the entrance to the house, and pulled the Alfa up just past them. Their two faces, frosty with disapproval, stared through the Volvo's windscreen at him.

'Shit, man! How do people *afford* these places?' Glenn said, staring at the steel gates between two columns topped with stone balls.

'By not being cops,' Grace retorted.

Money had never been a big factor in Grace's life. Sure he liked nice things, but he'd never had swanky aspirations and he had always been careful to live within his means. Sandy had been terrific at saving here and there. It always amused him that she used to buy the next winter's Christmas cards in the January sales.

But from these savings she was always buying them little *treats*, as she liked to call them. During the first few years of their marriage, when she worked for a travel agent and could get discounted holidays, she had twice saved enough for an entire fortnight abroad.

But no amount of scrimping and saving on his salary, even with all the overtime bonuses in the world that he used to get as a junior officer, would ever buy him anything close to the magnitude of the spread he was looking at now.

'Remember that film, *The Great Gatsby*?' Branson said. 'The Jack Clayton version, with Robert Redford and Mia Farrow, right?'

Grace nodded. He remembered it vaguely, or at least the title.

'Well that's what this place is, innit? That's a fuck-off house you're looking at.'

And it was: a dead straight tree-lined drive, several hundred yards long, opening into a circular car park with an ornamental pond in the middle, in front of a substantial white Palladian – or at least Palladian-style – mansion.

Grace nodded. Out of the corner of his eye he saw the doors of the Volvo open. 'Here comes trouble,' he said quietly. The DCs climbed out of their car.

Maggie Campbell, a dark-haired woman in her early thirties, and Vanessa Ritchie, a tall thin redhead, two years her senior, with a harder face – and demeanour – strode up to them, both in smart but sombre plain clothes.

'There's no way four of us can go in, Roy,' DC Ritchie said. 'It's too many.'

'I'll go in first with Glenn, and break the news. Then I'll phone you when I think you should come in and take over.'

He saw Maggie Campbell frown. Ritchie shook her head. 'It's the wrong way round – you know that.'

'Yes, I do, but that's the way I want to play this.'

'*Play* this?' she responded angrily. 'This isn't some kind of a bloody experiment. It's wrong.'

'What's wrong, Vanessa, is that a father shouldn't have to find out that part of his daughter has been found, short of a few important bits such as her head, in a bloody field with a beetle up her rectum. That's what's bloody wrong.'

The FLO tapped her chest. 'That is what we did our training for. We are specialists in all aspects of bereavement.'

Grace looked at the women in turn. 'I know all about your training and I know both of you – I've worked with you before and I respect you. This has nothing to do with your abilities. Your training gives you guidance, but at the end of the day there's also the policing aspect. On this occasion I have my reasons for wanting to break the news, and as the SIO on this case I set the rules, OK? I don't want any more sour faces from you, I want cooperation. Understood?'

The two FLOs nodded but still did not look comfortable.

'Have you decided how much you are going to tell the father?' Vanessa Ritchie said tartly.

'No, I'm going to play it by ear. I'll bring you up to speed before I call you in, OK?'

Maggie Campbell smiled in a half-hearted, conciliatory way. DC Ritchie gave him a reluctant *You're the boss* shrug.

On a nod from his boss, Branson pressed the bell, and moments later the gates swung jerkily open. They drove up to the house. Grace parked between the two cars outside, an old, rather grubby BMW 7 series and a very ancient Subaru estate.

As they approached the front door it was opened by a distinguished-looking man in his mid-fifties, with dark hair streaked with silver at the temples, wearing an open-necked white business shirt with gold cufflinks, suit trousers and shiny black loafers. He was holding a mobile phone.

'Detective Superintendent Grace?' he said in an upper-crust accent which was slightly muffled as he seemed to speak through his teeth, scanning both police officers uncertainly. He had a pleasant smile, but sad blue-grey eyes like a pair of little lost souls.

'Mr Derek Stretton?' Grace asked. Then he and Branson both showed him their warrant cards out of courtesy.

Ushering them in, Derek Stretton asked, 'How was your drive?'

'It was fine,' Grace said. 'I think we picked a good time of day.'

'It's a beastly road; can't think why they can't just make it motorway. Janie's always spending hours stuck when she comes down here.'

The first thing Grace noticed as he entered the hallway was how sparsely furnished the place was. There was a fine long inlaid table, and a tallboy and antique chairs, but there were no rugs or floor coverings, and he observed a row of shadows along the walls where paintings had clearly recently been removed.

Leading them through into an equally barren drawing room, with two large sofas on bare boards and what looked like a plastic picnic table put between them as a coffee table, Derek Stretton seemed in a hurry to explain, gesturing at the bare walls of the room and the large rectangular shadows, many with bare wires poking out, some with small lights at the top. 'Afraid I've had to let go of some of the family silver. Made a few bad investments . . .'

That explained the shadows on the wall, Grace thought. They'd probably gone to auction. Stretton looked so distressed, he felt genuinely sorry for the man, and that was without the bombshell he was about to drop.

'My housekeeper isn't—' He waved his arms helplessly in the air. 'Um, but can I get you some tea? Coffee?'

Grace was parched. 'Tea please, milk, no sugar.'

'The same, please,' Branson said.

As Stretton went out, Grace walked over to one of the few pieces of furniture in the room, an elegant side table covered in photograph frames.

There were a couple of much older people – grandparents, he presumed. Then one of a slightly younger Derek Stretton with an attractive woman of about the same age. Next to this was a young woman – Janie, he guessed. She was about seventeen or eighteen in the photograph, pretty and very classy-looking, in a black velvet ball gown, with long fair hair swept up and clipped by two diamanté barrettes, and an ornate silver choker around her neck. She bore a striking resemblance to a young Gwyneth Paltrow. She was smiling at the camera, but there was nothing self-conscious in that smile. To Grace it was a *Yes, I am gorgeous and I know it* smile.

There was another photograph next to it, also of Janie, a couple of years younger, on a ski slope, wearing a lilac anorak, designer sunglasses and a seriously cool expression.

Grace glanced at his watch. It was 11.30 a.m. He'd ducked out of the press conference, leaving it to the PRO Dennis Ponds to tell the pack that they now had the name of the victim, and would be releasing it the moment her next of kin had been informed – which would be in about an hour and a half or so. Then he wanted Ponds, in particular, to get her photograph out in as many places as possible, to see what sightings of her last hours might come in from the public, and to get the case on the next episode of *Crimewatch* on television, the following Wednesday, if they hadn't made progress by then.

Branson wandered over to the fireplace. A number of birthday cards stood on the mantelpiece. Grace followed. He stared at one with a cartoon of a proud-looking man in a suit and bow tie, with the wording above, 'To a very special Dad!'

He opened it up and saw the message: 'To my Darling Daddy. With all my love, tons and tons and tons of it. J XXX'.

Grace put the card back and walked over to a tall bay window. There was a fine view down to the Hamble River; Branson joined him and they stared at a forest of masts and rigging from a marina that looked as if it was just beyond the boundary of the property.

'Never been into boats,' Branson said. 'Never been totally comfortable with water.'

'Even though you live by the sea?'

'Not exactly *right* by it.' His phone rang and he pulled it out. 'DS Branson? Oh hi, yeah, I'm with Roy, down near Southampton. ETA about two o'clock back in Brighton. Roy wants a briefing at six thirty, so everyone there, OK? Yeah. Did we get the extra officers he requested? Only one so far? Who is it? Oh shit, you are joking! Him! I can't believe they've dumped *him* on us. Roy is going to be well pissed. We're going straight to her flat from here; Roy wants someone to go to her office, speak to her boss and the staff there. OK. Yeah. Six thirty. You got it.'

Branson slipped the phone back in his pocket. 'That was Bella. Guess what – your request for two extra officers for the team – know who they've given us?'

'Hit me.'

'Norman Potting.'

Grace groaned. 'It's about time he retired; he's older than God.'

'Hasn't exactly thrilled the ladies. Bella is not happy.'

Detective Sergeant Norman Potting was in his mid-fifties, a late joiner compared to some. He was an old-school policeman, politically incorrect, blunt and with no interest in promotion – he had never wanted the responsibilities – but nor had he wanted to retire when he reached fifty-five, the normal police pension age for a sergeant, which was why he had extended his service. He liked to do what he was best at doing, which he called plodding and drilling. Plodding, methodical police work, and drilling down deep beneath the surface of any crime, drilling for as long and deep as he needed until he hit some seam that would lead him somewhere.

The best that could be said about Norman Potting was that he was steady and dependable, and could get results. But he was boring as hell, and had the knack of upsetting just about everyone.

'I thought he was permanently up at Gatwick with the antiterrorist lot,' Grace said.

'They obviously had enough of him. Maybe they couldn't bear any more of his jokes,' Branson said. 'And Bella said he stinks of smoke from his pipe. Neither she nor Emma-Jane want to sit near him.'

'Poor precious souls.'

Derek Stretton came back into the room, carrying a tray with three china cups and a milk jug. He set it on the plastic table, then ushered them to one sofa, and sat down opposite. 'You said on the phone you have news about Janie, Detective Superintendent?' he asked expectantly.

Now Grace suddenly wished fervently he had sent the two FLOs in to do this task, after all.

25

Tom had done virtually no work all morning. He'd sat at his desk in his office with a pile of unanswered emails mounting up on his screen – at least his computer was working again now – and dealt with a few calls that had come in for him, as well as gone carefully through a list of costings for Rolex Oyster watches for Ron Spacks, but all the rest of the time he had been thinking.

Thinking.

His brain spinning but getting no traction.

The call last night at home from Chris telling him he had been burgled.

In fact there seems to be only one damned thing missing . . . Your CD . . .

Mind you, he had been in Chris Webb's office at his home, and it was cluttered beyond belief. It wouldn't be hard to lose a CD there – he had dozens lying all over the place.

Yet, Tom thought, someone was not happy that he had the CD, and they'd trashed his computer twice to tell him so. So now they'd taken it back? Had Chris Webb tried to play it and alerted them?

If whoever owned that CD – the dickhead from the train – now had it back, would that be the end of the matter?

Maybe the dickhead would be on the train again tonight? But Tom doubted it; in all the years he had been commuting he had never seen him before. Besides, he wasn't exactly sure what he would do – whether he would go up and shout at him, or whether he would be too nervous to say anything.

He had still not said anything to Kellie about it. Best to keep quiet, keep his head down. There had been no more calls, which meant, hopefully, he'd had his warning.

He sure as hell had got the message.

26

'The managing agents of the flat your daughter rents in Brighton let us in yesterday, Mr Stretton, and allowed us to take a couple of items belonging to her for DNA testing. We took some hair samples from a brush in the bathroom and a piece of chewing gum we found in a pedal bin,' Grace explained.

Derek Stretton held his cup without drinking, eyeing him warily.

'We sent these up to the Police laboratory at Huntingdon, and earlier this morning we received the results. The DNA from the chewing gum and from the hair is from the same person, and there was a complete match with the body that we found on Wednesday. I'm afraid the only conclusion we can come to, sir, is that the murdered young lady is your daughter, Janie.'

There was a long silence, and for some moments Grace thought that Derek Stretton was about to throw his head back and roar with laughter. Instead, all that happened was that the cup began to rattle in the saucer, louder and louder, until the man leaned forward and set it down.

'I – I see,' he said.

He looked at Grace again, then at Branson. Then slowly, like a complex folding chair, he seemed to collapse in on himself. 'She's all I have in the world,' he said. 'Please tell me it's not true. She's coming today – it's my birthday – we're going to dinner. Oh God. I – I . . .'

Grace stared rigidly ahead, avoiding Branson's eye,

wishing desperately that he could say it wasn't true, that it was a mistake. But there was nothing he could add, nothing that would make this man's grief any less.

'I lost my wife – her mother – three years ago. Cancer. Now I've lost Janie. I . . .'

Grace gave him some space, then asked, 'What kind of a daughter was she, sir? I mean – were you close?'

After a long silence Derek Stretton said, 'There's always a special bond between a father and daughter, I'm told. I've certainly found it so.'

'She was a caring person?'

'Immensely. Never ever forgot my birthday, or Christmas or Father's Day. She's – she's just – a – perfect . . .' His voice tailed away.

Grace stood up. 'Do you have a recent photograph of her? I'd like to get a picture out into circulation as quickly as possible.'

Derek Stretton nodded bleakly.

'And would you mind if we took a look in her bedroom?'

'Do you want me to come – or . . . ?'

'We can go on our own,' Grace said gently.

'First floor – turn right at the top of the stairs. It's the second door on your right.'

It was a young girl's room, a tidy, organized, methodical young girl. A row of cuddly toys lay back against the cushions. A U2 poster hung on the wall. There was a collection of seashells on the dressing table. Bookshelves stacked mostly with children's books, girls' adventure stories and a few legal thrillers from Scott Turow, John Grisham and several other American writers. There was a pair of slippers on the floor and an old-fashioned dressing gown hanging on the back of the door.

Grace and Branson opened all the drawers, rummaged

in her clothing, through underwear, T-shirts, blouses, pullovers, but they found nothing to remotely suggest what she had done to expose herself to a savage killer.

Then Grace picked up a velvet jewellery box and popped open the lid. Inside were some delicate amethyst earrings, a silver charm bracelet, a gold necklace, and a signet ring with an embossed crest. He closed the lid and held on to the box.

After fifteen minutes they went back downstairs. Derek Stretton did not seem to have moved from his chair, and he had not touched his tea.

Grace held up the box and opened the lid, showing Janie's father the contents. 'Mr Stretton, are all these your daughter's?'

He peered at them and nodded.

'May I borrow one of the items? Something that she might have worn recently?' He ignored the strange look that Glenn Branson gave him.

'The signet ring's probably the best,' he said. 'It's our family crest. She used to wear it all the time until quite recently.'

Grace removed a small plastic evidence bag from his pocket, which he had brought with him for this purpose, and, lifting the ring out of the box with his handkerchief, carefully placed it in the bag.

'Mr Stretton, is there anyone you can think of who might have had any reason to harm your daughter?' Grace asked.

'No one,' he whispered.

Sitting back down opposite Derek Stretton and leaning towards him, Grace cradled his chin on his hands and asked, 'Did she have a boyfriend?'

Staring at the carpet, Derek Stretton said, 'Not – not anyone special.'

'But she had a current fellow?'

He looked up at Grace, seeming to regain some composure. 'She was a fine-looking girl with a great personality. She was never short of admirers. But she took the law very seriously – I don't think she wanted too many distractions.'

'She's a lawyer?'

'A law student. She did a law degree here at Southampton University, and she's been studying for the past few years at Guildford Law School. Currently she's articled – or a trainee – or whatever they call it nowadays – with a firm of solicitors in Brighton.'

'And you've been supporting her during her studies.'

'As best I can. It's been a little tight these past months. Bit of a struggle. I . . .'

Grace nodded sympathetically. 'Can we just go back to the boyfriends, sir. Do you know the name of her most recent boyfriend?'

Derek Stretton seemed to have aged twenty years in the last twenty minutes. He was pensive for some moments. 'Justin Remington – she went out with him about a year or so ago. Very charming young man. He – she brought him down here a few times. Develops property in London. I quite liked him, but I don't think he had a big enough intellect for her.' He smiled with a faraway look. 'She has a – had a remarkable brain. Couldn't get near her at Scrabble from the time she was about nine.'

'Would you know where I could get hold of this Justin Remington?'

There was a silence as Stretton sat thinking, then furrowing his eyebrows he said, 'He was into real tennis. I don't think there are that many players. I know he played in London – I believe it was Queen's,' he said.

It was rapidly becoming clear to Roy Grace that he was going to get very little more from the man. 'Is there someone you can phone?' he asked him. 'A relative or a friend who could come over?'

After some moments, Derek Stretton said meekly, 'My sister. Lucy. She's not very far away. I'll give her a call. She'll be devastated.'

'Why don't you make the call while we're still here, sir?' Branson urged, as gently as he could.

The pair of them waited while he made the call, retreating as discreetly as they could to the far end of the room. Grace heard him sobbing; then he went out of the room for a while. Finally he came back in and walked over to join them, holding a brown envelope. 'I've put some photographs of Janie together for you. I'd appreciate them back.'

'Of course,' Grace said, knowing the poor man would probably have to make half a dozen calls over the coming months to get them back – they would inevitably get misfiled somewhere in the system.

'Lucy's on her way – my sister. She'll be here in about half an hour.'

'Would you like us to wait?' Grace asked.

'No, I'll be OK. I need some time to think. I . . . Can – can I see Janie?'

Grace shot a glance at Branson. 'I don't think it would be advisable, sir.'

'I'd really like to see her one more time. You know? To say goodbye?' He put out a hand and gripped Grace's firmly.

Grace realized he had not absorbed from the newspapers that Janie's head was missing. This was not the moment to tell him. He decided to leave that to the two FLOs. Vanessa Ritchie and Maggie Campbell were about to earn their keep and give some payback for the massive investment in their training.

'There are two women detectives who will be along to see you shortly, from our Family Liaison Unit. They'll be able to guide you on that.'

'Thank you. It would mean a lot to me.' Then he gave a sad little laugh. 'You know, officers, I – I never discussed death with Janie. I have no idea whether she wanted to be buried or cremated.' Wild-eyed he added, 'And her cat, of course.' He scratched the back of his head. 'Bins! She used to bring Bins here before she went away. I – don't know . . . it's all so . . .'

'They'll be able to help you with everything; that's what they are here for.'

'It never occurred to me that she might die, you see.'

Grace and Branson walked back out to the car in a deeply uncomfortable silence.

27

A community support officer, barely distinguishable from a uniformed constable, stood outside the front door of the building in Kemp Town where Janie Stretton had rented her flat, with a clipboard, logging all the people who entered and left the building. By contrast with the – albeit faded – grandeur of her father's house, this street with its run-down terraced houses, kaleidoscope of estate agents' boards, overstuffed rubbish bins, modest cars and vans, was real student bedsit land.

In the nineteenth century, Kemp Town had been aloof from Brighton, a posh Regency enclave of grand houses, built on a hill crested by the racecourse, with fine views out across the Channel. But gradually, during the latter half of the following century, with the construction of council estates and tower blocks and an increasing blurring of the boundary, Kemp Town became infected by the same seedy, tatty aura that had long corroded Brighton.

Parked at the far end of the street and sticking out much too much, Grace could see the tall, square, truck-sized hulk of the Major Incident Vehicle. He squeezed his Alfa Romeo into a space between two cars just past it, then walked back along the street with Branson, both men carrying their holdalls.

It was just before three o'clock, and Grace had stomach ache from having gobbled down two prawn sandwiches, a Mars bar and a Coke in the car on the way back from Janie's father. He'd been surprised he'd had any appetite at all after delivering the grim news, and even more so that he had actually felt ravenous – as if somehow in eating he was reaffirming life. Now the food was biting back.

A blustery, salty wind was blowing and the sky was clouding over. Gulls circled overhead, cawing and wailing; a Mishon Mackay *for sale* board rocked in a gust as he walked by. This was a part of Brighton he had always liked, close to the sea, with fine old terraced villas. If you closed your eyes, imagined the agency boards gone, the plastic entryphone boxes gone and a lick of fresh white paint on the buildings, you could picture wealthy London folk a hundred years ago, emerging from the front doors in their finery and swaggering off, maybe down to a bathing machine at the water's edge, or to a grand cafe, or for a leisurely stroll along the promenade, to enjoy the delights of the town and its elegant seafront.

The city had changed so much, even in his brief lifetime. He could remember, as a child, when streets like this were the domain of Brighton's seaside landladies. Now, after a couple of decades in the hands of property speculators, they were all chopped up into bedsits and low-rent student flats – cash paid, heavies sent round to collect the rent. And if anything went wrong, maybe you'd get it fixed, eventually, if you were lucky.

Sometimes, on a wet Sunday, Grace loved to go into the local museum and look at the prints and watercolours of Brighton in a bygone age, in the days of the old chain pier and hansom cabs, when men walked along in silk top hats wielding silver-handled canes. He used to wonder for some moments what life must have been like in those days, and then he would remember his father telling him how his dentist used to pedal the drill by foot. And suddenly he was glad he lived in the twenty-first century, despite all modern society's ills.

'Penny for your thoughts,' Glenn Branson said.

'I like this part of Brighton,' Grace said.

Branson looked at him, surprised. 'You do? I think it's skanky.'

'You've got no appreciation of beauty.'

'This part of town reminds me of that movie *Brighton Rock*. Dickie Attenborough playing Pinkie.'

'Yes, I remember. And I read the novel,' Grace said, for once trumping him.

'It was a *book*?' Branson looked at him in surprise.

'Christ, what stone did you crawl out from under?' Grace said. 'Graham Greene. It was one of his most famous novels. Published in the 1940s.'

'Yeah, well that explains it, old-timer. Your generation!'

'Yeah, yeah! You give me all this crap about knowing so much about movies, but you're just a philistine at heart.'

Branson stopped for a moment and pointed at a boarded-up window, then at the salt-burned paintwork above and below it, and then at the crumbling plasterwork. 'What's to love about that?'

'The architecture. The *soul* of the place.'

'Yeah, well I used to work at a nightclub around the corner, and I never found any *soul* here. Just an endless line of fuckwits out of their trees on E.'

They reached the bespectacled community support officer outside the front door and showed him their warrant cards. He dutifully wrote their names down on his log in the slowest handwriting Grace had ever seen. CSOs had been introduced to ease the workload of officers. They had been nicknamed *plastic policemen* and were perfect for duties such as this.

'You go up to the second floor,' he said helpfully. 'The stairwell and access have been checked – they haven't found anything forensically appropriate.' He talked as if he were running the show, Grace thought, privately amused.

Entering the front, the place reminded Grace of every low-rent building he had ever been in: the balding carpet on the floor, junk mail spilling out of the pigeonholes, the tired paintwork and peeling wallpaper, the smell of boiled cabbage, the padlocked bicycle in the hallway, the steep, narrow staircase.

A strip of blue, yellow and white Sussex Police crime scene tape was fixed across the door of the flat. Grace and Branson pulled their white protective suits out of their holdalls, put them on, then their gloves, overshoes and hoods. Then Branson rapped on the door.

It was opened after some moments by Joe Tindall, clad in the same protective attire as themselves. It didn't matter how many times Grace saw SOCOs at work, their hooded white outfits always reminded him of secret government officials cleaning up after an alien invasion. And no matter how many times he had seen Joe Tindall in recent days, he could not get over his colleague's recent makeover.

'God, we really get to meet in the best of places, don't we, Roy?' Tindall said by way of a greeting.

'I like to spoil my team,' Grace replied with a grin.

'So we've noticed.'

They went into a small hallway, and Tindall closed the door behind them. Another figure in white was on his hands and knees, inspecting the skirting board. Grace noticed that a radiator had been unbolted from the wall. By the time they had finished in here, every radiator would be off, half the floorboards would be prised up, and even parts of the wallpaper would have been removed.

A band of sticky police tape had been laid in a straight line down the centre of the hall, as the path for everyone to keep to. Tindall was meticulous at preserving crime scenes.

'Anything of interest?' Grace asked, glancing down at a ginger and white cat which had wandered out to look at him.

Tindall gave him a slightly strange look. 'Depends what you call *of interest*. Bloodstains on a bedroom carpet that someone's tried to scrub off. Spots of blood on the wall and ceiling. Car keys to a Mini outside. We've taken that in on a transporter – I don't want anyone driving it and contaminating it.'

'Good thinking.' Immediately Grace logged that Janie Stretton clearly had not driven to meet her killer. At least that eliminated one enquiry line. He knelt and stroked the cat for a moment. 'We'll get someone to take you to your granddad,' he said.

Tindall gave him that strange look again. 'Follow me.'

'You must be Bins,' Grace said to the cat, remembering Derek Stretton mentioning the cat.

It miaowed at him.

'Anyone fed this?'

'There's one of those automatic feeder things in the kitchen,' Tindall said.

Roy Grace followed the SOCO officer. In contrast to the exterior of the building and the shabbiness of the common parts, Janie Stretton's flat was spacious, in very good order and tastefully if cheaply decorated. The hall and the living room off it had polished wood floors thrown with white rugs, and all the curtains and soft furnishing covers were also white, with the hard furniture a shiny lacquered black, except for six perspex chairs around the dining table. On the walls were black and white photographs, a couple of them quite erotic nudes, Grace noticed.

To one side of the living room, in the recess of a bay window, was a small, rather flimsy-looking desk with a Sony laptop sitting on it and a telephone-answering machine combo. The message light was winking.

There was a minuscule kitchen, an equally minuscule spare bedroom, then a good-sized master bedroom, very feminine-feeling, with the lingering scent of a classy perfume Grace vaguely recognized and liked. It was strangely poignant to think that the wearer was now dead and yet this part of her remained. The room was carpeted wall to wall in white and there was a large central blotch, a good two feet in diameter, then several smaller blotches around it. Bloodstains someone had scrubbed, unsuccessfully.

Through an open door he could see into an en suite bathroom. He walked across, carefully skirting the bloodstains, and peered in. There was an empty plastic bucket and scrubbing brush on the floor by the bath.

His eyes roamed the bedroom, taking everything in, as another white-clad SOCO member busily dusted all surfaces for prints. He looked at the cedar chest at the end of the small double bed, the scattered cushions on the bed, the long antique wooden mirror on a stand, the closed Venetian blinds, the two bedside lamps, switched on, the mirrored wardrobe doors opposite the bed. He could see the spots on the wall which the killer had been too careless to wipe off. Or maybe the killer had just given up with the stains on the carpet – or been startled in the midst of his clean-up.

Yet the bucket looked spotless, as did the scrubbing brush.

Another enigma.

Bins came into the room and rubbed up against Grace's leg. He stroked the cat again, absently. Then, prompted by Tindall staring upwards, he suddenly noticed the mirrored ceiling above the bed.

'A little unusual, wouldn't you say?' the SOCO said.

'That's well kinky,' Branson commented. 'Yeah!'

'Maybe she had a bad back,' Grace offered, tongue in cheek. 'And it was the only way she could see to put on her make-up.'

'There's more,' the SOCO added, opening the chest at the end of the bed.

Grace and Branson peered in. To Grace's amazement it was full of artefacts he would have expected to have found in an SM dungeon.

Even without disturbing the contents he could see a whip, handcuffs, a full rubber face mask, several other restraints including a studded dog collar that had clearly not been designed with a dog in mind, a reel of duct tape, a bamboo cane and an assortment of vibrators.

Grace whistled. 'I think you've found her toy box.'

'Whatever floats your boat, right?' Joe Tindall said.

Grace knelt and peered in more closely. 'Anything else?'

'Yeah, in her bedside table about twenty recent porn magazines. Serious, hard stuff.'

Grace and Branson took a quick glance through the collection of magazines. Men on women, women on women, men on men and various permutations. Despite the circumstances Grace felt a prick of lust as he flicked through some of the women on women pages; he couldn't help it and in truth was quite pleased that at long last, after all these years, feelings, wants, were coming back to him.

'Is this kind of shit *normal*?' Glenn Branson asked.

'I've found porn in plenty of men's cupboards before,' Tindall said. 'Don't often find it in a woman's.'

Grace wandered away from the two men and walked around the whole flat on his own. He wanted to get the feel of the place. And the more he walked round, the more it did not feel homely.

He remembered the architect Le Corbusier saying that houses were machines for living in. That's what this place felt like. It was spotlessly clean. There was a fresh Toilet Duck freshener in the lavatory in the en suite bathroom; the sink was gleaming, all the toiletries, bar an electric toothbrush and a whitening paste, stored in the bathroom cabinets. The place was incredibly clean – for a student.

He contrasted her bedroom here with the one at her father's house, with the poster on the wall, the stuffed toys, the collection of shells, the books; you could form an image of the person from that room, but not from this one.

Grace went through into the living room and, using his handkerchief, pressed the last number redial on the phone. It rang a few times, then he got the voicemail of the firm of solicitors where Janie had worked. He then dialled 1471 to check the last incoming number, but it was withheld. Next he pressed the message play button on the answering machine. The cat stood near him, but he did not notice it. He was staring at a framed photograph of Janie on the desk beside the machine. She was in a long evening gown against a background of what looked like Glyndebourne opera house. Interesting, he noted, that all the photographs of her seemed to be very posed. The machine whirred for some moments, then he heard a rather bland woman's voice.

'Oh, er – hello, Janie, this is Susan, Mr Broom's secretary. It's quarter past eleven on Wednesday. Mr Broom was expecting you in at eight o'clock this morning to work with him on finishing the briefing notes to counsel. Can you please give me a call.'

Grace wrote the details down in his notebook.

There was another, similar message from the same woman, two hours later, then at three thirty in the afternoon a different woman, sounding younger and rather smart: 'Hi, Janie, this is Verity. Bit worried that you haven't turned up today. Are you OK? I might pop round later on my way home. Call me or text me or something.'

Then an hour later there was a different message from a woman with an overly jolly voice: 'Oh, hi, Janie, this is Claire. I have something for you. Give me a call please.'

The next message was from Derek Stretton.

'Hello, Janie, darling. Got your birthday card – you are so sweet. Longing to see you on Friday. I've booked at your favourite; we can go out and have a real seafood binge! Give me a call before if you have a mo. Lots and lots of love. Daddy!'

Then a rather coarse male voice: 'Oh, hello, Miss Stretton. My name's Darren. I'm calling from Beneficial to see if you'd like a quotation for household insurance from us. I will call you back.'

Then the jolly voice of Claire again, this time a touch concerned. 'Oh, hi, Janie, this is Claire again. I'm worried that you might not have picked up my last message. I will try your mobile again, it was for tonight.'

Grace frowned. For *tonight*? Wednesday night. When she had been dead for around twenty-four hours?

There were several more messages from her office the following day, Thursday. And from the woman called Claire again, sounding very irritated. There was also another message from her father, an anxious one this time.

'Janie, darling, your office have been in touch with me – they say you haven't been in since Tuesday and they are extremely worried. Are you all right? Please give me a call back. Love you lots. Daddy.'

Grace wound the tape back to the first message from the perky Claire.

'Oh, hi, Janie, this is Claire. I have something for you. Give me a call please.'

Something about this message bothered him, but he couldn't put a finger on it. He checked the machine to see if it logged incoming phone numbers, but it did not appear to.

'Glenn,' he said. 'You're the closest I have to a resident techie. Can you get into her address file on the laptop?'

The Detective Sergeant walked over to the computer and flipped up the lid. 'Depends on whether she's been a good girl or not. Whether we have any password to . . . Ah, no – brilliant! No password!'

He pulled out the chair and sat down. 'You want a name?'

'Claire.'

'Claire what?'

'Just Claire.' Grace could not be bothered to correct Glenn's grammar.

After only a few moments tapping at the keyboard, Branson lifted his head. 'There's just one. I tried different spellings.'

'Does it give an address?'

'Just a number.'

'OK, dial it.'

Branson dialled then handed Grace the receiver. It rang for a few moments then was answered by an abrupt male voice.

'Yes, hello?'

'May I speak to Claire?'

'She's on another line – who's calling?'

Grace did a quick calculation. They had dropped Janie's photograph off at the Major Incident Suite on their way here at the same time as they had picked up Glenn's holdall. It would be a good couple of hours before copies were out in the media so no one outside the police and Janie's immediate family would yet know she was dead. 'I'm calling on behalf of Janie Stretton,' he said.

'OK, hold a sec; she'll be with you in a minute.'

Grace heard a few moments of Vivaldi's *Spring*, then the voice he recognized as Claire. 'Hello?' she said, a little wary.

'Yes, hello. I'm returning a message you left for Janie Stretton on Wednesday afternoon.'

'Who exactly are you, please?' Very wary now. Too wary.

'Detective Superintendent Grace of Sussex CID.'

The phone went dead.

Instantly, Grace hit the redial button. The phone rang several times until the voicemail finally kicked in. 'I'm sorry, there is no one here to take your call at the moment—'

'Bullshit!' Grace said, hanging up. He pulled out his radio, dialled Bella, gave her the phone number and asked her to come up with an address. Then he phoned his assistant Eleanor and asked her to set up a press conference for later that afternoon. He was keen to get maximum exposure with the public before the world wound down for the weekend.

While he was waiting he checked the emails on his Blackberry, in particular for any news from the Suresh

Hossain trial – but that seemed bogged down in day after day of legal submissions at the moment.

Five minutes later, Bella, efficient as ever, radioed him back with an address near Hove station, about ten minutes drive away, going soberly, or ninety seconds with the blues and twos on. It was a business line in the name of BCE-247 Ltd. It meant nothing to him.

He turned to Branson. 'Bag the computer up and bring it; we're going to take a drive. I don't like people who hang up on me.'

28

Grace buckled himself in tightly, told Branson to do the same, then floored the Alfa Romeo's accelerator, driving as fast as he dared, weaving in and out of the traffic, horn blaring, flashing his headlights, wishing he was in a marked car.

As he crept over the line of his third red light in a row, all Grace could think was, *If I hit anything, anything at all, I might as well start flat-hunting in Newcastle.*

The address Bella had given him was in a parade of shops in the street that ran south from Hove station. Grace screamed into a tight left-hander, passing a busy car wash on the right, then another tight left-hander, cutting dangerously across the bow of a taxi exiting from the station.

He saw a woman dressed in a trouser suit emerging hurriedly from the door between a bathroom tiling shop and a newsagent's. She was about thirty, with a good figure, spiky red hair and a plain face with too much make-up caked on. She was carrying a large leather portfolio case.

Before the wheels of the Alfa had stopped turning, Grace was out of the car, running across the road, calling out to her: 'Claire?'

She turned, too startled to deny who she was.

He flashed his warrant card at her. 'Bit early to be knocking off for the day, isn't it?'

Her eyes darted furtively to the right then left, as if she was looking for an escape route. 'I . . . I was just – nipping out to get a sandwich.' She spoke in a coarse east London accent.

'We were talking on the phone a few minutes ago – I think we got cut off.'

'Oh,' she said evasively. 'We were?'

'Yeah, I thought it might be easier to nip round – you know what the phones are like . . .'

She watched his face warily, no hint of a smile.

'Mind if we pop into your office and have a chat?' Grace asked, watching Branson out of the corner of his eye walking across the road to join them.

Now she looked panic-stricken. 'Well . . . I – I think I need to speak to my business partner.'

'I'll give you a choice,' Grace said. 'We can either do this the nice way or the nasty way. The nice way is we go to your office now, have a cup of tea and a cosy chat. The nasty way is I stay here with you while my partner goes off to get a search warrant, and he'll come back with six police officers, who'll take your office apart, floorboard by fucking floorboard.'

Grace saw the panic in her eyes turn to fear.

'What exactly is all this about, officer?'

'You mean apart from the fact I don't like people hanging up on me?'

She blushed, not knowing what to say. A bus rumbled past, engine straining. Grace waited a moment. Then he said, 'I'll tell you exactly what it's about. Janie Stretton is dead.'

The woman's hand flew to her mouth in shock. 'Janie?'

Grace sensed it was time to apply pressure. 'On Tuesday night she was cut to ribbons by a maniac, stabbed to death and butchered. You've seen the news about the headless torso found in Peacehaven on Wednesday?'

All the blood was draining from the woman's face, leaving her make-up looking even more vivid. She nodded, her fingertips toying with her lips.

'Well, we've found out today that it's Janie Stretton. OK to have that chat now?'

*

The office of BCE-247 Ltd was a second-floor room overlooking the street with a small kitchenette leading off. Apart from the outlay for a couple of gallons of a lurid shade of purple paint, which covered every wall and clashed with the pea-soup-coloured carpet, it did not look to Grace as if any effort had been made with the place for the purposes of appearances.

There were three plain, old wooden desks, three clapped-out-looking executive-style swivel chairs, four tall grey metal filing cabinets. It all looked as if it had been bought as a job lot from a second-hand office supplies store. Additionally there was a cheap-looking CD player and an equally cheap-looking television set, switched off. In contrast, on each desk were up-to-date computers and modern phones. One was ringing now, but Claire ignored it. She seemed in shock.

Branson and Grace sat in two fake black-leather armchairs in front of the woman's desk, each nursing a mug of tea. Grace had his notebook out but he was watching her eyes really closely.

'So your full name is?'

He saw her eyes swivel to the left. To the memory side of her brain.

'Claire Porter,' she said.

Grace wrote it down. 'And this is your company?'

'Mine and my partner's.'

'And his name?'

Again her eyes swivelled to the left. It was unlikely she was lying about either her name or her business partner's, so the movement of her eyes to the memory side of her brain told him this was where her eyes would go each time she told the truth. Which meant if they went to the opposite side, she would be lying.

'Barry Mason.'

Grace thought for a moment. 'BCE-247 Ltd,' he said. 'Barry and Claire Enterprises?'

She shook her head. 'No, but close.'

Balancing the notebook on his knees, he held out his arms expansively. 'So, would you like to tell us?'

He watched her eyes swivel furiously to the right. Construct mode. She was trying to think of a convincing lie.

Then suddenly she buried her face in her hands. 'Oh fuck, I can't believe it. Janie. She was such a nice girl; I really liked her.'

'You left a message on her home phone at half-past four in the afternoon on Wednesday. You said' – he paused to read from his notebook – '"I have something for you. Give me a call please."' He paused. 'What was that about?'

She looked up, and again her eyes moved to the right and she appeared agitated.

Branson cut in, gentle, playing the classic soft man to Grace's hard. 'Claire, you might as well tell us. If you've got anything to hide, it will look much better for you if you tell us the truth.'

The words seemed to hit home. Her eyes raced around as if running for cover. 'God, Barry'll kill me. It stands for Barry and Claire Escorts Twenty-Four Seven. OK?'

Grace sat for some moments in stunned silence. 'Janie Stretton was an escort? A *hooker*?'

Very defensive suddenly, Claire said, 'We provide escorts for single men – and women. People in need of a date for a night out, that sort of thing. Not *hookers*.'

Grace noticed her eyes were still moving strongly to the right; they seemed to be trying to burrow their way as far to the right as they could get.

'All innocent?' Grace said.

She shrugged. 'For us, yes.'

'Yeah, yeah, yeah. Claire, I've heard it all before, OK? If the client wants to make a private arrangement with the young lady, that's not your problem, right?'

She was quiet for a moment. Then she said, 'I think I should call my solicitor.'

'I'm not interested in busting your squalid little business,' Grace said. 'Call your solicitor and then I will bust you, just for the hell of it, I'll bloody take you apart. I want to find Janie's killer; that's all I'm interested in. Help me with that and I won't touch you. Do we understand each other?'

She grimaced. Then finally she nodded.

'How much do you charge your punters?'

'Sixty quid an hour.'

'And how much do you get of that?'

'Forty per cent.'

'The girls keep the rest and any extras?'

'They keep their tips,' she said defensively.

'Right. Who was she with on Tuesday night?'

She turned to her computer and tapped the keyboard. After some moments she said, 'Anton.'

'Anton? Anton who?'

'I don't know.'

'You don't know the names of your punters?'

'Only if they want to tell me.'

'And how many of them tell you?'

'Quite a few. But I don't know if their names are real or not.'

Grace found himself getting increasingly angry. 'These girls sign up with you and you send them out on dates with single men – on which you get a fat commission – and you don't even bother to find out their bloody names?'

There was another silence. 'We always check on the girls, on a first date. We phone them after ten minutes. We have some code words; if they're not happy, then we have security we can send over to help them. This was her fourth date with Anton. I wasn't worried – I mean I didn't feel I had any reason to be worried.'

'It didn't bother you that she was a young, innocent law student?'

'We've lots of students on our books. They find it a good way to supplement their grants. Thanks to Tony Blair, most students leave uni with debts it will take them years to pay off. Doing escort work gives them an alternative. I like to feel we are doing our bit to help them.'

'Well of course,' Grace said, his voice corrosive with sarcasm. 'I mean, all that cash coming in . . . all your altruism, and her private arrangements with Anton the butcher none of your concern.' He was silent for a moment, thinking, then he asked, 'How many girls do you have on your books?'

'About thirty. And ten guys.'

'You have pictures?'

'Yes.'

'Let me see Janie's.'

She went to a filing cabinet, retrieved a folder, opened it, took out a photograph in cellophane, then handed it to Grace.

It wasn't like any of the photographs he had seen in her father's house or in her flat. This was a wholly different Janie Stretton, a Janie of the night.

She was lying seductively on a leopard-skin rug, dressed in the briefest of leather hot pants, a black lace blouse unbuttoned to the navel, with her breasts all but completely exposed.

Grace handed it to Branson. 'Just *escorts*,' he said to the woman sarcastically. 'Women companions for social functions, that sort of thing?'

'Yeah, that sort of thing.'

'Claire, I didn't just ride into town on the tailgate of a bloody truck, OK? She was on the game, wasn't she?'

'If she was, it was without our knowledge.'

'Where do you advertise?'

'Magazines, newsagents, on the internet.'

Grace nodded. 'And where do you get most of your clients from?'

'It varies. We get a lot from word of mouth.'

'And which magazines?'

Claire hesitated. 'Contact magazines, tourist ones, the local paper, one or two speciality mags.'

'Speciality?'

After some more moments of hesitation she said, 'Fetishes, mainly. People who are into rubber. Bondage. Stuff.'

'Stuff?' Grace questioned.

She shrugged.

'So do we have any way of finding out how this Anton first got hold of your number?'

She peered in the folder and pulled out an index card. 'May sixth. Anton. I wrote down, "Strong European accent".

He said he'd seen the advert in' – she squinted as if trying to read her own writing – 'the *Argus*.'

The local newspaper.

The phone rang again. She ignored it and continued squinting as if trying to decipher more notes. 'He wanted to see some pictures of the girls, so I directed him to the website. Then he rang back about half an hour later, saying he'd like a date with Janie. I have his number!'

Grace sat up and saw Branson's instant reaction also. 'You do?'

'I always take a call-back number for our clients. It puts them on guard.'

'Let me have it, please.'

He wrote it down as she read it out, then immediately dialled it on his mobile phone. Instantly he got the unobtainable signal. 'Shit.'

'Is there anything else at all you could tell us about this Anton?'

'I wish I could. Do you . . . think – that – that he might have been the one who . . . ?'

'If he wasn't her killer, he must have been one of the last people to see her. Do your girls ring in after their date's finished?'

'Sometimes, depends how late it is.'

'She didn't ring you on Tuesday night after her date with Anton?'

'No.'

'And you were ringing her about another date on Wednesday?'

'Yes.' She looked at her notes. 'Another gentleman. Do you need his name and number?'

Grace nodded. 'We'll check it out.'

'You'll be discreet?'

'I'll put my most discreet man on to it.' Grace grinned to himself. He'd delegate his new recruit Norman Potting to the task. The DS was about as discreet as a bull on roller blades in a china store.

29

By four o'clock Tom's office was starting to empty. Typical for a Friday, he thought. It was a fine, sunny afternoon in London, and the weather forecast was good. One by one his staff were clearing their desks, saying their cheery goodbyes and heading for the door.

He envied them their carefree weekends, and tried to remember when he'd last had a weekend in which he had really relaxed and not thought about work, not sat at his computer, poring over a spreadsheet of his outgoings and income, not peeked anxiously over Kellie's shoulder as she'd sat at her keyboard on the sitting-room floor.

His window was open a little despite the roar of the traffic and he felt the air, balmy and warm. Maybe this weekend he would switch off a little, as much as the dark cloud of that damned CD would allow. It was good news that Kellie had a job. The money wasn't great, but at least it would cover some of her spending extravaganzas – just as long as it did not encourage her to spend even more.

At four fifteen he decided, *To hell with it.* If he left now he might just make the next fast train, the 16.36, which would get him home comfortably in time for the barbecue he'd planned with Kellie, using the monster new piece of kit she had bought.

He shook his head at the thought of the barbecue. Insane. Yet he was curious to know what it looked like; curious to know how *any* barbecue could cost north of five hundred pounds.

In a fit of extravagance, minor compared to Kellie's, he took a cab instead of the bus to Victoria station, arriving with just minutes to spare. He grabbed an *Evening Standard* from a vendor, and without bothering to wait for his change sprinted for the platform, clambering aboard the train just seconds before the wheels began to turn.

Out of sheer determination, he struggled down the aisle of every single one of the train's crowded carriages, looking for the dickhead. But there was no sign of him. By the time he had finished, he had broken into a heavy sweat from the heat and from his exertion. He found one of the few empty seats, removed his laptop and his high-speed internet card from his bag, put the bag and his jacket up on the luggage rack, then sat down with his laptop on his knees and glanced at the front page of the newspaper.

THIRTY DEAD IN IRAQ BOMB CARNAGE.

He glanced through the article, about yet another suicide car bombing of police recruits, guiltily aware he had become almost numb to reports like these. There seemed to be so many, all the time. And he'd never really worked out where he stood on Iraq. He didn't care for Bush or Blair and every successive outrage had made him increasingly doubtful the world was a safer place since the invasion. Sometimes when he popped his head around the bedroom doors of his sleeping children he stared at them with a guilty helplessness, knowing just how responsible he was for their safety, but in terms of the politics of the world into which he had brought them, he felt woefully inadequate.

Then he turned the page, and it felt like an unseen fist had reached out from some other dimension altogether and was gripping his innards like a vice.

He was staring at a photograph of a young woman,

beneath a grisly headline running across the top of the third page: HEADLESS TORSO VICTIM NAMED.

Her face.

Reminding him again, just a little, of Gwyneth Paltrow, just as when he had first seen her, in his den, on Tuesday night.

It was *her*. For sure, for absolute certain.

His eyes jumped down to the words printed below.

> Sussex Police confirmed today that the badly mutilated body of a young woman, found on farmland in Peacehaven, East Sussex, on Wednesday, is that of missing law student Janie Stretton, 23.
>
> The Senior Investigating Officer leading the enquiry for Sussex CID, Detective Superintendent Roy Grace, said, 'This is one of the most brutal murders I have encountered in twenty years on the police force. Janie Stretton was a decent, hard-working and popular young woman. We are doing everything we can to apprehend her killer.'
>
> Derek Stretton, Janie's distraught father, issued this brief prepared statement from his £3m riverside mansion near Southampton. 'Janie was the most wonderful daughter a father could wish for, and was a great strength to me when my wife – her mother – sadly died. I beg the police to find her killer swiftly, before he destroys another innocent life.'

Then Tom's eyes jumped back up to Janie's face. And as he did so, the words of the threatening email burned back into his brain.

If you inform the police about what you saw, or if you

*ever try to access this site again, what is about to
happen to your computer will happen to your wife,
Kellie, to your son, Max, and to your daughter,
Jessica . . .*

For a moment he glanced nervously around at his
fellow passengers but no one was taking any notice of
him. A youth opposite was sitting plugged into an iPod; he
could hear the beat, an irritating raspy sound, too low to
recognize the music but louder than the *clackety-clack* of
the train. A couple of others were also reading newspapers,
while a woman was reading a well-thumbed copy of *The
Da Vinci Code*, and a man in a pin-striped suit was working on his laptop.

Tom stared back at the photograph. Was there any
possibility he was mistaken? Any at all?

But there wasn't. *It was her.*

So what the hell, he wondered, was he going to do?

30

At half past six, Roy Grace, Glenn Branson and all the other
members of the investigation team, including Grace's
newest recruit, Detective Sergeant Norman Potting, were
sitting at the large, rectangular table in the briefing room,
directly opposite MIR One, the Major Incident Room
where Operation Nightingale had been allocated its workstation.

Grace could smell the reek of pipe tobacco coming off
Norman Potting's clothes. The long-serving policeman was
dressed in a brown suit that was a good twenty years old, a
white shirt that looked like he had ironed it himself when
he was drunk, a green golf-club tie covered in food stains
and stout black shoes. He was a self-assured, rather cocky
veteran of three marriages, with a narrow, rubbery face
criss-crossed with broken veins, protruding lips, tobacco-
stained teeth and a thinning comb-over.

Grace formally welcomed Norman Potting, avoiding
eye contact with everyone else.

'Good to be on the team,' Potting returned in his deep
rumble of a voice, heavily tinged with his native Devon
burr. 'Especially pleasant to be working with some pretty
young ladies.' He winked broadly at Bella and then at
Emma-Jane.

Grace winced, then pressed on. He needed to be away
by seven if at all possible, just for a couple of hours. He
looked down at the briefing notes prepared by Bella and
Eleanor for him. 'The time is six thirty, Friday, June third,'

he read out. 'This is our second briefing of Operation Nightingale, the investigation into the murder of a previously unknown person, now identified as Jane – known as Janie – Susan Amanda Stretton, conducted on day two following the discovery of her remains. I will now summarize the incident.'

For some minutes Grace reviewed the events leading up to the discovery of Janie's headless remains, then the discovery of the beetle at the post-mortem. At which point Norman Potting interrupted him.

'Wasn't there something in the papers some years back about Hollywood stars putting gerbils up their bottoms, Roy?'

'Thanks, Norman; I don't think that has any currency here.'

'Mind you, there's a lot of them actors are queer and you don't know it.'

'*Thank you*, Norman,' Grace said firmly, trying to put him back in his box. He was about to continue, to tell the team about the discovery of Janie Stretton's secret life, when Glenn Branson put up his hand, interrupting him.

'You were telling me in the car earlier about the symbolism of the scarab beetle, Roy. I think that's useful to share with the team.'

'Yes, I was intending to. Briefly, in ancient Egyptian mythology, the scarab beetle was worshipped under the name Khepri – which translates literally as "he who has come into being" or, "he who came forth from the earth". Those Egyptians were great worshippers of the sun. In the same way that the scarab beetle pushed a ball of dung in front of it, the Egyptians imagined that Khepri rolled the sun – visualize it as a solar ball – across the sky from east to west each day – so they regarded Khepri as a form of the sun god, Ra. As a result the scarab became an important symbol of creation, resurrection and everlasting life in the religious mythology of ancient Egypt.'

'They were clever buggers, those Egyptians,' Norman Potting said. 'I mean how the heck did they build those pyramids? Mind you, I'd never trust one – have to watch those darkies.'

Grace, wincing, shot a sideways glance at Glenn Branson, then glared at Potting, wondering how on earth the man was still in the force and hadn't ended up in front of a sexual harassment or race relations tribunal. 'Norman, that language is totally unacceptable and I won't have it used in my briefings.'

Potting looked as if he was about to say something, then appeared to think better of it and sheepishly looked down at his papers.

'Have you figured out if the symbolism has any bearing yet, Roy?' Nick Nicholl asked.

'Not so far, no. I hope one of you geniuses will.' Grace grinned at him, then continued, telling the team of their discovery this afternoon of Janie Stretton's secret life. And, crucially, that they had the first name of a possible suspect. Anton.

It had already been established that the phone number for this Anton, which Claire at the agency had written down, belonged to an untraceable pay-as-you-go phone.

Grace paused to drink some water. 'Right. Resourcing. East Downs Division has been very positive in offering manpower. We instigated a search of the vicinity of the area where the torso and limbs were discovered on Wednesday morning, and have been widening and upgrading this further over the past forty-eight hours. I've brought in the Sussex Police Underwater Search Unit, and we are in the process of having the USU team drag all local rivers, lakes and reservoirs. I have also requested a further helicopter sweep.'

He went on through the headings. Meeting Cycles: Grace announced there would be daily 8.30 a.m. and 6.30 p.m. briefings. He reported that the Holmes computer team had been up and running since Wednesday. He read out the list under Investigative Strategies, which included Communications/Media, emphasizing the need to keep the discovery of the beetle out of the press, and that they were working on getting the murder featured on next week's *Crimewatch*.

Then Emma-Jane raised a hand. 'Are we going to release the information that Janie Stretton had a secret life on the game?'

Grace had been wondering exactly the same thing. He thought about Derek Stretton, already distraught, his life in ruins. What effect would that information have on the poor man? But would there be any value to releasing it? Would it prompt someone who had hired her services to come forward with some vital clue? Unlikely but possible. It was a tough call. Releasing it would greatly increase the press interest. Broader coverage might just mean that someone would come forward. Maybe a waiter or a barman might have seen Janie and this Anton together?

'Two family liaison officers are with Janie's father at the moment, DCs Donnington and Ritchie. I will discuss it with them first but my inclination is yes,' he replied to Emma-Jane. 'Unless they have very strong feelings that it would be too distressing to Mr Stretton at this stage, we will go ahead and release it.'

Next was Forensics. Grace reported that, apart from the beetle, there were no surprises from the post-mortem so far, apart from one: there was no sign of sexual assault on the victim. He had the report from Dr Frazer Theobald in front of him, but there was no need to read out the pages and pages of technical details. Janie had died from multiple stab wounds from a long, thin blade. *Having her head removed hadn't exactly helped her survival chances either,* he thought.

'At the moment, this scarab beetle is my main concern,' he said. 'Has anyone discovered any other murder where a beetle was found at the scene?'

'There was a woman found on Wimbledon Common in April,' Nick said. 'The victim was a twenty-six-year-old woman, also missing her head. She was wearing a silver charm bracelet that none of her family recognized. I had a jpeg emailed through. This is a printout.' He handed it to Grace. 'There was no sign of sexual assault in this murder either. And it is unsolved.'

Grace stared at the tiny silver beetle hanging on the bracelet. He recognized the markings instantly. It was a scarab. 'Good work,' he said. 'No others?'

'The Met are the only force to have responded so far,' Nick said.

Grace stared at the photograph. 'My hunch is there are going to be others. Can we get the file on this?'

Nick looked at his notes. 'The SIO is a Detective Inspector Dickinson; he's offered to meet me – or any of us.'

'He sounds unusually cooperative for a Met,' Grace said cynically. The Metropolitan Police tended to be a law unto themselves – arrogant, considering themselves the best, and not that cooperative with provincial forces. 'Can you arrange to meet him mid-morning tomorrow?'

'I was meant to be playing for Sussex CID in a police football friendly, but yes.'

'It's June now; this is the cricket season, not football,' Grace said in a chiding tone. 'We have a father I've just spent time with today, telling him his daughter has been butchered; I'm not sure he'd be that impressed to know the murder investigation had to be delayed because of a sodding football match.'

The Detective Constable blushed. 'No, sir – Roy.'

When he reached the end of his report, Grace summed up. 'We have now established a crime scene where the murder of Janie Stretton took place. Bella and Nick have conducted questioning of all Janie Stretton's neighbours, and this is ongoing. The alternative scenarios as I see them are as follows.

'One, this is a one-off killing by some very sick person.

'Two, we may be looking at a serial killer leaving a signature. We are waiting for more information from the Met on the other killing where a beetle was found to see if they may be connected. Our killer may therefore have killed at least twice, each time a young woman, and we can assume he is going to kill again.'

Then he asked his team if they had anything to report.

Potting said he had spent much of the afternoon at the firm of solicitors where Janie Stretton had been doing her training. He had interviewed her boss, a Martin Broom – who Grace had encountered in court once, over an assault during a particularly nasty divorce case – and several of her colleagues. Janie had checked out as a popular, hard-working and conscientious young woman.

Do we all have a hidden dark side? Grace wondered privately to himself. 'I've requested an additional team member. And I want someone from the High-Tech Crime Department to go through her laptop with a fine-tooth comb,' he said. Then he turned to DC Boutwood. 'Emma-

Jane, sorry to dump this on you, but I want you to organize a trawl through all the CCTV camera footage in the Brighton area on Tuesday night. You can draft in some help on this. What you are looking for is this young lady.' He tapped the photograph of Janie Stretton that had been circulated to the press. 'She went out on a fourth date with a man called Anton, or whatever his real name was, that evening. Someone must have seen them.' Then he turned to DC Nicholl.

'Nick, I want you to organize a team of Specials and PCSOs to take this photo to every restaurant, bar and pub in Brighton and Hove, and see if anyone saw her. OK?'

The beanpole nodded.

'Bella,' Grace said. 'Janie Stretton's father told me her last boyfriend was called Justin Remington – a property developer in London. Go find him and see what he has to say.'

She nodded.

'Emma-Jane, how did you get on with the tropical insect breeders?'

'I've located sixteen throughout the UK. Some are internet only, but I've found seven breeders. One, in Bromley, south London, sounds very interesting. He had a request to supply a scarab beetle just over ten days ago. To a man with an eastern European accent.'

'Magic!' Grace said. 'And?'

'I've arranged to see him tomorrow.'

'I'll come with you.'

Grace then looked down at his notes. 'Norman, we've removed the answering machine from the victim's flat. I'm having it examined by the Technical Support Unit. Whatever information they can extract I'd like you to check up on.'

'Any good-looking birds?'

'I'll find someone to help you if you find any.'

'I quite like the sound of this agency, if it's got birds of the calibre of Janie Stretton on its books.'

Grace ignored the man. His remark didn't even warrant an answer. 'I'll see you all here at eight thirty in the morning,' he said. 'Sorry to muck up your weekends.'

In particular he avoided eye contact with Glenn Branson. Glenn's wife was getting increasingly fed up with the hours that police work consumed. But that was his choice, Grace thought. When you signed up to Her Majesty's police, you took the Queen's shilling. And in return you dedicated your life.

OK, so maybe it wasn't actually spelled out in the contract. But that was the reality. If you wanted a life, you were in the wrong career.

31

It was windier down in Brighton than in London, but the air was plenty warm enough to be outside.

Girls Aloud were pounding out of the CD player built into the barbecue, and a digital light show flashed with the music. Jessica, dressed in baggy jeans, a black top and sparkly shoes, her long fair hair flailing, and Kellie, barefoot in white calf-length trousers and a striped man's shirt, were dancing on the lawn, gyrating wildly, laughing, having just the greatest time.

Max, in grubby grey shorts and an even grubbier Dumbledore sweatshirt, his blond hair hanging like a tousled mop over his forehead, had not yet finished inspecting the barbecue. He treated it with the reverence with which he might have treated a spaceship that had landed in their backyard. Which indeed was what it looked like.

It was vast, taking up a good chunk of the garden, eight feet from end to end, curved, with a futuristic design fashioned from stainless steel, brushed aluminium and some black, marbled material, complete with extremely comfortable fold-out stools. It looked more like the bar from one of those hyper-hip London hotels where Tom sometimes met clients for a drink than a device for grilling sausages.

The Giraffe must have walked past twenty times this evening. Tom saw Len Wainwright's head, craned forward way above the top of the close-boarded fence, bobbing steadily along, up and down, up and down, dying to catch Tom's eye and get into a natter about the machine. But Tom was in no mood for small talk tonight.

'What does that do, Daddy?' Max, pointing at a digital display, shouted above the sound of the music.

Tom set down his glass of rosé wine, then thumbed through the English section of an instruction manual the size of a London phone directory. 'I think it measures the temperature of the inside of the meat – or whatever you are cooking.'

Max's mouth opened and shut, as it always did when he was impressed by something. Then he frowned. 'How does it know that?'

Tom opened a compartment and pointed at a spike. 'There's a sensor in the spike; it reads the internal temperature. It's like a thermometer.'

'Wow!' Max's eyes lit up for a moment, then he was pensive again, and took a few steps back. 'It is a bit big, isn't it?'

'A little,' Tom said.

'Mummy said we might be moving, then we'd have a bigger garden, so then it won't be so big.'

'Did she?' Tom said.

'She said that 'xactly. Will you come and play Truck Racing with me?'

'I have to start cooking – we're going to eat soon. Aren't you hungry?'

Max puckered up his mouth. He always considered any question carefully, even one as basic as this. Tom liked that quality about him; he took it as a sign of his son's intelligence. So far he didn't seem to have inherited his mother's recklessness.

'Umm. Well, I could be hungry soon, I think.'

'Do you?' Tom smiled and stroked the top of his son's head fondly.

Max ducked away. 'You'll muck my hair up!'

'You reckon?'

He nodded solemnly.

'Well it looks to me like you have a bird nesting in it.'

Max stared at him even more solemnly. 'I think you're drunk!'

Tom looked at him in shock. 'Drunk? Me?'

'That's your third glass of wine.'

'You're counting, are you?'

'They said in school about drinking too much wine.'

Now Tom was even more shocked. Was the nanny state now sending kids home from school to spy on their parents' drinking habits? 'Who said that, Max?'

'It was a woman.'

'One of your teachers?'

He shook his head. 'A nothingist.'

Tom smelled sweet barbecue smoke coming from one of his neighbours' gardens. He was still poring through the manual, trying to find out how to fire up the gas grill. 'A nothingist?'

'She was telling us what was good to eat,' Max replied.

Now Tom got it, or thought he had. 'You mean a nutritionist?'

After some moments of deep thought, Max nodded. 'Can't we have one game of Truck Racing before you cook? Just one teeny game?'

Tom finally located the on–off switch. The instruction manual said to switch the grill on, then leave for twenty minutes. Kellie and Jessica looked well away, dancing to yet another track.

'One game.'

'Promise you won't beat me?' Max asked.

'That wouldn't be a fair game, would it?' Tom said, following him into the house. 'Anyhow, I never beat you; you always win.'

Max burst into giggles, and scampered on ahead of his father upstairs to his bedroom. Tom paused in the kitchen to glance at the television, in case the news was on, and to fill his wine glass up – finishing the bottle in the process. Unless Kellie had been helping herself, Max was wrong, he realized. It hadn't been his third glass, it had been his fourth. And on Monday he intended phoning Max's head-master and asking what the hell he thought he was playing at, indoctrinating kids into monitoring their parents' drinking habits.

But as he climbed the stairs, being careful not to spill any wine, he had something infinitely more important on his mind. He stopped at the top, thinking.

Max called out, 'You can have any colour you want except *green*, Daddy. I'm having *green*. OK?'

'OK,' he called back. 'You're having green!'

Max won the first race easily. Squatting on the carpet in his son's bedroom, holding the remote control, Tom could not get his brain to focus on the track. He crashed on the first bend in the second race, then went off again at the next opportunity, scattering tyres and bales of straw. Then he somersaulted into a grandstand.

For the past two hours, since he had seen the photograph of Janie Stretton in the *Evening Standard*, then seen her again on the *Six O'Clock News* when he'd got home, his brain had been mush.

He could not just ignore any more what had happened. Yet that email which had trashed his computer showed him this person or these people – whoever – were serious.

Which meant the threat was serious.

Was there really any useful information he could give to the police? All he had seen was a couple of minutes of the young woman being stabbed by a hooded figure. Was there really anything there which could help the police?

Anything worth risking the safety of his family for?

He played the argument over and over. And each time he came to the inescapable conclusion that yes, there might be something that could help the police. Otherwise why would the threats have been made against him?

He needed to discuss it with Kellie, he realized. Would she believe him, that he had innocently stuck the CD into his computer?

And if she was against him going to the police, what then? What would his conscience say to him?

The people he had always admired in his life, the true heroes, past and present, were those men and women who were prepared to confront things that were wrong. To stand up and be counted.

Tom watched Max for some moments, eyes alert, fingers expertly dancing around the controls, his truck hurtling around the track. Outside there was a lull in the music and he heard Jessica laughing gleefully.

Didn't they also have a say in the matter?

Did he have a right to put their lives in jeopardy over what he believed in? What would his own father have done in this situation?

God, it was at a time like this that he missed his parents so much. If he could have gone to them and asked their advice, how much easier that would have been.

He thought about his father, a decent man who had worked as a sales manager for a German company that manufactured industrial cleaning brushes. A tall, gentle man, and a verger at the local Anglican church, he worshipped every Sunday of his life, and was rewarded by God by having his head chopped off by the tailgate of a milk lorry on the M1 motorway at the age of forty-four.

His father would have given him a Christian perspective, no doubt the responsible citizen view, that Tom should report what he had seen and also the threat. But he had never been able to share his father's faith in God.

He would ask Kellie, he decided. She had a lot of wisdom. Whatever she said, he would abide by.

32

The clumsily handwritten poster Sellotaped to the glass pane of the door said: BRENT MACKENZIE. WORLD-FAMOUS CLAIRVOYANT. HERE TONIGHT ONLY! A large fluorescent yellow strip across it read: SORRY, SOLD OUT!

Outwardly the building did not look that promising. Grace had been expecting a fairly spacious hall, but the Brighton Holistic Centre appeared to occupy nothing grander than a small corner shop, with its exterior painted a rather garish pink.

A woman in her forties, wearing a black smock over a grey leotard and with slightly mad hair, stood on the other side of the door, collecting tickets. Grace took his wallet out of his pocket, dug his fingers into it and retrieved his ticket, which he had purchased several weeks earlier.

He felt nervous. A disconcerting jangling deep inside him seemed to strip away his natural confidence. It was always the same before he saw a medium or clairvoyant, or any other kind of psychic. The anticipation. The hope he held in his heart that this one might be different, that this one finally, after close on nine long years, would have the answer.

Either a message, or a location, or a sign.

Something that would tell him whether Sandy was dead or alive. That was the most important thing he needed to know. Sure, there would be all kinds of other questions that would then follow whichever answer he got. But first, please, he needed that answer.

Maybe tonight?

He handed over his ticket and followed three nervously chatting girls up the narrow staircase. They looked like sisters, the youngest in her late teens, the oldest in her mid-twenties. He passed an unpainted door marked QUIET, THERAPY IN SESSION, and entered a room that had about twenty assorted plastic chairs squeezed in, forming an L-shape with a gap where he presumed the clairvoyant would stand. There were blue blinds, pot plants on the shelves, and a print of a Provençal landscape on one wall.

Most of the chairs were already taken. Two young girls were with their mum, a pudding-faced lady in a baggy knitted top, who seemed to be fighting back tears. Next to them sat a long-haired earth mother of about seventy in a floral top, denim skirt and glasses the size of a snorkeller's mask.

Grace found a free chair next to two men in their late twenties, both wearing jeans and sweatshirts. One, grossly overweight, with ragged hair that reminded Grace of the comedian Ken Dodd, was staring blankly ahead and chewing gum. The other, much thinner, was sweating profusely and brandishing a can of Pepsi Cola in his hand as if it afforded him some status. Grace overheard some of their conversation; they were discussing electric screwdrivers.

Another mother and daughter entered the room and took the remaining two chairs, next to him. The daughter, thin as a rake and dressed to party in black trousers and red blouse, reeked of a scent that smelled, to Grace, of lavatory freshener. The mother, equally dolled up, looked like a computer-aged image of the daughter twenty years on. Grace was familiar with the technique; it was used frequently in the search for missing persons. A year ago he'd had a photograph of Sandy put through the process and been staggered by how much someone could change in just eight years.

There was an air of expectation in the room. Grace glanced around at the faces, wondering why they were all here; some because they were recently bereaved, he guessed, but probably most were just lost souls in need of guidance. And they had each forked out ten quid to meet a complete stranger with no medical or sociological qualifications, who was about to tell each of them stuff that could alter their entire approach to life.

Stuff that the spirits channelled through Brent Mackenzie, or so he would claim. Grace knew; he'd seen it all.

And yet he kept coming back for more.

It was like a drug: just one more fix and then he would stop. But of course he would never stop, not until the day he found out the truth about Sandy's disappearance. Maybe the spirits would tell Brent Mackenzie tonight; maybe the clairvoyant would do what all those before him had failed to do, and pluck it out of the ether.

Roy Grace knew the reputational risk he ran by pursing his interest in mediums and clairvoyants, but he was not the only police officer in the UK to regularly consult them, not by a long way. And, regardless of what the cynics said, Grace believed in the supernatural. He had no option. He had seen a ghost – two ghosts, in fact – many times during his childhood.

Every summer he used to go and stay for a week with his uncle and aunt, in their cottage in Bembridge on the Isle of Wight. In a grand town house opposite two very sweet old ladies used to wave at him from a bay window on the top floor. It wasn't until years later, revisiting Bembridge after a long absence, that he learned that the house had been empty for over forty years – the two old ladies who waved at him had committed suicide in 1947. And it hadn't been his imagination; other people had seen them also.

The audience were quietening now; the two men beside him seemed to have finished their discussion about electric screwdrivers. It was 7.45 p.m. exactly. Behind him he heard the hiss of a ring pull being tugged on a can of drink. A mobile phone beeped an incoming text message, and he saw the earth mother delve into her macramé handbag, pull the phone out and switch it off, her face reddening.

Then the medium sauntered in, with all the presence of a man looking for the door to a pub urinal. About forty years old, standing a good six foot four inches tall, he was dressed in a baggy orange T-shirt with a string of beads around his neck, fawn chinos and shiny white trainers. He had buzz-cut hair, a few days growth of stubble, a prizefighter's broken nose and a massive beer belly, and, Grace noticed, he was wearing a very expensive-looking watch. For some moments he appeared not to notice that he had walked into a crowded room. Grace even began to wonder whether this actually was the clairvoyant.

Then, facing the blinds, Brent Mackenzie spoke. His voice was thin and reedy, far too small for such a large man, but very earnest. 'I'm not using my memory tonight,' he said. 'I want to do my best for all of you. I will have a message for each of you tonight; that's a promise.'

Grace glanced around; just a sea of silent, rapt faces, waiting.

'My first message is for a lady in here called Brenda.' Now the clairvoyant turned and scanned the room. The pudding-faced mother put her hand up.

'Ah, Brenda, love, there you are! If I said there was a move imminent in your life, would that be right?'

The woman thought for a moment, then nodded enthusiastically.

'Yeah, that's what the spirits are telling me. It's a big move, isn't it?'

She looked at each of her daughters in turn, as if for confirmation. Both of them frowned. Then she looked at the medium. 'No,' she said.

There was an awkward silence. After a few moments the medium said, 'I'm being told it is a bigger move than you realize at the moment. But you are not to worry about it; you are doing the right thing.' He nodded reassuringly at her, then closed his eyes and took a pace back.

Grace watched him, feeling uncomfortable about the man. This was a typical ploy of a medium – to manipulate what he said when it did not resonate.

'I've got a message for a Margaret,' Brent Mackenzie said, opening his eyes and scanning the room. A rather mousy little woman in her late thirties who Grace had not previously noticed put up her hand.

'Does the name Ivy mean anything to you, darling?'

The woman shook her head.

'OK. What about Ireland. Does Ireland mean anything?'

Again she shook her head.

'The spirits are very definite about Ireland. I think you will be going there soon even if you don't realize it at the moment. They say you will go to Cork. There's someone who will change your life who is in Cork.'

She looked blank.

'I'll come back to you, Margaret,' the clairvoyant said. 'I'm being interrupted – they are very rude sometimes in the spirit world; they get very impatient when they have a message for someone. I'm getting a message here for Roy.'

Grace felt a jolt as if he had plunged his finger into an electrical socket. Brent Mackenzie was stepping towards him, staring hard at him. He felt his face burn and all his composure went; he stared back at the medium now towering over him, feeling confused, helpless.

'I've got a gentleman with me, I think he might be your father. He's showing me a badge he used to wear. Does that mean something?'

Maybe, Grace thought, *but I'm not giving you any clues. I'm paying you to tell ME things.*

Grace stared at him blankly.

'He's showing me his helmet. I think he was a police officer before he passed. He has passed?'

Grace gave him a reluctant nod.

'He tells me he's very proud of you, but you are having a difficult time at the moment. Someone is blocking your career. He is showing me a woman – with short blonde hair? Is her name Vespa, like the motor scooter?'

Now Grace was mesmerized. *Alison Vosper?* He desperately wanted to speak to the man, to tell him the name Sandy. But his courage had deserted him. And he did not want to lead him. Was Brent Mackenzie going to tell him something about Sandy? Some message from his father about her?

'Your dad's showing me something, Roy. It's a small insect. Looks like a beetle. He is quite agitated about this beetle. He's not very clear—' The clairvoyant cupped his head in his hands, turned round once, then again. 'I'm sorry, I'm losing him. He said it could save something.'

Grace, staring up at him, suddenly found the courage to speak. 'What exactly did he say it could save?'

'I'm sorry, Roy, I've lost him.' The medium looked at someone else. 'I've got a message for Bernie.'

Grace barely noticed. He was thinking. The man had got two hits. His father and the beetle. *He said it could save something.*

He would grab the clairvoyant at the end of the session, no matter how tired he was, and pump him for more.

What did the man mean? What the hell could it save? His career? Another life?

*

But he did not have to worry about getting hold of Brent Mackenzie when the evening ended. The clairvoyant, wearing a long anorak over his T-shirt, was waiting for him at the bottom of the stairs.

'Roy, isn't it?' he said.

Grace nodded.

'I don't normally do this, but could we have a word in private?'

'Yes, sure.'

Grace followed him into a tiny consulting room containing a desk, a couple of chairs and several dozen white candles, and the clairvoyant closed the door behind them. In this room he seemed even bigger, towering over Grace.

Remaining standing, Mackenzie said, 'Look, I'm sorry; we didn't have a very satisfactory session. I didn't want to say too much in there, in front of everyone, you know. Some things are private. This doesn't often happen to me, but I picked up some really bad feeling about you. I'm talking about this beetle thing I saw; I can't get it out of my head. Like one of those you see in ancient Egyptian writings.'

Tilting his head up at him, Grace said, 'A scarab?'

'Yeah, exactly. *Scarab* beetle.'

Grace nodded. 'Yes, that makes sense.'

The medium gave him a strange look. 'Makes sense?'

'It's to do with work. I can't really talk about it.'

'You're a copper, aren't you?'

'Does it show?'

The clairvoyant smiled. 'I was a copper myself, for ten years. Manchester CID.'

'You were?'

'Yeah, well. Long story. Save it for another day. The thing is, mate, they're telling me you are in real danger. Something to do with this scarab beetle. You need to watch your back.'

33

By the time Tom had figured out how to light the barbecue, it was already past the children's bedtime. And by the time he had finally cooked their sausages and burgers, Jessica was sound asleep and Max was grizzling.

And now he had drunk too much rosé wine, and he had to finalize the quotation for twenty-five Rolex Oyster watches engraved with a logo in a microdot, and email it to Ron Spacks. The DVD distribution giant had confirmed he was dead serious about placing the order, and Tom had promised the quotation would be with him no later than tonight. He had found a legitimate supply source that would give Spacks a bargain, and net him close to £35,000 profit on the contract. Not only a very sweet deal, it would be a massive help to his business – and his life – at this moment.

He stared fondly at Kellie, who was lying in front of the television, watching Jonathan Ross interview a rock star Tom had never heard of. Lady, as usual, was sitting by the front door with her lead in her mouth.

He hauled himself up the stairs, gripping the banister rail for all he was worth, as if he was climbing Everest the hard way.

Tom opened Jessica's bedroom door. Light from the landing spilled in, throwing shadows around. She was fast asleep, her face turned towards him, arm around her large, soft teddy, breathing in, a steady long and slow rhythmic hiss, then out with a sharp *phutt*.

Something gripped his chest like a vice, and his heart. He stood motionless, as if all time in the universe was frozen. This was his daughter. His child. His creature that he had brought into the world. His *little person*.

Jessica.

God, he loved her to bits. People said that parents had favourites but he didn't, he could honestly say that.

He blew Max a kiss, closed the door, and with a heavy heart went into his den to finalize the Ron Spacks figures.

When he had checked, then double-checked the email and sent it, he made his way back downstairs. Jonathan Ross on the television was talking about the size of willies. Kellie was now fast asleep, empty wine glass on the floor, a half-eaten box of Milk Tray on the sofa beside her.

After they had put the kids to sleep, he had told her about the website and the subsequent email, and then the photograph of Janie Stretton in the paper tonight.

They had watched the *Ten O'Clock News* together, and seen the poor young woman featured along with footage of the police search in Peacehaven, and a plea by a Detective Superintendent Roy Grace of the Brighton CID for anyone with information to step forward.

Kellie had really surprised him. He thought he knew her much better than he apparently did. He had imagined she would put the safety of her family first. Particularly after he told her about the threatening email.

She had taken less than a couple of minutes to make up her mind. 'Imagine that was Jessica in twenty years' time,' she had said. 'Imagine we were the parents, desperate for justice to be done. Now imagine, knowing all that, you are a witness, maybe the only witness. Your stepping forward might make the difference between the killer being caught – and being prevented from ever killing again – and destroying the lives of all those related to the victim. Imagine if Jessica was murdered by a killer who could have been stopped if only someone had been brave enough to step forward.'

He went through into the kitchen, took out a bottle of his favourite Bowmore whisky and poured himself several fingers. A few hours ago he had made the decision that he would abide by Kellie's view.

But then he had been expecting her to tell him that he needed to put the safety of the family first. And if that meant doing nothing, that would be preferable to anything that put them in jeopardy. Instead she was completely adamant he should go to the police, regardless of the consequences.

Sitting on a bar stool, he watched his reflection in the window. He saw a hunched man raise a glass of whisky to his lips and drink; he saw the man set the glass back down.

He saw the total despair in the man's face.

He drained his whisky, then went back into the living room to wake Kellie up. They had to talk more.

*

They talked long into the night, then finally, exhausted, Tom tried to sleep. But he was still awake at three o'clock. And at four. Tossing. Turning. Fretting, dry, parched, with a searing headache.

Tonight they were safe. Tonight he did not have to worry about threats. Kellie's view was that the police would protect them. Tom did not share her confidence.

Dawn was breaking. At five he heard a hiss of tyres, a whine, a clank of bottles. In another hour or so the kids would be stirring, running into their bedroom, jumping into their bed. Saturday. Normally he loved Saturdays, his favourite day of the week.

Kellie told him he could give the information to the police in confidence, and that the police would respect that. How would anyone find out he had been talking to them?

'Are you OK, hon?' Kellie spoke suddenly.

'I'm still awake,' he said. 'I haven't slept a wink.'

'Nor have I.'

He put out his hand, found hers, squeezed it. She squeezed back. 'I love you,' he said.

'I love you, too.' Then after a pause, she asked, 'Have you made a decision?'

He was silent for some moments. Then he said quietly, 'Yes.'

34

Roy Grace was having a sleepless night, also. An endless list of things he needed to check for Operation Nightingale churned through his brain. As well as the words of Brent Mackenzie.

The thing is, mate, they're telling me you are in real danger. Something to do with this scarab beetle. You need to watch your back.

What did he mean? Maybe he had just picked up the vibe of the scarab, which was preying heavily on his mind?

Then his thoughts went back to Janie Stretton. He pushed away all the emotion of her distraught father – he had become hardened to those things over the years. Perhaps more hardened than he liked, but maybe that was the only way to cope. He was thinking about what had been done to her. What was the sense in removing her head but leaving a hand? Other than that it was some kind of message? To whom? The police? Or perhaps a sick trophy?

And why the scarab beetle?

For the killer to show off his – or her – intellect?

Then his thoughts turned darkly to the warning from Alison Vosper, and the knowledge that this case was the Last Chance Saloon for him. To keep his job and his life here in Brighton, he needed to find Janie's killer with no fuck-ups, no newspaper headlines about cops dabbling in the occult and nobody killed in a car chase.

He had to walk on bloody eggshells.

Might be easier, he thought, to walk on water.

*

By six in the morning Grace had had enough of listening to the dawn chorus, to rattling milk bottles, to a barking dog way off in the distance, to all the damned stuff inside his head.

He pushed back the duvet, swung his legs out of bed and sat still for some moments, his eyes raw from lack of sleep, his head pounding. He had not slept for more than half an hour throughout the entire night, if that. And tonight he had a date. A really, really serious date.

And that too, he knew, was a big part of the reason he had barely slept. Excitement. Like a smitten teenager! He couldn't help it. He could not remember when he had last felt like this.

He walked to the window, opened the curtains a fraction and stared out. It was going to be a fine day; the sky was a blank, dark blue canvas. Everything felt very still. An enormous thrush was hopping clumsily around the dew-drenched lawn, pecking at the ground in search of worms. Grace stared at the Zen water garden Sandy had created, with its skewed-oval shape and its large, flat stones, and then at all the plants she had put around the borders of the lawn. A lot had died, and the ones that remained were wildly out of control.

He had no idea about gardening; that had always been Sandy's domain. But he'd enjoyed helping her create her own special garden out of the boring eighth of an acre rectangle of lawn and borders that they had started with. He dug in places she told him to dig, fertilized, watered, lugged bags of peat up and down, weeded, planted, a willing skivvy to Sandy as foreman.

Those had been the good times, when they were building their future, making their home, their nest, cementing their life together.

The garden that Sandy had created and loved so much was neglected now. Even the lawn looked ragged and weed-strewn, and he felt guilty about that, sometimes wondering what she would say if she returned.

Saturday mornings. He remembered how he used to go off for his early run, and come back bringing Sandy an almond croissant from the bakery in Church Road and her *Daily Mail*.

He drew the curtains right back, and light flooded in. And suddenly, for the first time in almost nine years, he saw the room differently.

He saw a woman's bedroom, decorated mostly in different shades of pink. He saw a Victorian mahogany dressing table – which they had picked up for a song at a stall in the Gardner Street market – very definitely covered in a woman's things: hairbrushes, combs, make-up and scent bottles. There was a framed photograph of Sandy in evening dress and himself in black tie finery, standing beside the captain of the SS *Black Watch* on the only cruise they had ever been on.

He saw her slippers still on the floor, her nightdress on a hook on the wall beside the bed. What would any woman make of this if he brought her back here? he thought suddenly.

What would Cleo think?

And, he realized, these thoughts had never occurred to him before. The house was a time warp. Everything was exactly the way it had been that day, that Tuesday, 26 July, when Sandy had vanished into thin air.

And he could still remember it so damned vividly.

On the morning of his thirtieth birthday Sandy had woken him with a tray on which was a tiny cake with a single candle, a glass of champagne and a very rude birthday card. He'd opened the presents she had given him, then they had made love.

He'd left the house later than usual, at nine fifteen, and reached his office at Brighton police station shortly after half past for a briefing on the murder of a Hell's Angel biker who had been dumped in Shoreham Harbour with his hands tied behind his back and a breeze block chained to his ankles. He'd promised to be home early, to go out for a celebratory meal with another couple, his then best friend Dick Pope, also a detective, and his wife Leslie, who Sandy got on well with. There had been developments on the case, and he'd arrived home almost two hours later than he had intended. There was no sign of Sandy.

At first he'd thought she was angry at him for being so late and was staging a protest. The house was tidy; her car and handbag were gone; there was no sign of a struggle.

Then, twenty-four hours later, her elderly black VW Golf was found in a bay in the short-term car park at Gatwick Airport. There had been two transactions on her credit card on the morning of her disappearance, one from Boots, and one from Tesco. She had taken no clothes and no other belongings of any kind.

His neighbours in this quiet, residential street just off the seafront had not seen a thing. On one side of him was an exuberantly friendly Greek family who owned a couple of cafes in the town, but they had been away on holiday. On the other side was an elderly widow with a hearing problem, who slept with the television on, volume at maximum. Right now, at 6.18 a.m., he could hear a muffled American voice through the party wall between their semi-detached houses; it sounded like John Wayne, addressing a bunch of bums he had just rounded up.

He went downstairs into the kitchen, wondering whether to make a cup of tea or go for his run first. His goldfish was drifting aimlessly around his circular bowl, as ever.

'Morning, Marlon!' he said breezily. 'Having your morning swim? Are you hungry?'

Marlon's mouth opened and closed a couple of times. He wasn't much of a conversationalist.

He filled the kettle, pulled up a chair and sat down at the kitchen table, looking around, wondering what signs of Sandy were in this room. Almost everything, except for the silver fridge, was red or had a red motif. The oven and the dishwasher were red, the handles on the white units, the hob, the doorknobs, were all red. Even the kitchen table was red and white. All Sandy's choice. It had been *the* fashionable colour at the time, but it all looked a little tired now; the ceramic surfaces were badly chipped. Some of the unit hinges had sagged. The paint-work was scratched and grimy.

The truth was, he knew, he would be better off in a flat. They rattled around in this place – himself, Marlon and Sandy's ghost.

He opened the cupboard door beneath the kitchen sink, ducked down, found a roll of black bin liners and tore one off. Then he picked up a photograph of himself and Sandy from a shelf and stared at it for a moment. It had been taken by a stranger, with Grace's camera, on their honeymoon. Right at the top of Mount Vesuvius. Sandy and he stood, looking sweaty from the exertion of the hard climb, both wearing T-shirts, against the backdrop of the crater partially masked by low grey cloud.

He placed the photograph in the bin liner, then stood still as if waiting to be struck dead by a thunderbolt.

But nothing happened.

Except a whole load of guilt crept up through him. What if it went really well tonight and he ended up bringing Cleo Morey back here after their dinner date?

He realized he needed to remove anything that was obviously Sandy's. And that was a huge milestone for him. A mountain.

But maybe it was time?

Then, having second thoughts, he took the photograph out of the bin liner and put it back on the shelf. It would look odd if he did not have photographs. It was her personal *things* he needed to reduce around the house.

Up in the bedroom, he looked at her hairbrush. There were still strands of her long, fair hair in the bristles. He pulled one out, held it up, his heart leaden suddenly. He let the strand drop and watched it float to the carpet, feeling a lump in his throat. Then he brought the brush to his nose and sniffed, but there was no scent of Sandy remaining on it, just a flat, dry smell.

He put the brush into the bin liner, and all the rest of her belongings from the dressing table and then from the bathroom. He carried the bag into the spare room used for storing junk, and placed it next to an empty suitcase, the box that his laptop had originally come in and several old rolls of Christmas wrapping paper.

Then he got changed into his shorts, singlet and trainers, folded a five-pound note into his pocket, and set off for his run.

His route took him straight down to the Kingsway, a wide dual carriageway running along Hove seafront. On one side were houses that would give way in half a mile or so to continuous mansion blocks and hotels – some modern, some Victorian, some Regency – that continued the full length of the seafront. Opposite were two small boating lagoons and a playground, lawns and then the promenade with stretches of beach huts, and the pebble beaches beyond, and just over a mile to the east, the wreck of the old West Pier.

It was almost deserted and he felt as if he had the whole city to himself. He loved being out this early on a weekend, as if he had stolen a march on the world. The tide was out, and he could see the orb of the rising sun already well up in the sky. A man walked, far out on the mudflats, swinging a metal detector. A container ship, barely more defined than a smudge, sat out on the horizon, looking motionless.

A sweeper truck moved slowly towards Grace, engine roaring, its brushes swirling, scooping up the usual detritus of a Friday night, the discarded fast-food cartons, Coke cans, cigarette butts, the occasional needle.

Grace stopped in the middle of the promenade, a short distance from a wino curled up asleep on a bench, and did his stretches, breathing deeply that familiar seafront smell he loved so much – the salty tang of the fresh, mild air, richly laced with rust and tar, old rope and putrid fish – that Brighton's elder generation of seaside landladies liked referring to in their brochures as *ozone*.

Then he began his six-mile run, to the start of the Marina and back again. For the final mile, he always turned inland, running up to the busy shopping thoroughfare of Church Road, Hove, to an open-all-hours grocery store, to pick up some milk and a newspaper, and maybe a magazine that took his fancy. Maybe this morning he would buy another style magazine. Something like *Arena*. Get some more ideas about what to wear tonight.

He stopped outside the shop door, partly refreshed by his run and partly exhausted from his lack of sleep, perspiring heavily. He did his stretches, then entered the store and walked over to the newspaper and magazine section. And instantly saw the headlines of the morning edition of the *Argus*.

BEETLE RIDDLE IN BRIGHTON LAW STUDENT MURDER

Seething with anger, he grabbed a copy of the paper from the stand. There was the photograph of Janie Stretton he had released yesterday. Inset below it was a small photograph of a scarab beetle.

> Sussex CID are refusing to say whether a rare scarab beetle, not native to the British Isles, might hold a vital clue to Janie Stretton's killer. When asked to confirm the discovery of the beetle during the post-mortem examination by Home Office Pathologist Dr Frazer Theobald, Senior Investigating Officer Detective Superintendent Roy Grace of Brighton and Hove CID was not available for comment . . .

Grace stared at the words, his fury growing by the minute. *Not available for comment*? No one had bloody asked him to comment. And he had given strictest instructions that the press were not to be told about the discovery of the beetle.

So who the hell had leaked it?

35

A few minutes before eight thirty, having showered, grabbed a quick bowl of cereal and, although it was Saturday, thrown on a dark suit, white shirt and plain tie – not knowing what the day would bring and who he might have to meet – Grace arrived at MIR One in the Major Incident Suite in a filthy mood, ready to skin someone alive.

His whole team was already there, waiting for him – and by the looks on their faces, all of them had seen the *Argus* headline too.

Just in case they hadn't, he thumped the paper down on the workstation. By way of a greeting he said, 'OK, who the fuck is responsible for this?'

Glenn Branson, Nick Nicholl, Bella Moy, Emma-Jane Boutwood, Norman Potting and the rest of the team all stared back at him blank-faced.

Grace fixed his accusatory gaze on Norman Potting as his first port of call. 'Any thoughts, Norman?' he said.

'The writer on the piece is that young journo, Kevin Spinella,' Potting rumbled in his deep rural voice. 'That bugger's always trouble, isn't he?'

Grace suddenly realized that in his anger he had neglected to look at the byline. It was because he was tired; he did not have his brain fully in gear after his sleepless night. A long run normally charged him up, but at this moment he felt drained and badly in need of a strong coffee. And the smell of the stuff was rising tantalizingly from several cups on the desk.

Kevin Spinella was a recent recruit to the paper, a young, sharp-voiced rookie crime reporter, fast carving a reputation for himself at the expense of the Sussex Police. Grace had had a previous run-in with this journalist, as had most of his colleagues.

'OK, Norman, your first task today is to get hold of this scumbag and find out where he got his story from.'

The Detective Sergeant pulled a face then sipped on his styrofoam cup of coffee. 'He'll probably just tell me he's protecting his sources,' he said with a smugness that really irritated Grace.

Grace had to restrain himself from yelling at the man because the truth was, Potting was probably right.

'The problem is, Roy,' Branson said, 'we've got a hundred Specials drafted in, searching for the victim's head. Could be one of them. Could be one of the SOCOs. Could have come from the Coroner's office. Or the mortuary.'

He was right, Grace knew. That was the problem with a major enquiry like this. Everyone was curious, that was human nature. It only needed one careless person to leak anything and it would spread in minutes.

But the bloody damage that could do. Or had done.

Parking the issue for the moment, he ran through the list that Bella Moy and Eleanor had prepared, and would continue to update, twice daily, throughout this enquiry. Then Norman Potting interrupted him.

'You never know, Roy; we might be able to pin something on this Kevin Spinella.'

'Like what?' Grace said.

'Well, I heard rumours that he might be a brown-hatter. You know, a turd-burglar.'

Grace, his heart sinking, felt another Potting moment coming on. 'Gay is the word we use.'

'Exactly, my friend.'

Grace stared at him sternly. Norman Potting was just so out of touch with the real world. 'And how exactly would that help us?'

Potting pulled a briar pipe, with a well-chewed stem, out of his suit pocket and stared at it with pursed lips. 'I'm wondering how the editor of the *Argus*, the voice of the City of Brighton and Hove, would feel about having a poof working for him.'

Grace could scarcely believe his ears. 'Norman, as the City of Brighton and Hove has the largest gay community in the whole of the UK, I think he'd be quite happy if the entire editorial team was gay.'

Potting turned to Emma-Jane and gave her a broad wink, a bead of spittle appearing in the corner of his mouth. Jerking his thumb at his own chest he said, 'It's all right, darling; lucky there're still a few *real men* around. Make the most of 'em.'

'When I find one, I will,' she said.

'Norman,' Grace said, 'the language you're using is totally unacceptable. I want to see you in my office straight after this meeting.'

Then to the team he said, 'OK, let's focus. E-J and I have an appointment at an insect farm in Bromley at eleven. Norman, you have your day cut out with Spinella and your follow-ups on Janie Stretton's answering machine.'

He continued on through the list of the day's tasks for each member of the team. All being well there would be a one-hour window this afternoon for himself and Glenn to meet in downtown Brighton, and do a spot of serious clothes shopping.

Then he tried to push aside the guilt he felt for just thinking this when all his attention should have been concentrated on Janie Stretton. Surely, after all the years of hell he had been through, he was allowed one treat, just occasionally?

Then, like a dark cloud slipping over the sun, he thought about Sandy again. She was always there, quietly in the background. It was as if he needed her approval for anything he did. He thought guiltily about her belongings that only a couple of hours or so ago he had dumped into a black bin liner. In case he brought Cleo Morey back home tonight?

Or just to try to clear his past, to make way for the future?

Sometime soon, when he had a moment to himself, he would go to an estate agent and put the bloody house on the market.

Even just the thought of that was like some giant weight lifting from his shoulders.

Glenn Branson's phone rang. He glanced at Grace, who nodded approval for him to answer.

'Incident room, DS Branson speaking. How can I help you?'

'Do you know why most men die before their wives?' Norman Potting suddenly said.

Grace, trying to listen to Branson's conversation, braced himself for what was coming next.

In response to a sea of shaking heads, Potting said, 'Because they want to!'

All the women groaned loudly in unison. Glenn Branson clapped the phone closely to his head and covered his opposite ear with his hand, trying to blot out the sound.

Potting, the only person who seemed to find his joke funny, was chortling away to himself.

'Thank you, Norman,' Grace said.

'Got a whole lot more where that came from,' the DS said.

'I'll bet you have,' Grace retorted. 'But it is a quarter to nine on a Saturday morning. Maybe you'd like to tell us some a bit later on, after we've arrested our killer?'

'Good plan!' Potting said, after some pensive moments. 'Can't fault you on that one, Roy.'

Grace stared back at the man. It was hard to tell sometimes whether he was being smart or just totally stupid. From past experience with the Detective Sergeant, he seemed, usually, to manage to be both simultaneously.

Branson, dressed today in an expensive-looking collarless leather jacket over a black T-shirt, was scribbling a number down on his pad. 'Ten minutes,' he said. 'I'll call you back. No, don't worry. Absolutely. Thank you.'

Everyone had suddenly fallen silent, watching him. As Branson hung up the receiver he said, 'Another possible lead.'

'Any good?' Grace asked.

'A man was calling me from a payphone – he was scared to talk from his home. Then he started worrying about a car parked down the street. He wanted to walk past it, check it out. I have to call him back in exactly ten minutes.' Branson checked his watch, a massive, stainless-steel rectangle that he liked to show off ad nauseam. It was a Russian divers' watch, he told everyone, which he had bought from some trendy shop in Brighton. It was meant to be the largest wristwatch in the world. Grace had seen grandfather clocks that had smaller faces.

They had logged over two hundred and fifty calls from the public since the story of the murder first broke on Wednesday afternoon. All of them had to be followed up, and all but a tiny percentage would amount to nothing.

Now with the information about the scarab beetle in today's *Argus* – and it would no doubt be in all the nationals tomorrow – the call rate would probably go up, and they would have a much harder time sorting the genuine from the cranks.

'Time waster or real?' Grace asked.

'He says he thinks he witnessed Janie Stretton's murder.'

36

Grace drove while Emma-Jane Boutwood, smartly dressed in a navy two-piece with a pale blue blouse, sat in the passenger seat of the unmarked Mondeo, with the directions she had printed off the internet on her lap on top of a large brown envelope.

Normally Roy Grace would have used an hour-long car journey as an opportunity to bond with a junior member of his team, but he had too much on his mind this morning, of which his anger at Norman Potting was just a small part, and their conversation was sporadic. E-J told him a little about herself – that her father had an advertising agency in Eastbourne and that her kid brother had survived a brain tumour some years back. Enough for Grace to get some sense of the human being behind the front of the young ambitious policewoman that he saw in the office. But she got very little back from him, and after a few attempts at engaging him in conversation she took the hint that he wanted silence.

He kept the car to a steady 75 mph, travelling anti-clockwise along the M25. It was one of his least favourite roads, its frequent heavy congestion causing many people to nickname it the world's biggest parking lot, but this Saturday morning the traffic was light and moving steadily. After a fine early start the weather was now deteriorating, the sky turning an increasingly ominous charcoal colour. A few spots of rain were striking the windscreen, but not enough yet to put the wipers on. He barely even noticed them; he was driving on autopilot, his conscious brain focusing on the case.

Janie Stretton had been murdered some time on Tuesday night and it was now Saturday morning, he was thinking. They still did not have her head, nor any motive, nor any suspect.

Not one damned clue.

And Alison Vosper had told him that on Monday the supremely arrogant Detective Inspector Cassian Pewe from the Met was joining Brighton CID at the same rank as himself. He had no doubt that the Assistant Chief Constable was waiting for him to put just one more foot wrong, and he would be off this case in a flash, replaced by Pewe, with his shiny blond hair, angelic blue eyes and voice as invasive as a dentist's drill.

Alison Vosper would be keen for her new protégé – which was how Pewe seemed to Grace – to make his mark quickly, and there could be no better showcase than a high-profile murder like this, where the existing team was getting nowhere.

What puzzled Grace most was the savage nature of the killing – the assailant must have been in a total frenzy – yet the absence of any apparent sexual assault. Did they have someone totally deranged, perhaps another schizophrenic like Peter Sutcliffe, the Yorkshire Ripper, on their hands? A man who heard voices from God telling him to kill hookers?

Or had Janie Stretton made an enemy?

Obviously her last boyfriend Justin Remington was a potential suspect, but from what Janie's father had said, he was a long shot. Bella Moy was a good judge of people – Grace would have a better feel about this man after she had interviewed him, which would be today, with luck, if she could get hold of him. If she felt any inkling of something not being right, he would then go and see the former boyfriend himself. But if, as he strongly suspected, it wasn't Justin Remington, then who? Why? Where was the killer now? Out there somewhere, about to strike again?

Last night, after he had been to see Brent Mackenzie, he had grabbed some fish and chips – and a pickled onion – and taken them back to the then almost deserted MIR One. He had washed the meal down with a tannic cup of vending-machine tea while poring over the case notes to date that Hannah Loxley, the team's typist, had prepared for him.

He had sat there a long time, staring at the photograph of Janie Stretton's face, then at the two large whiteboards. On one was pinned a section of an Ordnance Survey map of Peacehaven, with the two locations where her hand and the rest of her headless torso had been found ringed in red. There were also photographs of the body in situ, and a couple taken during the post-mortem, one showing the beetle in her rectum. He could picture, vividly, every detail of them now, and shuddered suddenly in revulsion.

What happened to you, Janie, on Tuesday night? And who was Anton? Did Anton do this to you?

His thoughts turned to Derek Stretton. Over 95 per cent of all murder victims in the UK were killed either by a member of their own family or by someone they knew. Was there anything he and Glenn Branson had missed when they had gone to see Janie's father yesterday? Something the man said that suggested he might have butchered his own daughter? Anything was possible; Grace had learned that much during his years in the force. But Stretton had seemed genuine, a sad father, down and lost. He did not have the aura of a man who had just killed someone.

The car radio crackled into life. They were out of range of Sussex Police airwaves now and were picking up a Bromley area controller, calling for a car to attend an RTA. Emma-Jane turned the sound down. 'Almost there,' she said. 'Go straight over the next roundabout, then it should be the second street on the left.'

Suddenly, as if the sky had been saving it all up, a torrent of rain exploded onto the windscreen, danced on the bonnet of Ford, rattling like pebbles on the roof. Grace fumbled to find the wipers, then got them on, slow at first, then faster; they smeared the rain into an opaque film, and for some moments he had to really concentrate until the screen cleared a little.

'Are you good with insects?' Grace asked.

E-J grimaced. 'Actually, no. How about you?'

'Not crazy about them,' he admitted.

He took the left turning she indicated, into a road of 1930s semi-detached houses – not unlike his own street, he thought. At the far end he saw a small industrial estate, beyond which the road went under a railway bridge. On the far side, on their left, were more semi-detached houses, then a busy parade of shops.

'It's here,' the Detective Constable said.

Grace slowed, looking for a parking space outside the shops. He saw a bakery, a chemist's, and a bric-a-brac shop with old chairs, a toy car, a pine table and some other arte-facts spread out on the pavement; there was a medical centre next to it, and a sports trophy shop next to that, and then he saw what looked like a pet shop, its window full of small, empty cages. The sign above the window read: ERRIDGE AND ROBINSON – IMPORTERS AND SUPPLIERS.

They parked the car in a bay a short distance further along, then ran back through the rain, Emma-Jane holding the large brown envelope over her head, and in through the front door of the premises – which set off a bell with a loud *ping*.

The smell hit Grace instantly: a sharp, intensely sour reek, toned down just a fraction with sawdust. They were in a dimly lit area, completely surrounded, floor to ceiling, by cages with ultraviolet backlighting, inside some of which he could see insects crawling around. He peered into one cage, only inches from where he was standing, and saw a pair of brown antlers twitching. A very large beetle, too large and too close for his comfort. He took a couple of steps back, wiped away some rainwater from his brow and gave the DC a *What the hell is this place?* frown.

Then he saw the spider, or rather its yellow and black hairy leg, followed by another leg, then another; it moved across its cage in three fast darts. It was enormous; with its legs outstretched and plainly visible now, the thing would not have fitted on a dinner plate.

Emma-Jane was watching it also; she looked very uncomfortable. Which was how he felt. The more he looked around, the more tiny eyes and twitching antennae he saw. And the stink was nearly making him retch.

Then an internal door opened, and a short, thin man in his late forties emerged, wearing brown overalls and a white shirt done up to the top button, but with no tie. He had small, wary eyes beneath massive, bushy brows that looked like two warring caterpillars. 'Can I help you?' he asked in a reedy voice with a tone that was distinctly aggressive.

'Are you George Erridge?'

His response was very hesitant and drawn out. 'Ye-es.'

'I'm Detective Constable Boutwood,' E-J said. 'We

spoke yesterday. This is Detective Superintendent Grace from Brighton CID.'

Grace held up his warrant card. The man peered at it, seeming to read every word, his face twitching, his eyebrows going hammer and tongs at each other. 'Yes,' he said. 'Right.' Then he looked at the two police officers in expectant silence.

E-J removed a colour photograph from the envelope and handed it to the man. 'We're looking for someone who might have supplied this creature to a customer in England.'

George Erridge gave the photograph just a brief glance and said almost instantly, '*Copris lunaris.*'

'You import tropical insects?' Grace asked.

The man looked quite offended. 'Not just tropical; European, pan-Asian, Australian; from all over the world, really.'

'You might have imported this one?'

'I usually keep some stock. Would you like to see?'

Grace was tempted to say, *No, I really would not*, but instead said dutifully, 'Yes, I would.'

The man led them through the internal door he had emerged from, into a shed a good hundred feet long. Like the shopfront, it was lined floor to ceiling with cages; the smell was even worse in here, much more sour and pungent, and the lighting just as dim.

'This is the roach room,' Erridge explained with a tinge of pride. 'We supply a lot of these to the pharmaceutical industry for tests.'

Grace, who had always had a loathing for cockroaches, stopped and peered into one cage in which there were about twenty of the brown creatures. He shuddered.

'One of the most resilient animals on the planet,' the

man said. 'Did you know that if you cut off a cockroach's head, it can live for up to fifteen days? It will still keep going back to its original source of food. Won't be able to eat it, of course.'

'Yech!' Emma-Jane gulped.

'I didn't know that,' Grace said. *Thanks for sharing it with me,* he nearly added.

'They would survive a nuclear holocaust. They finished evolving hundreds of thousands of years ago. Doesn't say much about the human race, does it?'

Grace looked at him, uncertain how to reply. Then he and E-J followed him through another internal door into an even longer shed. Halfway down, George Erridge stopped and pointed at one small cage. 'There you go,' he said. '*Copris lunaris.*'

Roy Grace looked for some moments before he saw one of the beetles with its distinctive markings, motionless.

'So, if I might ask, what exactly is your interest in these beetles?' Erridge said.

It was so tempting to tell him, and watch his expression, that Grace had to fight hard to restrain himself. 'I can't tell you the circumstances, but one of these beetles was found at a crime scene. What we would like from you is a list of any of your customers who have bought one of these from you recently.'

George Erridge went quiet, but his eyebrows jigged furiously at each other. 'I've only had one customer in recent months. Not much call for them, really; just the occasional collector and new museums – don't get many of those.'

'Who was the customer?' Grace asked.

Erridge dug his hands into his overall pockets, then pushed his tongue hard against his lower lip. 'Hmmn.

Funny bloke, sort of eastern European accent. He rang me 'bout two weeks ago, asking very specifically if I had any *Copris lunaris* in stock. Said he wanted six of them.'

'Six?' Grace said, horrified. His immediate thought was *Six murders like this one?*

'Yes.'

'Alive or dead?'

Erridge looked at him strangely. 'Alive, of course.'

'Who do you normally supply to?'

'Like I said, the pharmaceutical industry, natural history museums, private collectors, film companies sometimes; supplied a tarantula recently for a BBC production. I'll tell you a trade secret: insects are a lot easier to control than other animals. You want a docile cockroach, just put him in the fridge for four hours. You want an aggressive cockroach, put him in a frying pan on low heat for a few minutes.'

'I'll remember that,' Grace said.

'Yes,' Erridge replied intensely seriously. 'That's what you need to do. They don't suffer, you see. They don't feel pain the same way we do.'

'Lucky them.'

'Indeed.'

'What details do you have of this man who bought six of these?' Emma-Jane asked.

Looking a little defensive, Erridge said, 'I don't have any details. I only keep records on my regulars.'

'So you hadn't dealt with this man before?' she asked.

'No.'

'But you met him?' Grace asked.

'No. He phoned up, asked if I had them, and told me he would send someone to collect them. He sent a minicab and the driver paid cash.'

'A local firm?'

'I wouldn't know. I don't use minicabs; can't afford 'em.'

Grace's mobile phone suddenly beeped then vibrated. Excusing himself, he turned away from the insect expert and answered it.

'DS Grace,' he said.

It was Branson. 'Yo, old man,' he said. 'How you doing?'

'I'm shopping,' Grace said. 'Buying your birthday present. What's up?'

'The bloke who rang me during the briefing – the paranoid one I had to speak to in the phone booth who said he thinks he witnessed information about Janie Stretton's murder?'

'Uh huh,' Grace said.

'He said he saw it on his computer after inserting a CD he found on a train.'

'Is he letting us have a look at it?'

'I'm working on that now.'

37

Looking into someone's computer was like looking into their soul, Detective Sergeant Jon Rye believed, and he had had more than enough experience to make that observation. He had lost track of the number of computers he had examined in the past seven years – probably quite a few hundred, he had recently estimated. And today he had another one, a Mac laptop, fifteen-inch screen, about a year old.

He had never yet come across a computer that could hide its secrets from him and his team. Villains of every type – burglars, fraudsters, car-ringers, phishers, paedophiles – all thought they could wipe their hard disks and be safe. But there was no such thing as erasing a disk. The software that Jon Rye had at his disposal could recover just about every bit of deleted data from a disk, and could prise every digital footprint out of every nook and cranny of a computer's system, however complex, however well concealed.

At this moment, seated at his desk in the High Tech Crime Unit, which he ran, he was about to stare into the soul of a man called Tom Bryce. And there was no option but to spend the weekend at work because this man, who was a potential witness not a suspect, needed his machine back for work on Monday morning.

It was Jon Rye's boast, and it was no idle boast, that within an hour of looking at any man's computer, he would know more about him than his wife did. And invariably the computers which arrived in his bailiwick belonged to men rather than women.

The High Tech Crime Unit occupied a substantial space on the ground floor of Sussex House. To the casual observer, most of it didn't look any different to many of the other departments in the building. It consisted of an open-plan area densely packed with workstations; on the desks of several of these stood large server towers, and on some the entrails of dismembered computers as well. On one of the untidy shelves, between rows of tilted files, sat a bag of Tate and Lyle sugar. There was a Bart Simpson clock on the wall above one desk, at which Joe Moody, a large, pony-tailed man in a T-shirt and jeans, sat intently at his keyboard, logging the images of a bunch of dumber than usual young vandals, who had photographed themselves torching a car they had stolen.

One section of the room was caged off from the rest – this housed Operation Glasgow, a major child porno-graphy investigation which had been going on for two years and was on the verge of cracking one of the largest rings in Europe. The caging was to prevent cross-contamination of evidence with the rest of the department. Four people were at work in the cage today, and Rye did not envy them. Day in, day out, for the past twenty-four months they had had to spend their working hours looking at sickening pictures of sex acts involving children. Much of Jon Rye's work involved suspected paedophiles and nothing lessened the anger he felt every time he saw one of those pictures. God, there were some sick people out there in the world. Too damned many.

The Venetian blinds were drawn shut against the gloomy view of the cell block, made even more depress-ing by the pelting rain. But at least it was a tolerable temperature in his office today; most days in summer it was far too hot and stuffy, and the damned windows did not open.

A tough, wiry-framed man of thirty-eight with a boyish, pugnacious face and thinning, brush-cut fair hair, Jon Rye was dressed in a short-sleeved white shirt, navy suit trousers and black shoes, the kind of plain, near-uniform clothing he wore to work every day, and it made no odds to him that this was Saturday. These days it had become the exception for him not to work on Saturdays.

Jon had always been interested in technology and in gadgets, and when the use of computers had started to explode a decade back, he had seen the massive new opportunities for criminals they would bring, and how ill-equipped the police were at that time to deal with computer crime. He decided the best job security in the force would be in computer crime, and that after he retired from the police, with his background in the field, getting a well-paid job in the civilian world would be easy.

He had given up trying to convince his wife Nadine that this crazy job was only temporary and would not go on for ever; or maybe she had given up listening when he told her. He glanced around at some of the other members of his team who were also in today, and wondered how many of them had domestic grief over being here.

The simple fact was that they were overrun. They currently had a nine-month backlog of seized computers waiting to be forensically examined; as usual, it came down to resources. He suspected that the chiefs preferred to spend their money on making the police more visible – putting them out on the streets, nicking burglars, muggers, drug dealers, making the crime statistics look good – and that they regarded the High Tech Crime Unit as necessary but not something which won Sussex Police many brownie points.

Quite a few of his team were real geeks, recruited from outside the police – a couple straight from university, others from IT departments in industry and local government. At the workstation right behind him he watched the geekiest of all, Andy Gidney.

Gidney, who was twenty-eight, was just plain weird. Almost pitifully thin, with a complexion that did not look as if it had ever seen fresh air, hair that he surely cut himself, clothes and glasses that looked like they had come from a closing-down sale at a charity shop and a generally antisocial demeanour, the man was nonetheless utterly brilliant at his work – by far the cleverest member of his team. He spoke seven languages fluently, including Russian, and had never yet been defeated by a password.

They did not need passwords to actually get into a computer, because the software they used took them in through a back door, but some password-protected zipped files gave them grief. Andy had been working for most of the past week on a particularly intransigent file seized from a suspect in a massive phishing scam in which online banking websites were being cloned. He was refusing to give up and allow the machine to be sent to a specialist decryption facility.

Jon did not care for Gidney, but he admired his tenacity and respected his abilities. He had long come to accept that the people in this unit were very different to the petrol-head cops he used to work with on Traffic, where he had spent nearly ten of his twenty years to date with the force. In Traffic you saw mostly grim sights, and sometimes heart-rending tragedy. But here in High Tech Crime, you saw the true dark side of human nature.

He started as he did on every case, by carrying the computer through into the locked Evidence Room, where the walls were lined with wooden racks stacked with seized computers, all regarded as crime scenes and all bagged in shiny, translucent plastic evidence bags and tagged. Some of them had been here a long while. Several large plastic bins on the floor, piled high with more bagged computer equipment, carried the overspill.

Rye put Tom Bryce's laptop down on a work surface, unscrewed the casing and removed the hard drive, which he carefully connected to a tall, rectangular steel box with a glass front. This contained a write-blocking device, the Fastbloc, which would make a byte-by-byte forensic copy of the disk.

When that was completed, he reassembled the computer, carried it back to his desk, then plugged it in and began work. Out of habit, the first search command he entered was *Buffy*. Nothing came up. The second was *Star Trek*. Again nothing came up. Not proof, but a useful indicator that Tom Bryce was not a paedophile. The department had discovered a curious fact over recent years: a high percentage of paedophiles were simultaneously *Buffy the Vampire Slayer* fans and Trekkies. If you found both of those on a computer, you had your first alert.

Jon worked quickly and methodically. He scanned through the photograph album, with its many pictures of an attractive woman with wavy blonde hair and two kids, a boy and a girl, their development charted from the time each was a few days old, if even that, to now when the girl was about four and the boy about seven. Normal family pictures. Nothing to ring any alarms.

Then he started on Bryce's website bookmarks, but there was nothing remarkable there. He went back, following the man's footprints over the past year, looking at every website address he had visited. There were dozens of porn sites, as there were on just about any man's computer he had ever looked at, but apart from a few lesbian sites nothing to suggest the man was kinky.

Then he came across something that puzzled him. At first he thought it was traces of a virus, but then he realized it was source code for some self-installing spyware. The design of it rang a bell, but he could not immediately fathom why. He followed it carefully, allowing himself to be led through the links. And he saw that the software had recently generated a user name and password; he entered them but they had been invalidated, and he found his progress blocked.

He turned round. Andy Gidney, behind him, iPod plugged into his ears, was concentrating hard, his fingers moving over his keyboard with the speed and grace of a concert pianist. The Detective Sergeant got up, walked over to his colleague and tapped him on the shoulder.

'I need some help, Andy. Can you drop what you are doing for a few minutes and see if you can find a password and user name to get me through a firewall?'

Without saying a word, the geek huffily went over and sat down at Rye's desk. Jon went and got himself a coffee, and when he returned five minutes later Andy was back at work at his own desk.

'Did you manage it?' Rye asked.

'It's an eight-digit password, for God's sake,' Gidney said to Rye, as if the man was an idiot. 'Could take me days.'

The head of the High Tech Crime Unit sat back down at his desk, unpeeled the plastic lid of his coffee cup and set the cup down a safe distance from the computer. He went back through the footprints of the spyware and then, suddenly, he realized why the design of it had rung a bell.

He remembered exactly!

Moments later he was back in the Evidence Room, carefully removing the opaque plastic, marked POLICE EVIDENCE BAG, that encased a desktop computer and server tower which had been brought in just a few weeks ago.

38

'Come on! Jesus, we are *so* incredibly late! Jessica, get back into bed *right now*!' Tom Bryce yelled at his daughter, who had come running downstairs in her pink dressing gown for the third, or maybe fourth, time.

His nerves were all shot to hell and back.

Upstairs, Max yelled out, 'Daddeeeeeeeee!'

'Max, shut up! Go to sleep!'

'Noooo!'

Tom, dressed up and ready to go out in a black Armani jacket, white shirt, blue chinos and his suede Gucci loafers, was pacing around the living room gulping down a massive vodka martini. 'Kellie! What the hell are you doing? And where the hell is the babysitter?'

'She'll be here any moment!' she yelled back. 'I'm coming.' Then, louder, she shouted, 'Jessica, come back up here at once!'

'Daddy, I don't like Mandy. Why can't we have Holly?'

'Jessica! Come back up here!'

'Holly was already booked up,' Tom said to his daughter. 'OK? Anyhow, Mandy is nice; what's your problem with her?'

Jessica, proudly wearing two rubber bracelets to copy her brother, a pink one and a yellow one, plonked herself down on the sofa, picked up the remote and began to channel-surf the television. Tom snatched the remote back and switched the television off. 'Upstairs, young lady!'

'Mandy spends all the time on the phone to her boyfriend.'

'She has her own mobile; she can do what she wants,' Tom retorted.

Jessica, freshly bathed and pink-faced, pushed back her hair, tilted her face in a very grown-up ladylike manner. 'They talk about *sex*.'

'Jessica, firstly it is rude to listen to other people's phone conversations, and secondly you should be in bed, asleep, when she's here babysitting, so why does it matter?'

'Because,' Jessica said huffily.

Kellie came tripping down the stairs, looking stunning and reeking of a new Gucci scent Tom had bought her recently, which he found incredibly sexy on her. She was wearing a tight-fitting short black dress, which both revealed a daring amount of cleavage and showed off her terrific legs to their best, and she had on a huge Roman-style silver choker around her neck. She looked very classy.

Just perfect for tonight.

They had been invited to dinner by a new client Tom desperately wanted to impress.

Kellie looked at Tom. 'Drinking already?'

'Dutch courage,' he said.

Her eyes widened disapprovingly. 'I thought you were going to drive tonight, to save money on taxis.' Then she turned to Jessica. 'Upstairs to bed at once,' she said sharply. 'Or no television tomorrow, and I mean it.'

Jessica looked sullenly at her mother, then her father. She seemed about to say something back, then thought better of it and began to walk, infuriatingly slowly, out of the room.

'I'll only have one glass of wine when I get there, then I'll go on to water.'

'It's all right,' she said. 'I'll bloody drive, again.'

'I think we both need to drink tonight,' Tom said. He walked towards her, slipped his arms around her, held her tightly and kissed her on the forehead. 'You look beautiful.'

'You look nice, too,' she said. 'I always like you in a white shirt.'

Jessica was walking up the stairs now.

Tom nuzzled Kellie's ear. 'I'd just like to take you straight to bed.'

'Well you're going to have to wait. I'm not taking all this lot off and starting again.'

The doorbell rang. There was the thump of the dog flap, and Lady came bounding into the hall, barking loudly.

Tom stayed in the living room and drained his cocktail, the alcohol already starting to give him a buzz that was lifting his mood, giving him some confidence.

Then Mandy came into the room and his jaw almost dropped. The daughter of a friend of Kellie's from her keep-fit classes, Mandy had done some babysitting for them before on a few occasions over the past three years. And during that time he had noticed her progression from a little girl into something altogether more mature. And tonight she was – there were no other words for it – raw sex on legs.

She was seventeen now maybe even eighteen, short, blonde, a Britney Spears clone with a terrific figure, most of it visible. She was wearing an almost see-through glitter top, definitely the smallest miniskirt he had ever seen and patent leather boots that went up to her thighs. Her face was carefully made up, and he noticed she had glitter varnish on her nails and was clutching a very glitzy-looking mobile phone. She was a total mini-chav.

Her parents had let her go out babysitting like this?

And, he thought, dismayed, in not many years maybe Jessica would be dolling herself up like this.

'Good evening, Mr Bryce,' she said breezily.

'How are you doing, Mandy?'

'Yeah, all right. Got me exams this month, so I'm swotting.'

Grinning, he said, 'These are your swotting clothes?'

Not getting the joke, she said, very seriously, 'Yeah, that's right.' Then she added, 'I passed my driving test.'

'Brilliant. Well done!'

'Third time. Me mum said she'll let me borrow her car sometimes; she's got a brand-new Toyota.'

'That's very noble of her,' he said, mentally clocking another thing to not look forward to about Max and Jessica growing up.

Kellie came back into the room. 'We'll be back about half twelve or so, Mandy; is that OK?'

'Yeah, great. Have a brilliant evening.'

Tom raised his empty glass, took one more long, lusting look at the girl and suddenly realized he was feeling a bit drunk. He needed to be careful, he thought. Philip Angelides had been well up the rankings in the recent *Sunday Times* Rich List, with a personal net worth of over two hundred and fifty million pounds. He had a business empire that included a company making generic drugs, a chain of car dealerships, a group of travel agencies, a property company that built developments in Spain and a very successful sports management company – all areas that could use BryceRight products.

Tom had met him, as he met many of his potential clients, at the golf club, and he owned, by all accounts, a very serious house about half an hour's drive from Brighton in the country. Tonight's invitation to a dinner party was a big opportunity. Except Tom wasn't in any mood to go out tonight.

He had been fretting all day since going to the CID headquarters building up on the Hollingbury estate and telling his story to the tall black Detective Sergeant. DS Branson appeared to have taken everything he had told him very seriously, and had given him assurances that it would be treated with total confidentiality. Nonetheless it had made him extremely nervous when Branson had asked if they could borrow his laptop over the weekend to see what they could find from it. He had returned to the building with the laptop a little later that morning with many misgivings, although Kellie remained adamant he was doing the right thing.

This afternoon he had played a totally crap round of golf – one of the worst games of his life. His mind had just not been on it. He was scared; a deep, insidious darkness swirled through him. He could not stop thinking about what he had done: that he had put his wife and his kids in danger.

That maybe, just maybe, he had made the worst mistake of his life.

39

'A vodka and tonic, please,' Cleo Morey said.

The waiter turned to Roy Grace.

'I'll have a Peroni.' Then he changed his mind, suddenly deciding he was in need of a stronger alcohol hit than beer, despite the fact that he was driving. He would worry about that later. 'Actually, no, make that a large Glenfiddich on the rocks.'

They were seated at a table towards the back of Latin in the Lanes, an Italian restaurant just off Brighton seafront. There were newer, hipper restaurants he could have chosen, like the Hotel du Vin; smarter, more inventive ones, like Blanche House; there were a load of restaurants that he had never been to with Sandy.

So why had he chosen the one that had been his and Sandy's favourite?

He wasn't sure of the answer. Perhaps because the place was familiar to him he thought he might feel comfortable there, know the ropes. Or was it a further laying of her ghost to rest?

He recognized some familiar faces from way back among the staff, and a couple of them seemed to remember him – if not his name – welcoming him back like a long-lost friend. The place had a lively Saturday evening buzz to it, and at nine o'clock – later than Grace had planned on being here – every table was occupied.

The six thirty briefing had taken longer than he had anticipated, and he'd needed to stay on after, doing follow-ups, although there had really been only one development during the day.

Bella had tracked down Janie Stretton's previous boyfriend Justin Remington and discovered he had just flown back this morning from his honeymoon in Thailand. She had gone to see him, and it was now her opinion, supported by the visa stamps in his passport, that he could be crossed off the suspects list.

DC Nicholl's trawl of the bars, pubs and clubs in the Brighton and Hove area with a photograph of Janie Stretton had so far yielded nothing. It was Jon Rye in the High Tech Crime Unit who seemed to have come up with their first real lead.

DS Rye's examination of the computer belonging to the witness who had made a statement to Branson that morning had revealed that this witness – apparently unwittingly – had followed a complex internet routing to a server in Albania. This was the same routing, the same IP addresses and protocols found on the computer seized from a suspect in a major child porn ring investigation, which DS Rye had recently examined. Its owner, Reginald D'Eath, was already on the Sex Offenders List, with past convictions for a violent sexual assault and for trafficking child pornography.

D'Eath, now a key prosecution witness in a child pornography case being prepared against a Russian syndicate operating in the UK, was currently in hiding for his own protection in a safe house provided by the Witness Protection Scheme. Grace had spent a frustrating hour on the phone after the briefing, dealing with a jobsworth WPS duty officer, politely at first then losing his rag with her, trying to get the damned woman to put him through to someone who would sanction the release to him of Reggie

D'Eath's address. In the end he'd had to settle for a grudg-ing undertaking from the jobsworth that someone would call him in the morning by ten o'clock.

Cleo, facing him across the table, across the gleaming cutlery and the sparkling glasses, looked simply stunning. Her hair was shimmering in the flickering candlelight, and her eyes were the colour of sunlight on ice. She was wear-ing a perfume which was tantalizing Grace. It wafted over him, overpowering the tempting smells of hot olive oil, frying garlic and searing fish coming from the kitchen. He breathed it in, getting increasingly turned on.

In truth he was aroused by everything about her. By her cute turned-up nose, her rosebud lips, her dimpled chin. By her stylish cream jacket, the loose, low-cut silky grey T-shirt, the ocelot scarf slung around her slender neck, by her two huge, funky but classy silver earrings. He noticed more rings on her fingers: a gold signet ring with a crest on it, an ornate antique with a large ruby set in a clasp of dia-monds, and a modern-looking silver one with a square, pale blue stone.

She was a classic, English-rose beauty in every way. And she was here, on a date with him! The butterflies in his stomach were out of control. The waiters were all eyeing her. So were other diners. She was the most beautiful woman in this restaurant by a thousand miles. She was looking absolutely, bloody, drop-dead gorgeous!

There was just one problem. Suddenly he could think of absolutely nothing to say to her.

Not one word.

His mind was a blank, as if some geek had hacked into his brain and removed every thought from it. Smiling at her, trying to think of something that would not sound totally inane, he leaned forward to reach a packet of breadsticks and knocked an empty wine glass over in the process; it struck Cleo's side plate and shattered.

He felt his face reddening. Cleo immediately put her hand out to help pick up the larger shards, before a waiter intervened.

'Sorry about that,' Grace said to her.

'It's meant to be lucky, to break a glass,' she said.

'I thought that was at Greek weddings.'

'It's *plates* at Greek weddings. Glasses at *Jewish* weddings.'

He loved her voice; it was just so plummy and posh and confident. It was a voice that belonged to a different world to the one he had come from. The world of private schools, money, privilege. Society. She was way too upmarket to be working in a mortuary. Yet Janie Stretton had been posh too, judging from her family home. And she had worked for a sleazy escort agency.

Maybe being brought up posh gave you a veneer of being different. Scott Fitzgerald, a writer he liked, had written that the rich were different. But maybe they weren't so very different.

'I, er – love your rings,' he said lamely. It was all he could think of to say.

She looked genuinely delighted, holding her long, elegant and finely manicured fingers up one at a time, showing her seriously upmarket bling to him. 'You don't wear any?' she said. Then almost immediately she blushed, realizing she had put her foot in it. 'I'm sorry, that wasn't very sensitive.'

Grace shook his head. 'I never did wear one,' he said. Then he almost added, *when I was married.* But of course he was still married. Technically.

The drinks arrived. He raised his glass and chinked

Cleo's. 'Cheers!' he said, and something about her smile just suddenly, inexplicably, gave him a boost. 'You don't look bad for something that came out of a mortuary,' he added.

'Thanks a lot!' She sipped her drink, then after a few moments retorted, 'You know, you really look quite cool yourself – for a copper.'

Grace grinned, but for the second time today he suddenly had big doubts about the gear he had on. The first doubts had been in the trendy clothing store, Luigi's, which Glenn had insisted on taking him to this afternoon. The Detective Sergeant had gone mad, hauling stuff off the shelves like a deranged bargain-hunter on the first day of the January sales, and wheeling him in and out of the changing room.

Tonight he was wearing the outfit Branson had put together specially for this date: an unlined brown suede blouson from Jasper Conran, the most expensive black T-shirt he had ever bought, beige Dolce & Gabbana trousers, an insanely pricey belt, brown loafers and even brand-new yellow socks – which Branson insisted added a hip touch.

In addition he now had an entire new wardrobe for just about every occasion. The bill had come to over two and a half thousand pounds. He had never spent more than a hundred quid in a clothing shop in his life before.

But what the hell, he thought; these last few years he had barely bought any items of new clothing at all. Get it all over with in one big hit. And anything he didn't like he could go back and change.

'*For a copper?* Do I take that as a compliment?' he asked with a quizzical grin.

She smiled warmly, searching his face with her eyes. 'If you want . . .'

He gave what he hoped came over as a nonchalant shrug. 'Just some things I threw on. I—'

She was staring at his right shoulder. 'Is the price tag part of the design?'

He clamped his left hand onto his shoulder; immediately his fingers touched stiff card, attached to string. Under Cleo's wickedly amused gaze he traced the string back under the jacket collar, cursing his carelessness. 'Part of the design.' He nodded. 'Totally part of the design; it's the new thing in jackets, that – umm, sort of – umm, off-the-shelf look.'

She laughed, and he found himself laughing back. His nerves had disappeared, and suddenly his head was full of stuff he wanted to talk to this woman about. But she got in first, as he tugged the tag free, balled it and dropped it in the ashtray.

Swirling her drink in her glass, she said, 'I'm curious, Roy. About your wife; is it something you talk about? Tell me if I'm being nosy and it's none of my business.'

He reached hesitantly into his pocket for his cigarettes. Technically he had given up, but there were moments when he still needed one. Like now.

A waiter appeared with menus, two massive folded cards. Grace put his down without glancing at it, and Cleo did the same. 'No, you're not being nosy.' He raised his hands a moment, a little helplessly, unsure where to begin his reply. 'I've always talked about it openly, maybe too openly. I just want people to be aware – you know. I've always thought that if I talk about it to enough people, maybe one day I will jog someone's memory.'

'What was her name?'

'Sandy.' He offered the pack to Cleo but she shook her head. He took a cigarette out.

'Is it true what – what people say? She just disappeared?'

'On my thirtieth birthday.' He fell silent for a moment, all the pain returning.

Cleo waited patiently, then prompted, 'On your thirtieth birthday . . . ?'

'I went to work. We were going to go out with some friends for dinner in the evening, to celebrate. When I left home, Sandy was in a great mood; we'd been planning a summer holiday – she wanted to go to the Italian lakes. When I came back in the evening she wasn't there.'

'Had she taken her things?'

'Her handbag and her car were gone.' He lit the cigarette with the Zippo lighter Sandy had given him then gulped some more of his drink. Talking about Sandy didn't seem right on a date. Yet at the same time he felt he really wanted to be honest with Cleo – to tell her everything, to give her as much detail as possible. Not just about Sandy but about his entire life. Something about her made him feel he could be open with her. More open than with anyone he could remember.

He took a long drag on his cigarette, then blew the smoke out. It tasted so damned good.

Frowning, Cleo asked, 'Her handbag and her car? Were either of them ever found?'

'Her car was found the next evening in the short-term car park at Gatwick Airport. But she never used any of her credit cards. The last transactions were on the morning she disappeared, one at Boots for £7.50, one for £16.42 from the local Tesco garage.'

'She didn't take anything else? No clothes, no other belongings?'

'Nothing.'

'What about CCTV?'

'There weren't so many around then; the only footage we got was on the forecourt at the Tesco garage – she was alone and she looked fine. The cashier was an old boy; he said he remembered her because he always noticed the pretty ones and he'd had a bit of a laugh with her. Said she didn't seem under any duress.'

'I don't think a woman would just walk out of her life, leaving everything behind,' Cleo said. 'Unless . . .' She hesitated.

'Unless?' he prompted.

Fixing her eyes on him she replied, 'Unless she was running away from a wife-beater.' Then she smiled and said gently, 'You don't look like a wife-beater to me.'

'I think her parents still harbour a sneaking suspicion that I've got her buried under the cellar floor.'

'Seriously?'

He drained his glass. 'I suppose they figure every other avenue has been exhausted.'

'They actually accused you?'

'No, they're sweet people; they wouldn't do that. But I see it in their faces. They invite me over for the odd drink or Sunday lunch to keep in touch, but what they really want is an update. There's never much to tell them, and I can see they are looking at me strangely, as if they're wondering, *How much longer can he keep up these lies about Sandy?*'

'That's terrible,' Cleo said.

Grace stared at the cluster of gleaming bracelets around Cleo's wrist, thinking what great taste she had in everything. 'She was their only child; their lives have been destroyed by her disappearance. I've seen it in other situations, from work. People need something to cling to, something to focus their emotions on.' He took another drag on his cigarette and tapped the ash into the ashtray beside the price tag of his jacket. 'So, enough about me. I want to know about you. Tell me about the other Cleo Morey.'

'The *other* Cleo Morey?'

'The one you change into when you clock off from the mortuary.'

'Not yet,' she teased. 'I haven't finished with you yet, not by a long way.'

He saw she had finished her drink also, and hailed the waiter, ordering another for each of them. Then he turned to Cleo. 'I'm sorry, it's your turn to answer a question.'

She pulled a face, which made him grin. 'I want to know,' he said, 'why the most beautiful woman in the world is working in a mortuary, doing the most horrible job in the world.'

'I was a nurse – I did a degree at Southampton University. I wasn't a very good nurse. I don't know – maybe I didn't have the patience. Then I spent a couple of weeks working in the mortuary at the local hospital and I just found – I don't know how to describe it – I just felt that – it was the first place I had been to in my life where I could make a difference. Have you ever read the writings of Chuang-Tse?'

'I'm just a dumb copper from the backstreets of Brighton. I never got to read anything fancy. Who he?'

'A Chinese Taoist philosopher.'

'Of course. Silly me for not knowing.'

She dug her fingers into the ice at the bottom of her

glass, then flicked a droplet of water at him. 'Stop being horrid!'

He flinched as it struck his forehead. 'I'm not being horrid.'

'You are!'

'Tell me what this Chaung Tse geezer said!'

'He said, "What the caterpillar calls the end of the world, the master calls the butterfly."'

'So you turn corpses into butterflies?'

'I wish.'

*

They were the last to leave the restaurant. Grace was so engrossed in Cleo – and so drunk – he hadn't noticed that the last customers had left a good half an hour before, and the staff were waiting patiently to close up.

Cleo made a grab for the bill, but he snatched it off the plate, adamant.

'OK,' she said. 'I get the next one.'

'Deal,' he said, tossing his card down, hoping he still had some credit on it. A few minutes later they staggered out into the blustery wind, and he held the door of the waiting cab for her, then climbed in, his head spinning.

He'd lost count of how much they had drunk. Two bottles of wine, then sambucas. Then more sambucas. And they'd had several drinks to start. He slid an arm over the seat, and Cleo nestled comfortably against him. 'Ish been good,' he slurred. 'Like I shmean, really—'

Then her mouth was pressed against his. Her lips felt soft, so, so incredibly soft. He felt her tongue hungrily against his. It seemed just seconds later the taxi pulled up outside her flat, in the fashionable North Laines district in the centre of the city. Through the haze of alcohol he recognized the block, a recent conversion of an old industrial building. There had been a lot of publicity about it.

He asked the cab to wait while he got out and walked with her to the entrance gates, unsure suddenly when they got there, of the protocol. Then their mouths found each other again. He held her tight, a little unsteady on his feet, running his hands through her long, silky hair, breathing in her perfume, totally intoxicated by the night, by her scents, by her softness and warmth.

It seemed just moments later when he awoke with a start in the back of the cab, alone, to the beep of an incoming text. *Shit*, he thought. *Work*.

He fumbled with the keys to read the text. It was from Cleo. It read simply, *X*.

40

Kellie was quiet, the orange street lights strobing on her face as Tom drove the Audi down the London road back towards Brighton. The radio was turned down low; he could just hear the Louis Armstrong song 'We Have All the Time in the World', which always stirred him. He turned it up a little, tired out, struggling to stay awake and completely sober. The car clock read 1.15 a.m.

The evening at Philip Angelides' house had gone OK, but the atmosphere had been stilted. Some years ago he and Kellie had joined the National Trust and used to like driving out to visit different stately homes on Sunday afternoons. Some of the houses they had visited were smaller than the Elizabethan pile they had been in tonight.

There were sixteen of them seated around the antique dining table, served by a retinue of starchy retainers. Angelides forced each guest in turn to guess the provenance first of the white wine, then the red, starting with the country of origin, then going on to grapes, style, maker and year.

Caro Angelides, the tycoon's wife, was probably the most stuck-up woman Tom had ever had the misfortune to sit next to, and the woman on his right, whose name he had forgotten, was not much better. Their sole conversation was horses – it veered from eventing to hunting and back again. He could not remember either of them asking him one single question about himself throughout the entire evening.

Meanwhile, Kellie had had the man on her right brag to her about how clever he was, and the man on her left, an oily-looking banker who had got increasingly drunk, repeatedly put his hand on her leg and tried to move it up inside her skirt.

All the other guests were clearly seriously rich, and from an entirely different social stratosphere to Tom and Kellie, neither of whom had ever had any exposure to really fine wines, and it had particularly angered Tom to see Kellie's choices belittled by her host. And he'd had no chance to engage him in any kind of business conversation. In fact, as he drove he wondered why Philip Angelides had bothered to invite them at all. Except perhaps just to show off to them?

But it was bonding of a sort. He hadn't misbehaved; he'd managed to keep the conversation going with the two women on either side of him despite zero knowledge of the horse world – apart from an annual flutter on the Grand National. And he had at least guessed that the red wine was French – although that was a total fluke.

'What a horrible bunch of people,' Kellie said suddenly. 'Give me our friends any day! At least they are *real* people!'

'I think I'll get some good business out of him.'

She was quiet for a moment then she said, grudgingly, 'Great house, though. To die for.'

'Would you like to live in a place that big?'

'Yeah, why not, if I had all those servants.' Then as an afterthought she added, 'We will one day, I'm sure. I believe in you.'

Tom put his hand out and found Kellie's. He squeezed, and she squeezed back. He continued to hold it, driving with one hand as they lapsed back into silence. Into his thoughts. Heading home, heading back to reality.

His decision to go to the police hung like a dark shadow at the back of his mind. Of course he had done the right thing; what choice did he have? Could he have lived with his conscience? They had made the decision together; that's what you did as husband and wife. You were a team.

They were approaching the turn-off now. He moved into the left-hand lane on the almost empty road, freed his hand, needing both now, followed the sharp bend all the way round, then headed up the hill, coming off at the roundabout at the top.

Less than a minute later, dropping down into the valley, he made a left turn into Goldstone Crescent, then a sharp left into their road. He drove up the steep hill, pulled into the carport, switched off the engine and climbed out. Kellie remained strapped in her seat. Tom, holding the key fob, his finger on the electronic locking button, waited for her to get out. But she didn't move. He glanced around at the cars parked down either side of the road, all well illuminated by the street lighting. His eyes studied all the shadows. Looking. For what? A sudden movement? A solitary figure in a parked car?

Paranoid, he told himself. Then he opened Kellie's door. 'Home, sweet home!' he said.

Still she did not move.

He looked at her face, wondering for a moment if she was asleep, but her eyes were open; she was just staring ahead.

'Darling, hello?'

She gave him an odd look. 'We're home, I know,' she said.

He frowned. She seemed to be having a *Kellie moment*. And they were getting more frequent. He could not put his finger on exactly what these moments were, but every now and then for a few seconds, sometimes longer, she seemed to disappear into a world of her own. The last time he'd raised it with her she had snapped back at him that sometimes she needed space, thinking time. But she sure as hell sometimes chose odd places and times to do it.

Eventually she unclipped her belt and climbed out of the car. He locked the Audi, then walked to the front door, put his key in, pushed it open and politely stepped aside for Kellie to go in first.

The television was blaring. *Christ,* he thought, the children were asleep; didn't Mandy have any common sense? Then he looked around, surprised that Lady hadn't barked or come bounding out to greet them.

Kellie put her head through the lounge doorway. 'Hi, Mandy, we're back! Did you have a good evening? Turn the sound down, will you, love?'

The babysitter's reply was drowned out by the din of the television.

Tom walked into the lounge. Because he had been driving, he'd drunk very little and was now feeling in need of a stiff nightcap. Except it would be wise to wait until he had dropped Mandy home. It was a good couple of miles to where she lived; stupid to risk it.

On the screen a teenage girl was standing in a rain-drenched alleyway, screaming, as a shadow bore down on her. Mandy was sprawled out on the sofa, a teenage magazine open on the carpet, along with several sweet wrappers, an empty pizza carton and a Coke can. Engrossed in the movie, without taking her eyes from the screen she hovered her left hand over the carpet, searching for the remote, but she was several inches off target.

Just as the girl on the television screamed even louder, Tom knelt, grabbed the remote off the floor and muted the sound. 'Everything OK, Mandy?'

The teenager looked a little surprised by the sudden silence, yawned, then smiled. 'Yeah, fine, Mr Bryce. The children wasn't no trouble – good as gold both of 'em. I'm a bit worried about Lady, though.'

'Why's that?' Kellie asked.

Sitting up and putting on her boots, Mandy replied, 'She doesn't seem herself. She normally comes and sits with me, but she didn't want to leave her basket tonight.'

Tom and Kellie both walked anxiously into the kitchen. Lady, curled in her basket, did not even raise an eyelid. Kellie knelt down and stroked her head. 'Lady, darling, are you OK?'

Mandy followed them in. 'She drank quite a lot of water a while ago.'

'She's probably got a bug,' Tom said, glancing at half a congealed pizza lying on the work surface, along with a knife and fork, and a tub of melted Tesco caramel crunch ice cream with the lid off. He knelt and stroked the Alsatian as well. Cocking his head at the dog he asked, feeling very sleepy suddenly, 'Have you got a bug, Lady? Feeling grots?'

Kellie stood up. 'Let's see if she's any better in the morning. If not we'll have to call the vet.'

Tom gloomily saw a big bill coming, but it couldn't be helped. He loved the dog; she was a part of his family, part of his life. 'Good plan,' he said.

Kellie squared up with the babysitter, then told Tom she would drive Mandy home.

'It's OK, I'll do it,' Tom said. 'I deprived myself of all those fine wines – I might as well drive her.'

'I didn't drink much either,' Kellie said. 'I'm fine. You've done enough driving tonight. Have a drink and relax.'

He didn't take much persuading.

Tom poured himself two fingers of Armagnac, flopped down on the sofa and flicked the remote, changing from the horror film Mandy had been watching to a golden oldie comedy show, *Porridge,* and watched Ronnie Barker in prison for a little while, before changing again, this time to an American football game. He heard the front door close and the sound of the Audi starting up, and felt a good, warm sensation as the first sip of his drink slid down his throat.

Then he stared into the glass and swirled the dark liquid around pensively. He was wondering what the difference was between Philip Angelides and himself. What qualities had made Angelides such a financial success and himself such a failure? Was it luck? Genes? Ruthlessness?

Outside, Kellie reversed into the street, then began to drive down the hill, making small talk with Mandy. Even if she had looked more carefully in her mirror, she would never have noticed the car that pulled out to follow her.

It was more than a hundred yards behind and had no lights on.

41

Roy Grace, unsteady in his seat in the swaying taxi, stared at the display of his mobile phone. Stared at the single letter.

X

He was having serious trouble focusing and despite – or because of – his drunkenness his emotions were in turmoil. Street lights and headlights flashed past him. On the taxi's crackly radio some caller on a late-night phone-in programme was talking furiously about Tony Blair and the National Health Service. He looked at his watch. Ten past one.

How had the evening gone?

He could still taste Cleo on his lips. Could smell her perfume in the cab, on his clothes. God, she was lovely. He still had a hard-on. He'd walked out of the bloody restaurant with a hard-on. And if she had invited him in, would he have . . . ?

And he knew the answer.

But she had not invited him in.

He inhaled deeply, but this time all he got was the stale plastic smell of the cab's interior.

'Four hours bloody wait, me mum's sick with cancer, and they made her wait four hours with her head split open before anyone saw her!' the man on the radio said bitterly.

'Disgusting, innit?' the cab driver said.

'Totally,' Grace said absently, concentrating on the keypad of his phone.

'Nice lady you had there. I think I recognized her. Got a feeling I've met her somewhere.'

'Most people only get to meet her when they're dead.'

'Is that right?' the driver said, sounding bemused. 'An angel, is she?'

'Exactly,' Grace said distractedly, still concentrating on his phone. He tapped out *XX*. Then sent it.

When he reached home, several minutes later, he was disappointed that he'd had no response.

42

Tom woke with a start, feeling muzzy and confused, with a roaring sound in his ears, unable to think for a moment where he was. Motorbikes were racing on the television screen in front of him, he realized, starting to think a bit more clearly – that was the noise.

Looking around for the remote, he saw an empty brandy glass on the carpet at his feet and then it hit him with a jolt. He'd fallen asleep. What the hell was the time?

The clock on the DVD read 4.10 a.m. That could not be right. He looked at his watch. 4.09 a.m.

A cluster of motorbikes, all close together, were howling down a straight that he recognized as part of the Silverstone racetrack. He'd been on a corporate hospitality day there a couple of years ago, and had also been to the British Grand Prix a few times. They were braking now, heeling over into Copse. Finding the remote, he switched the television off and stood up slowly, feeling stiff as hell.

Why hadn't Kellie woken him when she came in? he wondered. Carrying his empty glass, he tottered out into the hall, his head feeling muzzy still, his whole body leaden. He set the glass down in the kitchen, then somehow found the strength to haul himself upstairs. Creeping along the landing, trying not to wake anyone – although the motorbike racing had already probably done that – he opened the door to his bedroom. Instantly something felt wrong.

The curtains were wide open, and there was sufficient grey, pre-dawn light to see that their bed was empty.

No Kellie.

And suddenly he was wide awake.

Very occasionally in the past when one of the children had had a bad dream, she'd crawled into their bed for a few hours. Wondering if she had done that now, he checked out each of their rooms in turn. But she wasn't there.

Then, cursing his stupidity, he ran downstairs, opened the front door and stared out at the carport. It was empty.

To be doubly sure he walked out to the pavement and looked up and down, in case for some reason she'd parked the Audi in the street and had fallen asleep inside it. But there was no sign of the car.

He looked at his watch again, trying to work out how long he had been asleep. What time had she taken the babysitter home? It had been about half past one. Two and a half hours ago. Two and a half hours to make a four-mile round trip?

An icy whorl of fear spiralled through him. Had she had an accident? Wouldn't someone from the police have been in touch by now, if that had happened?

Was she having a long Kellie moment on her own, out in the darkness somewhere? Surely she would have known he'd be fretting?

But that was the thing, part of Kellie's problem; she did the most irrational things sometimes without thinking of the consequences. She had never actually done anything to endanger the kids, but she often just did not think. Like the time she'd bought one of her endless 'bargains' on eBay, a week at a Champney's health farm, at the same time as he was going to be away in Germany at a trade fair. She had totally forgotten to consider what would happen to the children.

There had also been a couple of occasions when she had simply disappeared, once for a whole day, another time for over twenty-four hours. He had been in despair both times, ringing around every hospital in the south of England to see if she'd been in an accident, wondering if she was having an affair. Then she had turned up, apparently unconcerned that he'd had to take the day off to look after the children, telling him that she'd suddenly just felt she needed some *space*.

He thought back to earlier, when she had gone into one of her silent modes in the car. Is that what she was doing now, having some *space*? Nice of her to tell him.

He picked up the cordless phone in the bedroom and dialled her mobile number. Seconds later he heard her demented, Crazy Frog ringtone coming from downstairs and hung up. She'd left her phone behind.

Terrific.

He sat down on the bed, thinking. God, he loved her so much, despite her quirks. They had their differences, yet in many ways they were so comfortable together. He had loved watching her at the dinner table tonight. Yes, she was out of her social league in that vipers' nest – they both were – but she'd coped; she'd held her head up; she'd looked beautiful; she'd said nice things about him, building him and his business up to the people on either side of her.

Then he thought about the envy he'd detected in her voice tonight, in the car driving back, when he had asked her if she would like to live in a house as big as the Angelides'.

Yeah, why not, if I had all those servants. We will one day, I'm sure. I believe in you.

He hadn't yet had the courage to break the news to her that they might soon have to sell this house and downsize. He didn't know how to, didn't want to see the pain it would cause. And most of all he didn't want to seem a failure to her.

Christ, where are you, my darling?

He got up and paced around, his insides slippery with fear. It was twenty to five. He wondered whether to call Mandy Morrison's parents to ask if Kellie had brought her home safe. But if the girl was not home by now, her parents would have been on the phone, anxious.

Still fully clothed, he lay back against the headboard, his brain buzzing, listening for a car coming up the street. Instead, all he heard were the first twitterings of birdsong. After a few minutes, despite the hour, he rang Mandy Morrison's home number; the phone was answered by her very sleepy father, who assured him Mandy had been dropped safely home at about quarter to two.

He thanked him, then dialled Directory Enquiries and asked for the number of the Royal Sussex County Hospital. A few minutes later he was through to a tired-sounding woman at Accident and Emergency. She assured him that no one of Kellie's name had been admitted in the past few hours.

Next he got the main number for Sussex Police, from Directory Enquiries again, and rang that. But after being transferred to Traffic, then put on hold for several minutes, he was told there had been no reported road traffic accidents involving his wife or their car.

He did not know what to do next.

43

It was only Wendy Salter's second time on nights. The probationary WPC was three weeks out of Police Training College at Ashford in Kent, and had the best part of two years yet to serve before becoming a fully fledged officer like her colleague. PC Phil Taylor, a few weeks shy of thirty-seven, was at the wheel of the liveried police Vectra, driving fast, blues on, but on this empty road there was no need for the siren.

They were less than a mile from CID headquarters in Sussex House, and had driven almost the entire width of Brighton and Hove in the two minutes since they had picked up the emergency call from the Control Room. They had only just finished sorting out a drunken argument over a bill, which had turned into a fight, in the Escape night-club just off Brighton seafront.

Going at high speed through the city gave Wendy a massive thrill – she couldn't help it – it was like being on the best funfair ride in the world. And a lot of officers felt the same. The expression on Taylor's face showed he was among them.

It was 4.15 a.m. and, looking up through the wind-screen, Wendy could see a few cracks of grey dawn light appearing in the black canopy of the night sky. A terrified rabbit sprinted in the glow of the car's headlights across the road and vanished beneath the bonnet. She waited for the thud and was relieved when there was none.

'Bloody kamikaze bunny that was,' Phil Taylor said cheerily.

'I think you missed it.'

'I read somewhere that some bloke's published a book of road-kill recipes – in America.'

'Could only be in America,' Wendy said. She'd never actually been there, and had an image of the country heavily influenced by all the crazies in California she had seen on television, or read about, with a bit of Michael Moore thrown in for good measure.

They were passing woodland on their right and a sweeping drop to their left down to the lights of Brighton and Hove. Then, rounding a sharp right-hand bend, they saw the red glow ahead of them.

For a brief instant Wendy thought it might be the sun starting to rise, but dismissed that when she worked out they were travelling almost due west. The glow intensified as they drew closer, and then, suddenly, she could smell it.

The vile, acrid stench of burning paint, rubber and vinyl.

Taylor braked and pulled over a short distance from the blazing car, which was in a tarmac car park in a beauty spot with magnificent daytime views. But all WPC Wendy Salter could see as she unclipped herself and stepped out of the car, dutifully pulling on her hat, was dense, choking smoke as the strong breeze blew it straight towards them, making her eyes water. She turned away for a moment, coughing, then ran alongside her colleague as close as they could get to the vehicle before the heat stopped them.

In the distance she could hear the wail of a siren. Probably the fire brigade, she thought, the stench of burning paint and rubber one hundred times stronger now, and the fierce crackling and roaring of the inferno filling her ears.

She could see inside the car now, with most of the glass of the windows already burned out, and to her relief it was empty. It was an estate, and walking round to the front she recognized the radiator grille. 'An Audi,' she called out to PC Taylor.

'It's a recent model; you can tell from the grille,' he said.

'I know. The new A4.'

He gave her a glance. 'Bit of a petrol-head, are you?' he said with grudging admiration.

'Not as much as whoever did this,' she retorted.

'Kids,' he said, as if it were a swear word. 'Little bastards. Torching someone's brand-new wheels.'

'Joyriders?'

'Bound to be,' he said. 'Who else?'

44

Roy Grace woke at six thirty on Sunday morning to the beeping of his alarm clock, with a parched mouth and a blinding headache. Two paracetamol capsules he'd swallowed with a pint of water at about five in the morning had had about as much effect as the first couple he had downed a few hours earlier. Which was not a lot.

As he hit the snooze button, temporarily silencing the clock, the loud *chirrup* of a bird outside took over, incessant, like a stuck CD track. Light streamed in through a wide gap in the curtains, which he realized he had not closed properly.

How drunk was I last night?

Assembling his thoughts, his brain sluggish, feeling like someone had spent all night pulling wires out of it at random, he reached out for his mobile phone. But there was no further text from Cleo.

He could hardly expect there to be one, as it was only half six in the morning and she was probably sound asleep, but logic wasn't a major feature of his thinking just at this moment, with the pounding inside his head and the damned bird, and the knowledge that he had to get up and face a full day's work. No chance of a Sunday lie-in today, boyo.

He closed his eyes, thinking back. God, Cleo was lovely in every way, a really warm, gorgeous human being. She was very, very special – and they had got on so incredibly well! Then he thought back to their kiss in the back of the taxi, a long, long, amazing kiss. And he tried to remember who had started it. It was Cleo, he seemed to recall. She had made the first move.

He felt a pang of longing to speak to her, to see her. Suddenly, he thought he could smell her perfume. Just the lightest trace on his hand; he brought it to his nose and yes! It was strongest on his wrist; it must have come from when he had sat in the cab with his arm around her. He held his wrist against his nose for a long time, breathing in the musky scent, something stirring deep in his heart that he had thought, until these past few days, was long dead.

Then he felt a twinge of guilt. *Sandy*. But he ignored it, shut it out of his mind, determined not to go there, not to let it spoil this moment.

He looked at the clock again to double-check the time, his brain turning, reluctantly, to work. To the 8.30 a.m. briefing. Then he remembered he needed to collect his car.

If he got up now, he worked out, he would just have time to run to the underground car park where he had left the Alfa last night – the fresh air might help his head. Except that his body was telling him it did not need a run, it needed about eight hours more sleep. He squeezed his eyes shut, trying to crush the pain like cheese-wire cutting through his skull – and to ignore that sodding bird which he could happily have shot if he'd had a gun – and drifted for a few delicious moments back into thoughts about Cleo Morey.

It seemed barely a few seconds before the alarm started beeping again. Reluctantly, he hauled himself out of bed, opened the curtains the rest of the way, and padded naked into the bathroom to brush his teeth. The face that stared back at him out of the mirror over the basin wasn't a pleasant sight.

Roy Grace had never been a vain man but had until recently considered himself still young, or youngish, not handsome but OK-looking, with his best feature being his blue eyes (his Paul Newman eyes, Sandy used to tell him) and his worst his small but very broken nose. Now, increasingly, the face he stared at early in the morning seemed to belong to some much older guy – a complete stranger with a wrinkled forehead, slackening jowls and bags the size of oyster shells beneath his eyes.

It wasn't the beer or the fags or the fast-food diet or the crazy work schedule that got you in the end, it was gravity, he decided. Gravity made you a little bit shorter every day. It slackened your skin a little more, pulling it relentlessly downward. Half your waking life was a struggle against gravity but it always got you. It would be gravity that banged the lid down on top of you in your coffin. And if you had your ashes scattered to the winds, gravity would eventually bring them back down, every single bit of them.

He worried about his thoughts sometimes, which were becoming increasingly morbid of late. Maybe his sister was right; maybe he was spending too much time alone? But after all this time he was used to solitude. It was what he knew as normality.

It wasn't the kind of life he'd planned, nor the kind he'd ever remotely imagined he would be living, seventeen years back, when he had proposed to Sandy on a warm September day on the end of the Palace Pier, telling her that he'd taken her there because if she had said no, he would have jumped off. She'd smiled that beautiful, warm smile, tossed her blonde hair from her eyes, and told him – with her typical gallows humour – that she'd have considered it a much stronger test of their love if he had taken her to Beachy Head.

He downed a glass of tap water, screwing up his face at the taste of the fluoride, which seemed heavier than usual this morning. *Drink more plain water*, his fitness instructor, Ian, at the police gym told him repeatedly. He was trying, but the stuff just didn't taste as good as a Starbucks latte. Or a Glenfiddich on the rocks. Or just about anything else. He hadn't really worried about his appearance until now.

Until Cleo.

These years since Sandy's disappearance had taken a heavy toll on him. Police work was hard, but at least most coppers had someone to go home to at the end of their shift, and talk to. And Marlon, although company of sorts, just didn't do it for him.

He put on his jogging kit, gave Marlon some breakfast in case he forgot later, and eased himself out of the front door into the deserted street. It was a deliciously cool summer morning, with a clear sky holding all the promise of the day being a corker. And suddenly, despite his hangover and lack of sleep, he felt energized. With his heart humming, he set off down the street at a brisk pace.

Roy Grace lived in Hove, a residential district that had until recent years been a separate town to Brighton, although joined at the hip. Now both came under the joint umbrella of the City of Brighton and Hove. The Greek, from which the name Hove came – or Hove, Actually, as it had been nicknamed – was rumoured to translate as 'burial ground'.

This was not entirely inappropriate, as Hove was the quieter, more residential sister to the once brash, racy Brighton. The border began on the seafront at a spot marked by a war memorial obelisk and a coloured line across the promenade, but after that became increasingly obscure, with many people along its zigzag pathway north finding it ran through their houses.

Grace's own modest three-bedroom semi was in a street that went directly down to the Kingsway, the wide dual carriageway on the far side of which was the seafront. He crossed over, then ran across the dewy grass of the lawns, past the children's playground and the two boating ponds of Hove Lagoon where his dad, who enjoyed building model motor boats, used to take him as a child and let him hold the remote controls.

The Lagoon had seemed such a huge place to him then, now it looked so small and run-down. There was a worn-out-looking roundabout, a rusting swing, a slide in need of paint, and the same ice cream kiosk that had always been there. The boats were still locked away for the night, and several ducks drifted on the smaller of the two ponds, while a group of swans sat on the edge of the larger one.

He skirted the ponds and hit the promenade, just as deserted as it had been at this hour yesterday, and passed along a long row of blue bathing huts. As he ran, the landscape on his left changed. At first there was a row of drab post-war blocks of flats and a stretch of equally uninteresting houses. Then, after the King Alfred Leisure Centre, at the moment a major construction site, the view on his left turned into the one he loved: the long esplanade of grand, terraced Regency town houses, mostly painted white, many with bow windows, railings and grand porches. A lot of them had once been single dwellings, weekend homes for rich Regency and Victorian Londoners, but now, like most of the buildings in this city with its sky-high property prices, they had been carved up into flats or converted into hotels.

A few minutes later, approaching the boundary

between Brighton and Hove, he could see, ahead of him to the right, the sad, rusting spars rising from the sea which were all that remained of the West Pier. It had once been as lively and garish as its counterpart, the Palace Pier exactly half a mile further east, and visiting it had been one of the constant highlights of his childhood.

His dad, who was a keen fisherman, had taken him to the Palace Pier often, walking down to the exposed fishing platform at the far end, from where on a Saturday afternoon – out of the football season or when the Albion was playing away – they could come home with a good haul of whiting, bream, plaice and, if they were lucky, the occasional sole or even bass, depending on the tide and weather.

But it wasn't the fishing that had been the big lure of the pier for Roy as a child, it was the other attractions, particularly the bumper cars and the ghost train, and most of all the old wooden glass-fronted slot machines that contained moving tableaux. He had one favourite and was forever cajoling his father into giving him more pennies for the slot. It was a haunted house, and for a full minute, as gears cranked and pulleys whined, doors would fly open, lights would go on and off, and all kinds of skeletons and ghosts would appear, as well as Death itself, a hooded figure all in black holding a scythe.

Coming up on his left now – and his energy was starting to sag a little – was the hideous monstrosity of the Kingswest building, a grim, 1960s leisure structure totally out of keeping with the rest of the seafront. A few hundred yards further on and the handsome facade of the Old Ship Hotel loomed. He sprinted up the steps onto the upper promenade, crossed the almost deserted road, kept up his pace along the side of the hotel, and then entered the car park and glanced at his watch.

Shit. He realized he had badly miscalculated. If he was going to make the 8.30 a.m. briefing on time – and it was vital to his team's morale that he did – he had less than half an hour to get home, change and be out of the door.

He also now had a raging thirst, but there was no time even to think about stopping and grabbing a bottle of water from somewhere. He inserted his ticket in the machine followed by his credit card, then hurried down the concrete staircase to the level he had left his car on, crinkling his nose at the smell of urine, wondering why it was that someone had pissed in the stairwell of every single car park he had ever been into in his life.

45

At 8.29 a.m., with just a minute to spare, Grace approached MIR One, eating his breakfast, a Mars bar from a vending machine, and clutching a scalding cup of coffee.

He hurriedly finished his Mars, and popped a stick of mint chewing gum into his mouth to mask any residual alcohol from last night. Putting the rest of the packet back in his pocket, he was about to enter the room, when he heard footsteps behind him.

'Yo, old-timer, so how was the date?'

He turned to see Glenn Branson, in a leather jacket as glossy as a mirror, holding a cappuccino. He had a rim of its froth, like a white moustache, around his mouth.

'Fine,' he replied.

'*Fine?* That's all. Just *fine?*' His eyes searched Grace's mischievously.

Grace chewed on the gum and gave a coy smile. 'Well, probably a bit better than fine, I think.'

'You don't know?'

'I'm trying to remember; I drank too much.'

'Did you get laid?'

'It wasn't that kind of date.'

Branson looked at him strangely. 'Man, you're weird sometimes! I thought that was the purpose of dates?' Then he broke into a broad grin. 'I want a blow-by-blow account later. Did she admire your gear?'

Grace glanced at his watch, conscious it was now past eight thirty. 'All she said was that my tailor must have a terrific sense of humour.' He pushed the door open and entered the room, with Branson following.

'She didn't say that? Are you serious? Old-timer? Hey, come on!'

The whole team was seated around the workstation, all dressed casually except for Norman Potting, who appeared to be in his Sunday best – attired in a crisply pressed beige suit with a brightly coloured tie, and an even brighter handkerchief sprouting jauntily from his breast pocket.

Grace was dressed casually today also, partly because it was Sunday, partly because he was so damned tired he hadn't felt like putting a suit on, but mainly because he had a date. It was with a very special young lady – his god-daughter Jaye Somers – and he did not want to look like a boring old fart by wearing a suit.

So he'd put on some of the new kit he had bought yesterday – a white T-shirt, jeans that were too tight in the crotch but which Glenn Branson had assured him looked *well cool*, lace-up shoes that looked like football boots without studs, also apparently *well cool*, and a lightweight cotton jacket.

Jaye Somers' parents, Michael and Victoria, were both police officers and had been two of his and Sandy's closest friends – as well as being hugely supportive in those difficult months immediately following Sandy's disappearance. And they'd stayed just as supportive during the years that followed. With their four children, aged two to eleven, they had become at one time almost a second family to him.

He had taken Jaye out the previous Sunday, intending to visit Chessington Zoo because she had a thing about wanting to see a giraffe. But their outing had been cut short within half an hour when he had been called to attend the scene of a murder. He had promised to take her out this Sunday instead.

He liked Jaye a lot; she was the kind of daughter he would have loved to have had – extremely intelligent, pretty, interested in all and everything and wise for her years. He hoped he was not going to have to disappoint her a second time. Apart from anything else it would not give her a great deal of confidence in the reliability of adults.

The first item on his agenda was Reginald D'Eath, the sex offender whose computer had been seized. Grace reported that DS Rye at the High Tech Crime Unit had discovered there were identical routings on this computer to the ones found on the computer belonging to Tom Bryce. These routings might have taken Bryce to the website where, Branson believed after questioning the man exhaustively, it seemed likely he really had witnessed the murder.

Grace told the team he was expecting a call by 10.00 a.m. from someone from the Witness Protection Scheme with D'Eath's address. He delegated Norman and Nick to come with him to interview the man; for some reason he couldn't explain he had a bad feeling about this interview and thought that a show of strength might be needed.

Nick Nicholl reported he had continued the sweep of all the bars, pubs and clubs in Brighton late into the night with the photograph of Janie Stretton, but had still drawn a blank.

Norman reported on his trawl through the clients of the escort agency, BCE-247. So far, he told them, it had not yielded any client who admitted to knowing Janie and none who fitted the identity of the one called Anton. 'But,' he said, 'I have discovered something from another escort agency – it would appear Ms Stretton was registered with both of them.'

He held up a different, even raunchier, photograph of Janie Stretton to the one Grace had seen in the BCE-247 office. It showed her stark naked apart from tassels on her nipples, thigh-high patent leather black boots and studded leather wrist-cuffs, one hand on her hip, the other brandishing a cat-o'-nine-tails.

Grace was surprised at this sudden efficiency. Maybe he had misjudged Potting. 'Where did you get this?'

'From the internet,' Potting said. 'I did a search of all the girls on offer in the local agencies and recognized her face.'

Grace had imagined the net might be too much for an old-school detective like Potting to get his head around as a research tool. 'I'm impressed, Norman,' he said, quietly wondering whether Potting's trawl through the agency girls had purely been research for this case.

Blushing a little, the Detective Sergeant said, 'Thank you, Roy. There's life in the old dog yet, eh!' He directed a lecherous wink at Emma-Jane, who responded by looking down at her paperwork.

'Great pair on her,' Potting said, passing the photograph on to DS Nicholl, seated next to him, who studiously ignored the comment.

Apart from their workstation, MIR One had been almost empty when Grace arrived, but more people were coming in every few minutes, filling up the other two stations. Crime was no respecter of weekends. It would be business as usual for all the Major Incident Teams.

Emma-Jane reported on the overnight task she had been given by Grace. She'd contacted every minicab firm in the Bromley area, in search of the driver of the cab who had picked up a box of scarab beetles from Erridge and Robinson. But so far she'd had no luck.

They were interrupted by a loud burst of rap music. It was the new ringtone on Branson's mobile. Looking up apologetically he said, 'Sorry, my kid did that.' Then he answered with a curt 'DS Branson'.

A moment later, holding the phone to his ear, Branson stepped away from the workstation. 'Mr Bryce,' Grace heard him say, 'what can I do for you?'

Branson was quiet for some moments, listening, then he said, 'I'm sorry, it's not a good line . . . Your wife, did you say? She didn't come home last night? Still hasn't? Can you give me a description of the car she was driving?'

Branson came back to the workstation, sat down and began writing on his notepad. 'All right, sir. I'll check with Traffic. An Audi A4 estate, sport. I'll call you back – on this number?'

As he hung up, Nick Nicholl said, 'An Audi estate, did you say?'

'Yeah. Why?'

Nicholl typed on his keyboard, then leaned forward, scrolling up through the crime log on the Vantage screen. 'Yes,' he said, 'I thought so.'

Grace looked at him quizzically.

'Half past four this morning,' Nicholl said, still staring at the screen. 'An Audi estate was found torched up on Ditchling Beacon. The plates were burned off.'

Branson looked at him, his face a picture of deep unease.

46

Jessica, in her pink dressing gown, squatted on the kitchen floor stroking an extremely drowsy Lady. Max, standing above his sister – in a Harry Potter T-shirt which he had on the wrong way round – said very seriously, as if he were a leading authority in such matters, 'It's Sunday. I think she is having a Sunday lie-in!' Then for a few moments he turned his attention to a cartoon on the television.

'She's not going to die, is she, Daddy?' Jessica asked.

Tom, who had not slept a wink – unshaven, his hair a mess, barefoot in a T-shirt and jeans – knelt and put his arm around his daughter. 'No, darling,' he said, his voice shaky. 'She's just a little bit sick. She's got a bug or something. We'll see how she is in an hour or two. If she doesn't seem better we'll call the vet.'

He had phoned Kellie's parents, all her close friends and all his, just in case she had gone to one of them for the night. He had even phoned her sister Martha, who lived in Scotland. No one had seen her, or heard from her. He did not know who else to phone or what to do.

Jessica laid her face against Lady's and kissed her. 'I love you, Lady. We're going to make you better.'

There was no response from the dog.

Max knelt down also and laid his face against the Alsatian's midriff. 'We all love you, Lady. You'll have to get up soon otherwise you'll miss breakfast!'

None of them had had any breakfast, Tom realized suddenly. It was half past nine.

'When Mummy comes back she'll know how to make her better,' Jessica declared.

'Yes, of course she will,' Tom said flatly. 'You guys must be hungry – what would you like? French toast?'

Kellie always made the kids French toast on Sundays.

'You don't make it very well,' Max said. 'You always burn it.' He stood up, picked up the remote and began surfing the channels.

'I could try not to burn it.'

'Why can't Mummy make it?'

'She will do,' he said, struggling. 'I could make you some – to keep you going until she gets back?'

'Not hungry,' Max said grumpily.

'You want some cereal?'

'You always burn it, Daddy!' Jessica said, echoing her brother.

'Can we go to the beach today, Daddy?' Max asked. 'Mummy said we could if it was nice – and I think it is nice, don't you?'

Tom stared leadenly through the window. It looked glorious: blue sky, all the promise of a fine early summer's day. 'We'll see.'

Max's face fell. 'Awww. She promised!'

'Did she?'

'Yes.'

'Well, we'll ask her when she comes home what she'd like to do today, shall we?'

'She'll probably just want to drink vodka,' Jessica said without looking up.

Tom wasn't sure if he had heard correctly. 'What did you say, darling?'

Jessica continued stroking the dog.

'Jessica, what was that you said?'

'I saw her.'

'You saw Mummy doing what?'

'I said I wouldn't tell.'

Tom frowned. 'You wouldn't tell what?'

'Nothing,' she said sweetly.

The doorbell rang.

Max ran out into the hallway, shouting excitedly, 'Mummy! Mummy! Mummy's home!'

Jessica sprang to her feet and followed her brother. Tom was right behind them.

Max pulled the front door open, then stared up in glum surprise at the tall black man in the shiny leather jacket and blue chinos who was standing there. Jessica stopped in her tracks.

Tom did not like the expression on the detective's face one bit.

Glenn Branson knelt down to bring his face to the same level as Jessica's. 'Hello!' he said.

She fled back towards the kitchen. Max stood his ground, staring at the man.

'Detective Sergeant Branson,' Tom said, a little surprised to see him.

'Could I have a word with you?'

'Yes, of course.' Tom gestured for him to come in.

Branson looked at Max. 'How you doing?'

'Lady won't wake up,' the little boy said.

'*Lady?*'

'Our dog,' Tom explained. 'I think she has a bug.'

'I see.'

Max lingered.

'Why don't you get some cereal for you and Jessica?' Tom suggested.

Reluctantly Max turned and trotted back into the kitchen.

Tom closed the front door behind the detective. 'Do you have some news?' He was still puzzled by Jessica's remark about the vodka. What did his daughter mean?

Talking quietly, Glenn Branson said, 'We've found the Audi estate you said your wife was driving. It was burned out, torched, probably by vandals, up on Ditchling Beacon earlier this morning. We did a check on the chassis number – it's registered in your name.'

Tom stared at him open-mouthed in shock. 'Burned out?'

'I'm afraid so, yes.'

'My wife?' Tom started shaking uncontrollably.

'There was no one in it. Happens all the time at week-ends. Cars get nicked by joyriders, then they set light to them, either for fun or to get rid of their prints. Usually both.'

It took some moments for it to sink in properly. 'She was driving the babysitter home,' he said. 'How the hell could it have been nicked by joyriders?'

The Detective Sergeant had no answer.

47

The City of Brighton and Hove had so many different faces, Grace thought, and so many diverse people. It seemed that some cities were divided into different ethnic communities, but here in Brighton and Hove it was more like different sociological communities.

There were the genteel elderly, in their mansion blocks or sheltered housing, who on summer days could be seen watching the cricket at the County Ground or playing bowls on the Hove lawns, or sitting in chairs on the promenade, and the beaches in summer, and, if they had the funds, wintering in Spain or the Canaries. And the poorer elderly, shivering out the winter – and half the summer – imprisoned in their damp, dank council flats.

There were the in-your-face wealthy middle classes with their smart detached houses in Hove 4, and the more discreet, in the handsome seafront mansion blocks. And the more modestly off, like Grace, in homes spread out to the west to the suburb of Southwick, directly behind the commercial port of Shoreham Harbour, and in pockets all over the city and stretching well out to the Downs

Much of the colour and vibrancy of Brighton and Hove came from the very visible, and often brash, gay community, and the wall-to-wall students, from Sussex and Brighton Universities and the plethora of other colleges, who had colonized whole areas of the city. There were the visible criminals – the drug dealers lurking on the scruffier street corners, who would melt into the shadows at the smell of a police car – and the less visible ones, the rich ones at the top of their game, who lived behind high walls in the swanky houses of Dyke Road Avenue and its tree-lined tributaries.

Council estates fringed the city; the two biggest, Moulscombe and Whitehawk, had long had reputations for crime and violence, but in Grace's view these were not particularly deserved. There were crime and violence all over the city, and it made people feel comfortable to point a finger at these estates, as if there was an altogether different species of *Homo sapiens* living there instead of mostly decent folk who didn't have enough money to buy themselves smugness.

And there was the sad underclass. Despite regular attempts to remove them from the streets, the moment the weather warmed up, the winos and the homeless drifted back to the shopfronts, porches, pavements and bus shelters. This was bad for tourism and even worse for the city's conscience.

From the start of the festival in May and the arrival of spring, tables and chairs appeared outside every cafe, bar and restaurant, and the streets of the city came alive. Some of those days, Grace thought, you could almost imagine you were on the Mediterranean. Then a weather front would move in off the Channel, a howling south-westerly accompanied by punishing rain that would drum on the empty tables and lash the windows of boutiques filled with mannequins in beachwear, as if mocking anyone who dared to pretend that England ever actually had a summer.

The beating downtown heart of the city, through which they were travelling now, was concentrated in a square mile or so either side of the Palace Pier. There were the tightly packed Regency terraces of Kemp Town, in one of which Janie Stretton had lived; the Lanes, where the antique dealers were centred; and the North Laines district filled with small, trendy shops and tiny town houses, among which was the converted factory building where Cleo Morey had her flat.

Nick Nicholl drove the unmarked Ford Mondeo. Grace sat in the front passenger seat, busily making notes on his Blackberry. Norman Potting was in the back. They were driving down the London Road in the centre of Brighton. At most times of the day or night they would have been crawling along in dense traffic, but early on this Sunday morning, apart from a couple of buses, they virtually had the road to themselves.

Grace checked his watch. Hopefully this interview with Reggie D'Eath would not take long, and he could squeeze a couple of hours out of the day for his god-daughter. Enough to take her to lunch, if not to the giraffes today.

They were passing the Royal Pavilion, the city's most distinctive landmark, on their right. None of the three men looked at it – it was one of those places that was so familiar it had become all but invisible to them.

The turreted and minareted building in the style of an Indian palace was commissioned by George IV when Prince of Wales, as a seaside shag-palace for his mistress, Maria Fitzherbert, in the late eighteenth century. And as seaside shag-palaces go, nothing quite so grand had probably been built anywhere in the world, ever since.

They stopped at the roundabout at the intersection with the seafront, with the Palace Pier, garish even early on a Sunday morning, opposite them. A leggy blonde in a skirt that barely covered her buttocks crossed in front of them unhurriedly, throwing them a flirty glance and jauntily swinging a bag.

Potting, who had been quiet for some minutes, murmured, 'Come on, doll. Bend over; show us your growler!'

There was a gap in the traffic, and Nick Nicholl turned left.

'She's all right, she is!' Potting said, turning to watch her out of the rear window.

'Except *she* is a *he*,' Nick Nicholl corrected him.

'Bollocks!' Potting said.

'Yes, exactly!' the DS retorted.

They drove along Marine Parade, past the debris of broken glass and food cartons outside a nightclub, the über-trendy Van Alen apartment building, then the black and white flinted Regency facades that fronted the imposing crescent of Royal Crescent, where, Glenn Branson had told Grace a thousand times, Laurence Olivier had once had a home.

'You're talking through your arsehole,' Potting replied. 'She was gorgeous!'

'Big Adam's apple,' the DS said. 'That's how you tell.'

'Fuck me,' Potting said.

'I'm sure he would have done, if you'd asked nicely.'

'Shouldn't be allowed out on the streets looking like that, bloody fudge-packer.'

'You are so gross, Norman,' Grace said, turning round. 'You are quite offensive, you know.'

'Well I'm sorry, Roy, but I find poofs offensive,' Potting said. 'Never understood 'em, never will.'

'Yes, well, Brighton happens to be the gay capital of the UK,' Grace said, really irritated with the man. 'If you have a problem with that you're either in the wrong job or the wrong city.' *And you're a complete fucking prat, and I wish you weren't in my car or in my life,* he would have liked to have added, digging in his pocket for some more paracetamol.

On their left they passed terrace after terrace of imposing white Regency houses. On their right were the sails of a dozen yachts, fresh out of the Marina on a Sunday race.

'So this bloke we're going to have a chat with,' Potting said. 'Reginald D'Eath, is he one of *them*, too?'

'No,' Nick Nicholl said. 'He isn't – he just likes girls – as long as they're not older than about four.'

'That's something I really can't understand,' Norman Potting said.

Popping a pill from the foil pack, Grace thought grimly, *Great, at last we've found something in common.*

*

They drove up a steep hill at the back of Rottingdean, alongside a prep school playing field with a cricket pitch marked out in the centre and two large white screens on rollers, with pleasant detached houses opposite. Then they turned into a street with bungalows on either side. It was the kind of quiet area where anything out of the ordinary would stand out – as the bright yellow Neighbourhood Watch stickers, prominently displayed in each front window, warned.

A good choice of location for a safe house, Grace thought, except for one minor detail that appeared to have been overlooked. Who in their right bloody mind would put a paedophile in a house a few hundred yards away from a school playing field? He shook his head. Didn't anybody ever think?

'Is Mr D'Eath expecting us?' Nicholl asked.

'With morning coffee and a box of Under Eights, I

expect,' Norman Potting said, following this with a throaty chuckle.

Ignoring the terrible joke, Grace replied, 'The woman I spoke to from the Witness Protection Agency said they'd left a message for him.'

They pulled up outside Number 29. The 1950s bungalow looked a little more tired than the others in the street, its brown pebbledash rendering in need of repair, and repainting considerably overdue. The small front garden was in poor shape also, reminding Grace that he needed to mow his own lawn some time this weekend – and today was a perfect day for it. But when would he get the chance?

He told Norman Potting to wait in the street, in case Reginald D'Eath hadn't got the message they were coming and tried to do a runner, then, accompanied by DC Nicholl, he walked up to the front door. It bothered him that the curtains of the front room were still drawn at a quarter to eleven on a Sunday morning. But maybe Mr D'Eath was a late riser? He pressed the plastic bell-push. Dinky chimes rang out inside the house. Then silence.

He waited some moments, then rang again.

Still no response.

Pushing open the letterbox he knelt and called out through it, 'Hello, Mr D'Eath, it's Detective Superintendent Grace of Brighton CID!'

Still no response.

Followed by Nicholl, he walked around the side of the house, edging through the narrow gap past the dustbins, and pushed open a high wooden gate. The rear garden was in a much worse state than the front, the lawn weedy and badly overgrown, and the borders a sad riot of bindweed and nettles. He stepped over an upturned plastic watering can, then reached a kitchen door with frosted glass panels, one of which was smashed. Shards of glass lay on the brick path.

He shot a glance at Nick Nicholl, whose dubious frown echoed his own concern. He tried the handle and it opened without resistance.

They entered a time-warp kitchen, with an ancient Lec fridge, drab fake-wood units and Formica work surfaces on which sat a clapped-out-looking toaster and a plastic jug kettle. The remains of a meal sat on a dreary little table – a plate of half-eaten and very congealed eggs and beans and a half-drunk mug of tea – and a magazine, opened at a double-page spread of naked children, was propped against a serving bowl.

'Jesus,' Grace commented, disgusted by the magazine. Then he dunked a finger into the tea; it was stone cold. He wiped it on a kitchen towel hanging on a rack, then called out, 'HELLO! REGINALD D'EATH! THIS IS SUSSEX POLICE! YOU ARE SAFE TO COME OUT! WE ARE JUST HERE TO TALK TO YOU! WE NEED YOU TO HELP US IN AN ENQUIRY!'

Silence.

It was a silence Grace did not like, a silence that crawled all over his skin. There was also a smell he did not like. Not the smell of the stale, tired old kitchen, but a more astringent smell which he knew but could not place – except something in his memory was telling him it definitely did not belong in a house.

He needed D'Eath so badly. He was desperate to talk to him about what he had been looking at on his computer. He knew from Jon Rye that Reggie D'Eath had followed the same links as Tom Bryce and he had no doubt the paedophile would have information about what Tom Bryce had seen.

It was the best lead they had so far in the Janie Stretton murder enquiry. And, as he couldn't stop thinking, it wasn't just about driving the enquiry forward, it was about rescuing his career.

He bloody well had to succeed in this enquiry.

He nodded for Nick Nicholl to start looking around the rest of the house. The Detective Constable left the kitchen, and Grace followed him into a small sitting room, where the smell was even stronger. In here there was a cheap-looking three-piece suite, an old television, a couple of very badly framed Turner prints on the walls, and one solitary framed photograph on a mantelpiece above a fireplace containing an electric, fake-coal fire.

Grace stared at the stiffly posed couple in the photograph: a weak-looking, baby-faced man in his thirties, with thinning hair, dressed in a grey suit, a gaudy tie and a shirt collar riding too high, his arm around a hard-bitten blonde, outside the entrance of what looked like a register office.

Then he heard a shout. 'Roy! Jesus!'

Startled, he ran out of the room, and saw the DC a short distance down the corridor, hand over his face, coughing in an open doorway.

As he reached him, the sour, acrid smell caught the back of his throat. He held his breath and stepped past the DC into an avocado-coloured bathroom. And came face to face with Reggie D'Eath, through the choking haze.

Or at least what was left of the man.

48

And now Grace knew exactly what that smell was. A sick little ditty his science master had taught everyone at school sprang into his mind:

> Alas here lies poor Joe
> Alas he breathes no more.
> For what he thought was H_2O
> Was H_2SO_4.

Grace's eyes were stinging and his face was smarting. It was dangerous to stay in the room for more than a few seconds, but that was enough to see all he needed.

Reggie D'Eath was lying up to his neck in a bathtub, immersed in liquid that looked as clear as water. But it was sulphuric acid. It had already consumed almost all of the skin, muscle and internal organs below his neck, leaving a clean, partly dissolved skeleton around which a few pale, sinewy tendrils, still attached, were shrinking as he watched.

A metal ligature, around his neck, was attached to a towel rail above him. The corrosive fumes were working on D'Eath's face, blistering the skin into livid pustules.

Grace backed quickly out of the room, colliding with Nicholl. The two men stared at each other in stunned silence. 'I need air,' Grace gasped, heading unsteadily to the front door and out into the garden. Nicholl followed him.

'Everything all right?' Norman Potting asked, leaning against the car, puffing on his pipe.

'Not exactly,' Grace said, feeling very queasy, so disturbed he was unable to think clearly for some moments. He took several long, deep gulps of fresh air. A man a short distance up the street was washing his car. Close by was the *grind-grind-grind-whrrrrr* of a hand-pushed lawnmower.

Nicholl began a series of deep, hacking coughs.

Grace pulled his recently issued new phone out of his pocket, and looked down at the buttons; he'd practised with it a few times but never actually used the camera function before. Holding his handkerchief over his nose, he went back into the house, along to the bathroom, took a deep breath outside the door, entered and took several photographs in quick succession. Then he went back out of the room.

Nick Nicholl was standing there. 'You OK, chief?'

'Never better,' Grace spluttered, gulping down air. Then he pocketed his camera, not relishing what he had to do next.

He took another deep breath, dived into the bathroom, grabbed a large towel off a rail, wrapped it around Reggie D'Eath's head, and yanked hard.

After several brutal tugs, the head, along with a length of spinal cord, came free from the ligature. Surprised at how heavy it was and still holding his breath, Grace carried it out of the bathroom and laid it down on the hall floor.

The young Detective Constable took one look at the sight, keeled over, crashing into a wall, and threw up.

Grace, remembering something from his first aid training, ran into the kitchen, found a bowl in a cupboard, filled it with cold water then hurried back and emptied it over D'Eath's face, trying to wash away the acid. If there was any forensic evidence there, it might be saved, and in any case it would help with identification. The smell of the DC's vomit made him gag, and as he ran back for a refill he narrowly avoided throwing up himself.

Then he went back into the kitchen and radioed for a support team. He requested SOCO officers, a scene guard and some officers to do an immediate house-to-house. While he was speaking, he noticed a cordless phone lying underneath the vile magazine D'Eath had apparently been reading with his meal.

As soon as he had finished, he carefully picked up the phone, using his handkerchief, then brought it to his ear and pressed the redial button. A local number appeared on the display, then the phone rang. It was answered after just two rings by an almost obsequiously polite male voice.

'Good morning, Dobson's. May I help you?'

'This is Detective Superintendent Grace from Brighton CID. I believe a Mr Reginald D'Eath' (carefully pronouncing it deee-ath) 'called you recently; can you tell me your connection with him?'

'I'm awfully sorry,' Mr Politeness said. 'That name does not sound familiar. Maybe one of my colleagues spoke to him.'

'So who exactly are you?' Grace asked.

'We are funeral directors.'

Grace thanked the man, hung up and dialled 1471. Moments later he heard an automated voice: 'I'm sorry, the caller withheld their number.'

He hung up. D'Eath's last call had been to a funeral directors – who had no record of it. Had the phone been left like that as a sick joke by his killers?

Deep in thought, he went out, and invited Norman Potting into the house. It seemed mean to leave him outside in the glorious sunshine, enjoying his pipe, all on his own.

*

It was just under an hour before the first Scenes of Crime officers arrived, including a very disgruntled Joe Tindall. The man was becoming an increasingly disenchanted Roy Grace fan.

'Making this a regular Sunday habit, are you, Roy?'

'I used to have a life too,' Grace snapped back, suffering a sense-of-humour failure.

Tindall shook his head. 'Only fifteen years, eight months, seven days to my retirement, and counting . . .' he said. 'And I'm ticking off every bloody second.'

Grace led him into the house and along the passageway towards the bathroom, and the sight that greeted him really did not improve Joe Tindall's day one bit.

Leaving the SOCO officer, Grace went back outside, ducked under the police tape now securing the outside of the house, and eased his way politely through the fast-growing gaggle of curious neighbours, realizing that for over one whole hour he had not thought about Cleo Morey. Half a dozen police cars were now in the street, and the Major Incident Vehicle was reversing into a space.

Two uniformed Community Support Officers were knocking on the front door of the next-door neighbour, starting their house-to-house enquiries.

He walked a short distance up the street, out of earshot, and first dialled the Somers and apologized to Jaye that he was going to have to cancel again. The disappointment in her voice made him feel terrible. They would go next week instead, he promised her. But she didn't sound much like she believed him.

Then he dialled Cleo's number.

All he got was her voicemail.

'Hi,' he said. 'Just calling to say it was great to see you last night. Give me a call when you've got a moment. Oh, and I hope you're not on call today, for your sake. I have a seriously unpleasant cadaver on my hands.'

His headache – hangover – whatever – was back with a vengeance, and his throat felt as if it had been sand-papered. Feeling low as he walked back to the house, he went over to Nicholl and Potting, who were standing outside, chatting to the constable on guard. 'Either of you feel like a drink? Because I fucking well need one.'

'So long as it's not Mr D'Eath's bath water,' Potting said.

Grace almost smiled.

49

Kellie tried to move, but the pain in her arms worsened each time she struggled, the string, or wire, or whatever had been tied around them cutting deeper and deeper into her flesh. And when she tried to shout, the deep sound made her whole face vibrate and stayed trapped in her mouth.

'Mmmmnnnnnnnnnnnnnuuuug.'

She could see nothing, could not open her eyes. There was total bitumen blackness beyond the images inside her head. She could hear nothing except for the sound of her blood roaring in her ears. The sound of her own fear.

Shaking in terror and from cold. And from lack of alcohol.

Her throat was parched. She needed a drink. Desperately, desperately needed a gulp of vodka. And water.

Her crotch was cold and itchy. A while ago, when she had finally let go of the urine she could no longer contain, it had felt strangely, comfortably warm for several minutes. Until it had started to turn cold. Occasionally she could smell it; then it would just be the musty, chilly, cellar smell again.

She had no idea what the time was. Nor where she was. Her head pounded. Cold, sick fear swirled in the deep, black well of her insides, swirled in the blood inside her veins. She was so scared it was impossible to think clearly.

Just occasionally, she thought she could hear the very faint sound of traffic. An occasional siren. Coming to rescue her?

But she had no idea where she was.

Tears welled in her sealed eyes. She wanted Tom, she wanted Jessica and Max, wanted to hear all their voices, feel their arms around her. She tried to remember those moments, those confused, all-speeded-up moments.

She had driven Mandy Morrison home. Pulled up outside her parents' modern Spanish-style house in swanky Tongdean Lane, a steep hill near the Withdean sports stadium. She sat in the car, music playing on the radio, waiting to see that Mandy had let herself safely in the front door before driving on.

Mandy had opened the door, gone inside, turned and waved and closed the door.

Then the passenger door of her car had opened.

And the rear door behind her.

A hand as strong as steel had pulled her neck back. Then something wet and acrid was being held against her nose.

She whimpered at the memory.

Then she was here.

Shaking uncontrollably.

On her back on a rock-hard floor.

She struggled, trying to move her arms again, but the pain became unbearable. She tried to move her legs, but they felt cemented together. Her breathing was getting faster, her chest tightening.

She felt light pouring onto her. The darkness behind her eyelids became a red haze.

Then she emitted a muffled bellow of pain as tape

was ripped away from her eyes, taking what felt like half her skin. And she blinked, momentarily dazzled by the light. A squat man with a smug grin and wavy silver hair pulled back into a small pigtail, grossly overweight, in a baggy shirt open to the navel, was standing over her.

At first she felt relief; she thought this man had come to help her. She tried to speak to him, but all she could make was a gurgling sound.

He stared back at her without speaking, eyeing her up and down with an expression of deep thoughtfulness. Then, finally, he smiled at her, and her heart leapt. He had come to help her – he was going to get her out of here, take her home to Tom and Jessica and Max!

Suddenly his tongue slipped out of his lips and gave a quick flick, like a snake's, wiping all the way round them, moistening them. Then he said in an American accent, 'You look like a woman who takes it up the ass.'

He put his hand in his pocket and Kellie heard the clink of metal. As fear squeezed her, crushing every cell in her body, she saw a delicate silver chain swing from his fingers.

'I've brought you a present, Kellie,' he said in a voice that told her he was her new best friend. He held it up in front of her face; there was a small pendant hanging from the chain, and in the poor light she couldn't quite make out the design engraved on it. It looked like some kind of beetle.

'You can relax,' he said. 'We're just going to take a few pictures for your family album!'

'Grnnnngwg,' she responded.

'If you're a good girl and do exactly what I tell you, I

might even let you have a drink. Stoli vodka', he said. 'That's your favourite, isn't it?'

In his other hand he held up a bottle.

'I wouldn't want you to die of thirst,' he added. 'That would really be a waste.'

50

'So, an appropriate name for him then,' Norman Potting said. 'D'Eath.' Pronouncing it death.

Grace, Potting and Nicholl were seated in the oak-timbered saloon of the Black Lion in Rottingdean, each with a pint tumbler in front of him. Grace took a mouthful, holding the wide rim of the glass to his nose, breathing in the aroma of the hops, trying to get the reek of the sulphuric acid out of his nostrils.

His hand was shaking, he realized. From his hangover? From what he had seen this morning?

He remembered early on in his career when he had been a beat copper, out in a patrol car on nights, being called to attend a suicide on the London–Brighton railway line. A man had lain down on the track by the entrance to a tunnel, and the wheels had gone over his neck. He'd had to walk along the track and recover the head.

He would never forget the surreal sight of it lying there in the beam of his torch, barely any blood at all leaking and the almost surgically precise cut. The dead man had been about fifty, with a ruddy, outdoor complexion. Grace had picked the head up by the shaggy thatch of ginger hair, and had been surprised by just how heavy it was. D'Eath's head had been just as heavy.

He watched the kaleidoscope of lights on a fruit machine, which no one was using, go through their routine. He could hear the faint chimes that went with them. It was still early; there was just a handful of people in the place. A trendy-looking man, a media type, was seated by the fireplace, drinking what looked like a Bloody Mary and reading the *Observer*. An elderly, shapeless couple sat a couple of tables away, slouched over their drinks in silence, like two sacks of vegetables.

Thinking through the day's agenda – which had been thrown badly by D'Eath's murder – he was worrying about Nick Nicholl meeting the SIO of the murder investigation in Wimbledon, where a headless young woman wearing a bracelet with a scarab motif had been discovered two months earlier. It might be better to go himself, one SIO to another, rather than send a junior member of his team.

Turning to Nicholl, Grace asked, 'What time are you meeting the SIO of the murder in Wimbledon?'

'He's going to call me this afternoon. He has a brother in Brighton; he's coming down to have lunch with him.'

'Let me know and I'll come with you.'

'Yes, sir.'

Despite being in his late twenties, Nick still had something of a socially clumsy youth about him. And he still could not get his head around calling him Roy, as Grace liked all his team to do.

Grace checked the growing list of notes on his Blackberry. The smell of roasting meat coming from the kitchen was churning his already very queasy stomach. It would be a while, he thought, before he could swallow a morsel of food again. He wasn't even sure if drinking with all the paracetamol he had taken was very smart. But this was one of those moments when he needed a drink. On duty or not.

He took his phone out of his pocket and checked it was still on – just in case it had somehow got switched off and he had missed a call back from Cleo.

He wondered briefly how Glenn Branson was getting

on, worrying a little about his friend. Underneath the hulking frame that must have made him a formidable nightclub bouncer was a gentle guy. Too damned gentle and kindhearted for his own good, at times.

'Sulphuric acid,' Potting said pensively, raising his glass and taking a long draught.

Grace stared at him. The poor sod had not been blessed with good looks – in fact he verged on being plug ugly. Despite the ageing detective's failings, he suddenly felt a little sorry for his colleague, sensing a sad and lonely man behind the bravado.

Potting put his glass down on a Guinness mat, dug his hand in his pocket and got out his pipe. He stuck it in his mouth, then pulled a box of matches from the opposite pocket. Nick Nicholl watched in fascination.

'Ever smoked, lad?' Potting asked.

The young DC shook his head.

'Didn't think so; you don't look the type. Fit bugger, I suppose?'

'I try.' Nicholl sipped his beer. 'My dad smoked. He died at forty-eight from lung cancer.'

Potting was silenced for a second. Then he said, 'Cigarettes?'

'Twenty a day.'

He held up his pipe, smugly. 'There's a difference, you see.'

'Nick's a good runner,' Grace cut in. 'I want to poach him for my rugby team this autumn.'

'Sussex need some good runners at the moment,' Potting retorted. 'They've got a lot of bloody runs to get today. What a Horlicks yesterday! Three bowled out for ten! Against bloody Surrey!' He struck a match and lit his pipe, blowing out a cloud of sickly sweet smoke which billowed around Grace.

Potting puffed away until the bowl of his pipe glowed an even, bright red.

Normally Grace liked the smell of pipe smoke, but not this morning. He waved the smoke away, watching it curl heavily and lazily up towards the nicotine-decorated ceiling. Reggie D'Eath's murder could have been coincidental, he thought. The man was a key witness for the prosecution in the trial of members of a major international paedophile ring. There were several people who would have good reasons for wanting him silenced.

Yet what had been found on the two computers seemed to him to indicate another possibility. Bryce had been warned not to contact the police. He had – rightly – ignored the warning, and a police examination of his computer had connected it to Reggie D'Eath's PC. Less than twenty-four hours later D'Eath was dead.

There was an irritating chime from the fruit machine, then a series of further chimes like a xylophone. Potting and Nicholl were now deep into a conversation about cricket, and Grace drifted more deeply into his own thoughts. He remained so deep in thought that, even when they were back in the car, he barely registered the one piece of information that Norman Potting, changing the subject from cricket back to Reggie D'Eath, suddenly revealed.

51

The emergency vet, who had introduced herself as Dawn, a rather butch-looking Australian woman in her mid-thirties, was kneeling beside Lady, who was still very drowsy. She pulled down the Alsatian's left eyelid and examined it with the aid of a pencil torch. Max and Jessica watched anxiously. Tom stood with an arm around each of them.

The detective, Glenn Branson, had gone outside to make a phone call.

Tom stared down at the dog, his mind in turmoil. Yesterday morning he had gone to the police, defying the email warning that had been sent to him. Now Kellie was missing and the car had been found, burned out.

Oh Christ, my darling, where are you?

*

Standing in the brilliant morning sunshine out in the street, Branson held his mobile phone to his ear, talking to a family liaison officer, WPC Linda Buckley, arranging for her to come straight over to the Bryces' house.

Almost immediately after he ended the call, the phone rang. It was an officer from British Transport Police, PC Dudley Bunting, returning Branson's call. Glenn told him what he was looking for and that it was very urgent. Bunting promised to come back to him as quickly as he could.

'Today is what I need,' Branson said. 'Not three weeks time. That possible?'

Bunting sounded hesitant. 'It's Sunday.'

'Yeah, I know, I should be in church. And I'm with a geezer who would quite like to spend the day with his wife, and I'm with his two kids who'd quite like to spend the day with their mother – except it looks like someone abducted her in the middle of the night. So maybe you'd like to sacrifice the Sunday roast with your in-laws and pull your fucking finger out for me?'

Bunting assured him he would exert maximum digital extraction.

While he was talking, another call came in – from Ari. Branson ignored it. When he finished his call, a message signal appeared on the phone's display, accompanied by two sharp beeps.

The DS stared at the sign on the windows of the gym on the other side of the road. GYM AND TONIC. It was a good name, he thought. Yeah, he liked that. With a balled fist he tested his own stomach muscles. He still had a six-pack, but he needed to get back into the gym soon; there had been a time when he went to the gym every single day; now, he thought guiltily, he did well to make it twice a week.

But there was something else making him feel a lot more guilty, as he looked up at the clear blue sky and felt the glorious warmth of the sun on his face.

Ari, his wife – and his kids.

Sammy was just eight and Remi was three; he missed both of them every minute of the day he wasn't with them. Yet these days he hardly ever was with them. Work was increasingly consuming his life.

He pressed the message retrieval button and listened

to the voicemail Ari had just left – in a tone that was short and sarcastic, and growing shorter and more sarcastic by the day. 'Glenn, going to take Sammy and Remi onto the beach; be nice if you joined us as it was your suggestion. They'd quite like to see their father for at least one hour over the weekend. Perhaps you can call me back. My name's Ari, in case you've forgotten. I'm your wife.'

He sighed heavily. They rowed increasingly frequently about his hours. Ari seemed to have forgotten already that he'd taken the whole of last weekend off to drive up to Solihull for her sister's thirtieth birthday, dumping his work onto a broad-shouldered Grace.

Glenn Branson's problem was that he was ambitious; he wanted to rise through the ranks, like Roy Grace had done. But that meant long hours were not a temporary thing. This was the way it was going to be for the next twenty years.

A lot of his colleagues found the job tough on their marriages; it often seemed only those officers married to other police officers, who understood each other's crazy hours, had happy marriages. At some point he was going to have to make a decision about which was more important to him, his job or his family.

That was pretty ironic, really. Soon after Sammy was born, when Glenn Branson had been working as a nightclub bouncer, he had decided he wanted to have a career his son would be proud of, and that was when he had joined the Sussex force.

He was about to dial Ari when a voice behind him startled him. It was Tom Bryce, and the man looked in bad shape, his face pale, his eyes spooked.

'Could I have a quiet word with you, Sergeant Branson?' he asked.

'Of course.'

They climbed into Branson's pool Mondeo and closed the doors.

'What I want to ask you is if you think we're in danger – whether I should take my children somewhere? Go into hiding?'

The detective wasn't sure how to respond. He was quiet for some moments, thinking about Janie Stretton's vicious murder and the warning that Bryce said he had received on his email. Then his missing wife. He could not answer because he just did not have enough information yet. But what if this had happened to him and Ari had vanished? Could he honestly look Tom Bryce in the eye and tell him to stay put?

But what were the alternatives? A round-the-clock police guard? He doubted that could be swung unless there was much stronger evidence to persuade Alison Vosper to stand the cost. Move them to a safe house? Roy Grace had rung him half an hour ago to tell him about Reggie D'Eath. So much for safe houses.

'I think we need to consider the possibility that your wife has been abducted, Mr Bryce.'

This was what Tom had feared, although there was just one small nagging doubt in his mind. The words of Jessica came back to him repeatedly.

She'll probably just want to drink vodka. I saw her. I promised I wouldn't tell.

'I've arranged for a detective from the Family Liaison Unit,' the detective was saying. 'She's very competent – she'll move in here, if you agree. She'll organize a roster of herself and a colleague to give you and your children round-the-clock protection.'

'Is that what you would do in my situation, DS Branson?'

'Yeah,' he replied, hesitantly. 'Yeah. For the moment anyhow. Let's see what we learn today.'

Glenn Branson looked down, not able to look the man in the eye for more than a second. And as he said the words he was thinking to himself, *If this was me, would I want to have Sammy and Remi remain in the house?*

And he simply did not know the answer.

52

'Potatoes,' Norman Potting said suddenly.

The three police officers were in the car, Nick Nicholl driving, heading back from the pub in Rottingdean towards Sussex House. The pint of beer on top of the paracetamol and his late night was making Grace drowsy.

'Potatoes?' Nicholl echoed.

'I was brought up on a farm,' Potting said. 'My dad used to spray the potato crop with sulphuric acid. Dilute, mind you. Never did me any harm.'

'Sulphuric acid on potatoes? You're not serious?'

The words 'sulphuric acid' caught Grace's attention.

'My friend, I'm always serious,' Potting replied. 'The acid kills off the shoots and makes harvesting much easier.'

'And it kills anyone who eats the potatoes?' Grace questioned.

'It's all bollocks,' Potting said. 'All this organic crap. Nothing wrong with a few honest-to-goodness pesticides. Look at me!'

'I'm looking at you,' Nicholl said, glancing in the mirror.

'Never had a day's sickness in my life!'

You're just permanently sick, Grace thought.

'Harmless stuff in the right hands,' Potting continued.

'I don't think Reggie D'Eath would agree with you,' Grace retorted.

'Would you give your kids potatoes that had been sprayed with sulphuric acid?' Nicholl asked Potting.

'Wouldn't have a problem with it,' he said.

'Well, I would,' the young DC said.

After a moment's silence, Potting asked him, 'How many kids have you got?'

'First one on its way – any day now,' the DC said. 'How about you?'

'Two by my first marriage. One by my second. Two more by my third. The second by her, Suzie, has Down's syndrome. Not that I ever see much of the little buggers,' he said wistfully.

Nicholl was clearly affected by Potting's response. 'Down's?'

Potting nodded.

'I'm sorry,' Nicholl said.

Potting shrugged. 'That's the way it goes,' he said sadly. 'She's a good kid, always happy.' He shrugged again. 'Every family has something, don't they?'

'Are you still married? To your third?'

Potting's face fell. 'I gave up.' He pursed his lips. 'I'm a bachelor, footloose and fancy-free, like DS Grace here. Take it from me, lad, it's the best way.'

Nick Nicholl said, 'Actually, I'm very happily married.'

'You're a lucky man,' Potting replied.

'So if we're looking for someone who has enough sulphuric acid to fill a bath, we should be looking for a potato farmer?' Grace asked, turning his head.

'Or someone who supplies potato farmers,' Potting said. 'Or drugs companies. Or manufacturers of citric and lactic acids, and edible oils. Adhesives, explosives, synthetic rubber. Water and effluent treatment. Wood pulping. Leather tanning. Car batteries.'

'You should go on *Mastermind*,' Nicholl said, 'with sulphuric acid as your specialist subject.'

'I got involved in a case a few years ago. A chap in Croydon threw some in his girlfriend's face when she dumped him. Apparently it's common practice in one of the countries in Africa.'

'Nice guy,' Nicholl responded.

'A regular charmer. That's what you get with darkies.'

Now Grace was livid. 'Norman, in case you haven't noticed we have a black member on our team. If you make one more racist or homophobic remark I'm going to have you suspended. Any part of that you don't understand?'

After a few seconds' silence Potting said, 'I'm sorry, Roy. I apologize. Not very tactful of me. He's a good man, that DS Branson.'

Even though he's black? Grace was tempted to fire back. Instead he said, 'You'd have needed a few gallons of the stuff to fill that tub. The neighbours must have seen something. All those bloody Neighbourhood Watch stickers. Two tasks for you, Norman. First find out from the house-to-house team if any unfamiliar vehicles have been in the street in the past few days. Second, find out if there are any suppliers – or users – of bulk sulphuric acid in the area.'

'Before or after I finish working my way through the books of Barry and Claire Escorts Twenty-Four Seven, chief?'

'You'll have to multi-task like the rest of us, Norman.'

Two sharp beeps told Grace he had an incoming text. He looked down and saw it was from Cleo. Instantly his spirits lifted. Then, when he read it, they dropped. Or rather plummeted.

53

The video viewing room in the Major Incident Suite was a tiny, windowless cubicle, a few yards down the corridor from MIR One. With just Glenn Branson and Tom Bryce in there it felt crowded and claustrophobic. Yet another example, in Branson's view – and he was only an occasional visitor – of how poorly thought-out the conversion of the building had been.

Tom Bryce sat at the desk, with a monitor in front of him, and to his left a video and CD stack. The machine was loaded with CCTV footage from two cameras at Preston Park railway station, the first stop north from Brighton, regularly used by commuters both for its convenient location towards the outskirts and for the free parking in the streets all around. It was the station where the dickhead seated next to him on the train last Tuesday night, who had left behind the CD, had got off.

Constable Bunting had come up trumps. Within two hours of Glenn's call to British Transport Police, the officer had produced footage of the southbound platform of Preston Park at the time of the arrival of the train Tom had been on.

Tom forced himself to concentrate, but it was hard because he was beside himself with worry about Kellie. He had the shakes from having eaten nothing all day and drunk far too much caffeine. His stomach felt as if it was full of barbed wire. Suddenly his mobile phone rang.

He looked at the display but did not recognize the

number. 'I'd better answer it,' he said. Branson nodded his encouragement.

It was Lynn Cottesloe, Kellie's best friend who also lived in Brighton, wondering if there was any news or anything she and her husband could do to help. Could they bring some food over? Help out with the children? Tom thanked her and said that a rota of family liaison officers had been organized. She told him to call the instant he had any news, and he promised he would. Then he returned to his task.

The first camera showed the length of the platform, from a high vantage point. A train was just pulling out of the station. A counter in the top right-hand corner read 19.09.

'That's the Thameslink, the London Bridge service,' Glenn Branson informed him. 'Yours is coming in a couple of minutes.'

Tom fast-forwarded, then slowed when a new train appeared on the track. His nerves tightened. The train came to a halt. Doors opened and about thirty people climbed down onto the platform. He pressed the freeze-frame button, and looked at each character carefully.

No sign of the dickhead.

'This is the right train?' he asked.

'Definitely. The 6.10 fast service from Victoria – the one you told me you took,' Branson replied. 'Run it on a bit; might be that not everyone's off yet.'

Tom pressed the play button and all the people sprang back into life. He scanned the open doors of the train, many of which were being shut again, trying to work out the carriage where he had been sitting. It was about four back from the front – he estimated he was looking at it now.

And then he saw him.

The big-framed, baby-faced man, dressed in a safari-style shirt over shapeless slacks and clutching a small holdall, was stepping down onto the platform now, and looking carefully around almost as if to ensure the coast was clear before he got off.

Clear of what? Tom wondered, stabbing the freeze button.

The man stopped in mid-step, his left, trainer-clad foot in the air, his face angled slightly towards the camera but showing no awareness of it. Although the look of deep consternation on his face was clearly visible.

Tom pressed the play button again, and within moments the man's concerns seemed to be over, and he began walking, almost jauntily, towards the exit barrier. He froze the tape again, and said, 'This is him.'

Branson stared at the man in shock. 'Zoom in, will you, on his face.'

Tom fumbled with the controls, then zoomed in, a little jerkily, until he was tight on the dickhead's face.

'You're absolutely sure?'

Tom nodded. 'Yes. That's him. Absolutely.'

'You couldn't be mistaken?'

'No.'

'That's *very* interesting,' the Detective Sergeant said. 'Do you know who he is?'

'Yes,' Branson said, his voice turning grim. 'We do.'

54

Shortly before five o'clock, Sergeant Jon Rye was sitting at his desk in the High Tech Crime Unit, still working on Tom Bryce's computer, when his direct line rang. He picked up the receiver. 'Jon Rye,' he said.

'Hello. It's Tom Bryce. I'm actually in your building, up in the CCTV room . . . Just wondered if – if my computer was ready. I – could pop down . . . collect. I – I need to do some work tonight. I – I have – have to prepare for a very big meeting tomorrow. How are you doing?'

You sound terrible. You need to do some work, and I need to go home and salvage my marriage, Jon Rye thought. There was only himself and Andy Gidney, a short distance across the room from him, still there in the department late on this Sunday afternoon. Were the two of them sad or what?

Gidney, his iPod plugged as ever into his ears, was hunched over his keyboard, his desk littered with empty Coke cans and plastic coffee cups from the vending machines, clicking relentlessly away, working on cracking the code he had been trying to crack all week.

Rye worried about the geek – he seemed a lost soul. At least when Rye left the building, he had a home to go to. Maybe Nadine was sour sometimes, but there would be a meal on the table, the kids to talk to. Some kind of normality. What was Gidney's normality?

Mind you, he wondered, what was anyone's normality in here? Including his own? Most of their working weeks consisted of looking at porn on seized computers. And the vast majority of it was not your average titillating-but-cosy *Playboy* centrefold stuff; it was middle-aged men with children as young as two years old. Something he would never, not in a trillion years, really comprehend. How did that stuff turn people on? How could people do that with innocent children? How could a forty-year-old man sodomize a small child? And then live with the knowledge of what he had done?

The answer, sadly, was too easily and too often.

He knew exactly what he would have done if he'd caught someone meddling with his children when they had been young. It would have involved a razor blade and a blowtorch.

There was a sudden jangle of weird electronic noises which was becoming irritatingly familiar to Rye. Gidney's mobile phone. The geek removed an iPod earpiece and answered the phone in a flat tone, devoid of any emotion. 'Oh hi,' he said.

Rye knew roughly where Gidney lived – up off The Level, somewhere towards the racecourse, in a bedsit. It was an area of densely packed Victorian and Edwardian terraced houses, originally built as artisan dwellings, now largely monopolized by students and young singles. What did the geek go home to – if and when he ever did go home? A tin of beans on a single hob? Another computer screen? The *Guardian* newspaper – which he always carried under his arm into work but never seemed to read – and a pile of techie magazines?

'I need about another half-hour,' Rye said to Tom Bryce. 'You could wait, or would you like me to drop it back to you on my way home?'

'Yes. I – I have the children – I need to get back. Thank

you,' Bryce said. 'If you could drop it back I'd appreciate that.'

'OK, I have your address. I'll be there as soon as I can.' He checked his watch, wanting to make sure he left enough time to get home for the one television programme of the week he was addicted to, the motoring programme, *Top Gear*. Although it was some years since he had been a traffic cop he was still an unreconstructed petrol-head.

As he replaced the receiver, he saw Gidney, wearing his anorak and carrying his small rucksack, heading out of the door. No goodbye. God, he was always the same – no social graces at all!

*

It took Rye longer than he had planned to finish his examination, and he realized, just a little guiltily, that it was now over an hour and a half since he had spoken to Tom Bryce. He finally closed the man's laptop and was about to stand up when the phone rang.

It was an operator from the call handling centre in a building at Malling House, the police headquarters, where non-emergency calls from the general public were handled. 'Is that the High Tech Crime Unit?' the operator said.

Rye took a deep breath, resisting the temptation to tell the man he had the wrong number. 'Sergeant Rye speaking.'

'I have a caller who's complaining that someone is using his wireless internet connection without his permission.'

'Oh perrrlease?' Rye said, nearly exploding – he really didn't have the time for this. 'If he has a wireless internet connection, all he has to do is activate the encryption to protect it!'

'Would you mind talking to him, sir?' the operator said. 'It's the third call we've logged from him in the past month. He's a bit agitated.'

Join the club, Rye thought. Reluctantly he said, 'Put him on.'

Moments later he heard an elderly-sounding male voice, with a guttural Germanic accent. 'Oh yes. Hello there, my name is Andreas Seiler. I am an engineer; I am retired now but I was building bridges.' Then there was just the hiss of static. Rye waited a while.

Then to break the silence – and to see if the man was still on the line – he said, 'You are speaking to Sergeant Rye in the High Tech Crime Unit. How can I help you?' *I'm not hugely in need of a bridge*, he was tempted to add.

'Yes, thank you. Someone is stealing my internet.'

Rye looked at the clock on his computer screen. Twenty-five to seven. He just wanted to end this call and go home. And the operator might have mentioned the bloody man sounded as if he barely spoke English. '*Stealing* your internet. I'm not quite sure what you mean. Sir?'

'I am downloading a blueprint from a colleague from my old company, for a bridge they are designing in Kuala Lumpur Harbour. Then my internet slows down so much that the blueprint does not download. This is happening before.'

'I think you have a problem either with your internet service provider or with your computer, sir,' Rye said. 'You should start by contacting your ISP's technical support.'

'Well, I've done this, of course. And checked my computer. There are no problems. It is outside. I am thinking it is a man in a white van.'

Now Rye was just a little bit puzzled. And increasingly irritated by this bozo wasting his time. 'A man in a white van slowing down your internet connection?'

'Yah, that is right.'

'I'm sorry, Mr . . .' Rye glanced down at his notes. 'Mr Seiler. I'm a little confused. Where exactly are you?'

'I'm from Switzerland, but I am here working in Brighton.'

'Whereabouts in Brighton, sir?'

'Freshfield Road.'

'OK.' Rye knew that area well. An exceptionally wide street, on a hill, with two- and three-storey red-brick houses, many of the larger ones converted into flats. 'Your internet connection – you're on broadband?'

'Broadband, yes.'

'Do you have a wireless connection?'

'You are meaning Airport? Wi-Fi?'

'Yes, sir.'

'Yah, I have that.'

Rye grinned to himself, realizing what the man's problem probably was. 'Is your wireless network encrypted?'

Hesitantly, the man replied, 'Encrypted? I don't think so. I am staying in my son's flat, you see – this is his computer I am using.'

'You don't have to enter a password to use the wireless broadband?'

'No password, no.'

Without a password, any passer-by with a wireless internet card in their laptop could log on to the internet using someone else's wireless broadband. Rye had done it himself a couple of times, by accident, sitting in a patrol car with his laptop open. And, he thought a little guiltily, he had never bothered to password-protect his own wireless broadband connection at home. 'Is the van still outside?'

'Yes, that is right.'

'Can you read the registration number?'

The elderly Swiss engineer read it out to him. Rye wrote it down on his pad for no particular reason. 'My best advice is for you to activate the encryption, and that will lock him out.'

'I will speak to my son.'

'Good idea, sir.'

Rye finished the call and hung up. Then, because he was feeling fed up, he decided the rest of the force could know he was still in the office at twenty to seven on a bloody Sunday evening, and he decided to log the call as an official incident on the Vantage screen.

He typed his own name and department, entered the registration and description of the van, vague as it was, and logged the incident as 'War Driving. Sergeant Rye dealt with by phone.'

Childish, he knew, but it put him in one hell of a better mood.

55

'I've found a lasagne in the freezer,' the family liaison officer announced as Tom entered the kitchen, Jessica hanging on to one side of his trousers, Max the other, as if terrified that if they let go, he would disappear like their mother. 'Would you like me to cook that for your supper?'

Tom stared at WPC Buckley blankly; supper hadn't even occurred to him. All he could think about at this moment was the expression on Detective Sergeant Branson's face, when he had pointed out on the CCTV film the dickhead who had been on the train.

The strangely clipped response when he'd asked him if he knew who the man was: *Yes. We do.*

And then the detective's refusal to say any more about him.

Turning to the WPC, Tom said distractedly, 'Yes, thank you, that would be fine.'

'There are some bits in the fridge – tomatoes, lettuce, radishes. I could knock up a salad.'

'Great,' he said.

Lady came bounding in through the dog flap, looked at Tom and barked once, then wagged her tail, right as rain again.

'Are you hungry, Lady?' Tom asked.

She barked again, then looked at him expectantly.

'I don't like salad!' Max protested.

'I only like Mummy's salad!' Jessica said in a kind of solidarity.

'This is Mummy's salad,' Tom retorted. 'She bought it.'

'But she's not *making* it, is she?' Max said.

'This very nice lady is going to make it instead.' Tom picked up the dog's bowl and began to fill it with dried biscuits. Then he opened a can of her food. The vet had been unable to say what was wrong with the dog – probably just a bug, she thought. The detective had asked her whether she might have been drugged and the vet had responded it was possible. She would need to send a blood sample to the lab for analysis and it would take several days. Branson had asked her to do this.

'I've found some very yummy lemon ice cream in the freezer,' the WPC said breezily. 'You could have ice cream afterwards!'

'I want Mummy's ice cream,' Max said.

'I want chocolate, or strawberry,' Jessica demanded.

Tom exchanged glances with the police officer. She was in her mid-thirties, he guessed, with short blonde hair, a pleasant, open face and a warm but efficient nature. She seemed like someone who could cope with most situations. He gave her a *whatever* shrug, set the bowl down on the floor, then turned to Max.

'It *is* Mummy's ice cream. OK?'

Max looked up at him with big round eyes but they seemed completely devoid of expression. Tom could not read them, could not figure out exactly how his son was feeling. Or his daughter.

Or himself.

He desperately wanted to quiz Jessica some more about the vodka she claimed Kellie drank. What the hell was that all about?

'I don't like *lemon* ice cream,' Jessica said.

Tom knelt and put his arms around her. 'We don't have

any other flavours tonight. I'll get you chocolate and straw-berry for tomorrow – how's that?'

There was no reaction from his daughter.

'Give Daddy a hug, darling. I need a hug.'

'When will Mummy be home?'

He hesitated for a moment, wondering what he should say. The truth, that he just didn't know? Or a white lie? The lie was easier.

'Soon.' He scooped his daughter up in his arms. 'Bath time?'

'I want Mummy to bath me.'

'She might not be back until quite late, so Daddy's going to bath you tonight. OK?'

She looked away sulkily. In the living room he heard the volume of the television rise: tinkly music, the sound of car tyres squealing, a high-pitched American voice protesting about something. Max was watching *The Simpsons*. Good. At least that would keep him occupied until supper – or should he give him a bath, too?

He suddenly realized how little he knew about the kids' routines, about anything to do with the house. Dark, cold mist and a terrible fear engulfed him from within. Tomorrow morning he had to make a major presentation to Land Rover. Their marketing director was talking about a massive contract. If Kellie did not come back tonight, he just didn't know how he was going to cope with it.

Oh God, my sweet, lovely Kellie, please be OK, please come back. I love you so much.

At the top of the stairs, he carried Jessica into her bedroom then closed the door behind him and sat her down on the bed. He sat beside her.

'Jessica, can Daddy ask you about something you said this morning about Mummy? I said we would ask Mummy

what she would like to do today if she came back in time,
and you said, "She'll probably just want to drink vodka."
Remember?'

Jessica stared silently ahead.

'Do you remember saying that, darling?'

Pouting grumpily she said, 'You drink vodka, too.'

'Yes, I do. But why did you say that?'

Downstairs he suddenly heard Lady barking. Then
the doorbell rang. He heard Max shout out, 'MUMMY!
MUMMY! MUMMEEEEEEE! MUMMY'S HOME!'

Tom, his heart racing with sudden elation, tore down
the stairs. Max was already opening the front door.

Sergeant Jon Rye stood there, holding his leather
laptop case.

56

Roy Grace, sitting at the workstation in MIR One alongside most of his team, was running his eye over the latest incident reports log on the Vantage screen in front of him. It was a quarter to eight on Sunday evening, and although he still wasn't feeling hungry, he could feel himself getting shaky from lack of sugar or too much caffeine – or both, and was finding it increasingly hard to concentrate on his tasks.

Cleo Morey did not help either. Every few minutes his thoughts returned to her text of this morning.

He was checking the latest updates on Reggie D'Eath when he felt a thump on his back.

'Yo, old-timer!'

He looked up. Branson, who had popped out of the room a short while ago, and had returned with a massive carton of doughnuts from the supermarket across the road. He doled out one to each of the team members.

Grace took his and stepped away from the desk, deciding he needed to stretch his legs. Branson joined him as he walked across the room and out into the hallway. 'You OK, old man? You look like shit.'

Grace took a bite, licking the sugar off his lips. 'Thanks.'

Lowering his voice Branson said, 'So, a little birdie told me that you and Cleo Morey were cosying up to each other in Latin in the Lanes last night.'

Grace stared at him in surprise. 'Oh yes?'

'She's the one yanking your chain?'

'God, this is a small town!'

'It's a small planet, man!'

'How did you know who it was?'

The DS tapped the side of his face with his finger. 'Something you taught me – one of the first rules of being a good detective – build up your network of informants.'

Grace shook his head, half amused, half annoyed. 'That was before the regulations changed. *Sterile corridors*. All that crap.'

'Ever see that movie *Police*? Gérard Depardieu was a cop who leaned on his informants to get a drugs bust. Great movie.'

'I didn't see it.'

'It's well good. He reminded me of you. Bigger nose, though.'

'I look like Gérard Depardieu?'

Branson gave him a pat. 'Na, you're more like Bruce Willis.'

'That's better.'

'You sort of look like Bruce Willis's less fortunate brother. Or maybe his father.'

'You really know how to make a man feel good about himself. You look like—'

'Like who? Will Smith?'

'In your fucking dreams.'

'So tell me more about you and Ms Morey?'

'Nothing to tell. We had dinner.'

'Business, of course?'

'Totally.'

'Even in the back of your cab?' Branson pressed.

'Jesus! Is every fucking taxi driver in Brighton and Hove informing for you?'

'Nah, just a couple. I got lucky. Anyhow, they're not informants. They just keep their eyes open for me.'

Grace didn't know whether to be proud of his protégé for becoming such a proficient detective, or angry at him.

Interrupting his thoughts, Branson asked, 'So did she like your new gear?'

'She said I needed a new dresser and that you were total crap.'

Branson looked so hurt, Grace felt sorry for him. 'Don't worry – actually she didn't comment.'

'Shit, that's even worse!'

'We have two homicides and a missing woman; can we change the subject?'

'Don't change the subject! Cleo Morey! She's well gorgeous. Like, if I wasn't happily married, know what I mean? Except like – how do you stop thinking about what she does, man?'

'She didn't bring any of her cadavers with her to the restaurant, so it was easy.'

Branson shook his head, suppressing a grin. 'So, come on. Chapter and verse. Don't go all coy on me – tell me?'

'I don't have anything to be coy about. She has a boyfriend, OK? Actually, a fiancé. She somehow neglected to mention him.'

'You're shitting me.'

Grace pulled out his mobile phone and showed Branson the text he had received this morning.

Can't speak to u at moment. My fiancé just turned up. Will call later. CXXX

After some moments Branson declared, 'He's history.'

'That was midday. She still hasn't called.'

'Three kisses – trust me, he's toast.'

Grace crammed the rest of the doughnut into his mouth. Despite his lack of appetite, it was so good he could have eaten a second one. 'This another of your hunches?'

The Detective Sergeant gave him a sideways look. 'They're not all wrong.'

Cleo had not been on duty today. If she had, Grace would have attended Reggie D'Eath's post-mortem this afternoon, although it would not have been necessary as another detective had been appointed SIO of that case. 'We'll see,' he said.

Grace remembered an expression his mother used to use: *Time will tell.* Fate. She had been a great believer in fate but he had never totally shared that belief. It had helped her through her days dying from cancer. If you believed that some greater power was at work who had it all mapped out for you, then in some ways you were lucky. People who had deep religious faith were fortunate; they could abdicate all their responsibilities to God. Despite his fascination with the supernatural, Grace had never been able to believe in a God who had a plan for him.

He went back into the room and walked over to the workstation. On the large whiteboard was the photograph he had taken this morning of Reggie D'Eath in his bath, and a picture of Kellie Bryce – the photograph Branson had circulated to the press and to all UK police stations and ports.

Tomorrow morning Cassian Pewe, the arrogant shit of a Detective Inspector from the Met, was starting work with him on his cold case workload. And sure as hell if he did not have a result of some kind for her soon on Janie Stretton, the Assistant Chief Constable would have Pewe treading on the backs of his shoes.

Turning to Branson, Grace asked, 'Glenn, just how confident are you that Tom Bryce hasn't killed his wife?'

Whenever a woman went missing under suspicious circumstances, it was always the husband or boyfriend who was the prime suspect, until eliminated.

'Like I told you in the briefing an hour ago, I'm very confident. I interviewed him on tape in here – before we went through the CCTV footage – and I can get the tape profiled, but I don't think we need to. He'd have to have left his kids on their own in the house in the middle of the night, kill his wife, take her body somewhere, then drive to Ditchling Beacon, torch the car and walk five miles home. I don't think so.'

'So where is she? Do you think she might have done a runner with a lover?'

'I don't think she'd have torched her car, and I think she would have taken her handbag, some clothes, you know?'

'Could be good cover, torching the car.'

Branson was adamant. 'No. No way.'

'I'd like to see this Mr Bryce. Let's take a drive over.'

'Now? Tonight? We could go over but he's pretty distressed, trying to cope with his kids. I've got a rota of FLOs with him. I'd prefer to go back in the morning – if his missus hasn't shown up.'

'You've talked to the babysitter's parents?'

'Yeah. They were in bed when their daughter came home. She called out to them to say she was back, about 1.45 a.m. They heard a car drive off, that was all.'

'Their neighbours?'

'They don't have many in that street – up on "Nob Hill". I've been round them; no one saw or heard anything.'

'You've checked all traffic CCTV cameras?'

'I'm waiting – they've been looking through all the

footage from one a.m. until the call-out came in. Nothing so far.'

'Have you found out anything about them as a couple?'

'Talked to their neighbours on one side – elderly couple. He's about ten foot tall and she smokes so heavily I could hardly see her in the room. She seemed to have a bit of a friendship with Mrs Bryce – Kellie. Helps them out babysitting in emergencies, that sort of thing. What she said was that they have money troubles.'

Grace raised an eyebrow, his interest piqued. 'Oh yes?'

'You'd never know it from their house. They got a fuck-off barbecue that looks like Mission Control at Houston – must have cost thousands. They got a swanky kitchen, plasma telly, all the kit.'

'Probably why they've got money problems,' Grace said. 'Could she have torched the car for the insurance?'

Branson frowned. 'Hadn't thought of that. Does anyone ever make money out of a car insurance claim?'

'Worth finding out if they owned it or if it was on finance. Whether they've tried to sell it recently. The High Tech Crime Unit now have a copy of his laptop hard drive. Get them to check if he's posted any ads for his car on a website anywhere – someone like Autotrader. They could be in on this disappearance together.'

The more he thought about it, the more excited Grace got. *Money troubles*, he thought. Might be a red herring, but it needed to be explored. Sometimes people got up to ingenious tricks to reduce their debts. He watched Bella Moy reach for a Malteser; there was a trail of icing sugar from her doughnut to the edge of her keyboard. Nick Nicholl was on the phone, concentrating intensely.

Norman Potting was on the phone also, working his way through the client list of BCE-247, no doubt causing a few upsets, Grace thought a touch malevolently. Not that he took the moral high ground on prostitution – there had been a few occasions during the past nine years when he'd picked up the phone to call one of the numbers in the personal ads in the *Argus* himself. But on each occasion he had felt the shadow of Sandy over his shoulder.

The same thing had happened to him during a brief holiday romance on the one, disastrous, occasion he had gone on a singles holiday – to the Greek island of Paxos.

The door opened and the cheery face of Tony Case, the senior support officer for Sussex House, peered round. 'Just thought I'd pop in to see if there was anything you needed, Roy,' he said.

'Thanks, Tony, I think we're fine. I appreciate your coming in.'

Case raised a finger in acknowledgement. 'All part of the service.'

'Enjoy the rest of your weekend,' Grace said.

Tony Case looked at his watch. 'All four hours of it? That's almost funny, Roy.'

As the support officer headed off down the corridor, Grace stared at the bright orange lettering on the Vantage screen, scanning down it for the latest activity logged on the D'Eath murder. It did not take him long to find something. The house-to-house enquiries had turned up a vigilant neighbour who had clocked a white van parked outside Reggie D'Eath's house at around seven the previous evening. The neighbour had dutifully written down the van's number.

He double-clicked on the log to read the details. The PC who had interviewed the neighbour had requested a vehicle registration check, and it had come back as clean. The SIO appointed for Reggie D'Eath's murder was Detective Superintendent Dave Gaylor, a considerably more experienced officer than himself. No doubt Gaylor's team would be all over that van when they found it.

Nicholl came over and stooped beside him. 'Roy, I've just had a call from a bar manager I saw yesterday, at a place called the Karma Bar, down at the Marina. They've just been watching some CCTV tapes going back a couple of weeks – they're trying to stop a problem they have with a couple of drug dealers operating in the place – and he reckons he's got some footage of Janie Stretton.'

Grace felt a sudden bolt of excitement. 'How quickly can we get it here?'

'He'd rather I went there – he needs the tapes. He said I could watch them right away.'

'Now?'

'Yes.'

Grace thought for a moment. Nick Nicholl had not been in the CID long, and still had a lot to learn. The young DC was bright but he might miss something – and this promised to be the first lead they had in the case. If this was so, then it was crucial to get every possible piece of information from it.

'Bring her photographs,' Grace said. 'I'll come with you.' Turning to Branson, he said, 'We'll see Mr Bryce as soon as I'm back.'

'That's going to make it well late for him.' Glenn Branson was thinking, unprofessionally, he knew, but he couldn't help it, about the remnants of his own Sunday night. He longed to see his kids, even if it was just for five minutes before they went to sleep.

'Glenn, if Mr Bryce hasn't murdered his wife, or pulled off some scam with her, he's going to be wide awake all night long, trust me.'

Branson gave a reluctant nod, knowing Grace was right, and glanced at his watch. Grace would be an hour at the very least and probably much longer. By the time he was back and they'd gone to the Bryces' house it would be eleven at the earliest. He wasn't afraid of facing half a dozen knife-wielding thugs in a dark alley in Brighton, but at times he was bloody terrified of his wife, and at this moment he was terrified of picking up the phone to Ari and telling her he was unlikely to be home this side of midnight.

Grace was so fired up by the possible sighting in the Karma Bar that, running his eye down the rest of the incident reports log, he skipped over the report Sergeant Jon Rye had logged an hour earlier, headed War Driving, without even noticing it.

57

Tom read a few pages of *The Gruffalo* to Jessica. His heart wasn't in it, and she was not really listening. He didn't fare any better with Max.

All he could think was, miserably, that he must be a crap father. The children wanted their mother, which was completely understandable, but he was starting to feel beyond inadequate as a stand-in. They now even seemed to prefer the company of Linda Buckley to himself. The WPC was sitting downstairs, waiting for the replacement family liaison officer to arrive and take over from her for the night.

He put the book down, kissed his wide-awake son goodnight and closed the door, then went into his den and made another round of phone calls – to Kellie's parents, who had been ringing just about every hour, to all her friends, and again to her very worried sister in Scotland. No one had heard from her.

Then he went into their bedroom and opened the top drawer in the Victorian chest where Kellie kept her clothes. He rummaged through her sweaters, smelling her scent rising from them. But found nothing. Next he opened the drawer beneath, which was crammed with underwear. And his hand struck something hard and round. He pulled it out.

It was a bottle of Tesco vodka – sealed, unopened.

He found a second bottle, also unopened. Then a third. This one was half empty.

He sat down on the bed and stared at it. Three vodka bottles in her underwear drawer?

She'll probably just want to drink vodka. I saw her. I said I wouldn't tell.

Oh Jesus.

He stared at the bottle again. Should he phone Detective Sergeant Branson and tell him?

He tried to think it through. If he did tell him, then what? The detective might lose interest, thinking she was flaky and just might have gone off on a bender.

But he knew her better. Or did, until about a minute ago.

He rummaged through the rest of her drawers but found nothing further. He replaced the bottles, closed the drawer, then went downstairs.

Linda Buckley was sitting in the living room, watching television, a police series set in the 1960s. The station Sergeant had a box of cigarettes on his desk, which he offered to a harassed-looking woman with her hair in a bun.

'You like watching cop shows?' he said lamely, trying to make conversation.

'Only the ones set in the past,' she said. 'Don't like the modern ones. They get so many things wrong, it drives me nuts. I just sit there groaning, saying to myself, *They don't do it like that, for God's sake!*'

He sat down, wondering if it was wise to confide in her.

'You must eat something, Mr Bryce. Shall I pop your lasagne in the microwave for you?' she asked, before he had a chance to say anything.

He thanked her; she was right. Although all he felt like was a stiff drink. She got up and went out to the kitchen. He stared blankly at the screen, thinking about the vodka bottles, wondering why Kellie had the secret stash. How long had she been drinking? And, more importantly, why?

Did this explain her disappearance?

He didn't think so. Or at least did not *want* to think so.

The police series ended and the *Nine O'Clock News* came on. There was a smell of cooking meat, which churned his stomach. He had no appetite at all. Tony Blair was shaking hands with George Bush. Tom mistrusted both men, but tonight he barely noticed them. He watched jerky news footage of Iraq, then a photograph of a pretty teenage girl who had been found raped and strangled near Newcastle, followed by a plea from a clumsy-looking, inarticulate Chief Inspector with a haircut like a hedgehog, who had clearly never had any media training.

'It's on the table!' the family liaison officer called out bossily.

Meek as a lamb he went into the kitchen and sat down. The television in there was on, showing the same news.

He ate a couple of mouthfuls of the lasagne, then stopped, finding it hard to swallow. 'I think we should put a note on the front door,' he said, 'so your colleague doesn't ring the bell. I don't want the kids disturbed, thinking it's their mother arriving home.'

'Good plan,' she said, taking a scrap of paper from her briefcase and walking to the doorway. 'But I want to see that plate clean by the time I come back!'

'Yes, boss,' he said, forcing a grin, then forcing another mouthful down while she stood over him.

Then, moments after she had gone out of the room, a fresh news item was announced by the newscaster. 'Sussex Police are tonight investigating the murder of convicted paedophile Reginald D'Eath, who was found dead early today at his home in the village of Rottingdean in East Sussex.'

A photograph of D'Eath appeared on the screen. Tom dropped his fork in shock.

It was the dickhead from the train.

58

They had been building Brighton Marina for as long as Roy Grace could remember, far back into his childhood. They were still building it now, and maybe they always would be, he speculated. A large dusty area was closed off on which sat two cranes, a JCB digger and a caterpillar-tracked earth mover, amid towers of building materials beneath tarpaulins flapping in the strong breeze.

He'd never really worked out whether he liked the whole development or not. It was strangely positioned at the foot of tall, sheer white cliffs to the east of the city, and comprised inner and outer yacht basins around which the Marina Village, as it had been named, had grown – and was still growing. There were clusters of ersatz Regency town houses and apartment blocks, dozens of restaurants, cafes, pubs and bars, a couple of yacht chandleries, numerous clothing boutiques, a massive supermarket, a bowling alley, a multiplex cinema, a hotel and a casino.

But it always felt a little like Toytown to him. Like a grown-up version of something a child had assembled with Lego. Even after thirty years everything still looked new and felt a little soulless. The only part he really liked was where he and Nick Nicholl were walking now – the wooden boardwalk, built just a few years back, that ran along the entire waterfront.

On a warm evening like tonight the place had a great buzz, with people of all ages sitting out at its wall-to-wall cafes and restaurants, watching a few late yachts returning to their berths among the pontoons, talking, canoodling, listening to the pounding of music and the cries of gulls.

Grace, feeling more human after the sugar hit of the doughnut, experienced a deep pang in his heart as he passed a young couple seated at an outdoor table, staring into each other's eyes, clearly in love. Why hadn't Cleo mentioned that she was engaged?

Why hadn't he thought to ask whether she was in a relationship?

That long kiss in the taxi – all the way back to her apartment – that wasn't the behaviour of a woman in love with her fiancé, was it? Even with the alcohol talking?

With the sun sinking but still well above the horizon, Grace watched his lengthening shadow skim the planks ahead of him, Nicholl's considerably taller one bobbing along beside it. The DC, hands in his pockets with an envelope containing Janie Stretton's photographs tucked under his arm, loped along, slightly stooped as if he was embarrassed about his six foot six inches. He had been quiet as usual on the way here – which Grace was grateful for tonight as he wasn't in the mood for small talk.

They passed the cooler-than-thou Seattle Hotel, then reached the Karma Bar, with its roped-off outdoor seating area fronting the boardwalk, every table and just about every chair occupied.

Grace followed Nicholl inside. He had been dragged here on a few occasions during the past couple of years, by well-meaning friends who had insisted it was *the* place in Brighton for a man of his age to meet women. The exotic interior was different to anything else in the city: spacious, with a warm glow from oriental lanterns, inviting cushions strewn around recessed banquettes, a long bar, and decor influenced – to his eye at least – by India, Morocco and the Far East.

Nick Nicholl went up to a pretty girl behind the bar. 'Hi,' he said. 'I'm looking for Ricky.'

She looked around, then said pleasantly, 'I think he's in the office. Is he expecting you?'

'Yes. Could you tell him it's Detective Constable Nicholl and Detective Superintendent Grace to see him – we spoke about half an hour ago.'

She went off to find him.

'Your guy from the Met, this DI Dickinson, the SIO of the case in Wimbledon with the murdered girl wearing the scarab bracelet. It's tomorrow midday we're seeing him now, right?' Grace checked with Nick.

'Yes.'

'Probably just as well he didn't want to do it today – I don't think we'd have fitted him in.'

They both leaned on the bar. A Joss Stone song was playing. 'I like her,' Grace said.

Nicholl shrugged. 'Country and western's my thing, really.'

'Who do you like?'

He shrugged again. 'Johnny Cash is the man. Rachel and I were going to line-dancing classes – had to stop with the little one on its way.'

'They change your life, kids, so I'm told,' Grace said, staring down at a pile of *Absolute Brighton* magazines next to an ashtray.

'Prenatal classes aren't as much fun,' the DC admitted, with a glum nod.

A couple of minutes later the barmaid returned, and ushered them up some stairs into a comfortable office containing bland, functional furniture, in stark contrast to the bar. There was a desk behind which a young man with spiky hair dressed in a T-shirt and jeans was sitting, a sofa and a couple of armchairs, an elaborate sound system, and a bank of black and white monitors on which there were closed-circuit television images of the interior and exterior of the bar.

The young man stood up with a cheery smile and came round to the front of the desk. 'Hi, nice to meet you, Mr Nicholl,' he said, and shook their hands. Looking at Grace, he added, 'I'm Ricky, the manager. Read about you in the *Argus* – was it yesterday?'

'Could have been.'

'Thought they were a bit brutal, like. Can I offer you guys a drink?'

'I'd love a mineral water – still if possible.'

'A Diet Coke?' Nick Nicholl said.

The manager picked up his phone and ordered the drinks, then gestured to them to sit down. They sat on the sofa and Ricky pulled up a chair. 'Yeah, well,' he said, directing his remarks at the Detective Constable and tapping the side of his head. 'I got a good memory for faces – need to here, to remember the troublemakers. As I said on the phone, I'm sure that girl you was looking for came in here just over a week ago. Friday night, with a bloke. It was lucky – the tapes normally get wiped after a week – but we've had a bit of bother. You won't bust us or anything?'

Grace grinned. 'I'm not interested in busting you; I just want to find Janie Stretton's killer.'

'OK, we're cool.' Then Ricky frowned. 'What was that stuff I read about a beetle – a scarab?'

'It's not important,' Grace replied, a little more curtly than he had intended.

'Just interested, cos we got one in here on a shelf in the

VIP room – a little bronze, part of the decor. Pushing a ball of bronze shit. Yuk!'

'Where did you get it from?' Grace asked.

'Dunno, the interior decorator was responsible for all that stuff.' Ricky picked up a remote control and pressed a button. 'Watch the monitor in the centre,' he said.

There was a flicker that momentarily turned into a blur, then a series of images dropped down as if the horizontal hold was on the blink. The image stabilized, showing a wide-angle sweep of the very crowded bar, with the date and time running in the bottom right-hand corner.

'Watch the door, the one that goes out the front, now!' Ricky said, sounding excited.

Grace saw a muscular man in his thirties with a lean, hard face and a mean, king-of-the-jungle expression, walk in towing a girl with long hair, dressed in a tight-fitting miniskirt. It was Janie Stretton. No question.

He studied her companion carefully, watching his strutting gait which reminded him of the way Paras walked, as if ready to take on all-comers. The man had gelled spikes of short hair, sported a thick chain around his neck, and was dressed in a singlet and slacks. Holding Janie Stretton's hand all the way, he cut a swathe through the crowd and went straight up to the bar, at which point the camera, moving in a steady arc, lost them.

A few minutes later the camera picked them up again. The man was holding a pint glass of beer and she had a cocktail of some sort. The man clinked his glass against hers, then, in a curious movement, slid his free hand around her neck, appeared to grab a clump of her hair, pulled her head back and coarsely kissed her neck.

Nick Nicholl had the photographs of Janie Stretton on

his lap and was alternately looking down at them then up at the screen. 'It's her,' he said.

'No question,' Grace confirmed. 'Absolutely.' Looking at the manager, he asked, 'Who's her squeeze?'

'Dunno, never seen him before.'

'You're sure?'

'Not one hundred per cent, no – we get an awful lot of people in here. But I don't think so.'

Grace's mobile phone rang. Without taking his eyes off the screen, he pulled it out of his pocket and glanced down at the display.

It was Cleo Morey.

Excusing himself, he hit the button to answer and stepped out of the office.

She sounded very sweet and very humble. 'I just wondered if you were up for a drink tonight – if you'd like to come over here?'

He melted at the sound of her voice. 'I'd love to,' he said. 'But I have a good two hours' work to do.'

'So, come over after that – for a nightcap?'

'Umm . . .' he said, totally thrown. This was not the time or place for this sort of conversation.

'I've got wine, beer, vodka.'

'Any whisky?' he teased.

'Now that's a strange coincidence. I have a whole bottle of Glenfiddich I bought this afternoon.'

'Obviously synchronicity,' Grace said, trying to sound cooler than he felt – and not succeeding.

'Obviously.'

59

The family liaison officer who took over from Linda Buckley was a thin, overly polite young PC in his mid-twenties, called Chris Willingham. He carried a small suitcase in which he claimed to have everything he needed for his night's vigil, and within minutes was happily installed in the living room with an iPod headset plugged into his ears and a copy of the *Rough Guide to Croatia* open on his lap.

Glenn Branson had rung to say he was coming over again in an hour, making Tom wonder if he had any information. He was also determined to ask the detective why, when he had obviously recognized Reginald D'Eath as the dickhead on the train, he had not revealed this to him this afternoon at the CID headquarters.

Tom left Chris Willingham with a black coffee and a plate of chocolate digestive biscuits and retreated to the sanctuary of his den with the *Sunday Times*, which he had not yet opened. Normally, on a Sunday evening, he and Kellie would flop out on the sofa in the living room with all the sections of the *Sunday Times* and *Mail on Sunday* strewn around the carpet. He always started with the business pages, looking for high-profile companies to target as potential customers. Kellie began with the *Mail*'s *You* magazine.

But it was a waste of time even looking at a paper tonight; all he saw was a blur of newsprint. He felt so alone, so afraid. So totally lost and scared.

Scared witless for Kellie.

Reginald D'Eath, the dickhead on the train, the man who had left behind the CD, had been found murdered in his home. Strangled in his bath.

By?

By the same people who had threatened to kill his own family? Tom wondered.

On the news it had been reported that D'Eath – who had changed his name to Ron Dawkins – had done a deal with the prosecution in the forthcoming trial of a paedophile ring. So was it a professional hit? Or a revenge killing by a parent of a child he had abused?

Or, he speculated wildly, the coil of fear in his stomach darkening all the time, was it punishment for losing the disk? The same punishment he and his family were threatened with because he had found it?

Twenty-four hours ago they had been drinking champagne in the drawing room of Philip Angelides' house. Not a great evening, but at least life had been normal. Now he just did not know what to do. He was trying to get his head around tomorrow, Monday, but was finding it hard to think more than a few minutes ahead. He couldn't cancel the presentation to Land Rover and supposed he would have to delegate one of his team to do it for him – which would mean paying one of the two salesmen commission on the order if it came through, yet again reducing his margins and his ability to quote competitively. But at this moment that was the least of his worries.

Then he experienced a sudden flash of resentment towards Kellie. Irrational, he knew, but he couldn't help it. *How can you bloody do this to me at a time like this?*

Almost immediately he felt guilty for even thinking that.

Christ, my darling, where the hell are you? He buried his face in his hands, trying hard to think clearly through the fog of this nightmare and hating himself for being so damned helpless.

*

It was over an hour later a blue saloon pulled up outside the house. Looking out of his den window, Tom saw Glenn Branson climb out of the driver's door and another man – white, in his late thirties, with close-cropped hair, who looked every inch a copper – get out of the other side.

He raced downstairs, before they rang the bell and disturbed the kids, and opened the door. Lady came bounding out into the hallway, but he managed to calm her and stop her barking. She'd obviously recovered from the bug – or attempted poisoning.

'Good evening again, Mr Bryce. We're sorry to disturb you.'

'No. Thanks. I'm glad to see you.'

'This is Detective Superintendent Grace, the Senior Investigating Officer on this case,' Branson said.

Bryce stared briefly at the Detective Superintendent, surprised that he was so casually dressed, but then all he knew about the police was gleaned from the occasional episode of *Morse* or *Dalziel and Pascoe* or *CSI*, and, thinking about it, detectives on those shows were often very casually dressed, too. The man had a strong, pleasant face with laser-sharp blue eyes and a convincing air of authority.

'Thank you for coming over,' Tom Bryce said, showing them in, then leading them through to the kitchen.

'No developments, Mr Bryce?' Glenn Branson asked, pulling up a chair at the kitchen table.

'One, but I think you know that already. The man on the train was the paedophile who was found murdered today. Reginald D'Eath? I recognized his face on the news.'

Grace gave the room a quick sweep, absorbing the children's drawings on the wall, the swanky fridge with the built-in television, the expensive-looking units, then he sat down, keeping his eyes fixed on Tom Bryce's. 'I was very sorry to hear about your wife, Kellie, Mr Bryce. I'd just like to ask you a few questions, to help us do all we can to assist in locating her.'

'Of course.'

Watching Tom Bryce's eyes like a hawk, he asked, 'Can you tell me when you bought the Audi that was found burned out?'

The man's eyes swung immediately to the right. 'Yes, in March.'

'From a local dealer?'

Again the eyes went to the right, establishing his memory was on the right side of his brain. Which meant if his eyes swung left in response to a question, he would be accessing the creative side of his brain, and would be in construct mode. Lying. But at this moment he was telling the truth. 'Yes – from Caffyns.'

Grace pulled out his notebook. 'I'd like to start with some chronology. Can we run through the events leading up to the time when Kellie disappeared?'

'Of course. Can I offer you something to drink? Tea or coffee?'

The SIO opted for a black coffee, and Glenn Branson for a glass of tap water. Tom switched on the kettle and began to talk through in detail the events of yesterday evening.

When he had finished, Grace asked, 'You and your wife

didn't have a row or anything, either before you went out or on the way home?'

'Not at all,' Tom replied, his eyes briefly darting right again. He thought back again to the drive home last night from the Angelideses. Kellie had been in a slightly strange mood, but she'd had plenty of those before and hadn't vanished afterwards.

'Can I ask a rather personal question?' Grace said.

'Go ahead.'

'Do you have a good marriage? Or are there any problems in your relationship?'

Tom Bryce shook his head. 'We don't have a good marriage.' Then he said, emphatically, 'We have a *terrific* marriage.'

The kettle started boiling. Tom was starting to stand up when Grace's next question nailed him back down to his chair. 'Is everything all right with your finances, Mr Bryce?'

From the look in those laser eyes, Tom could tell Grace knew something about his problems. 'Actually they're not great, no.'

'Did you have any life insurance cover on Mrs Bryce?'

Tom stood up angrily. 'What the hell are you getting at?'

'I'm afraid I will have to ask you some very personal questions, Mr Bryce. If you would be more comfortable having a solicitor present, or if there are any you don't want to answer without one being present, that is your right.'

As the kettle switched itself off, Tom sat back down. 'I don't need anyone present.'

'OK, thank you,' Roy Grace said. 'So can you tell me if you have any life insurance cover on Mrs Bryce?'

The man's eyes darted again to the right. 'No. I had some on both of us – for the children's sake – but I had to cancel it a few months ago because of the cost.' He stood

up and went to make the coffee, and run Branson a glass
of water. Grace waited until he had sat back down, and he
could see his face clearly once more.

'Have you noticed any change in Mrs Bryce's behaviour
in recent months?'

And now Grace saw the flickering hesitation in Tom
Bryce's eyes; they darted very definitely to the left, to construct mode. He was about to lie to them. 'No, not at all.'

Then immediately after Tom had said this, he wondered whether it was time to come clean and tell them
about the vodka. And about her strange Kellie moments?

But he was scared that if he did they might lose
interest. So what the hell was the point in telling them?

Grace picked up his coffee cup, then set it down again
without bringing it to his lips. Again fixing on Bryce's eyes,
he asked, 'Do you have any concerns that Kellie might be
having an affair?'

Eyes securely right again. 'Absolutely none. We have a
strong marriage.'

Roy Grace continued with his questions for another
half an hour, at the end of which Tom felt the Detective
Superintendent had expertly and thoroughly – and at
times more than a little unpleasantly – filleted him.

He felt drained as he finally closed the door on them at
almost eleven o'clock, and also uncomfortable. It seemed
from the DS's questions – and the way he had reacted to
Tom's answers – that he was to the police a prime suspect.
This was something he wanted to change, quickly, because
all the time they were suspicious of him, they would be
focusing their energies in the wrong direction. And he
realized he had forgotten to ask DS Branson why he had
kept quiet about the dickhead's identity this afternoon.

Tom popped his head round the living room door, to

see the FLO engrossed in his book. He told him to help himself to anything he fancied in the kitchen, and apologized for not having a spare bed. DC Willingham told him he had had some sleep during the day and planned to stay up all night.

Then Tom climbed upstairs to his den, far too keyed up to contemplate sleep. He had some important emails to write about the morning's presentation and somehow had to find the strength to concentrate on them.

He tapped the return key on his laptop, to wake it up. Moments later a load of emails downloaded. Twenty, thirty, forty. The junk-mail filter picked up most of them, leaving just half a dozen. Three were from friends, no doubt containing jokes. One was from Olivia, his ever-efficient secretary, listing the week's appointments and reminding him what he needed for the presentation in the morning. One was from *Ivanhoe*, the Web-doctor site he subscribed to, but rarely had time to read properly.

The last one was from *postmaster@scarab.tisana.al*. The header read simply: Private and confidential.

He double-clicked to read the email. The text was brief and unsigned.

Kellie has a message for you. Remain online.

60

At 11.15 p.m. Emma-Jane Boutwood and Nick Nicholl were still at their desks at the workstation. The rest of the team had left, heading home to their lives, one by one, with the exception of Norman Potting, who was just getting to his feet now, straightening his tie and pulling on his jacket.

A handful of people remained at the other two stations. The surfaces were littered with empty coffee cups, soft-drink cans, food cartons, and the waste bins were overflowing. The room was always fresh first thing in the morning, Emma-Jane thought, and by late evening it smelled like an institutional canteen: a faintly sickly confection of aromas – onion bhajis from the deli counter of the Asda supermarket across the road, pot noodles, potato soup, microwaved burgers and fries, and coffee.

Potting gave a long yawn, then burped. 'Ooops,' he said. 'Pardon me. Them Indian things always do that to me.' He hesitated for a moment, getting no reaction. 'Well, I'm off then.' Then he lingered where he was. 'Either of you care for a quick jar? One for the road on the way home? I know a place that will serve us.'

Both shook their heads. Nick Nicholl was engrossed in what appeared to be, at least to Emma-Jane, a difficult personal call on his mobile. From the few words she had caught it sounded as if he was trying to pacify his wife, who was upset about something. Probably that her husband was still at work at this hour on a Sunday. In a way, although she missed having a boyfriend – it was a year since she had broken up with Olli – Emma-Jane was relieved that she had no one in her life at the moment. It meant she could concentrate on her career and not have to feel guilty about the crazy hours she put in.

Ignoring the fact that Nicholl was talking, Potting leaned closer to his face and asked, 'Don't suppose you heard the cricket score? I was trying to find it on the net.'

Nicholl glanced up at him, shook his head then focused on his call again.

Hesitating again, Potting dug his hands in his trouser pockets and repeated, 'Well, I'm off then.'

Emma-Jane raised a hand. 'Bye, have a nice evening.'

'Just about time to get home and back before tomorrow,' he growled. 'See you at eight thirty.'

'Look forward to it!' she said, a touch facetiously. Taking a sip of mineral water from a bottle, she watched him walk across the room, a shapeless man in a badly creased suit. Although she found him gross, in truth she felt a little sorry for him because he seemed so desperately lonely. She resolved to try to be nicer to him tomorrow.

She screwed the cap back on the bottle, then resumed working her way through the statements from Reggie D'Eath's neighbours, which had been taken down earlier today by the house-to-house enquiry team. She was also working on trying to find out more information about the white Ford Transit van that had been clocked outside his house the previous night by one of the dead man's neighbours.

Even though the D'Eath murder enquiry was being run by a different team, Grace believed it had enough relevance to Operation Nightingale for his team to be fully up to speed on all aspects of the enquiry at this stage.

On her desk was the licence number GU03OAG. Its registered owner was a company called Bourneholt International Ltd, with an address, a PO box number, that she would not be able to check out until the morning. When she'd shown it to Norman Potting, earlier, he'd told her that more than likely it was nothing more than an accommodation address. That seemed likely as nothing came up for the name in a search on the internet.

One of the phones on the workstation started ringing. Nick was still hunched over his desk talking into his mobile so E-J picked up the receiver. 'Incident Room,' she said.

The voice at the other end sounded brisk but courteous. 'Hi, it's Adam Davies here from Southern Resourcing Centre. Could you put me on to Detective Superintendent Grace?' Southern Resourcing was the call handling centre where all non-emergency calls were answered and assessed by trained handlers like Davies.

'I'm afraid he's out at the moment. Can I help you?'

'I need to speak to someone on Operation Nightingale.'

'I'm DC Boutwood, part of the Operation Nightingale team,' she replied, feeling proud at saying it.

'I have a gentleman by the name of Mr Seiler on the line phoning about a white van. I ran a registration check on the number he gave me, and it came up on the system that DS Grace has put a PNC marker on this vehicle. I thought he might want to speak to the gentleman.'

'Is he the owner of it?'

'No, apparently it's parked outside his flat. He made a complaint earlier this evening – it was logged at six forty p.m.'

'It was?' Emma-Jane said, surprised, wondering why this hadn't been picked up by anyone. 'Please put him on.'

Moments later she was talking to an elderly, irate man with a guttural Germanic accent. 'Hello, yes. You are not the police officer I am speaking with earlier?' he asked.

Jamming the phone against her ear with her shoulder, the young Detective Constable was tapping the keyboard furiously. Seconds later she found the 6.40 p.m. entry, logged by a Detective Sergeant Jon Rye of the High Tech Crime Unit.

War Driving. Sergeant Rye attended by phone.

What on earth did that mean?

'I'm afraid it is Sunday night, sir; a lot of people have gone home.'

'Yes, and the man in the white van is outside my apartment again, stealing my internet. It would be good if *he* went home.'

Stealing my internet? she thought. What on earth did that mean? But at this moment she was more interested in the van. 'Can you read the registration number of the vehicle to me, sir?'

After a moment, and agonizingly slowly, he said, 'G for golf, U for – ah – umbrella. Zero, three. O – Oscar, A for alpha, G for golf.'

She wrote it down.

GU03OAG

Suddenly, adrenalin coursing, Emma-Jane was on her feet. 'Sir, let me have your number and I'll call you straight back. Your address is Flat D, 138 Freshfield Road?'

He confirmed that it was and gave her the phone number. She tapped it straight into her mobile. 'Please don't go outside or frighten him off. I'll be with you in just a few minutes. I'm going to hang up and I will call you back in two minutes.'

'Yes,' he said. 'Thank you, thank you so very much.'

Nick was still engrossed in his call, and ignored her frantic gesticulations. In desperation she physically pulled his phone away from his ear. 'Come with me!' she said. 'NOW!'

61

Tom, shaking with nerves, sat in his den with a tumbler of Glenfiddich, trying to focus on the emails he somehow *had* to send to his team tonight about the presentation tomorrow morning. Every couple of minutes he clicked the send-and-receive button on his email. Followed by a large sip of whisky.

At eleven twenty his tumbler was empty and, in need of another, he went downstairs. PC Willingham was in the kitchen, making himself a coffee.

'Would you like one, Mr Bryce?' he asked.

Tom held up his glass and, aware his voice was slurring slightly, said, 'Thanks, but I need something a little stronger.'

'I don't blame you.'

'Would you like one?' Tom offered, uncapping the bottle.

'Not on duty, thank you, sir, no.'

Tom gave him an *it's your funeral* shrug, filled the tumbler to the brim with whisky, ice and water – but mostly whisky – and went back upstairs. As he sat back down at his desk, he noticed another email had come in from *postmaster@scarab.tisana.al*, with an attachment. The header said, simply,

Message from Kellie.

His hand was shaking so much he could barely steady the cursor on the attachment. He double-clicked.

The attachment seemed to take forever to open. Then suddenly the entire screen went dark. And Kellie's face appeared.

Harshly lit like a solo performer on a stage under the glare of a single spotlight, she was staring straight ahead, out of darkness. Still wearing her evening dress from last night, she was bound hand and foot and roped to a chair. A silver pendant Tom had never seen before hung from a chain around her neck. There was a large bruise below her right eye where it looked as if she had been punched, and her lips looked swollen.

She spoke in a choked, stilted tone, sounding as though she was attempting to recite from a memorized script.

Tom stared at her, totally numb with shock, as if this was not real, was just a bad joke, or a bad dream.

'Tom, please watch me carefully and listen to me,' Kellie said in a quavering voice. 'Why have you done this to me? Why did you ignore the instructions you were given not to go to the police? They are now punishing me because of your stupidity.'

She fell silent, tears flooding down her mascara-streaked cheeks. Steadily the camera zoomed in tighter and tighter on her face. Then even tighter, tilting down, favouring the pendant on the necklace. Until the necklace filled the screen completely.

And the design engraved on it was clearly visible. It was a scarab beetle.

'Don't tell the police about this film, darling. Just do exactly what they tell you. Otherwise it will be Max's turn next. Then Jessica's. Don't try to be heroic. Please do what they tell you. It's . . .' Her voice faltered. 'It's the only chance you and I have of ever seeing each other again. Please,

please don't tell the police. They will know. These people know everything.'

Kellie's voice ripped through his soul like barbed wire.

The screen went pitch black. Then he heard a sound. It started as a low whine, then steadily got louder and higher, more and more piercing. It was Kellie, he realized. She was screaming.

Then silence.

The film was at an end. The attachment closed.

Tom vomited onto the carpet.

62

Nick Nicholl drove the unmarked Vauxhall out of the security gates of Sussex House and floored the accelerator. Emma-Jane, on the radio, gave instructions to the Control Centre operator.

'This is Golf Tango Juliet Echo. We need uniform backup in the vicinity of Freshfield Road. The incident is at Number 138, but I don't want anyone there to see or hear the car until I say so – that is very important. Understood?' She was shaking with nerves. This was the first serious incident she had been in control of, and she was conscious that she might be exceeding her authority. But what choice did she have? 'Can you confirm?'

'Golf Tango Juliet Echo, dispatching uniform backup to vicinity of Freshfield Road. Requesting total silence and invisibility until further instructions. ETA four minutes.'

They were racing down a long, steep hill. Emma-Jane glanced at the speedometer. Over 70 mph. She dialled the number that Mr Seiler had given her. Moments later he answered.

'Mr Seiler? It's Detective Constable Boutwood; we are on our way. Is the van still outside?'

'Still outside,' he confirmed. 'Would you like that I go and speak with the driver?'

'No,' she implored. 'No, please don't do that. Please just stay indoors and watch him. I will stay on the line. Tell me what you can see.'

The flash of a Gatso speed camera behind them

streaked around the car. Still maintaining his speed, DC Nicholl continued down the hill, accelerating even harder as he saw a green light ahead of them. The bloody thing changed to red.

'Run it!' she said to him. She held her breath as he edged over the line and made a sharp right turn, cutting dangerously in front of a car, which hooted furiously at them.

'I am still seeing the white van,' Mr Seiler said. 'A man inside it.'

'Just one man?'

They were driving along a dual carriageway, a 40 mph limit, the speedometer nudging ninety.

'I only see one man.'

'What is he doing?'

'He has a laptop computer open.'

A second Gatso flashed.

'You'd better be right about this,' Nick Nicholl whispered. 'Otherwise my licence is toast.'

Street lights sped past them. Tail lights appeared like in a DVD on fast-forward. More lights flashed at them, angry drivers.

Ignoring her colleague, she was totally focused on the informant. 'We're only a couple of minutes away,' she said.

'So you want me outside now?'

'NO!' Her voice came out as a shriek. 'Please stay inside.'

Nick Nicholl braked, ran another red light, then made a sharp left up Elm Grove, a steep, wide hill with houses and shops on either side. The sign HARMONY CARPETS above a shopfront flashed past.

'What can you see now, Mr Seiler?'

'Nothing has changed.'

Suddenly the radio crackled. 'Golf Tango Juliet Echo, this is PC Godfrey. Uniform Delta Zebra Bravo. We are approaching Freshfield Road. ETA thirty seconds.'

'Stop where you are,' she said, suddenly feeling incredibly important – and very nervous of fouling up.

They passed the gloomy buildings of Brighton General Hospital, where her grandmother had died of cancer last year, then made a lurching, tyre-squealing dog-leg right into Freshfield Road.

Emma-Jane glanced at the street numbers – 256 . . . 254 . . .248 . . . Turning to Nick Nicholl, she said, 'OK, slow down; there's a mini-roundabout ahead. It'll be the other side of that.'

As they drove on she suddenly saw the white Ford Transit about 200 yards ahead of them, its tail lights glowing red. And now her heart really began to race. Within a few seconds she could read the number plate.

GU03OAG

She hit the radio button. 'Uniform Delta Zebra Bravo. There is a white Ford Transit outside Number 138 Freshfield Road. Please intercept.'

Then she turned to Nick Nicholl. 'Go for it! Pull up in front! Block it!' She unclipped her seat belt.

Within seconds they were sliding to a halt, angled in front of the van, and Emma-Jane had her door open before they had even stopped moving. She clambered out and grabbed the driver's door of the Transit.

It was locked.

She heard a siren. Saw blue flashing light skidding across the black tarmac. Heard the Transit's starter motor and the revving of its engine. Her arm was yanked almost out of its socket as the van jerked backwards. She heard the splintering crunch of metal on metal and glass. Then her arm was jerked forwards as the van accelerated, ramming the Vauxhall. The air was filled with the howling sound of an engine over-revving, the acrid reek of burning tyres, then a shriek of metal as the Vauxhall lurched sideways. She heard Nick shout, 'Stop! Police!'

Then another scream of bending metal. She hung on for grim life.

Suddenly her feet were swept away. The van was accelerating clear; it swerved sharply to the left and her legs trailed in the air, then to the right. Towards a line of parked cars.

She felt a moment of blind terror.

Then all the air was shot out of her. She felt a terrible pressure, then heard a dull crunching sound like breaking glass and metal. In the seconds of agony before she passed into oblivion, her hands giving up their grip, her body rolling into the gutter, she realized it wasn't glass and metal that had made that sound. It was her own bones.

Nick saw her lying in the road and hesitated for a moment. Glancing in his mirror, he saw the marked police car a long way back. Ahead of him, the Transit's tail lights were disappearing down the hill. In a split-second decision he accelerated after it, shouting into his radio, 'Man down! We need an ambulance!'

Within seconds he was gaining on the vehicle. He jolted over a speed hump. There were red traffic lights at the bottom of the hill, the junction with Eastern Road. The Transit would have to stop, or at least slow down.

It did neither.

As the van ran the junction Nick saw the glare of head-lights, and moments later a Skoda taxi strike the driver's door broadside. He heard a loud, dull metallic bang, like two giant dustbins swung together.

The Transit spun, and came to a halt, spewing steam, oil and water, its horn blaring, shards of glass and metal lying all around, one wheel buckled and at a skewed angle, almost parallel with the ground, the tyre flat.

The Skoda, slewing, carried on for some yards, making a high-pitched metallic grinding sound, steam pouring from its bonnet, then it mounted the pavement, hit the wall of a house and bounced a few feet back.

Nicholl halted his car, radioing for the emergency services, then jumped out and sprinted to the van. But as he reached it he realized there had been no need to hurry. The windscreen was cracked and stained with blood. The driver was slumped sideways, his body partially draped over the steering wheel, his neck twisted, his face, gashed open in several places, tilted up at the cracked windscreen, his eyes closed.

Steam continued rising and there was a stink of diesel. Nick Nicholl tried to open the buckled door but it was still locked. He pulled hard, nervous the van might catch fire, then harder, wrenching at it with all his strength. Finally it opened a few inches.

He was conscious of vehicles stopping; out of the corner of his eye he saw two people at the taxi, pulling the driver's door open, and another person struggling with the rear passenger door. Nick yanked harder still on the Transit door; it yielded a little more. And as it did so, he caught sight of a glow coming from the passenger footwell.

A laptop computer, he realized.

Squeezing through the door, Nick peered at the man's face closely. He was breathing. One of the principal lessons he had learned in first aid was never to move the victim of an accident unless it was to get them out of danger. He reached past the man and turned the ignition off. There was no smell of burning. He decided to wait, then went round to the other side of the van and removed the laptop – with presence of mind, only touching the machine through his handkerchief.

Then, desperately worried about Emma-Jane, he radioed to ask the status of the emergency vehicles. As he did so, he could already hear sirens.

And on top of his concern about the young Detective Constable, he had another worry. Roy Grace was not going to be a happy bunny when he heard about this crash.

63

At half past eleven, Roy Grace parked his Alfa Romeo on a single yellow line outside the unlit shop window of a dealer specializing in retro twentieth-century furniture.

He climbed out, locked the door and stood, in the orange sodium glow of the street lighting, in front of the wrought-iron gates of the converted warehouse where Cleo lived. For some moments he stared at the entryphone panel, feeling a confusion of emotions. Part of him was angry, part of him nervous about what she was going to say. And part of him was just plain low.

For the first time since Sandy had vanished he felt something for another woman. During brief moments when he had been awake last night and not thinking about Janie Stretton's murder, he had actually dared allow himself to think that it might be possible to start a new life. And that it could, maybe, have been with Cleo Morey.

Then her text had arrived.

Fiancé.

Just what the hell was all that about? Who was this man? Some dribbling chinless wonder from her posh background who *Mummy* and *Daddy* approved of? With a Porsche and a country estate?

How on earth could she have failed to mention that she was engaged? And why did she want to see him now? To apologize for last night, and tell him that the snog in the back of the taxi had been a terrible, drunken mistake, and they needed to be grown up about it as they had to work together?

And why had he come? He shouldn't be here. He should either be back at his desk in the Major Incident Suite or, at this late hour on a Sunday night, heading home to bed, to be fresh for the morning's briefing and all the follow-ups he needed to do on Janie Stretton. As well as keeping on top of the progress of the Suresh Hossain trial.

In his mind he was turning over the interview he had just come from with Tom Bryce. As part of Grace's training in recent years he had attended several psychological profiling courses, but he had never found them that helpful. They could give you useful clues if you were having to pick between three different suspects, perhaps, but nothing he had learned was helping him at this moment assess whether Tom Bryce was acting his grief and concern or whether it was real.

But the man had very definitely told one lie.

Have you noticed any change in Mrs Bryce's behaviour in recent months?

No, not at all.

What was that all about? Bryce was covering up something. Did he suspect she might be with a lover? Or have left him? And despite all his sympathy for the man, it was this moment of hesitation, this lie, that had sowed sufficient doubt in Grace's mind to prevent him from pushing all the buttons tonight for a full-scale hunt for Kellie Bryce. He would suggest to Assistant Chief Constable Alison Vosper, in the morning, that Cassian Pewe be put in charge of the woman's disappearance.

And, with luck, the smug little shit would end up with a lot of bright yellow yolk all over his face on his very first job. How sweet that would be.

He stared at the entryphone panel and felt butterflies in his stomach. *Get a grip, man!* Standing here on a doorstep like a pathetic teenager! At half past bloody eleven on a Sunday night!

He felt tired suddenly. Drained. For a moment anger flared up inside him – anger at Cleo and at himself for being so weak in coming here – and he was tempted to go back to his car and drive home. He turned, felt in his pocket for his keys, and was in the process of pulling them out when he heard her voice, sounding strangely distorted through the speakerphone. 'Hi!'

And that voice did something to him. It totally energized him. 'Pizza!' he said in a bad Italian accent. 'You have-a-order-a pizza?'

She laughed. 'Come into the courtyard and turn right. Number six, far end on the left! I hope you didn't forget the extra anchovies!'

The lock opened with a sharp click. He pushed the heavy gate open, digging in his pocket, suddenly remembering his chewing gum, and popped a stick in his mouth, as he walked across the spotless cobblestones illuminated by a row of lights inside glass domes. As he reached her door he put the gum back in its foil wrapper and balled it into his pocket.

The door opened before he had even pressed the bell, and Cleo stood there, barefoot, in tight jeans and a loose blue sweatshirt, some of her hair clipped up, the rest loose. Her face was pale, she was wearing hardly any make-up, yet she looked more beautiful than ever.

She greeted him with a meek smile, and a round-eyed guilty sort of look, like a child who has done something just a little bit naughty. 'Hi!' she said, and gave a little shrug.

Grace shrugged back. 'Hi.'

There was an awkward silence, as if each of them was waiting for the other to offer a kiss. Neither did. She stepped aside for him to come in, then closed the door behind him.

He entered a large, open-plan living room, softly lit with a dozen or more small white candles and some hip, ultra-modern lights; there was a strong scent in the room, faintly sweet, musky, feminine and very seductive.

The room had a good vibe; he felt instantly relaxed, could feel it was every inch Cleo. Cream walls and throw rugs on a polished oak floor, two red sofas, black-lacquered furniture, funky abstract paintings, an expensive-looking television and a Latino song from El Divo playing quietly, but assertively, from four seriously cool-looking black speakers.

There were several lush green plants, and in a square glass fish tank on the coffee table, a solitary goldfish was swimming around through the remains of a submerged miniature Greek temple.

'Still up for a whisky?' Cleo asked.

'I think I need one.'

'Ice?'

'Lots.'

'Water?'

'Just a splash.'

He walked over to the tank.

'That's Fish,' she said. 'Fish, meet Detective Superintendent Roy Grace.'

'Hi, Fish,' he said, then turning to Cleo, added, 'I have a goldfish, too.'

'I remember, you told me. Marlon, right?'

'Good memory.'

'Uh huh. It's better than a goldfish's. I read that they can only remember things for twelve seconds. I can sometimes remember things for a whole day.'

Grace laughed. But it was forced laughter. The atmosphere between them was strained, like two boxers in a ring, waiting for the bell for the first round to clang.

Cleo went out of the room, and Grace took the opportunity to take a closer look round. He walked over to a framed photograph which shared a small side table with a rubber plant. It showed a handsome, distinguished-looking man in his early fifties, dressed in top hat and tails, next to a fine-looking woman in her mid to late forties, who bore a striking resemblance to Cleo, in a stunningly elegant outfit and a large hat; there were dozens of people similarly attired in the background. Grace wondered if it was the Royal Enclosure at Ascot, although he had never been there.

Then he wandered over to a floor-to-ceiling stack of crammed bookshelves. He picked out a row of Graham Greene novels, a set of Samuel Pepys diaries, several crime novels, from Val McDermid, Simon Brett, Ian Rankin and Mark Timlin, a Jeanette Winterson, two James Herbert novels, an Alice Seebold, a Jonathan Franzen, *The Corrections*, a row of Tom Wolfe, bios of Maggie Thatcher and Clinton, an eclectic mixture of chick lit, an ancient copy of *Gray's Anatomy* and, to his surprise, a copy of Colin Wilson's *The Occult*.

Cleo came back into the room, holding two glasses, ice cubes clinking.

'You read a lot?' he asked.

'Not enough, but I'm a compulsive book buyer. Do you?'

He loved books and bought several every time he went

into a bookshop, but he rarely ended up reading them. 'I wish I had the time; I mostly end up reading reports.'

She handed him a hefty glass tumbler filled with whisky on the rocks, and they sat down together on a sofa, keeping a space between them. She raised her glass, of white wine. 'Thank you for coming.'

He shrugged, wondering what bombshell she was going to hit him with.

Instead, she said, 'Cheers, big ears.'

'Big ears?'

'Here goes, nose!'

He frowned.

'You don't know this?'

'No.'

'Cheers, big ears,' she said. 'Here goes, nose. Up your bum, chum!' She raised her glass and took a long swig.

Shaking his head in bewilderment, he took a swig of the whisky; it was dangerously good. 'What does that mean? "Cheers, big ears"?'

'Here goes, nose! Up your bum, chum!'

Grace shook his head, not getting it.

'Just a saying – I'll have to teach it to you.'

He looked at Cleo, then down at his drink, and sipped some more, changing the subject. 'So, do you want to tell me about, um – *Mr Right*? Your fiancé?'

Cleo took another gulp of wine. He watched her, loving the way she drank, no delicate prissy little sip but a proper mouthful. 'Richard?'

'Is that his name?'

'I didn't tell you his name?' She sounded astonished.

'Actually, no. It sort of escaped your mind last night. And on our previous date.'

She peered into her wine glass as if staring at ancient

runes. 'But, everyone – everyone knows about him. I mean – I thought – you *must* know.'

'I'm clearly not *everyone*.'

'He's been driving the team at the mortuary nuts for months.'

Grace rattled the ice cubes around in his glass. 'I'm not sure I'm on your bus.'

'Number forty-two,' she said. 'The meaning of everything? *The Hitchhiker's Guide to the Galaxy*?'

'Right,' he said, the penny dropping. He wondered for a moment whether Cleo was drunk. But she did not look drunk. Not even tipsy. 'I'm sorry, I'm lost. You have a fiancé who's been driving everyone nuts?'

'I thought you knew,' she said, looking very meek suddenly. 'Oh shit, you didn't, did you?'

'Nope.'

She drained her glass. 'Oh God!' Then she tilted the glass as if searching for a few more drops of precious alcohol. 'Actually, that's totally the wrong word to use, the God word.' She shrugged again.

'You want to fill me in?'

'You want the full Richard download?'

'Might be a good starting point.'

'Richard and I met about three years ago – he's a barrister. He came to the mortuary because he wanted to view a body in a murder case he was defending.' She raised her glass expectantly, then looked disappointed when she saw it was empty. 'I liked him; we started going out; my parents liked him; my brother and sister both thought he was lovely – and about a year and a half ago we got engaged. But about the same time I discovered I had a big rival. God.'

'God?'

She nodded. 'He found God. Or God found him. What-ever.'

'Lucky Richard,' Grace said.

'Very lucky,' she said with a trace of sarcasm. 'I envy anyone who finds God; how nice to be able to abdicate all your responsibilities to God.' Suddenly she stood up. 'You need any more whisky?'

Grace looked at his tumbler, which was still three-quarters full. 'I'm fine, thanks – I have to drive.'

Cleo went out of the room, returned with a full wine glass, and sat back down, much nearer this time.

'He started taking me to a charismatic church in Brighton,' she said. 'But it just wasn't for me. I tried it, because at the time I loved him, but all it did was start pulling us apart.'

'And his solution was to pray even more?'

'Right. Hey, you know you're quite astute – for a copper.'

Grace gave her a pointed look, but couldn't mask his grin. 'Thanks a lot.'

She chinked her glass against his. 'He started making me kneel with him, praying for an hour, sometimes even longer, asking God to make our relationship better. After a while I just couldn't hack it.'

'Why not?'

'Because I'm just not a believer.'

'Not in anything?'

'I spend my days cutting bodies open – you know what I do. I haven't yet found a soul in any of them.' She swigged some wine down. 'Do you believe?'

'I believe in some form of existence beyond death. But I have a problem with religion.'

'That puts us on the same bus,' she said.

'I saw Colin Wilson's *The Occult* on your bookshelf.'

'All that stuff intrigues me. I know you are into that, and that's fine. You can believe in ghosts, in some kind of spirit world, but you don't necessarily have to believe in some kind of monotheistic God. Right?'

Grace nodded.

'I broke it off with Richard six months ago, and he can't accept it. He's convinced God will fix it for us. It's hurt his career too. He spends more and more time praying for God to help him with his cases instead of reading up the briefs. I'm sorry; I look at all the shit that's happening in the world and mostly it's caused by people under some kind of delusion about their particular version of God. Sometimes I don't think Richard's obsession is that far removed from that of a Muslim suicide bomber. It's all part of the same damned belief system – that it's not this life that matters, it's the next one. What a crap idea! Shall we change the subject?'

Grace drank some more whisky. 'What would you like to talk about?'

She set her glass down, then removed his glass from his hand and put that down also. She wrapped her arms around his neck and whispered into his ear, 'How about we don't talk at all for a few minutes?'

Then she pressed her lips against his. They were soft, so incredibly soft; he breathed in her musky perfume, the smell of her freshly washed hair, felt her soft, sweet tongue deep inside his mouth, felt her pulling him deeper and deeper into her body, as if she was gathering him in like folds of silk.

And somehow, their bodies entwined, their lips never parting, they were climbing steep stairs – one flight, two flights, he was not counting – he was shuffling across a polished wood floor, then across a deep rug. El Divo were still playing, a soft jazzy song now. Candles, flames guttering, lined the walls, and she was still kissing him, exploring his teeth with her tongue, then the roof of his mouth, then duelling with his tongue, and he felt—

Oh Jesus, deep fire in his groin – bursting . . .

An electrical current was running inside his belly, shooting tiny, wonderful sparks through his body. He opened his eyes, saw her pale blue eyes smiling back at him. She was unbuttoning his shirt, and suddenly pressing her mouth, moist and soft, against each of his eyes in turn, and it was as if someone had turned up the current. She kissed his forehead, then his cheek, then his lips, again. Then again.

It was so good he was hurting.

Just a few times in the past nine years he had dialled a number in the personal ads in the *Argus*, and ended up in seedy basements in Brighton. One time he'd had a handjob from a fat Spanish girl. Another time he'd had oral sex from a Thai. And there had been a third, embarrassing time, when he had been barely able to raise it for a thin, local girl with a coarse voice and a flat chest.

Maybe because in his mind Sandy had been standing in that room. But she wasn't here now.

Cleo's slender fingers were fumbling with his belt. Another kiss, on his neck, right under his chin. He heard the clank of the buckle. Another kiss on his neck, lower now. Then suddenly he felt the release of his trousers opening, felt her hands inside his boxers, so warm and so incredibly – deliciously – sensually cold at the same time.

'Ohmygod.' He winced, feeling almost deliriously aroused. But he was determined to make this last a long, long time.

She smiled at him, the most totally, utterly dirty smile he had ever seen in his life. Then she was working on his shirt buttons again, undoing each one in sequence, pushing the fabric wider open.

Then she pressed her lips against his right nipple and he thought he was going to die of joy.

She continued working on him slowly, setting her own slow, so slow, so tantalizingly slow pace. She pinched his left nipple with her fingers, softly, then firmly, staring him in the face again now, smiling that wicked, beautiful, so incredible . . .

So incredibly . . .

Dirty . . .

Smile.

And he was so hard he could barely endure it one second longer.

Her tongue pushed deep in his belly button. Her hands were working his trousers and boxers together downwards, down over his calves, right down to his shoes.

Then she took him in her mouth.

Air shot out of his lungs, air from deep inside him, from some place or zone he did not know even existed any more, that he thought had long ago died. And he slid his hands under her sweatshirt, felt the flesh, the soft flesh of her toned midriff, pulled the sweatshirt slowly, steadily upwards, not wanting this moment to end, not wanting to remove it, just wanting to be here for ever, sliding her top upwards for ever, for all the days, hours, minutes, seconds, nanoseconds, picoseconds, femtoseconds of his life. Frozen in time.

Then he touched her breasts. No bra. Just large, much larger than he had imagined, firm, round, and she let out a moan as he touched them, then took him in her mouth again, deeper, far deeper.

Moments later, with his shoes still on and his trousers and boxers around his ankles, they were lying on a leopard-skin print throw on her bed. Staring at each other in silence. He slid his hand across her shoulders, feeling her strong shoulder blades, the contours of her back, her warm skin, and he was thinking – and he was trying not to think this, but he couldn't help it – how so different she felt to Sandy. Not better – just different.

Flashes of Sandy began coming into his mind. Comparisons. Sandy was shorter, her body fleshier, less well toned; her breasts were smaller, a different shape, her nipples larger, pinker. Cleo's were smaller, like crimson studs. Sandy's pubes were brown, a wild tangle. Cleo's were the winter-wheat colour of her hair, trimmed, neat. She was entwined around him, her fine strong limbs like some amazing pedigree racehorse, writhing, whispering, 'Roy, you are amazing. God, Roy, I've wanted this for so long. Make love to me.'

And he was gathering her up into him, not able to get enough of her, as if he was lost in some fairy tale. She was trying to pull him inside her, but he wasn't ready, not yet. It had been so long, he was trying to remember, had to hold back, had to remember how to hold back.

Had to slow everything down, somehow. Had to please her first. That had always been his private rule with Sandy, and with the small number of girlfriends he had slept with before her.

He moved down her body, caressing her breasts with his lips, then the contours of her stomach, running his tongue through the soft bristles of those winter-wheat hairs and then tasting her moistness, breathing it in, an incredible taste, smell, an even more intoxicating muski-ness than the perfume she was wearing.

She was moaning.

Oh God, she tasted so good, so good, so damned beautifully good.

His phone started ringing.

She giggled. The phone persisted. Then it stopped. He went in deeper with his tongue.

'Roy!' she murmured. 'Roy! Oh Roy! Oh my God, Roy!'

Two sharp beeps from his bloody phone. A message. He was beyond caring.

64

Chris Willingham stared at the hysterical man with puke spattered down the front of his T-shirt standing in the doorway of the living room, screaming at him, and tried desperately to remember from his recent training how to deal with a situation like this.

'YOU'VE GOT TO DO SOMETHING! PLEASE, YOU HAVE TO DO SOMETHING. YOU HAVE TO HELP ME FIND MY WIFE!'

Talk quietly, he remembered. That was the first thing. So, in a soft voice he said, 'What's happened, exactly?'

'SHE'S SCREAMING. SHE'S TERRIFIED OUT OF HER FUCKING WITS, OK?' Tom Bryce entered the room and grabbed him by the shoulders. 'YOU'VE GOT TO FUCKING *DO* SOMETHING!'

The young family liaison officer gagged at the stench of the vomit. Keeping his voice soft, he said, 'Tell me, Mr Bryce, what's happened?'

Tom Bryce turned and walked out of the room. 'Come on, come and see! She's on my computer!'

The PC followed Tom up the stairs and into the small den lined with books and files and framed photographs of his wife and children. He saw a laptop on the desk, the lid open, the screen blank. Tom Bryce tapped the carriage return on the keyboard and his email in-box appeared.

The stench of vomit was even stronger in here, and Willingham, concentrating on the screen, carefully stood clear of the mess on the carpet. He watched Bryce sit down, stare at the screen, frown, then search down through it.

'It was here,' Tom said. 'It was here, an email with a fucking attachment. Oh Jesus, where the hell is it?'

Willingham said nothing; Tom seemed a little calmer for a moment. Then he appeared to lose it again. 'IT WAS HERE!'

Tom stared in disbelief. The bloody email had vanished. He tapped in as a search key, one after another, every word from the email that he could remember. But nothing appeared. He sank forward, cradling his head in his hands, sobbing. 'Please help me. Oh please do something, please find her, please do *something*. Oh Christ, you should have heard her.'

'You saw her, on your screen?'

Tom nodded.

'But she's not there now?'

'Nooooo.'

Willingham wondered about the man's sanity. Was he imagining something? Flipping under the pressure? 'Let's take it from the top, shall we, sir?'

Trying to keep calm, Tom talked him through exactly what he had seen and what Kellie had said.

'If you received an email,' the PC said, 'then it must be on your computer somewhere.'

Tom searched the deleted folder, the junk mail folder, then the rest of the folders in his email database. It had gone.

And he began to wonder, just for a moment, whether he had imagined it.

But not that scream. No way.

He turned to the constable. 'You are probably thinking I imagined it, but I didn't. I saw it. Whoever these people are, they're clever with technology. It's happened before – I've had emails this week that vanished, wiping my entire database out.'

Willingham stood there, unsure what to believe or what to do. The man was in a bad state but did not seem mad, just in shock. Something had happened, for sure, but in his limited knowledge of computers emails did not just disappear. They might get misfiled; that had happened to him. 'Let's try again, sir. Let's go through all your files, one at a time.'

It was past midnight by the time they finished. Still they had not found it.

Tom looked up at him, imploring. 'What are we going to do?'

The FLO was thinking hard. 'We could try the High Tech Crime Unit, but I doubt if anyone will be there at this hour on a Sunday night. How about the technical support of your internet service provider – they might be twenty-four-hour?' Then he frowned. 'I, er . . . Actually, on second thought, I need to run this by DS Grace first.'

'Let me just try,' Tom said. He looked up the number and dialled it. An automated response put him on hold. After ten minutes of drecky music a human voice came on the line, an Indian accent, helpful and eager to please. After a further ten minutes that felt like ten hours he came back and reported that he could find no sign of the email or the attachment.

Tom slammed the phone down in fury.

In a tone that told Tom the FLO was becoming increasingly sceptical, Willingham asked, 'What were the exact words your wife said to you?'

Trying desperately to think clearly, Tom related her words as accurately as he could remember.

'She said, "Don't tell the police. Do exactly what they tell you, otherwise it will be Max next then Jessica. Please do exactly what you are told. You must not tell the police – they will know if you do."'

'Who are "they"?'

'I don't know,' he said, feeling so utterly helpless.

Willingham pulled out his digital radio. Tom immediately clamped his hand over it. 'NO!'

There was a long silence between them. Several more emails came in and the junk filter deleted them. Tom checked the folders. Nothing.

Finally, Willingham said, 'I think I should file a report on this.'

'No!' Tom snapped back.

'It will be secure, sir; I will only file it on the police system.'

'NO!'

Taken aback by the man's vehemence, the constable raised his hands. 'OK, sir, no problem.' He grimaced. 'How about I make a cup of tea for us both – or a coffee – and we have a think about what to do next?'

'Coffee,' Tom said. 'Coffee would be good, thank you. Black, no sugar.'

The constable left the room. Tom continued to stare at the screen; his entire life lay somewhere beyond its horizon.

A new email came in. It was from *postmaster@scarab. tisana.al.* Instantly, he clicked on it.

Congratulations, Tom! You are cottoning on fast! Now get out of the house, take Kellie's car, head north on the A23 London Road and wait for her to call you. I don't like you ignoring my instructions not to talk to the police. If you say one word, just ONE word to your new best friend, your rookie cop housekeeper, then my friend you will never see your wife alive again. Don't attempt to reply to this email. And don't bother searching for the hidden camera – you are looking at it.

65

Cleo smiled at him, her face so gentle and beautiful in the glow of the candlelight. Mellow jazz was playing in the background. Roy Grace could feel her warm, sweet breath on his face, saw strands of her tousled hair on her cheeks.

'That wasn't bad,' she whispered.

'For a copper?'

She gave him a playful punch. Then she cupped his face in her hands and kissed him on the mouth. The bed felt so comfortable, Cleo felt so comfortable, so good to be with, as if he had known her for years, as if they were the bestest-ever mates in all the world.

He caressed her skin, a deep warm glow inside him; he felt utterly, sublimely at peace. He was, for this fleeting moment at least, in a space he had never believed he could ever find again in his life. Then he remembered his phone ringing earlier, the beep of a message which he had ignored and should not have, and he looked at the clock, emitting weak blue light, on the bedside table.

1.15 a.m.

Shit!

He rolled over, groped on the floor, found his phone and pulled it to his ear, hitting the message retrieval button.

It was Glenn, telling him to call if he picked the message up before midnight, otherwise to wait until the morning. He put the phone back down, relieved.

'I'm glad you came over,' Cleo murmured.

'It was the lure of Glenfiddich, that was all. Can't resist it.'

'So you really are that shallow, are you, Detective Superintendent Roy Grace?' she teased. 'Anything for a free drink?'

'Uh huh. And maybe I was just a tiny bit curious about your fiancé. How shallow does that make me?' He took a sharp breath as she suddenly cupped his balls in her hands.

'Do you know what they say, Detective Superintendent?' She squeezed gently.

Gasping with pleasure – and just a tiny bit of pain – he said, 'What do they say?'

'When you have a man's balls in your hands, his heart and mind will follow.'

He exhaled sharply, deliciously, as she released the pressure a tiny bit. 'So talk me through your plans for the rest of the night?' he whispered.

She increased the pressure, then kissed him again. 'You're not in a very good position to negotiate, whatever my plans are!'

'Who's negotiating?'

'You think you are!' She removed her hands, rolled out of the bed and padded across the room. He watched her slender, naked body, her long legs, her firm, round, pale and gorgeous bum disappear through the doorway. Then he put his arms behind his head and lay back against a soft, deep, down pillow. 'Plenty of ice!' he called out.

She returned a few minutes later with two rattling glass tumblers, and handed one to him. Climbing back into bed beside him she raised her glass and clinked it against his. With a toss of her head she said, 'Cheers, big ears. Here goes, nose. Up your bum, chum!' Then she downed half her glass.

He raised his glass. 'Cheers, big ears!' he responded, then took a deep swig. Tomorrow was a million miles away. Her eyes, fixed on his, were sparkling.

'So you came over just because you wanted to know about my fiancé. Was that the only reason, Detective Superintendent Roy Grace?'

'Stop calling me that!'

'What do you want me to call you? The bonk at the end of the universe?'

Grinning, he said, 'That would be fine. Otherwise, just *Roy* would be fine too.'

She tilted her glass to her mouth, then leaned across, kissed him sensuously on his mouth, and pushed a whisky-flavoured ice cube in through his lips. 'Roy! It's a great name. Why did your parents call you Roy?'

'I never asked.'

'Why not?'

He shrugged. 'It never occurred to me.'

'And you're a detective? I thought you queried *everything*.'

'Why did your parents call you Cleo?'

'Because . . .' She gave a little giggle. 'Actually, I'm embarrassed to say, it was because my mother's favourite novels were *The Alexandria Quartet*. I was named after one of the characters – Clea – except my father spelled it wrong in the church register. He put an "o" on the end instead of an "a" – and it stuck.'

'I've never heard of *The Alexandria Quartet*.'

'Come on, you must have read them!'

'I must have had a deprived childhood.'

'Or a missspent one?'

'Could you play poker when you were twelve?'

'That's what I mean! God, you need educating! *The Alexandria Quartet* were four novels written by Lawrence Durrell – beautiful stories, all interlinked. *Justine, Balthazar, Mountolive* and *Clea.*'

'They must be if . . .'

'If what?'

'If they resulted in you.'

Then his phone rang again. And this time he answered it – very reluctantly.

Two minutes later, even more reluctantly, he was standing by the bed hurriedly and clumsily pulling his socks on.

66

'You scare easily, don't you, Kellie?'

Dazzled by the light in her eyes, Kellie squirmed against the bonds holding her, trying to move back in her chair, trying to move away from the wriggling legs of the hideous black beetle the fat, squat American was holding up to her face.

'Nooooo! Please noooooooooo!'

'Just one of my pets.' He leered.

'What do you want from me? What do you want?'

Suddenly he removed the beetle, and was holding out the neck of a vodka bottle. 'Drinkies?'

She turned her head away. Shaking. From terror. From hunger. From withdrawal. Tears rolled down her cheeks.

'I know you want a drink, Kellie. Have some, it'll make you feel so much better.'

She desperately craved that bottle, wanted to take the neck in her mouth and gulp it down. But she was determined not to give him the satisfaction. Out of the corner of her eye, in the glare of the light, she could still see the wriggling legs.

'Have one little sip.'

'I want my children,' she said.

'I think you want the vodka more.'

'Fuck you!'

She saw a shadow, then felt a fierce slap on her cheek. She cried out in pain.

'I'm not taking any shit from a little bitch – do you understand me?'

'Fuck you!'

The next blow was so hard it knocked Kellie and the chair over sideways. She crashed with an agonizing jar onto the rock-hard floor; pain shot through her arm, her shoulder, right along her body. She burst into tears. 'Why are you doing this to me?' she sobbed. 'What do you want from me? WHAT DO YOU WANT?'

'How about a little obedience?' He held the beetle up to her face, so close she could smell its sour odour. She felt its feet scratch her skin.

'Noooooooooo!' She writhed, rolling across the floor with the chair, crashing, banging, every bone in her body hurting. 'Nooo, nooo, nooo!' her breathing getting faster, gulping down air, hysterical. She felt a sudden wave of anger against Tom. Where was he? Why hadn't he come to find her, rescue her?

Then she lay still – spent, staring up into dazzling light, and darkness. 'Please,' she pleaded. 'I don't know who you are. I just want my children. My husband. Please let me go.'

This must be something to do with the email Tom had seen, that he had gone to the police with, she was certain. 'Why am I here?' she asked, as if for confirmation.

Silence.

'Are you angry with me?' she whimpered.

His voice was gentle suddenly. 'Only because you are misbehaving, Kellie. I'd just like you to cooperate.'

'Then un-fucking-tie me!'

'I don't think that's really possible at the moment.'

She closed her eyes, trying desperately to think clearly, to fight the terrible craving for alcohol. For just one tiny sip of that Stoli. But she was not going to give this fat

American the satisfaction. Never, no way in hell, no way, never, never, never.

Then the craving took over her brain.

'Please can I have a drink now?' she asked.

Moments later the bottle was inside her lips and she was greedily gulping the liquid down. Its effect on her was almost instant. God, it felt good. Maybe she was wrong about this man – maybe he was kind after all.

'That's good, Kellie! Keep drinking. That's really good, isn't it?'

She nodded in gratitude.

'See! All I want to do is be nice to you. You be nice to me, and I'll be nice to you. Any part of that you don't understand?'

She shook her head. Then felt bereft, suddenly, as he abruptly pulled the bottle away.

And suddenly she was thinking clearly again. And every scary movie she had ever seen started playing in her mind simultaneously. Who the hell was this man? A serial killer? What was he going to do to her? Fear squirmed like some wild creature loose inside her. Was she going to be raped? Tortured?

I'm going to die, here, in the darkness, without ever seeing Jessica or Max or Tom again.

How did you deal with a person like this? In films she had seen prisoners trying to establish a relationship, a bond, with their captors. It made it much harder for them to harm you if they got to know you a little.

'What's your name?' she asked.

'I don't think you need to concern yourself about that, Kellie.'

'I'd like to know.'

'I'm going to leave you now for a little while. With a bit of luck, your husband will be joining you soon.'

'Tom?'

'You got it!'

'Tom's coming?'

'Tom's coming. You don't want him to see you lying on the floor like that, do you?'

She shook her head.

'I'll get you sat upright. Want you to look good for the camera!'

'Camera?'

'Uh huh.'

Feeling a little drunk, she asked, her voice slurring, 'Sshwhy camera?'

'You're going to be a star!'

67

At 1.25 a.m. there was a sudden burst of Jay-Z as Glenn Branson's mobile phone rang in his bedroom. Hurriedly shooting his arm out, to answer it and silence the bloody thing before it woke Ari, he knocked over the glass of water on his bedside table, and sent the phone and his alarm clock thudding to the floor.

He sprang out of bed in the darkness, his brain a little scrambled, and scrabbled under the chair beside the table where the phone had fallen, the music getting louder. He finally grabbed hold of it and thumbed the answer button. 'DS Branson,' he said, as hushed as he could, crouching as if somehow that would make his voice even quieter.

It was Tom Bryce, and he sounded terrible. 'Detective Sergeant Branson, I'm sorry to call you so late.'

'No, no worries, Tom – just hold—'

'For Chrissake!' Ari said. 'You arrive home after midnight and wake me up, and now you're waking me up again. I think we should consider separate bedrooms.' Then she pointedly turned over away from him.

Great way to start the week, Branson thought gloomily, heading out of the room. He carried the phone into their bright orange bathroom and closed the door.

'Sorry about that. I'm with you now,' he said, perching naked on the lavatory seat for want of anywhere else. 'So tell me?' The room smelled of grout. He looked at the shiny new glass shower door, fitted only last week, and the crazy tiger-striped tiles Ari had chosen and which the fitter had only finished putting up on Friday. They'd moved into the house three months ago. It was in a nice position, a short distance from both sea and open countryside, in Saltdean, although at the moment, Ari had told him, the whole neighbourhood was on edge because it was less than a mile away that Janie Stretton's body had been discovered.

'I need to know this line is secure,' Tom Bryce said, sounding close to hysterics. There was a roaring sound, as if he was driving.

Branson looked at the caller display; the man was calling on his mobile phone. Trying to help keep Bryce calm, he said, 'You've phoned my police mobile – all its signals are encrypted. It's totally secure.' He decided not to mention that Tom's mobile, presumably a normal one, was open to anyone out there who tuned into its frequency. 'Where are you, Tom?'

'I don't want to tell you.'

'OK. You're not at home?'

'No, it's not safe to talk in my house – it's bugged.'

'Do you want to meet me somewhere?'

'Yes. No. Yes – I mean – I need you to help me.'

'That's what I'm here to do.'

'How do I know I can trust you? That it will be confidential?'

Branson frowned at the question. 'What assurance would make you feel comfortable?'

There was a long silence.

'Hello? Mr Bryce, Tom, are you still there?'

'Yes.' His voice sounded faint.

'Did you hear my question?'

'I don't know if I – if I should. I don't think I can take the risk.'

The phone went dead.

Glenn Branson dialled the number on the display, and it went straight to voicemail. He left a message saying he had called back, then waited a couple of minutes, wide awake, his brain racing, wishing Ari would be more understanding. Yeah, it was tough, but it would just be nice if she showed a little more sympathy. He shrugged. What the hell. Maybe he should read that book she'd bought him for Christmas, *Men Are from Mars, Women Are from Venus.* She'd told him it might help him understand how a woman felt. But he doubted he ever truly would understand what women wanted. Men and women didn't come from different planets; they came from different universes.

He dialled Bryce's mobile number again. It still went straight to voicemail. Next he dialled the man's home number, feeling a sudden deep dread that he could not define.

*

'Gone?' Roy Grace said, standing next to Branson in the hallway of Tom Bryce's house at ten past two in the morning, staring in bemused fury at the young family liaison officer. 'What do you mean, he's fucking *gone*?'

'I went up to see if he was all right, and he wasn't there.'

'Tom Bryce, his four-year-old daughter and his seven-year-old son leave the house and you didn't bloody notice?'

'I, uh . . .' Chris Willingham said helplessly.

'You fucking fell asleep on the job, didn't you?'

'No, I . . .'

Grace, chewing gum to mask the alcohol on his breath, glared at the young officer. 'You were meant to be looking after them. And keeping an eye on *him* as the prime fucking suspect. You let them walk out on you?'

The FLO talked both detectives through all that had

happened in the past few hours, in particular the email Tom Bryce claimed to have received and which had vanished from his computer.

Grace had come straight from the Royal Sussex County Hospital, where the young Detective Constable he had such high hopes for, Emma-Jane Boutwood, was on life support and about to be taken into theatre. He'd had the grim job of phoning her parents and breaking the news to them that their daughter was not expected to live.

He had dragged himself away from Cleo reluctantly and on a high, but after finding out the full scale of E-J's injuries, all memories of his time tonight with Cleo had been erased – at least temporarily – and he was now feeling very low, and desperately concerned for Emma-Jane.

The driver of the van, as yet unidentified, was still unconscious and in the intensive care unit at the same hospital. Grace had ordered a twenty-four-hour police guard on his bed, and left instructions with the constable who had turned up that, the moment the man regained consciousness, he was to be arrested for the attempted murder of a police officer. Grace could only hope they wouldn't have to upgrade the charge to murder.

Meanwhile DC Nick Nicholl was waiting for him back at the Incident Room with a laptop computer he wanted Grace to see, and dodgy Mr Tom Bryce had done a moonlight flit with his two kids – just what was that all about?

And the week was just over two hours old.

Turning to Branson he said, 'This phone call Bryce made to you – you said he sounded strange. Scared?'

'Well scared,' Branson confirmed.

Grace thought for a moment. 'Did you get him to fill out a missing persons report form for his wife yesterday?'

Branson nodded.

'You filed it?'

'Yes.'

'Phone Nick – he's at the Incident Room now. Ask him to look it up. It'll have the addresses of Mrs Bryce's close relatives and friends. A frightened man is not going to drive far with two small children in the middle of the night. Have you put out a description of the car?'

Both Chris Willingham and Glenn Branson stared at him blankly. It clearly had not occurred to either of them.

'What the fuck is going on?'

Glenn Branson, trying to calm him down, said, 'Roy, I didn't know how far we were supposed to go keeping tabs on him. Chris was just here to help him cope and to offer protection.'

'Yes, and if we circulate a description of the bloody vehicle he's in, we can get him even more protection – from every damned patrol car that's out there.' Which wasn't very many at this time of night, he knew.

'Shall I tell Nick to call out the rest of the team?'

Grace thought for a moment. The temptation to haul Norman Potting out of his bed was almost irresistible, but he had a feeling it was going to a very long day today. He would let as many of them as possible have a night's sleep, so at least he would have some fresh, alert people at the eight thirty briefing.

He needed to organize a replacement for Emma-Jane, he realized. And how was Alison Vosper going to react to yet another road traffic accident caused by a police pursuit? The taxi driver was in hospital with various minor injuries, his passenger, who hadn't been wearing a seat belt, had a broken leg. An *Argus* reporter was already down at the hospital, and they would be all over this story like a rash.

Fuck, fuck, fuck.

'One problem – I don't know the registration of the vehicle he's in,' Glenn Branson said.

'Well that shouldn't be too hard to find – there is probably the logbook somewhere in the house.'

Leaving Branson to make the call and the FLO to search downstairs for information on the car, Grace went upstairs, found the children's bedrooms then the master bedroom with its unmade bed. Nothing. Tom Bryce's den looked a lot more promising. He glanced at the man's desk, piled high with work files, and a webcam on a stalk. Crinkling his nose against the stench of vomit, he rummaged around in the drawers but found nothing of interest, then turned to a tall black metal filing cabinet.

All the information was in a file marked CARS.

Not all police work required a degree in rocket science, he thought.

*

Fifteen minutes later, Grace and Branson were in a grim elevator, with obscene spraypainted graffiti on every wall and a puddle of urine in one corner, in a tower block on the Whitehawk council estate.

They emerged at the seventh floor, walked down the corridor and rang the bell of Flat 72.

After a few moments a woman's voice called out, 'Who is it?'

'Police!' Grace said.

A tired, harried-looking woman in her early fifties, wearing a dressing gown and pompom slippers, opened the door. She looked as if she had been attractive in her youth, but her face was now leathery and criss-crossed with lines, and her wavy hair, cut shapelessly, was blonde, fading into grey. Her teeth were badly stained – from nicotine, Grace judged by the reek of tobacco. Somewhere behind her in the flat a child was screaming. There was a faintly rancid smell of fried fat in the air.

Grace held up his warrant card. 'Detective Superintendent Grace of Brighton CID, and this is Detective Sergeant Branson. Are you Mrs Margaret Stevenson?'

She nodded.

'You are Mrs Kellie Bryce's mother?'

She hesitated for a moment, then said, 'Yes. 'E's not here. You're looking for Tom? 'E's not here.'

'Do you know where he is?' Grace asked.

'Do you know where my daughter is?'

'No, we're trying to find her.'

'She wouldn't disappear – she wouldn't leave the children. She didn't never hardly bear to let them outta her sight. She wouldn't even leave them with us. Tom brung the kids here about an hour ago. Just rang the bell, bundled them in, then left.'

'Did he say where he was going?'

'No. 'E said 'e'd call me later.'

The screaming got worse behind her. She turned anxiously.

Grace fished a card out of his pocket and handed it to her. 'Please call me if you hear from him – the mobile number.'

Taking the card, she asked, 'Do you want to come in? A cup of tea? I must stop Jessica crying; my husband's gotta have his sleep. He's got the Parkinson's. 'E must have rest.'

'I'm sorry we disturbed you,' Grace said. 'Mr Bryce didn't say anything at all?'

'Nothing.'

'He didn't explain why he was bringing the children over in the middle of the night?'

'For their safety, that's what 'e said. That was all.'

'Safety from what?'

'Didn't say. Where's Kellie? Where do you think she is?'

'We don't know, Mrs Stevenson,' Glenn Branson said. 'As soon as we find her, we'll call you. Mr Bryce really didn't say where he was going?'

'Going to find Kellie, 'e said.'

'He didn't say where?'

She shook her head. The screaming got louder still. Grace and Branson exchanged glances – a question and a shrug.

'I'm sorry we disturbed you,' Grace said. He gave her a smile, trying to reassure her. 'We'll find your daughter.'

68

Tom, driving Kellie's Espace slowly north out of Brighton, holding his mobile phone in his hand, was shaking. The road was quiet, just occasional headlights coming the other way and, from time to time, lights appearing in his mirror, then passing him.

Indistinct thoughts flitted in and out of his mind, like the shadows made by his headlights. His whole body was clenched tight. He leaned forward, peering through the windscreen, shooting nervous, darting glances into the mirror, fear riddling his stomach.

Oh my God. My darling, where are you?

He did not know what he was doing here or what to expect. His brain felt locked; he was unable to think out of this box, unable to think beyond those words on his computer screen.

He had visions of the girl, Janie Stretton, in her room being butchered by the hooded man with the stiletto blade. But it wasn't Janie Stretton now, it was Kellie.

He couldn't imagine where Kellie was nor what was going through her mind. He just had to get to her, whatever it took, whatever it cost.

Money. That's what they would want, he suspected hazily. They had kidnapped Kellie and now they wanted money. And they would have to believe him when he told them he did not have very much, but he would give them everything he had in the world. *Everything*.

A road sign loomed up. COWFOLD. HAYWARDS HEATH.

Suddenly the display on his mobile lit up and it began ringing:

Private number calling

Nervously, he pressed the answer key. 'Hello?'

'Mr Bryce?'

It was DS Branson. *Shit.* He killed the call.

Moments later there was the double beep of a message waiting.

He played it. It was DS Branson, for the third time, asking him to phone him back.

Kellie, my darling, for God's sake call me!

Headlights loomed in his mirror. Although he was only doing forty on a dual carriageway, this time they stayed behind him, right on his tail. He dropped his speed to thirty. Still the headlights stayed behind him. His throat tightened.

His phone rang again. On the caller display was a number he did not recognize. He answered, a cautious, shaky, 'Hello?'

A male voice in a guttural eastern European accent said, 'Mr Bryce, how are you doing?'

'Who – who are you?' he said. The lights were right behind him, dazzling him.

'Your wife would like to see you.'

Finding it hard to see the road ahead, he said, 'Is she OK? Where is she?'

'She's fine, she's great. She is looking forward to seeing you.'

'Who are you?'

'There is a lay-by coming up in half a mile. Pull into it and turn your engine off. Stay in your car and do not turn round.' The phone went dead.

He did not know what to do. Some distance ahead, as he started down a long hill with signs to a garden centre on his left, his headlights picked up a blue P sign for a parking area.

Then he saw the lay-by.

His heart was thrashing like a crazed bird inside his ribcage, and his mouth was dry with fear. He tried desperately to think clearly, rationally. A voice somewhere inside his head was screaming at him not to pull over, to keep going, to call DS Branson back, to let the police handle this.

And another voice, a much quieter, more logical one, was telling him that if he did not pull over, Kellie would die.

Her scream of terror on his computer echoed all around him.

That scream had been real.

That woman on his computer last Tuesday night being cut to ribbons by the stiletto blade was real.

He indicated left, slowed, pulled over.

The headlights followed him.

He braked, switched off the engine, then sat rigidly staring ahead, frozen in fear but determined to stick this out, somehow.

The headlights in his mirror went off. Darkness. Silence. The engine pinged. He thought he saw shadows moving. Behind him tiny pinpricks of light appeared. They grew larger. A lorry roared past, shaking his car, and he saw its red tail lights fade slowly into the distance.

Then both rear doors of the Espace opened simultaneously. A hand, like a vice, gripped his throat.

Something was pressed over his mouth and nose, a damp cloth with a sharp, sour reek. He felt an instant, blinding headache, like a cheese-wire slicing through his brain.

Behind his eyes it was as if a television had been switched off: one small diminishing pinprick of light, rapidly fading to black.

69

The next Sussex police officer to get an early-morning call was Detective Sergeant Jon Rye of the High Tech Crime Unit. His alarm clock showed 2.43 a.m. as his mobile began to ring, and he cursed not having turned the damned thing off.

His wife stirred but didn't say anything as he snapped on the bedside light, waking up fast, looked at the caller display and saw only *Private number calling*. Almost certainly to do with work, he thought.

It was the SIO of the Janie Stretton case on the line. Rye glanced at his wife, asked Roy Grace to hold for a moment, then pulled on a dressing gown and hurried downstairs into the kitchen and closed the door.

'Sir?' he said. 'Sorry about that.'

'Sorry to disturb you,' the Detective Superintendent said. 'I need to ask you something urgently. Last night you logged an incident on the system – a "War Driving".'

Oh shite, Jon Rye thought blearily. He'd only logged that bloody phone call from that Swiss engineer out of cussedness. More as a joke than anything, really. Talk about something coming back to bite you!

'You put down the registration details of a white Ford Transit van. That van was outside a crime scene the previous night, and it has been involved in an accident following a high-speed pursuit tonight.'

'I see,' the head of the High Tech Crime Unit said.

'I've never heard of this expression, "War Driving", before. What did you mean by it?'

Rye explained.

When he had finished, Grace said, 'OK, if I understand correctly, you are saying that people with Wi-Fi – a wireless internet connection – can log onto any system that is not password-protected?'

'Correct, sir. The wireless router – a small bit of hardware that costs about fifty quid – puts out a signal, and anyone with Wi-Fi who's within range can log on to the internet through it, if they are not locked out by a password request.'

'So they can get a free high-speed internet connection doing this?'

'Exactly, sir.'

'Why would they bother?'

'If you are out and about, wanting to pick up or send emails, it can be just out of convenience. I've done it myself.' Rye, wide awake now, stepped over to the kettle, checked it had water and switched it on, deciding to have a cup of tea.

'You've done it yourself? How do you mean?'

'I've been a passenger in a car in Brighton, stopped at lights, with my laptop open, and suddenly I've realized I'm online – my Wi-Fi's picked up a signal from a wireless router. In a few seconds you can download and pick up a lot of emails – and web pages.'

Grace was quiet for a moment, digesting this. 'So Mr Seiler, who made the complaint, was angry about a man in a white van outside his house, connected to his wireless router by his Wi-Fi.'

'That's what it sounded like to me, sir.'

'But why would Mr Seiler have been angry? Would it have mattered?'

'Yes. If he'd been trying to send or download email, in particular large files, it would have slowed his connection speed down.' Rye searched for an analogy. 'If you imagine in your house you turn on every tap at the same time, water's going to come more slowly out of each of them than if you had just one running. It's not a perfect analogy.'

'So this man in the van realized he had found a good spot to surf the net from?'

'Yes, sounds like it; it's a way to use the net without paying.'

The Detective Superintendent was quiet for some moments. 'But the charges are pretty small now. Could there be another reason?'

The kettle was hissing, coming to the boil. It was pitch dark outside. On the fridge door was a crayoned drawing of a spindly man in a cap, in a boxy little car with four uneven wheels, and the word DADDY beneath it. It had been drawn by his daughter Becky a good ten years back, when he had been in Traffic; she must have been about nine. Strange what tiredness did to you, he thought. He probably hadn't looked at that drawing for the best part of a decade.

'Another reason?' Jon Rye said. 'Yes, if you had emails you wanted to send or receive that you wanted to make as hard as possible for anyone to track.'

'Thank you,' Grace said. 'You've been very helpful.'

'No problem. That information about the routings from the laptop I was given – from your Mr Bryce – was it helpful?'

'Incredibly, yes.'

'Good, we're still working on it.'

'Maybe talk later in the day.'

'I'll call you if we find anything more.' He sensed an anxiety in the Detective Superintendent's tone, as if the SIO was anxious to end the call – that it was now keeping him from something else he wanted to be doing. Something even more urgent than this call, which had woken his entire household up in the middle of the sodding night.

70

Grace, seated at the workstation in MIR One, hung up the phone and took a sip of the strong, sweet, white coffee he had just made himself. Since he had left the cleaners seemed to have been; the place was spotless, the smell of food replaced with the slightly metallic tang of polish, the bins emptied. Nick Nicholl, seated beside him, also hung up his phone.

'No news from the hospital,' the DC announced.

At this moment, Grace thought, no news was good news. No news meant that E-J was still alive. 'OK,' he said, nodding at the laptop that Nick Nicholl had taken from the van, which was now sitting in a plastic evidence bag in front of him. 'I want to check out the in-box and sent mail on this machine.'

He glanced at the Vantage screen, taking a quick look through the incident log for the night so far. Other than the flurry surrounding their own activities, it was a quiet night, typical of Sunday. Come Thursday and Friday nights, there would be ten times the activity.

The Detective Constable pulled on latex gloves, removed the laptop from the bag and popped its lid. It was still powered up, but had gone to sleep. For some moments the processor went through its wake-up checks, then it opened at the Entourage email program that must have been running, Nicholl realized, when they had approached the vehicle.

Branson, sitting opposite them, asked, 'Was Jon Rye helpful?'

'More helpful than I'd be to most people at this hour of the morning,' Grace retorted, blowing on the coffee to cool it.

'Yeah, well he used to be in Traffic. Serves him right to get a bit of payback. One of them bastards done me about ten years ago; could have been him.'

Grace grinned. 'Pissed? Breathalysed?'

'No, just speeding. Empty bloody road – I wasn't that much over. Bastard threw the book at me.'

'Yeah, I got done for speeding three years ago,' Grace said. 'By an unmarked car just up the A23. Told him I was a cop and that just made it worse. They seem to get sadistic pleasure out of nicking their own.'

'Know that old joke?' Branson said. 'About the difference between a hedgehog and a Traffic.cop car?'

Grace nodded.

'I don't,' Nicholl said.

'With the cop car, the pricks are on the inside,' Branson said.

Nicholl frowned for a moment as if his tired brain didn't get it. Then he grinned. 'Right! That's funny,' he said, moving the laptop so Grace could see the screen clearly.

'Start with the in-box,' Grace said. 'Anything that's come in since' – he looked down at his notes to check the time of Jon Rye's log – 'since six thirty yesterday evening.'

There was just one email sitting in the in-box, and it had a massive attachment, marked *SC5w12*. A symbol showed the email and attachment had been forwarded on to someone. The address of the sender was *postmaster@ scarab.tisana.al*. Grace felt a surge of adrenalin as he saw the word 'scarab'. 'We've hit the damn jackpot!'

'Dot al,' Branson wondered, now standing behind them, reading over their shoulders. 'What country is al?'

'Albania,' Nick Nicholl said.

Grace looked at him. 'Are you sure?'

'Yes.'

'You some kind of a closet geek, man?' Branson asked admiringly. 'How do you know that?'

The detective turned to Branson and grinned a little sheepishly. 'It was the answer to one of the questions at a quiz night down at our local a few weeks ago.'

'I've never been to one,' Branson said. 'Maybe I should go with Ari, improve our general knowledge.' *Might improve our marriage, more importantly*, he thought. *Try and find a few things to do together, other than argue.*

Grace was looking at the address again. 'Tisana,' he said. 'Did they have that one in your pub quiz too?'

Nicholl shook his head. 'Let's Google it.'

He keyed a search, but all that came up was an Italian website with a translator option. Nicholl clicked on that. Moments later they were staring at a long, detailed list of pathologies and plants. *Acne*, Grace read. *Carrot, soluble Tisana vitamins, Germ of Grain, Oil of Borragine, Burdock.* Then, more interesting to him at this late – or early – hour, he read, *Fatigue. Ginseng, Guarana, Elueterococco, Tisana vitamins and minerals. Lecitina di Soia.*

'Maybe he's a health nut,' Glenn Branson wisecracked. Nicholl ignored him, too weary for jokes at the moment.

'Go to the sent mail box,' Grace said.

Nicholl clicked on that. It contained just one email – the same one, with the same attachment.

'Can you see who it was sent to?' Grace asked.

'Strange,' Nick Nicholl said. 'There's no recipient showing.'

He double-clicked on it, and moments later the reason why became evident. There were hundreds and hundreds of recipients, all blind-copied. And all had email addresses that were just sequences of numbers combined with Tisana.

Grace read the first one: *110897@tisana.al*. Then the next one: *244651@tisana.al*.

'The first part looks like the name – obviously coded,' Nick Nicholl said. 'Tisana must be the internet service provider.'

'So why didn't Tisana show up on the search?' Grace queried.

'My guess is because someone doesn't want it to.'

'Can you hide things from search engines like Google?'

'I'm sure if you know what you are doing, you can conceal anything you want.'

Nodding, Grace said, 'Let's take a look at the attachment. See what that has to tell us.'

He stared at the screen as Nick Nicholl moved the cursor onto the attachment and double-clicked on it. Then, moments later, he was rather wishing he hadn't suggested it be opened after all.

All three of them watched in numb silence for the next four minutes.

71

At 6.30 a.m. Roy Grace rang Dennis Ponds, the senior Public Relations Officer, at home, apologetically waking him and asking him to come and see him at eight fifteen in his temporary office in the Major Incident Suite.

Grace had managed to snatch two hours of restless sleep, slumped, vaguely horizontally, across the two arm-chairs in the Interview Room, before heading back to his desk at the workstation shortly after 6 a.m. Branson had fared better, borrowing the sofa in the Chief Superinten-dent's office. Nicholl had gone home for a couple of hours, concerned at leaving his heavily pregnant wife on her own for too long.

At seven twenty Grace was standing outside the entrance to the Asda supermarket across the road and was the first customer when the doors opened, at seven thirty. He bought a packet of disposable razors, shaving cream, a white shirt, two croissants, six cans of Red Bull and two packs of ProPlus.

At eight he rang Cleo, but his call went straight through to her voicemail. He left her a brief message: 'Hi, it's Roy. Sorry I had to do a moonlit flit. You are amazing! Call me when you can. Giant hug.'

On the dot of eight fifteen, as Dennis Ponds entered the small bland office opposite the doorway to MIR One, Grace was feeling terrific. The wash, shave and change of shirt had freshened him, and two cans of Red Bull and four Pro-Plus were doing their stuff. The only thing not good was his back, which felt like it was burning. Cleo had scratched it to pieces. He couldn't believe it, standing in the men's room looking over his shoulder in the mirror at the long, raw red lines. But he grinned. It had been worth it. The fire on his back was nothing compared to the furnace burning in his belly for her. God, she was insane in bed.

'Morning, Roy,' Ponds said. He looked more like a city slicker than ever today, with his gelled-back hair, loud, chalk-striped suit, pink shirt with cutaway collar, and a blue tie that looked as if it was made of snakeskin.

Grace shook his hand and they both sat down. 'I apologize for calling you so early.'

'No problem,' Ponds said. 'I'm always up at sparrows; two young kids, three dogs.' He shrugged. 'So?'

'I want you to sit in on the eight thirty briefing with us – there's some video footage I need you to see.'

Looking at him a little uncertainly, Ponds said, 'Well, OK . . . I have quite a tight schedule this morning; I have to organize the press conference for Janie Stretton—'

'That's what this is about, Dennis,' Grace interrupted him. 'But it's also about something else. You may not have heard yet, but a vehicle my team was pursuing late last night was in collision with a taxi, in Kemp Town.'

Pond's face fell. 'No, I hadn't heard.'

'As a consequence of trying to apprehend the vehicle before it drove off, one of my best young officers is on life support at Sussex County. I just came off the phone. She's survived a five-hour operation but it still doesn't look good. She put her life on the line to stop that fucking vehicle – a Ford Transit. Do you understand that? She put her fucking life on the line, Dennis. She's twenty-four years old; she's one of the brightest and bravest young cops I've ever seen. She clung to the side of that vehicle to try to stop it, and the scumbag driving it smashed her into a parked car. She was trying to do her job, to uphold the law. Are you still with me?'

Hesitantly, Ponds nodded.

'I've got an officer on life support. I've got a scumbag suspect unconscious. I've got an innocent taxi passenger with a broken leg.'

'I'm not exactly sure what you are getting at,' Ponds said.

Grace realized all the caffeine might be making him seem a little aggressive. 'What I'm getting at, Dennis, is I want the editor of the *Argus*, and the editors of any other papers, radio news or television news that might pick up this story, to cut me some slack. I don't want to have to deal with a room full of braying vultures after another cheap let's-have-a-pop-at-the-police story about how reckless we are, endangering public lives, when actually we are trying to save lives, and risking our own in the process.'

'I hear what you are saying,' Ponds said. 'But it's not easy.'

'That's why you are coming to the briefing, Dennis. I'm going to show you something that I saw earlier this morning. Then I'm going to give you a copy of it. I think you'll find it'll make things a whole lot easier.' He gave Ponds an almost demonic grin.

They walked a few yards along the corridor and into the Briefing Room, which was quickly filling up, both with members of Grace's team and with the new team that had been assembled during the course of yesterday by Detective Superintendent Dave Gaylor for the Reggie D'Eath murder enquiry – there were several clear areas of crossover between the two.

Grace had decided to use the Briefing Room for this

session rather than MIR One partly because of the extra space, but mainly because there was a large plasma screen on the wall, into which DS Jon Rye, whom Grace had also summoned to the briefing, was currently plugging the laptop DC Nicholl had recovered from the crashed Transit.

Sitting down in front of the curved Crimestoppers display board, it felt at this moment as if his team couldn't stop a bloody bus, Grace thought, and remembered gloomily that today was the day Cassian Pewe started. How great it would be to get transferred to Newcastle just as he and Cleo were getting together, he thought. Putting them at opposite ends of the country. Three hundred bloody miles apart. Well it was not going to sodding well happen!

None of them would enjoy the four-minute show Grace was putting on. To start their week with the worst horror movie most of them would ever see in their lives was hardly a Monday morning treat. These were shock tactics, he knew, and they wouldn't make him any friends. But making friends was right at the bottom of his list of priorities at this exact moment.

He started the session in the way he always did. 'The time is eight thirty, Monday, June sixth,' he read out. 'This is our sixth briefing of Operation Nightingale, the investigation into the murder of Jane – known as Janie – Susan Amanda Stretton, conducted on day five following the discovery of her remains. I will now summarize events following the incident.'

For some minutes, mainly for the benefit of the newcomers from Detective Superintendent Gaylor's team, he went over the circumstances surrounding Janie Stretton's death, the investigations and actions that had been put in place subsequently and the key events. These he listed as: the theft of the computer disk which had enabled Tom

Bryce, apparently, to witness Janie Stretton's murder; the discovery that Janie Stretton had been supplementing her income as a trainee lawyer by working as a prostitute; the discovery of the link on Tom Bryce's computer with Reggie D'Eath's computer; Kellie Bryce's disappearance; her husband's disappearance; the recovery of a laptop computer from a crashed van last night, and what it contained, which they would all shortly see.

He looked at his watch. 'Whatever plans outside of work any of you have for the next thirty-six hours and forty-five minutes, you can forget. You'll understand why at the end of this briefing. OK, can I have your individual updates?' He looked first at Norman Potting.

'Can I just ask, is there any more news on Emma-Jane?' Potting asked.

'No, she's still on life support,' Grace answered curtly. 'I've organized flowers from our team to be sent to the hospital. What progress have you made on the two escort agencies Miss Stretton was registered with?'

'I went to take a formal statement from Ms Claire Porter, joint proprietor of BCE-247 escort agency, at seven thirty last night. She's about as much use as a chocolate teapot. I got nothing helpful from her.'

'And her clients?'

'I'm working my way through her clients, and also through her girls,' Potting said.

I'll bet you are, you dirty bugger, Grace thought, and could see from the expressions on several other faces, including the two FLOs assigned to Derek Stretton, Maggie Campbell and Vanessa Ritchie, that he wasn't alone in this view.

'So far, I haven't come up with anything.'

'And the second agency?'

'She had only just registered; they hadn't introduced any clients to her.'

Grace looked at his notes. 'What about the man called Anton who took Janie Stretton out on four dates from the BCE-247 agency?'

'I checked out the phone number. It was one of those pay-as-you-go jobs you can buy in just about any shop or petrol station. No record of the purchaser; won't get us anywhere.'

Grace circulated to the teams a dozen photographs of Janie Stretton with her date in the Karma Bar. They had been lifted off the CCTV tape and the quality was not great, but her face and the face of her muscular, spiky-haired date were clear enough. 'These were taken on Friday, May twenty-seventh, the night of Miss Stretton's third date with this Anton. I think we can presume this is him. I want these circulated to every police station in the country and we'll try to get it on *Crimewatch* on Wednesday night. Someone's going to recognize him.' Grace knew that this might raise identification issues in the future, but he would deal with them with the Crown Prosecution Service when he had to.

He turned to Maggie Campbell and Vanessa Ritchie. 'You said that Miss Stretton's father was talking about putting up a reward?'

'He confirmed last night,' Maggie Campbell said. 'One hundred thousand pounds for information leading to the arrest and conviction of her killer.'

'Good,' Grace said. 'That's helpful; that should test a few loyalties.' He looked at two of the new officers he had recruited from Dave Gaylor's team: Don Barker, whom Grace liked, a stocky, bull-necked detective sergeant in his mid-thirties, with a fuzz of fair hair and a pale blue shirt straining at the buttons, and a very confident, much

younger detective constable Grace had never seen before.
His name was Alfonso Zafferone; he had Latino good looks,
wet-look hair, and was dressed in an elegant houndstooth
sports jacket and a sharp shirt and tie. Addressing both
of them he asked, 'Any progress on the ownership of this
white van?'

Alfonso Zafferone replied. He had a cocky attitude,
making Grace take an instant dislike to him. He exuded a
demeanour that said he was cut out for higher things, and
menial tasks such as vehicle checks were way beneath him.
'As we already know, it's a company with a PO box address
in London. I checked out the company – it isn't registered
at Companies House.'

'Meaning?' Grace asked.

Zafferone shrugged.

His tiredness making him less tolerant than normal,
Grace snapped at him, deliberately getting his name wrong
– one of the best ways, he had learned over the years, to
put someone in their place. 'This is a murder enquiry,
DC Zabaglione. We don't do shrugs here; we do answers
verbally. Would you like to try again?'

The young DC glared at him, looking for a moment as
if he was about to answer back, then clearly thought better
of it. A little more meekly he replied, 'It means, sir, either
the company is registered overseas or the name is false.'

'Thank you. I want to know which is the case by our
next briefing, at six thirty. And where the mail to that PO
box is collected from. OK?'

Zafferone nodded sullenly.

You're not going to go far, my son, Grace thought. *Not
unless someone pulls the chain and flushes you down the
sodding toilet.* 'How about the identity of the van's driver?'

'He was starting to come round about ten minutes ago,

Roy,' Don Barker said. 'There was nothing on his clothes or in the van. He doesn't look English – may be central European. I'm going down to see him straight after this briefing.'

'Good,' Grace said. Then he turned back to Potting. 'OK, another task for you today, Norman, is to finish visiting all the wholesale suppliers of sulphuric acid in the area.'

'I'm on it,' Potting said.

Grace addressed Nick Nicholl. 'Remind me, Nick, what time are we seeing the DI from Wimbledon?'

'At half past eleven, sir.'

'And you're chasing up on any other force in the country that might have had a scarab beetle connected to a murder scene?'

'Yes, I'm working on that, sir.'

'Don't keep fucking sirring me, OK?'

The DC blushed.

Grace felt bad for having a go at him. He didn't need to snap at anyone. He needed to keep a lid on himself, he realized. He looked at the team and gave a smile. 'OK, we're now going to have a short movie. I apologize there is no popcorn.'

He got a ragged laugh.

After what you are about to see, you won't be feeling like eating popcorn, you'll be doing well just to keep down your breakfast, he thought to himself, nodding at DS Rye to close the blinds then start the video.

While Rye closed the blinds, Grace said, 'This video clip was found on this laptop computer, which was removed from the Ford Transit van last night. The hard drive we removed and is now in safekeeping, as a crime scene, in the

High Tech Crime Unit. What you are viewing is a cloned copy.'

Jon Rye clicked the keyboard to start the projection. Grace dimmed the lights.

On the screen appeared:

A SCARAB PRODUCTION

Here is a special bonus movie for all our customers,

'BATHTIME FOR REGGIE!'

The man is a convicted paedophile. Enjoy!

Moments later a slightly unsteady, hand-held camera showed, in wide angle, a small, rather old-fashioned avocado-coloured bath-room. The camera favoured the bathtub. Then a figure, wearing what appeared to be a full chemical-protection suit, with gloves, boots, a breathing tank and mask, struggled backwards in through the door, carrying something.

In a moment, it became clear it was the legs of a naked man, bound tightly together with cord.

A second man, in identical protective clothing, his face invisible behind his darkened-glass mask, held the shoulders of the naked man, Reggie D'Eath.

They deposited him in the empty tub.

A large, baby-faced man, with thinning hair and a flaccid body, he thrashed around in the bath like a fish out of water. His face was a mask of terror, but he was unable to speak because something, held in place with gaffer tape had been jammed in his mouth. His arms were tied tightly to his sides. All he could do was wriggle his body, heave himself up and down with his thighs and twist his head wildly from side to side, his eyes bulging, imploring, his small, thin penis flopping around between his hairless balls amid an untidy thicket of pubic hairs.

The men went out of the room, and returned with a large black plastic chemical drum which Grace estimated would hold about ten gallons. No markings were visible on it.

Reggie D'Eath was now thrashing so wildly that for an instant it seemed he would actually manage to leap out of the tub.

The men set the drum down. One then held D'Eath while the other produced a length of wire, wound it twice around his neck, then attached it to a towel rail high on the wall above his head. And pulled it tight.

D'Eath's eyes bulged even more. His movements became different after some seconds – convulsions rather than thrashing.

With some difficulty the two men moved him up a little, so he was reclining rather than lying flat. They adjusted the ligature so that it was now supporting him, clearly deeply uncomfortable and cutting into his neck but no longer strangling him.

An unseen hand tossed a wriggling scarab beetle onto his chest. The little creature tumbled over backwards almost comically, coming to rest on D'Eath's genitals. It started to right itself, but too late.

Without wasting any time the two men lifted the chemical drum, moving carefully out of the view of the camera, so as not to obstruct it, and tipped a good gallon of the liquid, which Grace knew to be sulphuric acid, straight onto D'Eath's genitals.

Steam rose.

Grace had never in his life seen a body shake and contort the way the unfortunate D'Eath's was doing now. The man's head was snapping from left to right, as if he was trying to saw the wire through his carotid artery; his eyes were strobing. As surreptitiously as he could, Grace glanced at the reactions of his colleagues. Ponds was holding his hand over his mouth. Every single one of them looked numb.

He turned back to the screen. The men continued pouring, emptying the entire contents of the drum into the bath. Within moments D'Eath's body ceased to move. The room slowly filled with a haze of chemical steam.

The video faded to black. Then appeared:

> DEARLY VALUED CUSTOMER, we hope you enjoyed our little bonus show. Remember to log in at 21.15 on Tuesday for our next Big Attraction – A man and his wife together. Our first ever DOUBLE KILLING!

Grace turned the lights back on.

72

From the parchment colour of Alfonso Zafferone's face, Grace guessed he wasn't going to have any more arrogance from this young DC for a while. He could not recall, in his entire career, when he had been in a room full of people so quiet.

Dennis Ponds was staring, bug-eyed and unfocused, as if he had just been told he was going to be put in the bathtub next.

It was Norman Potting who finally broke the silence. He coughed, clearing his throat, then said, 'Do we presume this is a snuff movie, Roy?'

'Well it's not his fucking family album,' Glenn Branson rounded on him.

There was no titter of laughter. Nothing. One of the female indexers was staring down at the table as if afraid to lift her eyes, in case there was more.

'Dennis,' Grace said, 'I'm going to give you a copy on your laptop to take to the editor of the *Argus*. Don't show him everything, but make him aware of just what we're dealing with here. I want him to run photographs of Mr and Mrs Bryce on the front page of the midday edition of his paper. We have a day and a half to find these people. Does everyone understand that? That they are going to be killed and video'd?'

Branson took a deep breath, then exhaled loudly. 'Man, who watches that kind of shit?'

'A lot of very ordinary people with sick minds,' Grace

said. 'It could be any one of us in this room – or your neighbour, your doctor, your plumber, your vicar, your mortgage broker. The same kind of people who slow down to rubberneck road accidents. Voyeurs. There's a little bit of it in all of us.'

'Not me,' Branson said. 'I couldn't watch stuff like that.'

'Are you saying that we are all potential killers?' Nick Nicholl asked.

Grace remembered something a psychological profiler who had lectured on snuff movies at a homicide convention in the States had told him late one night in a bar. 'We all have the capacity to kill, but only a small percentage of us have the ability to *live* with having killed. But there are plenty of us who are curious; we'd like to experience it vicariously. Snuff movies enable you to do that – to experience the killing of a human being. Think about it,' he said. 'There's no opportunity for normal people to actually kill someone.'

'I could have happily killed my mother-in-law,' Potting said.

'Thank you, Norman,' Grace said, silencing him before he could go on. Then he turned to Glenn Branson. 'Tom Bryce left his house in the middle of the night in a Renault Espace. There can't have been much traffic on the road. We don't know where he was going. We don't know how much fuel there was in the vehicle. I want you to call off the search for Janie Stretton's head and redeploy every single officer, all the Specials and all the CSOs to cover every CCTV camera – police, civic, petrol station, the lot – within a thirty-mile radius of this city.'

'Right away.'

Then, turning back to DS Barker, he said, 'Don, I want

someone to go through all of Reggie D'Eath's personal records – bank statements, credit card statements—'

'Someone's already on to that.'

'Good.'

Grace checked his watch. He had a nine thirty with Alison Vosper, then somehow had to get to a 10.00 a.m. appointment he had made on the other side of town. 'I'll see you all back here at six thirty p.m. Everyone know what they've got to do? Any further questions?'

Usually there would be plenty. This morning there were none.

Then a phone rang. It was answered by the secretary, who handed it after a few moments to Glenn Branson. Everyone watched him as if sensing there was some important news coming.

Branson asked the caller to hold for a moment, covered the mouthpiece with his hand. 'The Bryces' Renault Espace has been found down a farm track off the A23 at Bolney,' he said.

'Empty?' Grace asked, knowing the answer to the question, but asking it anyway.

'Burned out.'

73

Alison Vosper was power-dressed, as usual, when he entered her office on the dot of 9.30 a.m. And as usual he had an attack of butterflies. She scared him, he couldn't help it; the bloody woman's corrosive manner – and the power she wielded over him – affected him. And it didn't help that he knew she was out to get him with her new secret weapon, Detective *Superintendent* Cassian Pewe.

Sitting at her immaculate desk, exuding a pungent but unsexy perfume, she was dressed in a black jacket that made her shoulders look massive and an ivory-coloured blouse with a lace collar. Expecting a face of thunder, the Assistant Chief Constable surprised Grace by greeting him with a smile. Unscrewing the cap from a bottle of mineral water, she took a rather dainty sip. 'Good morning, Roy,' she said, her voice even more cordial than her smile. She gestured him to take one of the handsome Georgian carver chairs in front of her desk. 'Have a seat.'

Another good sign? he wondered. She rarely asked him to sit at these meetings. Or was this a very bad sign?

Still smiling, very definitely in sweet rather than sour mode today, she said, 'So, Operation Nightingale seems to be a bit of a fiasco, so far.'

'I – I wouldn't go so—'

She raised a hand to silence his defence. 'You still have no suspect. You haven't located the victim's head. One potential witness has been murdered and two others are missing. And last night, again, your team engaged in a high-speed pursuit which resulted in a serious accident.' Miraculously she was still smiling, but the warmth had gone and was replaced with apparent bemusement.

Grace nodded. 'It's not going our way,' he said. 'We need a lucky break.'

She replaced the cap on the bottle. It was a fine morning outside but the room felt dark and oppressive. 'You are tying up a massive amount of resources. It would be one thing if you could give me a result but all I seem to get is aggravation. Where are we at?'

Grace brought her up to speed. When he had finished, he waited for what he knew was coming: at best she was going to stick Cassian Pewe on this case with him, at worst she was removing him and replacing him with Pewe. To his surprise she did neither.

She pulled a slim black pen from the ammonite holder on her desk and tapped it thoughtfully on her blotter. 'You haven't got until nine fifteen tomorrow night, realistically, have you? If these people are going to kill Mr and Mrs Bryce and broadcast it to whoever their *customers* are, they're going to do it well in advance. They could be already dead.'

'I know.'

There was a brief silence. Grace looked down, feeling Vosper's eyes fixed on him. When he looked up he saw understanding in them. Despite her antipathy to him, she was at least professional enough to recognize – and accept – that the problems he was facing with this case were not necessarily of his making. But he was puzzled that she had not yet mentioned Cassian Pewe. Why was she holding back?

Very hesitantly, he asked, 'Is . . . ah . . . is this meeting with Cassian on? You wanted me to see him this morning.'

'Actually no, it isn't,' she said. Then she began tapping

the pen harder and faster on the blotter, without seeming to be aware she was doing this.

'OK,' he said, feeling a little relieved, but wondering what had changed her mind. Then he found out.

'Detective Superintendent Pewe was involved in a road traffic accident last night. He's in hospital with a fractured leg.'

Not only could Grace barely believe his ears, he could barely believe his eyes, either. She was smiling again. Just the very faintest of smiles, to be fair, but a smile nonetheless. Smiling as she conveyed the information that her protégé was in a bad way after a car crash.

'I'm sorry,' Grace said. 'What happened?'

'He was a passenger in a taxi in the centre of Brighton, late last night. It was in collision with a van being pursued by a police car.'

And the next moment Grace was smiling too; he couldn't help it. Gallows humour. It got to everyone in this job, eventually.

*

As he drove away from Alison Vosper's office, Grace phoned the Royal Sussex County Hospital to find out if the van driver from last night had come round yet. Right now that man was their best hope of getting to the Bryces' captors.

Just about their only damned hope.

Except for one long shot.

He drove to the Bryces' house, where DC Linda Buckley had just taken over from DC Willingham. She asked Grace if there was much point in her staying on in the house. After all, there was nothing to do except feed the dog. He suggested she wait a few more hours in case Tom Bryce turned up – which, he thought grimly, was unlikely.

He went upstairs and into the Bryces' bedroom, then hurried back downstairs. The Alsatian was standing in the hallway giving him a strange look, as if she knew he was the man who could bring her master and mistress home.

Despite his rush, Grace paused for a moment, knelt beside the dog and stroked her forehead. 'Hi,' he said. 'Don't you worry; I'll bring them back. Somehow. OK?' He stared into the dog's large, brown eyes and felt for an instant, just a fleeting instant, that the fine-looking creature had actually understood what he'd said.

Maybe it was his tiredness, or the stress, or whatever, addling his brain, but as he left the house and drove quickly away, heading for the eastern extremity of the city, the expression on that dog's face stayed with him, haunting him. She had looked so sad, so full of trust. And for a moment he wasn't doing any of this just for Mr and Mrs Bryce, and for their children. He was also doing it for their dog.

74

Tom woke with a start, with a blinding headache, badly in need of a pee, thinking there must have been a power cut. It was never this dark, normally; there was always the neon glow of the street lights, tinging the bedroom orange.

And what the hell was he lying on? Rock hard . . .

And then, as if a sluice had released cold water into his belly, he remembered something indistinct but bad.

Oh shit, bad.

His right arm hurt. He tried to raise it but it would not move. *Must have been lying on it*, he thought, *made it go to sleep*. He tried again. Then he realized he couldn't move his left arm either.

Nor his legs.

Something was digging into his right thigh. His jaw ached and his mouth was parched. He tried to speak and found to his shock he couldn't. All he could hear was a muffled hum, as he felt the roof of his mouth vibrate. Something was clamped over his mouth, bound tight around his face, pulling his cheeks in. Then a shiver ripped through him as he remembered the words last night. On his computer screen: . . . *get out of the house, take Kellie's car, head north on the A23 London Road and wait for her to call you . . .*

That's exactly what he had done. It was coming back now. Driving up the A23. The phone call telling him to pull over into the lay-by.

Now here.

Oh Christ, oh God, oh sweet Jesus Christ, where was he? Where was Kellie? What the hell had he done? Who the hell had—

Light suddenly appeared, an upright rectangle of yellow some distance away. A doorway. A figure coming through it, holding a powerful torch, the beam glinting like a mirror.

Tom held his breath, watching as the figure moved nearer. In the swinging beam of the torch he could see he was in some kind of storeroom stacked with massive plastic and metal drums that looked as if they contained fuel or chemicals.

As the figure came closer, Tom made out a very fat man in a loose-fitting open-necked shirt, his hair gelled back and squeezed into a short pigtail. A large medallion swung on a chain from his neck. There wasn't enough light to see his face clearly but Tom put him in his late fifties to early sixties.

Then the savage beam shone straight in his face; it felt like it was burning the backs of his retinas and he squeezed his eyes shut.

In a Louisiana drawl, and sounding sincere, as if it were a genuine question to which he was expecting an answer, the man said, 'So you think you're a bit of a hero, do you, Mr Bryce?'

Unsure how to respond and in any case unable to speak Tom kept silent.

He felt the beam move away and opened his eyes. The man squatted down in front of him, put out his hands until they were touching Tom's face, and then jerked them back, hard. Tom screamed. The pain was unreal. For several seconds he was convinced that half his face had been ripped clean off.

A length of gaffer tape dangled in front of his eyes. He could move his jaw again, open his mouth, speak. 'Where's my wife?' Tom said. 'Where is Kellie? Please tell me where she is.'

The man swung the beam across the room. And Tom's heart nearly broke as he saw, a short distance away, what at first he thought was a rolled-up carpet, then realized was Kellie. She was lying on the floor, trussed up, a manacle on her ankle, with a chain running from it up to a hoop on the wall, gaffer tape across her mouth, pleading at him with her eyes.

Tom's first instinct was to scream at the fat creep in fury, but somehow he managed to hold himself in check, trying to think clearly, to work out what had happened, just what the hell this nightmare really was. 'Who are you?' he said.

'You ask too many questions,' the man responded dismissively. 'You want water?'

'I want to know why I'm here. Why my wife is here.'

For an answer the man turned and walked away, back into the shadows.

'Kellie!' Tom called. 'Kellie, are you OK?'

He couldn't see her any more. Or hear her. 'Kellie, my darling!'

'Shut the fuck up,' the fat man said.

No, I won't shut up! Tom nearly shouted out. One second his insides were squirming with fear, the next blind anger seized him. How dare this bastard keep Kellie tied up? Or himself.

Got the most important presentation of my career in the morning. It could save my business. And I'm missing it because of you, you fat—

In the morning?

Was it morning?

It was coming back to him, unevenly, like trying to put sheets of paper strewn across a room by a gust of wind back into their proper order.

Kellie had gone. Her car had been burned out. Then he had responded to the email. And now she was lying across the room, all trussed—

He thought of the young woman on his computer screen, in her evening dress, the hooded man, the stiletto blade.

Pain welled in his bladder. 'Please,' he called out, 'I need to pee.'

'No one's stopping you,' the American said from the shadows.

Tom wriggled round. The man was stooped over Kellie. He ripped the tape away from her mouth. Tom winced at the sound.

Instantly she screamed at the man, 'Fuck you! Fuck you, you bastard!'

'Just be a little more ladylike; people will want to see you looking ladylike. Would you like a little more vodka?'

'Fuck you!'

Oh, God, Kellie! It was so good to hear her voice, to know she was alive, that she was OK, that she had fight in her. Yet this wasn't the way to deal with this situation.

He clenched his thighs together, and his abdomen, fighting the surge of pain from his bladder. Surely the man didn't mean him to relieve himself where he lay?

'Kellie, my darling!' Tom called out.

'Get this fucking bastard to get us out of here. I want Jessica and Max. I want my children. LET ME FUCKING GO!'

'Do you want the tape back over your face, Mrs Bryce?'

She rolled over onto her stomach and lay still, sobbing

hysterically, deep, gulping sobs. And Tom felt wretched, useless, so utterly, utterly useless. There had to be something he could do. Something. Oh God, something.

The pain in his bladder was stopping him thinking and his head felt like it had been split open. The torch beam was moving. As it did, Tom saw hundreds of dark-coloured drums, stacked floor to ceiling, huge bloody things, many bearing hazard labels. It was cold in here. There was a slightly sour smell in the chilly air.

Where the hell are we?

'Oh Tom, please do something!' she shrieked.

'Do you want money?' Tom called out to the man. 'Is that what you want? I'll rustle together whatever I can.'

'You mean you'd like to subscribe?'

'Subscribe?' Tom said, pleased at last to get some sort of response to his questions. Engage the man in conversation, reason with him, try to find a—

'You'd like to subscribe so you could watch yourself and your wife.' The American laughed. 'That's rich!'

Tom's spirits lifted a fraction. 'Yes, whatever, however much you want!'

The beam shone straight into his eyes again. 'You don't get it, fuckwit, do you? How are you going to be able to see yourselves?'

'I – I don't – know.'

'You're even more stupid than I thought. You want to pay money so you and your vain little drunk of a wife can watch yourselves looking good dead?'

75

Roy Grace was on the phone non-stop as he drove in his Alfa, making one call after another: checking on Emma-Jane, then the progress of each of his team members in turn, driving them as hard as they could be pushed.

He headed east along the coast road, leaving behind the elegant Regency facades of Kemp Town for the open country, high above the cliffs, passing the vast neo-Gothic pile of Roedean girls' school and then the art deco building of the St Dunstan's home for the blind.

Nine fifteen tomorrow night.

The time was lasered into his consciousness; it formed part of every thought that he had. It was now 10.15 a.m., Monday. Just thirty-five hours to the broadcast – and how long before then would the Bryces be killed?

Janie Stretton had been late at the vet with her cat for a 6.30 p.m. appointment, and she hadn't left until at least 7.40. In between then and approximately 9.15 p.m., when Tom Bryce claimed to have seen her on his computer, she had been murdered and the video of it broadcast. If the same pattern was followed now maybe they had until around 7.30 p.m. tomorrow. Just over thirty-three hours.

And still no live leads.

Thirty-three hours was no damn time at all.

Then he allowed himself just the briefest smile at the thought of Cassian Pewe in hospital. The irony of it. The incredible coincidence. And the fact that Alison Vosper had seen the funny side – showing him a rare side of herself, the *human* side. And the thing was – not a good thing, he knew, but he could not help it – he didn't feel even the tiniest bit bad about it, or sorry for the man.

He was sorry for the innocent taxi driver, but not for that little shit, Cassian Pewe, who had arrived in Brighton newly promoted and with every intention of stealing his lunch. The problem hadn't gone away, but with the man's injuries it was at least deferred for a while.

He drove through the smart, historic, cliff-top village of Rottingdean, along a sweeping rise then dip, followed by another rise, past the higgledy-piggledy post-war suburban sprawl of Saltdean, then to Peacehaven, near where Glenn Branson lived and where Janie Stretton's body had been found.

He turned off the coast road into a maze of hilly streets crammed with bungalows and small detached houses, and pulled up outside a small, rather neglected bungalow with a decrepit camper van parked outside.

He ended a call to Norman Potting, who seemed well advanced with his search for sulphuric acid suppliers, downed another Red Bull and two more ProPlus, walked up a short path lined with garden gnomes and stepped into a porch, past motionless wind chimes, and rang the door-bell.

A diminutive, wiry man well into his seventies, bearing more than a passing resemblance to several of the gnomes he had just passed, opened the door. He had a goatee beard, long grey hair tied back in a ponytail, wore a kaftan and dungarees, and was sporting an ankh medallion on a gold chain. He greeted Grace effusively in a high-pitched voice, a bundle of energy, taking his hand and staring at him with the joy of a long-lost friend. 'Detective Superintendent Grace! So good to see you again so soon!'

'And you, my friend. Sorry I'm so late.' It was just over

a week since Grace had last called on his services – when Frame had undoubtedly helped save an innocent man's life.

Harry Frame gripped his hand with a strength that belied both his years and his size, and stared up at him with piercing green eyes. 'So, to what do I owe the pleasure this time? Come in!'

Grace followed him into a narrow hallway lit by a low-wattage bulb in a hanging lantern, and decorated in a nautical theme, the centrepiece of which was a large brass porthole on the wall, and through into a sitting room, the shelves crammed with ships in bottles. There was a drab three-piece suite, the backs draped with antimacassars, a television that was switched off, and a round oak table with four wooden chairs by the window, to which Frame ushered him. On the wall, Grace clocked, as he did on each visit here, a naff print of Anne Hathaway's cottage and a framed motto which read, 'A mind once expanded can never return to its original dimensions.'

'Tea?'

'I'm fine,' Grace said, although he could have murdered a cup. 'I'm in a mega-rush.'

'Life's not a race, Detective Superintendent Grace, it's a dance,' Harry Frame said in a gently chiding voice.

Grace grinned. 'I'll bear that in mind. I'll put you on my card for a slow waltz at the summer ball.' He sat down at the table.

'So?' Harry said, seating himself opposite. 'Would you be here by any chance in connection with that poor young woman who was found dead here in Peacehaven last week?'

Harry Frame was a medium and clairvoyant, as well as a pendulum dowser. Grace had been to see the man many times. He could be uncannily accurate – and on other occasions totally useless.

Grace dug his hand in his pocket, pulled out three small plastic evidence bags and laid them on the table in front of Frame. He pointed, first, to the signet ring he had taken from Janie Stretton's bedroom. 'What can you tell me about the owner of this?'

Frame removed the ring, clasped it in his hand and closed his eyes. He sat still for a good minute, his wizened face screwed up in concentration.

The room had a musty smell – of old furniture, old carpet, old people.

Finally, Harry Frame shook his head. 'I'm sorry, Roy. Nothing. Not a good day for me today. No connection with the spirits.'

'Nothing at all from the ring?'

'I'm sorry. Could you come back tomorrow? We could try again.'

Grace took the ring back, put it in the plastic bag and pocketed it. Next he pointed in turn to the silver cufflinks he had taken from a drawer in the Bryces' bedroom and a silver bracelet he had taken from Kellie Bryce's jewellery box. 'I need to find the owners of these. I need to find them *today*. I don't know where they are but I suspect they are somewhere in the vicinity of Brighton and Hove.'

The medium left the room, and returned quickly holding an Ordnance Survey map of the Brighton and Hove area. Moving a candle in a glass holder out of the way, he spread it out on the table and pulled a length of string, with a small lead weight attached, from his trouser pocket.

'Let's see what we can find,' he said. 'Yes, indeed, let's see.' He held the bracelet and the cufflinks in his left hand, then, resting his elbows on the table, he inclined his face towards the map and began to chant.

'Yarummm,' Frame said to himself. 'Yarummmm. Brnnnn. Yarummm.'

Then he sat bolt upright, held the string over the map between his forefinger and thumb, and let the lead weight swing backwards and forwards, like a pendulum. After that, pursing his lips in concentration, he swung it vigorously in a tight circle, steadily covering the map inch by inch.

'Telscombe?' he said. 'Piddinghoe? Ovingdean? Kemp Town? Brighton? Hove? Portslade? Southwick? Shoreham?' He shook his head. 'No, I'm not being shown anything in this area, sorry.'

'Can we try a larger scale?' Grace asked.

Frame went out again and returned with a map covering the whole of East and West Sussex. But again, after several minutes of swinging the weight with fierce concentration, he produced no result.

Grace wanted to pick the man up and shake him. He felt so damned frustrated. 'Nothing at *all*, Harry?'

The medium shook his head.

'They're going to die if I don't find them.'

Harry Frame handed him back the links and the bracelet. 'I could try again later. I'm sorry. I'm so sorry.'

'This afternoon some time?'

Frame nodded. 'If you want to leave them with me? I'll spend all day; I'll keep working on it.'

'Thank you, I'd appreciate it,' Grace replied. He was clutching at straws, he knew, as he left with a heavy heart.

76

After the eight thirty briefing, Jon Rye had spent two and three-quarter hours working on the laptop that had been taken from the wrecked Ford Transit. But it was defeating him.

At twenty past eleven, feeling drained and frustrated, he went out of the department to get himself a coffee from the vending machine, then returned, deep in thought. With any computer he could normally find a way around any password protection by using forensic software to go in via a back door and then through the computer's entire internet history. But on this machine he was drawing a blank.

He held his security card to the door panel of the High Tech Crime Unit, then entered and crossed what he had jokingly christened the hamster's cage, the caged area housing the child pornography investigation, Operation Glasgow, nodding to a couple of the six people poring over their screens who glanced up at him, and walked through into the main part of his department.

Andy Gidney and the rest of his team were at their desks, well stuck into their day's work. He sat back down at his desk, the laptop itself secure in the Evidence Room, its cloned hard disk loaded into his computer.

Although he had been head of this unit for the past three years, Rye was smart enough to know his own limitations. He had been retrained from Traffic. Several of the younger members of his team were techies from the ground up, university graduates who had lived and breathed computers from their cradles. Andy Gidney was the best of the lot. If there was one person in here who could persuade this laptop to yield its secrets, it was Gidney.

He ejected the cloned hard drive from his processor tower, stood up and walked across to Gidney's workstation. Gidney was still working on cracking the pass code on an online banking scam. 'Andy, I need you to drop everything for the next few hours and help me out on this. We have two lives at stake.'

'Ummm,' Gidney said. 'The thing is, I'm quite close now.'

'Andy, I don't care how close you are.'

'But if I stop, I could lose this whole sequence! Here's the thing!' Gidney swivelled his chair to face Rye, his eyes burning with excitement. 'I think I'm just one digit away!'

'How long will it take you?'

'Ummm, right, ummm,' he said pensively. Then he closed his eyes and nodded furiously. 'Ummm. Ummm.' He opened his eyes again and looked down at the floor. 'I would *hope* by the end of this week.'

'I'm sorry,' Jon Rye said. 'You're going to have to park it. I need you on this right now.'

'Ummm, the thing is, there's nine of us in this department, Jon, right?'

Hesitantly Rye said, 'Yes?'

Concentrating hard on the carpet, Gidney asked, 'Why exactly me?'

Rye wondered if flattery would help. 'Because you're the best. OK?'

Gidney petulantly swivelled his chair, and, with his back now to DS Rye, raised his hand, sounding supremely irritated. 'All right, gimme.'

'The forensic image files are on the server under job number 340.'

'So what exactly am I looking for?'

Rye did not like talking to his junior's back, but he had learned from experience that there was no point trying to change this weirdo; it was best to humour him, if he wanted the best out of him. 'Postal addresses, phone numbers, email addresses. Anything that could give us a clue where a couple called Mr and Mrs Bryce might be – Tom and Kellie Bryce.' He spelled out their names.

'Do what I can.'

'Thanks, Andy.'

Rye returned to his desk, then was almost immediately called over to the far end of the room by another colleague, DC John Shaw, a tall, good-looking young man of thirty who he liked a lot. Shaw was extremely bright, also from a university background like Gidney, but the complete opposite of the other man in every way.

Shaw was working on a particularly harrowing photograph album on a hard drive seized in a raid on a suspected paedophile's house. He had noticed a pattern in the man's taste – bashing small children around before photographing himself having sex with them. It seemed similar to another case they'd handled recently and he wanted Rye's view.

Ten minutes later Jon Rye returned to his desk, deep in thought. He had become hardened to most kinds of vile stuff that he saw on computers, but hurting kids still got to him. Every time. He barely noticed, as he passed Gidney's workstation, that he wasn't there.

A short while later, taking a brief respite from his emails, Rye looked over his shoulder and was surprised –

and irritated, considering the urgency – to see that Gidney still had not returned.

He stood up and walked over to the geek's workstation. On the screen he saw:

> THE SHIPPING FORECAST ISSUED BY THE
> MET OFFICE, ON BEHALF OF THE MARITIME
> AND COASTGUARD AGENCY, AT 0555 ON
> MONDAY 6 JUNE 2005
>
> THE GENERAL SYNOPSIS AT 0000
>
> LOW WESTERN FRANCE 1014 EXPECTED
> SOUTHEAST ENGLAND 1010 BY 1300.
> LOW ROCKALL 1010 MOVING STEADILY
> SOUTHEAST. HIGH FASTNET 1010.
> DISSIPATING.

What on earth was the man doing looking at the shipping forecast when they were in the middle of an emergency? And where the hell was he? He'd been gone a good twenty minutes – if not more.

After a further twenty minutes had passed, it became evident to Rye that Andy Gidney had vanished.

And, he was about to discover, Gidney had securely deleted everything from the server and taken the laptop and the cloned hard drive with him.

77

Roy Grace drove away from Harry Frame's house suddenly feeling very low and very tired, despite the latest can of Red Bull and the caffeine tablets he had swallowed less than half an hour ago. It was too soon to take any more. He hoped to hell that the clairvoyant would suddenly get one of his sparks of inspiration.

Then his phone rang. He answered it hopefully. It was Branson, cheery as ever.

'Bearing up, old-timer?'

'I'm bagged,' Grace said. 'What news?'

'Someone from DS Gaylor's lot has been going through Reggie D'Eath's paperwork. They've found a monthly standing order on his Barclaycard to a company called Scarab Entertainment. The amount is one thousand pounds.'

'A thousand quid? A month?'

'Yup.'

'Where does someone like D'Eath get that kind of money?'

'By supplying small children to rich men as a sideline.'

'Where's the company based?' Grace asked.

'That's the bad news. Panama.'

Grace thought for a moment. There were certain countries in the world where the law guaranteed a company total privacy from investigation. He recalled from a previous case that Panama was one of them. 'That's not going to help us much in the short term. A *thousand* quid a month?'

'That's big business,' Branson said. 'Couldn't we get a court order to force all the credit card companies to tell us who else is paying a grand a month to Scarab Entertainment?'

'Yes, in these circumstances with lives at stake we could, but it won't help us. We'll get a list of nominee directors from some law firm in Panama that'll tell us to fuck off when we approach it.' How many subscribers did they have? It would not need many to make a very substantial business. One that they would go to great lengths to protect.

> DEARLY VALUED CUSTOMER, we hope you
> enjoyed our little bonus show. Remember to log
> in at 21.15 on Tuesday for our next Big Attraction –
> A man and his wife together. Our first ever
> DOUBLE KILLING!

For a thousand a month you would want to give the odd little freebie, wouldn't you? Just toss the occasional paedophile into an acid bath.

'You still there, old-timer?'

'Yes. Anything else your end?'

'We've got one sighting of Mr Bryce in his Espace, just after midnight, filling up with petrol at a Texaco garage at Pyecombe – from the CCTV camera.'

'Other vehicles on the camera?'

'No.'

'And nothing of use in the Espace?'

'Forensics are crawling all over it. Nothing so far.'

'I'm coming back to the Incident Room,' Grace said. 'I'll be about twenty minutes.'

'I'll have some coffee waiting.'

'I need a quadruple espresso.'

'Me too.'

Grace drove on, turning off the coast road and driving inland on the upper road through Kemp Town, past the posh girls' school, St Mary's Hall, the Royal Sussex County Hospital, then the Victorian Gothic facade of the mixed public school, Brighton College. On his left, a short distance ahead, he saw a muscular-looking man with a strutting gait walking into a newsagent's. Something about him looked familiar, but he couldn't immediately think what.

But it was enough to make him do a U-turn. He pulled over on the opposite side of the road, switched off the engine and watched.

After no more than a minute, the man emerged from the shop, a cigarette in his lips, carrying a plastic bag with a bunch of newspapers sticking out of the top, and walked towards a black Volkswagen Golf parked with two wheels on the kerb, its hazard flashers on.

Grace stared hard through his windscreen. The gait was distinctly odd, a curious rolling swagger that reminded him of the way some hard nuts from the armed forces walked. As if they owned the pavement.

Dressed in a singlet, white jeans and white loafers, the man had gelled spikes of short hair and sported a heavy gold chain around his neck. Where the hell had he seen him before? And then his – sometimes – near-photographic memory kicked in, and he knew exactly where and when he had seen this man before. Last night. On the CCTV footage in the Karma Bar.

He had been Janie Stretton's date!

Grace's heart was pounding. The Volkswagen drove off.

Memorizing the number, he gave it a few seconds, let a taxi followed by a British Telecom van pass, then pulled back out onto the road, made another U-turn and followed, dialling the Incident Room on his mobile. It was answered on the first ring by Denise Woods, one of the indexers, a very serious, very efficient young woman.

'Hi, it's Grace. I need a PNC check very quickly. I'm following the vehicle now. It's a Volkswagen Golf, registration Papa Lima Zero Three Foxtrot Delta Oscar.'

Denise said she would call him right back.

A short distance on, the Volkswagen, still in front of the taxi and British Telecom van, stopped at a red traffic light.

When the lights went green, the Golf turned left into Lower Rock Gardens, heading down to the seafront. The other two vehicles went straight on. Grace paused for a second, then turned left, keeping as far back as he dared.

Come on, Denise!

The lights at the bottom, at the junction with Marine Parade, were green, and the Golf turned right onto the coast road. Grace went over on amber, keeping as far behind the Golf as he dared, letting a Ford Focus and then an elderly Porsche overtake him, but keeping the Golf in sight.

As the Golf negotiated the roundabout in front of the Palace Pier, his phone rang. It was Denise. The registered owner of the car was a company called Bourneholt International Ltd, with a PO box number in Brighton. The car had not been reported lost or stolen and there were no police interest markers from anybody.

'Bourneholt International Ltd,' Grace said. 'I know that name.' Then he remembered why. 'Denise, quickly take a look at the registration of the van that crashed last night; I'll hold.'

The Golf continued heading west along the seafront, past the recently repainted facade of the Royal Albion Hotel. Then, as they approached the Old Ship Hotel, the Golf moved into the outside lane, its right turn indicator signalling.

To his relief, a blue S-class Mercedes in front of him was signalling right, also. Grace tucked in behind its substantial bulk. He saw the Golf head up, past the hotel, and make a right, down into the huge Bartholomew Square underground car park. So did the S-class. Grace was right on its tail, waiting behind it on the ramp.

Denise came back on the phone. 'It's the same, Roy. Bourneholt International Ltd.'

He clenched his fists in excitement. 'Brilliant!'

The automatic barrier swung up and he moved forward, waited for the ticket to emerge from the machine and grabbed it. 'Well done!' he said.

But there was no signal.

The barrier swung up again, and he drove the Alfa through. Just as he did so, a BMW 3 series reversed out of a space, blocking Grace's path.

It reversed slowly, a nervous man inching back, inch by sodding inch.

Come on! Grace screamed silently.

After what seemed an eternity, the BMW drove forward, then turned off onto the exit ramp. Grace accelerated. All the spaces on this level were taken. He took the ramp down to the next level. That was full too. So was the next level. But as he raced through it, a Ford Galaxy people carrier filled with children, a nervous mother at the wheel, reversed across his path.

Jesus, woman, get out of my way.

He had no option but to wait. And wait. And wait.

Finally he got down to Level 4, and saw several free spaces. He accelerated, looking for the Golf, and then he saw it. Parked in a bay.

The driver had vanished.

He braked behind it, cursing.

There was a blast of horn behind him. In his mirror he saw a Range Rover. He raised a finger, drove on a few yards, then turned into the first empty space he saw, switched off the engine and jumped out of the car. He sprinted towards the exit, up the steps two at a time, and out into the large open square with a Japanese restaurant in the middle, the Thistle Hotel on one side and rows of shops on the two other sides.

But there was no sign of the man with the rolling gait and the spiky hair.

There were three other exits he could have left by. Grace ran round, covering each of them. But the man had vanished.

Grace cursed, thinking hard, standing by the first exit, nearest the Golf and his car. He doubted the man had seen him tailing him. But how long it would be before he returned to the car was anyone's guess. It could be five minutes, or five hours.

Then he had an idea.

He dialled his former base, Brighton Central, and asked to be put through to an old mate, Mike Hopkirk, a Brighton Divisional Inspector. To his relief, Hopkirk was in and not on a call.

Hopkirk was a wise owl with many years of service behind him; he commanded a lot of respect in the force and was well liked. Grace had made his choice of who to call for this task very carefully. To get everything galvanized at the speed he needed, if Hopkirk agreed, he was the man.

'Roy! How are you? Keep seeing your name in the press! Glad to see your move to Sussex House hasn't blunted your appetite for pissing people off!'

'Very witty. Listen, I'll chat later. I need a big favour, and I need it right now. We're talking about two people's lives – we've reason to believe they've been abducted and their lives are in imminent peril.'

'Tom and Kellie Bryce?' Hopkirk said, surprising Grace.

'How the hell do you know that?' He was forgetting just how razor-sharp Hopkirk was.

The roar of a passing lorry drowned out Hopkirk's reply. Covering one ear and jamming the phone hard up against the other, Grace shouted, 'Sorry? Can you repeat that?'

'They're on the bloody front page of the *Argus*!'

The PRO had managed to pull it off. Brilliant. 'OK, Mike, here's what I want. I need you to close down Bartholomew Square car park for an hour – to give me enough time to search a car in here.'

He heard what sounded like a lot of air going backwards very quickly. 'Close it down?'

'I need an hour.'

'The biggest car park in Brighton, in the middle of the day. Close it down – are you out of your mind?'

'No, I need you to do this, now, right this minute.'

'On what grounds, Roy?'

'A bomb scare. You've had a call from a terrorist cell.'

'Shit. You are serious, aren't you?'

'Come on, it's a quiet Monday morning. Wake up your troops!'

'And if this goes pear-shaped?'

'I'll take the rap.'

'Won't be you, Roy, it'll be me, and you know that.'

'But you'll do it?'

'Bartholomew Square?'

'Bartholomew Square.'

'OK,' he said, sounding dubious but resigned. 'Get off my bloody phone; I need it!'

Grace needed his, too. He called Sussex House to arrange for a SOCO team to get down here immediately, and for the officer to be accompanied by someone from Traffic who was capable of getting past the locks and security system of a VW Golf.

Next he phoned a Detective Inspector called Bill Ankram, who was responsible for the deployment of the local surveillance team. In a rare stroke of luck, Ankram had good news for him.

'We were down to follow someone in central Brighton today and the job's gone short – we've had a no-show. I was about to pull the team out and have a training afternoon instead.'

'How quickly could you get them covering the Bartholomew Square car park?' Grace asked.

'Within an hour. We're not far away already.'

Grace made the detailed arrangements, gave him the vehicle registration and exact position of the Golf. Then he phoned the Incident Room and had them fax and email the photograph of the Volkswagen's driver to Ankram.

Next he spoke to Nicholl and told him he would have to see the officer from the Met on his own, after all. As he was speaking to him, there was a deafening explosion of wailing.

It sounded as if all the emergency vehicles in the entire City of Brighton and Hove had switched on their sirens simultaneously.

78

Kellie was scaring Tom. It was like being locked in the darkness with a total stranger. A completely unpredictable one. There were long periods of silence, then suddenly she would screech hysterical abuse at him. She was starting again now, her voice cracked and strained from so much screaming.

'You stupid bastard! You idiot man! You got us into this! If you had left the bloody CD thing on the train this would never have happened! THEY'RE NEVER GOING TO LET US GO. DO YOU UNDERSTAND THAT, YOU STUPID FUCKING FAILURE OF A MAN???'

Then she burst into a fit of sobs.

Tom felt all scrunched up inside. The sound of her crying was terrible, so harrowing. But there was nothing he could say that she seemed to take on board. He had been talking to her continuously since the fat man had left the room. Trying to calm her down, trying to boost her, to keep up their spirits.

Trying to do anything to distract himself from the searing agony in his bladder. From his raging thirst. And the pangs of hunger. And his fear.

He wondered if it was the vodka that was talking, making Kellie behave like this. Or the lack of it? Had she been on the edge, the way she had been for a few months after Jessica had been born, and this had pushed her over the cliff?

All that stuff with eBay – had that been some kind of a warning, or a cry for help that he had missed?

'YOU STUPID FUCKING FAILURE!' she screeched again.

Tom winced. *Failure*. Was that how she saw him? She was right. He'd failed in business; now he'd failed in the most important thing of all, protecting his family.

He clenched his eyes shut for a few moments and prayed to the God he hadn't spoken a word to in twenty-five years. Then he opened them again, but it made no difference; it was still totally black in here.

His legs were cramping from being bound together. He rolled over, but only did one complete loop before the chain around his ankle snagged tight and he cried out in pain as the manacle, or clamp, or whatever it was, cut into his leg.

Think, he said to himself. *Think!*

The wall and the floor immediately around him were smooth; he needed something jagged he could rub against to saw through the cords. But there was nothing, damned, damned, damned nothing.

'YOU HEAR ME, YOU STUPID FUCKING FAILURE!'

Tears welled in his eyes. *Oh, my darling Kellie, I love you so much. Don't do this to me.*

What did the fat creep want? Who the hell was he? How did you get through to someone like that? But deep down he knew who the man was, and why they were here.

Suddenly his fear deepened even further as his thoughts crystallized. He had dropped the kids off with Kellie's parents some while back, during the night; her mum was feisty enough, but her bedridden father was totally helpless, poor man. Was the fat man planning to seize the kids too? What if he or his thugs came when Kellie's mother was out?

In desperation Tom rolled over; the chain jerked tight. He pulled, ignoring the pain. Holding his breath, he pulled again, again, again.

But nothing gave.

He lay still for a while. Then he had an idea.

At that moment, some way in the distance, he saw the rectangle of light appear again: the door. Two figures came through, each with a torch. His pulse quickened; he felt a tightness in his throat. He tensed up, ready to fight, any way, any which way he could.

One figure was walking towards Kellie, the other towards himself. Kellie was silent. The next instant the beam, like quicksilver in his eyes, dazzled him. Then it swung away and lit a paper cup of water and a bread roll lying on the floor.

'Eat for you,' said a voice in broken English, a hard voice which sounded eastern European to his untrained ear.

'I need to urinate,' Tom said.

'Go on, piss in your pants like everyone else around here!' Kellie shouted out.

'You do no urinate!' the man replied.

'I have to go,' Tom implored. 'Please take me to the bathroom.'

The man was tall, lean, late twenties, dressed sharply in black, stern-faced with a short modern haircut. Tom could make out his features now. But, more importantly, he could see beyond him.

The nearest row of chemical drums.

'Eat,' the man said again, then walked away, joined by his companion. A few seconds later they had gone; the rectangle of light went out. Tom and Kellie were back in total darkness.

'Darling?' Tom said.

Silence.

'Darling, please listen to me.'

'Why didn't they bring me anything to drink?' she said.

'They brought water.'

'That is not what I fucking meant.'

How long had she been drinking? Tom wondered. How long had he not noticed?

'How am I supposed to drink with my arms tied to my side? Want to tell me that, Mr Smart Husband?'

Tom moved his head slowly towards where the water and the roll had been placed. His nose touched the side of the cup, and he cursed silently at the indignity of what he was being put through. Moving his lips gingerly over the rim, desperate not to spill any precious drop, he finally gripped the rim with his teeth, tilted the cup up, and drained it greedily.

Then, like some kind of blind nocturnal animal, he felt with his nose until he found the roll. He had no appetite, but forced himself to take a bite. He struggled to chew and swallow. Then he took one more bite, swallowed and spat the rest out.

'I think we should go home now,' Kellie announced. 'Do you think they'll give us goody bags?'

And for the first time in the last couple of days, Tom smiled.

Maybe she was calming down. 'I don't think much of their hospitality so far,' he said, trying to crack a joke back. But his words fell away into black silence.

The water and the food were already making him feel a

little better, giving him some strength. He decided to make his move.

Half rolling, half squirming, he eased his way slowly, painfully, across the floor, over to the left, in the direction he had memorized from the spill of the torch beam a few minutes ago.

Towards the line of chemical drums.

Then he panicked as the chain jerked tight on his ankle. *Please, just a little more, just give a little more.* He pulled hard, but the clamp bit in even harder, making him cry out in pain.

'Tom, are you OK? Darling?'

Thank God, she *was* calm now. 'Yes,' he hissed, suddenly concerned anyone might be listening in. 'I'm fine.'

Then his face touched something. *Please don't let it be the wall.*

It felt plastic, cold, round. It was a drum!

He tried to push his way up it. The drum wobbled. He slid down. Rolling onto his stomach, his legs tangled behind him, his ankle agony, he jerked himself up, then up again. Finally, taking a massive breath and exhaling and pushing himself at the same time with all he had, he succeeded. He got his chin over the rim.

And it felt beautifully, raggedly, sharp.

Slowly, inching back, keeping his chin clamped over it, he levered it back; it was heavy, much heavier than he had imagined, too heavy for him. Suddenly it toppled and fell to the floor with a loud, echoing boom.

'Tom?' Kellie cried out.

'It's OK.'

'What are you doing?'

'Nothing.'

Working as fast as he could, he moved up to the rim, felt

in the darkness where the cord strapping his arms to his sides was, and began to rub that against the rough edge.

After some minutes – almost as surprised that it had actually worked as relieved – he was able to move his arms away from his body. Just one tiny step, he knew, but he felt as if he had just climbed Everest. Relief surged through him. *He could do this!*

Now he swung his hands, still tied tightly together, through the darkness, feeling for the rim. He found it and began to rub the cord between his wrists furiously against the edge. Slowly, steadily, he could feel the strands giving and the binding loosening. And suddenly his hands were free. He shook off the last bit of slack cord from his wrist, pushed himself upright, stretching his arms and flexing his hands, trying to get the blood circulating in them once more.

'Are we going to die here, Tom?' Kelly whimpered.

'No, we are not.'

'Mum and Dad couldn't bring the children up. We've never thought about that, have we?'

'We're not going to die.'

'I love you so much, Tom.'

Her voice brought him close to tears again. There was so much tenderness, warmth, caring in it. 'I love you more than anything in the world, Kellie,' he said, leaning forward, feeling his way along the cords that bound his legs until he came to the knot.

It was tied incredibly tightly. But he worked on it relentlessly and after a short while it started to come loose. And suddenly his legs were free! Except for his shackled ankle. The thought was ever present in his mind that if the fat man came in now, there would be hell to pay. But it was a risk he had to take.

He knelt, gripped the rim of the drum, then stood up and, lifting as hard as he could, righted it. Then he felt along the top for the cap, and found it quickly, clasping his hands around it, moving them across it, trying to work out how it opened, for the first time in his life having some understanding of what it must be like to be blind.

There was a twisted wire and a paper seal over it. He worked his fingers underneath the wire and pulled. It cut into his flesh. Digging his hand in his pocket, he pulled out his handkerchief and wound it round his fingers, then tried again.

The wire snapped.

'Why are we here, Tom?' she asked plaintively. 'Who is that gross creep?'

'I don't know.'

'What did he mean, about us "looking good dead"?'

'He was just trying to scare us,' Tom replied, attempting to sound convincing, struggling to make the cap move, aware that his voice sounded considerably higher than usual, a vague, flimsy plan developing in his mind.

Slowly the cap began to turn. It took five, maybe six full turns before it came away in his hand. A vile, burning acrid reek instantly filled his nostrils. He lurched back, choking, dropping the cap and hearing it roll away in the darkness.

'TOM?' Kellie called out, alarmed.

He continued coughing, his lungs on fire. He was trying to think back to when he had done chemistry at school, a subject he had been crap at. There had been bottles of acid in the chemistry lab. Sulphuric and hydrochloric were the ones he could immediately remember. Would this stuff, whatever it was, eat through the chain attached to his ankle?

But how could he get it out of the drum in this

darkness? If the drum fell over and the stuff started pouring out, it could spread over the floor to Kellie. Or choke them.

Then his heart felt as if it had stopped. He saw the ray of light out of the corner of his eye. The rectangle in the distance. Someone was coming in.

79

Down on Level 4 of the Bartholomew Square car park a group of police officers was clustered around the black Volkswagen Golf. Outside, officers were blocking every entrance. There was not a soul anywhere else inside the entire building.

'I don't want the owner to know we've been in,' Grace said to the young PC from Traffic who was kneeling by the driver's door, holding a huge set of levers on a ring in one hand and what looked like a radio transmitter in the other.

'No worries. I'll be able to lock it again. He'll never know.'

Joe Tindall, in a white protective suit, stood beside Grace, chewing a stick of gum. He seemed in an even more grumpy mood than usual. 'Not content with ruining my weekend, Roy?' the senior SOCO said. 'Making sure you screw my week up right from the word go too, eh?'

There was a loud click and the Golf's door opened. Instantly its horn started blaring, a deafening, echoing *beep-beep-beep-beep-beep*.

The Traffic constable popped the bonnet open and ducked under it. Within seconds, the beeping stopped. He closed the bonnet. 'OK,' he said to Tindall and Grace. 'All yours.'

Grace, also in white protective suit and gloves, let Tindall go in first, and stood watching him. A quick check of his watch showed it had been twenty-five minutes since they had closed the car park. The scene outside the entrances was total chaos: police vehicles, ambulances, fire engines, dozens of stranded shoppers, business people, visitors. And the knock-on effect was that most of central Brighton's traffic was now gridlocked.

Grace was going to have a lot of egg on his face if nothing came of this.

He watched Tindall take print dustings in the most likely places first: the interior mirror, gear stick, horn pad, interior and exterior door handles. When he was done with those, Tindall picked a hair off the driver's headrest with tweezers and deposited it in an evidence bag. Then again using the tweezers, he removed one of several cigarette butts in the ashtray, and put that into a separate bag.

After a further five minutes he emerged from the car, looking marginally more cheerful than when he had arrived. 'Got some good prints, Roy. I'll get straight back and have the boys run them on NAFIS.'

NAFIS was the National Automated Fingerprint Information System.

'I'm coming up there myself,' Grace said. 'I'll be about ten minutes behind you.'

'I'll have a result waiting for you.'

'I appreciate it.'

'Actually, I don't give a fuck whether you appreciate it or not,' the SOCO said, staring hard at the Detective Superintendent.

Sometimes Grace found it hard to tell when Joe Tindall was being serious and when he was joking; the man had a peculiar sense of humour. He couldn't gauge it now.

'Good!' Grace said, trying to humour the man. 'I admire your detached professionalism.'

'Detached bollocks!' Tindall said. 'I do it because I'm

paid to do it. Being *appreciated* doesn't bang my drum.' He stepped out of his protective clothes, bagged them and headed off towards the exit staircase.

Grace and the Traffic constable exchanged a glance. 'He can be a tetchy bugger!'

'Cool glasses, though . . .' the constable said.

Grace checked the interior of the car, looking in the glove compartment, which contained nothing but an owner's manual, and in each of the door pockets, which were empty. He checked under the front seats, removed the cushion from the rear seat and looked under that. Nothing. There were absolutely no personal effects in the car at all; it felt more like a rental vehicle than a private one.

Then he checked the boot. It was spotless, containing just the toolkit, the spare wheel and a reflective warning triangle that he presumed came with the car. Finally, he crawled underneath; there was no mud, nothing to indicate anything out of the ordinary.

He hauled himself back to his feet, told the Traffic constable that he could lock it up and reset the alarm, and walked along to his car, anxious to get back to Sussex House. Hoping desperately the stroppy but brilliant Joe Tindall was going to produce a result with those prints.

And that the surveillance team did not lose the VW.

Bringing Brighton to a halt for no result was hardly going to improve Alison Vosper's opinion of him. Or his chances of avoiding relegation to Newcastle. Cassian Pewe or no Cassian Pewe.

Then, suddenly, he thought of Cleo. It was twelve twenty. She hadn't returned his call.

80

Tom threw himself down onto the floor and frantically scrabbled across the hard stone surface with his hands, trying to find the cords. A torch beam stabbed the darkness; it briefly fell on Kellie, then on his face, then jigged against the wall, lighting up a row of chemical drums.

Including the one with its lid removed.

Shit, shit, shit, shit, shit.

He lay on his side, very still, holding-his-breath still, hands rigidly to his side, legs clamped together, dripping perspiration. He heard the *clack, clack, clack* of footsteps approaching. His heart was thudding, the roar in his ears of his blood coursing through his veins. The bitter bile of terror rose in his throat.

This was going to be the moment. As soon as he was discovered. Christ, maybe he had been stupid all over again? Stupid to have left the house, stupid to have let them into his car. And now, stupid, unbelievably stupid to have tried to escape.

Kellie was right, what she had said earlier. Calling him a failure.

For an instant he shut his eyes, praying, fighting down vomit. Was this how it was going to finish? All the dreams? Never seeing the children again? Never—

There was a loud clatter. He heard something rolling across the floor. Whatever it was, it hit him on the side of the head. A hard object, but light.

He turned, remembering to stay in his trussed-up position. The beam shone directly into his eyes for a moment, blinding him. Then he heard the same broken-English voice he'd heard a short while ago.

'For urinate. No shit.'

The beam moved away from his face and onto an object lying on its side just a few feet away. It was an orange plastic bucket.

The footsteps receded. Tom turned to watch; he saw the flashlight beam swinging across the floor until the man reached the rectangle of light in the distance. He thought, fleetingly, that it did not seem to have occurred to the man how he was going to use the bucket with his hands trussed to his sides.

He heard the slam of a heavy-sounding metal door.

And then, once again, there was total darkness.

81

'Are you out of your fucking mind?' Carl Venner shouted, his face puce like his shirt with its buttons straining against his gut. Veins bulged at his temples. The scratch the young girl had made during his visitor's last call was still very visible. 'What do you think you are doing, coming here? I told you never, ever, *ever* to come here unless you are told. What part of *don't ever, ever come here unless you are told* do you not fucking understand, John?'

Andy Gidney stared down at the cheap beige carpet, his eyes fixed on one tuft; he was trying to calculate how many strands of fibre might be in the tuft.

Venner brought his index finger to his mouth and began to tear at the skin around the nail. A cigar smouldered in the ashtray on his metal desk on the top floor of the warehouse. 'And anyhow, just where have you been? I've been trying to call you for the past hour.'

'Ummm, I've been on my way here.'

'So why didn't you answer your fucking phone?'

'Because you told me never to bring it here.'

To the Weatherman's quiet satisfaction, that temporarily silenced Venner, who continued working on his finger for some moments, examined it, then worked on it some more. 'We have a major disaster on our hands, that's why I was calling you.'

Actually you have two, the Weatherman thought. *One you don't know about – yet.* Not that he cared. Carl Venner could have a thousand disasters and he wouldn't care. He continued counting the fibres.

Venner picked up his cigar, stabbed it between his lips, and puffed it back into life, blowing the smoke out of the corner of his mouth. 'A fucking disaster, OK?'

'Cromarty, Forth, south-west veering north four or five, occasionally six in North Utsire,' he informed Venner, still staring at the floor. 'Rain at times. Moderate or good.'

'What the fuck's with this weather forecast crap?'

'Ummm, actually – ummm – it's the shipping forecast.'

Venner shook his head. 'Jesus. One of our associates is in a coma and you're giving me the goddamn *shipping forecast*?'

'Umm, yes. Umm, that's right.'

Venner stared at him. This fuckwit was really beyond him. 'John, the disaster is that our associate had a laptop with him that he was using to upload our latest offering to our customers. The police have seized it. We need that laptop back.'

'I have it,' Gidney said. 'And the clone the High Tech Crime Unit made of the hard disk.'

Venner looked astonished. 'You have it?'

'Umm. Yes. Sort of exactly.'

'You have the laptop back?'

The Weatherman nodded.

The fat man's whole demeanour changed. He heaved himself up and shook the surprised Gidney by the hand. 'You are one smart motherfucker!' Then he sat back down, as if exhausted by the effort, clamped his cigar back between his lips and held out his hand, greedily, like a fat schoolboy wanting more sweets. 'So, gimme! You have it in your rucksack?'

'Umm, no, that's my sandwich.'

One of the two silent Russians entered the room; he was dressed as usual in a black suit over a black T-shirt. He stood a few feet behind Venner, silent and unsmiling.

The Weatherman stared back down at the tuft of carpet, ignoring the outstretched hand, trying to pluck up the courage to say what he had come here to say. He thought about Q in *Star Trek* again, and muttered the words silently to himself. *If you can't take a little bloody nose, maybe you ought to go back home and crawl under your bed. It's not safe out here . . . it's not for the timid.*

The Man Who Was Not Timid took a deep breath and, stammering, his face reddening, he blurted, 'I don't actually have them with me.'

Venner's face clouded over. 'Where do you *actually* have them?'

Gidney sensed an almost silent footfall behind him. He detected the faintest shadow on the carpet. Venner bringing in his team, the Russian in front, the Albanian behind, to intimidate him. But today he was The Man Who Was Not Timid.

He would stand his ground.

He was shaking, his face burning, rivers of perspiration rolling down inside his white shirt. But he was standing his ground. 'I have them in a safe place.'

'Exactly how safe?' Venner enquired coldly.

'Very.'

'Good. Sensible.'

'If you want them back, you have to pay me what you promised. And-and-and I,' he was blurting now, gabbling, 'I-don't-want-to-do-thisanymore.'

Then he stared at the carpet, gulping down air.

'Is that right, John?' Venner said calmly. 'You don't want to work in our team any more?'

'Ummm, no.'

'I'm really hurt! I figured we all got along so well! You know, John, I thought you and I were becoming real good buddies. I'm really hurt. Of course, you want to leave, you want your money, that's absolutely fine.'

The Weatherman was silent; he had not been expecting this reaction. He had expected Venner to explode.

'So exactly where is this very safe place you have the laptop and the cloned disk?'

Smiling proudly, Gidney looked up. 'You would never believe it. No one will look there; no one will find them in a thousand years!'

'That so?'

The Weatherman nodded excitedly.

'Not even the police?'

'Absolutely not!'

Venner beamed happily at the Weatherman, then swung his left hand sharply through the air.

The movement puzzled the Weatherman. It appeared to be some coded signal. But he did not have long to fret about it.

'Watch the birdie!' Venner said.

The Weatherman felt increasingly confused. The Russian standing beside Venner was holding up a small video camera.

The Albanian, standing behind him, took two swift steps forward and, with one chop of the side of his hand, snapped the Weatherman's neck and spinal cord in two.

82

The Fingerprint Department occupied one of the largest floor spaces in Sussex House. On the ground floor, a short walk along from the High Tech Crime Unit, it was a hive of quiet activity, and every time Grace went there, he noticed just the very faintest aroma of ink in the air.

Derry Blane, one of the senior fingerprint officers, sat at a workstation more or less in the middle of the labyrinth of desks and machinery. On his computer screen was the best print Joe Tindall had lifted from the Volkswagen, off the interior mirror. Grace and Tindall stood behind him, looking down over his shoulder at the screen.

Blane, a balding, bespectacled man, had avuncular looks and a quiet, learned manner which inspired confidence. He clicked the keyboard and a full set of ten prints appeared. He clicked again and Grace's heart skipped a beat. There on the screen was a police custody photograph of his man. And his name. The driver of the Golf. Janie Stretton's date at the Karma Bar.

'We've got a match,' Derry Blane said. 'I've run him through NAFIS, and he was printed just over a year ago, after a brawl at the Escape nightclub in Brighton. He was released with a caution. His name is Mik Luvic. He's an Albanian, of no fixed abode.'

'What else do you have on him?' Grace asked.

'Here's the thing.' Blane tapped his keyboard again. 'There's a PNC marker on him as someone to watch – at the request of Interpol.'

Grace's excitement increased. PNC was the Police National Crime database.

'So I ran an international search on his full set – we need a full set to do that – and it came up with a link to this charmer.'

Blane tapped another couple of keys and, after a moment, the head and torso of a grossly fat man appeared on the screen. He had a small head in comparison to the bulk of his body, with gelled silver hair pulled back into a tiny pigtail.

'His name is Carl Venner. Also goes under the name of Jonas Smith. He has an interesting history,' Blane continued. 'Venner was in the US military. He started out as a chopper pilot in Vietnam. Got a purple heart for being wounded in combat, then stopped flying for some health reason and became a radio operator. He later got promoted to a high position in military communications out there. After that he was involved in a scandal. You may remember it – a war cameraman and a couple of photographers were indicted on charges of filming the torture and execution of Vietcong, and then flogging the footage.'

'Snuff pictures?' Grace asked.

'Exactly. But Venner wormed his way out of the charges. He stayed with the US military and was moved to an intelligence posting in Germany. Then when Bosnia started up he was posted there. The same thing happened as in Vietnam. Eventually he was court-martialled for filming the execution of prisoners and selling the films into the international snuff movie market.'

'For real?' Grace asked.

'Yes, absolutely. This guy is lower than lowlife. He's your absolute bottom feeder. A smart lawyer got him off the charges, but enough mud stuck and he was slung out of the military. Next thing, his name crops up in an international child pornography ring based in Atlanta. Except it's not just men having sex with children; it's footage of kids being murdered. Mostly Asian, some Indian, some white too.'

'You really mix with the best, don't you, Roy?' Tindall said with a smile, his humour back.

'That's me all over. You should come to one of my dinner parties.'

'I keep waiting for the invite.'

'So what happened to him?' Grace asked, turning back to Blane.

'Seems he did a runner. Fell off the FBI's radar. Then . . . three years ago he popped up in Turkey. Then Athens. Then Paris. A cosy little snuff movie ring got busted there. The French police raided an apartment in the Sixteenth Arrondissement of Paris. They seized a load of equipment and a bunch of people who said Venner was the ringleader. He hasn't been seen since.'

'What's the link with Luvic?'

'Interpol have a desk man in London who knows about that. I have his number. His name's Detective Sergeant Barry Farrier.'

'Thanks, Derry, you've done a great job. And incredibly quick!' Because of the traffic, it had taken Grace twenty minutes longer to get back to headquarters than he had planned. But Joe Tindall must have had the same problem. Blane couldn't have had the prints more than fifteen minutes.

Back upstairs, in his private office opposite MIR One, Grace checked first with the surveillance team watching the Golf. The driver had not yet appeared. Then he was about to dial Detective Sergeant Barry Farrier when his mobile rang. As he answered he recognized Harry Frame's high-pitched, effusive voice.

'You have something?' Grace asked the clairvoyant.

'Well, I don't know if it means anything to you or not; I'm getting a watch.'

'A watch?' Grace said. 'Like a wristwatch?'

'Exactly!' Frame's enthusiasm mounted. 'A wristwatch! There is something very significant. A wristwatch will lead you to something very satisfying to do with a case you are working on. This case, I think.'

'Can you elaborate?' Grace asked, puzzled.

'No, I . . . No, that's all. As I said, I don't know if it means anything.'

'Any particular make?'

'No. Expensive, I think.'

'Expensive?'

'Yes.'

'A man's or a woman's?'

'It's a man's watch. I think there might be more than one.'

Grace shook his head, thinking hard. It really meant absolutely nothing at this moment. 'OK,' he said. 'Thank you, Harry. Let me know if you get anything else.'

'Oh, I will, don't you worry!'

Grace ended the call and immediately dialled the Interpol number in London. He had a two-minute wait for Farrier to finish a call, listening to 'Greensleeves' on what seemed a permanent loop, then heard a sharp Cockney accent.

'DS Farrier, can I help you?'

Grace introduced himself. Immediately, Farrier became excited.

'I've got detectives in Greece, Turkey, Switzerland and Paris who would like to have a chat with Mr Luvic.'

'I know where his car is,' Grace said. 'What do you have on Carl Venner?'

'Zilch. Hasn't been sighted in three years. And there's enough of him to see; he's a fat bastard.'

There was a knock on the door, and Norman Potting came in, clutching a sheet of paper. Grace signalled that he was busy. Potting hovered by the door.

'I'd be very interested in anything you can come up with on Venner,' Barry Farrier said. 'Got markers on him as long as my right arm. Right across Europe.'

'Could he be in England?'

'If Luvic is, there's a chance.'

'Tell me more about Luvic?'

'Albanian. Thirty-two. Smart boy. Studied technology at uni there, as well as becoming a kick-boxing champion and a bare-knuckle fighter. Typical of his generation – came out of uni, no jobs. Got involved with a bunch of students designing computer viruses for fun, probably out of boredom. Then he hitched up with another lot, blackmailing large companies.'

'Blackmailing?'

'Big business. Take a big sporting event here, like the Derby. The major bookies get threatened with attack by computer viruses, just a few days before, which will shut down their systems for twenty-four hours on Derby Day. Unless they pay up. So they pay up; it's the cheaper option.'

'I've heard of this happening,' Grace said.

'Yeah, it's big time. Anyhow, then somehow Luvic got hooked up with Venner. Probably recruited by him. They were involved in the French snuff ring together, for sure.

Both of 'em vanished at the same time. I can email you all the files.'

'Please.'

'Yeah, no worries. Right away. Tell you one thing. I seen some of the pictures. I'd like to get my hands on Venner and Luvic in an alleyway on a dark night. Just five minutes with them, I'd like.'

'I know how you feel. Tell me something, does a scarab beetle mean anything to you – in connection with these two?'

'Scarab? Scarab beetle?'

'Yup.'

After some moments' silence, Barry Farrier said, 'Their business in France – there was an insect, a scorpion, always present somewhere in the photos and films.'

'Alive or dead?'

'Dead. Why are you asking, can I enquire?'

'Sounds like he's well into his entomology,' Grace said. 'If it's the same man, he's now using scarabs – dung beetles.'

'Very fitting.'

Grace thanked him, agreed to keep him fully in the loop and hung up. Norman Potting immediately strode over to his desk and laid the sheet of paper he was holding down in front of him.

'Sulphuric acid, Roy. I've got what I think is a pretty comprehensive list of all the suppliers in the UK. There are five down in the south, two of them in our patch – one in Newhaven and one in Portslade.'

Grace, still absorbing the information he had been given by Barry Farrier, picked up the list and quickly scanned through the names and addresses. He clocked the two local ones.

Suddenly, the door burst open and Glenn Branson came in, his face lit up with excitement. 'I've got a result!' he said, his face inches from his SIO's.

'Tell me?'

Branson slapped the photograph of the VW Golf driver down triumphantly on the desk. 'I've just had a phone call from a taxi driver mate of mine.'

Frivolously, and for no real reason, Grace asked, 'Not the one who sneaked on me and Cleo to you?'

'The very same.' Branson grinned, then continued, totally elated, 'I circulated this photograph to all my contacts. He just belled me. He just picked up a fare who he says is a dead ringer for this fellow – in central Brighton twenty minutes ago. He's convinced it's this man. Dropped him off at a warehouse in Portslade. At this address.' He gave a handwritten scrap of notepaper to his boss.

Grace read it. Then he looked again at the list Potting had just given him. At the distributor of sulphuric acid based in Portslade.

It was the same address.

83

Tom remembered something. He did not have his mobile phone, but he had something else. He had felt the hard lump – he had been lying on it some of the time. Why the hell hadn't he thought of it before? he wondered.

He dug his hand into his trouser pocket and extricated his Palm Tungsten PDA. He pressed one of the four buttons on the bottom. Instantly the display lit up. The machine emitted a glow that, at this moment, suddenly felt as good as a thousand torches.

He could see!

'What's that?' Kellie called out.

'My Palm!' He could see her, actually see her face!

'How did – you – you can move?' she hissed.

'My hands.'

The beam did not have a long throw, it was wide and short, but for the first time he could begin to orient himself. They were in a huge store, with a ceiling maybe twenty feet high, stacked all the way round with racks of chemical drums; there were hundreds of them, if not thousands. There was a concrete floor, no windows, and the beam did not get as far as the door. From the temperature and the total absence of light, he guessed they were underground.

There must be a door big enough to get a forklift through for these drums, he thought. And almost certainly a lift.

He examined the shackle around his ankle. It looked like one of those police manacles for criminals he had seen in the movies: a wide metal clamp, locked, with a chain running off it secured to the wall by a metal hoop which was not going anywhere. Kellie was chained to another hoop some distance away. Her chain was fully extended. He stood up and moved towards her, but when his chain went tight there was still a gap of about ten feet between them.

'You can't dial with that thing, can you?' she asked.

'No.'

'What about email?'

'I could if I had my phone.'

He urinated into the orange bucket which had arrived a few minutes earlier with a relief that was, for a few fleeting moments, close to bliss.

'Don't forget to pull the chain,' Kellie said.

He grinned, suddenly loving her courage. If you could still smile, keep your spirits up – that was how people survived ordeals. 'I won't,' he said. 'And I'll put the lid back down.'

He took the few paces the chain allowed him over to the drum he had opened, then shone the light on its side, looking for the label he had felt earlier in the darkness. He found it.

It was white, with a yellow and black HAZARDOUS SUBSTANCE! warning label next to it. On the white part was written: H_2SO_4. CONCENTRATE. 25 LTRS.

Tom again thought back as hard as he could to his schoolboy chemistry lessons. Would this stuff eat through metal? How quickly?

There was just one way to find out.

He put the Palm down on the floor and picked up the bucket. As he did so, the display went out. For an instant his heart sank as he feared the battery had died, then he realized it was on an automatic power-down after two minutes. Quickly, he reset it to stay on permanently. Then he picked up the bucket and hurled its contents away from himself and Kellie, as far as he could.

He turned his attention to the drum. He had removed the cap earlier, and there was a fierce acrid smell as he neared it. He took a deep breath and, holding the drum as firmly as he could, very aware and scared of the consequences of knocking it over, tilted it so that some poured from the top and splashed on the floor beside the bucket.

'Shit.'

Steam curled up from the floor. The acid was reacting with something, which was a good sign.

'What are you doing?'

'Just trying an experiment.'

'What? What are you trying?' Kellie asked, her voice pitifully tight.

From his poor memory of chemistry some acids would not dissolve both plastic and metal. The fact that these drums were plastic told him they should not dissolve the bucket.

The burning acrid reek was getting worse; he could feel it right down his throat. He stepped back, took a deep breath, then eased the drum back a few inches and tried again. This time the acid rattled into the bucket. He kept going until it was just under half full, set the drum back down, upright, then picked up the Palm, examining the bucket carefully to make sure no acid was on the handle nor anywhere else he would touch.

He poured a small amount of the acid onto a couple of links of the chain.

Nothing happened. Wisps of vile-smelling steam rose from the floor on which the two links lay, and immediately around them, but there was no apparent reaction with the steel at all.

He stared down in agonized frustration, and swore. He might just as well have poured water onto them.

84

Carl Venner waddled up and down his office, a freshly lit cigar clamped in his mouth, wringing his hands, directing his anger alternately at Luvic, who was chewing gum and smoking a cigarette at the same time, and the Russian. 'Boys, this is not a good situation. It is just *so* not good.'

He raised his hand to his mouth, removed his cigar, then began biting the skin on the end of his index finger again. Tearing at it.

The Russian, who rarely spoke, said, 'We need get Yuri out of hospital before he wake.'

'Either get him out or silence him,' Venner said.

'I don't kill my brother,' he said darkly.

'You work for me, Roman; you do what I fucking tell you.'

'Then I no work for you.'

Venner strutted up to him. 'Listen, you piece of shit. You'd be fucking driving a tractor in the Ukraine if it wasn't for me, so don't ever threaten to quit, because I just might accept your resignation, and then what the fuck do you do?'

The Russian looked sullen but said nothing.

Luvic mimed a chop across his own neck with his hand. 'I fix.'

The Russian walked across to the Albanian and planted himself squarely in front of him; he stood a good head taller than the former bare-knuckle fighter. 'You kill my brother,' he said, 'I kill you.'

The Albanian stared mockingly back at the Russian, still chewing his gum. He brought his cigarette to his mouth twice in rapid succession, taking two quick drags, inhaling sharply and blowing the smoke out, then said, 'I do what Mr Smith say to me to do. I obey Mr Smith.'

'We have an even more urgent problem,' Venner said. 'That fuckwit creep John Frost – Gidney – with his god-damn weather reports, well there's one fucking report he got wrong!'

The two men looked at him quizzically.

'Acid rain! Bad-hair day for him today.'

The Russian grinned; the Albanian, who had no sense of humour, did not get it. He had put the Weatherman's body in the sulphuric acid tank, as was normal; in a couple of days he would move the bones to the hydrochloric tank. After that there would be no trace of him left.

'Our problem,' Venner went on, 'is we don't know what he did, what he said to anyone. And he lied about his phone, right?'

The Albanian nodded his confirmation. 'It was in his car, outside, switched on.'

'We know what that means, right?' Venner said.

Both his employees nodded.

'The police can get his phone company to plot his route across Brighton and Hove – exact times and places. Gentlemen, we need to bail, I'm afraid. We need to get out of here and go back to base in Albania until things calm down.'

'I prefer stay here,' the Russian said.

Venner tapped his chest. 'I'm fifty-nine. You think I want to spend any part of what's left of my life in that shit-hole country, if I don't have to? It's even got the world's ugliest women. We're here in this country because we like it here. But you guys have fucked up.'

'How?' the Russian said, looking angry now.

'How?' Venner said, as if astonished by the question. 'Mik gets followed from somewhere in Kemp Town to a car park in the centre of Brighton—'

Interrupting him, the Albanian said, 'Yes, but I lose him in the car park.'

'Yes – and your goddamn Golf and all.'

'I will get that back.'

Ignoring him, Venner turned his rage back to the Russian. 'Your idiot brother attracts the attention of the police, then gets in an automobile wreck and lets them get their hands on his laptop with our film of D'Eath on it, and you don't think that's a fuck-up?'

The Russian was silent.

'Here's what we do,' Venner said, his tone suddenly more conciliatory. 'We shoot the film of Mr and Mrs Bryce right now, and get rid of them. Then we're out of here. We'll go to Paris this afternoon. Then on from there. OK?'

Two silent, reluctant nods.

Then the Albanian said, 'Where we do the film?'

'Here,' Venner said. 'In this room. I have some very creative ideas. Mr Bryce has put us through a lot of grief; I want to hurt him. And I'd like to see him watch all the things we are going to do with Mrs Bryce first.'

He looked at the Russian. 'Roman, go bring them up here. Just untie their legs and gag them with gaffer tape – I always like tearing that stuff off.'

And suddenly, his mood buoyed by the thought of some very inventive things he was going to do to the Bryces, Carl Venner began to hum.

85

'Tom!'

The sudden, hushed urgency in Kellie's voice made Tom look up. *Shit!* The rectangle of light had appeared again at the far end of the room. Someone was entering, a tall, thin man in black. The eastern European.

Tom dived to the floor, on top of the Palm to smother the light. Quickly, groping with his hands, he found the PDA, located the power button and pressed it in hard to switch it off. Had the man come to empty the bucket? Tom wondered, a little irrationally. He pulled his arms tight to his sides and squeezed his legs together, faking the original position he had been trussed up in as best he could. He lay still, watching the torch beam steadily jig across the floor towards them.

Then it was right in his face.

'Mr Bryce, I take you upstairs now. We make you and Mrs Bryce movie stars!'

Tom, quaking with terror, was thinking that any second now the man was going to see that his cords had been removed. He *must* see that, unless he was blind!

'What do you mean, "movie stars"?' Kellie said, her voice cracking with fear.

The man swung the beam onto her face. 'We enough talk! Maybe you like quick fuck? Mr Bryce, you like watch me sex your wife for you?'

Tom's terror suddenly switched to fury. 'Touch her and I'll kill you,' he said.

The man rounded on him and shouted imperiously, 'ENOUGH TALK I SAY!' He stabbed the beam of the torch right into Tom's face. 'YOU QUIET. YOU ARE NOT THREAT ME!'

Then the man knelt down. Tom heard the sound of tape ripping and realized what was coming next. Blinking hard, he could see the man was leaning over him. He could smell cologne on him, a sharp, masculine tang.

Tom stiffened.

He knew he had just one shot at this, that was all. He hadn't thought it through, he just had to do it.

The man was holding a wide strip of gaffer tape between his hands. 'You close mouth,' he said.

'Can I just blow my nose?' Tom asked.

'No blow!'

'I'm going to sneeze!'

And in that moment he detected the hesitation, just the briefest wavering by the man. It was enough.

He sprang sideways, rolling over once, grabbing the bucket with both hands and lifting it, then turned and found the torch beam straight in his face. Kellie was safely to the left, well out of range. With all his strength he hurled the contents of the bucket straight at the flashlight beam.

He felt a few sharp pains on his hands like stings, droplets of the acid, but barely registered them as his ears filled with a terrible, piercing scream of agony.

The torch fell to the floor. Tom could just see the man staggering back clutching at his face. Had to get him! He had to grab him before he got out of reach!

Had to.

Tom lunged, launching himself forward in a full rugby tackle, aware there must be some acid on the floor but beyond caring. This was his only chance. Somehow, his arms almost leaving their sockets, he just managed to grab the man's right ankle before the chain snapped tight against his own, jolting him to a halt. Then, with a strength he did not even know he had, he yanked the ankle back towards him.

The man fell back across him, writhing, screaming, howling pitifully, clawing at his face with his hands. Kellie was screaming also.

'Tom! Tom! Tom!'

'HELP!' the Russian cried. 'HELP, YOU HELP, YOU HELP, PLEASE HELP!' Then he just started bellowing in agony, clawing at his face, at the same time writhing, trying to wriggle away from Tom.

The man had come to get them, which, Tom realized, meant he must have the keys to the shackles. He seized the torch and cracked it down with all his force on the back of the man's head. There was a tinkle of glass and the light went out. The man was silent, motionless, and for an instant the only sound in the room was the ghastly hissing coming from the man's head, accompanied by a new smell, a vile stench of burning flesh and hair. Tom retched; the acid seeming to fill the air with an invisible caustic haze. He could hear Kellie coughing too.

He found the Palm, switched it on and rummaged in the man's jacket pockets. Almost immediately he found a small chain with just two keys on it, and pulled it out. He stood up, shaking from shock and fear, not knowing if someone else was about to appear at any second, knelt and using the light of the Palm found the keyhole. But his hand was shaking so much he could not get it in.

Jesus, come on, please!

Finally it slipped in. But it would not turn. It must be the other one, he realized. Somehow he got the second one in straight away; turned it. The lock sprang open, and seconds later he was limping across to Kellie. His hands were really stinging now, but he had no time to think about that.

Crouching beside her, he kissed her and whispered, 'I love you.'

She was staring at him, wide-eyed, near motionless with shock. He unlocked her ankle shackle, then started working on the tight knot on the cord binding her legs. His hands were shaking again; the knot was so tight, so damned tight. It wasn't moving. He tried again. Then again. 'Are you OK, my darling?'

She said nothing.

'Darling?'

Nothing.

Then, in a tone that sent a shiver rippling beneath every inch of his skin, she said quietly, 'Tom, someone's coming into the room.'

He looked up. Straight into a torch beam coming from the doorway. Then he heard the chiding voice of the obese American.

'You are one silly boy, Mr Bryce. Very foolish indeed.'

The beam swung away from Tom's face, around the room. In seconds it would find the Russian on the floor. Tom, his nerves jangling, made a snap decision; he had no idea what the outcome would be, but it could not be any worse than waiting here, crouched down, for the American to come over.

He sprang up and ran at the doorway, aiming straight for the man in the puce shirt standing in it. He just ran, head down, screaming at the top of his voice, 'YOUUUUU HIDEOUS BASSTAAAARRRRD!'

He vaguely took in that the man was trying to pull

something from his pocket. Something black, metallic. A gun.

Then, running flat out, he struck the American full in the stomach with his head. It felt like hitting a massive cushion. He heard a winded gasp, felt a sharp jarring pain in his own neck, and a moment of blackness. The American tumbled backwards, and Tom fell with him, hitting the floor with his head between the man's legs.

Then a hand grabbed his neck from behind, a hand that felt cold and hard, more like a metal pincer than human flesh. It released his neck and a split second later grabbed his hair, jerking his head painfully up, then pulling him right over onto his back, thudding the back of his head down on the floor and holding it pinioned there.

Tom looked straight up into the stubby barrel of a handgun, and the eyes of ice behind it.

The man was stocky and muscular, with gelled spikes of short, fair hair and heavily tattooed arms. He was wearing a white singlet, with a gold medallion on a chain which was almost touching Tom's face, and he smelled of sweat. As he stared down expressionlessly, he was chewing gum, mashing it with small, intensely white incisors that reminded Tom of a piranha fish.

The American was staggering to his feet.

'You want I kill him?'

'No,' the American gasped, puffing and wheezing. 'Oh no. We're not going to make it that easy—'

Suddenly Tom heard a commotion a short distance away. A male voice shouted, 'POLICE! DROP YOUR GUN!'

Tom felt his hair released. He saw his assailant turn in shock, then without any hesitation raise his gun and fire several shots in rapid succession. The noise was deafening; Tom's ears went numb for a moment and his nostrils filled with the reek of cordite. Then his assailant, and the American, vanished.

An instant later he heard a different voice, English, cry out, 'I've been hit. Jesus, oh Jesus Christ, I've been shot!'

86

Grace, emerging from the large elevator, pushed past a partly open door labelled with a large yellow and black warning sign: PROTECTIVE CLOTHING MUST BE WORN BEYOND THIS POINT. Glenn Branson, first out of the elevator, rounded a corner head of him, and Grace heard him shout, 'POLICE! DROP YOUR GUN!'

Moments later he heard five shots in rapid succession. Then Glenn crying out.

Turning the corner he saw his colleague lying on the ground, clutching his stomach, blood all over his hands, his eyes rolling. Grace shouted into his radio, 'This is DS Grace. We have a man down! We need an ambulance! Send the firearms unit straight in. And all other units.'

He stopped, torn for an instant between staying with his colleague and wanting to catch whoever had done this. Waiting outside the building he had two vans of uniformed officers, an entry team from the Police Operations Department, a public order team armed with shields and batons, and a firearms team.

He turned to Nick Nicholl and Norman Potting, who were right behind him. 'Norman!' he yelled. 'Stay with Glenn!' Then he ran on. Ahead of him he saw a heavy metal door marked EMERGENCY EXIT ONLY swinging shut. He dived through it, then leapt up a stone staircase, two steps at a time, hearing Nicholl pounding up right behind him. He rounded a corner. Then another.

Round the next he caught sight of the man in singlet

and jeans with short, spiky hair who Derry Blane in the Fingerprint Department had identified as Mik Luvic. 'POLICE. STOP!' Grace shouted.

The man stopped, turned, pointed what looked like a gun at him. Grace, flattening himself against the wall and holding Nick Nicholl back with his arm, saw a muzzle flash, heard a *zing* then felt shards of cement dust strike his face. The man disappeared.

Grace waited for several seconds, then ran on up the steps, totally oblivious to danger, just angry – determined to get the bastard, to get him and tear him apart with his bare hands. He rounded another corner and stopped. No sign of Luvic. Up another flight, his heart pounding, round another corner. He paused again, inching forward cautiously. Still no sign.

They had to be near the top.

Up more steps and another corner. More steps. Another corner. Then a metal door ahead of them with a big red EXIT sign, swinging shut. Grace raced, panting, up to it, then turned to Nicholl. 'Careful.'

The young DC nodded.

They heard the roar of an engine, the clack of rotors. The helicopter he had seen on the roof, Grace realized.

He pushed the door open. A hugely fat, pigtailed man, who he recognized instantly from the photograph Derry Blane had produced as Carl Venner, was in the pilot's seat of the black helicopter. It was a small chopper, a four-seater Robinson. Luvic was untying a mooring rope attached to one of the helicopter's skids from a metal stanchion.

Bursting through the door, Grace yelled, 'STOP. POLICE!'

The Albanian raised his gun. Grace dived to the ground

as he saw the muzzle flash. A strong wind was blowing, worsened by the downdraught of the accelerating rotor blades. Sheltering from the wind and the Albanian's gun behind the structure next to him, the top of the lift housing, he presumed, Grace heard a *crack* close to his ear.

Seven shots, he had counted. How many in the magazine?

The mooring rope came free. Luvic ran round to the other side of the helicopter. Grace turned to Nicholl and yelled, 'Stay back!'

Then he began crawling forward on his stomach, looking around for something he could use as a weapon. A short distance to his right he clocked several bags of cement and a pile of bricks. Spiky Hair was working on the second rope. Grace got to his knees and launched himself at him.

Luvic raised his gun. Grace threw himself sideways just as he saw the muzzle flash, wishing to hell he'd had the sense to put on a flak jacket. An instant later he heard the crack of the pistol. The man pulled the trigger again.

This time nothing happened.

Grace went straight for him. The next thing he knew the Albanian's feet were flying at him, catching him full on under his chin. Grace was catapulted onto his back on the pitch surface of the roof, winded and stunned.

He heard the engine roar rise. He rolled over, blinking, still a little dazed, saw rooftops, the single tall chimney stack of what had once been Shoreham power station in the distance. Felt the wind increasing. Luvic was on board now. The helicopter's skids were off the roof.

In desperation he threw himself at the pile of bricks. Then he saw a length of scaffold pole lying beside them. He grabbed it and hurled it in a swirling arc, with all his strength, at the tail rotor.

For an instant, it sailed through the air in what seemed like slow motion. He thought he had thrown it wide. But, to his amazement, it was a bull's-eye, right in the middle of the rotor.

There was a grinding metallic sound and a shower of sparks. The helicopter lurched sideways.

Then he thought he had failed after all, as it rose sharply several feet in the air, before suddenly beginning to rotate on its own axis. And Grace saw that the entire tail rotor had gone.

The helicopter spun once, twice, then a giddying third time. It veered straight towards him, engine screaming, and he had to flatten himself on the roof to avoid being hit by the skids. The wind threatened to rip his jacket from his back and the hair from his head. Grace heard a huge bang and the next moment was showered with bits of metal and pieces of masonry, as the helicopter struck the side of the lift housing. Like some massive beetle crazed by fly spray, it skewed away, almost sideways, part of one of its main rotor blades clattering down inches from Grace, who rolled sideways to get out of its path.

He caught a glimpse of Venner in his puce shirt at the controls, saw the fear in his face as he struggled, saw the frozen white shock in the face of Luvic.

The helicopter tumbled over onto its side and did a complete flip, followed by another, tumbling towards the edge of the roof, reminding Grace of one of those cheap toys Brighton street vendors sold which were weighted and rolled over and over, propelled by their own momentum.

And suddenly there was a stench of aviation fuel in the air.

The stricken machine crashed into the lift housing for a second time, crabbed round, still under power, until the cockpit was hanging over the edge of the roof and the helicopter was prevented from going completely over only by its tail wedged against the base of the structure.

The engine stopped.

Grace scrambled to his feet and ran across.

The machine was see-sawing. Teetering on the brink. Luvic was unconscious, lying upside down on the glass bubble of the cockpit roof. Venner was struggling, upside down also, suspended by his harness. At any moment the helicopter was going to fall.

'Help me!' the pigtailed man implored, thrusting a hand out of the open, swinging door. 'Please, for God's sake, help me, man!'

Grace, who was not good with heights, knelt, staring at the car park a long way below, the wind threatening to blow him over the edge. He grabbed the man's wrist, which was greasy and thick as a ham.

The helicopter lurched. The stink of fuel was horrendous. Grace felt something bite into his hand. It was the man's wristwatch. He gripped the pudgy flesh just above it and met the man's tiny, terrified eyes, staring into his own. Imploring him.

'Help me! Get me out!' His medallion was hanging above his head.

The helicopter lurched again. Grace was pulled forward. Another few inches and he would fall over the edge. He realized what the man had to do. 'Your seat belt! Undo your seat harness!'

The man was beyond thinking in his panic. 'HELP ME!' he screeched.

'UNDO YOUR FUCKING HARNESS!' Grace screamed back.

There was a grinding sound. The helicopter lurched further. It was going. Only seconds left, Grace reckoned. 'UNDO YOUR BELT – YOUR HARNESS!'

Suddenly he felt his arm almost wrenched out of its socket. Grace clung on for dear life. But it was no good. Still he clung. Clung.

Clung.

Saw those tiny, desperate eyes once more.

Then Nick Nicholl was beside him, reaching down into the helicopter. Grace heard a faint click. Then, as if in a dream, the helicopter was dropping upside down, away from him. Like a huge toy. Until it hit the ground, straddling the roofs of a black Mercedes and a small white Fiat. Almost instantaneously there was a huge ball of flame.

And the wriggling, petrified, dead weight of Venner was suspended below him, over the drop, supported by nothing except the grip he and Nicholl each had on a wrist, the metal strap of Venner's watch cutting painfully into his hand.

Venner produced a long, gurgling whimper. The heat was burning Grace's face. Venner was slipping. He had to hold on to him. He wanted this creep to live; death was too damned good for him. Somehow, he did not know from where, he found some strength; Nicholl seemed to find it too, at the same time. And the next moment, like a huge, blubbery fish, the fat pigtailed man was hauled to safety, up over the edge of the roof.

Venner lay on his back, yabbering in terror; there was a

dark stain around his crotch where he had pissed himself. Moments later, with no time to spare, Grace roughly rolled him over onto his front, grabbed his hands and cuffed him. There was a vile stench; the creep had crapped himself as well, but Grace barely noticed; he was on autopilot now.

Yelling at Nicholl to get the man out of the building, Grace ran back to the fire exit, hurtled down the flights of steps and into the basement. Norman Potting, accompanied now by two uniformed constables, was kneeling beside Glenn Branson, who seemed semi-conscious.

'This whole fucking place is going up! Let's get him out!' Grace yelled.

He shoved his arms under his friend's shoulders, with a constable supporting his midriff and Potting and the other constable each taking a leg. They carried him up the stairs, then burst through a fire exit door into the car park, into a searing blast of heat from the blazing cars and the helicopter, the stench of burning paint and rubber, and a cacophony of sirens.

They carried Branson away as far as they could from the heat, until Grace saw an ambulance racing towards them.

They stopped. He looked down at Branson, bringing his face close to his mate's. 'How are you doing?'

'Remember John Wayne, when he got shot in that movie—' Branson said, his voice wheezy.

'Did he live?' Grace interrupted him.

'Yeah, he lived.'

'That how you feel?'

'Yeah.'

Grace kissed him on the forehead. He couldn't help it; he loved this man.

Then, standing back as the paramedics took over, he

felt something cutting into his hand. He looked down and saw a blue-faced Breitling watch on a broken metal bracelet. It was covered in blood. His own blood.

It was the watch, he realized, which had been on the pigtailed man's wrist. How the hell did he – ?

And he thought back to a couple of hours earlier today, to the phone call he had had from the clairvoyant Harry Frame.

I'm getting a watch.

A watch? Like a wristwatch?

Exactly! A wristwatch! There is something very significant. A wristwatch will lead you to something very satisfying to do with a case you are working on. This case, I think.

Can you elaborate?

No, I . . . No, that's all. As I said, I don't know if it means anything.

Any particular make?

No. Expensive, I think.

Sucking at his hand to staunch the bleeding, he turned to Nick Nicholl, who was closing a police car door on Venner. 'Do you know anything about wristwatches?'

His colleague was white, shaking. In a bad way. Seriously in shock. 'Not a lot. Why?'

Grace held up the watch he was holding. 'What about this?'

Norman Potting piped up, 'That's a Breitling.'

'What do you know about them?'

'Only that I could never afford one. They're expensive.'

A constable came running towards them, looking petrified. 'Please move away. We're worried the whole building might go up – it's full of chemicals.'

Suddenly seized with panic, Grace said, 'Christ, where the hell are Mr and Mrs Bryce?'

'It's all right, sir,' the constable said. 'They're in ambulances, on their way to hospital.'

'Good man.'

87

Five minutes later, just as the first fire engine pulled up outside, the warehouse exploded. The blast blew out windows from buildings up to a quarter of a mile away. It was over two days before it was cool enough for the forensic investigators to enter and begin their grim task.

Three sets of human remains were eventually found. One would be identified in a few weeks' time by his brother, still under police guard in hospital, from the partially melted gold medallion found around his neck. The second, just a human skull, would be identified from dental records as being Janie Stretton. The third would also be identified from dental records as being Andy Gidney.

The intense heat had made it impossible to determine, from what little remained of his bones, Gidney's precise cause of death. And no one was able to offer any explanation of what he had been doing on the premises.

In a couple of months, Detective Sergeant Jon Rye of the High Tech Crime Unit would provide a report for the Coroner's Court. And, for lack of evidence, the Coroner would have no option but to return an open verdict. More succinct but less informative than a shipping forecast.

*

It was half past four when Roy Grace finally left the blaze, which was a long way yet from being under control. He drove straight to the Royal Sussex County Hospital and went to find Glenn Branson in the emergency ward.

Glenn's pretty wife, Ari, was already there. She had never shown much warmth towards Grace, blaming him, he suspected, for keeping her husband away from home so much. And there was no thaw today. Glenn had been lucky. Only one bullet had hit, and it had gone through his abdomen, missing his spine by half an inch. He would be a little sore for a while, and Grace had no doubt he would enjoy much of his convalescence watching movies in which screen heroes took bullets and survived.

Next, in the intensive care unit, he met Emma-Jane's parents, her mother an attractive woman in her forties who gave him a stoical smile, her father a very quiet man who sat squeezing a yellow tennis ball in his hand as if his daughter's life depended on it. Emma-Jane seemed to be improving; that was the best they could say.

When he left the hospital, he felt depressed, wondering what kind of a leader he was to let two of his team come so close to death. He stopped off at a workmen's cafe, went in and had a massive fry-up and a strong cup of tea.

When he had finished, feeling considerably better now, he sat hunched over the Formica table and made a series of phone calls. As he stood up to leave, his mobile rang. It was Nick Nicholl, asking how he was, then telling him he hadn't had a chance to report on his meeting with the officer from the Met, about the girl who had been found dead on Wimbledon Common with a scarab design on her bracelet. It had turned out to be a dead end. A coincidence. The girl's boyfriend had confessed to her murder. Bella Moy, who had been working on all the other forces, had found no other murders with a scarab beetle at the crime scene.

Maybe we got lucky and caught them early? Grace wondered. But not early enough for poor Janie Stretton.

He told the young DC to go home, to put his arms around his wife, who was due to give birth any day, and tell her he loved her. Nicholl, sounding surprised, thanked him. But that was how Grace felt at this moment. That life was precious. And precarious. You never knew what was around the corner. Cherish what you had while you had it.

As he climbed back into his car, Cleo rang, sounding bright and perky.

'Hi!' she said. 'Sorry to be so long calling you back! Are you free to talk?'

'Totally,' he said.

'Good. I've had one hell of a day. Four cadavers – you know what it's like after a weekend!'

'I do.'

'One motorbike fatality, one fifty-year-old man who fell off a ladder, and two old ladies. Not to mention a male head that came in yesterday without much else left of him – but I think you know about that one.'

'Just a little.'

'Then I had to go into the centre of Brighton at lunchtime to buy an anniversary present for the aged Ps.'

'Aged whats?'

'My parents!'

'Ah.'

'And I got my damned car stuck in the Bartholomew Square car park. There was a bomb scare – can you bloody believe it?'

'Really?'

'When I finally got the car out, the whole bloody city was gridlocked!'

'I did hear something about that,' he said.

'So how was your day?' she asked.

'Oh, you know – average.'

'No big excitement?'

'Nah.'

There was a strange but comfortable silence between them for some moments. Then she said, 'I've been longing to speak to you all day. But I wanted to do it when we had some quality time. I didn't want it to be just a hurried, *Hi! Great shag last night. Bye!*'

Grace laughed. And suddenly it seemed an awfully long time since the last time he'd laughed. It had been a long, long few days.

Later, much later, after hours in the office making a start on the mountain of paperwork that would keep him occupied for the rest of the week and beyond, Grace found himself back in Cleo's flat.

That night, after they had made love, he slept in her arms like a baby. He slept the sleep of the dead. And for a few of those hours it was without any of the fears of the living.

88

On Thursday morning, his hands heavily bandaged and still hurting like hell from the acid burns, Tom Bryce went into his office for a couple of hours.

It was clear from the exuberant greetings from his staff and the stack of press cuttings on his desk that the front-page headlines he had made with Kellie, nationwide over the past couple of days, had done Bryceright Promotional Merchandise no harm at all. His two salesmen in the office, Peter Chard and Simon Wong, were over the moon – they couldn't remember when they had last had this level of enquiries, from existing and potential customers.

'Oh,' Chard added, standing over his desk, 'good news is that we've delivered the Rolexes to Ron Spacks. All twenty-five of them. Our margin is un-bloody-believable!'

'I never saw the final artwork,' Tom said, suddenly feeling a little concerned. If there had been a screw-up on the engraving of twenty-five Rolex watches, it would be a financial disaster.

'No worries! I rang him yesterday to check all was kosher. He's happy as Larry with them.'

'Get me the paperwork on them, will you?'

A couple of minutes later Chard put the file down on his desk. Tom opened it and stared at the order. The margin was fantastic, £1,400 profit per watch. Multiplied by twenty-five. That made £35,000. He'd never made that kind of a profit on an order before, ever.

Then his elation turned to gloom. Kellie had agreed to

go to a clinic, to dry out. Afterwards they would start afresh together. But the good places cost a fortune; for the top ones, you could be looking at the wrong end of a couple of thousand pounds a week – multiplied by several months. A good £30,000–40,000 if you really wanted a result. And the cost of childminders while she was there.

At least with this order he would have the dosh to cover it – and in the six years he had been doing business with Ron Spacks, the man had always paid on the nail. Seven days from delivery. Never a day late.

Looking at the paperwork, Tom asked, 'When were these delivered?'

'Yesterday.'

'Fast work,' Tom said. 'I only took the order last—'

'Thursday!' Peter Chard said. 'Yeah, well I found a supplier who had stock, and got our engraver to work through the night.'

'I never saw the design; he was going to send it through.'

Chard turned a couple of sheets of paper over, then tapped an A4 photocopy. 'This is a massive enlargement. It's actually a microdot, invisible to the naked eye.'

Tom looked down and saw a drawing of a beetle, a rather fine but slightly menacing-looking creature, with strange markings on its back and a horn rising from its head. He frowned.

'It's called a scarab beetle,' Peter Chard said. 'Apparently they are sacred in ancient Egyptian mythology.'

'Is that right?'

'Yep. Disgusting creature. Also known as a dung beetle.'

'Why would he want these on a watch?'

Chard shrugged. 'He's a DVD distributor, isn't he?'

'Yes, massive.'

'Maybe there's a record label with that name.' The salesman shrugged again. 'He's your client – I figured you knew.'

Tom felt a sudden cold shiver run through him. Maybe he should mention this to Detective Superintendent Grace when they next spoke – as a coincidence to have a laugh about, if nothing else.

But he decided it might be wise to wait until Ron Spacks had paid, first.

NOT DEAD ENOUGH

Read on for an exclusive extract from the
new Detective Superintendent Roy Grace mystery,
out now in Pan paperback.

1

Darkness took a long time to arrive, but it was worth the wait. And besides, time was not a problem for him. Time, he had come to realize, was one of the things you have in life when you have little else. He was time-rich. Near on a time billionaire.

Shortly before midnight, the woman he was following turned off the dual carriageway and drove into the lonely glow of a BP filling station forecourt. He halted his stolen van on the unlit slip road, fixating on her brake lights. They seemed to be getting brighter as he watched them. Glowing red for danger, red for luck, red for sex! *Seventy-one per cent of murder victims were killed by someone they knew.* The statistic was whizzing round and round inside his head like a pinball looking for a slot. He collected statistics, squirrelled them carefully away, like nuts, to sustain him through that long hibernation of the mind that he knew, one day, would come to him.

The question was: *how many of those seventy-one per cent knew they were about to be murdered?*

Do you, lady?

Headlights of vehicles flashed past, the slipstream of a lorry rocking his little blue Renault, making some of the plumbing implements behind him rattle. There were just two other cars standing by the pumps, a Toyota people-carrier that was about to drive off and a large Jaguar. Its owner, a plump man in an ill-fitting tuxedo, was heading back from the pay window, cramming his wallet back into his jacket. A BP tanker was parked up, the driver in a boiler suit uncoiling a long hose, getting ready to refuel the filling station tanks.

So far as he could ascertain in a careful sweep, there was just one CCTV camera scanning the forecourt. A problem, but he could deal with it.

She really could not have picked a better place to stop! He blew her a silent kiss.

2

In the warm, summer night air, Katie Bishop tossed her untidy blonde hair away from her face and yawned, feeling tired. Actually, beyond tired. Exhausted – but very, very nicely exhausted, thank you! She studied the petrol pump as if it was some extraterrestial creature put on Planet Earth to intimidate her, which was how she felt about most petrol pumps. Her husband always had problems figuring out the instructions on the dishwasher and the washing machine, claiming they were written in some alien language called 'woman'. Well, so far as she was concerned, petrol pumps came with an equally alien language – the instructions on them were written in 'bloke'.

She struggled, as usual, to get the filler cap off her BMW, then stared at the words *Premium* and *Super*, trying to remember which one she was supposed to put in, although it seemed to her she could never get it right. If she put in Premium, Greg criticized her for putting in petrol that was too low grade; if she filled up with Super, he chastised her for wasting money. But at this moment, nothing was going in at all. She held the nozzle in one hand, squeezing the trigger hard, and waved with the other, trying to attract the attention of the dozy night attendant behind the counter.

Greg's behaviour had been worrying her for some months now. He was going through increasingly violent mood swings, and obsessing about all kinds of stupid little things – like the position of his toothpaste on the bathroom shelf, and making sure all the chairs around the kitchen table were exactly the same distance apart. Talking millimetres, not centimetres. And he was becoming increasingly kinky, regularly bringing home carrier bags from sex shops filled with weird stuff – most recently a set of leather restraints and a rubber gas mask – which he insisted on trying out coarsely and harshly.

In truth, there were times recently when he had scared her.

She was so wrapped in her thoughts she didn't even notice the pump jigging away until it stopped with an abrupt *kerlunk*. Breathing in the smell of petrol fumes, which she had always quite liked, she hung the nozzle of the pump back up, clicked the key fob to lock the car – Greg had warned her cars often got stolen on petrol station forecourts – and went to the booth to pay.

As she came out, she carefully folded her credit card receipt, and tucked it into her purse. She unlocked the car, climbed in, then locked it again from the inside, pulled on her seat belt and started the engine. The *Il Divo* CD started playing again. She thought for a moment about lowering the BMW's roof, then decided against. It was past midnight, she would be vulnerable driving into Brighton at this hour with an open top. Better to stay enclosed and secure.

It was not until she had driven off the forecourt, and was a good hundred yards down the dark slip road, that she noticed something smelled different in the car. A cologne that she knew well. *Comme des Garçons*. Then she saw something move in her mirror.

And she realized someone was inside her car.

Fear caught the inside of her throat like a fish-hook; her hands froze on the wheel. She jammed her foot down hard on the brake pedal, screeching the car to a halt, scrabbling with her hand on the gear shift to find reverse, to back up to the safety of the forecourt. Then she felt the cold, sharp metal biting into her neck.

'Just keep driving, Katie,' he said.

Straining to see him in her rear-view mirror, she saw a sliver of light shear off the blade of the knife, like a spark.

And in that rear-view mirror he saw, reflected through the terror in her eyes, sweet recognition.